Of Truth and Beasts

"With several twists and surprises, this series is never predictable [and] the impressively shocking, climactic ending left me wanting more. . . . Don't miss this exciting series of magic, mythical creatures, and incredible lore."   —SciFiChick.com

"A crowd-pleasing mix of intrigue, epic fantasy, and horror."   —*Publishers Weekly*

"*Of Truth and Beasts* . . . once again allows the reader the rare opportunity to travel into the uniquely imaginative realms that only [the Hendees] can create with such power and grace. . . . These novels are an integral and enlightening part of the Noble Dead Saga, which in total is no simple myth but rather a true epic [that] stands at the highest levels of fantasy lore. . . . The Hendees' style of writing is verbally arresting, leaving the reader unable to put the novel down. They are a talented team of storytellers who are able to build a world that is both foreign and familiar. . . . This novel is a masterful conglomeration of manipulations, collusions, and deceits [that] allow for a situation where nothing is what it seems. . . . The only thing that could have topped the Hendees' whirlwind ending was their epilogue, which will undoubtedly make the Noble Dead Saga fans stand up and cheer. I, for one, am hooked and eagerly await the next incarnation [of] this hypnotizing series."   —BookSpot Central

"A fabulous thriller."   —*Midwest Book Review*

"The antagonists are strong, convincing forces with private agendas that add satisfying twists to another excellent addition to the series."   —Monsters and Critics

"Plenty of action. . . . Fans of the Noble Dead will enjoy the book."   —*Booklist*

continued . . .

"The Hendees excel at delivering action and intrigue."

Through Stone and Sea

"A textured canvas of tangled plots, hidden alliances, secret myths conjured from fantasy's best-known landscapes, and unique characters who will surely take their place in the annals of fantasy." —BookSpot Central

"Suspenseful adventure . . . incredible world building, and intriguing characters are the best part of this questlike fantasy." —SciFiChick.com

In Shade and Shadow

"The Hendees, if given a chance to complete their entire saga, may yet produce a combined fantasy masterwork that will surely stand on the highest pinnacles of literary fantasy lore." —BookSpot Central

"A nicely nuanced tale. . . . The authors use a deft touch to keep the pacing even and set the stage for future adventures in this endlessly intriguing horror-fantasy mix."

—Monsters and Critics

Child of a Dead God

"Readers who love vampire novels will appreciate the full works of Barb and J. C. Hendee, as they consistently provide some of the genre's best. . . . The audience will want to read this novel in one sitting." —*Midwest Book Review*

"Complex and bloody. . . . Interspecies distrust, grand ambitions, and the lure of dangerous secrets protected by the undead drive the action in this neat mix of horror with more traditional fantasy elements." —*Publishers Weekly*

Rebel Fay

"Entertaining . . . a hybrid crossing Tolkienesque fantasy with vampire-infused horror . . . intriguing."

—*Publishers Weekly*

"A real page-turner." —*Booklist*

Traitor to the Blood

"A rousing and sometimes creepy fantasy adventure . . . this is one of those books for which the term 'dark fantasy' was definitely intended." —*Chronicle*

"A unique tale of vampires and half-vampire undead hunters set against a dark fantasy world ruled by tyrants. The personal conflicts of the heroes mirror the larger struggles in their world and provide a solid foundation for this tale of love and loyalty in a world of betrayal."　　—*Library Journal*

Sister of the Dead

"[A] wonderful addition to the Noble Dead series . . . *Sister of the Dead* leads us on an amazing adventure that will keep you engrossed until the final chapter. . . . This is a series that will appeal to both horror and fantasy fans."　　—*SF Site*

"[An] intelligent dark fantasy series. . . . Much more than a medieval 'Buffy Does the Dark Ages,' *Sister of the Dead* and its predecessors involve readers on a visceral, highly emotional level and fulfill a craving for nifty magic, exciting action scenes, and a strong heroine who defies genre cliches."
　　—*Romantic Times* (4 stars)

Thief of Lives

"Readers will turn the pages of this satisfying medieval thriller with gusto."　　—*Booklist*

"Fans of Anita Blake will enjoy this novel. The characters are cleverly drawn so that the several supernatural species that play key roles in the plot seem natural and real. Supernatural fantasy readers will enjoy this action-packed, strong tale, because vampires, sorcerers, dhampirs, elves, fey-canines, and other ilk seem real."　　—*Midwest Book Review*

Dhampir

"*Dhampir* maintains a high level of excitement through interesting characters, both heroes and villains, colliding in well-written action scenes. Instead of overloading us with their world building and the maps and glossaries typical of so much fantasy, the Hendees provide well-rounded characters that go a lot further than maps in making a lively fantasy world."　　—*The Denver Post*

"An engaging adventure that is both humorous and exciting." —*New York Times* bestselling author Kevin J. Anderson

"An altogether compelling and moving work. . . . These are characters and a world worthy of exploration."
　　—Brian Hodge, Hellnotes

By Barb Hendee

THE MIST-TORN WITCHES SERIES
The Mist-Torn Witches

THE VAMPIRE MEMORIES SERIES
Blood Memories
Hunting Memories
Memories of Envy
In Memories We Fear
Ghosts of Memories

By Barb and J. C. Hendee

THE NOBLE DEAD SAGA—SERIES ONE
Dhampir
Thief of Lives
Sister of the Dead
Traitor to the Blood
Rebel Fay
Child of a Dead God

THE NOBLE DEAD SAGA—SERIES TWO
In Shade and Shadow
Through Stone and Sea
Of Truth and Beasts

THE NOBLE DEAD SAGA—SERIES THREE
Between Their Worlds
The Dog in the Dark

THE
MIST-TORN
WITCHES

BARB HENDEE

A ROC BOOK

ROC
Published by the Penguin Group
Penguin Group (USA) Inc., 375 Hudson Street,
New York, New York 10014, USA

USA | Canada | UK | Ireland | Australia | New Zealand | India | South Africa | China

Penguin Books Ltd., Registered Offices: 80 Strand, London WC2R 0RL, England
For more information about the Penguin Group visit penguin.com.

First published by Roc, an imprint of New American Library,
a division of Penguin Group (USA) Inc.

First Printing, May 2013

 REGISTERED TRADEMARK—MARCA REGISTRADA

ISBN 978-0-451-41415-1

Printed in the United States of America
10 9 8 7 6 5 4 3 2 1

PUBLISHER'S NOTE
This is a work of fiction. Names, characters, places, and incidents either are the product
of the author's imagination or are used fictitiously, and any resemblance to actual persons, living or dead, business establishments, events, or locales is entirely coincidental.
    The publisher does not have any control over and does not assume any responsibility
for author or third-party Web sites or their content.

ALWAYS LEARNING   **PEARSON**

For my beautiful daughter, Jaclyn, who was my first reader here . . . and who gave me hope.

PROLOGUE

My name is Céline Fawe, and I am a Mist-Torn witch.

By the age of fifteen, I had no idea what this meant, as none of my powers had manifested yet. I only knew that my mother had just died, that the apothecary shop she'd owned was now mine, and that I had to provide for my twelve-year-old sister, Amelie. My father had been killed long ago, and with my mother's passing, the two of us were alone.

What would you have done?

I did what anyone would do—I fell back upon my only strengths: the abilities to listen and to lie.

Of course, I didn't even know about those two skills until the week after Amelie and I had buried our mother and a young man came through the front door of our shop. His eyes were wild, shifting back and forth, reminding me of a colt locked in a stall for the first time.

But I was still so numb that I could barely draw

breath, and I didn't care what he wanted or why he'd come.

"I have an appointment," he said hesitantly, "with Eleanor."

Eleanor was my mother.

"She's dead," I answered.

To my surprise, the flash of disappointment on his face moved me, and for the first time, I really looked at him. He was medium height, with brown hair tucked behind his ears, wearing a burgundy tunic and a sword. I guessed him to be about eighteen.

"Dead?" he repeated. "No . . . She was going to tell me . . ."

He trailed off, but he didn't need to finish. My mother had been a seer, and he wanted to know something about his future. I was just about to tell him to go away when I spotted the small pouch of coins in his hand.

I tensed. I was no seer, not like my mother. I could grow healing herbs and cast small spells to stop bad dreams or ease the pain of unrequited love, but I was no seer.

Still, the cupboard was nearly bare, and that pouch beckoned. Curing bad dreams didn't exactly pay well.

A risky idea struck me, and at that point, I had little left to lose.

"I'm Eleanor's daughter," I said. "I have her gift. Sit down, and I can help you."

The relief washing over his face shamed me— but not enough to make me stop. I let him sit.

"What is it you wish to know?" I asked.

He sank down into the chair, facing me across my mother's faded table. "I . . . I want to marry, but my father doesn't approve."

"Why not?"

"Because Joselyn has no dowry. Her father has a title, but her family has no money, and my own father has been making arrangements with the Baron Driesè. Father expects me to marry the baron's daughter, Rhiannon."

"And you don't want to marry Rhiannon?"

He began to shake his head and then stopped himself. "I don't know! The baron controls half the silver mines in the northeastern province, and Rhiannon's dowry would bring my family great wealth. Joselyn would bring us nothing."

I cocked my head. This seemed a simple decision to me. Marry the rich girl. But I knew my mother would not see it so simply.

"Then what troubles you?" I asked. "Is Rhiannon ugly? Has her hair fallen out? Is she covered in pockmarks?"

He blinked, possibly finding my questions somewhat childish, which they were, but keep in mind that I was only fifteen. "No, if anything, most people would find her prettier than Joselyn," he said. "But when I'm with Joselyn, I don't feel alone."

I stared at him, and that was my first real glimpse into the adult world.

"If you don't marry Rhiannon, can your father

disinherit you?" I asked. Even at fifteen, I was pragmatic.

"No."

That was all he had to tell me. I'd seen my mother do this a hundred times. "Did you bring something of Joselyn's?" I asked, knowing my mother would have given him instructions.

"Yes, a lock of her hair."

I took it from him, holding the soft, light brown strands in my fingers. With my other hand, I reached out to grasp one of his. He almost pulled away, as if he didn't like being touched, but then let me grip his palm.

I closed my eyes. Although of course I saw nothing, I forced my body to jolt once, and then I swayed several times, breathing through my mouth. I opened my eyes again.

"Did you see it?" he asked, leaning forward. "Did you see my future?"

"Yes," I answered without wavering. "You marry Joselyn, and you are happy. I saw the two of you after your wedding, and everything was as it should be."

He sucked in a loud breath like a man saved from drowning and shoved the pouch across the table. "Thank you. Thank you so much."

That was how it started.

CHAPTER 1

"I didn't call you a liar," Amelie Fawe said flatly. "I said you were trying to cheat me. There's a difference."

Jareth, the village butcher, frowned at her while still holding two lamb chops in the air. They stood outside amidst the tables and booths of the morning market, with just a drizzle of rain coming down on their heads. But he was trying to overcharge her, and they both knew it.

Amelie sighed. It wasn't that she blamed him— or that she was even given to haggling over a few cuts of meat. But she and her sister, Céline, were among the dwindling number of people in She-tâna who had coins to spend. Most of the other villagers had been offering Jareth turnips in exchange for soup bones. Amelie had a feeling he was full up on turnips.

She had no intention of threatening him, but out of habit, her hand settled on the hilt of the short sword at her left hip. In truth, she was much better with the dagger sheathed on her right, but the sword made a stronger impression—and occasionally, she needed one.

Her sister, Céline, was slender and pretty, and Céline brought in most of the household's money. They were a fiercely independent team, and Amelie had long ago taken on the task of protecting them both. They needed no one but each other.

"All right," Jareth said, not appearing the least bit intimidated by her hand dropping to the sword. "A halfpenny, then, but you're robbing me blind."

She smiled at him and handed him a coin. "Céline asked after that rheumatism in your shoulder. Should I bring more of the bay leaf oil?"

His expression softened, and he was about to answer when the sound of hoofbeats stopped him. Amelie followed his gaze to the main path leading into the village, and she saw four riders coming from the tree line.

Three of them wore black tabards over chain armor, soldiers of Sub-Prince Damek. With distaste, Amelie recognized the man in the lead, Captain Kochè, the prince's chief bullyboy and tax collector.

"What do you suppose he wants?" Jareth said softly, putting the chops down and wiping his hands on his already bloody apron. "Taxes aren't due for two months."

All around them, villagers in threadbare clothing began slinking away as quickly as possible, but Amelie kept her eyes on the soldiers.

"Who's that with them?" she asked, squinting.

A fourth person—much smaller—in a full cloak rode just behind Captain Kochè.

"I can't tell," Jareth answered.

Amelie waited for the riders to come all the way into the village; then her stomach tightened when they began to pull their horses up just outside the village perimeter at a small two-story building with a painted sign that read, LAVENDER AND THYME.

It was the apothecary shop that she owned with her sister.

It was also their home.

All four riders stopped directly in front of the shop, and Captain Kochè swung off onto the ground.

"Oh, seven hells," Amelie gasped, forgetting about the lamb chops. "He's going after Céline!"

The smaller cloaked figure dismounted as well.

Jareth grabbed a meat cleaver off the table. "You want me to come?"

But Amelie was already running down the muddy path. "No," she called, "I've got it."

She and Céline didn't need anyone but each other.

Céline Fawe unfortunately had no appointments that day, so she'd planned to boil down some marshmallow leaves to make an astringent for in-

sect bites and bee stings, as midspring had arrived, and there would soon be an abundance of
insects. Humming, just a little off-key, she started
the fire, hoping Amelie wouldn't give Jareth too
much trouble over the price of a few lamb chops.
However, the two sisters didn't have many extra
pennies either . . . which was why she tended to
send Amelie to the village market. It was cow-
ardly and she knew it, but Amelie was much better at holding firm.

Céline also knew that even while just scraping
by, she and Amelie lived better than almost anyone in Shetâna. But they also lived slightly apart
from everyone else as well. Their little shop, with
the bedroom upstairs, had been built just outside
the village as if it didn't quite belong with the
other shops and dwellings. She and Amelie had
always felt that way about themselves, too.
Though their father had grown up in Shetâna,
their mother, Eleanor, had come from someplace
else, which she never spoke of. He'd been one of
the village hunters, and apparently, after an extended hunt one year, he'd come back with a
bride—and he'd promptly built her an apothecary's shop and home for them to share. Eleanor
could read and write, and she arrived with her
own texts and scrolls on herb lore. She made certain both her girls were literate, although Céline
had taken more willingly to scholarly pursuits.

As a result, both Céline and Amelie spoke differently than the villagers of Shetâna, saw the world a little differently, and sometimes used words no one else could understand. This set them apart.

Still, people came from nearby townships and villages just to see Céline, the seer, and have their futures read. Her reputation had spread as far north as the Vudrask River.

To count further blessings, their shop was warm, with a decent hearth, and although they had no front counter, the main room did boast several sturdy tables, and the walls were lined with shelves containing countless numbers of pots and jars.

Their little establishment looked the part.

The Lavender and Thyme apothecary shop was quite respectable—and Céline was proud of it.

Still humming, she was just about to head into the storage room for the marshmallow leaves when the sound of hoofbeats outside made her pause and half turn. The hoofbeats stopped, and then she heard booted feet landing with a squishing sound in the mud just in front of her shop. Who could that be?

Before she could wonder a moment longer, the door slammed open, and she froze in her tracks. Captain Kochè filled the open doorway with his wet tabard dripping water onto the floor. He looked at her, and his eyes moved up and down, just as they always did when he got within ten paces of her. He was revolting: tall but with a protruding belly, greasy hair, and a stringy mustache that stretched all the way down past his chin.

Céline, on the other hand, had learned from her mother that it was necessary for a successful seer to also look the part. She wore her mother's red velvet gown a good deal of the time, and it fit her slight body snugly. Her mass of dark blond curls hung to the small of her back, and both she and Amelie had inherited their mother's lavender eyes. Céline was well aware that in almost any circle, she'd be considered at least moderately pretty, but here in Shetâna, any girl with a halfway clean face and all of her teeth was viewed as a beauty.

It was rather tiresome.

The captain licked his lower lip, and Céline drew herself up to full height—which was still slightly shorter than the average woman.

"Can I help you?" she asked, pitching her tone to suggest she'd rather do anything than help him. She had no idea what he wanted. The shop's taxes were paid in full, and Sub-Prince Damek never paid an ounce of attention to Shetâna unless someone owed him money or he'd decided to have someone punished for insolence. The state of the roads was criminal, but no one here complained to him anymore.

"No, my dear," said a voice from behind the captain, "but you can assist me."

Kochè stepped aside, and a bent figure hobbled inside past him. One gnarled hand came up to push back the hood of a cloak, revealing the wrinkled face of an ancient woman who smiled, exposing yellow teeth. She closed the door behind herself. "I am Madam Zelinka. You might know of me?"

Céline did. She'd heard the name from several of her more prominent patrons, but no one who paid for Céline's services would ever be closely connected to Madam Zelinka. She was a marriage broker to the great noble houses, spinning a web of connections to increase wealth or bloodlines or to shore up weakening titles.

What could she possibly want here?

But Céline wasn't about to insult her and bowed politely. "Yes, ma'am. I'm honored by your visit. May I bring you some hot tea?"

The old woman's smile widened, chilling Céline to the bone. "What a dear girl you are," Madam Zelinka said, moving to a chair and sitting down. "Tea would be most welcome." She wore her white hair up in a simple bun on her head, and even through her wet cloak, she smelled like a dusty attic.

Captain Kochè remained standing to one side of the doorway, still dripping on the floor, with his gaze locked on Céline's waist. She tried to ignore him as she moved toward the teapot.

But before anyone else could say a word, the

door burst open again, and Amelie came running inside, panting, with one hand on the hilt of her dagger.

"Céline!" she cried and then calmed somewhat at the sight of her sister by the hearth.

A guard from outside appeared behind her, seeming surprised and looking to his captain for orders, but Kochè waved him away and the guard simply closed the door.

Turning to the captain, Amelie spat out, "What are you doing in here?"

Céline winced inwardly. Amelie and Kochè hated each other, and neither bothered to hide it. In fact, if the shop hadn't been the most lucrative tax source in Shetâna, Céline might have worried for her sister's safety.

The thing was, Kochè was the type who liked his women to look and behave . . . well, like women. At seventeen, Amelie was even shorter than Céline. But where Céline was slight, Amelie's build showed a hint of her strength and muscle. She insisted upon wearing breeches, a faded blue shirt, a short canvas jacket, and boots. She shared Céline's lavender eyes and small nose, but she'd inherited their father's straight black hair, which she'd cropped into a bob that hung just below her jaw.

When she and Céline had first been orphaned, they'd seemed easy targets for wandering soldiers, but Amelie had quickly proven that assumption wrong. She relied on speed and the element of surprise, and she could cut a man open in a matter of seconds with that dagger on her hip.

"*He* is doing nothing here," Madam Zelinka answered, sounding a tad less friendly now. "My business is with your sister."

Céline hurried over to stand between them. "Amelie, this is a marriage broker. She may have a task for me."

Amelie looked quickly between Céline and the woman. Although Amelie was overprotective and hot-tempered, she was certainly no fool, and this visit smelled of money.

"She'd like some tea," Céline went on. "Could you please get it for her?"

Their eyes locked, and then Amelie nodded once, heading for the hearth. Kochè was not making any threats. In fact, as yet, he hadn't said a word.

When it came to business, Céline always took the lead. She moved to the table and sat across from Madam Zelinka. "How is it that I might help you?"

The old woman's smile returned—along with her exposed yellow teeth—and she pulled three silver coins from inside the damp cloak. "Just a minor task, a trifle really."

The size of the payment hardly suggested a trifle, but Céline remained silent, waiting politely. She'd learned a long time ago that people tended to share more if they were left in silence for a while. Amelie set a steaming mug of the tea on the table.

"You'll have another visitor late this afternoon," Madam Zelinka continued, "a young noblewoman . . . a minor noblewoman, who will ask you about a pending marriage. She's heard of your reputation in these matters, and she will not consent to the betrothal until she's spoken with you and you have read her future. All you need do is assure her that the marriage will be a happy one and that she may accept without reservations."

"What is the girl's name?" Céline asked. "Just so I know who to expect."

"Rhiannon, eldest daughter of the Baron Driesè."

Something about that name was familiar . . . something from years past, but Céline couldn't remember what.

Zelinka pushed the silver coins across the table. "Can you manage this, my dear?"

The situation was blissfully clear to Céline. The old woman worked for the prospective groom's father—or perhaps the groom himself—and she wanted assurances that the wedding would take place, thus ensuring her own fat fee.

But if Kochè was escorting Zelinka, it meant the situation was also somehow connected to Sub-Prince Damek, so even if she'd wanted to, Céline was in no position to refuse.

"Yes, I can manage easily," she answered.

"Be sure you do," Kochè said in a low tone, speaking for the first time. "Be sure the girl says yes."

Céline blinked and glanced at Amelie. What interest could he have here? He was far from noble, so nothing that Madam Zelinka arranged could possibly be connected to him.

"Of course she will," the old woman said, standing up and hobbling toward the door. She hadn't touched her tea. "Good-bye, my dear. What a pleasant visit this has been."

Captain Kochè opened the door for her, but he kept his eyes on Céline, moving his gaze from her waist to her breasts. Now that his hair had dried partially, it looked even greasier. She fought to hold back a shudder.

Then, without another word, both Kochè and the old woman left as quickly as they'd come.

Céline shook her head, wishing she knew even a little more. "What do you suppose this is all about?"

Amelie shrugged. "At least he's gone." She walked over and looked down at the silver coins. "And *that* is easy money."

Yes, Céline had to agree. It was easy money.

Lieutenant Jaromir hid behind the tree line, peering toward the edge of the village. Though he'd grown up in the wet world of Droevinka, even he was becoming uncomfortable in the cold spring rain. His chain armor was dripping, and his tan tabard was soaked though.

"What are they doing in there?" he asked quietly. "They didn't even go all the way into the village."

He was about to say more, but when he looked at his companion, the words died on his lips. Sub-Prince Anton, his lord and closest friend, had gone pale.

"It's an apothecary's shop," Anton whispered. "They've gone to the seer who lives there."

"A seer?" Jaromir asked. "In that rat hole of a village? Are you sure?"

"Yes, I'm sure. I've been inside the place."

Jaromir peered through the trees again at the two-story shop, having a hard time picturing his prince inside such a dwelling. Two soldiers in black tabards waited outside the front door with the horses, while Captain Kochè and the old marriage broker went inside.

"Why would Damek send Zelinka here?" he asked.

"I don't know," Anton answered. "The last I heard, my brother's marriage was a sealed bargain." He shivered.

At least he was wearing a cloak, but Jaromir didn't like the thought of him being out for so long in this rain. At the age of twenty-three, Anton was already a good leader, but he was slight of build, and his health was not strong. His brown hair only made his skin look whiter, and the circles under his eyes didn't help.

"You think Rhiannon's having second thoughts about marrying your brother?" Jaromir asked.

"I don't know," Anton said again.

Jaromir wanted to sigh. The problem here was

that they didn't know much at all, and the situation was growing dire. He'd never been terribly interested in the arena of politics, but he did care about the people of this country, and he cared even more about Anton. Great changes were coming, and if Jaromir had any say in the matter, Anton would not only survive but also come out on top.

Droevinka had no hereditary king. Instead, it was a land of many princes, each one heading his own noble house and overseeing multiple fiefdoms. But . . . they all served a single grand prince, and a new grand prince was elected every nine years by the gathered heads of the noble houses. This system had served the country well for more than a hundred years. At present, Prince Rodêk of the House of Äntes was in rule.

But within two years, a new grand prince would be voted in.

Anton and Damek were sons of the House of Pählen. Their father, Prince Lieven, controlled a large province in the western region. He'd given Damek, who was the elder brother, an aging castle and seven large fiefs to oversee. He'd given Anton a better castle but six smaller fiefs. These "assignments" were a chance for each young man to prove himself. However, Prince Lieven had been aging rapidly in recent days, and it was rumored he would soon be naming a successor as leader of the House of Pählen. It was his right to choose between his sons, and should a victor be chosen within the next two years, then he would have the right to place his successor's name on the voting list for the position of grand prince.

As a result, Damek had been taxing his peasants near to death in order to increase the size of his military forces—which he viewed as a show of strength . . . but only because it was. Then two months ago, Anton had learned that Damek was negotiating to marry the daughter of a minor noble with an enormous dowry, large enough to dramatically shift the balance of power. This had come as a blow.

And yet, no wedding had taken place, nor had a date been announced.

So now Jaromir and Anton had been reduced to either depending upon spies or doing the spying themselves in order to learn the outcome, and they'd trailed Kochè and Damek's crone of a marriage broker this morning.

"Poor Rhiannon," Anton whispered. "Her father's trying to trade her off again."

Jaromir glanced at him in surprise. Why should Anton pity the daughter of a baron who controlled a ridiculous number of silver mines? Then again, Jaromir himself pitied anyone facing the prospect of marriage to Damek.

Anton looked up at the sky through the overhead ceiling of tree branches, as if trying to gauge the time. Then he turned to peer around the trunk of a tree behind him to see four of their own guards in tan tabards waiting with their horses a little deeper inside the forest.

"I should start back for Sèone," he said. "Both of us shouldn't be away from the castle for another night."

Jaromir didn't speak for a moment. They'd both been worried enough leaving their people for even one night, because in addition to Damek's machinations they had another problem rearing an uncomfortably ugly head back home.

"You want me to stay here?" he asked.

"Yes. I'll leave Corporal Pavel with you, but do what you can to find out what's happening, and . . ." Anton paused as if uncertain what he wanted to say. "Don't let anything happen to the seer. Keep her from harm if you can."

"The seer?"

"Yes, she's . . . Just don't let anything happen to her."

This unexpected order left Jaromir in a state of confusion, but he nodded. "I won't.

As Amelie had gone back out to finish her errands, Céline was alone that afternoon when a soft knock sounded on the door. She tensed, knowing that she was about to earn her silver coins. Going to the door, she opened it.

A small contingent of men on horseback waited a respectful distance away, and a lone young woman stood on the doorstep. She was lovely, with smooth red hair, wearing a dove gray cloak and matching gloves. Women such as her were seldom seen in Shetâna.

However, she appeared to be in her midtwenties, which surprised Céline. Noblemen tended to use their daughters like pawns on a chessboard, and that nearly always meant marrying them off by the age of sixteen.

"I . . . ," she began. "I am the Lady Rhiannon. I was hoping you would see me. I can pay you well."

Céline then realized that the young woman had no idea that she'd already been tipped off about the visit, so she stood aside and held the door open. "Of course. Please come in."

Rhiannon's tense face melted into such relief that Céline couldn't help asking her, "How did you learn of me?"

"A friend told me. Some years ago." But as Rhiannon said this, her tone held an underlying hint of bitterness. She came inside the shop and took off her cloak. Beneath it, she wore a sky blue gown of brushed wool.

Céline had never seen anything so new or so fine.

"You wish me to read your future?" she asked.

The fire crackled, filling the shop with a faint scent of smoke, and Rhiannon looked around at all the pots and jars on the walls. "Yes," she answered. "My father wishes me to marry."

"And you do not?"

"No, it's not . . ." Rhiannon trailed off and then said, "I have concerns. He is above my station."

Above her station? An alarm bell sounded inside Céline's mind before she managed to ask, "Who is the groom?"

Rhiannon turned and looked her straight in the face. "Sub-Prince Damek."

"Prince Damek?" Céline couldn't help gasping. A son of the House of Pählen would not marry the daughter of a minor baron. He would marry only the daughter of another great house.

But her open shock did not offend Rhiannon. Rather, the young woman stepped closer. "You see? I fear he only wants me for my dowry, and if that is the case . . . what will become of me once we are married? Will I be valued? Will I be happy?"

The first wave of guilt washed through Céline, but she remembered the hard look on Kochè's face when he'd said, *Be sure you do. Be sure the girl says yes.*

Was she really about to tell some unfortunate young woman that she'd be happy in a loveless marriage to a tyrant? Céline was gifted at telling people what they needed to hear, and at the same time, she'd tried to convince herself that she gave good, sound advice.

Left to her own devices, she'd have told this Lady Rhiannon to run for the hills.

But . . . the repercussions of doing *that* were not something she wanted to face. Sub-Prince Damek had sent Kochè to make sure she understood that Rhiannon's answer had better be yes.

"Please sit," Céline said. "Did you bring something personal of his?"

Rhiannon seemed eager to begin and held out a leather glove. "He often wears these, and he loaned me one. Will it do?"

"Perfectly."

Both women sat at the table. Céline took the glove in one hand and gently grasped Rhiannon's fingers with the other.

"Just sit for a moment and let me feel your spirit," Céline said. "It will guide me to your future."

"Thank you for doing this."

With a fresh stab of guilt, Céline closed her eyes. She didn't want to do this, so she prolonged her state of falling into a trance. Holding Rhiannon's fingers, she felt a strong energy. Rhiannon was possessed of a resilient spirit. Céline could feel it, as she often felt the spirit of those who came to patronize her shop.

But within seconds, she knew she would need to begin to sway and to pretend small jolts were passing through her body, and then she would be forced to open her eyes and probably ruin the rest of a young woman's life.

Then suddenly . . . without any warning at all, Céline felt a real jolt as if her body was being swept along a tunnel of mist, and she forgot everything but the sensation of speeding along through the mist all around her as it swirled in tones of gray and white.

The mist vanished and an image flashed before her. She saw a large bedroom with chipped stone walls.

A huge four-poster bed stood in the middle, and Rhiannon was sitting beside the bed in a chair, staring into space with a hollow look in her eyes. Just the sight of her filled Céline with alarm, as if Rhiannon had given in to despair.

The door creaked and opened, and Captain Kochè stood on the other side.

Rhiannon looked over at him absently. "Yes? Did you need something?" The tone of her voice suggested that whatever he needed didn't matter.

But he came inside and closed the door, and she stood up in mild alarm. "Captain, you should not be in here. This is my private bedchamber."

He crossed the room quickly and grasped the back of her neck, pulling her up against himself and pressing his mouth down onto hers. She tried to struggle but seemed halfway lost in shock.

Almost as if following a cue in a play, Sub-Prince Damek walked in with three of his own guards. His hair was long and dark. His skin was pale to the point of being white, and he wore a dark blue embroidered tunic.

He stopped cold at the sight of Kochè kissing Rhiannon, and then he said, "Harlot."

Kochè let her go, and she gasped. "No . . . my lord. I did not—"

"I have eyes!" Damek shouted. "You are an adulteress. I've suspected for weeks now." He moved closer. "The risk of placing a bastard as head of a noble house is treason." He turned back to his guards. "She is guilty. Have her strangled. Now."

As Céline watched this, she wanted to scream. She wanted to call for Amelie, but she had no voice. She was just an observer.

Rhiannon's eyes widened, and she tried to dodge around Kochè and make a run for the door. But one of the guards grabbed her easily and forced her to her knees. Another one wrapped a piece of rope around her neck and jerked it tight with both hands. She choked and struggled with a wild expression on her face, but he twisted the rope tighter and cut off her breath.

Damek looked on with a pleased smile.

Céline finally cried out, "No!"

The stone room vanished, and Rhiannon was sitting across the table from her, staring. Céline pulled her hand away and dropped the glove.

"What?" Rhiannon asked in alarm. "What did you see?"

Céline was still so lost, so horrified by what she'd just experienced, that all her defenses were gone. "He has you strangled," she blurted out. "He has you falsely accused of adultery and strangled right there in your bedroom. . . . I think it was only weeks into your marriage."

Rhiannon stood up. "Strangled?"

The women looked at each other, and Céline

tried to force herself into a calmer state. What had just happened? Had she just seen someone's future, like her mother had done? It had all been so real.

But then the actual scene began to make sense. Damek wanted Rhiannon's dowry—enough to marry her. Yet before having children, he'd want a bride from one of the great houses. For that, he'd need to be free.

"You cannot marry him," Céline said.

Rhiannon closed her eyes briefly. "I will have failed my father again."

Céline had no idea what that meant, but she didn't care. Rhiannon had been worried about being trapped in a loveless marriage, and Céline had been fully prepared to send her there, but *this* was something else. "If you marry him, he'll have you murdered."

Rhiannon opened her eyes and nodded. "I will send my answer this afternoon. I will tell him no." Digging into a pouch at her waist, she took out two coins. Feeling sick, Céline wanted to refuse them but knew that would appear strange.

"I suppose I should thank you," Rhiannon said, her voice shaking. "But I have no idea what will become of me now."

At least you'll be alive, Céline thought.

Rhiannon put on her cloak and went to the door. With her back turned, she said, "I do thank you. I suppose I knew. I always knew, or I wouldn't have come here."

She slipped out the door, leaving Céline reeling with her own thoughts.

Two questions rushed around inside her mind. First, was it possible that she might be a true seer? And second, what would Sub-Prince Damek do when he received Rhiannon's answer?

Lieutenant Jaromir had been watching the shop from inside the tree line all day. For hours, the only activity had been the sight of a pretty, short-haired girl dressed like a man—and well armed—leaving via the front door in the late afternoon. No one that young could possibly be a seer, so he assumed the seer was still somewhere inside.

But besides that, nothing had happened.

The rain was beginning to let up, though, and he began to seriously consider going back to his horse to get his cloak. He'd stuffed it in a saddle-bag that morning to try to keep it dry in case he ended up needing to use it as a blanket tonight.

"How long does the prince want us to stay here?" Corporal Pavel asked, standing beside him.

Although Anton's official title was sub-prince, most of his own people had been calling him "the prince" for years.

"Long as it takes," Jaromir answered. "Until we learn something useful."

Pavel grunted, clearly not happy with this assignment. But Jaromir was still glad for his company. Pavel was in his midtwenties, with cropped dark hair and a long, lanky build. To look at him, one would assume he'd be positively ungraceful, but that wasn't the case. He was good in a fight, and Jaromir often requested him for journeys away from Castle Sèone.

"Wait," Pavel said suddenly. "I hear hoofbeats."

A small contingent was coming down the road toward the village. Both Jaromir and Pavel dropped lower into crouched positions as they watched the riders pull up near the apothecary shop. It was a contingent guarding a single lady in a dove gray cloak. She dismounted, and part of her hood fell back, exposing a flash of brilliant red hair.

"That's Lady Rhiannon," Jaromir said. Of course he'd never spoken to her, but he'd seen her at a few state dinners while he'd been playing bodyguard to Anton. Her hair was unmistakable.

"So she's gone to visit that seer?" Pavel asked.

"Looks like."

They waited, but Rhiannon was not inside for long, and when she came out, she rushed for her horse so quickly that she tripped and nearly fell over the hem of her cloak.

"Something's wrong," Jaromir said in frustration. He wasn't going to learn anything hiding in these trees. "Come on."

"What are you going to do?" Pavel asked in alarm.

"Just hurry!"

They ran back for their horses and swung up. Jaromir's gelding was fast and sure-footed, even in the mud, and he pushed hard through the trees, coming out onto the main path a short ways outside the village. Then he slowed, as if he and Pavel were simply on a leisurely journey heading into Shetâna.

Within moments, he could see the contingent coming toward him, with Rhiannon in the lead, and he swallowed hard.

For most of his life, something about him had put women at ease. He wasn't exactly handsome, but he wore a small goatee and kept his light brown hair tied back at the nape of his neck. From his weathered skin to the scars on his hands, most elements of his appearance screamed "hardened soldier." But he could live with that. After all, he was a hardened soldier. He was comfortable inside his own skin, and he liked a good joke and a good story, and women seemed to respond well to his easy nature.

He was about to put that to the test now and fervently hoped Lady Rhiannon would not take offense . . . as he was going to try to speak with her.

When her contingent drew closer, he got a good look at her face and knew his instincts had been right. She was pale and appeared to be fighting tears.

Guiding his horse to the center of the road, he smiled. "My lady. It is good to see you again."

Her own guards pulled up, and one of them gripped the hilt of his sword, but Jaromir held his ground. True to her breeding, in spite of her distress, Rhiannon raised her eyes and seemed to be trying to place him. "Oh, you are Anton's man . . . Lieutenant . . . ?"

"Jaromir," he finished, widening his smile. "And I hear congratulations are in order. When will I be escorting my lord to your wedding?"

She winced, as if about to be sick, and gripped her reins more tightly. "There won't be . . . there will not be a wedding."

He knew he was already pushing his boundaries well past the limit, but she was in a moment of weakness, and he asked quickly, "Because of something that seer told you?"

She jumped slightly in her saddle, as he'd just given away the fact that he'd been spying on her, but he didn't expect a verbal answer. He wanted to see the expression on her face when she heard his question.

And that's how he got his answer. Her eyes widened, and her lips parted. That seer had told her something.

Then she drew herself up, with the demeanor of the lady that she was.

"You may tell your *lord*," she said coldly, "that he need not fear his brother's coffers will be filled with my family's money anytime soon. There will be no wedding."

Jerking her horse, she rode around him and went on her way.

He felt small and cheap to have taken advantage of her like that, but he'd do it all over again if necessary.

Once they were alone on the path, Pavel said, "Well, that's done. We can go home to Sèone now and tell the prince."

Yes, that would be the prudent thing to do, just head back now.

But Anton had told him to keep the seer safe . . . and Damek was about to get some very bad news.

"No," Jaromir said. "I think we'd better stay here a little longer."

Corporal Pavel sighed.

CHAPTER 2

"You did what?" Amelie asked that night over dinner, incredulous. "You told her to refuse him? Are you insane?"

Céline had been trying for hours to figure out a way to tell her sister what she'd done, and then she'd finally just blurted out that Damek was the intended groom and that she'd counseled Rhiannon not to accept him. But how could she explain it all? Amelie had often expressed unhappiness over the fact that Céline brought in most of their money by playing the seer. How would she feel if Céline told her that some of their mother's power may indeed have been passed down the line . . . directly to Céline. Such news might create a barrier between them.

The flames in the hearth cast shadows on the walls, and neither of them had touched the fried lamb chops on the table.

"I had to," Céline said lamely. "I couldn't advise her to marry him. Damek is dangerous."

"Isn't that the point?" Amelie nearly shouted.

"And who do you think he's going to blame now?" Her face was turning red. "After the way our father and mother both died, didn't we make a pact to look out only for ourselves?"

That stung, but Céline couldn't think about their parents. Not tonight. "Just listen," she said, getting up from the table. Hurrying to one of the shelves, she pulled out a sealed letter hidden between two jars. "I've written to Madam Zelinka, and I enclosed the silver coins she gave me. I told her that I counseled Rhiannon to marry Damek with all my best efforts, that I promised her she would be happy, but that she'd already decided against him before arriving, and there was nothing I could do."

Amelie looked at the letter with the coins sealed inside, but her expression was difficult to read.

"We'll pay one of the village boys to carry the letter tomorrow, first thing," Céline rushed on. "Zelinka can't fault me if she thinks I made my best effort, then returned the money when I failed. Damek probably won't be ready to give up on Rhiannon yet. He'll take at least one more run at her, maybe two. By the time he realizes it's a lost cause, he'll have forgotten all about us."

She could see her words calming her sister slowly.

Finally, Amelie nodded. "All right, maybe we can still come out of this alive." She leaned back in her chair. "But even so, that was a lot of money, Céline. Couldn't you have just told her to marry him?"

"No," Céline answered firmly. "I could not."

As things stood, she'd be having nightmares about Damek smiling while he watched one of his own guards strangling Rhiannon on the bedroom floor. But Céline pushed the image from her mind, went back to her chair, and sat down. She'd done her best to help Rhiannon, and life must go on.

"We should eat these chops before they get cold," she said. "Do you want bread?"

Amelie nodded, and her silky black hair swung forward and backward as if it had a life of its own. "And you really think we're safe? That Damek won't try to punish you?"

"Not if Zelinka shows him my letter, and anyway, punishing me won't get him what he wants, so why would he bother? This isn't like someone openly complaining about his lack of leadership. He might even want to keep my involvement hushed up."

As it turned out, however, she was wrong on all counts, and she never even had a chance to send the letter. Instead, just as she reached for the bread, the blade of a long sword smashed through the shutter of their one front window, and then something came flying inside, hitting the floor and rolling.

It was a bottle.

The bottle was filled with oil, and a rag had been stuffed in its mouth.

The rag was on fire.

A second burning bottle followed, but this one

shattered and oil spread across the floor, creating a long, running flame.

"Céline!" Amelie cried, jumping to her feet and grabbing her cloak off a peg, trying to put out the fire.

Céline cast about in panic, looking for anything she might grab to help her sister, but her own cloak and their blankets were all upstairs. No matter how hard Amelie beat at them, the flames kept spreading, and then a third bottle came flying through the window. This one smashed into a set of shelves and set the wall on fire.

"We have to get out!" Céline called over the growing roar. "Run for the back."

Amelie was not one to quit at anything, but the entire room was nearly engulfed, and smoke was filling the air; only a second after Céline's shout, they both bolted for the back door. Amelie stopped long enough to grab her sword. She almost never took off the dagger, so it was still on her hip.

Céline flew out into the night first, running through her beloved herb garden, jumping over the tall lavender and the catnip, with Amelie right on her heels. But even amidst the panic, amidst fleeing for her life, Céline could not help the horror washing through her that their shop, their home, was burning, and it was her fault.

Worse, she couldn't stop remembering the sight of the long sword crashing through their shutter, and she had a terrible feeling this wasn't over yet.

She stopped for a second to make certain Amelie was right behind her.

"Out the back gate and into the trees," Amelie said as quietly as she could and still be heard over the flames. Clearly, she was afraid the worst might yet be to come as well.

Céline ran for all she was worth, flying over more of her herbs and clutching at the handle of the back gate, pulling it open. With the roar of the fire behind her, she could think only of reaching the safety of the trees—and someplace to hide.

But she'd barely passed through when a strong hand grabbed her hair and she was jerked hard until her back was pressed up against someone's chest; he held the point of a knife to her throat.

"Amelie!" she screamed.

She couldn't see her captor, but she could feel his chain armor through her shoulder blades, and in the moonlight, she could clearly see two men in black tabards in front of her. One of them rushed through the gate, and then she heard Amelie's angry cry, followed by the clank of steel.

The other soldier didn't move for a few seconds. But when he turned to look at her, her heart nearly stopped. She could see the protruding belly and greasy hair of Captain Kochè. In the darkness, his eyes glowed as they moved slowly from her hips all the way up to her face.

"Don't kill that one yet," he told the guard holding her. "I want some time with her first."

She went cold and sick to her stomach at the same time, and over the roar of the fire, she could still hear the clanking of steel coming from the garden. Amelie was better when she had the element of surprise, and Céline didn't know how long she'd last in a stand-up fight against a trained soldier.

Céline cursed herself. What a fool she'd been.

But then, just for an instant, Kochè took his eyes off her and turned his head back toward the sound of the fight in the garden, perhaps wondering if he should go help his man end this quickly.

A loud thud sounded in Céline's ears, and she was freed so fast she stumbled forward. A flash of tan blurred past her, and as Kochè whirled to look back, a soldier in a tan tabard swung a club and caught him across the jaw.

Kochè, caught completely unaware, hit the ground like a sack of grain.

Céline glanced backward to see that the man in the black tabard who'd been holding her was now unconscious on the ground, and another soldier in a tan tabard stood there gripping a club. Panting and anxious, he was tall, with cropped dark hair.

But the man who'd clubbed down Kochè looked into the garden and then back at Céline. His sword was still in its sheath. "Where's the seer?" he demanded. "Is she still in that shop?" He had a muscular build and a goatee and wore his long hair tied at the nape of his neck.

Céline wondered if she could even speak, but she somehow got out, "I'm the seer."

He stared at her with a flicker of surprise, and then he ordered. "Pavel, get her on a horse! I'll get the other one."

"Sir, don't kill any of Damek's men," Pavel said back. "Or there'll be hell to pay."

"Go!"

Before Céline had time for a new wave of panic, her feet left the ground, and she found herself being heaved over Pavel's shoulder.

In Jaromir's mind, he'd pictured the seer as an old crone with a crystal ball, not a lovely young woman in a red velvet dress, and he was still trying to get his head around this as he ran through the back gate and almost raised a hand to his face to ward off the heat from the blazing apothecary shop.

But then the sight before him stopped him in his tracks.

The black-haired girl he'd seen coming out of the shop that afternoon was engaged in a desperate fight with one of Captain Kochè's men. Both of them were swinging hard, but most of the time, the girl was managing to duck instead of block, and her speed was astonishing. She had a short sword in one hand and a dagger in the other. But as her opponent was much larger and using a long sword, she couldn't seem to land a slash or a blow, and Jaromir was experienced enough to see she was getting tired.

As yet, they were both so absorbed, neither one had noticed him.

Quickly, he moved forward, and when the soldier finished a downswing—missing the girl—Jaromir swung hard with the club, striking the back of his head from behind. Unfortunately, he didn't go down right away, and the girl rushed in, ramming her dagger into an unarmored spot at the base of his throat. Blood squirted into the air.

"No!" Jaromir cried, too late. "Don't."

She jerked her dagger out, and the soldier fell, probably dead before he hit the ground.

Lost in rage and panic, the girl looked around wildly. "Céline!"

Her eyes stopped on Jaromir, and she rushed, swinging her short sword, which he managed to block with his club. "Stop it! I'm trying to help you."

She didn't even seem to hear him, and everything was happening almost too fast for him to keep up. She started to swing again, but he dodged to the inside, dropped his club, grabbed her wrist, and swung with his fist, catching her across the jaw. As the crack sounded, she collapsed against his arm, and he cursed under his breath.

He hadn't wanted to do that.

Worse, there was a dead soldier in a black tabard lying in the parsley patch.

But he could hear the voices of people from the village shouting out front now as they ran toward the burning shop. Crouching, he slid the girl's sword and dagger back into their sheaths. Then he threw her over his shoulder and rushed for the gate.

Once outside, behind him, all he could hear was the growing roar of the fire.

Céline was so numb she didn't even feel the cold. She was on a horse, sitting in front of the soldier called Pavel, while he held her tightly with one arm and held the reins in his other hand, pushing hard through the wet forest.

She could hear another horse moving behind them in the darkness, but as yet she'd not seen Amelie and had no idea what was happening. She only knew she'd brought the threat of death raining down on them . . . and that their home was gone.

More from instinct than hope, she'd struggled in Pavel's arm a few times, but he hadn't seemed to notice and just kept pushing his horse.

"All right," a deep voice called from behind. "That's far enough."

Pavel pulled up and turned his horse, looking back. "You sure, sir?"

"Yes, for a few minutes at least."

Céline wanted to weep in relief at the sight behind them. The soldier with the goatee was holding Amelie in front of himself on his own horse. She was unconscious but breathing and did not appear to be bleeding from any wounds. Then Céline saw that her hands were bound together by a small rope, and her eyes flew up to the soldier's face.

"A precaution I thought best," he said dryly. "For the rest of this night, you're both going to have to behave and do exactly what I tell you."

Still numb, Céline just stared at him. She had no idea who he was or what he wanted. She only knew that he'd tied Amelie's hands and that she was being held against her will on top of a stranger's horse . . . and that their home was gone.

The soldier's expression softened, almost to pity. "My name is Lieutenant Jaromir," he said, "and I swear I'm trying to help you."

Finding her voice, Céline whispered, "Why would you help us?"

"Because my lord ordered me to."

"And who is your lord?" she managed to ask, more confused than before.

"Sub-Prince Anton of the House of Pählen, Damek's younger brother."

CHAPTER 3

Sometime during the night, Céline's numbness began to wear off, and the cold night air began cutting through her dress.

She realized she had nothing left but the dress on her back, not even her cloak.

But Pavel must have felt her shivering because he stopped his horse long enough to pull his own cloak around them both. "Hold it closed with your hand," he said.

For some reason, this small act of kindness moved her, and feeling warmer, a few moments later, she let herself lean back against him and closed her eyes.

The horse moved on at a steady pace through the wet woods.

The next thing she remembered was the sound of Jaromir's voice saying, "All right, it's light enough. Wake her up."

She opened her eyes again and realized it was past dawn the next morning. Her first thought was of Amelie, and she cast about quickly to see her sister, wide-awake, sporting a dark bruise on her jaw, still sitting in front of Jaromir with her hands tied.

But Amelie's eyes looked like thunder, and Céline feared what she might do to Jaromir once her hands were free. The sisters locked eyes, and Céline tried to offer a short shake of her head, hoping Amelie understood. Although nothing was certain, these two men had at least *behaved* like protectors throughout the night.

But then Céline looked up beyond Amelie and nearly gasped. "Where are we?"

Pavel answered in her ear. "Home. Castle Sèone."

The sight was impressive. A moat the size of a river surrounded an enormous hill, almost a small mountain. Not far from where Céline was sitting, she could see a gatehouse with a closed portcullis at the end of a retractable bridge across the moat. A wall with numerous barbicans stretched from both sides of the gate all the way around the area at the bottom of the hill.

But she could see that on the other side of the gatehouse was a road leading about halfway up the hill to yet another gatehouse set against another stone wall that encircled the hill at that point. At the top of the hill stood a castle.

This place would be difficult to breach.

A creaking sound reached her ears, and then Jaromir said, "They're opening the portcullis. We should head inside now."

"In there?" Céline asked in alarm. The place had seemed impenetrable a second ago; once inside, how would she and Amelie ever get out again?

Without warning, Amelie rammed her head back and caught Jaromir hard on the chin, making him grunt with pain. She whipped one leg over the front of the saddle and tried leaping off, but he caught her and jerked her up against himself.

"Quit!" he ordered, sounding more annoyed than angry, and with her hands tied, she could do little more than struggle.

His chin was bleeding.

"My lord will just want to talk to you," he said. "He only wants to know what his brother is up to. Then you'll be free to go." He paused. "If you have anyplace to go."

Amelie stopped fighting him, but her face was still dark with rage.

"Good," he said, and he jumped off the horse, looking up at her. "I'm going to free your hands so we don't look like we're walking in with prisoners, but you'd better keep still and do what I say." Taking a knife from his belt, he looked at her and said, "You try to kick me or pull that dagger, and you'll regret it."

"She won't," Céline said quickly. "Amelie, tell him you won't."

It was possible Jaromir was telling the truth, that this Prince Anton simply wanted to know what was happening with his brother's impending nuptials, and he'd let them go once they'd told him everything they knew. Céline just hoped that Anton did not have much in common with his brother. His men were certainly nothing like Damek's.

Amelie just glared at her and then held out both hands. Jaromir cut her bonds, but he seemed ready for anything, watching her carefully.

"Amelie!" Céline said again. "We'll just go in and speak to their prince. Then we'll go . . ." She trailed off and the rage in Amelie's eyes faded. Where exactly would they go?

Pavel jumped off from behind her and landed on the ground.

Before Céline knew what was happening, he began leading his horse across the bridge to the first gatehouse, but Jaromir took the lead. Two soldiers in tan tabards standing inside the open portcullis came to attention at the sight of Jaromir.

"Sir," they said politely, almost reverently.

Jaromir just nodded and led Amelie past them, through the gatehouse tunnel and out the other side. Céline began to suspect that Jaromir was more than just a lieutenant in the prince's guard. But she had no time to wonder as they all headed up the road toward the second gatehouse.

As they reached it, the guards up there treated Jaromir with the same respectful deference, and Céline found herself being led through the second gatehouse to the inside of the high stone wall . . .

And there, even Amelie looked around in surprise.

They entered what appeared to be a thriving town built all around the castle above. People and animals and dwellings of all sorts stretched out as far as Céline could see. A smithy and a tannery stood just ahead. Cobblers, weavers, candle makers, bakers, and butchers hawked their wares. But more than that, Céline saw a vast number of what looked like homes to her left, and all the people looked well fed.

"They all live here inside the castle wall?" Amelie asked in shock, gripping the horse's mane. This was the first thing she'd said since last night, and Jaromir glanced up at her. "Of course. It's safest here inside the wall."

This seemed like a given to him, but to Céline it was not. Sub-Prince Damek lived quite differently. From what she understood, only his soldiers, his mistresses, his servants, and a number of minor nobles all currying his favor populated his home.

This Castle Sèone was more like a bustling town.

Jaromir kept moving onward and upward though the people and the shops and dwellings until they reached another bridge, this one shorter and leading across a gap to a huge wooden doorway at the front of the castle. It was unguarded, but Céline noted a pulley system on the other side that would allow the bridge to be raised, thus cutting off access to the castle.

"Here we are," Jaromir said, stopping at the beginning of the bridge and reaching his hand up to Amelie. "Hop down."

She ignored his hand and climbed off by herself. Céline admired her spirit, but when Pavel moved to help her down, Céline let him, and then she grabbed the stirrup to hold herself when her legs nearly gave way. She'd never in her life spent a whole night on the back of a horse. She was going to be sore for days.

"You all right?" Jaromir asked her, frowning.

"I'm fine," she answered, trying to straighten, and walking as quickly as she could to Amelie's side.

They crossed the bridge and entered the walled courtyard of the castle. Jaromir and Pavel were still leading their horses, but a boy appeared from nowhere to take their reins.

"Be generous with the grain," Jaromir told him. "They've both been going all night."

"Yes, sir," the boy answered, leading the horses away.

Then Jaromir and Pavel strode across the courtyard—leaving Céline and Amelie little choice but to follow. They moved through a large entryway inside the castle itself, down a stone passage, and emerged into what appeared to be a great common dining hall. An enormous burning hearth had been built in the wall directly across from the arched entrance. Servants and a few soldiers in tan tabards were milling around, but everyone came to attention when Jaromir walked in. The hall seemed alive with dogs as well, spaniels, bloodhounds, and wolfhounds. A wolfhound with a smattering of white on its muzzle had been lying by the fire, but it scrambled stiffly to its feet and attempted to run to Jaromir.

"Lizzie," he said when the dog reached him. "You're getting too old to run." He stroked her face while she continued to express great joy at his return by licking his hands.

Then he glanced at a servant carrying a tray and said, "Go and tell my lord I'm back, and that I brought the seer with me."

The servant set down the tray and hurried off.

Céline couldn't help wondering what it must be like to just give orders and have everyone run to do her bidding. She didn't think she would particularly like it.

Still petting the dog, Jaromir turned to Pavel. "You're dismissed. Go and find yourself something to eat."

As Pavel headed off, Jaromir walked over to a side table and poured two goblets of wine. The dog followed at his heels. Carrying the goblets back, he held one out to Amelie. "Here."

She didn't touch it.

"Oh, just take it," he said. "You haven't had anything all night. I'll arrange breakfast as soon as I can."

Céline reached out and took the other goblet. She hated depending on him, but it was looking more and more like he was in control here, and her own normal sense of survival was beginning to surface. "Thank you," she said.

He didn't answer her and just raised one eyebrow at Amelie, who finally reached out and took the goblet. "Thank you," she said, but her tone hardly suggested thanks.

To Céline's surprise, Jaromir flashed a grin, as if he found Amelie amusing. That was never a wise move.

But before Amelie could do anything stupid— like toss the wine in his face—the people around them began to bow, and Céline turned to see a young man in a burgundy tunic walking into the hall.

"My lord," Jaromir said, bowing slightly.

But Céline froze as the young man met her gaze. She knew him, and she could see that he remembered her, although his eyes flickered as if he was somewhat taken aback by the sight of her. He hadn't seen her since she was fifteen, and she had changed a bit. So had he. He was still pale, with brown hair tucked behind his ears, but now he had circles under his eyes. Without the circles, he would have been handsome.

He'd been her first patron five years before, and he'd asked her to help him decide if he should marry a girl he loved named Joselyn or a wealthy girl named . . .

Rhiannon.

Céline fought to keep her face still as the past and present collided. Damek and Anton were brothers, and Rhiannon's father had first tried to marry her to Anton, and he had refused in order to marry a penniless girl. What a blow that must have been to Rhiannon. Then her father had tried again five years later to marry her to Damek, and now Rhiannon was refusing the marriage. No wonder she'd been so worried about how her father would react.

Jaromir walked to Prince Anton quickly and leaned over, whispering in his ear. Anton's dark eyes widened as he glanced at the sisters.

"Burned?" he mouthed.

Jaromir kept speaking in his lord's ear, and Céline began growing nervous. What was he saying?

"What do you think this is really all about?" Amelie whispered.

"I'm not sure. But I think we have to play along." She choked once. "I'm so sorry about the shop."

"Why? You didn't burn it down."

But Céline could hear the cold anger in her sister's voice and hoped Amelie could hold herself together just a little longer. Amelie might not be angry with Céline, but she was angry and feeling trapped and needed an outlet.

Prince Anton turned from Jaromir and looked at Céline. "In there," he said, pointing to a small side chamber. "I would speak with you alone." His tone was haughty, as if he never expected anything but obedience.

"No," Amelie said flatly.

"It's all right," Céline said. "Truly."

Before Amelie could argue, Céline walked into the side room and found that she wasn't even nervous when Anton walked in behind her and closed the door.

Prince he might be, but for some reason, even after all she'd been through since last night, she wasn't afraid of him.

"Why did my brother try to kill you?" he asked.

This was not the first question she expected, and she looked at their surroundings. The room was small indeed, with a single table, two chairs, and no window. Several candles glowed from the table.

Anton was looking at her red dress. "Why?" he repeated. "Jaromir says you spoke to Lady Rhiannon? What did you say to her? And why did Madam Zelinka and Captain Kochè visit you that morning?'

So he knew some of the story already. She wondered how much.

Sighing, she realized she'd gain nothing by holding information back. "Madam Zelinka paid me three pieces of silver to read Lady Rhiannon's future and tell her that she'd be happy with your brother and to consent to the wedding. I agreed. I feared what might happen to me and my sister if I did not."

He shook his head, puzzled.

"I found that I could not keep my word . . . after I saw her future," Céline went on.

"What did you see?"

"He had her falsely accused of adultery and then strangled. I could not counsel her to marry him after seeing that."

Anton flinched and sank down into a chair. "Poor Rhiannon," he said softly. "Her father won't understand."

Really, this was not at all what Céline would have expected from Damek's brother. Anton seemed almost softhearted. But he certainly voiced no doubts that his brother was capable of murder.

Then his eyes narrowed, almost in anger. "You're speaking the truth to me? You really are a seer?"

This was shaky ground. The first time she'd spoken to him, she'd had no idea he was the prince of a great house. If he ever suspected that she'd been faking . . .

"Yes," she answered standing straight, "like my mother before me."

The anger in his eyes faded, replaced by what looked like pain. "But you told me to marry Joselyn. You told me I'd be happy."

At that, Céline had to call upon all her skills. Something had gone terribly wrong in his life, something to do with Joselyn, but when he spoke her name, only pain and sorrow rang in his voice, not anger. That suggested Joselyn had not made him miserable, nor had she run off with one of the castle guards.

He was in mourning.

Joselyn was dead. Céline would have staked her life on it.

Standing even straighter, she challenged, "And weren't you happy?"

His expression collapsed inward, and he looked away. "Yes," he answered after a long moment. "I was happy."

Abruptly he stood up and faced her again. All traces of sorrow were gone, and he was the haughty prince once more. Without another word, he turned and strode for the door, jerking it open and walking out.

At a loss, she followed him. Only a few paces into the great hall, he stopped and said over his shoulder, "You are free to go."

Go where? she thought in sudden despair, looking across the hall at Amelie.

But as Anton began walking toward the exit again, Jaromir stepped forward and stopped him. "My lord, I had another thought."

He leaned in and began speaking quietly in the prince's ear. Anton frowned at first, but then he began listening in earnest, and finally he turned to glance back at Céline.

"Very well," he said slowly. "But you'll have to show them everything." He paused, as if somehow the words Jaromir had whispered in his ear were beginning to take hold. "Show them the shop first, and then arrange a room for them in the castle."

He walked out.

What shop?

Jaromir smiled at Amelie, and Céline had a sinking feeling in her stomach. He wanted something more from them.

Amelie kept close to Céline as they both followed Jaromir back through the bustling town, but she almost couldn't believe how much her life had been altered in less than a full day. Their home was gone, and since she'd spent half the night unconscious, she had no idea where they were or how far they'd come.

Besides, after Damek's attempt to kill them—and her stabbing one of his men in the throat—they couldn't go home, even if someone there might take them in.

Worse, that bastard Jaromir kept smiling at her, as if sooner or later she'd find him charming. She wished she could run her dagger through his throat. Just thinking of how he'd knocked her out so easily and then trussed her up made her blood run hot. If he weren't so damn strong, she'd have gotten away from him outside the moat this morning.

But . . . since coming inside the walls, her opinion of the situation itself had altered. Cows, goats, and chickens added to the noise of people doing business here, and everyone seemed warmly dressed and well fed. This was nothing like their drab home village, nor was it like the grand city she'd seen on her one visit to Enêmûsk, which had been sharply divided between the rich and the starving.

She'd never seen anything like this place.

No one seemed afraid of the soldiers, and many people either nodded or called a greeting to Jaromir as if they liked him. He stopped in front of a solid one-story wooden building that had been stained a rich brown, with yellow painted shutters.

"This is it," he said.

Amelie barely glanced at the building and had no idea why he'd pointed it out, but then he opened the door and stepped inside. "Come on."

Once inside, Céline sucked in a sharp breath, but it took Amelie a moment to realize why. They were in the front room of a shop. There was a sturdy counter running half the length of the room, and the walls were lined with shelves of clay pots and jars. A dusty wooden table was littered with pestle and mortar, brass scales, small wooden bowls, and an open box of tinder and flint. A large welcoming hearth comprised the center of the south wall.

"This way," Jaromir said, and he led them behind the counter and through a set of swinging doors into a storage area. "There's a large bedroom through there," he said, pointing to a closed door, "but the best is out here."

He opened the back door of the shop and held it for Céline to see outside. She drew in another sharp breath, and Amelie looked over her shoulder at the remnants of what had once been a thriving herb garden.

Divided into eight large separate beds, the herbs were now either overgrown or dying from lack of care: cumin, fennel, mint, lovage, sage, rue, savory, foxglove, pennyroyal, rosemary, lilies, and roses . . . Amelie lost count. Faded red poppies lined the back fence, and an apple tree graced one corner.

Céline stepped out and knelt down in what was left of the foxglove patch. "Many of these plants are still alive," she said. "This could be brought back to its former state."

Céline had always loved herbs. She loved healing. But this was cruel, letting Céline sit like that in someone else's herb garden when her own was lost.

"Why did you bring us here?" Amelie demanded of Jaromir. "Why would you show this to her?"

"Because the owner's dead," he answered. He was standing so close she could see all the soft hairs of his goatee, and she backed up. "He died last summer," he went on, "and we've had no apothecary since. Ownership reverted to the prince, but the place has been standing empty."

Céline's eyes were sad. "Lieutenant, I hope you don't think we can purchase this place from your prince. We've no money hidden away." She sighed. "At present, this dress is all I have left to my name."

He shook his head. "No, I'm well aware you

lost everything last night. But the prince has given me leave to offer this shop to you if you can solve a problem for us."

Amelie stepped around him. "Offer us the . . . you mean let us live here, as members of his own people?"

Céline stood up, equally shocked.

This was a prosperous community, and the people here had goods to trade and money to spend . . . and daughters who'd be begging Céline to read their futures, daughters with coins in their purses.

And the shop was perfect, far superior to their old home. This was too good to be true. But nothing like this came easily. Amelie crossed her arms over the top of her canvas jacket. "Exactly what problem does he want us to solve?"

Céline listened with rapt attention, but for once, Jaromir didn't look even mildly amused. He'd gone deadly serious.

"I can't just tell you. I have to show you." He paused. "And I warn you, the sight isn't pretty."

That didn't sound good.

But Céline looked around at the large, neglected herb garden and then up at the beautifully stained wooden exterior of the shop. "Show me."

Céline stood amid countless barrels of ale in a cold-storage room below the castle larder, staring down into what had once been the face of a teen-aged girl.

"I warned you," Jaromir said.

The girl's body was lying on a table beside two others in the same state. All three had been desiccated—shriveled down to skin and bones. Two were dressed in fine gowns, but the third wore plain homespun. Their long hair was spread around them. As a healer in a village like Shetâna, Céline had seen her share of dead bodies, but she'd never seen anything like this.

"Was it plague?" Amelie whispered, standing beside her.

"No," Céline answered, and some of the numb feeling from the night before was returning to her hands. She needed time to recover between the fears and horrors and losses she'd experienced, but they just kept coming. The dead girls looked so fragile, so brittle, lying there with their hair spread around.

"How did this happen?" she asked Jaromir.

He, too, just looked down at the bodies, and Céline thought that even for him, a hardened soldier, this sight was difficult. "There was a fourth . . . I mean a first," he said. "She just vanished one night, and her father found her in the stable, hidden beneath some hay. He sent word to me because he did fear plague and thought I should know. We burned the body. Days passed and no one else got sick . . . but I still wondered what could do this to a girl her age. She was only sixteen."

He sounded so frustrated and so bereft that in

spite of everything, Céline wondered what it would be like to live in a community where the people could report a death to the soldiers and someone like Jaromir would take charge, would actually care.

"But then it happened again, about a week later," he went on, "only this time, the girl was found in her own bed." He pointed to the girl in the homespun. "She kissed her parents good night and went to bed, and they found her like this the next morning. At that point, I reported both deaths to my lord, and he ordered me to store the body. We have a royal physician at the castle, Master Feodor, and Prince Anton had him examine the body, but he could tell no more than me. The poor girl was just a dried husk."

Céline stared down at the body and shook her head. "But it happened twice more?"

"Again, about a week apart," he said, "and only at night. They'd just go to bed, and someone would find them like this the next morning. Only these two were from . . . wealthier families, merchants' daughters, but all of them were sixteen or seventeen years old and said to be uncommonly pretty. I managed to keep this hushed up for a while, but rumors are starting to spread."

Then his tone changed, and once again, he sounded like a soldier. "Sub-Prince Damek is known for his penchant toward brutal strength. As cruel as it sounds, his father, Prince Lieven, respects that. Anton is known as a good leader who takes care of his people. His father respects that, too, but I don't know which quality holds the most sway. I only know that if Anton loses his standing as a leader able to protect his people, it could destroy his chances of being named heir."

Céline shook her head. "What is it exactly that you wish me to do?"

"Use your powers," he said. "I can put together a list of young women this age who are thought to be pretty, and you can read their futures. If you can touch upon the next girl to die and see who or what is killing her, you can tell me. I can't fight what I can't see, but you can see for me."

"Read their futures?" Céline asked. "Won't that just set a blaze to more rumors?"

He hesitated. "I have a few ideas where we can make it look like a game . . . entertainment being provided by the prince."

"A game?" Amelic said, glancing at Céline. "That might work."

"You can do this, can't you?" Jaromir asked Céline, unashamed to be voicing doubt. "I mean, I know Prince Anton believes you are a true seer, but he has a trusting heart."

She looked down again at the three dead bodies, but Jaromir wasn't finished.

"Here's the bargain," he said. "If you solve this for us, help me put a stop to it, the shop is yours unconditionally. You can live here and conduct business under Anton's protection for as long as you like."

"And if I fail?"

"Then you're no seer and no use to us here. You can leave and go your own way."

Céline closed her eyes and saw the pretty shop with its yellow shutters and the herb garden out back. She imagined living in a world where the soldiers actually protected people and the prince cared for their welfare. She remembered the flash of ugly reality that had hit her when she'd read Rhiannon. Would it happen again? Had she inherited her mother's gift? And if it didn't happen again, how would she go about finding out whom or what was killing the young women here?

She only knew that she wasn't going to pass this chance by, and if she had to, she'd start looking for the cause herself . . . leaning upon her ability to read people and see the secrets beneath their faces.

"Can you do it?" Amelie asked, and Céline saw that her sister wanted to stay as badly as she did.

Céline looked straight into Jaromir's eyes. "Yes," she said. "I can do it."

CHAPTER 4

Céline hurried down an upstairs passage behind Jaromir, with Amelie following. It seemed that once the bargain had been struck, he was in a rush to get on with other business.

After leading them up from the cellars, where the bodies were stored, to the main floor of the castle, he'd bypassed the great hall and led them into a stairwell inside the north tower and then up three flights before stepping off the landing there and striding at a rapid pace down the chill stone passage, making several turns, until Céline felt hopelessly lost. This entire experience was making her more aware of just how little of the world she'd seen.

"Lieutenant," she breathed, trying to keep up. "Could you slow your pace?"

He stopped. "Oh . . . pardon." But he still looked distracted. Perhaps he wanted to report the bargain they'd made to Prince Anton. "Over there," he said pointing to a door. "That is an empty guest room. I'll have someone finish preparing it for you immediately. Go on in."

"Thank you," Céline answered for lack of anything else to say.

Without waiting to show them inside, he brushed past and headed back the way they'd come.

Amelie raised her thin black eyebrows at Céline. "Well, at least he's gone."

Uncertain if that was a good thing or a bad thing, Céline walked over and opened the door. While the room could hardly be described as "empty," it was certainly unoccupied, and she stepped inside.

Amelie followed her, drawing a loud breath. "Is this for us? He might have made a mistake."

"I don't think he makes many mistakes."

A four-poster mahogany bed waited across the room, covered in a sunflower yellow quilt. Interior shutters over the long window were open, letting misty light filter inside. Céline walked to the window and looked down, realizing they must be on the inner side of the tower, as they had a view of the courtyard below.

She turned back to take in the rest of the room.

A full-length mirror with a pewter frame stood in one corner and a mahogany wardrobe stood in the other. Dainty damask-covered chairs had been placed in front of a dressing table that sported silver brushes and a porcelain washbasin. A three-paneled dressing screen offered privacy for changing clothes. Best of all, the room contained its own small hearth.

Céline had never seen a room like this, much less been invited to sleep in one.

She walked over to the dressing table and noticed a miniature portrait leaning up against the mirror, of a lovely woman with chestnut-colored hair. Something about it made the room feel less their own, so she put it in a drawer. Then she touched one of the silver brushes, hoping for a few moments of peace, deciding she might not be able to handle even a mild event or encounter added to the long line since last night. And now . . . she had four deaths to solve. But she was also tired, sore, and hungry, having neither eaten nor slept, and she was sure Amelie must feel as weary as herself.

"Maybe we should rest?" Amelie said, as if reading her thoughts.

There was little else to do anyway. Even if they wanted to go in search of food, Céline doubted they could find their way back to the great hall. The only solid detail she could remember from the rushed journey up here was the sight of Jaromir's back.

"All right," she said, "but I'll have to sleep in my shift. I don't have anything else to—"

Without a knock sounding, the door burst open, and a stocky, stooped old woman came inside carrying a surprisingly large load of folded blankets and drying towels, with a wooden tray of food balanced on top, complete with a porcelain pitcher.

"Ah, here ye are," she announced. "His lord majesty lieutenant told me you were already in the room, but you never can tell with men. Half the time, they've no idea what they're saying."

At the irreverent reference to Jaromir, Amelie turned with some interest and took in the woman's measure. Céline followed suit, but the aging creature rambled on.

"Blankets I can see a need for, but there's no tub in sight, so what do you need with drying clothes, I ask? Men. Never know what they're about. Now, you both come and have some of this bread and cheese. He said you'd not eaten either. But Helga's here now. She'll feed you."

She appeared to be at least in her seventies, with thick white hair up in a bun that was partially covered by a green kerchief. Her wrinkled face had a dusky tone, and she wore a faded homespun dress that might have once been purple.

For Céline, another mystery of this castle was figuring out exactly who was who in the order of things. For one, Jaromir's rank was that of lieutenant, not even captain, so why did he appear to be second to the prince in the command structure here? This aged woman . . . Helga, appeared to be a lowly servant, but she'd called Jaromir "his lord majesty lieutenant" with enough sarcasm that it could not be missed.

Who was she?

"Don't just stand there, my girls," Helga went

on. "Come and eat." She set the blankets and towels on the bed and brought the tray to the dressing
table. Picking up a generous slice of soft, yellow
cheese and placing it on a piece of white bread,
she held it out to Amelie.

Céline had tasted white bread only a few times
in her life, as it was a delicacy afforded only by the
wealthy. "I . . . ," she tried to say, at a loss. "I . . ."

Amelie appeared equally uncertain, but she
reached over and took the offered food.

"Two seers," Helga murmured, prepping the
next helping of bread and cheese. "Good, good,
just what the castle needs now. From the line of
Fawe." She nodded in approval. "How many
years apart were you born?"

Céline's mouth fell open. What did she mean
by "two seers," and how did she know their family name? Well, Anton knew it, and he must have
told Jaromir. Jaromir must have told the woman.

"Three years," Amelie answered, biting into the
cheese.

Just then, a single knock sounded at the door—
which was still open—and all three women looked
over.

A fourth woman stood in the doorway, and
something about her caused Céline to tense.

She was young, perhaps eighteen, as slim as a
reed and standing stiffly, as if she'd rather be anywhere but in that doorway. The first word that
came to Céline's mind to describe her was "color-
less."

Her hair was that shade of grayish blond, like ditch water, and her eyes matched. She wore a plain gray dress with a high collar—but it was well made from good wool—and she had small gold hoops in her ears. Again, Céline was lost to place her position. She was hardly a lady of the castle, but servants did not normally go around wearing gold earrings. Although her features were small and could even be called attractive, her face was pinched, and her expression was nervous or worried. As she took in the sight of Céline, her eyes flashed clear dislike—possibly hatred.

Céline's gaze moved down to see that she carried two silk gowns in her arms, one a shade of rich amber and a second of midnight blue.

"That would be Inna," Helga announced, gesturing at the young woman with one hand, as if this should give Céline and Amelie an idea of Inna's place or position here.

Inna seemed hesitant to enter the room, and Céline glanced back at Amelie, who had put down her bread and cheese and was watching this new figure in the doorway with caution.

"What are you doing in here?" Inna demanded of Helga. "Get back to the kitchens."

"The maids are shorthanded today," Helga muttered. "His lord majesty lieutenant sent me to help."

"Do not call him that!" Inna ordered. But then the dislike on her face shifted to disgust. "Well, I suppose it is only fitting. Gypsies serving gypsies."

Céline's mouth nearly fell open, and she struggled to keep her expression still. What could they possibly have done to earn this young woman's contempt?

"How might we help you?" she asked.

At the sound of Céline's voice, Inna's attention shifted back.

Taking a breath, as if speaking to Céline was difficult, she said, "Prince Anton has invited a number of the better families to the great hall tonight for a banquet and entertainment. You and your sister are both expected to attend." She walked in brusquely and dropped both gowns on the bed. "The Lady Karina was kind enough to send you decent attire for the evening."

Although the suggestion that they were indecent posed a further insult, Céline could not help asking, "Lady Karina?"

But it was Helga who answered, "The prince's auntie." She nodded to herself again. "Yes, yes, his auntie."

"I don't wear gowns," Amelie said flatly, looking at Inna. "And there's nothing wrong with our clothes."

However, as she spoke, Céline couldn't help a flush of embarrassment. Her red velvet gown had once been her mother's. Though the color had held fairly well through many washings, the seams were worn and the material was thin. Although as yet she'd not seen many other women of the castle, she'd seen no one here wearing such a dress of such bright scarlet—or that fit quite so snugly.

Inna first stared coldly at Amelie and then Céline, looking them up and down. "Well, if you wish to grace Prince Anton's table dressed like a ruffian and a whore, that's none of my business. I was told to deliver the gowns and bid you to be in the great hall at sunset."

At the word "whore," Amelie made a fist and took a step forward, but Céline caught her arm. Inna did not appear to notice either movement as she turned and swept from the room.

Slightly shaken, Céline asked, "Who in the world was that?"

"That would be Inna," Helga said again, still nodding to herself. Then she clucked her tongue against the roof off her mouth. "Gypsies my big toe. Ignorant, rude girl. The Móndyalítko could teach her a thing or two."

Céline turned toward the dressing table. "Who are the Móndyalítko?"

Helga blinked. "You."

"Us?"

The poor old thing really was quite mad.

"Your mother's name was Fawe, was it not?" Helga asked. "And your father took it when they married?" She hung both gowns in the wardrobe and began talking to herself again. "Two? Two from the same mother? Born three years apart? The number three, the magic number, two sides of the same coin, the mind and the body, the future and the past. Yes, yes. It's good they've come now."

Céline glanced Amelie, who shook her head once as if to discourage any further conversation.

"All done," Helga announced, looking around with some satisfaction. "You both eat up, and if you need Helga again, just pull that cord over there, and I'll come straightaway. Don't want any scoldings from his lord majesty lieutenant. Certainly not."

With that, she half walked, half hobbled from the room and closed the door behind herself, leaving Céline and Amelie alone, looking at each other.

"Well . . . ," Amelie said, "the cheese is very good."

Céline's stomach rumbled and so she reached for a piece of the white bread, but even as she did this, her eyes were on the gowns hanging in the wardrobe and her thoughts were on how Helga could possibly have known that their father had agreed to take their mother's surname.

Just past sunset, Céline and Amelie walked into the great dining hall—after stopping twice to ask for directions.

Céline was feeling much more alert after having eaten and then slept for most of the afternoon, but she did not quite feel herself. From the moment Inna had delivered those gowns, Céline knew she was going to try on the one of rich amber and then look at herself in the full-length mirror. So she had.

She was still wearing the gown.

The square neckline was cut just above the tops of her breasts, with a point at each shoulder. The sleeves were narrow, and the slender waistline fit her perfectly. The skirt was full, draping about her in yards of fabric, and the color reflected just a hint of gold. It suited her dark blond hair, making the lighter tones glint under the braziers on the walls. She'd worn her hair loose, with its waves falling down her back.

She knew she had a part to play tonight, and somehow, this gown made her feel more like a seer who'd been hired by the likes of Prince Anton.

Amelie was still dressed her breeches, shirt, and canvas jacket. She wore her dagger but had thankfully left her short sword in their room. However, her breeches and jacket were dusty and covered in horsehair from a long night's ride.

"By the gods," Amelie whispered, looking around.

There were at least a hundred well-dressed people in the dining hall, perhaps more, milling around and visiting with one another with goblets in their hands.

Servants were preparing five long tables while the guests ignored their labors. At the top of the hall, near a dais, stood Prince Anton, surrounded by an assorted entourage. Jaromir and Pavel were just to his right, both having traded their chain armor and tabards for more comfortable-looking tunics. Jaromir's aging wolfhound, Lizzie, kept close to his leg.

Directly to Anton's left was a beautiful woman in her late twenties with ivory skin and chestnut hair piled high on her head. She wore a gown of light green satin that matched her eyes, and there was something vaguely familiar about her.

Next to her stood a slender man with a long, thin mustache, wearing a black silk tunic that would probably cost a peasant's yearly income.

"Oh, there's that woman," Amelie groaned quietly, and right away, Céline knew who she meant.

Inna, in her gray wool dress, hovered behind Anton with an eager, anxious expression, appearing for all practical purposes like a dog waiting for an order from its master, but she was still distinguished as neither a servant nor a lady of the castle.

A brief moment of panic coursed through Céline. Who were all these people? If she was to play a convincing seer here, she needed to know with whom she was dealing.

However, all of this noticing and pondering took place in the few moments when she and Amelie walked into the great dining hall, and then Prince Anton's eyes locked on Céline, drinking in the sight of her gown and moving up to her face and hair.

She fully expected him to look away after a second or two—out of sheer good manners—but he didn't.

Perhaps, for all his apparent breeding, no one

had taught him not to stare. With little idea what to do, she led the way toward him, with Amelie close behind.

They made their way easily through the throngs of guests, and on impulse, Céline made a small bow when they reached Anton. He looked even paler tonight than he had that morning, and the circles under his eyes held a hint of purple. She wondered if he wasn't well.

"My lord," she said.

He was still staring.

Thankfully, or perhaps not, Jaromir broke the moment with a single laugh as he turned to Amelie. "Seven hells," he said, looking at her dusty, horsehair-covered attire. "Couldn't Inna at least have found some boy with a set of clean clothes to loan you?"

Amelie's mouth tightened and her fist clenched, sending Céline into a state of alarm.

"Lieutenant," the beautiful chestnut-haired woman admonished. "Really."

Anton cast Jaromir a dark look and then seemed to find his own manners. He motioned to the woman. "Please allow me to present my aunt, the Lady Karina."

Céline hid her surprise. Karina couldn't be more than six years older than Anton. Up close, she was even more stunning, with a slender face and exotic slanted eyes. With little idea what a proper response might be, Céline simply bowed her head again. "My lady."

Karina smiled. "Anton has told me of your kind offer of . . . assistance. I am so glad for your presence here, and I must say you come as a surprise. I had no idea what to expect. You look lovely in that gown, my dear."

Céline was slightly taken aback, both at the lady's somewhat diplomatic use of the term "assistance" and at her open honesty about not having known what to expect and the kindness in her voice. She seemed sincere.

"Thank you for the gown, my lady," she answered. "I understand you had it sent."

"Well, I had two of them . . ." Lady Karina trailed off helplessly as she looked to Amelie, who stared right back.

"And this is Master Feodor," Anton put in quickly, gesturing to the slender man with the long mustache, "our court physician."

"Charmed," said Master Feodor, but his tone hardly suggested he was charmed in the slightest. Céline disliked him right away. He struck her as . . . oily.

Inna had moved a little closer to Anton's shoulder and was glaring at Céline with poorly disguised hatred. What in the world was wrong with that young woman?

A gong sounded throughout hall, echoing off the stone walls.

"The meal is ready," Anton said, sounding relieved, as if he realized this small, rather mixed party would not be capable of making polite conversation.

But that was also when Céline noticed that Anton had not been the only man staring at her. Pavel's mouth was slightly parted, his eyes fixed on her as well.

She wanted to sigh. This entire event hardly felt like a good start to a murder investigation.

Pavel was just as tall as she remembered, but he was clean and dry now, and the brown tunic he wore suited his tan face and cropped dark hair.

To her surprise, he stepped forward and offered his arm. "This way," he said.

Anton frowned but said nothing.

At a loss, Céline took Pavel's arm. He led her to the second table and then motioned her to a place on the bench. He sat on one side of her, while Amelie sat on the other.

Anton, Jaromir, Lady Karina, and Master Feodor all sat at the first table, up on the dais, with Anton in the center. Inna did not sit down, but rather stood behind Anton, again looking like a dog waiting for an order.

It seemed within moments, the tables were full of seated guests, most of whom were dressed in the gowns or quilted tunics of merchants or minor nobles, but there did seem an unusual number of pretty girls in their late teens among the families.

"Look at all this," Amelie whispered, gesturing to the food on the table, as if impressed in spite of herself.

"That's just the first course," Pavel said, and then

added, "But we don't eat like this every night, only when my lord calls for a banquet."

The spread laid out before them was indeed impressive, with long trenchers of mutton with gravy, roasted potatoes, and greens. Loaves of steaming white bread were abundant. Bowls filled with spring strawberries were being passed around, and everyone's goblet was kept full of red wine.

Without hesitation, Amelie took a gulp of wine and dove right into the mutton. Céline was a bit more stringent, especially with the wine, but she'd hardly taken two bites when a hoard of fresh servants came through the hall's entrance carrying huge trays of roasted turkeys over their heads—two for each table.

"Second course," Pavel said, taking a swallow of wine.

Céline had never seen anything like this. She wondered what Anton would think if he knew that she and Amelie had been considered beyond fortunate back home to have lamb chops and stale coarse-grain bread with tea for supper.

But Amelie was clearly enjoying herself, making small sounds of contentment with each new bite, murmuring about the delicious gravy, while Céline's mind could not help turning to the future. Perhaps Sub-Prince Damek had done them a favor.

If she could succeed here and become not only Castle Sèone's apothecary, but Anton's official "seer," then she and Amelie would never need to worry about scraping pennies together for a few bites of meat again.

Yet in order to make herself a permanent place here, she needed to know more about the people around Anton—who could be trusted and who was dangerous—if she was to understand how she might make herself indispensable.

Plus, she needed as much information as possible if she was to solve these strange deaths.

Watching Pavel take another swallow of wine, she said carefully, "I feel at a disadvantage here, not knowing anyone but you and the lieutenant."

He put his goblet down, eager to engage her in conversation. "Who would you like to meet?"

"Not so much meet"—she smiled—"but who is the Lady Karina to Prince Anton? Is she his father's sister?"

Her gaze moved to the woman sitting beside Anton, his aunt Karina, and even from here, Céline could see she had a comfortable relationship with Anton, close but not smothering.

Pavel appeared pleased to be speaking of Karina and shook his head. "No, she's his mother younger sister, but his mother died when he was just a boy." He paused. "Lady Karina came here about four years ago, after Prince Anton's wife, the Lady Joselyn, died. My lord was in a bad way, and Lady Karina came to help, all the way from the southern territories, down near the Everfen. He depends upon her now. She plans the menus and oversees the kitchen cooks, and she handles the household staff. My lord listens to her counsel in matters of state and the management of the fiefdoms."

Céline took this in quietly. So she'd been right about Joselyn being dead. That was a different kettle of fish best left for another time.

Amelie had been listening to the exchange and breathed out through her nose. "Jaromir seems to like being Anton's main counsel. How did he feel about Lady Karina coming here?"

Pavel paused. "The lieutenant came to serve Prince Anton shortly after the Lady Karina arrived, so he has never known the castle without her."

That pulled Céline's attention sharply. Jaromir had been in charge of the Sèone guard for only four years? He wore that mantle of power in the castle like he'd been born here.

She needed to know more—about everyone surrounding Anton.

Although she felt somewhat guilty using Pavel's obvious attraction in order to get information out of him, now that she'd started, she wasn't about to stop.

"And who is Inna?"

The pleased expression on his face faded, as if she'd spoken a sour word.

Inna was still hovering behind Anton. No wonder she was so thin. She never sat down to eat anything.

Pavel hesitated. "She came here about five years

ago as a girl, with the Lady Joselyn, as Lady Jose-lyn's personal maid. Folks say Lady Joselyn saved her from a bad home, and she was most grateful, maybe too devoted. But now . . . she takes care of my lord."

So Inna *was* some kind of servant who'd been here since she was only thirteen years old or so. Céline mulled over everything Pavel was saying, trying to interpret what he was not saying.

Joselyn had rescued Inna from some kind of un-fortunate situation and trained her to be a lady's maid, creating a possibly unhealthy devotion, which had now been transferred to Anton. She would definitely bear watching.

"What about Master Feodor?" Céline asked.

Pavel's mouth tightened, and he looked even less pleased. Céline noticed that his eyes were an unusual shade of green-blue.

"He . . . ," Pavel began and then stopped for a few seconds. "He's here at the request of my lord's father, Prince Lieven. They say . . ."

He trailed off again, and Céline wondered who "they" might be.

"They say my lord is not well," Pavel continued, lowering his voice. "And sometimes I think he fan-cies himself to be not well. But Master Feodor makes him *believe* he's not well, makes him rest too much and take draughts and bleeds him and the gods know what else." His voice dropped even lower. "But my lord's color has only gotten worse. I don't think Master Feodor knows what he's doing."

This got Céline's full attention, and she would have liked to know what was in the "draughts" Feodor was feeding Anton. She knew from experience that people tended to view physicians or healers with far too much blind trust, and she hoped Feodor was not some charlatan trying to make himself a place here at Anton's court by seeming indispensable.

Would that make him any worse than her?

She shook her head. Of course it would. She'd never give anyone medicine or advice unless it was in their best interests . . . Well, almost never.

But Pavel hadn't finished. "I'd not serve Sub-Prince Damek, not as one of his own men, I mean, but he is a harder man than my lord, and I think the grand prince of the land needs to be a hard man."

Something about this statement tickled the back of Céline's mind, though she wasn't sure why.

More servants bustled in and berry pies were being served just as the music started. She looked up toward the first table to see musicians with instruments behind the dais: a flute, a lute, and a harp. The tune was lively, and people began getting up from the tables, moving to the more open area of the hall in order to dance.

Several soldiers were gathering at an empty space at the end of one table, and a deck of cards came out. Amelie's eyes lit up. "Céline, do you mind if I—"

"Go," Céline said, glad her sister might find

some diversion here, as there wasn't much else for her to do.

But the moment Amelie was gone, Pavel stood up and held out his hand. "Will you dance?"

Startled, Céline fell back on honesty. "I don't know how."

Dancing was hardly a common pastime back in Shetâna. The people there were more interested in surviving either winter or the sporadic visits from Damek's soldiers.

"It's easy," he said. "I'll show you."

How could she refuse without insulting him? Still uncertain, she took his hand and let him lead.

As they approached the people dancing, she saw that everyone was swiftly sidestepping in a large circle while holding hands. Two dancers parted to let her and Pavel join, and a few seconds later, she found herself smiling.

The sensation was enjoyable . . . foreign but enjoyable.

Within moments, the steps changed, and she saw that all the women were supposed to skip to the man directly across the circle. Without hesitation, she skipped across, and a burly man with a fatherly face grabbed her hands and swung her around. The yards of fabric in the skirt of her gown swirled, and the strange sensation passing through her seemed to grow. She felt light. Happy.

Then she saw that she was supposed to continue moving and skip back to Pavel. As she did, he grasped one of her hands firmly and put his other hand on the small of her back, pulling her close. He was so tall she found herself staring at his left collarbone.

As suddenly as it had arrived, the happiness vanished, replaced by alarm. She continued the swift movement of the steps, letting him lead, but she was too aware of the strength in his hands and that she couldn't have pulled away from him had she wanted to.

She didn't like this and wondered how she'd let him get such a firm hold. She and Amelie both knew better.

Fighting for calm, she tried telling herself not to be such a coward. He was nothing like Damek's soldiers. Had she not spent the previous night sleeping in his arms on the back of a horse? But the music grew faster, and he swung her around, still gripping tightly with both his hands. The world began to spin, and she felt dizzy.

"Pavel," she tried to say.

Thankfully, with one last, sharp note, the song finished and the music stopped. As Pavel slowed, she attempted to disengage herself from his grip, but then she froze as her eyes landed on the pale, tense face of someone standing just beside the dance floor.

It was Anton.

His jaw twitched, and he walked directly to them. Pavel spotted him at the last second and came to attention.

"Corporal," Anton said coldly, "this lady is here

to assist Lieutenant Jaromir, *not* to dance with
you."

Pavel's face blanched, and he stepped backward. "Pardon, my lord," he stammered.

In spite of her recent distress, Céline found herself tempted to spit a retort at Anton—that such a
reprimand was hardly necessary. But in truth, she
was here for a reason, and it was not to pass the
evening dancing with soldiers in her fine borrowed gown.

"Thank you for the dance, Corporal," she told
Pavel. "As I mentioned to you earlier, such an act
will help me fit among the guests better."

Pavel blinked in surprise and then nodded. "It
was my honor."

Then he was gone, and Céline stood alone with
Anton, who was observing her with caution, as if
trying to figure her out.

Well, she might as well get started. "How do
you want to do this?"

But he had no need to answer, as she noticed
that two cushioned chairs had been set up in one
corner of the hall, near the enormous hearth.

Lady Karina used the moment in between
songs to stand up from the table and smile.

The hall fell silent as everyone looked up at her.

"Good friends," she said, as if born to address
halls filled with people, "Prince Anton has arranged for a special entertainment this evening."

Céline glanced at Jaromir up on the dais, but he
was listening to Karina politely.

"He has engaged a seer to tell the futures of our daughters," she went on, still smiling. "They might ask her anything they wish . . . of a future betrothed, perhaps, and she will answer."

This last was said almost as a joke, and so the people in the hall tittered with good humor, but for the first time since walking into the hall before dinner, Céline sensed a strain—almost a fear— beneath the pleasant expressions of those around her. These people weren't fools, and four of their young women were dead, and now Anton had engaged a seer to read the futures of unmarried girls.

"Who would like to go first?" Karina asked, pitching her tone to suggest the first girl would have a great honor.

The fathers and mothers in the hall all seemed to glance at one another at once.

Sensing the unease growing stronger, Céline walked through the crowd with her head high, over to one of the cushioned chairs by the fire.

She sat with her back straight.

A plump girl of about fifteen, wearing a pink gown, stood nearby, watching her.

Céline held out one hand. This much she knew. She knew how to play the part.

"Come and sit, my dear. Would you like to know something about the man you will marry?"

The girl flashed a smile and nodded. "Yes."

Céline smiled back.

And so it began.

*   *   *

While watching Céline, Jaromir kept his face as polite and impassive as possible. He'd certainly not missed seeing Anton's unexpected and abrupt dismissal of Pavel. What was that about?

But at present, he had his own dilemmas to deal with. He was a good deal more worried about the deaths of these young women—and all the possible repercussions—than he was willing to let on.

Various concerns swirled in his mind. His own success and position depended on Anton's success, but not all his motivation was mercenary. He'd cared about few individuals in his life to date, but he did care about Anton. He cared very much. Anton saw him as he'd always wanted to be seen: trustworthy and capable. Jaromir would do anything to maintain Anton's high opinion— and to protect him.

More important, Jaromir cared about this country, and he wanted the petty princes constantly in the throes of civil war, constantly at each other's throats, to be reined in. If Anton became grand prince, he would fight to establish peace, fight for the welfare of the people.

Why couldn't Prince Lieven see this? The House of Pählen and the people of Droevinka would be far better served by a leader like Anton than by a self-serving warlord like Damek.

Jaromir was determined to help prove Anton a superior prince, and that meant showing that the people of Castle Sèone were safe—were protected. There could be no rumors of pretty young girls murdered in their beds. He hated to even think of the ramifications of that in regard to Anton's reputation. Anton could lose any standing he'd gained in his father's eyes for promoting a *different* method of governing from his brother.

Could Céline help them?

Watching her, too far away to hear her words, he could see how easily she'd captured the plump girl's fascination and eagerness. Holding the girl's hand, Céline closed her eyes and whispered in the girl's ear as if the room was empty and no one existed but them. Jaromir wondered if that unto itself was not part of the draw of Céline's gift. Few people ever experienced having the complete attention of someone else. Céline was giving the girl her undivided attention.

Who wouldn't enjoy that?

A few moments later, the girl rose, smiling and nodding, and Jaromir knew that she was not the next victim of this unseen murderer. He had no idea what Céline had told her, but it didn't matter. Many people in the hall had been surreptitiously watching, and when the "reading" ended, the girl looked so happy that Baron Tarook's youngest daughter hurried over to take her place . . . and Céline began again.

Jaromir wanted to shake his head at these girls' eagerness to have their fortunes told. The young never think evil will befall them, and they simply wish to know more about their bright futures.

Looking down, he saw that Lizzie was still at

his side. She'd been in his life longer than anyone he knew, since she was a puppy. He'd once taken her everywhere he traveled, but now her traveling days were over, and her favorite place was by the great hearth in this hall.

"Go lie down, girl," he ordered, pointing toward the fire.

She obeyed instantly and made her way over.

He stood there watching Céline read through two more girls, both of whom left nodding and smiling when their turn was finished. Then he did wonder what she was telling them, and he hoped fervently that she could do what she claimed. If not, he would remain in the dark.

But in addition to all these worries and doubts swirling in his head, he also found himself unsettled by the effect Amelie had upon him. Why did he continue to tease her, to antagonize her? Worse, why was he worried about his penchant for teasing and antagonizing her? She could not be further from the type of woman who attracted him.

His current mistress, Bridgette, was now crossing the hall to visit with Lady Karina, who had risen from the table to mingle with guests. Bridgette was a young widow with red-gold hair and a long, graceful neck, and she was a favorite of Lady Karina's. Her dead husband had been a wealthy silk merchant, but she'd not hesitated to fill Jaromir's bed when he expressed interest. Few women at Castle Sèone would hesitate, and he wasn't vain enough to attribute this to his charm or muscular build—or his goatee.

Just like men, women enjoyed power, and at present, he held power here.

So why could he not keep from looking in Amelie's direction? At thirty-one, he was too old for her . . . or maybe she was too young for him. She was coarse and bad tempered and had grown up in a filthy village ruled by Sub-Prince Damek.

He chose only women who were personally ambitious, who had no interest in sowing a close relationship, but rather who followed his instructions in order to keep him pleased, in order to pursue their own advancement at court though him. He never allowed a mistress to come to his rooms unless he sent a summons first. He insisted on full control over when they saw each other.

Something told him Amelie was not a woman who would ever submit to such an arrangement. She probably couldn't care less about a social position at court, and if she ever did become involved with a man, it would be for love, and she'd expect to be loved in return. She wouldn't sit around and wait for him to summon her, nor indeed would she agree to live apart.

He had no place in his life for such a woman. His task was to protect Anton and the people of Castle Sèone.

And yet . . . the music was lively, and standing there, watching her playing cards with some of his men, he was struck by an overwhelming urge to dance with her, to see her smile at him while he held her tightly and whirled her around the floor, her short black hair flying and her lavender eyes focused on him.

He shook his head hard to clear it.

She was dressed in dusty breeches covered in horsehair. The idea of him being seen dancing with her was ridiculous. He'd be a laughingstock.

And yet . . . he found himself moving toward her table. He couldn't seem to stop.

She saw him coming but only glanced at him before winning a hand while the soldiers groaned or growled.

"Not again," one of them said.

"Pay up, boys," she answered.

There was a small pile of coins in front of her, and he wondered what she'd used for her initial bet to enter the game. She must have had a few pennies stored away in her clothes.

He knew full well that he should be watching Céline, but he told himself that one dance wouldn't distract him.

As the hand of cards had just finished, and the musicians were beginning a new song, he decided this would be a good time to interrupt. When he stepped up to the table, his men jumped to attention, but he waved them back onto the bench and held out his hand to Amelie.

"Will you dance?"

She looked briefly at a line of barrels along the north wall and then picked up the deck of cards.

"There's not enough wine in this entire castle to get me to dance with you."

Several of his men started choking, and he flashed them a look of anger, wondering if they were smothering laughter.

The choking sounds ceased.

Even back when he'd been a lowly sword for hire, no woman had ever spoken to him like that, and he had no idea how to respond, how to save face in front of his men.

Realizing any response at all would probably just result in another insult on her part, he started to turn away, but then Amelie dropped the deck and called out, "Céline!"

Following her line of sight across the hall toward the hearth, he saw Céline tightly gripping a young woman's hand. Céline's eyes were wide open, staring at nothing. She was completely silent, and she'd gone pale.

Jaromir began to run.

After five years of practice, Céline was quite skilled at telling people exactly what they wanted to hear without providing too much detail. Her descriptions of future husbands or wives often *sounded* detailed but in truth could be applied to a broad number of people.

The real trick was gleaning proper bits of information from the one being read and then guessing correctly about hopes, dreams, or needs. Céline had a gift for this.

Most sixteen- or seventeen-year-old girls were easy targets and only too happy to answer her initial questions.

However, when she'd sat down tonight, she could not help feeling trepidation, almost dread. What would she see? Would the mists rush around her again as she witnessed the death of some innocent young woman?

But upon taking the hand of the plump girl in the pink gown, she'd felt nothing out of the ordinary, and within a few seconds, she'd gone into her usual act. It was second nature.

However, what she was doing tonight was different from when someone had a specific question—when they brought her a personal object or possession to "assist" in her reading. This was more general and therefore easier.

"What kind of man do your parents have in mind for you?" she asked.

"Someone of good family, with a dependable income."

Typical.

"And what do you have in mind for yourself?"

The girl blushed. "Well, someone not too much older than me . . . tall, with a pleasing face."

Also typical.

Céline closed her eyes, pretended to feel the jolt, and then began weaving stories of the girl's future.

"He'll come from a town inside the provinces ruled by the House of Pählen . . . ah, he does have a pleasing face. He is the son of a prosperous merchant . . . but I cannot see his name."

She went on with more general descriptions. What she told the girl would most likely be the truth. This girl didn't seem to be one of the nobles here tonight, so her parents would probably choose a merchant's son within this province of Droevinka.

But once Céline finished, the girl was positively glowing.

After that, the other young women in the hall seemed eager for Céline's services, and she no longer had to encourage anyone to sit down. They were practically lining up.

She read two more girls, leaving them with hopeful visions of their lives to come, and then she looked up to see a pretty girl about sixteen years old watching with interest. Her chocolate brown hair was so long it hung down past her hips, and she wore a gown of forest green.

The girl smiled. "I'm Sybil," she said. "It was kind of Anton to arrange this. I'm bored to death with dancing, and he never thinks of providing other entertainment."

The fact that she'd just called her prince by his first name meant she was probably from a noble family—of high rank. But she also might be somewhat sheltered, as she seemed to have no knowledge of any other reason for why Céline might have been hired.

Céline nodded politely. "Come and sit."

Sybil moved to join her, holding out her hand with complete trust. "I'm already betrothed, but I haven't met him yet. My parents arranged it." She didn't look entirely happy about the situation. "You're not married, are you?"

The question startled Céline. It was an unusual question. "No."

Sybil sighed. "I wish I could be a seer like you. Earn my own living."

Céline was moved by her words and suddenly wished she could tell the girl a different future from the one probably laid out for her.

She grasped Sybil's hand. "Well, let me try to look ahead. I'll tell you what I see."

"Thank you."

Something about Sybil pulled at Céline. She was so trusting and yet clearly wanted more out of her life than to marry the man her parents had arranged for her. Closing her eyes, Céline let her thoughts roll, searching for something else she could tell this girl, something that might give her hope.

And that's when the first jolt hit.

As a second one hit, Céline felt herself being swept along a tunnel of mist again, and she lost all sensation of anything besides speeding along through the mists swirling all around her in tones of gray and white.

The mist vanished, and an image flashed before her.

She saw a room with gray stone walls. She was

standing beside a bed, but she could see only one side of it.

Sybil lay there sound asleep. Her chocolate brown hair was spread out like a curtain across the pillow, and she was covered in a yellow-and-red-checked quilt. She looked so peaceful, so deep in slumber.

Céline began to relax at the sight.

Then . . . two slender hands wearing long black gloves came in from the side of the image, reaching down toward Sybil.

On instinct, Céline cried, "No!" and she tried to knock the hands away. But she wasn't really there. She was only an observer, and she could do nothing. The black gloves continued to move. One of them settled on the side of Sybil's face and the other on her throat.

Céline wanted to scream, to fight, to stop this, but she was locked inside the vision, just watching.

The hands didn't grip down or do anything besides touch Sybil's face and throat, but the flesh on Sybil's cheek began to move, rippling of its own accord. It began to shrivel.

"No," Céline choked.

Beneath the black-gloved hands, Sybil's face continued to shrivel, to wither, sinking in upon itself until her face was nothing more than a dried husk. Inside the vision, the black gloves pressed harder on her cheek and throat. It went on and on as Sybil's body seemed to shrink beneath the quilt.

Céline could feel herself choking in horror.

"Stop it!" someone ordered. "Come out!"

Strong hands had ahold of her arms, shaking her once, and the small room vanished. She found herself back in the great hall, staring up into Lieutenant Jaromir's alarmed eyes.

"Let go of her," someone else said, someone familiar, and Céline saw Amelie standing behind Jaromir.

"Amelie," Céline whispered.

Anton was striding toward them, and half the hall was staring. The music had stopped. Perhaps realizing how this must look, Jaromir let go of her.

"Pardon," he said.

Reality was rushing back to Céline as she tried to recover from the nightmare she'd just witnessed. Sybil was on her feet, frightened. "What did you see?"

Céline fought for control. The poor girl. The event in the vision had to be changed. Sybil had to be protected.

"Oh, I do beg your forgiveness," Céline heard herself saying, astonished at her own self-control. Somehow, she smiled reassuringly at Sybil. "Sometimes my sightline into the future becomes crossed, and I see my own." She moved closer to Sybil. "I saw something unpleasant, but it had nothing to do with you. Please forgive me. I think I sought too many visions, too quickly, in a short span of time. Perhaps I might rest?"

Sybil's fear vanished, replaced by concern. "You

saw something unpleasant for yourself? I'm sorry."

She was kind.

"It's all right," Céline answered, still smiling but casting her gaze toward the small chamber at the bottom of the hall where she'd spoken to Anton that morning. She could feel his eyes upon her. "I just need to rest."

With that, she began walking, head still high, toward the small chamber, hearing two sets of footsteps behind her.

"I will go and attend to the seer myself," Anton announced. "I fear she has overtaxed herself. My Lady Karina, have the musicians play on." A third set of footsteps sounded.

The walk felt long, but Céline finally reached the chamber, made her way inside, and collapsed in a chair. Jaromir, Amelie, and Anton followed her in. She didn't see which one closed the door.

"What?" Jaromir demanded instantly. "You tell me what in the seven hells just happened out there."

"She's not your dog or one of your soldiers," Amelie told him. "Don't give her orders!"

They both sounded far away.

"Both of you stop!" Anton ordered. His voice softened, but the circles under his eyes looked black. "Céline, what did you see?"

"It's her," Céline whispered. "Sybil. She's next."

"What does that mean?" Jaromir asked.

"She was asleep, in a bed," Céline went on, almost feeling as if someone else spoke. "Gloved hands . . . like a woman's or a slender man's, came in from one side and touched her. She just shriveled away, like those girls on the table in the cellar. I couldn't do anything to stop it. I just had to watch."

"Who?" Anton demanded, sounding far less soft now. "Who did this?"

"I don't know. I only saw the gloved hands . . . black gloves."

"You must have seen more than that!" Jaromir insisted.

"Leave her alone," Amelie said, but she looked puzzled, as if wondering about Céline's game here.

"No, I didn't," Céline said quietly. "I only saw the gloves, and I saw her die."

Jaromir sighed and turned to Anton. "What do you want to do?"

Anton stared at the wall for a few moments and then said, "Tell her parents the truth and place her under guard." His eyes locked with Jaromir's. "I'll talk to her father. You get a room set up."

"Yes, my lord."

CHAPTER 5

Less than hour later, Amelie found herself inside a guest room, watching as Céline inspected the bed—which looked like a simple bed with a plain white comforter. The room sported no hearth or window, and it felt overly small with Anton, Jaromir, Sybil, and both Sybil's parents also crowded inside.

Inna was hovering in the doorway, her mouth set tightly.

"All right," Céline said, turning from the bed. "I think this will be safe."

"Why do I have to stay in here?" Sybil asked, sounding frightened. "Why can't I go back to our own apartments?"

"Because you are safer here," Anton answered. "Lieutenant Jaromir will stand guard."

Amelie had no idea what the game was, so she kept her mouth shut. Apparently, Sybil's father was Anton's second cousin, a middle-aged minor noble named Lord Cirren. The family had apartments inside the castle, and Cirren held a place on

Anton's council. The man's mouth was set tighter than Inna's, suggesting he didn't approve of this entire situation, and his wife, Lady Edith, wouldn't stop wringing her hands.

Earlier, Anton's words about notifying the girl's parents and placing her under guard had sounded sensible: clean and simple.

Reality was proving a tad messier.

"You told me your vision was about yourself," Sybil accused Céline, "not about me."

"I know," Céline answered, standing straight. "I didn't wish to alarm you until I'd spoken with Prince Anton and heard his decision in the matter."

Amelie held her tongue. What was Céline up to? Yes, she was making herself appear useful, but it seemed dangerous to actually pick out a girl and claim she would be the next victim. What would happen if someone else were killed? Céline would look a complete charlatan.

"This is absurd," Lord Cirren sputtered. "Anton, I can keep my own daughter protected."

Anton shook his head. "No. She's safer with Jaromir."

"But she can't stay in here alone," Lady Edith insisted, coughing twice as she spoke, "with soldiers at her door, on the word of some . . . forgive me, my prince, of some gypsy seer you hired." She paused, looking at her daughter, and Amelie could see love in the woman's eyes. "I will sleep in here with her." She coughed again, but Sybil's expression melted in relief at the prospect of her mother remaining.

"No," Anton said. "You need to be in your own rooms, where it's warmer."

Was Lady Edith not well?

Anton wasn't finished. He looked to the doorway. "But I agree that Sybil shouldn't be left alone. Inna, will you sleep here with her?"

Inna's eyes flashed hatred at Céline, and she opened her mouth as if to spit out her opinion of these proceedings, but then she looked to Anton. "Of course, my lord."

"Everyone else to bed, then," Anton said. He was pale and exhausted. "Jaromir, you're in charge."

Céline was still standing by the bed, staring at its white cover, and Amelie moved to her. "Let's go."

Céline relented, allowing herself to be led out into the passage. Amelie was finally getting her bearings here and knew their own room was just down the corridor. As they left, Jaromir began giving orders as the room behind them was being secured.

However, once they'd stepped inside their room, Amelie closed the door and looked at the four-poster bed with its extra blankets and at the dressing table with its fancy damask covered chairs. A freshly lit fire burned in the hearth, and she took a moment to ponder how all this had come to be. So much had happened in such a short span of time.

Someone—probably Helga—had closed the

shutters over their single long window. The fire in the hearth provided yellow light. Helga had probably built the fire, too.

Céline walked to the bed and sank down, her expression bleak.

"What . . . ," Amelie began, not certain how to word this. "What exactly is the plan here? What are we going to do if another girl is murdered in the next few days? How are we going to find the killer before someone calls you a fake?"

Céline looked at the floor. "Amelie, I'm tired. Could we discuss this in the morning?"

Frustrated, Amelie took in her sister's weary face. "All right, but I can't help if I don't know the plan. You need to tell me what you're thinking."

She took off her breeches and boots, leaving on her long, faded blue shirt—which reached halfway to her knees. Then she unlaced Céline's borrowed gown, and Céline let the dress fall to the floor, so that she wore only her comfortable cotton shift. They both crawled under the piled covers, and soon the bed felt warm.

Neither spoke for a while, and then Céline said, "Lady Edith needs a rose petal syrup for her cough. If I had access to the herb garden and the apothecary's equipment, I could make her a vial."

"You really want that shop, don't you?" Amelie whispered.

"Yes, I do."

Céline said no more.

Still troubled, unaccustomed to feeling shut out

of her sister's plans, Amelie burrowed deeper into the covers, listening to Céline's soft breathing.

But sleep would not come to Amelie. Her body was too tired and her mind was too busy, which was never a good combination. Doubt often came to her in the night, and she couldn't help wondering what she and Céline would do, where they would go, if they failed here.

Time crept by, and she still couldn't sleep. She just lay there, thinking and worrying.

It must have been halfway to dawn when the sound of a loud cry down the passage made her shoot up from the covers, looking toward the door. The cry was followed by shouting and pounding.

"Céline," she said, but her sister was already awake.

Diving from the bed, Amelie grabbed her breeches. She was pulling them on while Céline ran out door wearing nothing but her white cotton shift.

"Céline!"

Buttoning her breeches, Amelie ran, and they both came upon the sight of Jaromir unlocking the door of the room where he'd placed Sybil. He had two soldiers standing guard with him, but Amelie didn't recognize either one. The pounding from inside continued.

As he got the door unlocked and shoved it open, Inna came rushing out, gasping for breath. "She's dead! Dead!"

Jaromir ran past her into the room, and Amelie followed with Céline at her heels.

There, lying in the bed, was the dried husk of what had been Sybil. Her lovely brown hair was spread on the pillow, but her face was nothing more than shriveled skin adhered to bones.

"Oh, no," Amelie whispered.

None of this made sense. Céline walked to the bed and looked down at a yellow-and-red-checked quilt.

"Inna!" she nearly shouted. "Where did this come from?"

Amelie blinked. The quilt? Why would Céline care about that?

"What is it?" Jaromir asked, his eyes moving to the quilt.

"This wasn't here before," Céline said. "Where did it come from?" She sounded brittle.

One of the other soldiers dragged Inna back inside, and she simply pointed at a chest across the room. "We were cold. I took it out."

Céline closed her eyes. "It wasn't here before," she whispered.

Jaromir turned on Inna, his expression dark, almost threatening. "What happened? No one could have entered this room."

Frightened, dressed only in her shift, with strands of her grayish blond hair sticking to her face, Inna raised a hand, as if in defense. "I don't know. I was asleep and then I just . . . I felt something was wrong, and I turned up the lamp and I . . . saw her!"

"The door was locked," Jaromir answered coldly, "and there is no window. You were the only one here."

"I was asleep!" Inna cried. "I heard nothing."

"Look for a pair of gloves," Céline said quietly. "A pair of long black gloves."

Perhaps realizing he'd get nothing sensible out of Inna, Jaromir called in another of his men, and they began searching the room.

The next half hour or so followed with a mix of confusion and activity. Céline stood at the end of the bed, staring down at the quilt, while the room was searched—revealing no black gloves. Soon, Master Feodor arrived. Amelie was surprised to see him still dressed in his silk tunic from dinner. He also seemed vaguely displeased to see Céline there, nothing overt, just a flicker of distaste passing across his features when he walked in.

"Well?" Jaromir asked, but the question was unnecessary.

Feodor conducted a brief examination of Sybil's body and sighed. "Yes. Just like the others."

"Someone should wake Anton," Céline said, her first words in quite a while.

"No!" Inna cried.

Feodor glanced at her and said, "Inna's right. My lord needs his sleep and should not be disturbed. This can wait until morning."

Jaromir put a hand to his mouth, as if thinking, and then he nodded. "I'll go inform the girl's parents myself."

"If not Anton, then the Lady Karina should be the one to tell them," Céline whispered. "It should be a member of the royal family." She looked up at Jaromir. "You promised to . . . protect Sybil. This isn't your fault, but the girl's parents should be told by Anton or Karina."

A muscle in his jaw twitched, and Amelie realized Céline was right.

Jaromir nodded once, tightly. "I'll wake her."

A guard in the doorway approached hesitantly. "Sir, what should be done with the body?"

If possible, Jaromir stiffened further. "Put it in the cellar with the others."

Deciding that enough of this was enough, Amelie steered Céline toward the door.

Out in the passage, she asked, "How did you know?"

"I couldn't change it," Céline whispered. "I should have changed it. She was kind. She wanted more out of life than to marry a stranger her parents picked out."

She fell silent again, and Amelie was nearly overwhelmed by a wish that they could go back to the day before, and Céline could tell Rhiannon to marry Damek, and the Lavender and Thyme would not be burned, and she and Céline had never come here.

*   *   *

An hour past sunrise, Jaromir woke up naked in his bed with Bridgette sleeping on his chest.

Looking down at her closed eyes and her breasts as they rose and fell, he was almost ashamed of having called her to him in the night, but after the painful task of telling Lady Karina the news of Sybil's death—and then giving her the task of informing Sybil's parents—he could not face the thought of going to bed alone, of lying there thinking on all he'd seen in that small, windowless room.

So he'd sought oblivion in Bridgette's body, using her as a method of release.

It hadn't helped.

She was lovely, with creamy skin and even features. But they had little in common and even less to say to each other. He couldn't tell her what he'd been through—and she certainly wouldn't be interested in hearing it.

Now he wished he hadn't called her here.

Carefully, trying not to wake her, he slipped out from under her head and crawled from under the covers. The floor was cold on his bare feet, and he put on his discarded clothing from the night before, as if he couldn't get out of his own room fast enough.

He wanted to be alone with his thoughts, with his own self-recrimination.

Once out in the passage, he shut the door behind himself and took a long breath. He'd failed Anton last night. He had failed to save Sybil, and

in doing so, he'd made Anton look like an ineffectual leader—someone who could not protect
his own people.

Jaromir would do anything for Anton. No one
could possibly understand what he owed
Anton . . . no one.

Jaromir did not like to view himself as a man
who ever needed or wanted to be saved.

But Anton had saved him.

Standing there in the passage alone, outside his
room, nearly shaking from a mix of helplessness
and unwanted guilt, he couldn't help his mind
from slipping back to a place he'd much rather
have forgotten . . .

CHAPTER 6

FOUR YEARS IN THE PAST

Jaromir stood at attention in the great hall of Prince Lieven. He wore the deep brown tabard of Lieven's castle guard, but the tabard was a lie. He wasn't one of the prince's soldiers. He was just a hired sword, engaged for a week to help exaggerate Lieven's show of force for a "family gathering" at the castle.

No one in the hall spoke to Jaromir or even noticed him.

He was nothing.

Yet he couldn't believe his good fortune at having achieved even a week's worth of employment here. His wolfhound, Lizzie, was pressed up against his leg. His sword, his chain armor, and his dog were all he had left in the world.

Looking around the great hall, he thought on how most he'd seen before were rectangular, but this one was an enormous square. Heavy chairs, tables, and benches were haphazardly strewn around, but a fire burned in the hearth, and he reveled in the comfort of being warm. He wished he'd been able to borrow a razor from someone to shave his face. Beneath his armor and clothing he was filthy from having slept outdoors for too long, and he knew that his appearance was not working in his favor.

Prince Lieven sat in a chair on a dais at the top of the hall. A stocky man with a graying beard, he was in his midfifties but as yet showed no signs of slowing down. Jaromir was desperate to impress him, to find some way to gain a permanent place among the Castle Pählen guards, even if it meant standing night watch for the rest of his life.

Lizzie whined, and he reached down to stroke her back. There were at least twenty other soldiers in brown tabards placed around the hall, but still, no one glanced Jaromir's way. They didn't believe he'd be here long.

He hoped they were wrong.

Once he'd thought himself far too proud to grovel for a humble position as a night watchman, but pride was a tenuous thing that could be worn down bit by bit over a period of years.

Looking back at the dais again, Jaromir thought on everything that had brought him to his current state.

Five years before, at the age of twenty-two, he'd already achieved the rank of lieutenant by serving among the military forces for the House of Hilaron in the eastern provinces. His lord was an older prince named Phillipos, and Jaromir was loyal. Something about the aging prince stirred his sense of protection.

But tired of waiting to be the head of the house, Phillipos's son raised a contingent of men and waged war on his own father. Prince Phillipos himself was killed and his soldiers were nearly decimated. Jaromir survived . . . his horse did not.

In his mercy, the victorious son offered any surviving soldiers a place in the new military for the House of Hilaron. Most of them gratefully accepted.

Lieutenant Jaromir refused to swear fealty.

He decided he would rather live by his sword as a hired mercenary than serve his dead lord's traitorous son. This seemed the only path of honor. So he headed west, on foot, with his wolfhound, Lizzie, for company.

To his shame, within a year, he began to regret his decision. Life as a hired sword in a nation like Droevinka turned out to be worse than he could have imagined—with him taking on jobs that once would have sickened him. He was often forced to keep company among men who were little better than animals, who understood only hunger and strength. He lived well sometimes and nearly starved at others. He and Lizzie often slept outside.

It rained a good deal of the time.

Upon deciding to better his situation, he found that because he'd relinquished his place with the House of Hilaron, it was nearly impossible to find a proper post with another lord or prince. They wanted only men they knew, men who had come highly recommended, or men they had reason to trust. No one had a reason to trust him.

The years passed.

Then, by sheer luck, one night he was drinking ale in a tavern, and he overheard that Prince Lieven of the House of Pählen was hiring extra men for a family gathering that involved his two sons. Jaromir didn't need to ask a reason for the extra security—as both sons would be bringing their own men. The elder princes in Droevinka tended to foster competition and hostility between themselves and their sons. They viewed it as healthy for the future survival of the house—if not always for themselves.

Castle Pählen had been a two-day walk from the tavern, but Jaromir started off immediately.

Upon arriving, he'd been hired, and now . . . he counted his good fortune to have gained even short-term employment with the prince of a house, and a powerful one at that.

He was determined not to waste this chance.

He had no pride left.

So he stood at attention in the great hall of Castle Pählen while his mind mulled over how he might distinguish himself.

Conversation in the hall had been soft, but the

entire chamber fell silent as Sub-Prince Damek walked through the archway. He and his men had arrived at the castle the day before and had been taking their leisure.

"You called for me, Father?" he asked.

"Yes, your brother has arrived in the courtyard and will be joining us directly."

"Good news indeed."

Where his father was stocky, Damek was slender. He was pale and handsome and rarely said a word without meaning to land a verbal cut. But Jaromir no longer held illusions about the nobility. Damek was exactly what he'd come to expect from a typical sub-prince: cruel, greedy, brutal, and self-serving. His brother, Anton, would be just like him.

A servant entered the hall, and Jaromir expected Sub-Prince Anton to be announced. Instead, the servant called, "The Lady Karina, of the House of Yegor."

A lovely woman with chestnut hair floated into the hall, walked to the dais, and bowed. "My lord. Anton will be in directly. I traveled with his entourage, and he is seeing to the horses."

Lieven studied her for a moment, taken aback. "Ah, yes, Lady Karina. One of my late wife's sisters? It is good to meet you. I'd been informed you had arrived at Sèone." He continued his visual appraisal in a manner that bordered on impolite. "You bear little resemblance to my Bethany . . . just your hair."

If Karina was offended, she didn't show it and smiled. "No, I believe she took after our mother, but I was only a child when she was sent west to marry you. I look more like our father."

Jaromir couldn't help noting that this was the first time Prince Lieven had met his dead wife's sister.

"It was kind of you to come all the way from the southeast provinces," Lieven responded. "How fares my son?"

She hesitated. "He is bearing up. I will continue to be of assistance to him."

"Perhaps you should come and be of assistance to me," Damek said, sinking lazily down into a chair. "I'd no idea we had such an *aunt* in the family."

She turned cold eyes upon him. "Your brother is in mourning."

Jaromir had heard through conversations taking place around him that Anton had recently lost his wife, but Jaromir scoffed at the idea of a sub-prince in mourning. The poor young wife had probably come with too small a dowry, or she'd otherwise displeased him, and he'd had her poisoned or strangled.

"Sub-Prince Anton, of the House of Pählen," a servant announced loudly.

At first, Jaromir barely glanced at Anton, but then something about the sub-prince pulled his attention back. Anton was young, maybe nineteen. Although pale like his brother, as opposed to merely slender of build, Anton looked as if he hadn't been eating. His eyes were haunted, and Jaromir was struck by the impression that he'd been ordered here by his father—and that it was the last place he wished to be.

It seemed foolish for Jaromir to form these impressions in the matter of a few seconds, but he couldn't help it.

A tall man in a tan tabard walked beside Anton. They both wore long swords.

"My son," Lieven said, "and Captain Nazar. Welcome. Come and sit."

Anton seemed to sleepwalk toward the top of the hall, and Damek watched his every move as if gauging him somehow. Still sitting in his chair, Damek casually pulled his own sword from its sheath and began wiping it with a cloth.

Jaromir tensed.

But then he realized that he no longer felt Lizzie against his leg. Looking around, he spotted her sniffing the floor near the arched entrance to the hall. He couldn't call her back or make a sound. The hall guards were to remain silent.

"How was your journey, my son?" Lieven asked Anton, but his voice was strained, as if he had no idea what else to ask.

"Fine, Father. Thank you."

Anton's response sounded obligatory, polite but without thought, and it occurred to Jaromir that the young man might truly be in mourning. He looked fragile . . . wounded, and Jaromir was astonished at the compulsion to protect someone else surging through him. He hadn't felt this in a long time.

Damek stood up and yawned.

With his sword in his hand, he walked casually toward the dais. "Well, now that we're all here, perhaps we might finally settle some matters of importance."

Lieven raised an eyebrow. "What matters would those be?"

"Naming me official heir, of course. I assumed that was why we'd all been called to home and hearth."

Prince Lieven's face began to redden. Damek must be the greatest of fools to blindside his father like this—and in front of witnesses.

"I'm sure Anton is in agreement," Damek went on, "aren't you, my brother? You think it's time Father officially names me heir?"

Anton was staring toward the burning logs in the hearth. "What?" he asked, seeming to speak through a fog. "Oh, of course. Whatever you both decide. Father, could I please be excused to my rooms? I'm weary from the journey."

Without waiting for permission, he got to his feet and headed for the archway. His guard captain, Nazar, followed him.

"You see?" Damek said to his father. "He's tired. He's always tired. He's not fit to rule. Let us stop this charade of you 'choosing' between us and give our people some assurances that I will follow you."

Lieven was on his feet. "Anton! You stop right there."

The Lady Karina hadn't said a word, but neither did she seem the least intimidated, and she was watching this play out with close attention.

Anton stopped near the left side of the archway.

Lieven turned on Damek. "I am head of this house, and *I* will decide who follows me."

Damek lost all his seemingly bored composure. "I am the eldest! The title is mine by right." He pointed at Anton. "Look at him. Can he hold our lands together?"

Anton indeed looked to be the shadow of a ghost standing there by the arch. He didn't say a word to defend himself.

"Get out of this hall until dinner," Lieven ordered Damek. "And do not broach this subject in my presence again. I will name my heir when I so choose."

Damek's expression flattened in open hatred, and he whirled on one foot to stride from the hall. Just then, Jaromir saw Lizzie in the center of the archway. Damek saw her in the same instant, and his eyes narrowed. His sword was still in his hand, and he gripped the hilt tighter. He was enraged, and he wanted to hurt something, to kill something.

Jaromir fought from crying out. If he made a

sound, if he challenged a sub-prince in this set-ting, he'd be dismissed immediately. Panic flooded through him that he was about to lose the only friend he had.

Finally, unable to just stand there and watch, he took a step forward, ready to shout.

But Sub-Prince Anton appeared to awaken from his fog. He saw Lizzie and he saw his brother's face—and the sword in his brother's hand. In a graceful movement, Anton crossed the archway and used his knee to nudge Lizzie to the other side. She obeyed and followed him.

By the time Damek reached the archway, Lizzie was out of his path. He kept on walking, ignoring both his brother and the dog.

That evening, Jaromir was granted a few hours off duty—as he'd been appointed to help with the night watch later. As he wouldn't be paid until the end of the week and he wasn't allowed in the great hall during the dinner hour, he made his way to the kitchen to try to charm a meal from the women there.

Thankfully, he looked better. He'd been able to borrow a razor an hour ago. Using a bucket of well water, he'd shaved and washed and tied his hair back at the nape of his neck. When he walked into the kitchen, he found it abuzz with activity, but a few scullery girls glanced his way. Lizzie sniffed the air and drooled.

"You get that dog out of here," said a squat middle-aged woman in an apron, "or I'll cook it."

Jaromir flashed her a grin. "You'll get us both out of here fast if you can spare some chicken."

"Food's up in the great hall," she said, leaning over to examine the crust on a pie.

"Yes, but there's no invitation up there for the likes of me, and I'm starving. I'll trade a kiss for your trouble."

She looked up from the pie, taking in his face. Most women liked his face when it was clean and properly shaved. "You can keep your kiss." However, she grabbed a wooden plate and piled on a few pieces of roasted chicken and potatoes. "Now, out back with you. And take that dog!"

He thanked her and headed through the back door, sitting down on some crates outside, tearing some chicken off the bone for Lizzie. "Here, girl."

It was a cool night with a clear sky. The potatoes were excellent, and he knew that if he could land himself a permanent place here, he'd never go hungry again.

Lizzie had finished her first bites of chicken and began whining for more. "Hold on," he said, tearing more off the bones.

When he looked up, he saw someone walking toward the stables. A moment later, he realized it was Sub-Prince Damek. What was he doing out there? All the nobles should be up in the great hall stuffing their faces, gulping wine, and dancing.

Damek vanished inside the stable and didn't come out.

Jaromir waited, keeping to the shadows of the back door and the piles of crates. Not long after, another figure came into sight, heading for the stable as well . . . a tall man wearing a tan tabard.

Captain Nazar.

He too vanished inside the stable.

"Stay here," Jaromir told Lizzie.

Looking for an open window in the stable, he spotted nothing that might help him, but then he noticed a slight crack in the wall with a large knothole in the adjoining board. Slipping up silently, he crouched to see if he could hear what was going on inside.

Two low but clear voices could be heard through the hole.

"I'll give you the Westlake fiefdom and a quarter of the rents," Damek was saying.

"Half the rents," Captain Nazar countered. "What's one fiefdom to you when you'll be named heir to your father's lands?"

A pause followed. "All right, half, but only if this succeeds.

Jaromir took a sharp breath.

"There's an old gazebo down by the river," Damek went on. "My father liked to have us meet him there when we were boys, for talks with him or sometimes for training. I have a scribe in my employ who can imitate my father's handwriting perfectly. Tonight after Anton retires to his rooms,

I'll have a note delivered to him, asking him to meet my father at the gazebo tomorrow at dawn. He'll not find that strange. Father often asked us to meet him quite early or late, probably as a test of obedience."

"And when he arrives, your own men will kill him?"

"Yes, you need not take part in the act. Just make certain he's unprotected. But his body must be dumped into the river afterward. The current is fast this time of year, and he'll be swept downstream. I will still be abed, with witnesses to speak for me, and Anton will simply not appear for breakfast. It may be weeks before he's found. If ever."

Jaromir pulled away from the outer wall, thinking over everything he'd just heard, wondering how he could use it to promote himself, and in the end decided that protecting Anton took precedence. It was the only path of honor.

The next morning, before dawn, Jaromir was crouched behind an oak tree growing near the gazebo. As a hired guard he had access to the castle amory, and in the night, he'd borrowed a few extra weapons. Now he had a loaded crossbow in his hand, a second loaded crossbow on the ground, and his sword and dagger in their sheaths.

Anton and Captain Nazar arrived first. It was a misty morning and the sun was just cresting into view.

"Father?" Anton called. He looked exhausted, as if he hadn't slept.

"You're sure he told you to meet him here?" Nazar asked.

"Yes, of course."

Four soldiers in black tabards came out of the mist, walking toward the gazebo. Anton wasn't alarmed. He probably assumed they'd been sent with a message. Then all four drew their swords.

"Nazar, look out," Anton called, drawing his own blade and taking a defensive stance.

But Captain Nazar simply stepped away, and the leader of the black-clad soldiers charged.

"Nazar!" Anton called, confused now.

Jaromir didn't rush himself. Carefully, he aimed the first crossbow, and when he was sure, he fired. The quarrel struck the lead assassin in the back with a sucking sound. The man fell forward. Jaromir dropped the empty crossbow and snatched up the second one. The next soldier in line turned in panic to see where the quarrel had come from, and Jaromir shot him square in the chest.

Dropping the second crossbow, he drew his dagger and charged. He thought it was possible that the last two of Damek's men would turn and run, but apparently they feared Damek more than a fight against unknown odds, and they kept coming.

By that point, Anton had recovered from his initial shock, and he was running forward into the fight, engaging one of the assassins.

Jaromir caught the other one—a middle-aged

man with a scarred face. His opponent swung hard, missed, and drew his arm back, overconfident at the prospect of fighting a man who'd chosen a smaller weapon. But Jaromir dashed inside his guard, grabbed his sword arm, and drove the dagger up into his torso, between his ribs. The man's eyes widened briefly, but it happened so fast it might not even have caused much pain.

Jaromir jerked out his dagger, knowing that if the man were still alive, that act would cause pain. He whirled to see Anton fighting the last soldier in a black tabard, but Captain Nazar was closing on Anton fast. He must have realized the consequences of failure at this point.

Jaromir ran to intercept Nazar, dropping the dagger and pulling his sword.

The captain swung at him in desperation. Jaromir dodged and faked a strike from the right, and when Nazar moved to block, Jaromir swept with his leg, knocking Nazar off his feet. The instant Nazar's back hit the ground, Jaromir struck downward with the point of his sword, driving it through the man's stomach with both hands on the hilt.

Nazar cried out, and a few seconds later, blood flowed from his mouth.

Jaromir whirled again to find that Anton had sliced through the throat of his own opponent. The assassin fell backward.

Then Jaromir and Anton stood alone, panting, surrounded by dead or dying men.

Visibly shaken, Anton stared at Jaromir's tabard, perhaps trying to figure out what had just happened. "You're one of my father's guards?"

"No, I'm a hired sword . . . for this gathering."

"Why did you save me?"

"Because you saved my dog."

Anton was silent for a moment, and then he glanced down at his dead captain and back. "So you're a man of no rank, then?"

"I was a lieutenant under Prince Phillipos of House Hilaron, but I would not serve his son."

Anton nodded. "Phillipos. I see."

Jaromir wondered what it was that he saw.

Five days later, the "family gathering" was officially over, and the castle was alive with activity as Damek's and Anton's entourages were preparing to leave. Jaromir waited to see if there would be repercussions from the attack at the river, but it seemed that Anton never told his father, and Damek was quite skilled at cleaning up behind himself.

However, as a result, Jaromir had done nothing to distinguish himself to Prince Lieven and would be out of work again tomorrow.

He'd been asked to help load some of Lady Karina's baggage. As he could hardly refuse, he was in the guest quarters waiting outside her rooms with a few other men when he looked up to see Anton coming down the passage toward him.

"Walk with me," Anton said.

Jaromir had no idea what to think, but he fell into step beside Anton, and they went all the way to the end of the passage, where they stopped and looked down through tall archers' slits in the wall, observing the activity in the courtyard below.

Anton's eyes were still haunted.

"I seem to be short a captain," he said.

"I'm not a captain."

"You could be."

Jaromir shook his head. "I'd not be named to a rank I hadn't earned."

Anton kept gazing through the slit in the wall. "You are a strange man. Would you come back with me and head my guard at Castle Sèone?"

Jaromir didn't need to be asked twice.

CHAPTER 7

Still leaning against the wall in the passage outside his room, Jaromir ran a hand over his face, remembering the journey "home" with Anton.

By the time they'd reached Castle Sèone, he and Anton had become friends, but Jaromir had no idea how highly he'd been placed until they entered the castle and he began his duties—with full authority over everyone in Sèone except for Anton and the Lady Karina. After that, he became *the* Lieutenant, like the title of a lord.

He owed Anton more than he could ever repay, and now he had to stop these bizarre murders.

He didn't blame Céline for his failure last night. She'd done exactly as he'd asked. She'd read the girls at the banquet, and she'd given him the name of the next victim.

After that, it had been his job to save Sybil.

And he'd failed.

Opening his eyes, he began walking again, not really knowing where he was heading, only knowing that he wanted to know something more, anything, before he spoke to Anton. A few moments later, he found himself moving downward through the castle's passages until he reached the larder . . . and then the cellars.

The bodies of four girls lay on the tables now that Sybil's had been added. They looked so fragile, almost like a mix of paper and straw, like macabre dolls being sold at a village fair. He stared down at them, one by one, desperate for one of them to tell him something, to give him one piece of information he might use to stop this from ever happening again.

His mind slipped backward through the night before. How could the killer have entered the room? He'd chosen it specifically for security. There was no window, no hearth, and he'd been standing guard at a locked door.

Moving to Sybil's body, he reached down and touched her silky brown hair. This loss hurt him more than the others—because he should have stopped it.

"I'm sorry," he said.

But as he spoke, a sharp intake of breath sounded from behind a stack of barrels, and his hand moved instinctively for the hilt of his absent sword. Casting about, he spotted a rusty kitchen knife left behind on a table and he grabbed it. "Who's there?"

When no one answered, he strode over, gripping the knife, and looked behind the barrels. Then he halted in surprise.

"Inna?"

She stood there with her arms crossed, and he realized she must have been viewing the bodies herself and then hidden when she heard him coming.

"What are you doing down here?" he asked.

Her eyes shifted back and forth, and she didn't answer.

"Come out of there," he ordered.

Something about her had always left him unsettled. In her own way, she was not without attractions, still young and slender, with clear skin and an efficient manner. He'd seen more than one of his men casting looks after her when she walked past them. But her ceaseless sycophantic manner with Anton gave Jaromir the shivers.

Had he been able to find a diplomatic method of sending her away, he would have done it a long time ago. Unfortunately, although Anton did not appear to welcome her attentions as his personal servant, he would not hear a word spoken against her either, so Jaromir's hands were tied.

At his order, she moved from behind the barrels out into the cellar, her gaze turning instantly to the bodies.

"You were looking, too?" he asked. "Do you see anything that I don't?"

At this point, he was willing to take assistance from any corner. But she only drew her arms more tightly around herself. She wore her usual gray dress but had no shawl. He'd have offered her his cloak had he been wearing it, but he was dressed in only the breeches and tunic from last night.

Her silence frustrated him. "Inna, you must have seen something more in the room last night. Think hard. Can you tell me anything else? Anything to help me keep this from happening again?"

Her eyes flashed up to his face. "Why?" she asked sharply. "Why would you waste your time? Waste Anton's strength with *this*?" She motioned to the dead bodies, and the venom in her voice grew. "If you had an ounce of honor, you'd bury this baggage and do your job, protecting Prince Anton! If it happened again, you wouldn't bother him with it." She leaned forward, breathing harder. "These girls' deaths are nothing compared to Lady Joselyn's, and he is still in pain, still recovering. He should be left in peace to mourn, and what do you do? You counsel him to hire some whore of a gypsy seer, tiring him out, wearing him out." She stepped back, motioning to the bodies again. "These are nothing compared to Anton's health. Get rid of them and do your job."

He stared at her, at a loss for words. Although he'd always suspected a hint of madness ran just below her skin, he'd never heard her speak like this.

Before he could recover himself, she whirled and ran for the archway, fleeing toward the stairs leading up to the kitchens. He let her go, but his mind was reeling.

Was she overwrought by having woken in bed with a dead girl, or was she truly as unhinged as she sounded? A cold feeling washed over him as he suddenly wondered if the killer had not figured out a way to enter a locked, windowless room after all.

Maybe the killer had been in there all along.

Céline and Amelie slept late that morning, but upon waking, Céline rose almost instantly and dressed in her old red gown, leaving Amelie awake but still huddled beneath the blankets. The fire had long since gone out.

They hadn't spoken about what occurred last night, and Céline was desperate not to be faced with questions—at least not yet.

Glancing at the dressing table, she noticed that the miniature portrait of the chestnut-haired woman was leaning against the mirror again. Helga must have found it and put it back.

"You in a hurry?" Amelie asked, sitting up.

The moment was awkward. They'd survived their orphan years together by never keeping anything from each other. Amelie deserved answers. But Céline felt stretched thin, too shaken, too guilty, too confused to start making confessions about her recently surfaced ability.

"I'm going to go check in with Jaromir," Céline said. "See if anything else has happened."

Amelie leaned back with hurt in her eyes.

Céline fled toward the door. "I promise we'll talk later." She jerked it open, desperate for a few moments to herself. "I promise."

Stepping out, she closed the door behind herself and took a long breath. She had no intention of going anywhere near Jaromir. He was the last person she wanted to face—well, second to last. Facing Amelie right now would be worse.

The castle was huge. So she decided to just walk for a little while and gather herself, gather her strength.

But she'd taken only a few steps when the sound of muttering and stumping echoed up the passage, and she saw Helga coming toward her, carrying a tray of tea. The old woman stopped at the sight of her.

"Up and about?" Helga asked. "Fire's gone out, and you've had no breakfast." This morning, her head scarf was a shade of dirty orange, and it was more than slightly askew, having slipped down over one side of her head, causing her to look lopsided. She squinted, taking in Céline's face.

"Ahhhh," she said, nodding, setting the tea tray down on the floor, pouring a mug, and holding it out. "The night was too much, I see. But you can't get around that. Comes with the gift."

Céline stiffened. The things this woman said disturbed her, as if she somehow knew more than she should. But Helga continued to hold the mug out, and Céline could see it steaming and smell the sweet spice. She hadn't eaten or drunk since dinner last night, and finally she reached out for the tea.

"Good girl," Helga said. "You'll get your bear-

ings soon enough. So will your sister, but she's
farther to go. Two sides of the same coin. The future and the past."

What did that mean?

For some reason, Céline always felt tongue-tied
in the midst of Helga's babbling, and she suddenly wanted to say something, anything, but
didn't know what. The old woman pointed beyond her, in the other direction down the passage.
"Go that way, my girl, till you reached a stairwell
leading up. A pretense for dawdling covers the
walls up there. You'll have an excuse."

Céline blinked. She had no idea how to converse with Helga, but she longed to be away from
this passage, on her own. "Thank you," she managed to say, and then she turned and fled, still carrying the steaming mug of tea.

She didn't want to think about last night, about
her own failure to alter a future that'd she clearly
seen . . . that she should have been able to change.

Just as promised, she found a stairwell down
the passage and stepped inside, heading up, sip-
ping her tea along the way. The stairwell wound
in a few circles, and it was darker than she expected, with no braziers on the walls at all, but
soon enough, she saw dim light at the top and
then stepped out into a much wider passage, almost a hall. There were tall, narrow windows to
her left—possibly slots for archers—and the wall
to her right was covered in enormous portraits,
some larger than herself, in ornate frames wider

than her hand. Taking a last swallow, she set the mug down and moved forward to explore.

Dusty spiderwebs covered the ceiling and even some of the paintings, but the late morning light filtering in allowed her to see far too many details of the neglect of this hall. A few corners of the frames had teeth marks, as if rats had chewed upon them.

Did none of the servants care for this hall?

Walking slowly, she looked up at the first portrait. The background was dark, but it depicted a proud-looking middle-aged man with a close-trimmed silver beard. He wore a sword on his hip and had a cream-colored dog standing at his side. Was he one of Anton's ancestors?

Moving farther down the wall, she took in each one of the portraits, ladies and noblemen and finely dressed soldiers, all larger than life, all so serious of expression—no one was smiling. While the sight of all of them in their state of sad decay might have been cloying to some people, Céline rather welcomed their presence.

As if she were alone and yet not alone.

Then she stopped, looking up at portrait that struck her as different from the others. It depicted a young woman dressed all in black, even to her boots. Her hair was black and hung in loose waves, and she'd been painted out of doors, beside a burning campfire, on a dark night. The outline of evergreen trees graced the background. What an odd choice of scene for a noblewoman of the House of Pählen. Her skin was ivory and seemed to glow by the light of the fire. Céline could not stop studying this one painting. It seemed so much more alive than the others.

A footstep sounded behind her, and she whirled, perhaps jumpy after all from being in the presence of so many imposing life-sized portraits.

Anton emerged from the stairwell. He walked halfway to her and stopped. Although finely dressed in a quilted tunic and polished boots, he looked even paler than he had last night, and his eyes were bleak.

"Helga told me you'd come up here," he said raggedly.

Although she'd wanted to be alone, for some reason, his was the only company she thought she might be able to stand. But the sight of his face brought all her guilt rushing back.

"You know about Sybil," she said.

He nodded, and if it were possible, his expression grew bleaker. "She was kind."

Céline wanted to choke, and she turned away. "I'm so sorry."

"Why are you sorry?"

When she turned back, he seemed genuinely puzzled. She knew it was a mistake to speak openly with him. He was her patron, and she needed to maintain the aura of mystique, but again, for some reason, he was the only one to whom she felt able to show any pain, any doubts.

All the horror of the night before came bubbling to the surface.

"Because I should have been able to change it! To stop it! I made sure that the bed Jaromir put her in was not covered by a yellow-and-red-checked quilt. I should have searched the room. I should have stayed with her." She paused, and then her true fear came pouring out. "What if my vision is what placed her in that room? What if just by speaking up, I'm the one who caused her death?"

Anton was staring at her from where he stood, and in the light of his full attention, more bottled fears poured from her mouth. "And what about Rhiannon?" she said. "What if her father threatens to cast her out if she won't marry Damek, and so she marries him after all, and part of the reason he has her killed is from spite at her initial refusal?" She drew a harsh breath. "A refusal that I counseled! What if all my prophesies of death only serve to ensure those deaths? If so, I should just keep silent."

Unable to go on, she put a hand over her eyes, not wishing to see anything, real or envisioned.

But his footsteps sounded as he closed the distance between them and grasped her wrist lightly. His hand was cold as he slowly pulled her fingers away from her eyes. "Listen to me. Because of you, Jaromir and I know more than we did yesterday. We don't know precisely how this is being done, but we know that someone with slender hands wearing black gloves is murdering the girls by nothing more than touch. Maybe it's some kind of unknown poison on the gloves. Maybe it's something more . . . arcane. But you cannot stop telling us what you see."

His face was close enough that she could see every swirl in the dark circles beneath his eyes. His thick hair had been carefully brushed and tucked behind his ears. His features were narrow, and she thought he would be handsome without the circles. But he looked so tired, so exhausted, and again she wondered what was wrong with him, what Master Feodor was supposedly doing to help him.

That last thought made her realize she had ahold of herself again. He seemed to realize it, too. Letting go of her wrist, he stepped back. "Don't worry about Rhiannon. I'll write to her today. I'll tell her she has a place here if her father disowns her. I'll make sure she's not forced to marry Damek."

As his words sank in, the rush of gratitude that hit Céline was almost too much to take in amidst everything she was going through. He seemed so different this morning. Gone was the haughty arrogance. He seemed just like . . . a man honestly trying to comfort her.

She wasn't used to anyone besides Amelie trying to help her.

"You will?" she asked.

"This morning," he promised. "But you can't

stop reading our young women and telling me and Jaromir what you see." He took another step back. "All right?"

Reluctantly, she nodded. If she didn't help him solve this, what would become of her and Amelie? After the release of her outburst, she seemed able to begin shoving the ragged emotions back into a corner of her mind.

She wanted that apothecary's shop as much as she'd wanted anything in her life.

"This hall has been badly neglected," she said to change the subject.

His breeding prevailed, and he fell into step beside her, looking up at a painting of a tall, hawkish man in chain armor. "I don't think I've ever been up here. I rarely enter the guest wing. I'm not sure who these people are."

"Truly?" Céline asked in surprise. "These aren't your ancestors?"

"Not that I know. My grandfather took this castle from a rival in a siege. Most of the portraits of my ancestors are with my father, at Castle Pählen." He paused. "But the only ones I recognize there are my grandfather and my mother."

His tone had altered slightly, becoming thinner at the mention of his mother.

"When did she die?" Céline asked.

"I was only eight, but I remember her. I'm glad Father had her portrait done, though. Sometimes I forget what she looked like, and when I visit him, I can be reminded." He continued looking up. "I once had a miniature of just her face, but it was lost some time ago. Sad really. It was one of the few possessions I valued."

Later, Céline had no idea what possessed her to ask the next question. It just came from her mouth as if of its own accord. "Did you have a portrait done of Joselyn?"

He stopped walking and turned white.

"Oh, forgive me . . . ," she stammered. "I didn't mean to . . ." What would ever possess her to remind him of *that*? Here she was, trying to prove herself indispensable, and she'd just called attention to the fact that she'd counseled him to wed a woman who'd died—apparently less than a year into their marriage.

"No, I didn't," he answered quietly. "I meant to, but she was gone too soon." He wasn't angry, and to both her alarm and relief, he almost seemed eager to broach the subject of Joselyn. "Why did you tell me that I'd be happy?"

She felt cornered and regretted that they'd managed to go from discussing the portraits into this verbal quicksand. If he didn't believe in her ability to read the future, he might set her and Amelie outside the gates by noon.

Her mind raced. "Because I only saw one image," she answered. "It was shortly after you and she were wed. You were in the great hall below, and I could see your faces clearly. You were happy."

This seemed safe enough.

But he looked as if he'd been kicked in the stomach, and she knew that if she possessed an ounce of sanity, she'd switch topics immediately. To her shock, she found herself asking, "How did she die?"

"I killed her," he answered quietly, almost inaudibly, and she froze, very aware that she was alone with him up here.

As if in response to her earlier outburst, words began pouring from his mouth, words she felt must have been bottled up for a long time.

"You were right," he said, "and we were happy. I'd never been so happy. I could talk to her. I wasn't alone." The words were clipped and quiet. "Only two months after we were married, she told me she was carrying our child. After that, even my father seemed to accept her. We planned a nursery, and I thought on all the years to come, spending them with her, watching our children grow."

Warning bells began sounding in Céline's mind. She knew exactly what was coming, and his voice was so raw, so full of pain, she didn't think he could stop himself if he wanted to. But she understood human nature too well. He had no one he could talk to of these things, not Jaromir, not Lady Karina. For them, he had to play the capable prince. Right now, he was caught up in the moment, sharing pain with someone who had shared her pain with him.

But what of later in the day? Would he suffer a bout of horror and embarrassment that he'd let down his guard and bared his soul? Would he be so regretful that he'd not even be able to face her? Then what would happen?

"My lord—," she tried to cut in.

He didn't seem to hear and rushed on in his quiet voice. "When her time arrived, the castle rejoiced and the midwife came . . . but the hours passed, and more hours. They wouldn't let me see her, but I stood outside the door, and I could hear her screaming."

Céline wanted to close her eyes. He might never forgive her for having heard this.

"Then she stopped screaming. I ordered the door opened, and I went in. She was dead. The child was dead, and the bed was covered in blood. I'd killed her."

In spite of her fears, Céline whispered, "Oh, Anton."

She knew she should have called him "my lord" or "prince," but neither felt appropriate.

"Afterward, I thought I'd die, too." He looked into her face. "I blamed you at first, thinking you'd lied to me, but that passed, and I knew well enough to blame myself."

How surreal. She'd not given him a moment's thought once he'd walked out of her shop five years ago.

"I wanted to die," he said. "But then Karina came, and then I found Jaromir . . . and I just went on, living each day as her killer."

"You didn't kill Joselyn," Céline said, throwing

caution to the wind. "Men die in war and women die in the childbed, and that is the way of things. All of life is a risk, and she wanted that baby just as much as you did."

His eyes fixed on her face, and this time, a different warning bell sounded. She'd seen lust on the faces of enough men to know it, but he looked at her with longing, loneliness, and hunger. His hand began to rise toward her. It was pale and slender, and she was astonished by the thought that his touch would be soft, that she might even welcome it. She was also almost certain he hadn't reached for a woman like this since Lady Joselyn had died . . . and yet he reached for her.

But the bells turned into a scream. Tragic or not, men like Anton burned hot for a mistress and could cool just as quickly. Once they were finished, they normally got rid of her as fast as possible, even unto sending her off so they wouldn't have to be reminded every day.

Céline wanted to be his seer, his village apothecary, not his mistress. Although a part of her longed to feel his hand on her cheek . . . moving down her throat, she was not about to trade her future for what would probably be a few weeks of pleasure at best.

Taking a step back, she said, "I should go and check on Amelie. She didn't get much sleep last night. You and Jaromir should plan how you want to proceed. It's possible we might just tell some of the parents and girls what I'm really doing here."

He blinked and his hand dropped. All traces of longing vanished from his eyes, but so did his open demeanor. The haughty prince returned.

"Very good," he said. "I will speak to Jaromir."

Turning, she walked swiftly toward the stairwell, glancing up once at the portrait of the black-haired woman by the campfire.

CHAPTER 8

The next few days passed in a blur.

Céline suffered through several regrets, such as her continued inability to tell Amelie the truth. She'd managed to put her sister off by claiming that she'd made a guess while attempting to make herself appear useful in the investigation and then had been overwrought when Sybil had actually been killed.

Amelie had appeared to accept this on the surface, but she also told Céline they'd better come up with a much better plan than simply guessing and trying to look useful.

Céline couldn't fault that logic, but she was also mildly alarmed by how quickly she was adapting to castle life. Lady Karina continued her kindness and had sent up more clothing: gowns, clean shifts, stockings, and even a pair of dark breeches for Amelie.

Helga brought breakfast to their room every day, and she built the morning fire. She also made their bed and laundered their clothing. Lunch was served in the dining hall in a buffet fashion, and there were sit-down suppers with meat, root vegetables, white bread, early spring strawberries, and wine every night—not as lavish as the banquet, but still fine meals.

Céline had no duties other than reading any young women Jaromir brought to her, and Amelie spent much of her time playing cards with off-duty soldiers. The sisters were both living like ladies of leisure.

But Céline couldn't help feeling these quiet days were like a lull before a violent storm. That something was about to happen. Jaromir had apparently made her true purpose here more widely known, and he'd asked for volunteers among families with daughters. But so far only a few parents had brought their daughters to be read, and Céline had been relieved not to have found herself pulled along in the mists, forced to witness an ugly death.

At the same time, she felt she was making no progress.

Anton had kept his distance after their rather raw exchange in the upstairs portrait hall.

On the fourth day, however, he sent out announcements for another banquet at the castle set for the following night, and he made it clear a refusal would be perceived as an insult.

The following day, castle cooks and servants bustled with the preparations.

As Céline dressed for this banquet, she knew

she would be on display again and that Jaromir and Anton both expected results. Jaromir had been growing more and more restless, and he wanted something he could fight.

The wardrobe in her room now contained a number of gowns, and she chose one of soft lavender wool with a scoop neck and a fairly straight skirt. It matched her eyes and accentuated her slim hips.

As she stood before the mirror, her mind flashed back to the way Anton had looked at her in the portrait hall, and she wondered if she should change into her own threadbare red dress. At least she felt like herself in that dress . . . and could keep her sights on the end goal.

"Céline, who do you really think is doing this?" Amelie asked, pulling on her boots. "Killing the girls, I mean. It has to be someone who wants to discredit Anton, but I've been talking to the soldiers for days, and everyone here seems loyal."

Céline turned from the mirror. "You've been talking to the soldiers? Trying to gain information?"

"What did you think I'd been doing? Amusing myself with cards?"

Actually, that was exactly what Céline thought she'd been doing.

After seeing the black gloves and the sight of Sybil's life draining away, Céline had been wallowing in fear that the killer was indeed, as Anton so politely put it, "more arcane" in nature.

But he'd also mentioned the possibility of an unknown poison. She knew of nothing to make flesh shrivel so quickly, but that didn't mean it didn't exist.

"And none of the maids claim to know anything of secret passages in the guest quarters," Amelie went on. "Not even Helga, and I think she'd tell me if she knew."

"Secret passages?"

"How else could the killer get inside that room? There's no window, and Jaromir was standing on the other side of a locked door. But I haven't been able to do a search of the room."

Céline stared at her. "Why don't you just ask Jaromir for permission?"

"What? And let him find it? Let him solve this? No, we have to solve it ourselves and make you look like the 'seer' in the process."

Céline turned away. "We're late," she said, realizing dusk had fallen.

They stepped out into the passage, walking side by side, but Céline's thoughts were churning. What if Amelie was right? What if the killer was simply someone trying to discredit Anton? A perfect way to discredit a respected leader would be through a series of deaths of pretty, unmarried girls—which he was unable to stop.

"Do you remember Pavel saying something odd at the table at the last banquet?" Céline asked, murmuring in case they passed someone unexpectedly.

"No . . . just him telling you about the people closest to Anton. What else did he say?"

"That he'd never serve Prince Damek, but he thought Damek would make a better grand prince, that Anton was too kind . . . or rather that Damek was a harder man and therefore better qualified to protect the country."

"Oh, I do remember. So even someone loyal to Anton might be working against him, just because the person thinks Damek could better protect Droevinka?" Amelie shook her head. "That could leave a lot of people here to choose from."

A flush of shame passed through Céline. Amelie had been actively looking for suspects, questioning soldiers and castle maids, while she had wallowed in self-pity and guilt, certain she was chasing a shadow and at the same time worrying that she might even be accelerating the murders.

That would stop right now.

"We need to make a list," she whispered as they walked down the stairs, "of everyone who thinks Anton is too soft to rule the country."

"Good." Amelie nodded. "I'll see what I can find out."

Their discussion stopped as they entered the great hall.

It was crowded with milling guests as before, but now few people bothered with any pretense of attending an enjoyable dinner offered by their prince. More than half the guests in the hall glanced at Céline as she entered, and the rest preferred to pretend she was not a reality.

But she could hardly blame them.

At the last banquet, she'd read a lovely young woman who'd wound up lying dead on a table in the cellars only a few hours later.

Anton stood at the top of the hall near the dais with his usual entourage, and Lady Karina smiled at Céline from her place beside him. Céline smiled back. But then she shifted her gaze back to Anton as he took in the sight of her lavender gown. After only a second or two, he looked away.

Master Feodor had donned his usual black silk tunic, but he drank down a large goblet of wine rather quickly and signaled to a servant to pour him more. Was something bothering him? Or did he always drink that much?

Inna was hovering behind Anton, and Jaromir was dressed in his chain armor again, along with his tabard and sword, wearing an expression dark enough to make Céline wish she could avoid him for the remainder of the evening. Even his loyal wolfhound, Lizzie, kept her place by the fire instead of at his side. He looked as if he could kick a small kitten across the hall.

"I like that dress," someone said from beside her, and she turned to find Corporal Pavel towering over her and Amelie. His familiar face and cropped dark hair were a welcome sight. He might be slightly besotted, but at least he was a simple man with simple needs. She knew how to handle him.

"Thank you," Céline said. "Lady Karina has nearly packed our wardrobe, and she has good taste."

"I haven't seen you in a few days," Amelie told him. "Where have you been?"

He hesitated. "My lord saw fit to have the lieutenant place me on night watch at the lower gates. But I'm off duty tonight."

Céline tried not to wince. Anton had ordered Pavel on night watch at the outside gate? She hoped that hadn't been due to his attentions to her.

But if so, it didn't appear to daunt him. The gong for dinner sounded, and he lowered his arm for her to take. "Come and eat with me," he said.

She took his arm.

Once dinner had ended, Jaromir wasted no time getting Céline set up in her chair near the hearth, and then he practically ordered Baron Medev to go fetch his youngest daughter. Jaromir no longer felt he had the luxury of pretending these readings were some sort of entertainment, and no one would believe such a sugarcoated illusion anyway. Not after Sybil's death.

In part, this lack of pretense was a relief, as it allowed him to use his power and give the necessary orders, but it also drove him even harder to

find a way to make these murders stop. He wanted
Céline to pinpoint the next victim, to get him the
next name, and then he was going to try a different tactic to catch the killer.

Baron Medev's daughter came over and sat
across from Céline. The girl looked frightened, but
Céline took her hand, murmuring reassurances.

Jaromir couldn't help liking Céline. She was
good at her job.

However, he also had a feeling this was going
to be a long night, and he hoped it would not be
fruitless. Many daughters of the minor nobles and
local merchants were present tonight, but that was
no guarantee the next victim was here among
them. There were other pretty young women in
the village outside.

And he badly wanted a name tonight. He
needed to *do* something.

For now, all he could do was keep an eye on
Céline and let her go to work.

Turning around, his gaze moved to Amelie, as it
often did when she was in the vicinity. She'd made
some friends among his men and earned a reputation as a good card player. Now she was sitting on
a bench, waiting for a few soldiers to join her and
get a game going. She wore the same faded shirt
and jacket, but with clean breeches. Her hair shone
in the candlelight, and he liked how it swung
along her jaw when she moved her head.

Then . . . a flash of sapphire blue silk caught the
corner of his eye, and he turned a little further to

find Bridgette watching him. He had not spoken to her or called her to his bed since the night Sybil was murdered. She'd sent him a few sympathetic notes, telling him to take heart and reassuring him that he'd have this solved soon. But he knew she was just playing a part, and he hadn't answered the notes; she was probably beginning to suspect there was more to his cooling off than this murder investigation.

Now she'd just caught him staring at Amelie.

Bridgette's expression was hard, but when she found him looking at her, she smiled and curtsied in playful humor. He nodded and turned around to watch Céline again. He didn't wish to encourage Bridgette to approach him. Not tonight.

After a few moments, though, he glanced back to see if she'd engaged someone else in conversation, but she was no longer where she'd been standing. He continued his search . . . and to his shock, he saw that Bridgette had walked straight to Amelie and was talking to her.

Knowing he should stay in place and watch Céline, he still couldn't help himself. Bridgette's back was to him, and he moved slowly up behind her, just close enough to hear what she was saying. Bridgette's finery and pretty face would be enough to daunt most women, but Amelie was turning ashen.

"I suppose you learned to play cards in that hovel from where you came?" Bridgette was asking. "Where was it?"

"Shetâna," Amelie answered tightly.

"Oh, yes, one of Damek's mud pits. Did you farm pigs there? I heard almost all the peasants under Damek's rule farm pigs for a living."

Her tone was regally polite but held such a cutting edge of cruelty that Jaromir almost couldn't believe it. He knew she could be haughty. He even liked that side of her, as it reminded him how far he'd come. But he'd not known she could be cruel. She was intentionally trying to make Amelie feel small, and for all Amelie's skill with that dagger on her hip, she had no idea how to fence with someone like Bridgette.

"No," Amelie said. "We had a shop."

Several of the soldiers around her were beginning to look uncomfortable.

"A shop?" Bridgette said brightly. "How charming. So then you must have kept the pigs out back? Else why would you dress in that manner?" She motioned toward Amelie's clothes.

"Bridgette!" Jaromir said, and when Amelie looked up and saw him standing there, her ashen face went pink.

Bridgette, however, turned pale. "Lieutenant," she said, "I didn't hear your approach."

"Apparently not," he answered coldly. "Why don't you go and attend the Lady Karina."

She stiffened at his dismissal but attempted a smile. "Of course."

Turning in her sapphire gown, she swept away. Jaromir knew better than to apologize for her, so he simply said to Amelie, "I'll go keep watch on your sister."

She nodded, but for all her tough exterior, he could see she'd been cut—probably most by not knowing how to fight back in this polite verbal arena.

Walking toward Céline, he felt embarrassed by his mistress, and he wished he could somehow take back the words she'd spoken to Amelie.

After reading six young women in immediate succession, both Céline's smile and her calming assurances were beginning to tire. Worse, Jaromir was pacing the stone floor like a restless wolf watching for any sign of unusual movement, but after each girl, when she shook her head at him, his expression grew darker.

He wasn't helping.

Looking up, Céline saw a young woman of about eighteen standing near the opposite chair. She was tall, with a strong build. Blond braids hung forward over her shoulders. Though well made, her gown was of dyed cotton as opposed to silk, satin, or brushed wool. Her face was plain, but her blue eyes were bright, and she seemed almost eager to speak with Céline.

"I think I am next," she said. "My name is Erin."

"Come and sit," Céline said, resummoning her smile.

To her surprise, the young woman grabbed the other chair and pulled it even closer, so that when she sat down, their knees were touching. She leaned forward and whispered, "I don't care about this matter you're handling for the prince. I wish to know something else."

In spite of her weariness, Céline's interest was piqued.

"I'm engaged to be married," Erin said quickly.

Céline's interest faded. Weren't they all by her age? Most were married already.

Her face must have given her thoughts away, because Erin waved a hand. "No, I don't want you to paint pretty stories of a handsome knight. I've known my betrothed since we were ten. Cecil is a fine man."

"Then what is it you wish to know?"

Erin lowered her voice. "I need to know if I will bear him a son. My mother could only give my father one child . . . me. Cecil is his family's only son. They have no other male heir and are anxious to ensure a male grandchild. His parents have doubts about him marrying me if I prove to be like my mother, not a good breeder." She straightened. "But I won't spend my life accepting their blame, suffering their accusing looks and words. Can you look into my future and tell me if I will bear a son?"

Céline hesitated. This was a very specific question, nothing she could dance around with vague details, and in truth, she didn't believe this young woman's happiness should hinge upon pleasing her betrothed's parents.

But Erin leaned even further forward, so close she was breathing on Céline's cheek. "Please. I love Cecil. I would be his wife. But only if we will both be happy."

Well, that was a better reason than the first she'd given.

"Here," Erin said, holding out her hand. "I brought something personal of his and mine—locks of our hair."

One chunk of hair was carrot red, and the other blond.

Céline pursed her mouth, wondering how to proceed. She could hardly refuse to read the girl. Taking both locks of hair, she grasped Erin's hand with her free one and closed her eyes, wondering how she could handle this without making promises or creating disappointment. With her eyes shut tightly, she was about to pretend the first jolt . . . when a jolt actually hit her, and she found herself rushing down the corridor of mists.

Oh, no, not this young woman.

Fear and anguish flooded through her at the thought that Erin was the next victim, but the mists vanished and she found herself standing in a sun-drenched bedroom, near an open window, listening to the sound of harsh grunts, followed by a brief scream.

Erin lay atop a bed, soaked with sweat, and attended by a midwife. She was giving birth.

"Good," the midwife said, sweating herself. "One more push. You're almost there."

Erin bore down, gritting her teeth and grunting hard, and the baby slipped out, landing in the midwife's arms.

Céline looked on, wishing she could help. She had delivered babies in Shetâna and knew the many duties that must be attended to quickly, from cutting the cord, to cleaning the child, to seeing that all the afterbirth came out and massaging the mother's abdomen.

"Is the baby all right?" Erin panted.

The child began to cry, and the midwife brought it up for Erin to hold. "A healthy boy," she said.

The birthing room vanished.

Unfortunately, Céline instantly found herself back in the great hall with her eyes wide open, and Jaromir was standing behind Erin's chair, ready to pounce. She waved him away. He frowned and didn't move.

"What?" Erin asked anxiously. "What did you see?"

"I saw you lying in the childbed," Céline answered without hesitation. "You have a healthy son."

Erin leaned back and breathed in through her mouth. "Thank you," she whispered.

But Céline was still awash in the realization that she'd just witnessed a future that did not involve horror or death. This girl had asked her a question, and she'd focused on the answer . . . and she'd seen it.

Erin was rising. "If I can ever do anything for

you, please ask me. My father is the village blacksmith." Then she was gone, hurrying back to a
young man with red hair. Gripping his hand, she
whispered in his ear, and he smiled broadly.

"What exactly was that?" Jaromir snapped,
moving closer.

"I saw her future, and she is not the next victim."

He ran a hand over his face. "Well, then, who
is? I need something, Céline. Should I bring you
another girl?"

But Céline's gaze moved to Anton, and more
specifically, to Inna hovering behind him.

"Lieutenant . . . ," she began, "how old is Inna?"

"Inna?" he repeated in surprise. "I don't know;
eighteen or so, I'd guess. Why do you—?"

"Some men might find her pretty, and I haven't
read her yet."

He followed her gaze. Watching his face, she
could almost see his mind working. "I don't think
she's the next victim. In fact, I've even wondered . . ." He trailed off.

"Wondered what?"

"No, you're right. You should read her." He
seemed determined now. "And tell me anything
you see, even if you don't think she's in danger."

Céline had no idea what he was after, but she
had other concerns when it came to Inna. "You'll
have to go to Anton first and have him order her.
I don't think she'd submit to this otherwise."

He glanced down at her and nodded. "I won't be long."

Although Céline was fully prepared for some opposition, the unfortunate scene that followed astonished her. Jaromir went straight to Anton and spoke in his ear. Anton's brows rose briefly, and a short conversation ensued. Finally, Anton turned to Inna and said something to her that caused her features to twist.

"No!" she cried.

Nearly everyone in the hall turned toward the front. Anton appeared both stunned and discomfited as he leaned closer to her, speaking more forcefully. But she shook her head in refusal until he grabbed her arm and began dragging her toward the hearth.

"No!" Inna shouted again. "My lord, let go of me."

He didn't even slow down, and Jaromir followed him like some man at arms.

Everyone was watching, and Céline sat in helpless horror, thinking there was no way Anton could have handled this in a worse fashion. Inna looked like an angry lamb being led to the slaughter. This would hardly ensure the trust of Anton's people when it came to their daughters being read by the seer.

Then Anton was standing directly in front of her, still gripping Inna's arm. "Sit," he ordered.

"My *lord*," Céline whispered, "this is hardly necessary. Nor is it helpful."

He ignored her and stared hard at Inna. "Sit," he repeated.

Then it occurred to Céline that for all his kindness and concern for his people, he was accustomed to being obeyed. When he was refused, he reacted like any other warlord.

That was a piece of information worth storing away.

Inna's face was wild, torn between fear and anger and the pain of having refused him. Perhaps realizing he would not relent, she changed tactics and began begging, "Please, my lord, do not make me do this. I cannot sit in this audience and submit to such indignity. Please."

He stood there like a stone.

"Inna," Céline said, with genuine pity. "It's all right. I promise this won't take long."

Inna flashed her a look of pure hated. "Do not speak to me."

"*Sit* down," Anton ordered, "and stop this foolish behavior."

He watched while Inna sank into the chair.

Céline sighed. "Inna, I have to touch your hand."

She was beginning to regret having suggested this. The hall was quiet, and Anton turned around. "Musicians," he said, "play something cheerful."

For Céline, this macabre order was the last cherry on the cake of her self-control, and she glared at him. "You're the one who should stop playing the fool!" she whispered.

He might have flinched, but she couldn't be sure. "Inna," he said, "give her your hand."

The hostility on Inna's face was so affecting that Céline hesitated, but she had to do this. Reaching out, she grasped the fingers of Inna's left hand and then closed her eyes. She let her mind go still, trying to forget Anton and Jaromir standing there like sentinels. She focused only on Inna . . . on what was to come.

A hard jolt hit her, and then another. The great hall vanished, and she was swept away on the white mists, rushing forward, blind and bodiless until the mists vanished, and she found herself once again inside a small, darkened bedroom.

Why was it always bedrooms?

But then she looked down. Inna lay sleeping beneath a white quilt. She looked younger with her face so relaxed. Panic hit Céline immediately . . . as this was all too familiar.

"Inna, wake up!" she said, but she wasn't really there. Inna couldn't hear her.

Slender hands covered in black gloves came into view, moving slowly toward the bed, and Céline began to choke.

The black gloves continued to move. One of them settled on the side of Inna's face and the other on her throat. Again the hands did not grip down, or do anything besides touch Inna's face and throat, and the flesh on Inna's cheek began to ripple . . . and then to shrivel.

Beneath the black-gloved hands, Inna's face

withered, sinking in upon itself until it was nothing more than a dried husk. Inside the vision, the black gloves pressed harder on her cheek and throat, and as with the other young victims, Inna's body seemed to shrink beneath the quilt.

Céline began to weep, sobbing in gulps.

"Come out of it!" someone ordered.

The dim room vanished, and she found herself in Anton's grip, looking at his pale chin. He had ahold of her upper arms. Though his voice was harsh, he also sounded worried. "Céline, come out of it."

Without thinking, she leaned in, pressing her face into his shoulder.

"It's Inna," she choked. "Inna's next."

Within the hour, Jaromir had secured a small, windowless room just down the passage from his own apartments. He wasn't taking any chances this time. He had Pavel and two other men, Guardsmen Rurik and Winshaw, whom he knew well, gathered around the outside of the door.

"No one closes the door," he ordered. "We'll run a two-man watch in three-hour shifts so no one gets tired. Just stand in the doorway and keep your eyes on her while she sleeps. Don't look away for a second, understand?"

"Yes, sir," his men answered in unison.

He had full control out here. But the scene playing out in the interior of the room was another matter—involving Céline, Inna, and Amelie. Inna

was still stunned by having been rushed here, and
she kept going on and on about not having laid
out Anton's bedclothes or his nighttime snack or
his goblet of wine. She was nearly hysterical.

Anton himself had already retired for the night,
leaving the arrangements to Jaromir.

"Please, please," Inna begged, "you must let me
go! My lord needs me to attend his sleeping preparations."

Amelie appeared to have little patience with
such a display and seemed close to knocking the
young woman senseless—to which Jaromir might
not have objected.

While Céline was normally calm and sensible,
the experience from her vision had left her rattled,
and to his consternation, she seemed bent on arguing with his strategy. For the third time, she
came at him.

"Lieutenant, you must see this won't work,"
she insisted. "By placing her inside this room in
the castle, you're signing her death warrant. If you
wish to keep her safe, you'll take her outside the
city gates, somewhere far from here, somewhere
the killer cannot reach her."

She'd been pressing this point since only moments after having read Inna in the great hall, and
he had no intention of voicing the main flaw of
her argument: that he needed Inna for bait. To this
point, he'd simply ignored Céline, but now she
was questioning him in front of his men.

"Mistress Fawe," he said quietly, pulling her

aside, "I am not just trying to save Inna. I am trying to catch a murderer. Inna will not be left alone, but you need to leave me to this. Go back to your own room."

"But, Lieutenant, you cannot just—"

"Now!" He looked back into the room. "Amelie, please come take your sister back to your room."

He had no idea how Amelie would react, as she didn't tend to follow orders, but she seemed relieved at the prospect of flight and came out quickly, grasping her sister's hand. "Come on, Céline."

"Amelie, we can't leave her like this!"

"Do you require an escort?" Jaromir asked, not bothering to keep the threat from his voice.

"No," Amelie answered, dragging Céline away.

Jaromir regretted having been so harsh, but he turned back to the task at hand, walking to the doorway of the room. "Inna, you can sleep in your clothes. I'm not shutting the door, even for a few moments."

She stared out at him with hollow eyes but didn't argue. Perhaps the reality of her situation was beginning to set in.

"Sir," Pavel said, "Rurik and I should take the first watch. That way, you can sleep for a few hours. The last attack occurred halfway between the mid of night and dawn. If you and Winshaw take the watch in three hours, that'll most likely be when the killer appears anyway." He paused.

"Plus, I've been on night watch this week, and I'm not tired."

Jaromir hated to just go to sleep, but Pavel's words made sense, and Jaromir was determined to count only upon these three men he trusted, spelling each other in teams, in short three-hour shifts in order to keep alert.

"All right." He nodded. "Have me woken in three hours, and remember my apartments are within shouting distance." He turned to look inside the room. "Don't take your eyes off her . . . I mean it. One of you keeps a watch on her if she has to use the chamber pot. Understand?"

"Yes, sir."

Still reluctant to leave, he headed down the passage to his own rooms. Pavel was right, and he'd be in better form if he at least rested for a few hours. But only when he slipped inside his rooms and found himself alone did he relax enough to let doubts begin to flow. There was no guarantee the killer would strike tonight. This night vigil could be repeated for some time. He had to make sure his men remained alert.

Worse, what would happen when the killer realized he or she couldn't attack Inna without being seen by two armed soldiers? Would the murderer choose another victim? No, Jaromir had to rely on Céline's vision. It was all he had.

Running a hand across his jaw, he tried to remember the last time he'd shaved properly. His goatee was turning into a beard, but he was too exhausted to care.

A knock sounded on the door.

With a sigh, he went to open it, wondering if Pavel or Rurik had forgotten to ask him something.

But it was Bridgette standing on the other side, wearing nothing but a silk dressing gown with a half-tied sash. Had she walked from her own apartments like this? Her red-gold hair was hanging loose, and his eyes fixed on her face, moving down her throat to the V in the dressing gown between her breasts. He knew that her body was delicate and soft at the same time.

"I fear I offended you this evening," she said. "If so, I have come to apologize."

She hardly sounded apologetic, but her coming here—without him sending a message—must be humiliating on her part. She'd been married to one of the wealthiest silk merchants in the province, and now she was sharing a bed with an ex-mercenary.

A part of him thought on her earlier cruelty to Amelie tonight, and he wanted to send her away. Another part kept looking at the V in her dressing gown. He was tired, but he also needed release, and they'd always served each other well in that capacity.

Stepping back, he held the door, and she entered with the hint of a triumphant smile. By the time he'd closed the door and turned around, she'd untied her sash and let her dressing gown drop to the floor.

He couldn't help a sharp intake of breath. Her skin was flawless, and he took in the sight of her high-set breasts and the small red-gold triangle at the tops of her thighs. Without waiting, he moved to her, grabbing her bare back with one hand and moving his other hand between her legs.

She gasped and said urgently, "Don't take off your armor."

He knew she liked all elements of the act of having sex with a soldier. He'd never minded before. But something about the way she'd said it hit him wrong. He didn't know why. Pulling her in tightly, he pressed his tongue into her mouth and waited for his body to respond.

In his mind, he kept hearing the same brightly spoken but cutting sentences over and over.

Did you farm pigs there? I heard almost all the peasants under Damek's rule farm pigs for a living.

The cruel tone of it echoed in his ears.

Sliding his hand from her back up to cup one of her breasts, he kissed her deeper, willing himself into arousal.

It didn't work.

A shop? How charming. So then you must have kept the pigs out back?

He stopped and took his mouth from hers. This wasn't going to work. For all her beauty, the memory of her trying to hurt Amelie was branded onto his brain.

"What is it?" she asked.

He reached for her dressing gown and handed it to her. "I'm tired. Go back to your own rooms."

Alarm—possibly fear—flickered across her face. She was wealthy enough, but her place here at court, and her choice apartments, were due to him.

"Jaromir?"

He could see any number of questions developing on her lips, and he hoped she wouldn't ask them. He was too weary to lie to her tonight, and once spoken, the words could not be taken back. That was a great tragedy of life. Words could never be taken back.

She seemed to realize this as well, and managed a brittle smile while reaching for her gown. "Of course. You only need call on me, and I'll come directly."

After tying her sash, she made a graceful exit.

Looking at the closed door behind her, he didn't think he'd be calling upon her again.

Amelie didn't know what to do.

She'd led Céline back to their room, thinking that some time alone together by the crackling fire would help set things right, but Céline continued to tremble while pacing the floor.

"He's wrong," she kept whispering. "Why can't he see that? He needs to get her away from here, but Anton won't listen to me. He only listens to him."

"Céline! What is wrong with you?"

Amelie had never seen her sister like this. Once again, she thought Céline pointing a finger at the next victim—and Inna at that—was a mistake. Last time, by a fluke, the poor girl she'd named had turned out to be the next victim. But Amelie doubted such an event occurring again. This strategy of Céline's seemed to lack any sort of plan.

Céline looked over at her. "Jaromir is wrong, and he's going to get Inna killed."

"You can't possibly know that. Are you starting to believe your own game?"

After standing there a moment longer, Céline went to the bed, sitting on the edge. "Come and sit with me. I have something to tell you. Something I should have said days ago, but I haven't known how."

Amelie moved slowly to join her sister. She didn't like this. "What?"

Céline opened her mouth and closed it again. Whatever she had to say, she truly didn't know how to say it.

"We've never had secrets from each other," Amelie said.

"No. No, we haven't." But Céline paused again. "I've been seeing the future when I read some people . . . really seeing their futures. It started back home when I read Rhiannon. I saw Damek having her falsely accused of adultery and strangled. I saw Sybil die. I saw black gloves reaching for her face and throat. Tonight, I saw Inna die the same way."

Amelie froze. "No, I know Mother could see for real, but we . . . we live by our wits."

Céline stared at the floor and shook her head. "I was afraid to tell you. I was afraid of what you'd say. But it's true. I'm becoming like Mother." Her eyes flew up. "It doesn't change anything. It could even help us. I'm giving the correct answers once I have a true vision . . . or I think I am." Her voice grew intense. "But so far, I haven't been able to change anything I've seen, not for certain! Jaromir is wrong for keeping Inna in the castle. She should be taken far away."

Amelie sat there, still frozen. For the past five years, she and Céline had lived by their wits and their strengths, with Céline playing the seer and Amelie making certain they were both safe, protected. At times, the money Céline earned made the partnership feel less than equal, but Amelie had worked hard at her contributions, and as sisters, they treated each other as equals. Now Céline was becoming like Mother? A true seer?

"It won't change anything," Céline insisted. "But tonight, you have to help me."

"With what?"

"To save Inna. We have to try and alter the future I saw for her."

Amelie shook her head in confusion. "Save her? We'd never get near her. Jaromir's got two armed guards on her door."

Céline stood up. "I can get near her. As we were heading back here tonight, I heard Pavel volunteer for the first watch." She paced toward the hearth. "But we need to get down into the village and break into the apothecary's shop first."

"Why?"

Céline turned around. "Because I saw poppies growing in the herb garden."

CHAPTER 9

Céline had a bad feeling that her three hours were almost up. It had taken longer for them to get down to the village, break through a window at the shop, and harvest the poppies than she'd expected. Only the youngest, nearly unripe heads would work for what she needed.

Then she'd had to go back inside the shop to boil the heads down properly to make a white, milky syrup.

She knew she was endangering her chances of ever achieving ownership of the shop, and the thought pained her, but Inna's life mattered more. And for all his good intentions, Jaromir was wrong.

Once back inside the castle, she and Amelie had hurried up to their room. Helga always left a jug of cold spiced tea and two mugs on their dressing table, in case one of them should become thirsty in the night. Without hesitation, Céline poured two mugs of the tea and unstoppered the vial she'd carried from the village.

"How much will you use?" Amelie asked.

"All of it."

She poured half the vial of the milky substance into one mug and the rest in the other.

"All of it?" Amelie repeated, watching her.

"It has to put them to sleep."

Amelie glanced down at a chair. "We could just break a leg off this, and I could put them to sleep."

"Both of them? I doubt you could reach Pavel's head. And anyway, it would just give Jaromir an excuse to lock you up if he catches us."

"Oh, and drugging them is so much better."

Strangely, even after her painful confession, things between her and Amelie seemed unaltered. They might argue, but they had always worked together. Perhaps nothing would change after all.

"So how are you going to get them to drink it?" Amelie asked. "Use your charm?"

"That's the general idea. But we need to hurry. If Jaromir takes watch, we won't have a chance. Not even if you offered it to him."

"Not even if I . . . ," Amelie stammered. "What does that mean?"

"Come on," Céline said. "We need to go."

Carrying both mugs, she led the way back downstairs, past the great hall, and to a stairwell leading up again, inside the west tower, toward a section of the castle that housed permanent residents.

Before stepping off at the first landing, she steeled herself. "You'd better stay here out of sight," she told Amelie, "and let me handle this first part."

Without waiting for an answer, she started down the passage, spotting Pavel outside the assigned door in the same moment he spotted her coming.

His face registered shock at first, and then a flush of pleasure. She was still wearing the lavender gown.

Céline had little understanding of feminine wiles, but she didn't need them here. She knew what most men responded to, what most people responded to really: nurturing kindness. Pavel's predisposed attraction to her should do the rest.

As she approached, the other guard turned to face her as well . . . What was he called? Rurik?

"It's late, miss," he said.

She offered them both a tired smile. "I know, but I couldn't sleep." Holding out the mugs, she said, "You've been here for hours, and I thought you might be thirsty. It's just cold tea, but it's spiced, with a little milk added. Helga left it for us to drink in the night."

Rurik hesitated, but Pavel seemed in charge here and told him, "It's all right."

After that, the ease with which both men reached out surprised even her. Under normal circumstances, Jaromir would not have hesitated to accept a mug of tea from a pretty face, but he'd never have taken one from her hand or Amelie's tonight. He'd have suspected they were up to something—which they were.

Pavel seemed so pleased by her attention that she felt a stab of guilt.

"Has all been quiet?" she asked, looking into the room where Inna lay sleeping.

He took a swallow of tea and nodded. "The lieutenant's lady came by, but otherwise we've seen no one."

Jaromir had a lady? That was news.

But she listened politely, watching him take another swallow.

"All right," she said. "I just wanted to check on you and bring you something to drink."

His face softened at the words "check on you," and another stab of guilt hit home.

"What time will you breakfast?" he asked.

"Probably midmorning," she lied.

"I'll meet you in the dining hall."

Though she had no intention of being anywhere near this castle by midmorning, she said, "Be sure you get some sleep first. You've had a long night."

He seemed so taken aback by her concern that he couldn't speak.

"Both of you, drink up," she said, "so I can take the mugs back to our room."

They tipped their mugs and swallowed down the rest of the tea. With a motherly countenance, she gathered the mugs and bid them both good night. After walking gracefully down the passage, she stepped back onto the landing and moved out of sight, where Amelie was hiding around the corner inside the stairwell.

Amelie stared at her and whispered, "I was watching. They were like little boys in your hands."

"That was the easy part. You wait until we have to get Inna out of the room. You'll have to keep her quiet."

Amelie raised one eyebrow. "What's the plan after that?"

"I'm not entirely sure," Céline whispered back. "You might have to steal us a pony and cart. We'll get her at least a day away from the village and find a safe place to keep her. You can stay with her—keep her there. But I can't be away too long if I'm to continue to help catch the killer. I'll come back and explain to Anton what we've done and that I am still willing to keep seeking information about the murderer . . . short of letting Jaromir use the girls as bait. I won't stand for that."

"I don't know, Céline. That means you'll be traveling for at least a day by yourself, getting back here."

"Well, let's just get Inna out of the village and then decide what to do next."

Sighing, Amelie asked, "How long till Pavel and Rurik fall asleep?"

"I'm not sure. I've never drugged anyone before."

Although she hadn't said anything, Amelie hardly expected Céline's plan to go smoothly. For one, Pavel and Rurik weren't likely to both fall over in a dead faint at the same moment. And two, she wasn't convinced they should be doing this at all.

She didn't disagree with Céline's viewpoint. If Inna indeed was the next victim, then she should be taken as far from danger as possible . . . but Amelie wasn't quite as willing to risk their own future and place here in order to help the likes of Inna.

There seemed to be something else driving Céline onward, a need to prove to herself that she could change what she'd seen in her vision.

So, Amelie hid there with her on the landing for a while, just waiting and listening. All was quiet. In light of what they were attempting tonight, she'd strapped both her dagger and her short sword to her belt.

"Maybe I should go and check?" Céline whispered. "See if they're asleep."

But before she'd finished her sentence, a slurred voice sounded from down the passage.

"Pavel . . . Pavel, wake up!"

Amelie dashed out from the landing. Looking down the passage, she saw Rurik weaving on his feet, standing over the unconscious body of Pavel laid out on the floor.

"Pavel!" Rurik slurred again. All she could see of him was his exposed back.

Knowing it was possible that his voice might soon reach Jaromir, Amelie jerked her short sword from its sheath and held it point up, hilt down.

She flew down the passage, running up behind the disoriented Rurik and hitting him as hard as she could on the back of his head with the hilt.

He dropped like a sack of grain, landing on top of Pavel's chest.

Turning, Amelie found Céline right behind her.

"We need to get Inna. Quick!" Céline breathed.

Amelie rushed into the room just as Inna was beginning to stir, probably awakened by the activity outside her door. Without hesitation, Amelie sheathed her sword, grabbed Inna's mouth, and dragged her out of bed. Eyes wide, Inna struggled and fought, but she wasn't strong, and Amelie had no trouble holding her.

"You try and get us caught, and I'll bash the back of your head in," Amelie hissed in her ear, positioning her so she had a clear view of Rurik.

She had no intention of doing this—but Inna didn't know that.

Céline hurried in. "We're trying to help you, to save you. Just come with us."

Inna struggled harder and tried to cry out, this time sounding enraged as opposed to frightened, and this time, her anger made her feel stronger. Amelie's grip slipped. With little choice, she let go with her right hand and used her left to jerk Inna around and punch her across the jaw.

Like Rurik, she dropped.

"What did you do that for?" Céline whispered in panic.

"What did you expect?" Amelie whispered

back. "That we could drag her out the castle's front doors kicking and screaming?"

Hoisting Inna's unconscious form over her shoulder, Amelie carried her down the passage and down the stairwell, weaving only a few times under the extra weight. Céline followed anxiously but didn't say anything more.

Once on the main floor, they made a beeline for the castle's entryway and the open doors leading out into the courtyard—which led to the short bridge into the village. At night, two guards were usually in attendance at the entryway, but the castle was always open to anyone of the Sèone community, and as the taverns and eateries and gambling dens were out in the village, the guards were accustomed to nobles, merchants, or other soldiers coming and going around the clock. They were mainly posted to question strangers attempting to enter in the late hours.

It appeared Anton trusted his own people, and the stronger security had all been focused on the outer gates.

"Pretend you're drunk," Amelie told Céline, and they both weaved on their feet—with Amelie still carrying Inna—as they approached the entryway.

Both guards on duty had played cards with Amelie over the past few days, and so they knew her. One of them, Guardsman Stiva, smiled ruefully when she approached.

"Are you ever going to bed?" he asked.

She'd passed them both earlier when she and Céline had gone to make the poppy syrup and come back. Amelie patted Inna's bottom. "We had a little gathering in our room, and my friend here had too much wine. I think she needs some air."

Glancing at Inna's backside in mild concern, he asked, "You want some help?"

"No, we're good."

Amelie staggered past him, not entirely faking, as Inna was starting to get heavy. Céline followed. Once they were outside the castle, cool night air blew across their faces, and they hurried across the courtyard, out the gates, and over the bridge into the village.

"Down here," Céline said, moving out ahead and trotting toward the path, turning and heading to the back outer wall of a stable, out of sight of the castle. Amelie went after her as quickly as she could, relieved to lower Inna to the ground once they were safely hidden in the shadows.

"She's not as light as she looks."

Inna began to stir. Her eyes opened. For a moment they were blank, and then she hissed like a cat, sitting up, pressing her back against the stable wall and looking around. "What have you . . . Where am I?"

"You're almost safe," Céline said. "Stop fighting and trust us!" She leaned closer. "I saw you die, and you were in a room with gray stone walls. We're going to get you all the way out of this village, just to be sure."

"Out of the village?" Inna was so taken aback, her words didn't even sound venomous. Then bitter poison began leaking into her voice as her eyes narrowed. "You fools. Prince Anton orders both the inner and outer portcullises to be closed at night. He began that some time ago to avoid a night attack when the civil wars increased in the north."

"Yes, but they'll let us out," Céline said. "I can see no one being allowed inside, but surely the guards will allow villagers or merchants who wish to leave to get out."

Inna shook her head with great satisfaction. "No, they have orders not to open either portcullis until dawn for any reason. Some other prince hiding his men outside might take advantage. The way the castle is positioned, anyone approaching the gates in daylight hours can be seen for leagues, but Prince Anton is cautious at night."

Amelie let her mind go back to that first day they'd arrived here. She remembered Jaromir saying something at dawn about it getting light enough to enter, just as she'd looked ahead to see a gatehouse with a closed portcullis, set inside a stone wall, on the other side of a bridge stretching over the moat. Beyond that gatehouse had been a road leading about halfway up the hill to another gatehouse set against another stone wall.

Even Jaromir had waited for dawn before trying to enter the exterior gate.

Even Jaromir.

She closed her eyes. "Then we can't get out of the village tonight."

"And by morning," Inna said smugly, "the lieutenant will have every man under his command searching for you, and all the guards on the gates will have been warned." Her expression shifted slightly, more to a demeanor of begging. "But we can go back inside now. If you let me attend to my lord, I swear I'll say you were only trying to help me do my duties, not trying to steal me away. Prince Anton would understand that. He wouldn't punish you for freeing me to attend him."

Her eyes were glassy, with a hint of madness, and Amelie wondered if perhaps they shouldn't give up on this venture and take her back inside.

"No," Céline said flatly. "We'll hide somewhere until morning, and then I'll think of a way to get us out those gates. Inna, if you go back inside that castle, or even if you stay in this village, I think you will die."

Inna leaned back, hissing like a cat again.

"Céline . . . ," Amelie began, not certain how to voice her doubts. "Where are we going to hide? As soon as Jaromir finds Pavel and Rurik, he'll get a search going. We can't go to the apothecary's shop. It's the first place he'll look. We don't know anyone in the village. We have no friends here to help us."

At the word "friends," Céline stiffened. She was quiet for a moment and then looked up. "I think I might know where to go."

*   *   *

Exhausted from five days of too little rest and too much strain, Jaromir slept on his bed, still wearing his chain armor and tabard. But after a while, his internal instincts began to expect a knock at the door, a call for him to take watch.

His eyes opened.

He lay on top of the blankets for a moment, feeling that something was wrong . . . the time of night felt wrong. As he sat up, the feeling increased, and he got out of bed, hurrying for the door.

Out in the passage, he looked left. "Pavel," he called, expecting an answer. None came.

He'd taken only a few steps when he spotted the bodies on the floor, and he started running, panic flooding through him.

"Pavel!"

When he reached them, though, he didn't stop. Instead he jumped over the top of them and skidded into the room, expecting the worst. But to his puzzlement, no shriveled corpse lay in the bed. It was empty. Whirling back around, he noticed the lump on the back of Rurik's head, and he strode back to the doorway, lifting Rurik from where he lay over Pavel's chest. Rurik was breathing, but he was like a deadweight. Pavel moaned.

What had happened here?

Where was Inna?

Kneeling by Pavel, Jaromir shook him, none too gently. "Wake up!"

Pavel's eyelids cracked a slit. He sported no visible injuries, and yet his hand went to his head and he moaned again.

"Get up!" Jaromir ordered, needing information right now. "What happened here? Where's Inna?"

Using both hands, he grabbed the front of Pavel's tabard, pulled him up, and leaned him against the wall. In Inna's frantic devotion to Anton, had she somehow managed to overcome her guards and escape?

The young corporal's eyes opened in confusion. "Inna? I . . . I . . ." He coughed a few times, and then he saw Rurik lying on the floor. "What happened?"

"That's what I'm asking you!"

Pavel's eyes moved to Jaromir's face, and they cleared slightly. "Sir, I . . ."

"What's the last thing you remember?"

Pavel blinked. "Céline . . . she brought us some tea."

Jaromir went cold. "Céline brought you tea and you drank it?" He could feel the anger building beneath the surface of his skin, and he fought to hold it back. "Céline, who was earlier arguing with me to have Inna moved outside the village? Who is a skilled apothecary? She handed you a cup of tea while you were standing guard and you drank it?"

Realization began dawning on Pavel's face, followed by anger, as he seemed to be piecing together what must have happened. "Sir, I didn't think—"

"No, you didn't! You didn't think at all, did you?"

Jaromir rocked back on his heels, considering options. No one could leave the village at night, so the sisters would have to try to hide Inna someplace until morning, and it was unlikely they'd do so inside the castle.

But they had his only bait, his only way to lure and trap the murderer.

His first instinct was rouse every available man under his command and launch a full-scale search, but he rejected that idea as quickly as it came. The people of Sèone were already frightened enough by this series of unexplained deaths. Soldiers flooding the village in a search would hardly help mend the fraying illusion of peace and security here.

"All right, Corporal," he told Pavel. "You clear your head fast, because this is what we're going to do." He paused. "The two of us are going down to the village ourselves, and we're going to keep this quiet. They can't have gone far, and we're going to find them and bring them back here. Can you walk?"

The rage, the darkness in Pavel's eyes surprised him. "I can walk."

So the young man felt betrayed by a woman. Well, it wouldn't be the first time, and this was a lesson he wouldn't soon forget.

Jaromir offered him no pity. "This is your fault, and we'd better find them before morning and Prince Anton hears of this." He glanced down at Rurik. "Help me get him onto the bed first."

Céline followed a trail of smoke rising high into the night sky. She knew from experience back in Shetâna that blacksmiths would often keep the forge smoldering all night to make life easier the following morning when work began.

In the spring, most peasants let their fires go out at night to keep from burning unnecessary fuel during hours of sleep. The weather wasn't exactly warm, but it wasn't frigid either.

"Where are we going?" Amelie whispered, dragging the unwilling Inna along behind.

"You'll see," Céline answered, too focused on the trail of rising smoke to stop and explain. She didn't even know if this would work, but she couldn't think of anything else to try, and they had to find someplace to hide until she could think of a way to get Inna past Jaromir's soldiers and out the gates.

They passed a number of closed shops and dark dwellings and seemed to be heading straight toward the south side of the Sèone wall. Most of the eateries and taverns were on the other side of the village, so the street was quiet.

After passing another small stable, it didn't take Céline long to find the blacksmith's forge—with a well-constructed house attached.

"Keep her quiet and wait here," Céline instructed.

"What are you doing?" Amelie asked.

"Just trust me."

With a quick breath, Céline hurried over to the front of the house and knocked. Nothing happened, and she knocked again. This time she heard heavy footsteps, and a large middle-aged man opened the door. "What in the name of the gods . . . ," he mumbled, rubbing one hand over his eyes, and then he saw her. She didn't recognize him from the banquet that evening, but he seemed to recognize her, so he must have been there.

"I know it's late," Céline rushed to say, "but could I please speak to Erin?"

"Father," a soft voice said, "who is it?"

Erin stepped from a room in the back out into view, her blond braids coming loose from their ties. She saw Céline in the doorway.

"I'm sorry for this," Céline said, "but I need help."

"So you just let the prince's seer walk in and out of here twice?" Jaromir asked in short, clipped words. "And the second time, her sister was carrying *his* personal attendant over one shoulder?"

He was at the entryway of the castle, questioning the guards there, making certain that Céline had gone outside.

"I never saw their friend's face," Guardsman Stiva protested. "Amelie told me they'd all been drinking and needed some air. We've no orders to stop castle guests from coming and going."

He sounded defensive, and in truth, Jaromir couldn't fault him. Castle guests and residents had always been allowed to come and go as they pleased. He was just frustrated, and he wanted to take it out on someone.

"We should go, sir," Pavel said, his voice deadly quiet.

Jaromir nodded, and they headed across the courtyard, through the gates, over the bridge, and out into the village spreading all around them.

"Will this do?" Erin asked, holding a lantern up to the door of a small shack out back of the forge.

She still seemed uncertain about hiding Anton's clearly unwilling personal attendant from Jaromir, but Céline had explained the situation carefully and honestly and managed to convince Erin that Inna's life was at stake. Erin's gratitude to Céline had done the rest.

She'd taken them out of the forge house, around the back, and into a run-down area that sported a small faded shack. A small grove of untended aspen trees grew on the west side. "I think my grandfather stored tools in here once, before my father made improvements to the forge." She looked back at Céline. "No one will look for you here."

"It's perfect," Céline said, stepping up to the door. "Thank you."

"When Prince Anton learns of this," Inna spat at Erin, "your father won't be blacksmith in Sèone anymore."

Erin winced, but Céline cut in quickly. "That's not true. If Anton decides to punish anyone, it'll be me."

Lowering her voice, Erin whispered, "Why do you risk yourself to save this woman who does not wish to be saved?"

Céline didn't want to mention her attempt to alter a future that she'd seen—especially not to Erin. "I have to try," she answered simply.

Shaking her head, Erin handed her the lantern and then pushed the door further open to let her inside. Céline entered, holding the lantern high and glancing around. The place was cold and dusty, with a back door but no windows. At least they were out of sight. That was all that mattered. "You'd better go back to the house," she told Erin.

Amelie dragged Inna through the door and shoved her down into a sitting position. "Stay there," she ordered.

Céline sighed. There were only a few hours until dawn, but she felt they would be long ones.

"They're not here, but they were," Jaromir said, walking through the main room of the apothecary's shop. "There are still embers in the hearth. Céline must have come here to make whatever she fed you." He picked up some loose poppy petals on the floor. "Some kind of opiate."

Pavel didn't answer at first and then said, "She's not here now."

No, and Jaromir hadn't expected to find his quarry here. But he'd had to at least look. What now? Sèone was a large community, almost a town.

"Where would they hide?" Pavel said, almost to himself, as he walked across the floor, looking at the web-covered jars and pots along the wall. "They don't know anyone outside the castle. They have no friends out here. Where can we even start?"

Jaromir's memory for verbal exchanges was sharp, and he recalled a softly spoken sentence from earlier that evening.

If I can ever do anything for you, please ask me.

He started for the door. "I can think of one place."

Time seemed to drag. As Amelie crouched on the floor of the filthy shack, she was growing less and less certain of this undertaking. Success seemed nearly impossible—and failure could come at a high personal price.

As if reading her face by the dim light of the lantern, Céline said, "Please don't give up on me, Amelie. I have to see this through. What use is my gift to anyone if I can't prevent a tragedy or a death?"

Her voice was so tight that Amelie scooted closer, feeling guilty for her doubts. Céline had openly asked very little of her in their lives to date.

"You're with me, aren't you?" Céline asked. "You'll help me?"

"Yes," Amelie answered, and she meant it. "I'll help."

Inna was leaning up against a stack of wooden boxes. She hadn't spoken since they'd entered the shack and settled to wait. "I need to relieve myself," she said. "And I won't do it in here."

"Just hold it," Amelie said.

"I can't."

What an impossible pain this woman was. Amelie could barely stand the thought of spending days in her company. How had Anton put up with her turning down his bed, laying out his nightclothes, preparing food and drink in his rooms, and hovering around him? Just the thought made her shudder.

"We could take her outside for a moment," Céline suggested. "She's right about not . . . going in here. The smell would be unbearable after a while."

Amelie stood up. "Oh, very well, but you stay in here, Céline. The fewer people moving around out there, the better." She reached for Inna. "If you yell out or try to run, I swear you'll be sorry."

After pulling Inna out the door, she closed it behind them and looked around, spotting the grove of aspen trees growing on the west side of the shack. "Come on," she whispered. "Over there."

Jaromir approached the forge carefully with Pavel right behind him. "We'll do a full sweep before we start knocking on doors," he said quietly.

Pavel nodded, but he'd been strangely silent since leaving the apothecary's shop, and Jaromir worried he might be taking Céline's betrayal too hard.

"This way," Jaromir said, moving west. He wanted to get an idea what types of buildings or possible hiding places lay around the forge. He was still hoping they could handle this situation quickly and quietly.

"We'll question the family if we have to," he whispered, "but first I'd rather—"

He froze as movement ahead caught his eye. Amelie came out of a decaying shack and began leading Inna into a small grove of aspen trees. Moonlight bathed both women, glinting off Amelie's black hair.

He pulled back, motioning to Pavel and ducking around the corner of the forge.

"Céline's probably still inside the shack," he said. "You get her, and I'll get Amelie and Inna."

Pavel nodded.

Céline wrapped her arms around herself, wishing she'd been more sensible about a few things—like tracking down some cloaks before they'd left the castle. But Lady Karina had sent only indoor clothing for their wardrobe, and Céline wouldn't have known where to find any cloaks.

Still, the fact was that they had no warm clothing and only the money Amelie had won playing cards.

As insistent as she'd been that they keep going, so far no ideas had come to her of how they might disguise themselves to get through the gates. She had no doubt that by morning Jaromir would have given the guards orders to detain anyone fitting her and Amelie's descriptions.

She gripped herself tighter, rocking back and forth.

That was when the door burst open, as if it had been kicked. It slammed against the sidewall with a bang.

Pavel was standing in the doorway.

Céline jumped to her feet, alarmed but not afraid . . . until she got a clear look at his face. Instinctual terror—from all her years in Shetâna—shot through her. Whirling, she darted for the back door, running wildly to get through it before he caught her.

As her hand reached the latch and pulled, two arms shot past her head, one on each side, slamming the door closed and holding it.

"Don't!" she cried without thinking, turning around inside his arms to push against his chest. He didn't move. He just stood there, breathing hard, his body trapping hers against the door. She could feel the chain armor beneath his tabard and found herself staring at the hollow of his throat as he continued breathing in and out loudly.

He was angry, beyond angry, and she was afraid of him.

Slowly, she tried to look up, only to find him looking down at her. Even in the dim lantern's light, she could see the danger in his face. She cursed herself for falling into the illusion that he was nothing like one of Damek's men, for thinking him to be safe.

Pavel was a soldier.

"You played with me," he whispered. "Made me look a fool to the lieutenant."

She had.

Still, he hadn't hurt her, and at least he was talking.

"I'm sorry," she answered, staring at the hollow of his throat again. "I didn't have a choice. I had to save Inna . . . I had to see if I could change my vision. I still think the lieutenant is wrong and that Inna will die if she remains here." The speed of her words picked up. "I know I embarrassed you, but isn't her life worth that much?"

He didn't move, and he didn't answer. She was still trapped against the door.

"And what about Prince Anton?" she rushed on. "If we don't start saving some of these girls, his reputation will suffer, and he could be overlooked to head the House of Pählen."

He answered softly, "Maybe it's best if he is overlooked."

Jaromir was surprised when Pavel kicked open the door of the shack. He hadn't expected that.

But a few seconds later, he had his hands full as Amelie came running from the aspen trees and saw him. She stopped beside a stack of firewood, her eyes moving between him and the door of the shack.

"Don't move," he ordered.

Inna came running from the aspens, her loose hair sticking to her face, her breaths coming fast. "Lieutenant, you're here. Please, please take me to my lord. I never laid out his bedclothes."

She sounded mad, but he kept his eyes on Amelie—whose right hand flashed down to the short sword on her hip. She didn't pull it. She just grabbed the hilt.

If she'd been anyone else, he would have drawn his sword, but he just couldn't bring himself to pull it, not on her.

"It's over," he said. "Pavel has Céline, and we're all going to back to the castle."

"To my lord," Inna cried, "not that room. To my lord!"

He ignored her, keeping his gaze on Amelie's hand. He didn't want to hurt her. "I'm coming over. Don't draw that blade. We're just going back to the castle."

Slowly, she took her hand off the hilt. He relaxed just a bit and walked toward her. She hadn't spoken, but she seemed calm. Maybe she'd finally seen some sense and knew they had no way out of the gates.

He never saw her next move coming. Just as he drew close enough to touch her, her body became a blur as she grabbed a small log from the wood-pile and rammed the end of it into his stomach. When he doubled forward, she drew it back and clubbed him across the jaw. Pain exploded in his head, and he nearly fell.

She was coming around for another hard blow as he roared and grabbed her wrist, wrapping his other arm around her waist and picking her up. She dropped the log, but she kicked his leg once before he slammed her feet against the ground and whipped her body around, pinning both her arms with his own and lifting her feet off the ground again, with her back to his chest. His stomach hurt, and the pain in his jaw was blinding, and he held her hard enough to hurt her—without caring.

"Quit!" he managed to say.

She fought a few moments longer and then went still. She wouldn't win this on strength, and they both knew it.

"Put me down," she said finally.

He didn't.

"Inna!" he ordered. "Stay right there."

Carrying Amelie, he strode to the doorway of the shack and stopped just inside.

Pavel had Céline trapped against the back door, and something about his stance unsettled Jaromir . . . or maybe it was the look on Céline's face. She was afraid.

"Corporal," Jaromir barked, ignoring the pain in his stomach. "Stand down. We're going back to the castle."

CHAPTER 10

The sisters spent the remainder of the night locked in their guest room with a guard posted outside.

Céline had no idea what to expect next, but she wasn't surprised when Guardsman Winshaw opened their door about two hours past dawn and told her she'd been summoned to Prince Anton. She'd already washed and brushed her hair and donned her old red dress.

"I'm coming, too," Amelie said.

"No," Winshaw answered.

"She's not going alone."

Seeing an ugly confrontation brewing, Céline turned to her sister. "It's all right. Just stay here. I probably won't be long."

She had no idea if anything would be all right, but Amelie would do them no service here by attacking another castle guard. Hurrying out to the passage, she was relieved when Winshaw closed the door, with Amelie still inside, and one small crisis had been averted.

Another guard was posted outside, which suggested that Amelie was still going to be kept in their room.

But then Céline found herself being rushed along the passage, and her fears began to return.

In Shetâna, Damek's subjects could be slaughtered for complaining about the state of the roads. She knew things worked differently here on the surface, but Anton's behavior at last night's banquet and the threat of violence she'd seen on Pavel's face were beginning to convince her that the men here didn't like being defied any more than the ones back home.

While she didn't think Anton would resort to violence himself—or probably not—he could certainly dismiss her and Amelie, which would be a polite term for throwing them out of the village with no food and no home. Worse, if he was truly angry at what he might construe as betrayal, he could turn them back over to his brother.

She and Winshaw reached the main floor, and she expected him to take her through the great hall, to the small side chamber where Anton had spoken with her several times before. But Winshaw motioned her to keep going, and he led the way to the stairwell inside the west tower leading up into the quarters for permanent residents.

"Where are we going?" she asked.

"The prince's apartments."

She halted. "No." She had no intention of being

trapped alone with Anton in his private rooms, especially not if he was already angry.

Winshaw turned around impatiently and reached out for her wrist. When she pulled back in alarm, he stopped with his hand in midair and said, "My lord is not well this morning but still wishes to question you. The lieutenant is with him."

Céline wavered, feeling foolish. "Oh . . ."

He turned and began walking again. She followed. He went past the landing on the first floor, curving around to the next flight, and he stepped off at the second landing, moving all the way to the end of the passage there and knocking once.

"Lieutenant?"

The door opened instantly, and Jaromir looked out. The left side of his jaw sported a black and purple bruise from where Amelie had clubbed him with a log last night.

"Inside," he ordered Céline. His face was unreadable.

Standing straight, she walked past him. She heard him dismiss Winshaw and close the door, but she couldn't help looking all around . . . at Anton's sitting room. She'd not known what to expect—if she'd expected anything at all—but the place was rather austere. There were tapestries on the walls and a large hearth. The furnishings consisted of a messy writing desk, a few heavy wooden chairs, and rows of bookshelves along the walls. It looked more like the chambers of a scholar than those of a prince. A closed door stood on the same wall as the hearth, and she suspected it led to his sleeping chambers.

Anton himself sat himself sat in one of the heavy wooden chairs, wearing a burgundy dressing gown. His feet were bare. But Winshaw had not been exaggerating. He didn't look well. As opposed to pale, his face was tinged green this morning, as if he was nauseated, and his hands were twitching.

Jaromir moved over to stand beside him, and neither one invited her to sit down. They both seemed to expect her to speak first, and for some reason, in her nervousness, the first thing that came out of her mouth was, "Please don't punish Pavel. I used him. It wasn't his fault."

Jaromir's face flickered in surprise, and Anton sighed, using one hand to try to hold the other still. "Céline, no one is going to *punish* anyone. But you cannot ever again disregard Jaromir's decisions and go off on larks of your own. There is a chain of command here, and in matters of security, he is at the top."

Both men looked at her expectantly, as if they anticipated a profuse apology, possibly even a little begging of their pardons.

She stared at Anton. Instead of feeling relief that he wasn't going to banish her and Amelie or turn them over to Damek, she felt a touch of anger beginning to rise. She wouldn't stand here and be scolded like a child.

"Jaromir's decision was wrong," she said flatly.

"It's still wrong. I am assuming Inna survived the night? If she remains in this castle, she won't survive much longer."

"Céline!" Jaromir barked, his expression growing dark.

Anton lifted a hand to stop further argument, but when he lowered it, he began scratching at his forearm, and she noticed the skin was reddened. She wished she could ask permission to examine it, but he was talking again.

"I understand why you did what you did last night," he said to her, "and I know we have already asked a great deal in forcing you to be witness to these murders before they happen."

She calmed a little. At least he sounded less condescending now.

"So I'm willing to overlook everything," he went on, "you drugging my guards, stealing Inna away, Jaromir and Rurik's injuries . . . all of it. We will proceed with the original bargain, but only if you only agree to continue helping us and to abide by Jaromir's decisions from now on."

"I won't let him use the young women I name as bait."

Jaromir sucked in an angry breath. "This isn't going to work."

Still scratching his forearm, Anton said with less patience, "It *will* work, but we need more information, a good deal more. Céline, I'm afraid we need to ask you for something difficult."

"What?" she asked cautiously.

He hesitated, and again she was tempted to ask to be able to examine him—at the risk of insulting Master Feodor's skills—but then Anton said, "I want you to read Inna one more time."

Of all the things she might have expected him to say, this wasn't among them. The thought of watching Inna die again was almost more than Céline could face.

"I know what I'm asking," he rushed on, "but I had a thought. This time, neither Jaromir nor I will interfere no matter how distraught you become. I want you to stay inside the vision as long as you can, long enough to see as much as you can . . . perhaps the killer's face."

She let the words sink in.

The annoyance on Jaromir's bruised face vanished. He was looking at her with concern now, possibly regret. "Will you do it?" he asked.

Clearly, they had been discussing this before she arrived. "Is my sister still under house arrest?" she asked.

"No," Anton answered. "We'll have the guard at your door removed at once."

She felt deflated somehow and looked away. "Of course I'll do it. You knew I would do it."

No matter what had happened here, she still wanted the shop. She wanted to stay in this prosperous village inside the safety of a wall. She wanted to stop these murders.

"Good," Jaromir said, walking across the room and opening the door by the hearth.

Inna was on the other side, looking out with wild eyes. Behind her stood an enormous bed covered in a dark blue comforter.

A fresh flash of irritation passed through Céline. They must have certainly believed she'd say yes if they'd already brought up Inna and stored her away in Anton's bedroom.

Am I that predictable? Céline wondered.

"Inna," Anton said in his haughty prince voice, "come out here and sit down."

Why did he always have to speak to her like that?

"You will allow Mistress Fawe to read you again," he ordered.

Inna stepped out slowly, carefully. She still wore her soiled gray dress from last night, and half her hair had come loose, making her look more unhinged than usual. She watched Céline and Jaromir as if they both posed a threat, and then her eyes settled on Anton. She sank down to the floor on her knees.

"My lord, I would do anything you asked, but I beg you, leave me to do my duties in the daylight hours. All the deaths occurred at night, all of them. If you let me serve you in the day, I will gladly sit here and let this gypsy whore touch me and make up any story she likes."

Her voice had a hysterical edge, and Anton didn't seem able to look at her, as if the sight of her kneeling there embarrassed him. Céline wondered why he'd not arranged another position for her long ago.

He asked Jaromir, "May she work without guards during the day?"

Jaromir nodded tightly, looking as if he wanted to leave the room. "If you wish."

"Agreed, then," Anton said, scratching his forearm harder. "Céline, you may proceed."

Although she had agreed to do this, suddenly the thought of touching Inna's hand, of going through this again, made her waver. Perhaps sensing weakness, Inna moved to one of the chairs and sat down, watching Céline with her usual hatred. Jaromir pulled another chair close, and Céline realized she had no choice, not if they were to continue moving forward. Anton's idea was not without merit. Both times before, when she'd seen a young woman die, either he or Jaromir had shaken her out of the vision.

Gritting her teeth, she sat down opposite Inna and reached out, closing her eyes and touching Inna's hand. Clearing her mind, she sensed for the spark of Inna's spirit, focusing all her attention on Inna's future.

The jolt hit her hard this time, almost painfully, followed by another, and then she was rushing forward through the corridor of mists, steeling herself for the grotesque scene that was to come.

The trip was not long.

But when the mists vanished, she didn't find herself inside the small room with the stone walls, looking down at Inna's sleeping face. She was in a bedroom, but tapestries covered the walls and the bed was enormous, covered by a dark blue comforter.

She was in Anton's bedroom. Glancing out the narrow slit of a window, she gauged it to be just before dusk.

Upon hearing a soft muttering, she turned to see Inna at the bedside table pouring a goblet of wine and setting it on the nightstand. She looked much the same, in her soiled gray gown with her hair only half-dressed, and loose strands of it sticking to her face.

"He missed last night's draught," she murmured, "my poor lord. He'll need more."

Reaching into the pocket of her gown, she withdrew a square of folded paper. Laying it on the nightstand, she unfolded it and took out a small packet, which she opened and held over the goblet of wine. White powder fell into the liquid. Inna hesitated and then added another packet, mixing it into the wine until it vanished. "He needs more, my poor lord. So he can rest."

Céline watched in shock. Inna was drugging Anton, and from hints in her murmured words, she'd been doing so for some time.

But at least Céline was not watching Inna die. Had the future been altered?

Then the bedroom vanished and Céline was rushing along on the mists again. She felt dizzy and disoriented when the mists cleared. Only now she found herself again in the small room with Inna asleep in the bed.

The future had not been changed.

Inna was sleeping with her face toward the wall, and Céline trembled, knowing what was to come, but she was determined to remain here, to focus upon seeing as much as possible. Almost instantly, the slender black-gloved hands moved in from the side of the image, reaching down toward Inna.

Summoning all her strength, Céline fought to look up, to half turn inside the vision and see who was standing beside the bed. Her gaze moved up the slender black-clad arms, up and up to the sight of a pale face . . . and when she recognized the face, she thought perhaps she was going mad herself.

It was the young woman from the painting in the upper portrait hall, the pale, dark-haired one beside the campfire, dressed all in black.

The woman continued reaching for Inna.

"No!" Céline cried, trying to push her away. "Don't touch her!"

But Céline wasn't there and could do nothing.

The woman placed one hand on Inna's face and the other on her throat, and Inna's flesh began to shrivel inward on itself.

"No," Céline whispered.

As Inna turned to a dried husk, the woman's face began to take on color, as if she was draining Inna's life away and absorbing it.

Céline forced herself to watch, to glean anything she could from this nightmare scene . . . and the woman began to speak.

"Forgive me," she whispered to Inna's dead body. "Forgive me. I cannot stop. I must obey. I have no choice."

She turned and walked across the small room, vanishing right through the wall like a ghost. She was gone, and Inna was nothing more than a dried husk lying on the bed.

Céline began to weep.

The room vanished.

Still crying softly, she found herself back in Anton's apartments, looking into Inna's suspicious face. But now Anton was out of his chair and kneeling beside Céline.

"Shhhhhh," he said, handing her a handkerchief. "What did you see?"

His voice was urgent.

Céline tried to speak and failed. After wiping her face with the cloth, she tried again. "I saw her. It's the woman in the painting in the upper portrait hall. The one dressed in black, standing by the campfire. She murders Inna . . . drains Inna's life as if taking it into herself."

Anton jumped to his feet. "What?"

"Liar!" Inna spat. "Your lies go too far this time."

"It's her." Céline spoke directly to Anton. "Do you remember that portrait? We were looking right at it."

Anton was staring at her, and Jaromir rushed up beside him, so close their shoulders touched.

"What is this?" Jaromir demanded. "What is she talking about?"

"A portrait," Anton said, "of a young woman . . . wearing long black gloves."

His eyes hadn't moved from Céline's face.

"It's her," Céline insisted. "I saw her drain Inna and then walk right through the wall like a ghost."

Jaromir turned on his heels and began striding toward the door.

"Where are you going?" Anton asked.

"To the upper portrait hall, to burn that painting. To finish this."

"No!" Céline called after him, and he stopped. How could she explain what she'd heard, what she'd felt. "You can't do that. I think . . . I think she is somehow enslaved. I could be wrong, but after killing Inna, she said something about being forced to obey. You can't burn the portrait until we know what's happening here. If the portrait is possessed by a spirit and someone else is controlling it, we must find out who."

Jaromir was looking to Anton for instructions now, and Anton raised a hand. "Hold off. I need to think."

Inna leaned forward in her chair. "Do not listen, my lord. She weaves lies as others weave cloth."

And then Céline turned her attention fully upon Inna, remembering the first vision. "Anton," she said slowly, not caring if anyone was offended by her use of his given name, "this woman has been drugging the wine on your nightstand. I think she's been doing so for some time."

Inna's mouth fell open, and her eyes widened.

Anton took four steps away, as if to put distance between them.

But Jaromir came striding back. "What?"

"It's a white powder stored in paper packets," Céline went on calmly, "that she keeps in the pocket of her dress. I think my vision was of the late afternoon today, before dusk. I saw her stirring it into his wine. I think normally she would do this at a different hour, before he goes to bed, but tonight she'll be under guard again."

Later, she wondered if she shouldn't have broken this news differently, as she should have foreseen the effect such a statement would have on Jaromir. The lieutenant's face hardened, and he grabbed Inna's arm, jerking her out of her chair.

It happened so fast.

Inna cried out in pain, and Céline called, "Jaromir, don't!"

But his other hand was already digging inside the pocket of Inna's dress, and he pulled out a large piece of folded paper, passing it to Céline.

"What is it?" he demanded, keeping Inna in his grip.

Anton stood watching all this without a word.

Céline laid the paper in her lap and unfolded it, taking out one of the packets. Licking her finger, she touched the powder and tasted it.

Her mother had spent years teaching her the various tastes of the proper strengths of components used in powders or elixirs so that if there were ever a question, she would know if she had a correct mix.

"It's an opiate," she said, moving her tongue to the roof of her mouth. "I can taste the poppies . . . but something else, too." Still uncertain, she touched the powder and tasted it again. Then her eyes flew up to Jaromir's face. "There's hemlock in this."

With a roar, he threw Inna back into her chair and leaned over it, placing both his hands on the arms. "Where did you get that? Who gave it to you?"

Inna stared at him, terrified, and shook her head. "It's medicine to help him sleep! He needs it to rest!"

In one swift movement, Jaromir pulled a dagger from his belt and held it to her throat. "Where did you get it?"

Still, Anton did nothing. He just watched in silence.

But Céline was on her feet. She hadn't meant to incite this. "Lieutenant, stop!" She grasped his right arm, trying to pull the blade away. He shoved her backward with his elbow and then put the point of the blade to Inna's cheek. "Where?"

Once again, Céline cursed herself for having become lost in the illusion that justice functioned differently here. She'd never seen Jaromir like this, but she had no doubt he'd start cutting Inna if she didn't give him what he wanted. Céline feared there were few lines he wouldn't cross when it came to protecting Anton.

Inna must have realized this, too, because she said, "Master Feodor."

"Feodor?" Jaromir asked in confusion.

"My lord stopped taking his draughts!" she cried. "He would not drink what Master Feodor gave him. I had to do it! I had to help him rest. Master Feodor said he must have rest."

Jaromir pulled the blade away.

"It's true," Anton said quietly. "I felt Feodor's draughts were not helping me, and I told him I'd take no more."

Céline absorbed the repercussions of this. For some reason, Master Feodor had been feeding Anton a mix of opiates and hemlock. Hemlock could be used in small doses for someone with severe insomnia, but it was certainly not meant for long-term use, and it was also a poison that could kill in larger doses. When Anton stopped taking the draught, Feodor had used Inna to put the powder in Anton's wine.

The expression on Jaromir's face frightened Céline—or at least frightened her for Master Feodor. "You don't know why he did this," she said. "He might have believed he was helping his prince."

Jaromir looked to Anton. "What do you want me to do?"

Anton didn't hesitate. He pointed to Inna. "Take her back to that room you prepared and keep her under guard. Then go have a talk with Master Feodor."

"Yes, my lord," Jaromir answered, grabbing Inna's arm again.

"No!" Inna wailed, trying to pull away. "You promised! You promised I could serve him during the day."

Jaromir dragged her from the room and closed the door behind himself, leaving Céline and Anton in an awkward silence. How could he have allowed someone as sick in her mind as Inna to serve him in such a personal capacity?

Her thoughts must have shown on her face, because he said, "You don't understand."

No, she didn't.

"Inna came with Joselyn," he said simply.

"I know. Pavel told me. He told me that Joselyn helped to keep her from an unfortunate situation."

"Unfortunate? You could say that. Her father sold her to a brothel when she was thirteen years old. Joselyn knew the family, and she saved Inna. When they came here, I could see that Inna was not . . . right. But she loved Joselyn, and I couldn't fault her for that. When Joselyn died, Inna nearly went mad from grief, and I nearly went mad from grief, and she began to do small things for me, as she had for Joselyn. I should have stopped it, but I didn't. I couldn't. I made sure to keep a distance between us, but the only thing keeping her from falling back into grief was being able to care for me." He ran a shaking hand over his face. "Do you think me so wrong?"

"No," Céline said, and she meant it. How could empathy be wrong? "Of course not."

He took his hand away from his face and looked at her.

Amelie had been pacing the floor of their room, and she nearly melted in relief when Céline came back through the door, announcing that their guard had been dismissed and the bargain for the apothecary's shop was still in place.

But her relief was short-lived as Céline began telling her everything else that had happened in the last hour.

"A woman from a painting?" Amelie asked, sinking down on the bed. "How is that possible?"

"I don't know. I only know what I saw."

The door opened, and Helga hobbled in, carrying a tray of food. But Amelie was too caught up in their current dilemma to stop talking.

"What do you mean that you think someone else is controlling her? Who could control an image from a portrait?"

Helga set her tray on the dressing table. "Probably a kettle witch," she said.

Both sisters fell quiet for a moment as they turned toward the dressing table.

"What's a kettle witch?" Amelie asked.

"You know," Helga rattled on, pouring tea. "Not one of the Mist-Torn. A witch who learns from books, who casts by throwing bits of this and bits of that into a kettle."

"You mean a cauldron?" Céline asked.

"Cauldron, kettle." Helga waved her hand. "It's all the same. They're not of the Mist-Torn." She paused. "But that doesn't mean they aren't dangerous. I've known a kettle witch or two with some power. Hate the Mist-Torn, they do."

Amelie and Céline looked at each other helplessly. Helga seemed to know a good deal more than they did, but she seldom made any sense.

"Helga," Céline began, "who are the Mist-Torn?"

"Who are the . . . ? Did your mother teach you nothing?" Helga set down the pot. "You."

"Us?" Amelie asked.

Helga peered at her closely. "You truly know nothing?" She sighed. "Your mother must have broken with her people."

"I don't think she had any people," Céline said.

"Course she did. The Móndyalítko. Your mother was Mist-Torn, from the line of Fawe."

Amelie's discomfort and frustration grew. She didn't like the idea of their mother having had some secret life among a pack of gypsies. Their mother had been an apothecary and a respected seer. Their father had been a village hunter in Shetâna, and a good man, maybe too good. Amelie didn't remember him well, but she remembered the day he died. Three soldiers had ordered a Shetâna farmer to turn over his entire herd of goats. The farmer objected and a fight broke out. Amelie's father tried to stop it and ended up with a dagger through his stomach. Six years later, their mother had gone to take medicine to a family with the fever. She'd caught it herself and died a week after.

After that, both Amelie and Céline had made a pact to protect themselves first, to put themselves first. Over the past few days, that pact had been put to the test, but Amelie still believed in it.

Helga tilted her head to one side, as if considering how to proceed. "The Móndyalítko command no wealth and no power in the sense of the princes and lords, but they have their own bloodlines of power, the shape-shifters, the Mist-Torn, and the like. A Mist-Torn witch is born with her power. She's a treasure to her people. She will take a lover when she pleases, but few of the Mist-Torn ever marry. Your mother must have wanted your father very much."

"She did," Céline said quietly.

"But the kettle witches," Helga rambled on, "they have to study, to learn from books or other kettle witches. That's why they hate the Mist-Torn. Jealousy."

"So . . . if we're looking for a kettle witch here," Céline said, "we should seek someone who's educated, someone capable of learning from books, and who understands spell components?"

"That sounds about right," Helga answered, nodding.

"Can it be either a man or a woman?"

"Course. They're not Mist-Torn."

"How do you know all this?" Amelie challenged. For she herself was no Mist-Torn witch. She'd been born with no power, and this entire discussion made her feel ordinary . . . mundane.

Helga straightened. "How? I am Móndyalítko; that's how."

"Then what are you doing here? Why did you leave your 'people,' as you say?"

"That is *my* business," Helga snapped, surprising her. "And you'd best look to your own. Two sides of the same coin, you are. The future and the past."

Amelie huffed. Not that nonsense again.

But Céline was studying Helga closely, thoughtfully. "The future and the past," Céline whispered.

After depositing Inna in the small room near his own apartments and posting two guards at her open door, Jaromir debated on the best place to blindside Master Feodor before he sent a request for the meeting.

He considered going down to the prison beneath the old barracks—just for psychological effect. But then he had a better idea. He was well aware that he could not physically threaten Feodor as he had Inna. Master Feodor was still Anton's court physician, appointed by Prince Lieven. Jaromir would have to tread carefully here and yet still get some answers.

So now he was back in the cellars beneath the

castle larder, looking down at the bodies of the four dead girls again.

He didn't have to wait long before hearing the sound of light, clicking footsteps. Master Feodor walked in with an annoyed expression. "You sent for me, Lieutenant? I do assure you that I cannot tell you anything more about how these girls died, and I'm a busy man this morning. The prince is not well."

"I'm aware the prince is not well."

Something in his voice caught Feodor's attention—as the man stopped walking. Jaromir looked him up and down, noting how Feodor clearly appreciated the finer things in life: silk tunics, heeled boots, jeweled rings. Jaromir had never paid much attention to this before, but he did now.

"The prince has just had Inna placed under house arrest," he said.

"Arrest? Don't you mean protection?" Feodor's lower lip twitched, and he glanced around, as if looking for anyone down here besides Jaromir and the four dead bodies.

"No. She was caught with a powder that contained opiates and hemlock. She's been putting it into his wine every night, and she said you gave it to her." Jaromir said this calmly but did not bother keeping the hostility from his voice. "Conspiring to poison the prince is a capital offense."

Feodor stiffened and looked back the way he'd come, seeking an escape. Jaromir had succeeded in blindsiding him. He'd been caught completely off guard.

But to Feodor's credit, his expression shifted to one of righteous indignation. "Poison? How dare you. I gave the powder to Inna because she's the one who sees to him at night. I also gave her instructions to only use it on the nights when he had trouble sleeping. If she abused the privilege, then your quarrel is with her, not me, but the prince does need his rest."

"From hemlock?"

"It is commonly used in sleeping powders, as you would know had you spent time studying anything other than how to use that sword on your belt."

Jaromir tensed, but the taunt didn't rattle him. He'd known men like Feodor before. They always tried to turn the tables with insults. This man standing before him was frightened.

"Anton said he'd stopped taking any of the draughts you assigned him," Jaromir went on, "that they weren't helping. Is that you why you had Inna feeding him the powder? Because he wouldn't take it from you anymore?" He dropped one hand to the hilt of his sword. "What exactly did you tell her to make her start putting it into his wine?"

Feodor sputtered and took a step back. "Touch me and I'll report you to Prince Lieven! You have no authority to tell me how to best care for the prince's health. I gave Inna instructions which she did not follow." He half turned toward the doorway. "Am I under arrest, Lieutenant?"

The question was mocking.

To Jaromir's anger and worry, he'd not managed to learn anything by which to justify Feodor's arrest. But he didn't believe the physician's story about having told Inna to use the powder sparingly and only on nights when Anton truly couldn't sleep. There was something more going on here.

Master Feodor had been slowly weakening Anton on purpose. Jaromir was convinced of it. "No," he admitted. "You aren't under arrest."

Feodor turned on heel to stride toward the stairs.

Jaromir couldn't help adding, "Not yet."

CHAPTER 11

As Céline and Amelie walked into the great hall that evening, Céline quickly noted that an unusually small crowd of castle residents had turned out for dinner.

Lady Karina was in attendance, but Anton was conspicuously absent—as were Inna and Master Feodor.

Jaromir and Corporal Pavel were standing near a table chatting with a few soldiers who were just beginning a game of cards.

Amelie walked over, and Jaromir moved easily to give her room to take a place at the bench. His great wolfhound shoved her nose under Amelie's hand, seeking attention.

"Hello, Lizzie," Amelie said, scratching the dog's ear.

Although Amelie and Jaromir could hardly be considered friends, Céline marveled at how nothing had changed in their treatment of each other. His jaw looked worse than it had that morning, and Amelie had bruises up and down both arms—hidden under her shirt—from the fierce way he'd had to pin her the night before. But she'd given him little choice, and he'd simply fought back. They both seemed to accept this, and a bit of mutual violence did not appear to have affected them much.

However . . . Pavel was staring at Céline with an almost wistful expression. There had been no military repercussions for him from the events of last night. He'd not been punished or demoted.

In fact, Jaromir seemed to have forgotten about the whole event—though Céline knew he hadn't. Jaromir was smart enough to know Pavel's lesson had been learned and any further words were useless. The relationship between the two of them remained unchanged as well.

Not so for Pavel and Céline.

Last night, in his anger, he'd used fear as a weapon, and he'd shown her a side of himself that he normally kept hidden. She had seen it.

Nothing was the same between them.

He took a step toward her, and she took a step back. His expression changed to open regret, but he couldn't change the past. That was the tragedy of the past. It couldn't be changed.

"Céline," a smooth voice said.

She looked to the left to see Lady Karina coming toward her. Karina was especially lovely tonight, with her chestnut hair piled high, a few loose curls hanging around her face, wearing a silk gown of seafoam green.

"Will you walk with me to the fire?" Karina asked.

"Of course, my lady." Céline welcomed the interruption and fell into step, heading toward the hearth and the typical crowd of wriggling dogs that always seemed to gather there.

"Anton has informed me of what occurred this morning," Karina said, "about Inna, I mean."

Céline kept silent. She didn't know if Anton had informed his aunt about the other discovery—the woman in the painting that Céline had seen in her vision.

"I wanted to tell you that I've never been comfortable with Inna as his personal attendant," Karina went on. She sounded slightly defensive, as if perhaps Céline might blame her for not having taken action herself. "This business of her putting hemlock into his wine has left me most distressed."

"There is no way you could have known, my lady," Céline said diplomatically.

Karina stopped walking when they reached the hearth, and she looked into the crackling logs. "Anton has given me great license in the decision making here at court, but I've never interfered with his personal choices. I came here . . . a great distance from the south, when his wife died and he was unable to manage things."

Listening to her, Céline realized that life could not have been easy for Karina when she'd first arrived four years ago—functioning neither as Anton's wife nor as his mother—and yet she'd launched into managing a vast household for a grief-stricken nephew. The fact that she was beautiful and only five or six years older than him probably hadn't helped.

"It must have been difficult," Céline said, "you being . . . well, so young and filling the role of his aunt."

Karina nodded. "Yes, I was still a child myself when he was born. I was what you might call a 'late surprise' to my parents, when my siblings were reaching adulthood and my mother thought herself past conceiving."

Céline couldn't help wondering why Karina herself had not married. Could she be content to go on living with her nephew, basically filling in for his dead mother? But that question was far too personal.

"I simply didn't want you to think that I've been neglectful of Anton's welfare," Karina said. "I should have found a way to send Inna off years ago." Something in her green eyes changed as she spoke these last words. There was an anger, a hardness that Céline had not seen before. Karina always appeared so composed, so serene that she seemed above real anger.

"The prince would have objected had you tried," Céline said, thinking on her conversation with him that morning. "There's nothing you could have done."

Karina turned from the fire and left the topic

behind as she looked across the hall at Amelie playing cards. "I do wish your sister would let me lace her into a proper gown and put up her hair."

Céline tried not to laugh. "That would be a feat indeed, my lady."

Jaromir was walking toward them.

Upon reaching the hearth, he gave Karina a short bow. "May I have a word with the seer, my lady?"

Karina looked him up and down. "To do with castle security?" Her tone was colder than Céline had ever heard it.

"Yes, my lady."

"Then I should be informed as well."

His jaw tightened ever so slightly, possibly in surprise. Perhaps Karina had never asked such a thing before.

But he bowed slightly again and turned to Céline. "If I gain permission from Anton to detain Master Feodor, will you read him for me? I don't know what you can tell me by looking at his future. But I need to know what he's really doing here."

"Tonight?" she asked.

"No, tomorrow. It's already dark out, and tonight I don't want to get far from Inna's room. We're going to run watches in three-hour shifts."

She bit the inside of her mouth, trying not to argue with him. She still felt they should get Inna out of the castle and away from the village.

"Will you read him for me?" Jaromir asked.

Céline studied the bruise on his jaw and his somewhat outgrown goatee. Helga's words echoed in her mind. *Two sides of the same coin. The future and the past.*

"I may have a better idea," she said.

Lady Karina watched her carefully but said nothing.

Jaromir and Pavel stood through the first, un-eventful three-hour watch at Inna's door that night. Though Jaromir had filled Pavel in on the story of Céline's vision, he remained skeptical that the murderer was an illusory ghost woman who could step outside of a portrait or walk through walls.

It wasn't that he doubted Céline's word. He believed she'd described exactly what she'd seen in the vision, but it just wasn't in him to accept her descriptions at face value. What if someone had dressed up like the woman in the painting? Some-one who knew how to use tricks of light for ap-pearing and disappearing? He'd heard of such things. How the woman could get past him or his guards was something else, but he didn't believe they were dealing with a spirit.

However, he didn't discount Céline's belief that the woman was being controlled or driven on-ward by someone else, for he was still certain that someone here was determined to undermine An-ton and make him appear weak.

"Reporting for duty, sir," a voice called up the passage.

He turned to see Guardsmen Winshaw and Stiva coming toward him. Rurik was still recovering from the blow to his head—delivered by Amelie—and so Jaromir had enlisted Stiva, whom he knew to be a steady man.

Pavel glanced through the open door at Inna, who had been lying on the bed with her face to the wall since she'd been delivered here earlier in the day.

"All quiet, sir?" Stiva asked.

"Yes, but stay sharp," Jaromir answered. "One of you keep your eyes on her at all times." That afternoon, he'd already filled them in on Céline's vision. "Remember, you're watching for a pale young woman dressed in black who may know tricks of light that can make her seem able to appear and disappear."

Both men nodded. "Yes, sir."

Then Stiva asked Pavel, "Have you got the money you owe me? You lost that last hand on credit."

He grinned, and Pavel grinned back. The young corporal might have a hot temper beneath the surface, but he was always good-natured about paying his gambling debts. "Not on me, but I'll go to my room and come back with it."

"Don't get lost," Stiva joked, moving to the open door with Winshaw.

"You two stay sharp," Jaromir said again. He

normally didn't mind an easy camaraderie among his men, but right now, he wanted Stiva and Winshaw at full attention, watching Inna. "Pavel and I will relieve you again in three hours."

"Yes, sir."

Pavel headed off, and Jaromir went down the passage to his own apartments. Although he'd never admit it, he was looking forward to lying down for a while. Both his stomach and his jaw still hurt from last night, but he'd been impressed with the speed at which Amelie had moved. If she'd landed that last blow, she would have put him down. There weren't many men who could get the jump on him like that.

Once inside his rooms, he took off his sword but left on his armor and lay down on the bed, not intending to go to sleep, just to rest for a while . . . so he wasn't certain how much time had passed when he was awakened by the sound of Pavel pounding on his door and shouting.

"Sir! Sir, wake up. Get up! They're dead. Sir!"

In a flash, he was off the bed and across the room, jerking the door open.

"What are you saying? Who's dead?"

But Pavel was running back down the passage. Confused and still groggy, Jaromir ran after him and saw two forms lying prone outside Inna's door. Shades of the previous night flashed by him, but he could tell this was different even before he skidded to a stop.

"I wasn't gone long," Pavel babbled, "and I

came back with the money I owed Stiva." He dropped to his knees. "Look at him. Look at Winshaw."

Both Winshaw and Stiva were lying faceup, their flesh shriveled and dried against their bones, just like the dead girls in the cellar. Jaromir couldn't let himself feel anything. He ignored Pavel and walked into the room.

Inna lay on the bed, dead, dried to a husk.

Strangely, the first thought in his mind was that Céline would blame him.

The next thought was that he blamed himself.

By noon the next day, Amelie felt as if she'd lost all control of her own world. Jaromir was escorting her and Céline down to the great hall, and she still couldn't believe what Céline was asking her to do.

The tension between the three of them was so thick she could have cut it with her dagger.

Céline had taken the death of Inna rather hard, and she refused to look at Jaromir or speak to him unless necessary. His face was haggard, and his eyes were hollow. While Amelie wasn't prone to jumping to his defense, she knew he'd only been doing what he thought was right. He'd lost two of his men, who might have been his friends, and Céline was treating him as if their deaths were his fault.

That was hardly fair.

He led them both through the great hall to the small side chamber—where the door was closed and locked. He unlocked it with a key and ushered them both inside. A few servants who were milling about, laying out the midday meal, glanced in their direction, and Jaromir closed the door behind himself, shutting off any view from outside.

Inside the chamber, Master Feodor was sitting in a chair with Corporal Pavel standing directly behind him, towering over him like hostile guard dog. Feodor had always given Amelie the shivers. She didn't care for his long mustache or his politely veiled contempt. But Jaromir and Pavel were tall men, wearing swords, daggers, and chain armor. Feodor was a slender, almost fragile-looking man. He was unarmed, and it appeared Pavel had been keeping him in that chair.

"Lieutenant!" Feodor said angrily. "I demand to know the meaning of this. Your . . . *man* has refused to let me leave this room. The prince will hear of this."

"The prince ordered it," Jaromir answered.

Feodor's jaw twitched, and he was perspiring enough for Amelie to see a few beads of sweat on his face.

He's afraid, she thought.

"Where is the prince?" Céline asked, not looking at Jaromir or Pavel.

The tension felt just as thick in here, only now it held a hint of threat.

"He isn't well," Jaromir answered shortly. "Can you do this?"

Céline refused to look at him and instead turned to Amelie. "Please try this for me. Helga seems to . . . know things. Just try."

Amelie was nearly trembling. She wanted this suspicion of Céline's to be true more than she'd ever admit, but she was terrified of failing if she tried, of condemning herself to the mundane forever.

"All you need do is touch his hand and focus on the past," Céline said, "on what brought him here."

"What is this?" Feodor demanded. He began to stand up, but Pavel shoved him back down into the chair.

"This girl is going to read you," Jaromir said, gesturing to Amelie. "She's going to read your past."

The whites of Feodor's eyes showed bright around his irises. "I will not submit to such indignity!" He started to rise again, and this time Pavel held him down, with both hands on his shoulders.

"That isn't necessary," Céline said raggedly.

"Just do it!" Jaromir barked at her.

Amelie got the feeling he was nearing the end of his tether and probably blaming himself for the deaths of Inna, Winshaw, and Stiva. Céline was not helping here, but she was also pale and stretched tightly herself.

"How do I start?" Amelie asked, trying to move this forward, even if she failed.

Céline closed her eyes briefly and opened them again. Without having to be told, Jaromir dragged a chair across the floor, directly in front of Feodor, who was perspiring more freely now. Amelie almost pitied him. But Jaromir and Pavel were both acting like bullies, and she'd never cared much for bullies.

Sitting down, she looked to Céline, who crouched beside her.

"Take his hand and close your eyes," Céline said. "Then try to sense for the spark of his spirit and focus on what brought him here, on what he's doing here."

"Prince Lieven will hear of this!" Feodor protested weakly.

"Shut up," Jaromir told him.

If Feodor turned out to be guiltless, Jaromir had probably gone too far and there would be repercussions . . . but if he were guiltless, why would he have instructed Inna to secretly drug Anton?

Suddenly, Amelie's curiosity, her need to seek information and know what Feodor was doing here, overrode her discomfort with all the tension and edge of threat filling the room.

Reaching out, she touched Feodor's hand. He flinched but didn't pull it away, as if realizing he had no choice.

Amelie closed her eyes, trying not to tremble visibly, experiencing for the first time what it must feel like to be Céline, to have everyone watching expectantly, wondering what the "seer" might actually reveal.

Pushing such self-absorbed thoughts away, she focused all her energy on Feodor, on seeking the spark of his spirit . . . and she felt something, a hint of his essence. Focusing harder, she pinpointed the questions in her mind on what he was doing here, on why he had come.

Nothing happened.

She saw nothing.

This went on long enough that panic began to set in. What if Céline and Helga were wrong? What if she and Céline were not two sides of the same coin and Céline was the only one who'd inherited the powers of the "Mist-Torn," as Helga called their mother's line.

With her eyes still closed, Amelie thought on the white powder Céline had described, laced with hemlock, being poured into Anton's wine goblet.

Then . . . a sharp jolt struck her, almost painful. A second one hit, and the small room around her vanished. A whooshing sound rushed in her ears, and she was being swept backward down a corridor of white mist. For all her courage, the sensation was terrifying. Amelie liked control, and she'd lost control of her own body.

The white mists swept and swirled around her, and she couldn't stop or escape them.

Without warning, they vanished, and she found

herself standing in a large room with polished pine walls and a burning hearth. How could this be?

Looking around, she realized she was no longer in Castle Sèone. By the antlers and boar heads on the walls, it appeared to be some sort of hunting lodge, but soldiers in black tabards stood at attention all around.

Frightened, she reached automatically for the sword on her hip, but none of the soldiers reacted. It was as if they couldn't see her.

There was a rough-edged table at the top of the room, along with a man sitting in an ornate chair. He looked to be about twenty-five, handsome and slender. His hair was long and dark. His skin was pale to the point of being white, and he wore a sleeveless blue embroidered tunic. He looked like Anton—only with darker, longer hair. But his eyes were cruel, and he was gazing downward at someone over the top of the table.

Amelie followed his gaze to see Master Feodor kneeling on the floor.

"My father has finally made arrangements to send you to my brother, as his personal physician," said the man in the ornate chair. "This has taken no small effort on my part."

Amelie drew a sharp breath. She knew who he was: Sub-Prince Damek. In her time living under his rule in Shetâna, she'd never once seen him.

"Yes, my prince," Feodor said in oily voice. He didn't appear remotely frightened, only expectant.

"So you understand what I'm asking you to do?" Damek asked.

"Fully, my prince. I will send regular reports of everything occurring at Sèone, and I will endeavor to . . . hinder his progress as the master of his fiefdoms."

"He must appear weak," Damek said, "both in body and mind, in strength and his ability to lead. Can you manage this?"

"Easily, my prince, and in return . . . ?"

"You'll be well rewarded, do not fear, but do not disappoint me. He must appear weak."

Feodor bowed low. "I will not fail."

"See that you don't."

Amelie was breathing hard, trying to take this in. She was here, but not here—present but unable to be seen or heard. Just the sight of Damek in his chair filled her with revulsion.

And Feodor was a traitor.

The hunting lodge vanished, and she found herself back inside the small chamber with her eyes open, staring at Master Feodor sitting in his chair across from hers. He was staring back, his terrified eyes fixed on hers.

Céline crouched beside her. "Amelie, are you all right? What did you see?"

But she was still breathing hard, overwhelmed by the reality of what had just happened, of her experience, the knowledge of her ability . . . and of what she'd just witnessed.

"Jaromir!" she cried without thinking, and he

grabbed the arm of her chair, pulling it around effortlessly to face him.

"What?" he asked. "Amelie, what did you see?"

"He's in the pay of Sub-Prince Damek," she choked. "He came here to hurt Anton."

CHAPTER 12

A short while later, Céline and Amelie were hiding out in their room. The scene following Amelie's revelations had not been pretty, culminating in Jaromir ordering Pavel to take Master Feodor down beneath the old barracks and lock him in a prison cell.

Feodor had not taken this with bravery or good grace, subjecting the servants in the great hall to quite an unseemly display as he was dragged from the chamber.

As soon as possible, Céline and Amelie had both fled for the stairs, hurrying to the solitude of their room.

"What do you think will happen to him?" Amelie asked, sinking down onto the bed.

Céline understood what she was going through—the latent responsibility for having spoken up about the events in a vision. "I suppose it depends on whether or not Jaromir can find any proof. I know he believes you, but right now, all he has is the word of a 'gypsy seer,' as Feodor will state in his own defense."

"Yes," Amelie said, nodding. "There has to be some kind of hearing, right? Even if it's just Anton and his council presiding? And Jaromir has to find proof, doesn't he? It won't all rest on what I saw."

"No, of course it won't." With mild annoyance, Céline then noted that the miniature portrait of the chestnut-haired woman was back on the dressing table. She picked it up. "How does this keep getting back out here?" She didn't know why the sight of the portrait bothered her, only that it did.

The door opened and Helga hobbled in carrying a plate of bread, ham, and sliced carrots. "I know you've had no lunch," she said, "either of you."

She left the door open, but Céline didn't mind. Few people ever came down this passage, and the open door made their space feel bigger. But as Helga set the tray on the dressing table, Céline asked her.

"Helga, are you taking this miniature from the drawer and setting it back out again?"

Helga blinked. "Of Lady Bethany? No, I've not touched it. I thought the prince must have given it into your keeping for some reason."

That made no sense at all.

"Who is Lady Bethany?"

"Who is . . . why, she was the prince's mother. He used to have that picture in his bedroom, and

I would sometimes dust it when I helped the
housemaids."

"What?" Amelie asked, hopping off the bed
and coming closer.

"You didn't know?" Helga responded in genuine surprise.

And then Céline realized why the face in the
miniature seemed vaguely familiar. Her face was
round, and she looked more cheerful than exotic,
but her chestnut hair and skin tones were similar
to Lady Karina's.

"This is Anton's mother?" Céline asked,
alarmed now as she remembered something else.
"He told me he'd lost this. How could it have
ended up in here?"

"Should we try and give it back to him?" Amelie asked, sounding reluctant.

Céline understood why, and she herself didn't
care for the idea of simply walking up to Anton,
handing him a miniature of his mother, and saying, "Oh, by the way, we've had this in our room
since we arrived."

How would that look?

"No . . . ," she said. "Let me think of something
else. I'll try to put it someplace where he'll find it."

Amelie nodded. "Good. I think that's best." She
studied the tiny portrait. "She was pretty. Helga,
do you know how she died?"

"Of the rupture, when his lordship was only
eight years old."

"The rupture?" Amelie asked.

"You know," Céline said quietly, "that pain that starts in the right side, like Jareth's oldest son back in Shetâna."

Amelie fell silent. She and Céline had both seen people die this way. Normally, it began with someone feeling sick to their stomach, followed by a sharp pain in the right side of the abdomen that turned to agony, followed by an organ erupting inside them, followed by death. Once it began, there was nothing the finest physician could do to stop it, and it was a terrible way to die.

"Poor lamb," Helga said, still gazing at the portrait. "I heard the pain started in the morning, and she was gone before the next day."

And poor Anton, to have lost his mother so young.

No one spoke for a moment, and then Céline put the portrait back in the drawer.

As if eager to change the subject, Helga began slapping ham onto slices of bread and glanced at Amelie. "I heard what happened downstairs with Master Feodor," she told Amelie. "So you found your side of the coin."

Amelie didn't respond. Perhaps she wasn't ready to talk about her new ability yet.

Sitting on the bed again, Amelie leaned back against the headboard and said to Céline, "I wanted to stay here so badly . . . but now I'm not sure. I thought this place was different from home, but you saw Jaromir and Pavel down there. Maybe it's not so different."

Céline wasn't surprised that her sister had been

suffering the same doubts. "Well, we could set up someplace else. With me reading futures and you reading pasts, I doubt we'd starve."

"You could go and find your own people," Helga suggested. "Always a place for the Mist-Torn with the Móndyalítko."

A sound in the doorway caught Céline's attention, and she turned to see Anton standing there. Two male servants stood behind him, carrying *the* portrait from the upstairs hall. Anton looked terrible. His hands were trembling and his skin was tinged green. She had a fairly good idea of what was wrong with him, but she feared offending him by speaking up.

However, his expression was stricken, and she wondered how long he'd been there. She knew he hadn't been there when they'd spoken of his mother, but had he heard them discussing the possibility of leaving Sèone?

"My lord," she said, for lack of anything else to say.

Thankfully, Amelie broke the moment by climbing off the bed and moving closer to the door. "Is that it?" she asked, fixating with a kind of awe on the image of the pale, dark-haired young woman by the fire—wearing long black gloves.

Anton recovered his composure. "Yes, I'm having it moved to my rooms. I want to keep it close to myself and away from everyone else."

Céline wondered about the wisdom of that but knew better than to challenge him. Why had he stopped at their door? It was unusual for him make any sort of visit. If he wanted to speak to someone, he normally sent a messenger and had the person summoned.

"Did you need anything from us?" she asked.

"Yes." He hesitated. "The lieutenant has arrested Master Feodor, pending some . . . unsettling charges. I want you and Amelie to both do readings of Master Feodor with me inside the room, for her to see what else she can learn of the past, and for you to try and see his future. And I want to hear both your reports immediately afterward."

Although Céline thought he should be in bed, she answered, "Of course."

But Amelie spoke at the same time. "Again? So soon? I just read him."

Anton frowned and Céline tensed. He wasn't used to having his orders questioned.

To his credit, he answered, "It would be a great service to me, Amelie."

With her mouth set tightly, she nodded once. "All right."

"My thanks." He waved off his two servants holding the large portrait between them. "Take that up to my apartments." Then he stepped back from the door, motioning to Céline and Amelie. "Come, then. It's a bit of a walk down to the prisons."

Jaromir strode through the old guard room of the castle prison to find Pavel waiting outside a locked cell door.

After conducting a full search of Master Feodor's rooms and finding nothing he could use for proof, Jaromir decided he would have to rely on other methods. Taking off his sword, he handed it to Pavel, but he kept the dagger on his hip and a second one in his boot.

"Don't let anyone inside," he ordered Pavel. "Not anyone."

"Yes, sir."

"Unlock the door."

The prison at Castle Sèone was rarely used except for the occasional petty thief or anyone else Jaromir thought worthy of a lockup. Last fall, an old woman had come to him complaining that her daughter's husband had badly beaten the girl. When Jaromir went down into the village and saw the young wife, he'd ordered the husband locked up for six months.

He was the law here, and everyone knew it.

Master Feodor clearly knew it, and he backed up against the dank wall of the cell when Jaromir entered. Pavel remained outside, locking the door again.

"You cannot keep me in here without evidence," Feodor said. "I demand that Prince Anton be informed."

"He's been informed."

Feodor didn't seem surprised. He must have known Jaromir wouldn't keep someone of his status locked up without Anton's consent.

"How are you doing it?" Jaromir dove in without hesitation. "Murdering the girls, using some woman who pretends to be a ghost? How is it done? Poison on the gloves?"

At that, Feodor's face went completely white. "Murdering the . . . ?" he sputtered. "You can't possibly believe I have anything to do that."

Jaromir walked closer, keeping Feodor backed up against the wall. "Who else has a reason to discredit Anton?"

Shaking his head wildly, Feodor insisted, "No! I've murdered no one. My only task was to . . ." He trailed off in horror, aware of what he'd almost said.

"To what?"

"To care for Prince Anton's health." Feodor collected some control of himself again. "And you have no proof otherwise. You've nothing but the word of a gypsy who dresses like a boy."

Jaromir jerked the dagger from his belt and pressed the sharp edge below Feodor's left eye. "How long have you been working for Damek? Since before Prince Lieven decided to send you here?"

Terror twisted the physician's features. "You cannot do this! You have no right."

In a quick movement, Jaromir sliced the man's cheek open, watching blood run down his face. "My duty is to my prince," Jaromir whispered. "I can do anything I want."

Feodor's eyes widened in fear and pain.

"How long have you been working for Damek?" Jaromir repeated.

"Two years," Feodor blurted out.

"And Damek somehow convinced his father that Anton needed a court physician?"

"Yes, but not on his own word. He did it through the counsel of others. His father would never believe him to be concerned for Anton's health."

Jaromir put the blade back to Feodor's face. "And he told you to poison Anton slowly, with hemlock?"

"I never intended harm! Only to weaken him, to make him appear unfit to rule."

The rage inside Jaromir kept growing. He'd left Anton's health in the hands of this piece of filth . . . and he'd not even suspected. He should have routed this out long ago.

"Have you sent word to Damek of the murders here?"

Feodor breaths were coming quickly. "Yes."

"Have you informed him of Anton's recent downturn in health?"

"No."

Jaromir stepped back, thinking. If he left Feodor alive long enough for an official hearing, there was a chance Damek might find some way to interfere. Feodor was clever. In the process, the physician could even find a way, some way, to keep feeding Damek information about what was happening at Castle Sèone.

No, this needed to stop here. Jaromir had overlooked a spy and a traitor in their midst. Such an act could not be forgiven on his part, but it could be amended.

Reaching down with his left hand, he jerked the other dagger from his boot and held it out, hilt first.

"Take it."

Realization dawned in Feodor's eyes, and he tried backing further against the wall. "No! I'll not give you an excuse to murder me."

"Take it or I'll kill you and put it into your hand after you're dead. At least this way you have a chance."

Nothing happened for the span of a few breaths, and then Feodor went for the dagger, grasping the hilt. Jaromir rammed forward with his right hand, driving the other dagger through the hollow of Feodor's throat, grinding it in a half circle.

Moving back, he watched the body fall.

It was done.

Céline walked quietly beside Anton down a dank, wet stairwell and through what must once have been a guardroom. Now the entire prison gave off an eerie, lonely sensation, and she wondered what tragedies must have taken place down here over the past hundred years or so.

Amelie came just behind them, and as they passed from the guardroom into a larger area sporting six wooden doors with narrow slits at the bottom, Céline saw Pavel standing at attention, and Jaromir was just coming out from one of the cell doors.

At the sight of Anton, he froze in the open door-way, and Céline's gaze moved down to the dripping dagger in his hand. She went cold.

"I came to question the prisoner myself," Anton said. "Is there a problem?"

"Yes, my lord," Jaromir answered. "I obtained a full confession, but as I finished, he managed to pull a dagger from my belt and attack me. I had to defend myself."

"Is he dead?"

"I fear so. I don't believe he was involved in the deaths of the girls, but he confessed to his betrayal of you."

At the calm, detached manner of this exchange, a roar began growing in Céline's ears. As if Feodor would ever attack Jaromir. She was having trouble breathing.

"Unfortunate," Anton said, "but if he gave a full confession, your word will not be questioned."

The roar in Céline's ears grew louder, and she rushed past Jaromir into the cell. He whirled to come after her, but she was already looking down.

Master Feodor lay there on the damp floor of the cell with a dagger gripped in his right hand. His eyes were still open, and his cheek had been sliced. Blood flowed from a hole at the base of his throat, forming a pool around his head.

"You murderer!" she cried, turning on Jaromir.

"Céline," Anton said in alarm.

The roar in her ears was almost deafening now, and her lunch threatened to come back up.

"You just came in here and killed him," she went on, unable to stop. "Judge and executioner. And your lord and master isn't going to say a word."

The cell was going dark around her.

"Corporal Pavel," Anton said, his voice tight, "Mistress Fawe is not well. Please carry her back up to her room."

When she saw Pavel coming toward her, she dodged deeper into the cell, nearly slipping on the pool of blood. "No," she told him. "You just stood outside that door and listened. You didn't even try to stop it."

Then suddenly, Amelie pushed past Pavel and ran inside the cell, grasping Céline's arms, holding her up, and glaring back at the men with an expression that gave even Jaromir pause.

"I've got her," Amelie said. "We don't need your help. We don't need anyone but each other."

Something in those words caused the roar to quiet.

"Céline, come on," Amelie whispered in her ear. "Don't make Anton order Pavel to carry you again."

Still sick to her stomach, Céline let Amelie lead her toward the door. All three of the men got out of their way.

*   *   *

Amelie took Céline directly back to their room and forced her into the bed, beneath the covers, to rest.

Thankfully, Helga was still there, and she dampened a cloth, pressing it gently to Céline's forehead. Céline stared blankly out into the room, her gaze fixed on nothing.

"I can't do this anymore," she whispered.

"I know," Amelie answered.

"Shhhhhhh," Helga said to Céline. "Go to sleep, my girl. You'll feel better when you wake."

Amelie didn't think so, but she kept quiet, sitting down on the end of the bed, wishing she knew how to stroke Céline's forehead like that.

A soft knock sounded on the door.

Oh, what could anyone here possibly want from them now?

Annoyed, Amelie hopped off the bed and jerked the door open to find Pavel standing on the other side. He was the last person she wanted to see—well, second to the last. And he was sadly mistaken if he thought she'd let him in.

"What?" she asked, blocking the doorway.

"Is Céline all right?" As he'd made no move to enter and he looked genuinely concerned, she softened a bit. "No. She's not."

"If she hadn't caught him off guard, the lieutenant would never have let her slip past him and see that. I'd never have let her see it."

"Oh, and so her not seeing it means it didn't happen?"

He winced and she sighed.

"What is it you want, Corporal?" she asked.

He held out a piece of paper. "Read this and don't refuse. Please don't refuse, Amelie."

Then he was gone, walking down the passage for the stairway that led down. Amelie moved back into the room and unfolded the paper.

Inside was a message to her:

> *I'm in the upstairs portrait hall, alone.*
> *Please come up.*
>
> *Jaromir*

She tossed the note on the dressing table and shook her head.

"What is it?" Helga asked.

"His lord majesty lieutenant wants me to come up to the portrait hall and see him."

"Then you should go."

Amelie turned. "You're not serious?"

For once, Helga wasn't rambling or speaking halfway to herself. "Things were different here before he came. He's kept this place safe for a good while now, but he keeps himself apart, alone. If he's so wounded that he's asked for help, you should give it."

"I don't owe him anything."

"Don't you?"

Unbidden, a memory erupted in Amelie's mind of her home burning behind her, of her arms growing weary in a fight she couldn't win . . . of Jaromir clubbing a soldier in a black tabard.

Helga turned back to Céline. "You go to him. I'll care for her."

Amelie stood watching the bed for a moment. Without completely knowing why, she turned and left the room, heading for the other end of the passage, with an odd, dark stairwell leading up. She'd not ventured there herself before, but Céline had described it.

After climbing the stairs, she walked out into a long hall with tall archers' slits along its outer wall, serving as windows, and a line of enormous portraits down the inner wall. Even from here, she could see an empty space where a painting had been removed.

Jaromir was sitting on the floor with his back to the wall. An unexpected wave of pity passed through her, but if he'd called her up here to offer comfort, he would be disappointed. She didn't even know how to comfort Céline.

"I'm here," she said weakly, walking toward him. "What do you want?"

He kept his eyes on the opposite wall. "To make you understand why I did what I did."

"I already know why, to protect Anton. I'd probably have done the same for Céline."

Then he looked up at her, with a hint of relief. Maybe she could give him some comfort. The thing was . . . she did understand why he'd killed Feodor, and she wasn't even sure he'd been wrong.

"Sit down," he said.

Cautiously, she crouched beside him. While she didn't enjoy watching him play the bully, she found that she didn't like seeing him like this either. He seemed diminished somehow.

"No, I mean that I want you to *understand*," he went on. "I want to show you why I'd do anything for Anton."

She frowned. What was he talking about?

"I want you to read my past," he said.

She started to rise. "No."

To go inside his head? To look at his past? That was too intimate.

In a flash, he had ahold of both her wrists and wouldn't let her get up. "Don't go."

On instinct, she jerked hard once, but she knew the strength in his hands only too well by now, and she couldn't even make his arms move. Instead of kicking him, she said, "This is why Céline is so tired of this place! You get us to trust you. You behave like our friend . . . until one of us doesn't do exactly what you want, and then you act like one of Damek's men."

He let go as if her skin burned his hands. "Don't leave. Please."

That was the third time in about the last ten minutes that he or Pavel had used the word "please."

"I'm no good with words," he rushed on, "and you're the only one who can see, who can know why I'd do anything to protect Anton." He was silent for a moment. "I want somebody to know."

She breathed out through her nose and sat down on the floor. Maybe Helga was right, and he had cut himself off from everyone. He needed some kind of connection after the horrors of the past few days. But she couldn't bring herself to touch him and try to look at his memories. She feared it would create too much of a . . . connection.

"Couldn't you just tell me?" she asked. She could give him that much. He deserved that much.

His eyes fixed on her face as he appeared to be considering the option of truly talking to someone, and she suddenly wondered about the wisdom of her offer. Perhaps Jaromir never *talked* to anyone—or at least not about anything that mattered. Would letting him unburden himself to her be even more intimate than trying to read his past?

She was well aware that he often looked at her with more than a passing interest, and she'd been determined to keep him at arm's length. It wasn't that she didn't find him attractive. She could finally admit that to herself. What woman wouldn't find him attractive? He was tall, strong, and comfortable with himself. He looked out for those he cared for, and he was one of the most capable men she'd ever met.

But . . . she'd met his mistress, and while playing cards, she'd heard casual talk from the guards about his previous mistresses. He liked wealthy, beautiful, shallow women who followed his orders, and he never kept one woman for very long.

Since Amelie was a far cry from his usual type, she might hold his interest a little longer, but how much longer? She had no intention of becoming just another cast-off mistress on Jaromir's list.

Still, he was in pain, and for better or worse she did want to help him.

"Talk to me," she said. "If you want me to understand, you'll have to tell me. I'm not going to try to read your past." Settling more comfortably on the floor, she asked, "When did you and Anton meet?"

Still staring at her, he answered, "Four years ago . . . at Castle Pählen."

She sat, just waiting, until he opened his mouth again, and he began to talk, weaving a story in which he'd given up his place as a lieutenant for the House of Hilaron, out of loyalty for a fallen prince, without having any idea what life as a mercenary on the open road would be like.

"You wouldn't believe some of the things I did to survive," he whispered. "I wouldn't want to tell you."

She just listened.

"Then I heard that Prince Lieven was hiring guards for a family gathering and I went to beg for anything he'd give me," he went on. "I had no pride left. I was filthy and starving . . . even once I was hired, I had to beg food and a razor, and I was facing being turned out as soon as the gathering had ended."

He was quiet for a moment. "But then Anton . . .

he saved Lizzie from his brother, and so I saved him from a group of his brother's assassins."

In spite of her determination to keep quiet and listen, she couldn't help blurting out, "What?"

He nodded and went on speaking quietly, telling her of a dirty deal Damek had made with the captain of Anton's guard, of a bloody fight, of Anton's tragic surprise that anyone would go as far out of his way to help as Jaromir had.

"He was so alone," Jaromir whispered. "I didn't realize at the time, but I did later."

"And he asked you to come back with him? To head up the guard here?"

Jaromir was breathing fast now, lost in the past, and his eyes were glassy.

"Yes. By the time we reached Sèone, he and I had become friends. But I didn't understand how high he'd placed me until we entered the castle and he assigned my apartments. I became *the* Lieutenant, like the title of a lord. Soon, almost no one used my name. I was either 'sir' or 'the Lieutenant.'" He leaned back against the wall. "Can you imagine how that would feel? To be nothing one day . . . *nothing*, and then suddenly find you'd become more than you thought possible?"

Amelie leaned back on her hands. "Yes, I can imagine how it feels."

A few hours past sunset, Céline was still beneath of the covers of their bed, listening as Amelie told her Jaromir's story, of all that he had told her.

Helga was gone now, and the two sisters were alone.

Without wanting to be, Céline was moved by Jaromir's story, but it wasn't enough.

"It doesn't excuse what he did to Feodor."

"He's protective of Anton."

"To the point of judicial murder?"

Amelie didn't answer, and Céline wondered what her sister was thinking. But Céline was drained, tired. Everyone that she or Amelie had pointed out as a possible victim or villain was dead.

Helga had been right, though, and after sleeping through the afternoon and early evening, she was calmer.

"I'm still not sure I can do this anymore," Céline whispered.

"Do you want the shop?"

"I don't know."

Before Amelie could answer, a pounding on the door made them both jump. The pounding continued, and Amelie hurried to the door, pulling it open.

Jaromir leaned in over the top of her head. If he'd looked haggard earlier, he looked positively aged now. "Céline, you have to come. Anton's worse."

She sat up. "How much worse?"

"I think he's dying."

Up in Anton's bedroom, Céline sponged the sweat off his face. He was unconscious, but his body was shaking. Amelie sat beside her, and Jaromir sat on the side of the bed, almost ill himself. If Céline hadn't known him better, she would have said he was frightened.

Pavel stood by the door with his arms crossed, little better off than Jaromir. The oversized portrait of the dark-haired woman by the campfire leaned against the wall beside him.

"Was he vomiting before he fell unconscious?" Céline asked. All the broken ties between them didn't matter in this moment.

"Yes," Jaromir answered. "I thought it was a good thing. I thought if Feodor had managed to give him some kind of poison before he was locked up . . . that Anton was purging himself. Is that possible? Could Feodor have fed him poison?"

Céline chewed on the inside of her lip. She knew what was wrong with Anton. She'd known that afternoon. But men of his status—and the people around them—did not like to acknowledge a dependency upon elixirs or wine or anything but their own power. Even suggesting such a thing could be construed as insulting. That was why she hadn't said anything earlier. She'd simply hoped he wouldn't get worse.

"Céline!" Jaromir insisted.

The room was dim, with only a few candles glowing. Anton groaned in pain, sweating into his bedsheets.

"No," she said as matter-of-factly as she could.

"He's having the opposite problem. Master Feodor had been finding a way to feed him an opiate for a long while. His body has become dependent upon the opiate, and now the lack of it is making him ill. His organs can no longer function properly without it, and I'm afraid the dependency is so severe that he may continue to grow worse."

Pavel tensed in the doorway, and Jaromir sat up straight.

But then, to her great relief, the lieutenant asked, "Can anything be done?"

"Yes, but you're not going to like it."

"Just tell me!"

"He'll need small, weakened doses of the opiate for a while, possibly weeks, decreasing in amount until he's weaned away from it. Then he'll need a tonic made from colewort to help his liver cleanse the toxins from his body."

She knew the thought of giving Anton more of the drug that had made him ill in the first place probably went against every instinct Jaromir possessed, but she could see the pain on his weathered face. Jaromir viewed Anton as far more than a means to position and power.

"And you can make these potions?" he asked.

While she hardly considered either the poppy syrup or the cleansing tonic to be a potion, she nodded. "Yes, but only if you give me full access to the apothecary shop and its herb garden, and if you want this done quickly, I'll need some assistance."

Her words had an almost magical effect on him. He stood up, some of the haggard lines vanishing. He was a man who needed a plan, a mission. He was only truly miserable when he felt helpless.

"What kind of assistance?" he asked.

"I'll need Amelie with me, and we'll need several lanterns if we're going to harvest poppies at night. Oh, and a good deal of firewood, as we'll need to make a blaze in the hearth."

Looking down at Anton, Jaromir seemed torn for a second or two about something, and then he said, "I'm staying here with him. Pavel, you gather lanterns and firewood. Take Céline and Amelie down to the apothecary's shop. Keep them safe, and give Céline any help she needs."

Pavel jerked the door open, as if equally glad for something to do, for some action to take. "Yes, sir."

As Céline hurried toward the door, she called over her shoulder to Jaromir, "Send someone to wake the Lady Karina."

Making a vial of the weakened poppy syrup went much faster this time. Pavel proved useful, both in helping her and Amelie gather the best poppies and in building the fire while they prepared the components.

But somewhere during this process, Céline was struck by a startling thought: She had altered a vision. When she'd read Inna the day before, she had clearly seen Inna putting a double dose of the powder into Anton's wine that same afternoon.

By speaking up, Céline had caused Jaromir to trap Inna inside the small guest room, preventing her from drugging Anton's wine.

As a result, Anton was now suffering, but there was no denying that Céline had changed an event she had seen in a vision, changed the future. It could be done.

This was a revelation.

But she wiped the sweat from her forehead and worked faster on the poppy syrup.

Sooner than she expected, she was back in the castle, nearly running back down the passage to Anton's rooms carrying a spoon and a vial. Amelie and Pavel trotted behind. Upon reaching the door, Céline knocked, and Jaromir opened it.

Lady Karina was inside the room now, her expression unreadable. "How bad is he?" she asked instantly.

Céline had no idea how to answer, so she didn't. Instead, she hurried to the bed. "Jaromir, come and lift him up. He should be sitting so he won't choke."

The lieutenant moved in quickly, putting one arm beneath Anton's back and lifting him into a sitting position. "Get his mouth open," Céline instructed. She hoped Anton wasn't so far gone that he couldn't help a little.

"Anton," she said, touching his face with two fingers. "You must swallow. Do you hear? You need to swallow this."

She poured a spoonful of the poppy syrup over

his tongue and then closed his mouth with her hands. He sputtered and convulsed once, but he swallowed it.

"Again," she told Jaromir. "One more."

When they'd finished, she sat beside Anton, still holding the spoon.

"How long till we know if it works?" Jaromir asked.

"Not long, but it will work. I've seen this before . . . with ex-soldiers back in Shetâna. My mother taught me what to do."

Karina came over to sit on the bed, her lovely face a mask of calm, but her eyes gave her away; she was beyond worried. Both Amelie and Pavel hovered in the doorway. Jaromir began to pace back and forth across the room. But about a half hour later, Anton stopped moaning in pain, and he stopped sweating. Céline felt the temperature of his face and listened to his breathing.

"All right, he's just sleeping now, not unconscious. He's not in pain, and he should keep his food down once he wakes."

Karina lowered her head and closed her eyes, as if finally allowing herself to express emotion.

Jaromir let out a shaky breath and leaned over, putting his hands on his knees. "Céline, I didn't know you could . . . I had no idea you were a physician. You should have told me."

"I'm not a physician. I'm an apothecary."

Amelie came closer to the bed. "He'll really be all right?"

"I think so."

Amelie, Jaromir, and Pavel all looked about done in, and Céline had no idea what time it was. "The three of you should all go get some rest. I slept this afternoon, so I can sit with him."

"I'll stay, too," Karina put in. "Céline's right, Jaromir. You should all go and rest." This last suggestion sounded more like an order.

Relenting, Jaromir nodded. "Send for me if there's any change."

Moments later, Céline and Lady Karina were alone with the sleeping Anton, and Céline had time to struggle with her own feelings, her own realization that the futures she saw could be changed. But also, to her partial shame, she'd loved working in the shop tonight, perhaps more than she had back home at the Lavender and Thyme. Even neglected, the herb garden promised a wealth of life, and the shop was so well equipped . . . and it seemed to need her. Silly thought.

"Thank you," Karina said, breaking the silence. "I've some knowledge of herb lore, and yesterday I was informed what Master Feodor had been giving him. But I'd no idea this could happen." Her mouth tightened, and she stood up, pacing the room. "I should have routed Feodor out long ago. How could I not have seen?"

"You cannot blame yourself, my lady. Jaromir is a virtual watchdog, and he didn't catch Feodor either. The man was sent by Anton's father. How could either of you have guessed?"

Karina stopped pacing and studied Céline. "I cannot tell you how glad I am that you've come to us. In spite of Anton's . . . illness, I've seen a change in him since your arrival, as if he wants to live now, to rule, to best his brother. I've hated to see Anton alone these years, but I knew another marriage would be a terrible mistake, and with you, there are no worries on that score."

Céline stiffened, caught off guard and offended on several levels. First, did Karina believe she was—or would be—Anton's mistress? A plaything to provide him with entertainment and keep him from marrying again? Second, Céline had never thought this lady given to typical noble snobbery, but the words "with you, there are no worries on that score" made Céline want to flinch.

For all Karina's apparent kindness, it seemed she viewed Céline as one or two notches above a castle servant.

"Jaromir and Pavel dragged us here," Céline said, trying to keep the anger from her voice, "and I remained to help Anton solve the murders of these poor young women . . . and to keep Anton from appearing as a weakened leader to his father. I fear for this entire region should Damek be named heir."

Karina waved one hand in the air. "Damek will never be the heir. Though tragic, the unsolved deaths of a few girls would mean nothing to Prince Lieven. I've met him, and I can see how his mind works. I've understood the situation for years. No, Lieven is simply waiting until Anton is ready, but you need not worry. Anton will soon enough be head of the House of Pählen, and then he will be the grand prince of Droevinka."

Perhaps Karina was still shaken from her fears that Anton might have been on his deathbed. But the words coming from her mouth were startling. Céline had no idea she was so ambitious for Anton. Was she equally ambitious for herself? Seeking at least partial power to help rule through him? Pavel had clearly said she was given a voice here in matters of state.

Karina ceased her pacing near the bed. "But the deaths of these girls will have no impact on Prince Lieven's decision, and I fear the murders will not be solved, even with your good help."

"They must be," came a whisper from the bed.

Anton's eyes were open, and he'd been listening. Though probably as weak as a puppy, he wasn't sweating or shaking. He was looking at his aunt. "We must stop these murders. My lady, arrange another banquet, for tomorrow night. Céline must continue reading the young women. At present, we have nothing else to try."

The thought of even one more reading was almost more than Céline could face, but she had other worries.

"You won't be on your feet by tomorrow night," she insisted.

His quiet voice was firm. "I will."

*   *   *

Although she was weary to the bone, Amelie couldn't sleep. Finally, she climbed out of bed and stood on the cold floor, wondering if perhaps she shouldn't just go and sit with Céline and the Lady Karina. Here, alone in this room, she had too much time to think. Much too much.

Her mind kept going over her experience that afternoon with Jaromir, how he'd told her of his past. It was difficult to admit, but she felt differently about him now. She understood him better.

And she didn't want to understand him.

She certainly didn't want to be standing by the firelight from the hearth, thinking about him.

Sighing, she reached for her breeches and then noticed that the miniature of Lady Bethany was back on the dressing table, leaning against the mirror. How did that thing keep getting out of the drawer?

Walking over, she picked it up. With everything that had happened in the past day and night, they'd completely forgotten to try to get it back to Anton. Pausing, she looked down into the pretty face of Lady Bethany. Poor woman, to have died so young, leaving her sons without a mother.

Bethany's face was rounder than Karina's, and so were her eyes. Their thick chestnut hair was the same, though, even the manner in which they wore it, piled high with a few loose curls hanging down.

Then suddenly, even in the light of the fire, Amelie felt cold, and she looked up. The room appeared to be filling with white mist. Her eyes dropped back to the portrait just as the first jolt hit.

"No!" Amelie said aloud, speaking to the portrait.

But she was jerked backward, rushing down the corridor of swirling mists, almost unable to believe what was happening. The journey was long, and she grew light-headed, fighting to break free from the mists, to get back to her room.

The mists cleared, and she was outside, in broad daylight, with a cluster of red apples hanging over her head.

Half turning, she saw that she was standing only a few paces from a young woman, perhaps sixteen years old, who knelt on what appeared to be damp ground beneath an apple tree, inside an orchard. The day was clear and the sun shone bright in the sky, but beyond the orchard, Amelie could see pools of still water filled with more cattails than she could count.

The Everfen?

"Bethany?" a smooth voice called. "Are you out here?"

The young woman raised her head. It was Anton's mother . . . only younger than the image in the miniature. She was little more than a girl, wearing a muslin gown, soaked through the skirt where she knelt.

At first she didn't answer the call, and then finally said, "I'm here, Karina, over here."

The sound of sweeping skirts answered, and

another woman came around a tree. Amelie gasped. It was the Lady Karina . . . but she appeared to be in her late twenties. She looked exactly the same as when Amelie had seen her in Anton's rooms less than an hour before.

"Whatever are you doing? Father is waiting to tell you good-bye," Karina said as she stopped walking. "You've ruined that dress."

"I don't care."

"Oh, stop playing the martyr and get up."

"I don't want to go." Bethany seemed near to tears. "Can't you go for me? Can't you take my place?"

"Would that I could," Karina answered coldly, and then her face softened. "Forgive me . . . I'm . . . I know this isn't your fault. But Prince Lieven is determined to expand his territories here in the south, and he wants a bride from the House of Yegor. The head of any southern house would jump at the chance to connect with Pählen. Father wrote to offer him a daughter, with some lands thrown in for a dowry, and Lieven agreed. That's all there is to it."

"But Father has four daughters. Why did he have to pick me?"

"Because of your youth. Because princes like Lieven tend to prefer sixteen-year-old girls; that's why. Father says I'm too old, that if I arrived at Castle Pählen as the sacrificial lamb, Lieven might send me back. He won't send you back." This last was spoken with bitterness.

"Yes, but you've rebuffed every man who's asked for you."

"Because there's been no one from a great house!" Karina answered. "Which is why Father never tried to force me . . . and now it may be too late." She moved closer to her sister. "But it's not too late for you. Prince Lieven's influence and his lands are growing. You'll have sons. Lieven may not be the grand prince in his time, but if the power of Pählen continues to grow, you could be the mother of a grand prince, enjoy power through him. Try to imagine that far ahead, Bethany. It will sustain you."

Bethany stared at the damp ground. "Father claims to love me, but he knows nothing about Lieven. He's sending me to the west, to share a bed with a man he's never met. Is that love, Karina?"

"Yes," Karina answered. "In this case it is. And I wish I was your age and you were mine. I'd take Father's brand of love in a heartbeat." She reached down. "Come on. You'll need to change that dress before the caravan leaves."

Bethany gripped her sister's hand. "You'll write to me? We'll share everything that happens to us both?"

Karina nodded. "Oh, yes. I will follow everything that happens in your life."

Bethany climbed to her feet, still holding Karina's hand.

The scene of the orchard vanished, and Amelie

was back in the glowing firelight of her room staring down into Bethany's face. How had that just happened? How had touching the miniature pulled Amelie back through the mists?

But immediately, a more important revelation hit her. If the vision had been real . . . then Lady Karina had not aged a day in more than twenty-five years, since before Sub-Prince Damek was even born.

CHAPTER 13

Jaromir lay on his bed, trying to sleep and failing. He couldn't stop thinking on those terrible hours with Anton tonight, watching his friend vomit and convulse and finally fall unconscious.

He'd feared that Anton had been further poisoned, but once Céline had voiced the truth, he'd chastised himself as an idiot. He should have figured it out himself. He'd seen enough men who loved strong drink, who had fallen on hard times, and then suffered from a lack of gin. He'd seen the shaking and sweating and sickness.

But the way Céline had stepped in and taken over had given him more relief than he could express, and now it seemed Anton would recover.

But Jaromir couldn't fall sleep. He was still recovering from the experience himself.

A knock sounded on the door. Sitting up, he hesitated, hoping it wasn't Bridgette. He wasn't about to let her in, and he wasn't up to sending her away. But he couldn't ignore the knock, so he walked over and opened the door.

Amelie was standing in the passage, pale and shaken.

"What is it?" he asked, thinking this must be about Anton. "Is he worse?"

"The prince? No, I think he's . . . I haven't heard anything more."

Jaromir moved aside, opening the door further. "Then what's wrong? Come inside."

She shook her head and wouldn't cross the threshold. "No, I just . . . I was thinking about earlier, about what you told me . . . and a few things that Pavel told me and Céline."

After all they'd been through tonight, he didn't feel like speaking of his past anymore. "What about it?" He knew he sounded short, but he couldn't help it.

She didn't notice his tone. "The Lady Karina was already with Anton before you came here?"

He frowned. "Yes, but just before."

"How well did Anton know his mother's family?"

This was indeed becoming odd. Puzzled, he said, "I don't think at all. From what little I know, the marriage of his parents was arranged between the families via proxy, and his mother was sent up from the south in a caravan to marry Prince Lieven. Common enough among the great houses. I don't think Prince Lieven ever met her family."

"But years later, long after Bethany was dead, Lady Karina learned that Lady Joselyn had died and that Anton had fallen into mourning, and she came here to offer him her help. How would she have known he needed help? And why would he have accepted?"

"Amelie, I'm tired. Why are you asking these things?"

"Could they have been writing to each other, Anton and Karina?" she asked. "Maybe she wrote to him once he was given Castle Sèone, or even before, and she worked to establish a connection between them?"

"I don't know. It's possible. Anton has always been good about answering letters, and Karina is his mother's sister." He stepped forward. "What is this about?"

But she drew away from him, and he was reluctant to grab her arm after what she'd said to him up in the portrait hall.

"I don't know. I need to talk to Céline . . ." She turned. "Good night, Lieutenant."

And then she was hurrying down the passage. He knew better than to follow.

Upon returning to her room near dawn, if Céline thought she'd get any sleep, she was sadly mistaken.

For she walked in to find a very distraught Amelie pacing the floor.

Amelie then rushed to her and spilled out an astonishing story, speaking in fits and starts from the moment she'd picked up the miniature of Lady Bethany to her visit to Lieutenant Jaromir

for any possible extra information. By the time
she'd finished, Céline was more than skeptical,
but she knew she'd need to tread carefully.

Drawing Amelie over to the bed, Céline motioned her to sit down. "Are you sure it wasn't a
dream? We've been through so much in the past
few days and nights."

Amelie's expression moved from shock to anger. "It wasn't a dream! How would I have known
what to ask Jaromir? How would I have known to
get him to confirm that Prince Lieven knew nothing of Bethany's family?"

Suddenly, the weight of what Amelie was saying began to touch Céline. "You really saw a vision of Bethany when she was sixteen . . . and
Karina was the same age she is now?"

"Yes!"

"But that would been at least twenty-six years
ago."

Amelie nodded vigorously. "Before Damek was
even born."

Céline sank onto the bed beside her sister. "She
said something tonight, something about being
certain Anton would be named heir to the House
of Pählen and then become the grand prince. Do
you think she's seeking power through him?"

"Maybe, but how has she not aged?"

"I don't know." Céline's mind began turning
over their options. "We can't go to Anton or Jaromir with this. All we have is your word—from
a vision you saw by touching a portrait that

shouldn't even be in this room. And then what would we accuse her of? Looking younger than she should?"

"She should look about fifty-five."

"We can't prove that."

"Then what do you want to do?"

Céline looked around the room, at the silver brushes on the dressing table, the gowns in the open wardrobe, and the wooden screen in the corner.

"Set a trap," she answered.

The following evening, as Amelie stood before the full-length mirror, she was beginning to regret how easily she'd agreed to Céline's plan.

"Céline . . . I don't know about this."

"Oh, will you stop?" Céline answered. "You look lovely, and this is the only thing I could think of to get her up here alone. Surely you can stand wearing a gown for an hour or so?"

But Amelie wasn't so sure. She didn't feel like herself. Céline had laced her into the silk midnight blue gown that Inna had initially brought the day they'd arrived. It was tight at the waist and the skirt felt heavy, and she looked like a stranger to herself in the mirror.

"I'll bet Jaromir would pay a year's wages to see you in that," Céline said, straightening the brushes on the dressing table.

An angry retort formed on Amelie's lips, but she managed to bite it back. She wished Céline would stop teasing her about Jaromir. She was conflicted enough about him as things stood. "I doubt he earns a wage," she answered. "He probably has the run of the castle treasury and just takes whatever he wants."

The fire burned brightly, but the spring night was unusually warm, and the room felt hot and stuffy. Moving to the window, she opened the shutters and breathed the night air, looking down into the courtyard.

"All right," Céline said from the dressing table. "I think we're ready."

"What makes you think she'll come herself?" Amelie asked. "She might just send one of her maids."

"Oh, she'll come. Trust me."

A short while ago, Amelie had a written a note—dictated by Céline—that read:

> *Dear Lady Karina,*
> *   For the banquet tonight, I have put on one of the gowns you had sent to us, but I waited until Céline had already gone downstairs. Because of my past refusals in this matter, I was embarrassed to ask for her help. Would you please come to my room and help me to dress my hair? I would be so grateful.*
> *   Your servant,*
> *   Amelie Fawe*

They'd given the note to a castle maid and had it sent directly to Karina's room. Amelie objected strenuously to the wording of the note, as it sounded nothing like her.

But Céline continued to insist that it would appeal to Lady Karina and bring her here directly. "For all her polite ways, I suspect your breeches and dagger offend her. Women like her are forced into a role by their birth and station, and most of them can't stand the thought of another woman escaping that role. I know for certain that she's been dying to put you into a gown and to dress your hair since we first arrived."

"But my hair is too short for her to dress," Amelie said, turning away from the open window.

"Oh, you'd be surprised what a lady like Karina can do with—"

A soft knock sounded on the door, and Céline froze for an instant. Then she hurried over to crouch down behind the dressing screen, completely hidden from sight.

This was part of the plan, too.

Still uncertain about the entire strategy, Amelie walked across the room. It was too late to turn back now. She opened the door.

Céline's instincts must have been right, as the Lady Karina stood on the other side, and she smiled at the sight of the midnight blue gown. "Oh, my dear, how beautiful you are. Let me do your hair, and we'll walk down to the hall together."

She swept inside, wearing emerald green silk that rustled gently. Her own hair was elaborately dressed . . . but she had so much of it. Amelie thought when it was down, it probably reached the small of her back.

"I brought some pins," Karina said. "Come and sit."

"How is Anton?" Amelie asked, moving to the dressing table and sitting down.

"Weary, but on his feet. I did object to this banquet tonight, but he is determined." She looked down at the table. "Will you hand me that brush?"

Looking into the mirror, Amelie studied Karina's reflection, her lustrous hair, her glowing skin. She looked exactly as she had in the vision from so long ago.

How was that possible?

Céline had counseled Amelie to wait until after Karina had finished with her hair, ensuring that she was relaxed and pleased with her own work, but Amelie decided not to wait another moment.

Turning in the chair, she grabbed Karina's hand and gripped it tightly.

Karina's slanted green eyes widened in surprise, and she tried to jerk away, but Amelie was stronger and held fast while focusing all her internal energy on Karina's past, on how she had not aged.

She felt for the spark of Karina's spirit.

The jolt hit her as before, but this time the experience was different. Karina was fighting her, fighting to break free, and Amelie fought back. Within seconds, Amelie's spirit began overpowering Karina's, but as a result, she could feel their spirits mingling and meshing together.

The room around them vanished.

Another jolt hit, and then Amelie was rushing backward through the mists, only Karina's spirit was still with her. Their spirits sped along, blending together until Amelie couldn't separate them. She thought Karina's thoughts and saw what Karina saw.

She *was* Karina.

And then the mists began to fade . . .

CHAPTER 14

TWENTY-SIX YEARS IN THE PAST

The summer after Bethany left for her marriage and new life as the wife of a prince in the west, Karina's sorrow and disappointment with her own life came to feel like a weight around her neck. She was not remotely sorry that she'd never married. No one worthy had asked her.

She was only sorry that her father had not been able to arrange a great match for her, as he had for her youngest sister. Oh, he was in the process of making "acceptable" matches for their other two sisters, but nothing on the scale that he'd made for Bethany.

And Karina would accept no less.

For women of their class . . . youth, beauty, wealth, and land were the only bargaining chips to be offered. Her father possessed abundant land, and she was well aware that she still possessed beauty, but at the age of twenty-nine, she was considered on the edge of losing her youth—possibly over the edge.

Father was nothing if not honest, and he'd told her that if she wished, he might able to arrange a match with a noble widower; an older man who'd lost his wife might agree to take Karina if a sweet enough dowry was offered.

But she did not wish this.

She wanted to run a great household. She wanted fiefdoms with fat rents under her charge. She wanted to be the beautiful mistress to one of the most powerful houses in Droevinka, to be worshipped by her peasants as kind and generous, to be valued by her husband as indispensable in helping him with decisions of state.

She wanted to be the mother of princes.

It cut like a sharp knife that her silly younger sister had been handed the opportunity for all these things . . . only because she was so young.

Karina considered herself to be clever, but she cursed herself that she'd never before realized the absolute importance of youth in a woman.

Looking into the mirror every night, she saw a lovely face staring back, with smooth skin, slanted green eyes, and glossy hair. The nobles who visited her parents here and the people of her father's villages and the household servants still gazed at her with admiration when she entered a room or rode down the streets, but how long would this last? Next year she would be thirty.

Thirty.

How long before the glow of her skin faded and her hair grew dull like her mother's and she woke up one day to find creases around her eyes? The prospect filled her with a dread she couldn't bear. Once that happened, she'd have nothing to place on the bargaining table but her father's land.

Worse, no one would gaze at her in admiration when she floated into a room. How could she live without that? It was all she had.

Her sorrow and fear of the future continued to grow.

Thankfully, she had one comfort and refuge to which she sometimes escaped, for some peace from her own thoughts. Her father had felt his girls should be accomplished in more skills than proper taste in gowns and hairstyles and good manners, and he'd encouraged them to pursue talents or interests. Bethany had proven herself quite skilled at the lute, and she'd chosen to study music.

Karina found joy and solace in painting. She loved to do a sketch of an object or a person and turn the sketch into an oil-painting likeness. Her father said she had skill, and he didn't offer his favor lightly.

He displayed some of her better work, and it was admired by all.

Karina needed to be admired.

So in the months after Bethany's departure toward a future of power and admiration, Karina took to her own room more and more, where she'd set up her easel and brushes.

One afternoon, she was in her room, working on a still life of a flower arrangement she'd put together herself—with short-cut roses and white pansies—and she was so absorbed in the work that it was too late before she remembered that she'd forgotten to change out of a new gown.

Father had paid quite a sum for the gown, a sky blue satin, and with some alarm, she saw that she'd spotted the sleeve with white paint. After a few moments of panic, she decided to go down to the kitchens and see if Martha, their head cook, could help. Martha had once managed to get every drop of spilled red wine out of light pink silk. It was possible she might be able to do something with few spots of paint.

Karina had no idea that this one small accident would alter the course of her life. But as she approached the kitchens, she heard a number of female voices and the word "Móndyalítko," and she stopped outside the open archway, not allowing herself to be seen.

The paint on her sleeve was already dry, and a few more moments would make no difference. She loved to hear the kitchen gossip, and she knew that if she walked in, the women would cease talking.

"Wagons with houses built on top?" someone asked. "I should like to see that." Karina didn't recognize the voice, but she was familiar with only a few members of the kitchen staff.

"Well, they've set up camp just outside the village." This was a voice she did know: Eveeta, a beautiful scullery maid of about sixteen. She had red hair and a charming smattering of freckles at the top of her breasts.

"You can go and have your fortune read or buy baubles or watch the entertainments," Eveeta went on. "I was just down there. They have a man who can swallow fire if you pay him half a penny. Oh, and they have one of the Mist-Torn in their company."

"What's a Mist-Torn?" Martha asked.

"You know, one of their women who's born with some sort of power," Eveeta said.

Martha snorted. "Good gods, girl, you'll believe anything. You can't listen to a thing those Móndyalítko tell you. They're born tricksters and liars."

The chatter went on, but Karina drew back from the archway, forgetting all about her ruined sleeve. For the first time since Bethany had left, she found herself interested in something outside of her room.

The Móndyalítko.

She'd heard stories of them . . . that women among them often carved out positions of power in the community through skills or abilities. Yet they were surrounded by mystery—perhaps self-created mystery.

Karina wanted to see them.

Perhaps she would go and have her fortune told.

*   *   *

About an hour past sunset, Karina arrived at the Móndyalítko encampment with four of her father's men riding beside her.

Her entourage made its entrance among the quaint wagons with brightly painted houses built into their beds. Campfires seemed to be glowing from the ground near every wagon, but as she dismounted, she heard music and looked to see a girl singing a haunting tune for a small crowd.

The girl's waving black hair hung like dark cloud around her glowing ivory face. More than merely pretty, she was exotic and alluring. No one could take their eyes from her. Karina felt a rush of envy worse than anything she'd ever felt toward Bethany, but she couldn't explain why.

Why should she envy some gypsy girl?

"How might we serve you, my lady?" asked a voice from behind her. "A love potion perhaps? Or would you like to hear your fortune?"

Karina turned to find a quite different woman, late middle-aged, with skin ravaged by disappointment and time, deeply wrinkled. The woman's hair might have once been long and glossy, but now it hung in dried-out lanks going gray.

"Who is that?" Karina asked, turning back toward the singing girl surrounded by enraptured admirers.

The hag didn't answer at first but then finally said, "My sister, Jaelle." Hatred and venom dripped from her voice.

"Your sister?" Karina repeated, unable to keep the surprise from her voice. This woman looked old enough to be the girl's grandmother.

"She is Mist-Torn," the hag answered simply, as if this would explain everything.

Then Karina remembered Eveeta mentioning something about this . . . something about a gypsy born with power.

The girl, Jaelle, was so lovely, so fresh, with her flawless skin and warm smile as she sang.

"What is your name?" Karina asked the hag. Her stomach felt tight. Somehow, she knew that she was standing at the crux of her life. She didn't know how she knew this, only that she did.

"I am Lucrezia."

"And *that* girl is your sister?"

"Yes."

"How?"

Again, Lucrezia did not speak for a moment. Hatred and envy emanated from her eyes. "She does not age. Her body draws small bits of youth from any girl around her, just bits, but it keeps her from aging a day."

At those words, Karina almost couldn't breathe. She fought to maintain her noble demeanor.

"That is the truth?" she demanded. "She's not just some girl your people use to lure in villagers? And don't lie to me. I can find out if you're lying, and my father can have your entire company banished from this province."

Lucrezia didn't react to the threat. " 'Tis true,

my lady. She stopped aging over thirty years ago, a gift from the line of the Mist-Torn."

"But you are her sister, and you received no such gift?"

Lucrezia's expression closed up, and Karina could see the scars of jealous poison deep inside her eyes. If there was one thing Karina understood, it was jealous poison.

"Is there something I might do to serve you?" Lucrezia asked.

But Karina was reeling and needed time to think. Calling to her guards, she rode back to her father's manor.

There, she spent a sleepless night.

The following afternoon, she returned to the gypsy encampment. As she dismounted, a handsome young man holding a violin looked her up and down without bothering to disguise his interest.

"Can I be of service, my lady?" he asked. His tone was insolent, almost suggestive, but inwardly she could not help being pleased at his clear approval of her beauty.

"Which wagon belongs to Lucrezia?" she asked coldly.

With a flourishing bow, he pointed. "That one."

Without bothering to thank him, she moved away from her contingent of guards toward the wagon.

"Hello?" she called.

The bed of the wagon was covered by what appeared to be a small house. The door opened, and Lucrezia looked down in surprise. "My lady . . . what did you . . . Do you wish to have your fortune told?"

Wishing for a more private discussion, Karina nodded and then turned her head. "Wait out here," she told her guards. After that, she made her way up a few steps and stepped inside a tiny dwelling with two bunk beds attached to the walls and a cushioned bench behind a table. Crystals hung from the ceiling, and balls of colored glass lined a makeshift window.

"Please sit," Lucrezia said.

But Karina did not. Instead, she reached into her cloak, took out an emerald necklace, and dropped it on the table. Lucrezia couldn't hide her shock. To her, the emeralds in the necklace would bring a fortune.

"My lady?"

"I'm not here to have my fortune told. I seek information . . . knowing you might not have it but are able to attain it."

To Karina's joy, Lucrezia's eyes narrowed in cunning, in the light of opportunity. "However I might help, my lady."

Karina wasted no time mincing words. "This power of your sister's. You say she was born with it, but can it be stolen, can it be taken by another?"

Again, Lucrezia could not contain her shock.

"Stolen? Given to another? No," she said emphatically. "The power of the Mist-Torn is sacred. It cannot be used by another."

"Are you certain?" Karina went on. "You must have women with arcane knowledge here . . . kettle witches, as they are called by our villagers. Perhaps you're one yourself? Find a way to take your sister's power and give use of it to me, and this emerald necklace will be but a small token of your reward. You can name your price, and I assure you I will pay it."

Lucrezia slowly reached a gnarled hand toward the table.

But Karina grabbed her wrist. "Has the thought of stealing her power never occurred to you?"

Lucrezia's shock only seemed to increase. "To steal from the Mist-Torn? Even if such a thing were possible, I would be cast out from my people . . . not just by those here, but by all of Móndyalítko."

She appeared so terrified of that prospect that Karina began to relax a little. This Lucrezia might be jealous and greedy, but perhaps she would not dare try to take what Karina wanted.

"Will you look into this for me? Seek information among the crones of the kettle witches?"

Lucrezia's eyes were locked on the emeralds. "It may take a bit of time, my lady. May I take the necklace now?"

"Yes."

*   *   *

A week later, Karina received a message asking her to meet Lucrezia a half league from the mill, down the village creek.

Karina slipped out alone and rode by herself. She knew this wasn't safe, but the reward was worth the risk, and she also understood why Lucrezia had chosen such a secret meeting place. At this point, they shouldn't be seen plotting together.

Past the mill house, she steered her horse down the creek until she was well outside the village, surrounded only by trees, the creek, and the calling birds.

The ground was damp, and her horse had some trouble with its footing, but soon enough, she spotted Lucrezia standing alone between the tree line and the rushing creek. Karina dismounted.

"I wasn't sure you'd come," Lucrezia said.

"Can it be done?" Karina demanded without preamble.

Lucrezia's eyes were alight with cunning again. Now that she'd had time to absorb what Karina was asking, it stood to reason that her mind would be fully focused on how she might serve herself. But Karina had no worries about that. She wanted Lucrezia to be self-serving.

"It can be done, my lady, but it's no simple matter." She unrolled a scroll in her hand; it was written in a language Karina couldn't read. "I stole this from one of our elders," Lucrezia said. "The power of a Mist-Torn witch can only be taken from her and used if she is killed and her spirit is trapped. A spell is then cast to enslave the spirit . . . but the spirit must be visible to the master."

"Visible?"

"Yes, the spirit must be held someplace, contained someplace where it can still be seen and commanded."

The hint of an idea began forming at the back of Karina's mind. Excitement began to build.

"Also," Lucrezia continued, "wielding the power of an enslaved ghost will not work the same as it did for the Mist-Torn herself. You will be able to force her to use her power for yourself, but it may work quite differently coming from the hands of a ghost and being transferred to you . . . and I'm not sure what to expect. You may need some trial and error to harness the ghost's abilities properly."

That didn't matter. Karina would figure it out. What mattered was enslaving Jaelle in the first place.

"Can you cast the necessary spells?"

At this, Lucrezia's wrinkled, ugly face twisted with an expression of greed. "Perhaps we should speak of terms."

"By all means. What is your price?"

"To be free of groveling for pennies reading fortunes. I want a house of my own. Servants of my own. To be my own mistress."

"Done," Karina said instantly.

The quick response put Lucrezia on her guard. "Where is the house?"

"In the prosperous village of Góra. My grand-mother left it to me in her will, and it is mine to give. I will give you more jewels to sell, but that emerald necklace alone should keep you comfort-able for years."

"You mean to do this, don't you? You're not some spoiled noble hoping to help play the kettle witch."

"Don't insult me. Can you cast the proper spells?"

"I can . . . but, my lady, if you are the one to en-slave Jaelle, you must be the one to end her life. Can you drive a dagger through her heart with your own hand?"

For eternal youth? Karina could slaughter half the village. "Have no fear on that score."

"Then we only need to a find a prison, a place where her spirit can be trapped."

Karina nodded. "I have an idea for that, as well."

Another week later, and Karina was ready.

She'd worked night and day painting a back-drop large enough for a life-sized portrait. The scene had come to her when she'd thought on Jaelle by the campfire at night, with large ever-green trees just behind her. Jaelle had looked so pleased with herself by that campfire.

Karina would put her in such a setting forever.

Near midnight, she slipped out and went down to her mother's rose garden. Lucrezia was already there, with a campfire burning and a cauldron on a hook bubbling over a fire.

The whole scene was like something from a dark fairy story.

However, Karina was dragging the canvas with the backdrop, and as it was as tall as herself, she was having some trouble. Lucrezia came to help her lean it against the stone wall of the garden.

"Is the oil completely dry?" Lucrezia asked.

"Yes."

Karina had chosen this spot, as it was close to the house but always deserted at night. She knew she'd not be able to drag the painting far, and she couldn't ask for help.

Lucrezia had a dagger in her right hand. "Stand still." Reaching up, she sliced off a thick lock of Karina's hair. Keeping the hair, she held out the dagger. "Take it. It's razor sharp."

Karina took it. "When will your sister arrive?"

"Soon. I told her we were being well paid to entertain the lord's daughter by helping her cast a love spell out here in this garden. We've done such things before, many times. Most young women enjoy the thrill of pretending." Looking at the dagger in Karina's hand, she said, "But most young women are nothing like you."

"No, they are not."

Then, to Karina's worry, Lucrezia's expression wavered slightly. "You must swear to me that no word will ever reach my people of my part in this . . . should it be discovered."

Karina relaxed again. She could easily promise that.

"I swear."

A few moments later, footsteps sounded outside the wall, and a lovely visage came walking through the gate. Karina couldn't keep in a soft gasp as the envy hit her. What was it about Jaelle that caused everyone to gaze upon her with such admiration? What is her glowing skin? Her wavy black hair? Or was it her complete assurance that she was worthy of such worship?

"My lady," she said, smiling, nodding to her sister first and then taking in the sight of the rosebushes. "What a perfect setting. Did you bring a personal object from the man whose love you hope to gain?"

She was dressed all in black, even to her gloves, and Karina wondered if this was typical or part of the "show" she'd intended to perform tonight.

"Yes," said Karina, showing Jaelle the dagger. "I have something right here."

Gripping the hilt, she stepped up and drove the sharp blade right through Jaelle's rib cage, upward toward her heart. The girl's expression shifted to horror as her body jerked once.

"Quickly!" Lucrezia shouted.

Karina jerked out the knife and watched the body fall. But Lucrezia grabbed the dagger from her hand and held the bloody blade over the cauldron, letting three drops fall. Then she dashed back to the body and cut a lock of Jaelle's hair, again rushing back and dropping the black lock, along with the chestnut one she'd taken from Karina, into the cauldron.

"By the heart's blood of the Mist-Torn," she whispered, "this gift is enslaved."

Karina watched with fascination as Lucrezia took a ladle from the cauldron and dipped it into the boiling substance. Then she threw the ladleful of liquid against the painting, watching as it splashed across the surface.

"Inside!" she shouted. "Forever inside."

A glow rose from Jaelle's body, swirling and solidifying until her exact form appeared to be floating above the dead body.

"What have you done?" the ghost cried, but then she was swept toward the stone wall of the garden . . . and inside the painting, standing by the campfire, looking for all purposes like a life-sized portrait of a lovely gypsy girl.

Karina breathed in and out, with blood dripping from her right hand. But then she was struck by doubt, by disappointment. So she had murdered Jaelle, and then Lucrezia had trapped the spirit in the painting. But now what?

"You must command her," Lucrezia said, breaking the silence. "You need to have her use her power to drain life from a living body and pass it to you. She is your slave now and cannot refuse anything you ask."

Could it be so simple? Karina's heart beat fast.

She would not turn thirty. She would not age an-other day.

Lucrezia strode toward her. "But the keys to my house first, and the title of ownership. You prom-ised."

Karina glanced at her briefly and then back to the painting. "There is no house," she said calmly. "Anything I inherit instantly belongs to my fa-ther, and those emeralds you took are family heirlooms, well-known throughout the province. If you try to sell them, you'll be hanged."

Lucrezia hissed and stepped back. "No!"

But Karina was still staring at the painting.

She pointed to Lucrezia. "Jaelle, drain her."

A black-and-white form blurred from inside the portrait, and the spirit of Jaelle flew toward her sister. The painting was now nothing more than the backdrop again. Lucrezia screamed and tried to run, but Jaelle caught her quickly, touching her with both hands.

Lucrezia screamed again as her wrinkled flesh began to shrivel, sinking toward her bones, and she fell to the ground, nothing more than a dried husk. Jaelle's spirit stood beside the body, looking whole and solid.

Karina remembered what Lucrezia had said about learning to use Jaelle's power.

"You will feed me her life," Karina ordered.

But Jaelle looked over at her in confused sor-row. "Won't work," she said as if finding speech difficult. "It must be youth. Must be beauty."

Youth and beauty?

"Come with me," Karina said.

She slipped back into the kitchens, which were silent and dark, and made her way to the servants' quarters. She knew which room was Eveeta's. The door was unlocked, and she silently entered, looking down at the sleeping girl.

Jaelle floated just a few inches off the ground beside her.

"Her," Karina ordered quietly. "Take only what you need."

With reluctance, Jaelle floated forward and touched Eveeta's face with her black-gloved hands. Eveeta's soft skin lost its luster, but only a little.

"Pass the youth and beauty to me," Karina whispered.

Jaelle floated back to Karina and touched her.

Nothing happened.

"What is wrong?" Karina demanded.

"Not enough."

Steeling herself, Karina pointed to Eveeta again. "Then take her life. Take it all."

Jaelle moved to Eveeta, touching her face and throat. Her smooth skin began to shrivel and sink into itself, and soon, like Lucrezia, she, too, was a dried husk.

Jaelle floated back and touched Karina. This time, warmth and life flowed into her, giving her a feeling of euphoria, of unbelievable well-being.

A small cracked mirror hung on the wall, and when Jaelle had finished, Karina rushed to the mirror. She didn't look any younger than her twenty-nine years, but her face glowed and her hair was unusually glossy. She was beautiful. She felt beautiful, worthy of admiration.

Joy flooded through her.

"Back into the painting," she told Jaelle.

The spirit of Jaelle vanished.

Karina walked through the house and out to the rose garden, finding Jaelle back inside the portrait, in her pose by the campfire. Karina tilted the canvas and picked it up, to try to carry it back to the house, but she left all three bodies where they lay, a mystery for her father's guards to solve. No one would ever connect the dead bodies of two gypsies and a kitchen girl to the beautiful Lady Karina.

For the first decade no one noticed anything truly unusual about Karina, or at least no one said anything. Some women aged better than others. But although she did not turn thirty physically, she did have a birthday, and then a thirty-first . . . and a thirty-second . . . so on.

As the years passed, her focus slowly began to pinpoint on only two things.

First was her sister Bethany. As promised, the sisters corresponded regularly. Karina became obsessed with everything that involved the House of Pählen. She was not surprised—and was possibly a little pleased—to learn that her sister had almost no relationship with Prince Lieven. The two rarely spoke and knew little about each other. However, within the first year of marriage, Bethany gave birth to a healthy son, named Damek. This news was like a knife in Karina's stomach. Two years later, Bethany gave birth to a second son, named Anton.

After that, Karina found that Bethany's empty, chatty letters weren't enough by way of information, and she began to hire spies and send them across Droevinka. She soon managed to get a maid employed inside Castle Pählen, who sent her regular reports.

Through this maid, Karina learned a great deal. Even as a child, Damek proved himself to be sly and cruel, sometimes torturing castle dogs or tormenting servants if he could.

Anton was gentle and quiet and loved to read.

But when Damek was ten and Anton was eight, Bethany took ill one morning and died within a day. She'd been gone nearly a month before Karina was informed by her spies.

Prince Lieven had been left with no wife, and two boys with no mother.

For a moment, just a moment, Karina allowed the spark of a fantasy that she might find a way to replace her dead sister, but that notion passed almost as soon as it had surfaced. Prince Lieven expressed no interest in taking a new wife. Why should he? He had claim to all his dead wife's lands and two healthy sons to follow him.

Karina's interest began to focus on Anton, who

by all reports missed his mother and was lost in a lonely fog with only his cruel brother and overly busy father.

She waited until he was twelve years old before she wrote to him:

> *My dear nephew,*
> *I am your mother's younger sister, but I have felt for you these past years, and how you must miss her. I would have written you sooner, but I thought that only now would you care for an aunt to be writing you letters . . .*

She went on to subtly offer him sympathy and a motherly shoulder to lean upon, not knowing what to expect in return. Her instincts proved infallible. He wrote a long letter back, thanking her and telling her a bit about his daily life and interests. But she read the letter four times in succession, as it touched her deeply, echoing the voice of a boy starving for love, starving for an adult in his life who cared for his thoughts and feelings.

A connection was formed, and she rejoiced.

But it was also at this time that her second obsession became an issue: how to remain youthful and beautiful indefinitely without being labeled some sort of sorceress. By trial and error, she'd learned how to best use Jaelle's power. Greedy for the experience of euphoria in the early days, she'd had Jaelle drain five more young women and pass their youth to her. But of course the deaths caused some local alarm, and though Karina did not fear she would be connected, she stopped . . . waiting to see how long the infusions would last.

They lasted five years.

She did not note a single change in either the glow of her skin or the gloss of her hair for five years.

But one day, she did notice a change, just a hint of dullness in her complexion, and so she had Jaelle take and pass on only one life. To Karina's dismay, the infusion lasted less than a month.

Deciding to try what had worked the last time, she had Jaelle take six lives over a period of a few weeks and transfer them in quick succession. This lasted another five years. Karina was not certain why the power worked in this fashion, only that it did.

However, by the time Anton had turned twelve years of age, and their correspondence had begun, in the southeast, the people around Karina were beginning to talk—as she was in her midforties.

She debated on the best course of action.

But that was an eventful year around her, and both her parents passed away. As her father had died with no male heir, both his title and the family estate went to his younger brother. However, Karina came into her own inheritance money, and it was substantial. She let her family know that she didn't wish to remain on the estate and live with her uncle but would prefer to travel.

She rented a villa far from her childhood home and hired a staff of new servants. After that, the only constant in her life was Anton—but only through a regular exchange of letters. Still, she felt she knew him well. As yet, he was only a seedling, so she did not try to visit him, nor invite him to visit her. She was waiting for the right time. If he saw her in his youth, and then saw her again later, he would wonder why she'd not aged.

But she swelled with pride when he was given charge of Castle Sèone—and then she managed to keep herself from chastising him when he thwarted his father and married a minor noble with no money named Joselyn . . . out of love. He soon wrote to her that his young wife was expecting a child. This news filled Karina with a strange longing, that somehow she had missed out on an essential element of life, though she wasn't quite certain what it was. Shortly before Joselyn was to deliver, Anton wrote to Karina, expressing that he was missing the help and advice of a mother, and would Karina consider coming to live with them?

The idea stunned her at first, but then . . . she began to grasp hold of many possibilities—that this might be the *right* time. She was well aware that Lieven had not named Damek as heir and was in the process of choosing between his two sons. Could she help influence this? Suddenly, she found herself enjoying the image of stepping into a position as Anton's surrogate mother at Castle Sèone.

Writing back, she asked him for his thoughts on when and how this transition might best take place.

He didn't answer.

She waited.

Then one of her spies sent a message that Joselyn had died in the childbed, and Anton appeared to have gone mad with grief, locking himself away and refusing food.

She sent word to the castle that she was coming.

In a matter of days, Karina began her journey west.

While the death of Joselyn was indeed tragic, Anton's need for a mother figure was now even greater. Karina would arrive awash in sympathy and step in to help him. He would be named heir. She would become his strong right arm and live out her dream as mistress of a great house—then mistress of a nation.

Traveling with a caravan, as her sister had done so many years ago, Karina arrived in the courtyard of Castle Sèone on a cloudy afternoon in the autumn. Upon dismounting, she was greeted by a tall, silver-haired woman in an apron.

The woman's expression of relief was profound.

"My lady," she breathed. "I can't tell you how grateful we are that you've come. I manage the maids and kitchen girls. But with the mistress . . . gone, and the young prince in mourning, the household is going to ruin."

Karina reached out and touched her hand. "I will do my best to assist you and to help the prince."

"Thank you, my lady. We've had rooms prepared. Is there anything you wish brought up directly?"

"Only a few small chests for now, but I have another . . . concern." She motioned to the tall painting wrapped carefully in canvas. "I have a family heirloom with me, a portrait, but I'd rather not hang in it my rooms. It's not good enough for a family portrait hall, but might there be a lesser hall, someplace out of the way where it might be hung?"

She wanted it hidden in plain sight, but someplace where it might go unnoticed, finally forgotten by anyone but herself.

If the aging housekeeper found this an odd request, she didn't show it. Instead, she pursed her mouth a moment and said, "Oh, yes, there's a small hall above the guest quarters in the north tower with some old portraits. I could have it hung there."

Karina smiled. "Thank you. That would be perfect."

CHAPTER 15

The white mists vanished and Amelie found
herself still gripping Karina's hand. She let go
and jumped up off the dressing table chair, backing away, trying to clear her head from the years
and years of events she'd just lived through, as if
she was Karina.

A sensation of sickness, like worms crawling in
her mind, made her choke as she backed away.

"You . . . you murdered those girls . . . Sybil . . .
Inna. You took their lives!"

Karina was staring at her with wild eyes, more
stunned than angry or guilty. "You *know*," she
breathed. "No one has ever known. No one could
suspect me."

As Amelie's mind cleared slightly, she realized
that Karina had viewed herself as untouchable.
She'd not objected to Anton using Céline in this
search, as she never believed anyone would learn
her secrets or connect her to the murders.

"You're mad," Amelie said, shaking her head.
"All those deaths for nothing more than a pretty

face." Her hand went to her side instinctively, but the dagger wasn't there. She was wearing the midnight blue gown.

Karina drew herself up. "Far more than a pretty face, as you know if you lived through everything I just felt in that vision." Though her expression was still wild, she almost seemed to find satisfaction in speaking of these things, and Amelie fervently hoped that Céline would remain hidden behind the dressing screen, just listening. As yet, she would not know the extent of the danger Karina posed.

"Anton will be named grand prince," Karina said, "and when that happens, I will be at his side."

"For how long?" Amelie shot back. "Even if all your plans come true? You've already been with him four years. What if he does become Lieven's heir, and then he is named grand prince in the next election? What happens at the end of another nine years and you haven't aged a day? Do you think you'll still be at his side?"

Karina grew calm. "You are not as shortsighted as you appear." She paused. "Yes, I will still be at his side because I will have aged. My place is with Anton now, and my reward will be the power I reap with him. Right now, I need my beauty to help influence the other princes in his favor . . . but after that, I can live without it. I've decided that in another five years, when this infusion fades, I will not use the painting again. I will be content."

Amelie didn't believe her. But it didn't matter.

"You're not going anywhere near Anton. Not ever again. Once Jaromir hears of this, you'll be lucky if you only wind up in a prison cell."

But Amelie was only trying to lull her into a false sense that they were engaged in a fight of words, in the common battle of women, when all the while, Amelie looked for an opening, for the right instant to move.

"Jaromir will hear nothing," Karina answered.

"Oh, yes, he will."

Amelie moved like lightning, relying on the element of surprise—as always—to dash forward and strike out with her right fist, intending to knock Karina unconscious with one blow. But somehow, Karina must have seen what was coming and managed to pull back just enough that Amelie's fist glanced across her jaw.

"Jaelle!" Karina called. "Come to me!"

Anton was ashamed of himself.

He stood in the great hall with Jaromir and Pavel. Guardsman Rurik was present as well, his head wound having healed enough for him to resume his duties.

Anton was waiting to greet his guests, waiting to see Céline enter through the archway.

But she did not.

He wondered what was keeping her, but his eagerness was not the source of his shame. His arm itched. His hands were trembling. He could not stop thinking of how he'd felt earlier that day when he'd taken his small dose of the poppy syrup and all the pain went away and he'd no longer felt like clawing off his own skin.

The bottle of poppy syrup was up in his rooms. Céline had told him not to take another dose until tomorrow, but this was going to be a long night. He told himself that he needed to be at full strength tonight, not some weakling with shaking hands. His people needed to see him as a leader.

Turning to Jaromir, he said, "Neither Céline nor the Lady Karina have arrived yet, and I just remembered that I left a half-written letter to my father on my desk. I'd prefer any servants coming in to clean did not see it." He began walking away. "You wait here. I will return directly."

Jaromir frowned but would never question Anton. "Yes, my lord."

Still ashamed, Anton hurried out of the hall and up the stairs of the west tower, nearly jogging off the second landing and down the passage to his apartments. He tried not to let himself think, beyond making internal assurances that this would be the only time he'd circumvent Céline's instructions. Tomorrow he would begin to wean himself off the opiate as planned.

Tomorrow.

After opening the doors to his front room,

which mainly served as an office and a library, he hurried through to his bedroom, to his bedside table, and picked up the bottle of poppy juice, hating himself but knowing he wasn't going to stop.

Then he thought that he should at least be cautious enough to use the spoon and not just swallow straight from the bottle. But the spoon wasn't on the night table. Turning, he glanced around to see where Céline had left it . . . and his eyes fell upon the portrait leaning against the wall beside the door.

The pale-skinned woman was no longer in the painting. Only the dark backdrop and the evergreen trees and the campfire remained.

And Céline had not arrived at the banquet.

"Céline."

Dropping the bottle of poppy syrup, he ran from his rooms and back downstairs, panting from exhaustion by the time he reached the main floor and cursing how weak he'd allowed his body to become. Once, he'd been strong and swift, skilled with a sword. He would be so again.

Just outside the archway of the great hall, he put his hands on his knees and managed to shout, "Jaromir!"

Céline was crouched behind the dressing screen, peeking out through a crack.

She'd seen Amelie grab Karina's hand and then watched as both their bodies froze, their minds lost in the mists of the past.

But when they'd both come out of it, nothing either one said made any sense . . . except that Amelie believed Karina was the killer.

Céline's first instinct had been to rush out and protect her sister, but she was no fighter and was uncertain what she might do. And she had so often seen Amelie prevail in physical conflicts by relying almost entirely on speed and the element of surprise.

This was the thought that held Céline back. Karina had no idea she was in the room, and she still held the element of surprise.

But the exchange between Karina and her sister was growing heated.

"You're not going anywhere near Anton," Amelie said. "Not ever again. Once Jaromir hears of this, you'll be lucky if you only wind up in a prison cell."

"Jaromir will hear nothing."

"Oh, yes, he will."

Then Amelie's body became a blur as she dashed forward and struck out with her right fist. At the last second, Karina moved back just an inch, and Amelie did not catch her with enough force.

"Jaelle!" Karina called, sounding like a madwoman. "Come to me."

Céline tensed, but something told her not to move—not yet.

A black-and-white form whooshed in from the wall above the hearth, and the pale-skinned young woman from the portrait floated there in the air, tendrils of her black hair dancing around her face.

Karina pointed at Amelie. "Drain her."

As Amelie turned to run, the floating woman flew straight toward her.

Céline had already seen enough of what this ghostly creature could do, and it was clear that Karina was controlling it. In less than a second, two facts solidified in Céline's mind. One, the shutters to the window were open, and two, Karina was standing directly in front of it.

Céline charged.

She didn't think or hesitate, and it was possible that Karina never saw her coming. Céline ran from behind the dressing screen and across the room as fast as she could, using both hands when she crashed into Karina and pushing with all the strength in her arms and shoulders.

Karina fell through the window, three stories down from the tower, and smashed against the cobbles of the courtyard below. Céline stopped only long enough to lean out and make certain she was dead. Karina lay still, with her limbs at twisted angles. Torches from the courtyard wall showed a dark pool spreading out around her head.

Then Céline whirled.

Amelie was on the floor with her eyes closed, and the ghostly creature had one hand upon her face and was reaching toward her throat with the other.

"Stop!" Céline commanded.

The ghost-woman stopped, looking up at her in confusion, perhaps at the fact that she was able to stop.

"Karina is dead," Céline said. "You serve her no more. Get away from my sister."

But the confusion in the ghost's eyes only grew, and she wailed once, sounding like an animal in pain.

The door burst open, and Jaromir came running in, casting about to try to see what was happening. His gaze reached the wailing ghost first, and then Amelie on the floor in her midnight blue gown.

"Amelie!" He ran to her.

Anton came on his heels, pale and exhausted. He, too, saw the ghost, but then the creature floated higher, staring at the men in the room with a kind of puzzled fear, and she whooshed back through the wall above the hearth, leaving only silence in her wake.

Jaromir knelt down and lifted the top of Amelie's body with one arm. He shook her gently. "Amelie?"

Her skin did not look shriveled or altered, and Céline hoped she'd been able to stop any damage in time. Amelie's eyelids opened. "Jaromir?"

"Don't talk," he said.

But Anton was staring at Céline with a tight expression on his face, as if wondering what she was doing there at the window. Slowly, he walked over, and for Céline, the reality of what she had done began to sink in.

He leaned out the window and looked down at the courtyard floor.

Céline had just killed his aunt, and she did not possess a shred a proof.

"Anton, it was her," she rushed to say. "Karina was controlling the ghost."

His body was rigid, and he didn't answer. She felt the first trickle of real fear.

"Where's the ghost?" Jaromir asked, as always thinking first of any danger to the castle.

"In the painting," Amelie whispered.

Jaromir stood in front of the painting in Anton's bedroom as Amelie spun out a horror story of murder and twisted vanity stretching back twenty-six years. The pale-skinned, dark-haired ghost was back inside the portrait, frozen in her pose, as if she'd never left.

Amelie's quiet voice went on.

Anton and Céline both listened in silence, Anton's face still tight and unreadable. He had loved his aunt. More, he had depended upon her.

But Amelie's story . . .

Had it been Céline doing the telling, Jaromir might have harbored a hint of doubt as the tale grew more and more difficult to absorb. While he judged Céline to be a basically good person, he also believed she was a highly skilled liar.

However, in recent days he'd assessed Amelie's

character numerous times, and he was convinced that she possessed little capacity for open deceit or fantastical imagination. Perhaps Anton knew this, too, and he neither interrupted nor tried to deny what she was saying. He just listened.

As she finished, she said, "I knew Jaelle would go back inside the painting once Karina no longer commanded her, but I'm still not sure why. It's been her prison for so long."

In a wooden voice, Anton answered, "When I lived with my father, I sometimes saw men being released after many years of imprisonment . . . men who would beg to be allowed to go back inside, to their cells. It was all they knew."

Jaromir had seen this phenomenon, too, but at the moment he was more concerned with whatever Anton was going to do next. Céline was frightened. She hid it well but not well enough. Jaromir's gut told him that Anton believed Amelie's account. The details were too pronounced: Anton's age when Karina began writing to him, specific lines from her letters, his invitation to her during the late months of Joselyn's pregnancy. Jaromir had never been told any of this, and he suspected the only ones who'd known such things were Anton and Karina themselves. Had Amelie gotten anything wrong, Anton would have interrupted her.

He had not.

But Anton's conscience would fight. He would not want to accept that his beautiful, beloved young aunt was an aging serial murderess.

Would he go so far as to deny the truth and punish Céline?

Finally, Jaromir turned to Anton and asked, "What do you want me to do, my lord?"

Anton was quiet for a moment, just looking at the painting. "Take this thing out into the courtyard and burn it."

CHAPTER 16

The gathering down in the courtyard was solemn.

Karina's body had been quietly removed, leaving only the pool of blood from where she'd fallen.

Although Céline stood beside Anton, she had no idea how he felt toward her anymore. His body was stiff. Between his current struggle with a dependency on opiates and the death of Karina—combined with the other revelations of this night—she could almost see the waves and waves of pain coming off his skin.

Guardsman Rurik had come out with them, and he'd brought firewood, which he was placing in a long pile. He'd also brought a flask of lamp oil, which he'd set down on the ground while he worked. Jaromir and Amelie held the portrait between them. Amelie looked recovered from her brief touch by the ghost. At least that was something.

But she was still wearing the midnight blue gown, and Céline could not help but notice Jaromir casting puzzled glances. He had the good sense not to ask.

Céline could hear Anton breathing, as if with effort, and she wished he would say something, anything, to give her a chance to comfort him. She couldn't bring herself to speak before he did—lest she try to offer comfort and discover he blamed her for tonight's events. She didn't think she could bear that.

"The apothecary's shop is yours," he said suddenly.

Why would he be thinking of that?

"You completed your side of the bargain," he went on. "You . . . you found the murderer, and I always pay my debts. The shop is yours."

"Anton," she whispered.

"Unless you want to do as Helga suggests, and go find your own people, go away and live with the gypsies."

And then she understood why he'd mentioned the shop. With the exception of Jaromir, everyone Anton cared about seemed to leave him. Did he fear Céline would leave, too?

She'd be a liar if she told him she hadn't considered it. This was a world beyond her understanding, of people seeking position and power, capable of great violence when they felt threatened and great kindness when the spirit moved them. But perhaps she'd come to understand that at least Anton and Jaromir were neither villains nor saints, only men who did what they thought was right at the time and muddled through as best they could like everyone else. Anton had lost his mother and his wife, and an aunt who he thought loved him. He didn't have much luck with the women in his life.

"Do you want me to stay?" she asked.

"Yes."

"Then I will."

In that moment, had he asked, she might have sworn to stay forever.

Rurik finished laying the long pile of firewood, and Jaromir and Amelie lay the portrait, face up, on top of the wood. Jaromir picked up the flask of lamp oil and poured some of it over the painting.

"I'll get a torch," he said.

Although Jaromir was struggling with the painful guilt that he'd missed routing out yet another dangerous individual in the castle—and never suspected Karina for a moment—he took relief in the act of doing something, anything. He'd wanted to burn this portrait days ago, from the moment Céline described the actual killer from her vision.

Self-recrimination would come later. For now, at least he could take solid action.

After pouring half the oil in the flask over the portrait, he switched the flask to his left hand, walked to the courtyard wall, and lifted a torch from its bracket.

Going back to the painting, he lowered his torch but glanced over at Anton for the final order.

Anton nodded. "Do it."

Amelie and Rurik both took a few steps back, and Jaromir ignited the portrait, watching the flames burst. The act brought relief as he tossed the torch onto the fire and moved away from the growing heat.

Karina was dead, and the portrait would be gone soon. No more girls would be drained to husks in their sleep.

This was over.

"Jaromir . . . ," Amelie said from beside him. "What is that?"

Squinting, he looked through the flames to see something rising from the painting, a muted blur of black and white.

A pain-filled wail exploded in the night air. In disbelief, Jaromir watched as the black-and-white blur solidified over the top of the portrait . . . into the form of the ghost.

She wailed again and screamed, "No!"

Her face was wild with terror, and she cast around madly until her gaze fixed on Céline. Jaromir stood helpless and useless as the ghost sailed through the air, straight toward Céline, and vanished inside of her.

The ghost was gone.

"Céline!" Amelie cried.

But Céline's features twisted to mimic the same

panic Jaromir had just seen on the ethereal woman. Céline wailed, echoing the same sound.

Anton grabbed hold of her, shouting. "Get out! Get out of her."

Lost, Jaromir had no idea what to do until Céline snarled and clutched Anton's face with both her hands. Anton gasped, and his skin began turning gray.

Jaromir drew his sword.

Amelie was running the instant Jaromir's hand went for the hilt of his sword. She had no idea how far he'd go to protect Anton . . . but she had no intention of finding out.

Beating him to Céline, she threw herself through the air, using all the strength in her body to knock Céline away from Anton and then pin her to the courtyard floor. Céline screamed and fought, trying to latch her hands onto Amelie's face, but Amelie grasped her hands and tried to feel for the spark of a spirit, for whatever might still be left of Jaelle.

She felt something, connected with something.

And then . . . she began meshing her spirit with Jaelle's, focusing on the past, on the last moment that Jaelle was truly happy.

The courtyard vanished.

Amelie and Jaelle were rushing backward down a corridor of white mists, on and on, while Amelie held on tightly to the spirit mingled with her own. The mists vanished, and she found herself standing in the Móndyalítko encampment near the Everfen, only this time, she did not see through Jaelle's eyes. She was only an observer, with the ghost of Jaelle beside her.

"Where are we?" Jaelle asked.

"Home," Amelie answered. "Safe at home."

Her panicked, rapidly executed plan was to just keep Jaelle calm long enough for Jaromir to finish destroying the painting. It was all she could think to do.

But in the vision, the real Jaelle stood by a campfire with a small crowd of admirers. She was lovely, with glowing skin and waving, glossy hair. She began to sing, her light but haunting voice floating through the night.

The ghost sighed. "That was me."

Leaving Amelie's side, she walked through the crowd, and no one appeared to see her. Upon reaching her living self from the past, she stepped into her body. The ghost vanished, and the singing went on.

Back in the courtyard, Jaromir skidded to a halt as Amelie knocked Céline away from Anton, and the sisters began to struggle.

Anton dropped to the courtyard floor, but his eyes were open, and he tried struggling up to his knees. Suddenly, while rolling on the ground, Amelie grabbed ahold of Céline's hands and pinned her, and both women went still.

"What's happening?" Anton choked.

Jaromir didn't know, but he stood ready with his sword drawn for whatever might happen next, and Rurik came up beside him, blade in hand.

"Don't either of you touch Céline," Anton ordered, still on his knees.

Jaromir didn't know if he could obey that order—only that he would have to be the strong one here. This was all uncertain territory, and it seemed the ghost had taken possession of Céline. His priority was to protect Anton.

But then, a white-and-black blur rose from Céline's body, and the ghost of Jaelle appeared again, this time walking across the courtyard as if she were alive. She stopped near the fire, and to Jaromir's astonishment, she began to sing. It was beautiful.

The painting was about halfway burned, and he realized what Amelie must be attempting—to just hold the ghost at bay until the painting was gone. He also realized that he was still clutching the half-empty flask of lamp oil in his left hand.

"Stay with the prince," he ordered Rurik.

Dropping his sword, he turned and ran to the fire. Jaelle did not see him. She seemed to believe she was somewhere else. But he didn't hesitate. Holding out the flask of oil again, he splashed what he could on the painting and dropped the flask. Then he began stomping on the painting with his boots, stoking the flames, using his hands once to break off pieces to be burned at a faster pace.

The singing echoed over the flames.

He burned his hands and one of his legs, but he just kept stomping until the last of the painting was consumed by fire.

Jaelle stopped singing.

She turned slowly toward him.

The Móndyalítko encampment around Amelie vanished, and she found herself kneeling on the courtyard floor, pinning Céline's hands. She let go of Céline and looked back just in time to see Jaromir crushing and stomping the last of the portrait into the flames, but the sight was alarming. One of his pant legs was on fire, and he didn't appear to notice.

Jaelle's voice trailed off, and she, too, was staring at Jaromir.

"No," she said, as the last of the portrait was devoured.

Then she wailed again, with the pain-filled, ear-splitting sound. But her feet began to dissipate, and the blurred dissipation moved upward, through her legs and her waist.

Jaromir leaped from the fire, using his already injured hands to put out the flames on his leg.

Jaelle continued to vanish until only her head remained, and then that dissipated as well. She was gone. The wailing echo lasted a few seconds longer than she did.

Anton crawled over to Céline, who was cough-ing and trying rise, and he helped her sit up. But Amelie couldn't take her eyes from Jaromir.

He'd known exactly what to do.

Somehow, he'd known.

CHAPTER 17

Two weeks later, Céline was out back of the apothecary's shop, working in the herb garden. Amelie had gone to the baker's to buy some bread.

In different ways, they were both still recovering from the events up at the castle, but it had been a rapid two weeks, and throwing themselves into a surge of industry had helped to heal some of their wounds.

The sisters had salvaged all the plants in the garden that they could, and today, Céline was trimming back the lavender to help encourage new growth.

The herb garden was looking much better, and they'd started a kitchen garden of root vegetables as well, planting potatoes, onions, and carrots.

Upon leaving the castle, they'd taken nothing except the same possessions with which they'd arrived—except for the coins Amelie had won playing cards. But the shop itself, and a home in Sèone, had been the promised payment, and neither sister had any intention of laying claim to anything else.

Céline had made quiet arrangements for Helga to sneak the miniature of Bethany back into Anton's bedroom. The question of the miniature itself remained a mystery, how it had ended up in their room in the first place, not to mention how it kept coming out of the drawer into plain sight, as if waiting for Amelie to pick it up.

Céline had no answers and decided not to dwell on the possibilities. Having faced down one ghost had been trial enough.

She and Amelie had left the castle as soon as possible.

They'd set to work immediately, cleaning the house first and taking inventory of the pots, jars, vials, and equipment. They'd made friends with their nearest neighbors, and Amelie soon learned which butcher and which baker to patronize. Making their money last had been a concern, but Céline had been able to harvest enough herbs and flowers to make up some simple cough syrups and liniments for sore muscles and cleansers for cuts. These had sold quickly, as the people of Sèone had been without an apothecary for some time.

Céline and Amelie were made to feel welcome.

They even had a new addition to their household.

The blacksmith's daughter, Erin, had visited last week, and when Céline had complained to her of mice having overtaken the inside of the shop, Erin had gone home and come back with a large orange cat named Oliver. She insisted that Céline keep him, as they had an overabundance of cats at the forge.

Oliver had gone to work immediately, but he had a bad habit of bringing his dead trophies to either Céline or Amelie so they could praise him for his hunting prowess.

Céline wished he would stop doing that.

Sometimes, she still had a hard time accepting the magnitude of the changes in her life. She missed some people back in Shetâna, and even had moments of mourning her mother's burned shop. But she loved the new shop and the feeling of safety that she and Amelie enjoyed here. It seemed so strange that if they ever had a concern, they could go to Anton's soldiers for help.

A few people from the village had approached her, asking for a reading, but she'd politely declined—as yet. She was not healed enough to see another future. Perhaps in time.

Clipping another dead lavender stem, she noticed Oliver torturing a worm wriggling on some overturned earth. He batted it with his paw again, watching it move with great fascination.

"Stop that," she told him. "Leave the worm alone."

Without warning, he looked toward the back door of the shop and leaped to his feet, hissing and spitting with his orange hair standing on end.

"Oliver! What in the world is wrong with . . . ?"

But then she followed his eyes to the open doorway and saw Lieutenant Jaromir standing there with a large wooden box in his arms. He must have come in the front door and walked through the shop. She noticed he wore gloves, and she wondered about the burns on his hands and his leg.

"It seems you've hired some new protection," he said, "while I've been demoted to playing a delivery boy."

Céline stood up cautiously. "Oliver, stop hissing. It's all right."

She hadn't seen Jaromir or Anton since leaving the castle. Right away, she'd made more of the weakened poppy syrup for Anton, along with a salve from some wild-growing orpine that she'd found and boiled down to mix with goose grease, to help heal Jaromir's burns. Later she'd made a cleansing tonic from colewort for Anton, but she'd sent all these up to the castle with a local boy.

"How is the prince?" she asked.

"Better." His tone was uncertain. "He has a good deal of healing to do."

Yes, she understood that.

"Come and look at this, Céline." He set the box down. "Helga brought it to my attention that you left a good deal behind in your room, and she wasn't good-natured about insisting that I bring it all down here."

Céline went over and looked into the box. All of their gowns and stockings and underwear and Amelie's new breeches were folded inside—along with the silver brushes and two thick cloaks, which had not previously been hanging in the wardrobe.

"Oh, Jaromir, these things weren't ours."

He shrugged. "Take them. No one else has any use for them, and maybe you can get Amelie back into that blue dress."

"That would be a feat indeed."

While the amber silk gown was hardly useful here, the cloaks, stockings, breeches, and lavender wool dress would make life easier next winter. And she'd never used anything so fine as those silver brushes.

"Just keep them," he said, moving further out into the garden. "This is looking quite polished."

"Thank you. Did you come only to deliver the clothing? Does the prince need more of the cleansing tonic?"

"No, I came bearing an invitation." He paused. "To a banquet at the castle tomorrow night."

"A banquet?" she asked quietly.

"Don't worry, you and Amelie are just invited as guests. You'll sit at the first table with me and Anton."

Céline glanced away, feeling on uncertain ground again, caught somewhere between the village dwellers and the castle dwellers.

"So . . . am I to come as the prince's apothecary?" she asked.

"No, as the prince's seer."

She didn't speak for a moment.

"Will you come?" he asked.

"Yes, we'll come."

National Bestselling Authors
Barb & J.C. Hendee

BETWEEN THEIR WORLDS
A Novel of the Noble Dead

Wynn Hygeort is stunned when Magiere and Leesil, along
with the elven wolf Chap, show up at the Guild of
Sagecraft. But Wynn cannot leave with her friends—
she still must access the texts within the Guild's archives
which may help her divine the locations of the last two
Orbs sought by the Ancient Enemy. To complete her
task—and protect the Orbs—Wynn must remain
sequestered from her friends.

But she's essentially a prisoner. One of the Guild's
superiors is just as eager for Wynn to translate the ancient
texts, but she knows the others will not permit her to
share that knowledge—knowledge Magiere and Leesil
desperately need if they're going to stop the Ancient
Enemy from unleashing war on the land…

"Impossible to put down."
—SciFiChick

facebook.com/acerocbooks

Available wherever books are sold or at
penguin.com

R0155

National Bestselling Authors
Barb & J.C. Hendee

OF TRUTH AND BEASTS
A Novel of the Noble Dead

Wynn has returned safely to the Guild of Sagecraft with her companions, the vampire Chane Andraso and Shade, an elven wolf. Though Wynn had managed to regain her seized journals, she only received a glimpse of the ancient texts penned by forgotten vampires, and once again, the volumes have slipped from her grasp. The price for her brief success may prove costly.

For the animosity of her guild superiors has grown even more fierce. This time, instead of cloistering her, they purposefully give her a mission so tedious it will keep her out of the way for as long as possible. But Wynn has her own plans...

facebook.com/acerocbooks

Available wherever books are sold or at
penguin.com

R0061

The Ordeal of Thomas Hutchinson

———————————————

Thomas Hutchinson, age 30. By Edward Truman.

Bernard Bailyn

The Ordeal of
Thomas Hutchinson

The Belknap Press of
Harvard University Press
Cambridge, Massachusetts
1974

To Charles and John

Preface

This book, which depicts the fortunes of a conservative in a time of radical upheaval and deals with problems of public disorder and ideological commitment, was not written as a tract for the times, nor is its purpose to illustrate general ideas about law and order and the causes or consequences of civil disobedience and insurrection. It is part of a general effort I have been making over the past few years to develop a fuller picture of the origins of the American Revolution than we have had before, and also to exemplify an approach to history that emphasizes balance over argument, context over consequences, and the meaning of the past over the uses of the present. But it would be foolish to deny that I have been influenced in writing it by the events of the late 1960's, when the original drafts were written. I am quite certain, in fact, that my understanding of Thomas Hutchinson's dilemma in using troops to quell public disorders and my recognition of the reasons for the ultimate failure of this otherwise successful and impressive politician and historian—his calculatingly pragmatic approach to politics; his insensitivity to the moral ingredients of public life and to the beliefs and passions that grip people's minds; and his incapacity to respond to aspirations that transcend the ordinary boundaries of received knowledge, prudence, and common sense—my understanding of all of this has undoubtedly been sharpened by the course of American politics in the 1960's and early 1970's. Nevertheless the structure and substance

vii

of the book, and the issues it discusses, developed from considerations of Hutchinson's time, not of our own. This is a book about the eighteenth century, and its purpose is to throw light on aspects of the origin and character of the Revolution that have hitherto been obscured.

For there is in fact a whole area of the Revolution that has been almost completely submerged in the historical literature and that hardly enters at all into our general understanding of what that formative event was all about. And it is not a secondary or incidental part of the story. It is fundamental, and the omission of so basic a part of the story did not come about and was not perpetuated accidentally. The gap in the historiography of the Revolution to which this book is directed is a natural outcome of the way in which historians approach such an event as a revolution and of the relationship they bear to the event itself. For there is something like a regular pattern in the succession of historical interpretations that follow great public events, a pattern that has been most fully explained by Sir Herbert Butterfield, first in his *Whig Interpretation of History* (1931) and then in the many essays that followed that remarkable little book.

As Professor Butterfield explained, the earliest historical writings that follow a great and controversial event are still a significant part of the event itself. At that near point in time the outcome is still in some degree in question, the struggle in an extended form is still alive, emotions are still deeply engaged; and because of this immediacy, indeterminacy, and involvement, attempts at explanations of what happened tend to be *heroic* in character. That is, they are highly moral: the struggle they present is between good and bad; and they are highly personified: individuals count overwhelmingly; their personal qualities appear to make the difference between victory and defeat.

Then in the course of time the historian's angle of vision shifts. This change in viewpoint is a logical one, part of an almost inevitable alteration in the historian's relation to the event. For a second or third or fourth generation of writers, the outcome of the event is no longer in question as it was for the first generation. The episode appears now not to be something whose meaning remains to be determined but rather a familiar link in a long chain of events that stretches from the distant past to the present. The personalism therefore fades and in its place the relatedness of the whole flow of events from the past into the present—the fit and interconnectedness of events—stands out. The historian is struck not so much by the personal decisions and personal qualities of the actors as by the inevitability with which the past flowed through the event and became the present, and by the natural way in which people and conditions that sought to impede this flow into the present were swept away. The historian at this stage is consequently attuned to early premonitions of what became mighty developments, he seeks the seeds of future events, dwells on cognates and analogues, and strives to show how the future was implicit in the past. This is the *whig* interpretation in its essence—abstracted from the peculiar British locale from which the name was derived.

And then at last there is a third and final turn in the relation between the viewer and event, which leads to a third and, so it seems to me, an ultimate mode of interpretation. At this point the distance has become so great, the connections so finely attenuated, that all of the earlier assumptions of relevance, partisan in their nature, seem crude, and fall away, and in their place there comes a neutrality, a comprehensiveness, and a breadth of sympathy lacking in earlier interpretations. Not a new objectivity nor a new precision in the use of facts—a fiercely partisan, heroic view can be as objective and accurate in the use of the facts it chooses as any other—but an inclusiveness of sympathy and a degree of comprehensiveness in data that distinguish this interpretation from its predecessors. Now the historian, in his analysis and description, is no longer a partisan. He has no stake in the outcome. He can now embrace the whole of the event, see it from all sides. What impresses him most are the latent limitations within which everyone involved was obliged to act; the inescapable boundaries of action; the blindness of the actors —in a word, the tragedy of the event.

Heroic; whig; tragic—these words have meaning, I believe, for describing the kinds of interpretations that are put forward at the major stages of historians' removal from the events they interpret. This is more a logical than a strictly chronological scheme. Though distance in time is a major determinant, a multitude of forces impinging on historians' minds determine the duration of such phases, and a phase once past can be recovered when the circumstances shift. But I know of no clearer way of explaining my approach to the subject of this book than to note that it falls at the end of a long phase of whig partisanship—a phase that included such different writers as George Bancroft, G. O. Trevelyan, and Charles Beard—and at the point where we may begin to see the tragedy of the Revolution. I do not mean the sadness of it; and I certainly do not mean the error or wrongness of it. I mean simply that we have knowledge enough of all the circumstances—material, cultural, political, even psychological—to enable us to catch glimpses of the whole of that distant globe and to note the limits within which men struggled. *All* men—the famous and the obscure, the best and the worst, the winners and the losers. They were all equally real, equally bound by the circumstances of the time, and are equally necessary to understand if we are to make sense of the Revolution.

It is this consideration that shapes the chapters that follow. For if recent historical writings have allowed us to see with some clarity the pattern of fears, beliefs, attitudes, and perceptions that became the ideology of the Revolution—which alone, in my judgment, explains why certain actions of the British government touched off a transforming revolution in America—they have not yet made clear why any sensible, well-informed, right-minded American with a modicum of imagination and common sense could possibly have opposed the Revolution. And until that is done, until we look deliberately at the development from the other side around, we have not understood what the issues really were, what the struggle was all about. It is as clear an example as may be found of what Professor Butterfield described forty years ago: a situation in which it is essential to understand the efforts that had no future if one is to explain the victory of what, in the retrospect of later history, became the forces of progress.

My purpose, then, is to convey something of the experience of the losers in the American Revolution. And I do this not because I agree with them or judge them to have been right or because I find them more appealing people than their opponents. Quite the contrary: most of the finest human qualities, to which one instinctively responds—the desire to eradicate the cruelties people inflict upon one another; the spirit of hope and enterprise; confidence in the future; above all, the passion to cast off restraints and in some enduring way to release pent-up aspirations—all of this seems to me to have been on the side of the victors. I turn to the losers sympathetically in order to explain the human reality against which the victors struggled and so to help make the story whole and comprehensible.

But who *were* the losers in the American Revolution? Not in the end the British people or the British government. They were of course defeated in war and they lost an empire, but their losses were superficial next to those that other defeated peoples have suffered. The British monarch and the structure of government survived the war; English commerce with and profit from America flourished after the war; the country was not invaded; and the lives of the common people were scarcely affected. The real losers—those whose lives were disrupted, who suffered violence and vilification, who were driven out of the land and forced to resettle elsewhere in middle life and died grieving for the homes they had lost—these were not the English but the Americans who clung to them, who remained loyal to England and to what had been assumed to be the principles of legitimacy and law and order which the British government embodied. They were the American loyalists, and it is their history that allows us to see the Revolutionary movement from the other side around, and to grasp the wholeness of the struggle and hence in the end to understand more fully than we have before why a revolution took place and why it succeeded.

It is, I think, a peculiarly difficult thing to do, and likely to be misinterpreted. For while, as I have said, I think we are approaching a maturity, fullness, and depth in our understanding of the Revolution that we have never had before, the American nation is built on the outcome of the Revolution and partisanship is an instinctive part of our approach to the events. It is extremely difficult to put two hundred years of history aside and refuse, for purposes of historical understanding, to choose among the contenders of that distant struggle and to see it just as it was—an event full of accident, uncertain in outcome, with good and bad, sense and nonsense, distributed on both sides. For in the end we do instinctively care and we do choose, since we inherit the victory; and on perhaps no topic in the history of the Revolution does our instinctive partisanship come so naturally to rest as on the loyalists. It would seem to be almost impossible to avoid using them in one distorting way or

another. And indeed when one looks at the record of what historians have said about the American loyalists,[1] the likelihood of escaping partisanship of some distorting kind seems extremely small,
and the effort I am making to do precisely that seems doomed to
failure from the start. Nevertheless, my aim in what follows is to
probe, in the case of the most important loyalist of all, the origins of
the Revolution as experienced by the losers, and thereby restore, in
some small degree, the wholeness of that event.

The first problem I encountered in attempting to understand
Thomas Hutchinson's career was to gain some kind of control over
his huge correspondence and the other manuscript sources relating
to his life, which I have described in the Note on the Hutchinson
Manuscripts. In that difficult preliminary work I had the invaluable
assistance of Dr. Patricia King. Her informal calendar of the main
correspondence and her survey of certain other sources were of
immense help. At the very end of the project I was still referring
back to her early work, and I remain grateful to her for her care
and thoroughness in preparing those surveys. Later, I had the
assistance of Judith A. Ryerson, who, besides typing the main drafts
of the book several times and transcribing hundreds of pages of
notes, worked out a number of special research problems. It was
she who tracked down the scattered newspaper publications of
Hutchinson's letters, and it was she who identified him in the political cartoons that are reproduced in this book. It is a pleasure for me
now to acknowledge her long and patient assistance.

At every stage of the research and writing I had the benefit of
the advice of Malcolm Freiberg, who began studying Hutchinson's
life long before I did and whose knowledge of the Hutchinson
manuscripts, which he has so generously shared with scholars visiting the Massachusetts Historical Society, is expert. It was Mr. Freiberg, working with an original transcription by Catherine Barton
Mayo, who prepared the typescript of the main Hutchinson correspondence that is now available at the Massachusetts Historical
Society. That splendid transcription saved me many months of work,
and I am happy now to thank Mr. Freiberg for allowing me to use
it, for his patient help on difficult technical problems, and for his

---

1. See the Appendix below: "The Losers: Notes on the Historiography of Loyalism."

generous aid in reading proof and locating material for the illustrations. Jacob M. Price, drawing on his extensive knowledge of eighteenth-century Anglo-American manuscript sources and bibliography, responded willingly to many queries. And Caroline Jakeman provided expert help in tracking down references and documents in the Houghton Library, Harvard University.

The whole of the book was read in various drafts by Lotte Bailyn and John Clive. Their criticism was thorough and pointed, and if I could have satisfied them completely I would have written a much better book; but as it stands it has been immensely improved by their perceptive comments. And I had the advantage of Donald Fleming's criticism of a draft of the first chapter, which too led to substantial improvements.

I am grateful to the British Library Board for permission to refer to and quote from various manuscripts in the British Museum, particularly those among the Egerton Manuscripts; to the Rt. Hon. the Earl of Dartmouth, for permission to quote from the Dartmouth Papers in the Staffordshire County Record Office; to the Chapin Library, Williams College, for permission to quote from Hutchinson's unpublished "Account and Defense of Conduct"; to the Harvard College Library, for permission to cite the Sparks Manuscripts and other papers in the Houghton Library, Harvard University; and to the Massachusetts Historical Society, for permission to quote from a large number of unpublished papers in its collection.

A preliminary sketch of the book was presented in November 1969 as the Anson G. Phelps Lectures on Early American History at New York University. I deeply appreciated the honor of delivering those lectures, which gave me the opportunity of formulating the main problems of Hutchinson's life as I have understood them. I wish to thank my hosts in the History Department at New York University, and especially Professors Bayrd Still and Paul Baker, for the many kindnesses I received from them on the occasions of those lectures.

An invitation to deliver the George Macaulay Trevelyan Lectures at Cambridge University in 1971 led me to expand the book considerably and to consider aspects of the story I had not studied before. The environment in which those lectures were delivered led me to shift the proportions of the resulting book and to note implications throughout the story that I would not otherwise have seen. The generous hospitality of my hosts at Christ's College, where I lived during my stay in Cambridge, particularly that of the Master, Lord Todd, and of Professor J. H. Plumb, made the experience especially memorable for me.

As for the two gentlemen to whom the book is dedicated, they have been hearing about Hutchinson for so long and have for so long suffered from the attention he has received that they deserve the fullest thanks that I can give.

B.B.

Contents

Illustrations

xvii

The Ordeal of Thomas Hutchinson

————————————

Abbreviations

AAS *Procs.*	*Proceedings of the American Antiquarian Society*
Adams, *Diary and Autobiography*	Lyman H. Butterfield *et al.*, eds., *Diary and Autobiography of John Adams*. 4 vols. Cambridge, Harvard University Press, 1961.
Add. MSS	Additional Manuscripts, British Museum.
Bernard Papers	Francis Bernard Papers (Sparks MSS 4). 13 vols. Houghton Library, Harvard University.
CO	Colonial Office Papers, in Public Record Office, London
Diary and Letters	Peter Orlando Hutchinson, ed., *The Diary and Letters of His Excellency Thomas Hutchinson, Esq.* ... 2 vols. Boston, 1884–1886.
Eg. MSS	Egerton Manuscripts, British Museum
Gipson, *British Empire*	Lawrence H. Gipson, *The British Empire before the American Revolution*. 15 vols. Caldwell, Idaho, The Caxton Printers; N.Y., Knopf, 1936–1970.
History of Massachusetts-Bay	Thomas Hutchinson, *The History of the Colony and Province of Massachusetts-Bay*. Ed. Lawrence Shaw Mayo. 3 vols. Cambridge, Harvard University Press, 1936.
MA	Massachusetts Archives, State House, Boston
MHS	Massachusetts Historical Society
MHS *Colls.*	*Collections of the Massachusetts Historical Society*
MHS *Procs.*	*Proceedings of the Massachusetts Historical Society*
Quincy, *Reports of Cases*	Josiah Quincy, Jr., *Reports of Cases Argued and Adjudged in the Superior Court of Judicature of the Province of Massachusetts Bay between 1761 and 1772*. Ed. Samuel M. Quincy. Boston, 1865.
W.M.Q.	*William and Mary Quarterly*

Note on Modernization

Eighteenth-century documents quoted in the text have been modernized in three ways. Spelling has been altered to conform to current American usage but not so as to affect the choice of words: *steared* becomes *steered,* but *amongst* does not become *among.* Punctuation has been modernized when doing so would assist in conveying the writer's thought; for the most part this has meant eliminating commas and standardizing terminal punctuation. And capitalization of initial letters has also been changed to conform to modern usage. However, other typographical peculiarities—particularly italics and small or full capitalization of whole words—have been retained.

Chapter I

Success of the Acquisitive Man: Portrait of the Provincial Bourgeois

On the fourth of July, 1776, Thomas Hutchinson, the exiled loyalist governor of Massachusetts, was awarded an honorary doctorate of civil laws by Oxford University. "Probably no distinction which Hutchinson ever attained was more valued by him," his nineteenth-century biographer wrote; certainly none so fittingly symbolizes the tragedy of his life.[1] For he was honored as an American—the most distinguished as well as the most loyal colonial-born official of his time. Provincial assemblyman, speaker of the Massachusetts House of Representatives, councillor, lieutenant governor, chief justice, governor, he had gone through the entire course of public offices and of official honors, and he was in addition America's most accomplished historian. But to the people who on the day of Hutchinson's award proclaimed their nation's independence, he was one of the most hated men on earth—more hated than Lord North, more hated than George III (both of whom, it was believed,

1. James K. Hosmer, *The Life of Thomas Hutchinson* (Boston and N. Y., 1896), p. 337. Hutchinson's brief factual account of the event is in *Diary and Letters*, II, 75. The exiled chief justice, Peter Oliver, similarly honored that day, described the scene more dramatically and more romantically in his diary: scarlet gowns, time-honored ceremony, over 2,000 spectators, "the ladies seated by themselves in brilliant order, the theatre in a most noble building, the ceiling painted in elegance . . . an *orchestra* for vocal and instrumental music, three orations . . . a most agreeable entertainment." Eg. MSS, 2672, pp. 82–85.

he had secretly influenced), and more feared than the sinister Earl of Bute.

The distrust and the animosity Thomas Hutchinson inspired surpass any ordinary bounds. The reactions he stirred are morbid, pathological, paranoiac in their intensity.

John Adams was transfixed by him: for fifteen years, suspicion, fear, and hatred of Hutchinson were ruling passions. He first recorded his suspicions of Hutchinson in 1760 when he was twenty-five. Five years later he poured out the first of a series of rhetorical cascades against Hutchinson's "very ambitious and avaricious disposition," condemned his taking "four of the most important offices in the province into his own hands," and spoke with bitterness of his secret network of officeholding kin who together created the "amazing ascendency of one family, foundation sufficient on which to erect a tyranny." Hutchinson, he said, had not only "monopolized almost all the power of the government to himself and his family" but "has been endeavoring to procure more, both on this side and the other side of the Atlantic." He was a "courtier," Adams said, slyly manipulating "the passions and prejudices, the follies and vices of great men in order to obtain their smiles, esteem, and patronage and consequently their favors and preferments"; he was a dissembler, a man of a thousand disguises, hungry for power, for office, and for gain: from him "the liberties of this country [have] more to fear . . . than from any other man, nay from all other men in the world." A decade later Adams's hatred of Hutchinson had become obsessive: "the mazy windings of Hutchinson's heart and the serpentine wiles of his head," he wrote, were primary sources of the Anglo-American conflict, and in his "Novanglus" letters of 1774–75 he wrote an impassioned history of Hutchinson's "tyranny in the province" and his advancement of the ambitions of "Bute, Mansfield, and North," to which could be traced the entire source of the Anglo-American conflict.[2]

2. Adams, *Diary and Autobiography*, I, 168, 260–261, 281; II, 53, 39, 55; III, 430 (see also, among innumerable references to Hutchinson's evil influence, I, 233, 305–307, 310–311, 332; II, 34–35, 81, 82, 86, 119); "Novanglus" papers of Feb. 20 and March 6, 1775, in Charles F. Adams, ed., *Works of John Adams* (Boston, 1850–1856), IV, 57ff., 99ff. (see also IV, 28, 91ff., 141, and X, 243). For the general context of Adams's thought, see Bernard Bailyn, *The Ideological Origins of the American Revolution* (Cambridge, Harvard University Press, 1967), chap. iv, esp. pp. 121–123.

Adams's opinions, in this case as in so many others, were extreme, but in differing degrees they were widely shared. Josiah Quincy, Jr., convinced "that all the measures against America were planned and pushed on by Bernard and Hutchinson," went to England in the winter of 1774, with the support of the provincial leadership, in large part to counteract the malevolent influence of Hutchinson and other Tories on administration policy. In the same year John Dickinson lumped together "the Butes, Mansfields, Norths, Bernards, and Hutchinsons" as the "villains and idiots" whose "falsehoods and misrepresentations" were inflaming the people and creating hostilities. John Wilkes was informed from Boston that Hutchinson had inherited "a strange kind of attachment to what is called the King's prerogative, but being a man of the greatest duplicity, he had art enough to conceal it from the public"—art enough, apparently, to conceal it for no less than thirty years until finally, early in the reign of George III, he had felt safe to profess it. Samuel Adams, whose political life was formed in struggles with Hutchinson, denied that Hutchinson had true greatness even in evil, for while he was as mad with ambition and lust for power as Caesar, he lacked the courage and intrepidity needed to reduce a free people to slavery. And Mercy Otis Warren in her history of the Revolution devoted page after page to the pernicious influence of that "dark, intriguing, insinuating, haughty, and ambitious" man—so diligent a student of "the intricacies of *Machiavellian* policy," so subtle a solicitor of popular support, so hypocritical in his sanctity and ruthless in his lust for power—and to the fatal consequences of "his pernicious administration."[3]

3 *Ibid*., pp. 122–123 (cf. George II. Nash, III, "From Radicalism to Revolution . . . Josiah Quincy, Jr.," AAS *Procs.*, 79 [1969], 263–265, 268, 287); [John Dickinson] to Arthur Lee, Philadelphia, Oct. 27, 1774, in R. H. Lee, *Life of Arthur Lee* (Boston, 1829), II, 307; Samuel Adams to James Warren, March 25, 1771, *Warren-Adams Letters*, I (MHS *Colls.*, LXXII, 1917), 8–9; Mercy Otis Warren, *History of the Rise, Progress and Termination of the American Revolution* . . . (Boston, 1805), I, 79–85, 96–99, 112–126. The only credits she would allow Hutchinson were fair-mindedness as a judge and consistency in political conduct and principle—though the principle, of course, was that of passive obedience and reverence for monarchical authority (pp. 125–126). These backhanded compliments, hardly noticeable in the general excoriation, may have been the result of James Winthrop's urging, upon reading the manuscript, that Mrs. Warren soften her characterization of Hutchinson—justified though Winthrop believed it to be—with a bit of "undeserved praise" in order to gain the approval of the ex-Tories for her *History* as a whole. Winthrop to Warren, Feb. 26, 1787, *Warren-Adams Letters*, II (MHS *Colls.*, LXXIII, 1925), 282–283.

A "tool of tyrants," a "damn'd *arch traitor*," Hutchinson was hissed *in absentia* at the official dinner to welcome his successor, General Gage, and when later the Revolutionary mob found his portrait in his house in suburban Milton, they stabbed it with bayonets and tore out one of the eyes. The judicious Franklin spoke openly of Hutchinson's duplicity, and in 1772 decided that he would have to be destroyed politically if the British empire were to be preserved. The London merchant and Member of Parliament William Baker prided himself on having denounced Hutchinson to the House of Commons as "a parricide who has attempted to ruin his country to save his own little narrow selfish purposes."[4] And though Hutchinson was a hero to most of the loyalists,[5] some of them too, like the former New York judge William Smith, believed him to be "a mere scribbling governor" and relished the nastiest scraps of gossip about him that came their way.[6]

His official patrons distrusted him. Governor Thomas Pownall, who in 1757 recommended Hutchinson's appointment to the lieutenant governorship in a letter of elaborate praise—"He has (and deserves, I will pawn my credit and honor upon it) universally the best character of any man in this continent, both as to his head and

4. John Andrews to William Barrell, May 18, 1774, MHS *Procs.*, 8 (1864–1865), 328. *Diary and Letters*, I, 565, for the portrait episode; the information on the treatment of the portrait given to P. O. Hutchinson, the nineteenth-century editor of the *Diary and Letters*, is confirmed by the latest restorer of the painting, who reports the original right eye completely gone and "various holes and breaks in canvas throughout" (Report of Nov. 1972, in MHS). The frequently restored painting is reproduced as the frontispiece, above. Franklin to William Franklin, London, Oct. 6, 1773, in A. H. Smyth, ed., *Writings of Benjamin Franklin* . . . (N.Y., 1905–1907), VI, 144; to same, Sept. 1, 1773, *ibid.*, p. 117; to Joseph Galloway, Feb. 18, 1774, *ibid.*, p. 195; to Samuel Cooper, Feb. 25, 1774, *ibid.*, p. 204; and more generally, *ibid.*, pp. 258ff. Baker to Charles Lee [London, Sept. 3, 1774], *Collections of the New-York Historical Society . . . 1871* (N.Y., 1872), p. 132.

5. E.g., Richard Lechmere to Lane, Son, and Fraser, Sept. 28, 1774, in MHS *Procs.*, 2d ser., 16 (1902), 290, explaining the dilemma of the "humane and good Governor Hutchinson," who, out of "the real goodness of his heart and love of his native country" had made such favorable representations of his countrymen that when the truth becomes known—that they "are not such quiet, peaceable, and orderly beings as he has represented them"—he will lose all credit with the King and ministry.

6. Adams, *Diary and Autobiography*, II, 110; William H. W. Sabine, ed., *Historical Memoirs [1763–1776] of William Smith* . . . (N.Y., 1956), pp. 207, 235, 236; L. F. S. Upton, ed., *The Diary and Selected Papers of Chief Justice William Smith, 1784–1793* (Toronto, The Champlain Society, 1963–1965), I, 78, 263 ("I told the story of his falsehood in the letter from Boston after the interview at Hartford in 1773. Temple says he was one of the vilest of men."). For Smith's peddling of Temple's more circumstantial gossip, see below, p. 371. Every effort was made to obliterate Hutchinson's name from public recognition: the town of Hutchinson became Barre in 1776, and Boston's Hutchinson Street became Pearl Street.

heart"[7]—left Massachusetts three years later enraged at the conduct of his associate; for fourteen years thereafter the former governor sparred with Hutchinson from England, and he renewed their quarrel directly when Hutchinson arrived as an exile in England in 1774. Both Sir Francis Bernard, who succeeded Pownall as governor in 1760 and who served as Hutchinson's personal agent in London in 1769–1771, and Lord Hillsborough, secretary of state for the colonies during the same years, who appointed Hutchinson to the governorship, disapproved of his conduct at several points, and at least on one occasion found his activities acutely embarrassing. Even Hillsborough's benign successor, Lord Dartmouth, the soul of Christian charity, who was extremely well disposed to Hutchinson and eventually became a friend of his, came to believe that Hutchinson had blundered badly as governor and in a bizarre episode attempted, at great cost to his official dignity as secretary of state, to correct what he considered to be Hutchinson's most costly error. And no less an authority than Lord North, according to the contemporary annalist George Chalmers, believed that Hutchinson, through his indiscretions, had personally precipitated the outbreak of the Revolution.[8]

Thus the great men of the day: but what of more ordinary opinion? One of the most remarkable documents of the age survives to testify. Through the decade that followed the Stamp Act a Boston shopkeeper with the unlikely name of Harbottle Dorr, unknown to history except for a passing involvement with the Sons of Liberty, carefully collected the leading Boston newspapers as they were published and preserved them for posterity in four huge volumes. Not only collected them but, "at my shop amidst my business &c., when I had not leisure to be exact," annotated them, elaborately, with pungent personal comments on the news of the day and with cross references in his own pagination, backward and forward to documents supporting or refuting the charges printed in the newspaper columns. And more than that: Dorr bound into the volumes the most important pamphlets of the time, which he also annotated in

7. Thomas Pownall to the Earl of Halifax, Sept. 4, 1757, Peter Force Papers, ser. 9, box 7, Library of Congress.

8. Memorandum by George Chalmers, July 15, 1783, reporting Samuel Danforth's knowledge that "Lord North blamed very seriously Governor Hutchinson for his letters . . . and said these brought on the war." New England Papers (Sparks MSS 10), IV, 33, Houghton Library, Harvard University.

his distinctive style, together with miscellaneous documents of the history of British liberty—Magna Carta, the Petition of Right, the Massachusetts charter; and then in conclusion, indexed it all, volume by volume, with analytical categories that reveal as clearly as any document of the time the compelling concerns of an ordinary man.

Hutchinson is among the first of these concerns. Dorr's index and commentaries catalogue Hutchinson's errors, correct his misstatements, and warn at every turn of his evil intentions. An anonymous columnist's claim that the colonies "had no *rights* of our own" is identified by Dorr in the margin as "Hutchinsonian doctrine." When Hutchinson's zeal is praised, Dorr scribbles, "no compliment to him; quite the reverse, as coming from such an infamous ministry or their tools." It is Hutchinson, he explains in a marginal gloss, who is meant by the customs commissioners' "nestor," and the word "pension" is supplied for "p----n" lest the reader mistake the object of Hutchinson's desire. When a writer in the *Boston Gazette* wonders "if our governor is a *mere tool* of an arbitrary minister of state," Dorr instantly removes the doubt: "He certainly is one!" He footnotes a vague newspaper reference to government advisors known to be "supple eno' to bow the *knee of servility* to the tool of a tool of an haughty Thane" with the explanation, "Hutchinson (governor) is a tool to Lord Hillsborough, Lord Hillsborough a tool to Bute, and the Earl of Bute a tool of the Devil!" Dorr will hear nothing of Hutchinson's professed desire to promote the prosperity of his country: "words," he scribbles in the margin, "are but wind; actions speak louder." When Hutchinson as governor in a message to the House explains his aversion to unwanted innovations, Dorr laughs, "Hah! Hah!" and to document the contrary triumphantly cites the governor's letters of 1768 supposedly recommending authoritarian changes in the colony's government. He jubilantly records a report that "Governor Hutchinson attempted to cut his throat"; explodes in the margins when the hated name appears—"vile hypocrite! and slanderer," "arch fiend," "traitor!"—; and at one point writes simply, in smoldering indignation, "Oh the villian!"[9]

9. Of Dorr's marvelous collection, the first three volumes are in the MHS and the fourth is in the Bangor, Me., Public Library. Microfilms of all four volumes are available at the MHS. Dorr, the son of a leather dresser who died insolvent in 1746 but whose assets included 33 bound books and 44 pamphlets (Suffolk County Probate file #8542), died in 1794 with net assets of £323 16s. 6d. His estate included two dictionaries and

There were some, of course, who disagreed. Hutchinson's protégé, in-law, and colleague Peter Oliver, in his "Origin & Progress of the American Rebellion," wrote a lyric apostrophe to Hutchinson's virtues, which he summarized as "an acumen of genius united with a solidity of judgment and great regularity of manners"—qualities, he pointed out, that nature only sparingly confers. Some who knew Hutchinson only by reputation were amazed when they actually met him. The Bostonians, William Eden wrote in 1774, shortly after Hutchinson arrived in England, "thought Hutchinson a tyrant—I met him on Thursday last, at the Attorney General's—they might as well have taken a lamb for a tiger." Both Jonathan Mayhew and Andrew Eliot, Boston ministers of liberal views, spoke well of Hutchinson's "capacity and erudition" in their correspondence with the English libertarian Thomas Hollis and believed "he certainly wishes well to his country."[10] But these were minority opinions. The feeling was widespread among well-informed Americans that Thomas Hutchinson had betrayed his country; that for sordid, selfish reasons he had accepted and abetted—even stimulated—oppressive measures against the colonies; that he had supported them even in the face of a threat of armed resistance; and that in this sense his personal actions lay at the heart of the Revolution.[11]

---

various printed sermons and pamphlets, in addition to the "newspaper books," which were sold for £7 10s. (*ibid.*, #20299). The quotations in the two paragraphs above are from: Dorr's Preface to vol. II (where he apologizes for his misspellings); I, 588; II, 557; III, 78, 377, 363, 489; IV, 321, 433, 758; III, 187; IV, 1148, 1156. Dorr's volumes, esp. III and IV, teem with references to Hutchinson, who seems to have obsessed Dorr as he did John Adams.

10. Douglass Adair and John A. Schutz, eds., *Peter Oliver's Origin & Progress of the American Rebellion* (San Marino, Henry E. Huntington Library, 1961), pp. 29ff.; Michael G. Kammen, *A Rope of Sand* (Ithaca, Cornell University Press, 1968), p. 264 (cf. *Diary and Letters*, I, 197); Mayhew to Hollis, March 19, 1761, MHS *Procs.*, 69 (1947—1950), 118 (for Mayhew's putative involvement in the riotous destruction of Hutchinson's house in 1765 and his effusive assurance to Hutchinson that he had had nothing to do with such "unparalleled outrages . . . God is my witness . . . [I] have a deep sympathy with you and your distressed family," see Bernard Bailyn, "Religion and Revolution: Three Biographical Studies," *Perspectives in American History*, 4 [1970], 115); Eliot to Hollis, Jan. 26, 1771, MHS *Colls.*, 4th ser., IV (1858), 454. On Eliot, Hutchinson's lifelong friend, who rescued Hutchinson's manuscripts from the mud after the 1765 riot and who regretted his appointment to the governorship only because it might "destroy his comfort and affect the purity of his heart," see Bailyn, "Religion and Revolution," pp. 87–110, where the ambiguity of Eliot's attitude to the Revolutionary movement is discussed in detail.

11. Controversy over Hutchinson's role in the origins of the Revolution continues with astonishing heat into our own time. No loyalists ever wrote as elaborate a panegyric of Hutchinson or as bitter a blast at Hutchinson's enemies as did C. K. Shipton in his 68-

So it was said, again and again and again. Was it true? Of what in fact was he guilty? He asked himself this question repeatedly discussed it endlessly with himself, his friends, associates, with anyone of any importance who would listen, and left behind a voluminous record of his replies. Twice he drew up formal, official justifications of the whole course of his administration and of the character and effect of his opinions. One, written in 1775 in response to attacks made on him in the House of Commons, is his "Account and Defense of Conduct," which he called a "brief vindication of my character" and which he circulated privately to those he thought mattered most. The second he intended to be more public, the final volume of his *History of Massachusetts-Bay*, which he wrote in the leisure of his exile and left for posthumous publication, carefully pruned of all antagonistic phrases, all invidious portraits, anything that might detract from its central purpose of explaining what had happened and of clearing his reputation of slander.[12]

But his fullest testament was written indeliberately. Hutchinson was a voluminous letter writer and, after 1774, a faithful diarist. His correspondence from 1765 until his departure for England in 1774, comprising hundreds of letters, drafts of letters, and notes related to his correspondence, survives intact—rescued accidentally from

---

page biography of the governor in volume VIII of *Sibley's Harvard Graduates* (Boston, MHS, 1951), for which he was courteously but roundly attacked by Bernhard Knollenberg (*W.M.Q.*, 3d ser., 10 [1953], 117–124). Hutchinson appears as a hapless victim of Sam Adams's propaganda and demagoguery in John C. Miller's *Sam Adams: Pioneer in Propaganda* (Boston, 1936); is stoutly defended as an able and far-sighted administrator and politician in Gipson's *British Empire*, vols. X–XII; and is the hero of *The Boston Massacre* (N.Y., W. W. Norton, 1970) by Hiller Zobel, whose interpretation of that event, centering on the idea of a radical plot against the troops, is almost indistinguishable from Hutchinson's own view. In response to Zobel's book the New Left historians have risen in rage and indignation, denouncing Zobel for a bias equivalent to what Mayor Daley's would be if he were to write a history of the Democratic Convention of 1968; see Jesse Lemisch, "Radical Plot in Boston (1770): A Study in the Use of Evidence," *Harvard Law Review*, 84 (December 1970), 489–504. In this latest "radical" blast, the ancient charges against Hutchinson, first propounded by the Adamses, Otis, and the other leaders of the Revolutionary movement, are cited as if they were fresh and conclusive evidence (e.g., *ibid.*, pp. 194n27, 502n39).

12. On the writing of the "Account and Defense of Conduct" and the third volume of the *History*, see below, Chap. IX. The final portion of the *History of Massachusetts-Bay* was published by Hutchinson's grandson, the Reverend John Hutchinson, in London in 1828. In Lawrence Shaw Mayo's modern edition of the *History* (Cambridge, 1936), the text of volume III is a collation of the 1828 edition with Hutchinson's final manuscript, but it does not include the very revealing material that Hutchinson eliminated from an earlier draft. These suppressed passages and phrases have been published by Catherine Barton Mayo as "Additions to Thomas Hutchinson's *History of Massachusetts-Bay*," AAS *Procs.*, n.s., 59 (1949), 11–74.

the oblivion to which Hutchinson assigned it at his departure from America. In addition, Hutchinson's personal correspondence and much of the correspondence of his immediate family survive in notebooks preserved in the British Museum. And finally, his diary, from his arrival in England until the year before his death, exists both in manuscript and in print, in an edition, only slightly expurgated, published by a loyal descendant.[13]

The written record is therefore remarkably complete. The letters and diary form a documentary history not only of Hutchinson's administration but of his private life over the course of his last twenty years. In them one can find a detailed self-portrait, and the truth of the claims laid against him.

ii

It is hard to imagine anyone less disposed by background and heritage to betray his countrymen than Thomas Hutchinson.[14] His family had helped to found New England, and they had prospered with its growth. Until Thomas, only one of the family had been famous: the notorious seventeenth-century Anne, who had refused to adjust her singular convictions to the will of the community (she was the last in the family—until Thomas—to do so) for which she had been banished, to die in exile. But the family's main interest had never been hers. The Hutchinsons had been tradesmen in Lon-

13. On the Hutchinson manuscripts, see the Note, pp. 409–412. The recovery of his correspondence and its use by the patriots is discussed below, pp. 334ff.

14. Unless otherwise noted, the genealogical and biographical material that follows is drawn from Shipton's "Hutchinson," William H. Whitmore, *A Brief Genealogy of the Descendants of William Hutchinson* . . . (Boston, 1865), Malcolm Freiberg, "Thomas Hutchinson: The First Fifty Years (1711–1761)," *W.M.Q.*, 3d ser., 15 (1958), 35–55, and above all, Hutchinson's own history of his family and his autobiographical notes entitled "Hutchinson in America," written in the reversed back pages of the volume of his diary that commences Aug. 1, 1777 (Eg. MSS, 2664). This 99-page family memoir, discussed below, Chap. IX, is published in part only, scattered through the two volumes of the *Diary and Letters* (in chronological order, the main fragments, mixed in with excerpts from letters and other material, appear in II, 456–478, and I, 45–152, the latter section being a pastiche documentary biography of Hutchinson taking him from his birth to June 1, 1774, when his diary begins with his departure for England). As is indicated at various points below, the editor of the *Diary and Letters*, Thomas Hutchinson's great-grandson, Peter Orlando Hutchinson, omitted as "personal remarks . . . not material in a historical point of view" (I, 60) some important passages of the manuscript—which Hutchinson "intended' for my own children and no part to be published to the world" (Eg. MSS, 2664, p. 1 from end [see Note on the Hutchinson Manuscripts, below, p. 411 n1, for explanation of the pagination of this volume of Eg. MSS]).

don before the Puritan migration; in New England they became merchants, and remained merchants, with remarkable consistency, generation after generation. In the course of a century and a half they produced, in the stem line of the family, not a single physician, not a single lawyer, and not a single teacher or minister. The entire clan devoted itself to developing its property and the network of trade, based on kinship lines at every point, that Anne's brothers and nephews had created in the mid-seventeenth century. They prospered solidly, but not greatly. Their enterprises were careful, not grand. They were accumulators, down-to-earth, unromantic middlemen, whose solid, petty-bourgeois characteristics became steadily more concentrated in the passage of years until in Thomas, in the fifth generation, they reached an apparently absolute and perfect form.

He was born in Boston in 1711. His father, Colonel Thomas Hutchinson, had risen somewhat, though not greatly, beyond the level of his two prosperous merchant-shipowner relatives, Elisha and Eliakim.[15] The colonel served on the provincial Council for over twenty years, donated the building for a Latin grammar school (which his son would attend), and improved into provincial magnificence the imposing town house bequeathed to him by a widowed aunt.[16] The colonel's marriage fitted perfectly the pattern of his classically bourgeois existence. His wife, Sarah Foster, ten years his senior, was the daughter of John Foster, the Boston merchant to

15. For a summary of Thomas and Elisha Hutchinson's shipping investments, 1697–1714, see Bernard Bailyn and Lotte Bailyn, *Massachusetts Shipping 1697–1714: A Statistical Study* (Cambridge, Harvard University Press, 1959), pp. 128, 130, and for the pattern of the family's partnerships in shipping during those years, pp. 36–37. The establishment in the seventeenth century of the Hutchinson-Sanford "family commercial system" is analyzed in detail in Bernard Bailyn, *The New England Merchants in the Seventeenth Century* (Cambridge, Harvard University Press, 1955), pp. 88–90.

16. This famous house, or mansion as it was commonly called, built between 1689 and 1692 by John Foster, Colonel Thomas's father-in-law, who was also the third husband of Colonel Thomas's aunt Abigail Hawkins, descended to Governor Hutchinson and was severely damaged in the Stamp Act riot of August 26, 1765. Governor Bernard, who noted particularly its solid cupola and fine brick walls "adorned with Ionic pilasters," thought it had been designed by Inigo Jones or his successor. FB (Francis Bernard) to Earl of Halifax, Castle William, Boston, Aug. 31, 1765, Bernard Papers, IV, 152. Lydia Maria Child, who knew the house as it was rebuilt after the riot (it was demolished only in 1834), wrote a vivid description of its interior as she pictured it in the 1760's in the opening pages of her novel about Thomas Hutchinson and the origins of the Revolution, *The Rebels* (1825). For a detailed account of the appearance and history of the house—"the first developed example of provincial Palladianism in New England"—see Abbott Lowell Cummings, "The Foster-Hutchinson House," *Old-Time New England*, 54 (1963–1964), 59–76.

whom he had been apprenticed in trade, of status identical to the Hutchinson family's, who engaged in the same kinds of trade as they did, and to whom, by force of the remarkable endogamy that characterizes the family history, Colonel Thomas became triply related by other marriages between the two families.[17]

Colonel Thomas set the pattern for young Thomas's life. He was industrious (until prosperity and personal problems led him to relax his attention to business), charitable, unaffected, unworldly, and clannish. A strait-laced, pious provincial, he read the scriptures to his family mornings and evenings and devoted himself to trade and to the welfare of his kin and community. For over thirty years, his son later recorded, Colonel Thomas "kept a table on Saturdays with a salt fish or bacalao [cod fish] dinner." To this unpretentious feast he regularly invited only four close friends, all of them merchants, two of them relatives; only "now and then," his son recalled, was a clergyman added to the group. The colonel's life and young Thomas's boyhood were deeply scarred by family tragedies, quite aside from the financial losses that severely reduced the family fortune. The colonel's eldest son, Foster, *"a most lovely son,"* an "amiable youth, the delight of [Harvard] College," died of a smallpox inoculation at seventeen; his death, young Thomas recalled, "was a heavy stroke" to his father. And then an infant son died, followed by a young daughter, of consumption; and finally in 1739 the twenty-three-year-old Elisha died of a fever, a loss which, coming as it did in the decline of the father's life, "broke his heart." Colonel Thomas himself had never been strong. For many years, his son candidly recorded, he had suffered secretly from a rupture, and all his life he had been subject to "indigestion and flatulencies at his stomach." More important for the legacy he may have passed on to his son, the colonel, young Thomas noted many years later, had had "two or three turns . . . of nervous disorders, which confined him several weeks at a time and deprived him of his sleep." He died soon after the loss of his son Elisha, of a "hectic fever" that followed "a languishing illness."[18]

17. Colonel Thomas's aunt Abigail, twice a widow, married Foster when he was himself a widower, and his half-brother Edward married another of Foster's daughters.

18. Samuel Mather, *The Faithful Man Abounding with Blessings* . . . (Boston, 1740), p. 21; Eg. MSS, 2664, pp. 41–45 from end (passages omitted in *Diary and Letters,* II, 468–470). For Colonel Thomas's will, which specifies not only his real estate holdings in Boston but the rental income from them, see Whitmore, *Brief Genealogy,* pp. 18–19.

For young Thomas, the future governor, there was no break in the continuity of family and community life. He entered Harvard at the age of twelve, where he developed not so much the intellectual interests that later became important to him as his ability and resources in trade. At the time he entered college, he recalled half a century later, his father undertook his proper education by presenting him with "two or three quintals of fish." From this humble capital he managed to build, by "adventuring to sea" through his college years, a fund of £4–500 sterling, which, combined with an inheritance from his father, became a fortune, by provincial standards, by the time of the Revolution: in cash, fifteen times his original capital, and in real estate, eight houses, including the Boston mansion he had inherited, two wharves and a variety of lots and shop properties in Boston, and in suburban Milton a country house universally admired for its simple beauty and splendid setting, and a hundred acres of choice land.[19]

Additional property in cash and real estate came to him through his marriage, which served for him as it had for his father to reinforce the family's dominant characteristics. The Sanfords of Rhode Island had been related to the Hutchinsons by marriage and in business for four generations; as early as the 1640's the two families had worked together to build the first important New England commercial network, the Hutchinsons controlling the primary London-Boston link and the marketing to the west, the Sanford in-laws handling the secondary routes to the south and, through cousins in Barbados, the links to the West Indies and the Wine Islands. Margaret Sanford, daughter, granddaughter, and great granddaughter of New England merchants, was seventeen in 1734 when Hutchinson married her. At their marriage, the governor of Massachusetts wrote in a business-like letter of introduction for their honeymoon trip, the couple could claim a joint fortune of £5–6000 sterling; Thomas, he said, was "a young gentleman of exact virtue [and] of good natural sense," a bit too modest, perhaps, but a successful merchant and universally esteemed.[20]

19. In 1770 Hutchinson reported that his Boston properties brought him £140–£150 a year. TH to FB, March 25, 1770, MA, XXVI, 471. On the Milton property, see Malcolm Freiberg, *Thomas Hutchinson of Milton* (Milton, Mass. 1971), pp. 3–10. Its importance to him in his years of exile is discussed below, pp. 327–330, 372.
20. Jonathan Belcher to Francis Harrison, June 27, 1734, MHS *Colls.*, 6th ser., VII (1894), 77. For the kinship relations between the two families, see Whitmore, *Brief Genealogy*, p. 11n; for the commercial associations, see above, note 15.

Four years later, at the age of twenty-six, Hutchinson entered politics. He was never thereafter out of it, and he maintained an altogether consistent policy in defense of what, until the great issues of the 1760's intervened, were widely considered to be the basic interests of the colony. As representative of Boston to the Massachusetts House from 1737 to 1749 (with the exception of a single year) and a councillor for the succeeding seventeen years, he distinguished himself by his effective defense of a hard money policy and by his equally determined defense of the territorial integrity of Massachusetts and of its chartered rights. As a leader of the hard-money forces, he inevitably made enemies, though no more than others on his side of that savagely divisive issue. His mastery of the economics involved was universally acknowledged, and while he was firm in his advocacy, he was never unreasonable, never fanatical. So convinced was the community of Hutchinson's "disinterestedness and integrity," Pownall reported in 1757, that even those who most sharply disagreed with him continued to respect him, even to revere him. In the end Hutchinson's views on the money question prevailed, in part because of the shrewd use that Massachusetts, led by Hutchinson, was able to make of the specie it received from the English government as repayment for its contribution to the war against France; and in part because when in 1741 the issue developed into a crisis that threatened violence, Governor Belcher had seized the initiative and stamped out the incipient rebellion by force. There was no limit, Belcher wrote Hutchinson in a portentous letter of 1741, to what political fanatics would do; they would even defy Parliament, for the common people were told by their leaders that they were out of the reach of the government of England, and the Assembly was made to think they were as big as the Parliament of Great Britain. "They are grown so brassy and hardy as to be now combining in a body to raise a rebellion. . . . I have this day sent the sheriff and his officers to apprehend some of the heads of the conspirators, so you see we are becoming ripe for a smarter sort of government."[21]

21. Pownall to Halifax, note 7 above; Belcher to TH, May 11, 1741, *Belcher Papers*, II (MHS *Colls.*, 6th ser., VII, 1894), 388. For general accounts of Massachusetts politics and imperial affairs in this period as they involved Hutchinson, see Herbert L. Osgood, *The American Colonies in the Eighteenth Century* (N.Y., 1924–25), III, pt. 2, chap. xvi, and pt. 3, chap. iv; Gipson, *British Empire*, III, chap. i; V, chaps. iv, v; X, chap. iii; Robert Zemsky, *Merchants, Farmers, and River Gods* (Boston, Gambit, 1971), chaps. v, vi; and John A. Schutz, *William Shirley* (Chapel Hill, University of North Carolina Press, 1961).

But if Hutchinson's views on monetary matters were controversial, his defense of the colony's political and territorial rights was not. His service to Massachusetts as agent in all matters affecting its external relations was sustained through thirty years and was almost uniformly successful. He was turned to repeatedly, and year after year he extended himself in the public behalf. In 1740 he was sent by the colony to England to plead the case of certain Massachusetts landowners whose property had fallen to New Hampshire in a crown ruling on the colony's boundary, and though, through no fault of his own, his official efforts came to little, he did not return empty-handed; the Holden bequest, which led to the construction of that superb miniature of Georgian architecture, Holden Chapel, still standing in the Harvard Yard, was obtained by him for the College.[22] He negotiated repeatedly, almost annually, with the border Indians in the interest of his native colony, managed the province's lottery, supervised the financing of the Louisbourg expedition of 1745, dealt with other colonies on joint military efforts, adjudicated boundary disputes with Connecticut and Rhode Island; and in 1754 represented the Bay Colony at the Albany Congress, where he played a major role.[23] Before his appointment as lieutenant governor in 1758 he served as the Massachusetts agent of the commanding general of the British forces during the climax of the Seven Years War, and when he quarreled with Governor Pownall it was in defense of the political interests that had maintained stability in Massachusetts for a decade and in opposition to what he felt were corrupt practices in handling the colony's war effort. Through all of this Hutchinson served on the bench as judge both of the inferior court of common pleas and of the probate court of Suffolk County.

It is hard to see what more he could have done to serve his coun-

22. Documentation for this important episode in Hutchinson's early political career, in which Hutchinson carried out "secret service" for Governor Belcher as well as the official mission (and which in the end cost him "5 or £600 out of pocket") will be found in *Belcher Papers*, II, 335ff. (esp. pp. 386–390, 409, 426); William Shirley to Samuel Waldo, June 27, 1740, Henry Knox Papers, MHS; and Thomlinson-Atkinson Correspondence, MHS.

23. Lawrence Gipson's exhaustive research on the authorship of the Albany plan of union reveals that the final version was a combination of drafts submitted by Hutchinson and Franklin. Gipson, "Thomas Hutchinson and the Framing of the Albany Plan of Union, 1754," *Pennsylvania Magazine of History and Biography*, 74 (1950), 5–35. See also Gipson's "The Drafting of the Albany Plan of Union," *Pennsylvania History*, 26 (1959), 290–316 (and discussion, *ibid.*, 27 [1960], 126–136); and his "Massachusetts Bay and American Colonial Union, 1754," AAS *Procs.*, 71 (1961), 63–92.

trymen or how, as a leader of the establishment in trade and politics, he could have been more enlightened. It had been Hutchinson, more than anyone but Franklin, who saw at the Albany Congress the benefits of restructuring imperial and intercolonial relations, and he did what he could to implement these advanced ideas. Unlike many colonials in his position, he had never been a "courtier": as a young man in London he had "found it very tiresome work to attend upon a British court," Isaac Watts reported, and he was never thereafter tempted to forsake local interests for advancement "at home."[24]

Yet in the end his services were forgotten and he was cursed as a traitor in the land of his birth—cursed not merely by the wild men, the alarmists, the political paranoids, and the professional agitators, but by some of the most stable, sensible people of the time, many of whom knew him personally. There was, they said, some deep flaw in his character, some perversion of personality, some profound "malignancy of heart," that had turned his patriotism into treason, and led him to sacrifice the general good for the most sordid, selfish gain.[25]

iii

What do we know of the personality of Thomas Hutchinson, his character, his style and sensibility?

Surprisingly little. Of all the people who worked with him, struggled against him, cursed and denounced him, not one left a sketch of his character or even of his appearance more detailed or perceptive than James Otis's remark that he was "a tall, slender, fair-complexioned, fair-spoken, 'very good gentleman.' " John Adams, who wrote voluminously about him and was capable, beyond any other American of the eighteenth century, of casting a character, left polemics, but no account of his person. Edward Gibbon, who sought Hutchinson out in London in 1775 and knew him well, refers to him in his otherwise wonderfully expressive letters without a single adjective, without even the faintest shading of phrase that might re-

24. Watts to Benjamin Colman, Epsom, Aug. 19, 1741, MHS *Procs.*, 29 (1894–1895), 386; see also pp. 337, 396.
25. E.g., James Warren to John Adams, Sept. 7, 1777, *Warren-Adams Letters*, I, 367.

veal his perception of the man. Only one authentic portrait of Hutchinson exists, painted in London when Hutchinson was thirty. It is superficial but incidentally revealing. It shows a person dressed in utmost simplicity, slim in form, with a narrow face and undistinguished features. The lips are full but slightly compressed and pursed. There is a wisp of a smile, but no real attempt at expression. The overall effect is that of constraint, simplicity, and an almost total lack of emphasis, flair, or style.[26]

It is not much to go on, but it is suggestive. For his prose conveys the same qualities. He wrote easily, abundantly, and logically. But the style is not only unaffected and unadorned in the extreme, devoid of images, figures of speech, thin even in adjectives, but so lacking in emphasis, so unpunctuated, so *still*, as to seem at times inarticulate. The reader finds himself again and again having to go back and re-read passages because the thread is lost. The point, he invariably finds, is in fact there, but the stress is insufficient; the necessary emphases are missing. Hutchinson seems not to be attempting to reach the reader directly, not trying to convince him of what he is saying. One even-paced, unassertive paragraph follows another. This paragraph from the *History of Massachusetts-Bay* is typical:

They distinguished civil subjection, into necessary and voluntary. From actual residence within any government, necessarily arose subjection, or an obligation to submit to the laws and authority thereof. But birth, was no

26. *Boston Gazette*, Jan. 31, 1763, quoted in Leslie J. Thomas, "Partisan Politics in Massachusetts during Governor Bernard's Administration, 1760–1770" (Ph.D. diss., University of Wisconsin, 1960), p. 102. For Gibbon's references to Hutchinson, supported by Hutchinson's own references to encounters with the historian recorded in the *Diary and Letters*, see J. E. Norton, ed., *Letters of Edward Gibbon* (London, 1956), II, 51, 57–58 ("I think I have sucked Mauduit and Hutchinson dry"), 70–71, 72–73, 75; and below, p. 289. The authentic portrait, now in the MHS, is reproduced as the frontispiece to the present volume. The features that appear in that painting are easily recognizable in the political cartoons drawn more than thirty years later, which appear following p. 204. The "Copley" portrait, thought for many years to have been of Hutchinson and reproduced as such in Shipton's "Hutchinson," has been proved to be a portrait of Chief Justice Peter Oliver, and in any case is not by Copley (Andrew Oliver, *Faces of a Family* [p.p., 1960], no. 8D; and documents kindly supplied the author by Mr. Andrew Oliver). Copley did make a pencil drawing of Hutchinson "some years" before 1774; shortly after Hutchinson arrived in London the painter, who had left America earlier that year and whom the ex-governor saw frequently, wrote his half-brother Henry Pelham in Boston to send the drawing to Hutchinson and make a copy for himself. But neither Copley's original nor Pelham's copy has been located. Copley to Pelham, London, Aug. 25, 1774, *Copley-Pelham Letters* (MHS *Colls.*, LXXI, 1914), 242. Hutchinson was apparently six feet tall (*Diary and Letters*, I, 440); and the political squibs refer commonly to his thin figure ("Tommy, skin and bones").

necessary cause of subjection. The subjects of any prince or state had a natural right to remove to any other state, or to another quarter of the world, unless the state was weakned and exposed by such remove, and even in that case, if they were deprived of the right of all mankind, liberty of conscience, it would justify a separation, and upon their removal, their subjection determined and ceased.[27]

Not only are there almost no figures of speech and few adjectives, but the nouns are frequently abstract and the word order inverted ("From actual residence within any government, necessarily arose subjection")—a combination perfectly calculated to trip the reader up and force him to retrace his steps. His narratives, his arguments, his explanations are bland in content and blandly told. Personalities rarely come into focus: "It is a delicate thing to hit off characters with justice," Ezra Stiles wrote Hutchinson upon reading volume I of his *History*. "[Yet] the business of an historian is to paint, that we know the man and see him as he is. You have sometimes taken occasion to contrast the good and evil of character, without pointing out the result, the prevailing and ultimate complexion." The events themselves, Stiles concluded, were narrated with perspicuity and impartiality, but there was too much "cautiousness in character and motives."[28]

The same could be said of almost every expression of Hutchinson's personality. He was by instinct political not philosophical, inductive not deductive; he sought to succeed in the world he knew, not transform it. At least as to his own career, he once wrote, he felt himself to be what he called "a quietist, being convinced that what is, is best." So he counseled a too-stubborn political ally to "strive to be more of a willow and less of an oak. We don't live in Plato's Commonwealth, and when we can't have perfection we ought to comply with the measure that is least remote from it." He was circumspect in everything he did. Caution, control, and prudence were the guiding principles of his life "My temper," he wrote in a characteristic understatement, "does not incline to enthusiasm." Everyone recognized it. You are, Governor Bernard wrote Hutchin-

27. *History of Massachusetts-Bay*, I, 216. In this quotation, the spelling and punctuation have been left as originally written, but otherwise quotations from the *History* and from Hutchinson's correspondence are modernized according to the general rules explained in the Note on Modernization on p. xviii above.
28. Stiles to TH, Newport, Jan. 8, 1765, *New-England Historical and Genealogical Register*, 26 (1872), 163.

son in 1769 after handing over to him the colony's government, "a much prudenter man than I ever pretended to be," and, he added, with more of a double meaning than he might have admitted, you "will take care of yourself." Hutchinson knew that his administration would be very burdensome and very precarious, but that, he said, would only "excite in me the more caution and circumspection." He tried never to overextend himself—"I don't love to promise too much"—and "never chose to give an opinion suddenly" on a matter of importance. Often he lectured others—his children, his colleagues, the constituted bodies of government—on the need for caution, at times lapsing into unappreciated moral discourses. To a correspondent seeking his approval of an unconventional marriage he pointed out that it was not enough to argue that in terms of "abstract morality" there was nothing wrong with it; "is not prudence a part of morality?" he asked with characteristic abstractness and underemphasis. Consider the consequences, he urged, consider your position, consider the use your enemies would make of such an obvious indiscretion.[29]

Hutchinson himself never neglected such considerations—with results that his colleagues occasionally found disturbing. At one important point in his career, as we shall see, he was officially consulted by the secretary of state on possible alterations in the constitution of Massachusetts which he was believed to have urged unofficially in the past. But his reply was said by the secretary, in words almost identical to Stiles's critique of the *History,* to be "like a lawyer's opinion, in which doubts and difficulties are stated but no conclusion is drawn." A great opportunity to strengthen government had been irretrievably lost by this too judicious, too cautious response, he was informed; an excess of caution, he was warned, could destroy the possibility of action.[30]

It was not something Hutchinson could easily change in himself. Constraint was too deep a part of his nature. He rarely wrote an important letter only once. Drafts, notes, and revisions of letters

29. TH to Israel Williams, Oct. 28 and Aug. 8, 1759, Israel Williams Papers, MHS; TH to Richard Jackson, Oct. 15, 1770, MA, XXVII, 24; FB to TH, London, Nov. 17, 1769, Bernard Papers, VIII, 24; TH to Thomas Whately, July 29, 1769, MA, XXVI, 359; TH to [?], Aug. 27, 1771, MA, XXVII, 221; *Diary and Letters,* II, 258; TH to [?], Nov. 12, 1771, MA, XXVII, 254.
30. FB to TH, London, Nov. 10, 1770, Bernard Papers, VIII, 138–142. See below, pp. 189–192.

abound in his papers; in them one can trace successive alterations and excisions that soften the edge of his original thought. Richard Jackson was one of his most intimate correspondents; he was the only person, in England at least, to whom, for a brief period, Hutchinson expressed his more or less unqualified opinions. Yet in 1762, when affairs were in fact placid in Massachusetts, he carefully removed from a letter to Jackson the sentence: "We have violent parties in our little mock Parliament, and sometimes the public interest gives way to private piques and prejudices, as well as with you." Whole letters on important topics are drafted, redrafted, and then, if the sentiment is found still to be injudicious, or likely to be thought so, left in draft and filed away with the notation "not sent." Very little, however, was ever thrown away, and sometimes a passage eliminated from one piece of writing turns up in another, safer context. Hutchinson had originally drafted a lengthy paragraph for volume II of his *History* critical of what he felt was the anarchic democracy of the Massachusetts town meetings, but then he "considered the times, and thought it would do more hurt than good." He therefore struck it out of the book and used the passage in a draft of a letter to Jackson explaining what must happen to society when every member of the town meetings "thinks it hard to be obliged to submit to laws which he does not like"—but then, thinking such a comment indiscreet even in a private communication, eliminated it from the letter too and suppressed the passage altogether. His *History* as a whole had originally been planned, he confessed to a friend (in a paragraph he deleted with a large X in his draft copy but which the Revolutionary leaders later published in full in the newspapers), as a history of his own times similar to Bishop Burnet's: "I shall paint characters as freely as he did, but it shall not be published while I live, and I expect the same satisfaction, which I doubt not the bishop had, of being revenged of some of the r[ogue]s after I am dead." But in fact he permitted himself no such indulgence. Partly, he explained to Stiles, it was simply that he knew he had "no talent at painting or describing characters." Partly too he had decided to take no chances: "My safest way was to avoid [personalities] and let facts speak for themselves. I was astonished after reading Robertson's *History of Scotland*, and having settled Mary Stuart's character in my own mind as one of the most infamous in history, to find him drawing her with scarce a blemish." But the great challenge came in volume III, which Hutchinson wrote only for posthumous publication. Here if anywhere self-assertion would be justified and personal opinion might be spread upon the record. But it is one of the most impersonal, bland, and circumspect accounts of revolutionary events ever written by a participant—and not by accident. The chance survival of the heavily revised first draft shows how carefully and deliberately Hutchinson pruned his naturally unacerb style, how thoroughly he curbed his spontaneous thought, to achieve the final result.[31]

He was cautious and temperate in everything he did. He permitted himself no ostentation in clothes. A laced coat, he said, was "too gay for me"; he preferred "a grave, genteel waistcoat," for, he wrote, he "would not be singular." As governor he had hoped to make do with his father's old carriage, but his friends told him his station required a more fashionable one. He agreed, then wrote his agents in England to get him one—secondhand, at a substantial saving: "it can't be too plain if neat and light," he wrote.[32] None of this was senseless penny-pinching or dour prudery, and he was no misanthrope. He had no objection to stage plays, banned by the General Court of Massachusetts; he collected statuary (in cheap reproductions); and he hung in his hall a variety of paintings and fashionable prints, among them Hogarth's "Marriage à la Mode" series, in "rich frames and glass." He allowed himself at least one substantial extravagance, in furnishing, enlarging, and beautifying the Milton house, which was a joy to him from the time he built it in 1743 until he left for England thirty-one years later. Situated on a hilltop overlooking the Neponset River, with an unobstructed view north to Boston Bay, it was a "long, low structure with a central section rising a story and a half, flanked by dependent wings on either side each only one story high," and it has aptly been called "a Monticello in Massachusetts." Hutchinson spent as much time there as he could—every summer after 1754—and there he fully

31. TH to Richard Jackson, Nov. 15, 1762, and Nov. 19, 1767, MA, XXVI, 29, and XXV, 226–27; TH to Colonel [John] Cushing, Jan. 3, 1763, MA XXVI, 39 (cf. *The Remembrancer . . . Part II, For the Year 1776* [London, 1776], p. 62); TH to Stiles, Jan. 15, 1765, *New-England Historical and Genealogical Register*, 26 (1872), 164; Mayo, "Additions," cited in note 12 above.

32. TH to Peter Leitch, Oct. 5, 1769, MA, XXVI, 386; TH to James Fisher, Nov. 24, 1772, MA, XXVII, 417; TH to Peter Leitch, March 29, 1766, MA, XXVI, 222; TH to FB, Feb. 7, 1771, MA, XXVII, 116.

indulged what taste he had for physical, sensual refinement.[33] It was a simple, modest taste. The habits of a lifetime were never overcome, even in Milton. Restraint and calculation had been part of his way of life since early childhood. "All the time he was at college," he wrote of himself with Franklinesque pride some fifty years later, he

kept a little paper journal and ledger, and entered in it every dinner, supper, breakfast, and every article of expense, even of a shilling; which practice soon became pleasant, and he found it of great use all his life, as so exact a knowledge of his cash kept him from involvement, of which he would have been in danger. And having been a very few instances negligent in this respect for a short time only, he saw the consequences of this neglect in a very strong light, and became more observant ever after.[34]

In religion too he was rational, circumspect, and cool. He honored his family's traditional commitment to the Congregation church, joining at the age of twenty-four the so-called New Brick Church of his college tutor and brother-in-law, the Reverend William Welsteed, to which he remained faithful, in formal terms at least, until he left America in 1774, and in which he baptised his children. He was closer in spirit, however, to his lifelong friend, the tolerant, rationalist, non-doctrinaire Reverend Andrew Eliot and to the Episcopal preacher Henry Caner, whose Anglican church he frequently attended, than he was to Welsteed or his Calvinist successor, Ebenezer Pemberton.[35] For he despised the fanaticism of the Puritans, either in its ancestral form, laced as it was with those fine-spun doctrinal subtleties that led men to torture each other in passionate self-righteousness, or in its more modern, more pietistic form whose

33. "Remarks upon the Laws . . . 1770," MA, XXVII, 86; for his order to his son to purchase in London small bronze busts of 18 named classical and modern figures, chiefly literary, and for the initial order for the secondhand coach, see invoice accompanying TH to TH, Jr., April 14, 1766, MA, XXVI, 226; TH to FB, Dec. 22, 1770, MA, XXVII, 82; inventory of furnishings in the Milton house (including, besides the Hogarths, 3 large landscapes, 2 portraits, 10 framed prints, and 3 glazed mezzotints), *Diary and Letters*, I, 559ff.; Freiberg, *Hutchinson of Milton*, pp. 3, 5, 9. Among the losses that Hutchinson enumerated to Secretary of State Conway after the Stamp Act riot that destroyed his Boston house were 4 paintings, 2 of them portraits of his grandparents, and 4 large prints "newly framed and glazed." CO5/755/373.
34. *Diary and Letters*, I, 46.
35. On the Hutchinson family's membership in the New Brick Church, see *New-England Historical and Genealogical Register*, 18, (1864), 344; on Welsteed and Pemberton, see C. K. Shipton, *Sibley's Harvard Graduates*, VI (Boston, MHS, 1942), 153ff., 535ff. On Eliot, see note 10 above.

crankish adherents "scarce ever settled an account with anybody without a lawsuit."[36] The career of his great-great-grandmother Anne fascinated and chilled him. Her sincere religious passion, he felt, was in itself no more humane than the destructive fervor of her enemies. Through the whole of the famous Antinomian controversy, which he recounted in a passage of his *History* that is the very essence of the Enlightenment's indictment of bigotry, "the fear of God and love of our neighbor seemed to be laid by and out of the question." At the end, he wrote, Anne no doubt held in reserve "some fine spun distinctions, too commonly made use of in theological controversies, to serve as a subterfuge, if there be occasion; and perhaps, as many other enthusiasts have done, she considered herself divinely commissioned for some great purpose, to obtain which she might think those windings, subtleties, and insinuations lawful which will hardly consist with the rules of morality. No wonder she was immoderately vain when she found magistrates and ministers embracing the novelties advanced by her."[37]

A true religious life to Hutchinson meant simply the worship of God and rectitude. He judged the practice of religion by its results, in human terms: "the longer I live the less stress I lay upon modes and forms in religion, and do not love a good man the less because he and I are not just of the same way of thinking." For himself he

36. TH to TH, Jr., London, May 13, 1775, Eg. MSS, 2661, p. 150. Hutchinson expressed his religious beliefs most candidly in the letter to FB cited below, note 38, and in a letter to an unnamed correspondent, Aug. 27, 1772 (MA, XXVII, 377–380), acknowledging receipt of a pamphlet favoring an American bishopric. In the latter letter he recalls reading Locke on toleration as a college student and wondering how anyone who thought at all could have thought differently; he tells of his pity for the destructive intolerance of his Puritan ancestors and his fear that if unrestrained the majority of people even in his own time would act in the same way; he speaks openly of his belief that the clergy of all denominations are bigots; and he describes the catholicity of his preference in worship. This letter, found among his papers at Milton, was published by the Revolutionary leaders with interpolated editorial comments as conclusive proof of Hutchinson's treachery, hypocrisy, and infidelity. *Remembrancer, 1776, II*, p. 58. See below, pp. 334ff.

37. *History of Massachusetts-Bay*, I, 51, 62–63. For Hutchinson's less formal account of Anne's personality and career, see *Diary and Letters*, II, 461; but significant passages of this segment of Hutchinson's account of his ancestors were omitted by the editor. Hutchinson believed, for example, that if Anne had lived another ten years she would have become a Quaker and would have restrained that sect from some of its most extravagant tenets. Of her chief persecutor, the Reverend John Wilson, Hutchinson wrote that "though he thought himself hardly used in being forced to leave England for nonconformity there, [he] could not think it a hard thing to banish Mrs. Hutchinson and all her friends for nonconformity here." He concluded that Anne "was a sincere woman, though of a deluded imagination." Eg. MSS, 2664, pp. 13–20 from end.

would have chosen the Anglican church if he had had the opportunity to choose: "had I been born and bred there," he wrote Bernard in 1771, "I would never have left it for any other communion." Its rational, tolerant views were his own, and he could see no particular objection to the establishment of an American episcopate if its jurisdiction were limited to the spiritual lives of Anglicans. But he felt no need to change formal church affiliations to express his point of view. Most clerics, he believed, of all denominations, were bigots of one sort or another, and his own pastor, Pemberton, though a Calvinist in an erratic way, was at least a "friend of government" and tolerant of other denominations. Besides, it was politically more useful for him to remain in his family's church and share to that extent the religious life of the mass of the people.[38] For he did not think that integrity and virtue ultimately depended on a belief in the supernatural; such a belief, he felt, as often bred stupid superstition and cruel bigotry as it did decency, tolerance, and justice in human dealings.[39]

None of this rationality and circumspection was a strenuous achievement for him. Caution, temperance, and tolerance were natural for him. There is no evidence, as there is for John Adams, of a struggle between nature and nurture, between powerful erratic impulses and the constraints of culture. Hutchinson did not respond deeply to the physical qualities of life; his sensuous apprehensions were never keen, and he felt no inner promptings, as Adams did, to follow a wayward course. He spoke fearfully to others, especially to the young, of the temptations of dissolute living and of its disastrous consequences. But there is not the slightest shred of evidence, implicit or explicit, that he himself had ever in any way been tempted.

38. TH to Pemberton, London, n.d. [Dec. 1774?], Eg. MSS, 2661, p. 92; TH to FB, Dec. 24, 1771, MA, XXVII, 265. For Hutchinson's explanation of the circumstances that led him to write as he did of his pragmatic approach to church affiliation, see TH to Jonathan Sewall, July 8, 1775, Eg. MSS, 2661, pp. 158–159, discussed in its context below, pp. 338–339. The characterization of Pemberton was made to George III, July 1, 1774, *Diary and Letters*, I, 168.

39. TH to Thomas Flucker, London, Oct. 17, 1774, Eg. MSS, 2661, p. 69 (a passage deleted in draft). Hutchinson's indignation at the ignorant superstition of Anne's devout persecutors spills over into a footnote to the episode in his *History of Massachusetts Bay* (I, 64n): "Some writers mention the manner of her death as being a remarkable judgment of God for her heresies. . . . Mr. Weld says she was delivered of as many unformed foetuses at a birth as she maintained errors, and that another actress [i.e., partisan of Anne's] was delivered of a monster, and that all the women were seized with a violent vomiting and purging—stories as credible as that of the Flanders countess who is said to have as many children at a birth as there are days in the year."

He maintained without a struggle a correct and honorable code of conduct.[40]

Virtuous but not stylish, intelligent but didactic, heavy-spirited and self-absorbed, he judged people, and often found them wanting. He had no great admiration for mankind in general. He had found it useful to assume that each man presented to the world not his true self but what he called a "persona" and that it was best therefore to "absolutely suspend all determination upon the real state of his mind" until long acquaintance and a careful matching of external appearances and modes of expression with true motives as they were revealed allowed one to establish the authentic character. For not only were appearances deceiving, but "words you know are arbitrary, a little use would soon cause them to convey quite contrary ideas." This was the way of the world; it had always been so. The great Pompey's friends had said of that man of high character that he "never spake as he thought." Cicero had been a man of even higher character, and he was in addition an incomparable moralist; but a comparison of his writings while Caesar was alive with the orations he delivered after Caesar had been killed shows "what a part he was acting." No doubt some men appeared to be virtuous, wise, and disinterested and in fact were so, but not many. Most lied or at least hid their true intentions as they jostled for position and scrabbled for gain.[41]

The world was a moral tragedy not a human comedy, demanding firmness not subtlety. Hutchinson could see the good and evil in people but seldom their ridiculousness, and so he had no sense of humor. His attempts at humor, almost nonexistent in the mass of his papers, turn for their effect on rather heavy-handed irony, and quickly slip over into moral or political preachments. "I am at Milton," he wrote in 1771 to his recently departed friend Commodore Gambier (one of the few people outside his family with whom he seems to have had a light-hearted relationship),

40. For typical warnings to the young, especially against the dangers of London's corruptions, see TH to Nathaniel Rogers, Dec. 14, 1761, MA, XXVI, 1; to TH, Jr., n.d. [April 1766?], *ibid.*, p. 223; to James Gambier (to help protect young Billy Hutchinson against the "*illecebrae* of the most dangerous place in the world"), May 7, 1772, MA, XXVII, 331. For Adams's very different response to the world, see Bernard Bailyn, "Butterfield's Adams: Notes for a Sketch," *W.M.Q.*, 3d ser., 19 (1962), 241–256.
41. TH to Richard Saltonstall, Aug. 22, 1759, Robert E. Moody, ed. *Saltonstall Papers*, I (MHS *Colls.*, LXXX, 1972), pp. 429–430.

You would have made some humorous remarks upon the company if you had been present among us today. About one half had been yesterday at the turtle feast at The Peacock, which they did not quit until between 3 and 4 this morning . . . Lady William has changed in one evening a tolerably healthy Nova Scotia countenance for the pale, sickly complexion of South Carolina, Mrs. Robinson her natural cheerfulness and fluency for an unusual gravity and taciturnity. Poor Paxton's usual refreshing nap after dinner was turned into a waking coma, more insensible with his eyes open than he used to be when they were shut. In short, there was no need of a nice discerner to ascertain who had and who had not been of the party. The physicians, parsons, and sextons may very well afford to contribute to the support of The Peacock. I only wish, instead of my good friends, the company might consist of Otis, Adams, Cooper, Hancock, Molineux, and half a hundred more of the same cast.[42]

Pale shades of Horace Walpole! Yet this is the gayest, most gossipy passage Hutchinson left behind, probably that he ever wrote, at least to anyone outside his family. It marks a partial, passing relaxation of restraint. But how faint the whole effect. There is no burst of laughter, no sting of malice. The imagination is austere, local, prosaic. And so, it seems, was the whole of Hutchinson's mind and sensibility.

Deeply bred—locked tight—in the culture of an intensely Protestant, mercantile province of the British world and heir to its establishment, he felt no elemental discontent, no romantic aspirations. He sought no conquests in a larger world but steady gains in the one he knew. Like his ancestors before him, he was an accumulator, a slow relentless acquisitor, and he remained such, even after his formal retirement from business in the early 1760's. But though the desire for gain was an essential part of his nature, he was never crudely avaricious—he was too intelligent and too much a neo-Puritan ascetic for that. His lifelong search for profits, like his quest for power and influence and status, was never ruthless and never flamboyant, and it was deeply conservative in that it presumed the structure of life as it was. Like so many ambitious and modestly creative people, he needed a stable world within which to work, a hierarchy to ascend, and a formal, external calibration by which to measure where he was.

His correspondence radiates respect for status and an instinct for

42. TH to James Gambier, Oct. 31, 1771, MA, XXVII, 249.

small passages through the complexities of the world. So he wrote the son of an earl who sought his daughter Peggy's hand, that such a marriage would do "the greatest honor to me and my family," but "it cannot be approved of by the noble family to which you belong. In my station, restrained from respect to My Lord Fitzwilliam, I should think it my duty to do all in my power to discourage any of his sons from so unequal a match with any person in the province, and I should certainly be highly criminal if I should countenance and encourage a match with my own daughter." So too he declined a baronetcy, when it was offered to him in 1774, for prudential reasons, but then—prudence within prudence—he "thought it not amiss, however, to ask His Lordship, [that], if I should be reproached with being slighted in England, whether I might say that I [had] had the *offer* of such a mark of honor." To which Dartmouth, he reported, immediately replied (and one can picture the patronizing smile), " 'Most certainly.' " Just so, a decade earlier, in sending Richard Jackson copies of volume I of his *History* to distribute where they might do the most good, he specified certain particularly important recipients, and then instructed Jackson to present a half-dozen other copies "where you think they may be acceptable, as high up as may be in character for me, and order the binding according to the quality of the person."[43]

Sensitively attuned to a world of status and degree, bland, constrained, realistic, unromantic, ambitious, and acquisitive, he was, for all his hatred of religious zeal, the Puritan *manqué*. For he retained the self-discipline and seriousness of the colony's stern founders and something of their asceticism; but he lacked their passion, their transcendent vision, and above all their inner certainty.

For he was never fully confident of his abilities. He was, for

43. TH to William Fitzwilliam, April 6, 1771, MA, XXV, 475; TH to Foster Hutchinson, London, Nov. 1, 1774, *Diary and Letters*, I, 283 (emphasis added); TH to Richard Jackson, Dec. 20, 1764, MA, XXVI, 125. For the reasons behind Hutchinson's refusal of the honor, see below pp. 290–292. Hutchinson had hoped to dedicate volume I of his *History of Massachusetts-Bay* to the Earl of Halifax, but before presuming to do so he wrote to Jackson inquiring about the appropriateness of this step; when Jackson failed to respond, he dropped the idea. TH to same, Oct. 15, 1764, MA, XXVI, 104. For Jackson's distribution of copies to the chancellor of the Exchequer, the speaker of the House of Commons, the attorney general, the solicitor general, the first lord of the Treasury, and the chief justice, see Jackson to TH, March 3, 1766, MA, XXV, 64–65. He could not locate the Earl of Kinnoul and Sir Henry Frankland, to whom TH had also wanted copies sent.

example, a good jurist: commentators, even some of his most severe critics, testified to his skill as adjudicator and fair-minded enforcer of the law.[44] But he was keenly sensitive to his lack of formal legal training, worked at self-improvement, and readily confessed his own inadequacy. When he visited the great chief justice, Lord Mansfield, and fell into a discussion of the Somerset case and the laws governing slavery, he "wished to have entered into a free colloquium and to have discovered, if I am capable of it, the nice distinctions he must have had in his mind . . . but I imagined such an altercation would rather be disliked and forebore."[45] He was a genuine if modest intellectual, with a true feeling for history—any history—the history of England, which he knew well; the history of continental Europe, which he studied partly from French sources; the history of Japan, which he came upon by accident and read with interest; above all, the history of his native Massachusetts, which he knew better than any man alive, which he chronicled in full, and whose historical documents he carefully preserved, edited, and published. His mind was remarkably historicist. When the famous Scottish historian William Robertson told him he had put aside his history of the English colonies because "there was no knowing what would be the future condition of them," Hutchinson informed him that the future had nothing to do with it: the outcome, he said, "need make no odds in writing the history of what is past." A true account of the history

44. Even Mercy Warren conceded that he had acquired knowledge of the common law and "generally decided with equity in his judicial capacity." *History of the American Revolution*, I, 79–80. His careful attention to equity, in very human terms, in handling difficult cases of intestacy bears this out. He had never stuck simply to the letter of the law, he explained, but judged "from the nature and necessity of the thing, it not being supposeable that a man's house can be cleared the day of his death, and I always allowed reasonable time for the family to separate. When a widow and whole family have continued together for a twelve month or more and she had spent the produce of the small estate for the common support of the whole as [had been] usual in the intestate's lifetime, I have excused her from accounting for the profits and minuted at the bottom of the account that they were spent in support of the family. . . . When part of the children only remained and the rest were scattered, I used to take care that in some way or other they all had justice done them in proportion to their shares in the estate." TH to Israel Williams, Dec. 2, 1771, Williams Papers, MHS. William Gordon too, in his general assessment of Hutchinson's career, conceded that among his credits was the equity of his decisions as judge of probate. *History of the Rise, Progress, and Establishment of the . . . United States of America . . .* (N.Y., 1789), I, 356–357.

45. *Diary and Letters*, II, 277. "I never presumed to call myself a lawyer," Hutchinson wrote. "The most I could pretend to was, when I heard the law laid down on both sides, to judge which was right." TH to John Sullivan, March 29, 1771, MA, XXVII, 136.

of the colonies ought to be written, Hutchinson said, and handed down to posterity. But he always regretted his lack of deep learning and never ceased belittling the virtues of his *History*.[46]

Weaknesses of health, to some extent perhaps hereditary, added to his uncertainties. Never very robust, he began around 1762 to follow a careful regimen of exercise, walking and riding at regular intervals, controlling his consumption of food and drink, and guarding against excesses in work. But in April 1767, well before the major crisis of his career had developed, he suffered what appears to have been a nervous breakdown—he was, as he put it, "paralytic" for six or seven weeks—and only gradually regained his health.[47] He was never thereafter free of worry, about himself as well as about the world. Night after night as governor he lay awake struggling to find the proper path for the authority he represented, worrying if he had the wisdom and the physical and psychic strength to guide the colony to peace. Repeatedly, in the ordeals of the seventies, his energy ebbed, his spirits flagged, and he hovered at the edge of collapse.[48]

His refuge in the increasing turmoil of his life remained what it had always been, his family. He was deeply affectionate with those closest to him, and profoundly involved with their lives. However convenient and inevitable his marriage to Margaret Sanford may have been, it proved to be a relationship of intense intimacy. Only scraps of evidence remain, but they gleam in the bulk of his correspondence. After their marriage in 1734, they were parted only once

46. For his early and general interest in history, including work in Latin and French, see *Diary and Letters*, I, 47. For his reading of Jean Levesque de Burigny, see below, pp. 369–370; for his translation from the French of accounts of Champlain's voyages, see Bernard Papers, IX, 303–305 (1762); on his interest in Japanese history, see *Diary and Letters*, I, 588; for the conversation with Robertson, see II, 194.

47. TH to FB, Jan. 13, 1772, MA, XXVII, 277. For references to this illness, see TH to Israel Mauduit, June 6, 1767, MA, XXV, 186, specifying a nervous disorder during the previous six or seven weeks; to William Bollan and Richard Jackson, June 2, 1767, MA, XXVI, 238, 276, explaining that his nerves, "always weak," had recently been badly affected by the political abuse he had received, but that a total cessation of business for several weeks and long rides in the country had partly restored his health; and to FB, March 30, 1772, MA, XXVII, 307, upon hearing that his former chief had suffered a stroke, suggesting as a cure long horseback rides, a change of scenery, and mental diversion, which had restored him when he had once been "unstrung."

48. Thus, after the Massacre, fearful that Captain Preston would be lynched, he "sat up until midnight and until the scouts which had been sent to different quarters made return that all was quiet." TH to General Gage, June 23, 1770, MA, XXVI, 511. Years later he recalled "my lying awake whole nights in America, fearing I should be called to account in England for neglect of duty to the King." *Diary and Letters*, II, 203.

for any length of time, in 1741, when Hutchinson was in England. His one surviving letter to "My Peggy" from that trip tells of his anxiety at being so long separated from her, begs for news from home, implores her to take care of her health, and expresses the fervent hope that "you will never pass another winter alone as long as I live." They spent in all eighteen years together and she bore him twelve children. Such was his attachment to her, he later wrote, "that she appeared in body and mind something more than human." Her death after childbirth in 1754 was the worst thing that ever happened to Hutchinson, worse even than the political catastrophe that later overwhelmed him. "From the first of her danger I never left my house," he recalled in later years, "and seldom her chamber." Her final words, " 'best of husbands,' " uttered "with her dying voice and eyes fixed on me," tore him to pieces; he could never forget that agony. Her death, he wrote, was the loss of more than half his soul. Neither religion nor philosophy, to which he turned, could help him. The only comfort he could find was Pliny the Younger's austere consolation that acceptance of the inevitable, the lapse of time, and a surfeit of grief would gradually heal the wound. But in fact the memory of his wife never left the surface of his mind. For years after her death he withdrew from all social activities and lived, Thomas Pownall recorded in 1757, "retired in the country with his children." She had given him, Hutchinson wrote ten years after her death, "the greatest happiness, too too short, I ever enjoyed." Three months before his own death in 1780, and after twenty-six years without her, he said of her that "of all earthly objects ever known [she was] deservedly the dearest."[49]

He was close to all of the five children who survived infancy, but closest of all to his youngest, a daughter, whose birth had occasioned

---

49. TH to Margaret Sanford Hutchinson, London, April 13, 1741, Eg. MSS, 2659, p. 1; *Diary and Letters,* I, 54–55 (I have changed Hutchinson's third person narration to the first person); memorandum of letter to Israel Mauduit, Sept. 22, 1777, Eg. MSS, 2661, facing p. 179; Pownall to Halifax, letter cited above, note 7; TH to David Cheeseborough, March 9, 1763, MA, XXVI, 47; *Diary and Letters,* II, 342. I wish to thank my colleague Professor Ernst Badian for identifying Hutchinson's reference to Pliny's letter from an almost totally illegible scribble in Hutchinson's memo. In the letter that Hutchinson was referring to—to Rosianus Geminus, *Letters,* bk. VIII, v (Loeb ed., II, 11–13)—Pliny tells of the terrible blow one Macrinus has suffered in the death of his wife, and praises the wife and the marriage in terms that apply to Margaret Hutchinson and her marriage with extraordinary aptness. Hutchinson never considered remarrying and in 1775 advised Peter Oliver, whose wife had just died, that remarriage would be a mistake. TH to Peter Oliver, May 25, 1775, Eg. MSS, 2661, p. 153.

his wife's death, to whom he gave his wife's name, and whom he called by the same pet name, Peggy. She stayed with him, unmarried, as companion, amanuensis, and hostess until her agonizing death of consumption in London at the age of twenty-three. Of his three sons, the two oldest, bearing the ancestral names Thomas and Elisha, followed their father in trade; only the youngest, Billy, failed to pursue the familiar course, but he could find no other, and remained uncertain—a student from time to time, a dabbler, and a source of worry to his father always.

The family group was extraordinarily close: the force of cohesion that bound them fits no ordinary description. It was not merely that they lived together harmoniously until the older children married; not merely that as adults they gathered to watch together the ship carrying one of them overseas until it passed over the horizon; nor that their family letters over a period of almost fifty years express continuing affection, intimacy, and trust.[50] More than that: they could not bear to break away, and sought to keep the group intact, to tighten the bonds, even in the centrifuge of marriage.

At the height of the family's prosperity, in the early 1770's, the extent of endogamy, already visible in the Foster connection in the previous generation, had become a public phenomenon. For the fact was undeniable, however false—and natural—the political purposes imputed to it, that by successive intermarriages the Hutchinsons had become a large and tight-knit tribe with an extraordinary accumulation of high offices.

The genealogy is important. Three family groups—the Sanfords, the Hutchinsons, and the Olivers—were involved. Margaret Sanford, Thomas Hutchinson's wife (distantly related to him by birth), was the second of three sisters. Her younger sister, Grizell, came to live with the Hutchinsons after Margaret's death, and remained with them, unmarried, ever after, serving as Hutchinson's housekeeper. The older sister, Mary, married Andrew Oliver, who became secretary of Massachusetts when Hutchinson became lieutenant governor, and lieutenant governor when Hutchinson became governor. But

50. TH to TH, Jr., April 14, 1766, MA, XXVI, 225. On the family ties, see, besides Hutchinson's many letters to members of his family in the MA and Eg. MSS collections and the selections scattered through the *Diary and Letters*, the extensive Hutchinson Family Correspondence and the letters of Thomas's son Elisha to his wife before she was able to join him in England, 1774–1777: Eg. MSS, 2659–2660, 2668.

that is only the start of the relationships between the Oliver and Hutchinson families. In the year of Hutchinson's accession to the governorship and Oliver's to the lieutenant governorship, their children—Hutchinson's eldest son Thomas, Jr., and Oliver's daughter Sarah—married. But these two were already related in their own generation, for in the previous year, 1770, another Hutchinson child, Sarah, had married an Oliver, Dr. Peter Oliver, Jr., Andrew's nephew. And then to conclude the series, the families were related yet again in 1772 when a third Hutchinson child, Elisha, married Mary Oliver Watson, Peter Oliver's granddaughter. And political relationships kept pace with the development of kinship ties. Andrew Oliver's brother Peter—brother, that is, of the lieutenant governor and father-in-law of one of the governor's children—had been associate justice of the superior court since 1756, and became chief justice when Hutchinson resigned that post to assume the governorship. Thus, all of the three Hutchinson children who married, married Olivers, and they did so during the first three years of Hutchinson's governorship. And thus, too, three brothers and brothers-in-law occupied simultaneously in the 1770's the governorship, the lieutenant governorship, and the chief justiceship of Massachusetts. No one but a Hutchinson or an Oliver had been lieutenant governor of Massachusetts after 1758 or chief justice after 1760.

Your children, the Sanfords' business agent David Cheeseborough wrote to Hutchinson in 1771, "seem to marry just as you could wish."[51] But why they did—what explanation there might be for such extraordinary inbreeding—is a question that eludes the historian's grasp as it did contemporaries'. But its effects cannot be doubted. It created a family situation of maximum reinforcement for Hutchinson, upon which he relied heavily in the great ordeal he faced. But at the same time it helped isolate him from the community at large and intensified his clashes with other, competing family groups which, like the Otises, the Adamses, and the Bowdoin-Temple-Erving clan, reacted bitterly to the exclusiveness of Hutchinson's family ties. More important, it resulted in an immediate environment of thoroughly like-minded people who would support him in his views without criticism or serious discussion. The importance of this cannot be exaggerated, for nothing in Hutchinson's

51. Cheeseborough to TH, Newport, May 6, 1771, MA, XXV, 482.

own range of sensibilities disposed him to understand or equipped him to deal with the new currents that were moving Anglo-American politics in the 1760's.

iv

At the start, in the early 1760's, the changes that were slowly over-taking American politics were far from evident. The outward pattern remained what it had been for fifty years or more: a delicately poised, unsteady balance between, on the one hand, executive authorities equipped with archaic powers theoretically supported by the crown and, on the other hand, popular assemblies whose members were chosen by a broad electorate and which were relatively unaffected by that "influence" of patronage and corruption that had brought stability to England since the days of Robert Walpole. The governors were felt to be legally too powerful, their opponents politically "overgreat"; the one threatened tyranny, the other anarchy; struggle was the inevitable result. And struggle there had been in most colonies, whenever the two powers were active—yet in the end not lethal struggle, nor ultimate conclusions. For the overall structure of the English government had been too weak, too flexible and manipulable, to sustain ultimate confrontations. The lines of authority from Whitehall to the colonies had been too easily turned aside, too sensitive to pressure from various sources, and too devoid of policy or principle to support conclusive struggles.

This looseness and unsystematic, seemingly random, disjointedness had kept in check the political passions that lay beneath the surface in America. For while the surface was that of the age of Walpole—hard, cynical, unsentimental, pragmatic, venal—below were the passions of an age of ideology. They were not unique to America. Fervent commitment to freedom—of the mind and of the person—and to the possibility of the betterment of the lives of men freed from the fear of arbitrary force, had been part of the life of Britain itself at least since the great upheaval of the Civil War. But in Britain, in the eighteenth century, these flows of doctrine and belief had moved most powerfully not in the central stream of political life but in its deep undercurrents and at its wide margins—among radical nonconformists nourishing ancient sources of anti-authoritarianism; among doctrinaire libertarians guarding the pure principles of liberty; and among disaffected politicians seeking leverage against the powers that were. But in the colonies the ideological forces of the age had flowed freely in the mainstream, for it had been there, in the apprehensions caused by what often seemed an alien and hostile executive, that they seemed most urgent—it had been there, in the naturally free condition of life, that they seemed most capable of fulfillment—and it was there consequently that deprivation had been felt to be most galling. The flow of opposition, libertarian, and nonconformist thought, moving everywhere below the surface of the English-speaking world and capable of endowing ordinary political events with high moral and ideological meaning, had entered the colonies in the earliest years of the eighteenth century and had threatened again and again to turn ordinary political conflicts into passionate confrontations. But each time in the end accommodation had been reached and the pattern of conflict blurred. So public men like Hutchinson—hard-headed and pragmatic, eager for profits, appointments, and influence and versed in the means of acquiring them—had been able to govern with only passing, usually dismissive, acknowledgment of the force of political belief.[52]

But in the early 1760's this unstable balance was shifting. The accession of George III transformed the basic conditions of American politics. The pursuit of colonial revenue introduced new stringencies and new sanctions in the colonial administrative system. The dismissal not only of Pitt's war ministry but of the pliant Newcastle, who for a generation as secretary of state had been chief custodian of colonial patronage, threatened the established network of colonial influence in England and with it the possibility of breaking the official chain of command, mollifying official rigor, and disengaging the lines of conflict. When policy was added—that the colonists assume responsibility for partial repayment of the burden of their keep; that customs be collected and regulations enforced; and that the settlement of new lands proceed within regulations laid down in Whitehall—the world had truly changed.

In 1760, as these changes began, Thomas Hutchinson was at the height of his powers. Forty-nine years of age, an experienced, successful, and influential public figure who prided himself on his

52. Bernard Bailyn, *The Origins of American Politics* (N.Y., Knopf, 1968).

ability to withstand the savagery of politics, he was moving toward the fulfillment of his career at the center of colonial affairs, where it was expected that his abilities would once more gain him success. And so they would have, if times had not changed—if politics had not entered a new phase. Never having felt deep personal discontent—never having passionately aspired—never having longed for some ideal and total betterment—never having found in some utopian vision a compelling and transforming cause, he had never understood the motivations of the miserable, the visionary, and the committed, and he was unprepared to grapple with the politics they shaped.

Chapter II

The Face of Revolution

On the night of August 26, 1765, a mob, more violent than any yet seen in America, more violent indeed than any that would be seen in the entire course of the Revolution, attacked the Boston mansion of Thomas Hutchinson, chief justice and lieutenant governor of Massachusetts. Hardly giving Hutchinson and his family time to flee from the supper table into the streets, the rioters smashed in the doors with axes, swarmed through the rooms, ripped off wainscotting and hangings, splintered the furniture, beat down the inner walls, tore up the garden, and carried off into the night, besides £900 sterling in cash, all the plate, decorations, and clothes that had survived, and destroyed or scattered in the mud all of Hutchinson's books and papers, including the manuscript of volume I of his *History* and the collection of historical papers that he had been gathering for years as the basis for a public archive. The determination of the mob was as remarkable as its savagery: "they worked for three hours at the cupola before they could get it down," Governor Bernard reported; only the heavy brickwork construction of the walls prevented their razing the building completely, "though they worked at it till daylight. The next day the streets were found scattered with money, plate, gold rings, etc. which had been dropped in carrying off." Hutchinson was convinced that he himself would have been killed if he had not given in to his daughter's frantic pleading and fled. He estimated the loss of property at £2,218 sterling.[1]

People of all political persuasions, everywhere in the colonies, were shocked at such "savageness unknown in a civilized country." Hutchinson appeared in court the next day without his robes and, as the young lawyer Josiah Quincy, Jr., who would later pursue him like a fury, reported, the chief justice, "with tears starting from his eyes and a countenance which strongly told the inward anguish of his soul," addressed the court. He apologized for his appearance: he had no other clothes but what he wore, he said, and some of that was borrowed. His family was equally destitute, and their distress was "infinitely more insupportable than what I feel for myself."

Sensible that I am innocent, that all the charges against me are false, I cannot help feeling—and though I am not obliged to give an answer to all the questions that may be put me by every lawless person, yet I call GOD to witness (and I would not for a thousand worlds call my *Maker* to witness to a falsehood)—I say, I call my *Maker* to witness that I never, in New England or Old, in Great Britain or America, neither directly nor indirectly, was aiding, assisting, or supporting, or in the least promoting or encouraging what is commonly called the STAMP ACT, but on the contrary, did all in my power, and storve as much as in me lay, to prevent it. This is not declared through timidity, for I have nothing to fear. They can only take away my life, which is of but little value when deprived of all its comforts, all that is dear to me, and nothing surrounding me but the most piercing distress.

I hope the eyes of the people will be opened, that they will see how easy it is for some designing, wicked men to spread false reports, raise suspicions and jealousies in the minds of the populace and enrage them against the innocent. But if [they are] guilty, this is not the way to proceed. The laws of our country are open to punish those who have offended. This destroying all peace and order of the community—*all will feel its effects.* And I hope all will see how easily the people may be deluded, enflamed, and carried away with madness against an innocent man.

1. TH to William Bollan, [Sept. 1765], MA, XXV, 151–152; TH to Richard Jackson, Aug. 30, 1765, in James K. Hosmer, *The Life of Thomas Hutchinson* (Boston and N.Y., 1896), pp. 91–94; FB to Earl of Halifax, Aug. 31, 1765, Bernard Papers, IV, 149–152; FB's "Observations on the Proceedings . . .," CO5/755/573–574. TH's official valuation of his losses is based on an exhaustive enumeration of the entire contents of the house which he sent to Secretary of State Conway on Oct. 27, 1765: *ibid.*, 372–380.

I pray GOD give us better hearts![2]

People flocked to see the ruins: Hutchinson estimated that ten thousand in all came to look; and they took away a sense of alarm for the security of their property and lives. The best friends of government and law, he reported, were "intimidated and utterly dispirited." Fears of general anarchy swept through the town and province. "It was now become a war of plunder," Governor Bernard wrote, "of general leveling and taking away the distinction of rich and poor." The customs house and the residences of "some of the most respectable persons in the government" would go next, it was said. The attorney general, Hutchinson wrote confidentially, simply disappeared for ten days after receiving a threat of treatment similar to Hutchinson's, and an unknown number of others followed him after taking steps to secure their goods.[3]

What had caused the riot? Resistance to the Stamp Act had generally been violent; and individuals, especially the would-be stamp distributors, had commonly been attacked.[4] But no one in America had been as deliberately and savagely assaulted as Hutchinson, though he had not been appointed a stamp master and though, as he said, he had opposed the Stamp Act. What was the meaning and what would be the ultimate effect of the attack?

People groped for explanations. Some said that intercepted letters had revealed villainy on Hutchinson's part that had otherwise been hidden. Governor Bernard noted, among other causes, the im-

2. FB to Lords of Trade, Nov. 30, 1765, in Quincy, *Reports of Cases*, p. 416n (the complete letter is in Bernard Papers, IV, 174) and pp. 170–173. Typical of the general shocked reaction is Jane Mecom's comment to her brother, Benjamin Franklin, that Hutchinson's suffering "was never equalled in any nation, our Saviour's only excepted; and like Him, I am told he bore it praying for his enemies at the instant they were persecuting him." She suggested that Franklin and TH should compare notes and "console one another." Jane Mecom to Benjamin Franklin, Boston, Dec. 30, 1765, in Carl Van Doren, ed., *Letters of Benjamin Franklin and Jane Mecom* (Princeton, Princeton University Press, 1950), pp. 86–87. For the later relationship between TH and Franklin, see below, Chap. VII.

3. TH to Richard Jackson, Sept. 1765, MA, XXV, 150; FB to Halifax, Aug. 31, 1765, Bernard Papers, IV, 155. On Sept. 7 Bernard wrote again to Halifax on the likelihood of anarchy when the Stamp Act went into effect if "persons of property and consideration" did not unite in support of government; in the "anarchy and confusion which will ensue, necessity will soon oblige and justify an insurrection of the poor against the rich, those that want the necessities of life against those that have them." *Ibid.*, pp. 158ff.

4. Edmund S. Morgan and Helen M. Morgan, *The Stamp Act Crisis* (Chapel Hill, University of North Carolina Press, 1953), chaps. viii–xi.

portance of the fact that the level of violence in Boston had been raised by the merging of the so-called North End and South End gangs in earlier agitations. Hutchinson himself observed that the day before the riot the Reverend Jonathan Mayhew had preached an inflammatory sermon, not the first of his career, on the text "I would they were even cut off which trouble you," and years later in his *History* he recorded that one of the rioters confessed "that he was excited to [the riot] by this sermon, and that he thought he was doing God service." So too Hutchinson noted that the rioters had been inflamed by a dozen pipes of wine they had found in his cellar, and in addition he pointed out the attraction to the rioters of destroying *his* house, which was private property, rather than the governor's, which was public property and which one way or another the town as a whole would have to replace.[5] But none of this, he knew, sufficiently explained what had happened on August 26 nor the growing hostility to him generally that had developed in provincial politics during the previous five years and of which that riot had been the destructive culmination.

The fierceness of the resistance to the Stamp Act generally had taken him by surprise, as it had Franklin and other experienced and observant politicians. Not that violence as such was a new experience for any of them. There had been violence before in Boston—frequently, in fact. As well as any man in Massachusetts, Hutchinson knew the force of inflamed mobs and shared the widespread fear of disorder in the fluid society of colonial America. Nor was this the first time that challenges to English authority had been made. But nothing had prepared him for the wave of disorders that swept like a firestorm over America in the summer of 1765. Two months before the destruction of his house, he wrote that the populace was receiving the Stamp Act "as decently as could be expected. . . . The act will execute itself. . . . The scarcity of money will be the greatest difficulty."[6]

5. TH to Jackson, Sept. 1765, MA, XXVI, 150; FB to John Pownall, Nov. 26, 1765, New England Papers (Sparks MSS, 10), I, 97–98, Houghton Library, Harvard University; *History of Massachusetts-Bay*, III, 89; Bernard Bailyn, "Religion and Revolution: Three Biographical Studies," *Perspectives in American History*, 4 (1970), 113ff.; TH to Thomas Pownall, Aug. 31, 1765, MA, XXVI, 149; TH to H. S. Conway, Oct. 1, 1765, MA, XXVI, 155–156.
6. TH to Richard Jackson, June 5, 1765, MA, XXVI, 140.

Somehow, in ways he did not understand, the world had greatly changed. While in formal terms he had reached a point of public eminence close to his highest aspirations, he had also become the target of a political opposition more passionate, less rational, and less manageable than anything he had known before. From time to time, even in the years before the Stamp Act, it occurred to him that he was in the midst of a revolution that would destroy the British empire and the structure of public life as he had known it. But he dismissed such fears as irrational and hence groundless. The colonists, he confidently informed alarmists in the late fifties, "must be stark blind if they could not see that an independence upon Great Britain must prove their ruin, and therefore they would not aim at it for centuries to come."[7] But the problem of what seemed to be irrational opposition to constituted authority would not disappear, nor would the personal animosity that accounted for the destruction of his property. The political opposition was in its essential characteristics new, and Hutchinson was fated to be its victim.

ii

The set of circumstances that by 1765 would make Hutchinson the primary victim of the developing revolution in Massachusetts began to form in the mid-1750's and especially during the brief governorship of Thomas Pownall (1757–1760). It was then that the structure of what would become Revolutionary politics in Massachusetts, and Hutchinson's unique role in it, first took shape; and one must glance back to Hutchinson's career in this late colonial period to understand the explosion that rocked his world in 1765 and the animosity against him that grew steadily thereafter.

Until 1757 Hutchinson had been one of a number of establishment figures who knew how to find their way successfully through the paths of factional intrigue. As a young man he had had Governor Belcher's favor when that native son had been governor, and when in 1740 Belcher had been dislodged by a band of rivals intriguing in London, Hutchinson had gravitated to his successor, the ambitious

---

7. TH to Thomas Pownall, March 8, 1766, MA, XXVI, 215 (for a somewhat different phrasing in an earlier draft of the same letter, see *ibid.*, p. 207).

and well-connected English lawyer, William Shirley.[8] For almost two decades thereafter Hutchinson had remained a leader of Governor Shirley's unusually stable political coalition. He had been appointed to local offices by Shirley, had risen to the Council under his patronage, and had taken on a peculiar, informal role of influence during the early years of the Seven Years War as a coordinator of the war effort, to which he was deeply committed, when Shirley himself had been drawn into the high command of British military operations in North America.[9]

By 1756 Hutchinson had emerged as the prime figure in Shirley's administration and the governor's chief agent for military affairs in Massachusetts. When Shirley left America in that year to defend his weakening interests in England, Hutchinson became the quasi-official liaison in the colony to the new commander in chief of British forces, Lord Loudoun, with whom, as with his successor General Abercromby, he worked devotedly to bring the Bay Colony and the adjoining provinces to full support of the war. Communicating with Loudoun over the head of the aged and ineffective lieutenant governor, Spencer Phips, with "no other design . . . than to promote the service and approve myself," Hutchinson worked in every way he could to stimulate troop recruitment, procure supplies, and coordinate efforts with other colonies. His views of Britain's and America's stake in the international war were imaginative—"the affairs of America are become very extensive and the several parts of them great and important"—and his frustration with the inferiority of the military commanders sent to the American theater grew intense as successive campaigns faltered and failed. "What we want is one great genius to direct and conduct [American affairs]," he wrote in August 1758. "This, like the sun in the heavens, would spread its influences. But they at home either do not see the necessity of it or they have it not to send us." But though his perspective as an amateur military strategist was broad and his frustration with

8. John A. Schutz, "Succession Politics in Massachusetts, 1730–1741," *W.M.Q.*, 3d ser., 15 (1958), 508–520. Hutchinson's transition in loyalty had been swift: he left for England in 1740 in the interest of Governor Belcher and returned in the company of Governor Shirley. Jonathan Belcher to Richard Waldron, Nov. 30, 1741, MHS *Colls.*, 6th ser., VII (1894), 549.

9. John A Schutz, *William Shirley* (Chapel Hill, University of North Carolina Press, 1961), esp. pp. 168ff.; John J. Waters and John A. Schutz, "Patterns of Massachusetts Colonial Politics . . .," *W.M.Q.*, 3d ser., 24 (1967), 550n.

successive military failures intense, he made no effort to intrude himself into grand planning, devoting himself rather to the humble, complicated, and wearing task of coordinating the general strategy, such as it was, with the minutiae of local factionalism. So, in 1757, he confidentially drafted for Lord Loudoun a message for him to send to the Massachusetts General Court chiding the colony "in a language acceptable to our people" for its ineffectual effort in raising troops for the Crown Point campaign of the previous year; reported on the intricate relation between troop recruitment and local political rewards and punishments; warned of the colony's excessive appointment of commissioned officers; explained the relation between possible military appropriations and the limits of local taxation; and, when Lieutenant Governor Phips fell ill and weakened, pleaded for the quick appointment of a successor since, in the absence of both governor and lieutenant governor, the executive authority in the colony would devolve on the Council, and that, he explained to Loudoun, would mean the end of the colony's effective prosecution of the war. For these important services Lord Loudoun was grateful, and he marked Hutchinson for official advancement. When Phips died in 1757 Hutchinson received from Loudoun the promise of a "personal reward" for his efforts, a commitment Shirley's successor as governor, for his own reasons, soon honored.[10]

Governor Thomas Pownall, who elevated Hutchinson to the lieutenant governorship and with whom Hutchinson would struggle, directly or indirectly, for the rest of his life, is one of the most interesting minor figures of the Revolution; and his career forms a counterpoint to Hutchinson's. A bachelor not yet thirty-five years of age when he arrived as governor, vain, short-tempered, and ruthlessly ambitious, he had powerful connections in London through his older brother John, who had been secretary of the Board of Trade for a decade. In a series of maneuvers that began in 1754, Thomas Pownall had used all of his influence to dislodge Shirley

10. Stanley M. Pargellis, *Lord Loudoun in North America* (New Haven, Yale University Press, 1933), pp. 214, 216; Gipson, *British Empire,* VII, 93–94, 164, 316, 321; TH to Lord Loudoun, March 7 and Jan. 21, 1757, Photostat Collection, MHS (Hutchinson's letters to Loudoun in this collection, which are copies of originals in the Huntington Library, express his attitude to the empire, and to American politics in relation to it, extremely well); TH to Israel Williams, Aug. 11, 1758, J. Davis Papers, MHS (the letter concludes with a sharp critique of the failings of the successive commanders in chief).

from both the military command and the governorship. When he arrived in Boston as governor, therefore, he was well known to be an enemy of the controlling Shirleyan group that had actively supported the war. Three consequences followed almost inescapably: first, Pownall became an active political partisan of the former opposition forces in the colony that were increasingly localist and populist-libertarian; second, both because of this political affiliation and because he hoped to succeed to the military high command himself, he fell out with successive commanders in chief, Loudoun, Abercromby, and Amherst; and finally, he turned for support to Hutchinson, hoping through him to reconcile the Shirleyan establishment.[11]

Pownall was no stranger to Hutchinson. They had corresponded earlier about military affairs, and Hutchinson had distrusted him from the start. Once installed in office in Boston, the young governor, Hutchinson recalled years later, cultivated Shirley's enemies, "not considering that most of them were enemies to the governor as well as to Mr. Shirley"—enemies, that is, to the office as well as to the person—and kept away from those who, in Hutchinson's view, had assured stability in the Massachusetts government for over a decade. At the very beginning of his administration Pownall embarrassed Hutchinson by insisting that he help remove William Bollan, Shirley's son-in-law, from the sensitive position of Massachusetts agent in London. Hutchinson had helped get Bollan appointed in the first place and had supported him over the years; he believed Bollan's representations in the capital could be relied on for accuracy and loyalty to the Massachusetts administration, and he flatly refused to desert his associates at "the caprice of the governor."[12]

The estrangement was quickly confirmed. When Pownall told

11. Pownall's career through the period of his governorship is traced in John A. Schutz's sympathetic biography, *Thomas Pownall, British Defender of American Liberty* (Glendale, Calif., Arthur H. Clark, 1951), pp. 15–180. The view presented here is quite different from Schutz's, though the information contained in his book has been taken into consideration, and closer to Waters and Schutz's "Massachusetts Colonial Politics," pp. 555–558. The same years are covered, with some excellent documentation, in Charles A. W. Pownall, *Thomas Pownall . . .* (London, 1908), pp. 1–163.

12. Malcolm Freiberg, "Thomas Hutchinson: The First Fifty Years (1711–1761)," *W.M.Q.*, 3d ser., 15 (1958), 53; Eg. MSS, 2664, pp. 63–64 from end; *Diary and Letters*, I, 60; *History of Massachusetts-Bay*, III, 41–42; Waters and Schutz, "Massachusetts Colonial Politics," pp. 550, 556–557; TH to Israel Williams, Feb. 10, March 28, and Oct. 28, 1759, and March 4, 1760, Williams Papers, MHS.

Hutchinson that he had decided to recommend him for the lieutenant governorship, Hutchinson at first declined on the ground that he might not be able to hold that post and remain a member of the Council, where, he pointed out, support for the government was particularly important and particularly needed—a forceful argument, Pownall confessed to Halifax, "that must ever lay me under obligations" and which he proposed to solve by declining actually to deliver the commission to Hutchinson until he himself should leave the province physically, which in fact he never did in the two years of his active tenure. After Hutchinson's appointment to the lieutenant governorship was finally announced, Pownall failed to support him in a dispute that arose with the councillor Sir William Pepperrell, who claimed the right to preside at the Council by virtue of his rank as baronet, a right that had traditionally been accorded to the lieutenant governor. The clash with Pepperrell was "a most trifling affair in itself," Hutchinson admitted, but it made him wish he had never accepted the lieutenant governorship, for if he insisted on his right to preside he would alienate a significant group of merchants with influence in the Council, but if he failed to do so, "it will be said I had not spirit enough to assert the right the King's commission gave me." A vote of the Council, but not a word from Pownall, in the end gave him the precedence he felt himself entitled to.[13]

Pownall continued in other ways to slight Hutchinson while using him—to round up deserters, to obtain housing for returning veterans and provide them with supplies, and to rally the votes of the Shirleyans—and Hutchinson continued to distrust the governor's judgment and purposes and to withhold his full support. But the fundamental differences between them grew out of Pownall's close affiliation with the populist elements in the colony, whose interests, material and political, and whose ideological sensibilities led them increasingly, if not to oppose the war effort directly, at least to evade the strict enforcement of trade regulations that had been imposed to support the war by the King's first minister, William Pitt.

These popular leaders were merchants, who profited by government contracts for military supplies but fought the embargoes and

13. Pownall to Earl of Halifax, Sept. 4, 1757, Peter Force Papers, ser. 9, box 7, Library of Congress; TH to Israel Williams, June 5, 1758, Williams Papers; Eg. MSS, 2664, pp. 64–65 from end.

other wartime trade regulations, and a few non-merchant politicians who warned of the danger of tyranny in the growing influence of the military on public policy. Pownall sought them out, entertained them well, appointed them to offices of trust, and solicited their support; he also joined with them in business schemes, especially land speculation in eastern Maine. As his involvement with these former opposition figures grew, his difficulties with, and alienation from, the successive military commanders increased. By 1759 he had broken with Abercromby, who charged him with deliberately undermining the war effort and, according to Hutchinson's later recollections, with tampering with official mail. Bogged down in local factionalism, dependent on Hutchinson but resentful of him, vulnerable to charges of malfeasance in office, and frustrated by his lack of influence in the higher councils of the now increasingly successful war, he appealed to London to be relieved, and on June 3, 1760, he left America permanently. He was bruised, resentful of the Shirleyans whom he had tried to use, allied to the group that would lead America to Revolution, and convinced of his own capacity, so far frustrated, to play an effective role in Anglo-American affairs.[14]

Pownall's administration was a brief interlude between the long, late-colonial era of William Shirley, which had nourished the young Thomas Hutchinson's success in trade and politics, and the disastrous decade of Sir Francis Bernard, in which Hutchinson's failure began; but though brief, it was a critical interlude. For in these years Hutchinson's devotion to the welfare of the empire and his identification of America's well-being with the strength of Great Britain had become an intense commitment.[15] At the same time his differences with the momentarily triumphant opposition forces had become charged with more than ordinary political meaning. They were of course his rivals in quite traditional factional contests for

14. Schutz, *Pownall*, pp. 153ff.; Waters and Schutz, "Massachusetts Colonial Politics," pp. 557–558. Pownall's most active participation in the war effort lay in supervising the defense of the Maine frontier; the key fort there was named after him. He knew the region well and actively promoted its settlement. In Dec. 1759 the proprietors of the Kennebec Purchase granted him 500 acres in the shire town of "Pownallborough" and ever after he retained an interest in the possibilities of land speculation and settlement there. In the 1760's he corresponded with his successor, Governor Bernard, on the subject. Fannie S. Chase, *Wiscasset in Pownalborough* (Wiscasset, Me., p.p., 1941), pp. 61–65. The towns of Pownal, Maine, and Pownal, Vermont still bear his name. On Hutchinson's later recollection of Pownall's break with Abercromby, see below, p. 369.

15. For General Wolfe's recognition of TH's "zeal for the public service," see Wolfe to William Pitt, June 6, 1759, cited in Gipson, *British Empire*, VII, 317n.

the control of public offices. But beyond that, he had been shocked by their pursuit of private gain at the expense of the general welfare, which he took to mean the welfare of the pan-Atlantic polity that had protected the infant colonies for a century and a half. He distrusted the glib libertarianism by which they justified their resistance to appeals for wartime sacrifices. And he felt a danger in their seemingly deliberate misrepresentation of the motives of those like himself who argued that constraint and regulation in trade and politics were necessary if America was to survive and flourish in a world of warring states. None of this was publicly expressed, nor did he privately draw general conclusions from these growing apprehensions. But within a few months of the arrival of the new governor, Francis Bernard, he found his worst fears justified.

iii

In later years, in exile in England, when he saw much of Francis Bernard, then crippled by a stroke and living in retirement on a government pension, Hutchinson felt warmly toward his former superior; but in the decade of Bernard's governorship, though he served him loyally and was well rewarded for his service, he had cause again and again to resent him, both personally and politically. Bernard was the ideal type of the patronage appointee in the first British empire.[16] A well-educated barrister whose only administrative or political office in England had been the recordership of the town of Boston in Lincolnshire, he had practiced law until the financial needs of his ten children drove him to seek more lucrative employment in the colonies. Through the patronage of his wife's influential uncle, Viscount Barrington, who was secretary at war almost continuously from 1755 to 1778 and connected with the most powerful figures in the early ministries of George III, he was

16. There is no modern biography of Bernard, but useful information in his son Thomas's *Life of Sir Francis Bernard* . . . (London, 1790) and in the sketch in *Diary and Letters*, II, 320–323. The events of his governorship in Massachusetts are chronicled exhaustively in Leslie J. Thomas, "Partisan Politics in Massachusetts during Governor Bernard's Administration, 1760–1770" (Ph.D. diss., University of Wisconsin, 1960). The account that follows in this and successive chapters is largely based on the Bernard Papers, a selection from which appears as *The Barrington-Bernard Correspondence* . . . *1760–1770*, ed. Edward Channing and A. C. Coolidge (Cambridge, 1912), and on the Hutchinson MSS.

appointed to the governorship of New Jersey in 1758, and then, feeling socially and culturally isolated there and seeking a better-paying position, managed to have himself transferred, at the age of fifty, to Massachusetts. He was a decent man who had simple, uncomplicated desires: peace and quiet, the respect of those he ruled, some comradeship in literary matters, appointments for his six sons, and a substantial income—from salary, from fees, and from lucrative investments. As far as he knew the prospects in Massachusetts were excellent. "I am assured," he wrote shortly before he arrived in Boston, "that I may depend upon a quiet and easy administration. I shall have no points of government to dispute about, no schemes of self-interest to pursue. The people are well disposed to live upon good terms with the governor and with one another, and I hope I shall not want to be directed by a junto or supported by a party, but that I shall find there as I have done here that plain dealing, integrity, and disinterestedness make the best system of policy." True, he had heard from Pownall the discouraging news (along with accounts of investment opportunities in northern New England land) that the total income of the Massachusetts governor, from salary and "all advantages and contingencies," was only £1200 sterling; but he thought he could live more cheaply in Boston than in many other places, and in addition he would have far better opportunities for educating and providing jobs for his children there than he had had in Perth Amboy. Moreover, in Boston, "perhaps the most polished and scientific town in America," he was sure he would find the "refined conversation and the amusements that arise from letters, arts, and sciences . . . many very conversable men, tolerable music, and other amusements to which I had bid adieu not without regret." Finally, he had heard that the Massachusetts governor had (in the fortress to which he would repeatedly flee in the years to come) "a very pretty place to retire to, a pleasant apartment in Castle William, which stands in an island about three miles from the town at the entrance of the Bay."[17]

He was thus a well-disposed and ordinary man, with ordinary

17. FB to Lord Barrington, April 19, 1760, *Bernard Papers*, I, 201–203. Bernard had originally expected an income of at least £1500 (*ibid.*, pp. 194–196). But he had received a warning, from Welbore Ellis in London, who told him that he was at the head of a people "difficult to manage, and this difficulty principally arises from an absurdity in the situation of the governor, who is to depend in a great measure for his subsistence on those whom he is instructed from hence to contradict and control." *Ibid.*, IX, 116.

desires, but he was no politician and he was innocent of the arts of governance. "Open in his behavior," Hutchinson wrote of him, "regardless of mere forms, and inattentive to the fashionable arts of engaging mankind," he was destined by his manner alone to offend the sensibilities of the proud Bostonians.[18] But it was not simply a question of manner and sensibilities. He was determined to get every penny to which his office entitled him. It was this mainly that led him to his fatal decision to appoint Hutchinson to the vacant chief justiceship; and it was this—well before the Stamp Act raised fundamental questions of principle—that first pitched Hutchinson into open conflict with the Pownallite faction of merchants and populist politicians.

Hutchinson had not sought the chief justiceship, which fell vacant when the incumbent, Stephen Sewall, died five weeks after Bernard arrived in Boston, nor had he attempted to solicit Bernard's patronage or to forge a political alliance with him. He had declined even to offer the new governor his judgment of the leading local politicians: "if he be a wise man he will suspend his judgment of men . . . until he can settle it either from a personal acquaintance with them or else—which is the next best way of doing it—from their general characters [i.e., reputations]." He contented himself with assuring the new governor of his support and filling him in on the business pending in the Assembly. But if Hutchinson did not seek Bernard's support, Bernard had reason to seek his. Though the Assembly quickly granted the new governor a substantial salary and then gave him the gift of Mt. Desert Island, off the southeast coast of Maine, he quickly discovered the difficulty of maintaining the "quiet and easy" administration he had expected. The province, he found, was "divided into parties so nearly equal that it would have been madness for me to have put myself at the head of either of them." In this situation, "management and intrigue," he wrote to Barrington, were required to preserve the force of government and at the same time convey at least "the appearance" of respect for the colonists' cherished liberties, "of which they formed high and sometimes unconstitutional ideas."[19]

18. TH to Richard Jackson, [May 5, 1765], MA, XXVI, 138.
19. TH to Israel Williams, Aug. 25, 1760, Williams Papers; FB to TH, June 15, 1760, and to Barrington, May 1, 1762, Bernard Papers, I, 264, II, 189. For the history of the

The appointment of the new chief justice was crucial to the success of this delicate balance. For it was the superior court in the end that would largely determine whether the interest of the state would be sustained in general, and in particular whether the trade regulations would be enforced, and whether therefore the governor would receive his statutory third of the income from forfeited goods. In the immediately preceding years the superior court, influenced particularly by the tough-minded associate justice, Chambers Russell, who also served as admiralty court judge, had been forceful in assigning customs cases to the admiralty courts, where the judges were likely to convict if the evidence warranted it, rather than to the common law courts, where juries were likely to acquit. The superior court had recently been willing, too, to issue writs of assistance mobilizing public support for customs officers searching for contraband goods. The problem for Bernard was how to assure the continuation of this essential support for government.

He knew that Governor Shirley had promised the next court vacancy to the venerable Barnstable lawyer James Otis, Sr., then speaker of the House and, in Shirley's time, a political colleague of Hutchinson's. But word reached Bernard that Otis's appointment at this juncture would be inadvisable, perhaps because his brilliant but unstable son James, Jr., was leading the family into doubtful political alliances and was reluctant to use his office as deputy advocate-general of the vice-admiralty court to prosecute violations of the navigation laws. Hutchinson's commitment to maintaining close ties between England and America, on the other hand, was beyond question, as was his reputation with all parties for integrity, industry, judiciousness, and devotion to public service.

The day after Sewall died "several gentlemen" (Bernard said they were "the best men in the government") told Hutchinson they were proposing him for the vacancy. He was pleasantly surprised, but he immediately expressed what he called "a diffidence of my own abilities," for he was no lawyer and he was not at all certain "that it would be advisable for me to undertake so great a trust." He re-

---

Mount Desert grant (Feb. 27, 1762), whose confirmation in England took nine years and from which Bernard received no profit whatever (it was confiscated by the state of Massachusetts in 1779), see William O. Sawtelle, "Sir Francis Bernard and His Grant of Mount Desert," *Publications of the Colonial Society of Massachusetts*, XXIV (*Transactions*, 1920–1922), 197–254.

peated these same doubts "of my abilities to give the country satisfaction" when young James Otis called on him to seek his support for the elder Otis's appointment; and while he did not promise the Otises his help and said merely that the whole question was new to him and that he would have to think about it, he went out of his way to praise the elder Otis and to register his own lack of enthusiasm for the appointment. By the end of the month Hutchinson was still doubtful of his own qualifications; he was "so diffident of his own fitness," his brother-in-law Andrew Oliver wrote confidentially, that while he might accept the position if it were thrust on him, he would not take the ordinary steps to seek it. And his passivity persisted even though most of the judiciary assured him of their support. When, after a month, Bernard finally broached the subject to him, explaining that "the major voices seemed to be in my favor," Hutchinson replied that while recognizing the importance of the position, he knew "the peculiar disadvantages I should be under" in following so distinguished a jurist as Sewall. And when some weeks later Bernard told him that he had definitely decided to appoint him and indicated that even if he refused he would not turn to Otis, Hutchinson "still expressed my doubts of the expediency of it, and assured [Bernard] that if he thought proper to appoint some other person I would take no offense, but would endeavor every way in my power, consistent with the public interest, to contribute to the ease of his administration."[20]

Bernard was well aware of the problems: years later he would apologize to Lord Mansfield for having appointed a chief justice "not . . . bred to the law";[21] but he knew that the essential qualifications were as much political and intellectual as strictly legal, and he

20. This account is largely reconstructed from Hutchinson's recollection of the details of the appointment, which he published in the *Boston News-Letter*, April 7, 1763; nothing in that account is contradicted by any of the other explanations, including the younger Otis's (*Boston Gazette*, April 4 and 11), and it makes clear the ambiguity that lay behind so much of the subsequent trouble: that Otis, Jr., understood Hutchinson's honest but cautious remark that he was not seeking the appointment to mean that he would not accept it. John J. Waters, Jr., *The Otis Family in Provincial and Revolutionary Massachusetts* (Chapel Hill, University of North Carolina Press, 1968), p. 119. The letter that FB promised to write to Lord Halifax explaining his motives in appointing Hutchinson (Nov. 17, 1760, Bernard Papers, I, 283) has not been found. Six years later he did explain it, to Lord Shelburne (Dec. 22, 1766, *ibid.*, IV, 276), and that account is compatible with Hutchinson's. Oliver's comment on TH's diffidence is in Oliver to Israel Williams, Sept. 30, 1760, Williams Papers.
21. *Diary and Letters*, I, 195.

could count on Hutchinson's diligence in perfecting his knowledge of the law. So Hutchinson, still concerned about his lack of technical qualifications and having refused to solicit actively for the appointment but always eager for advancement, prestige, and a major public role, accepted.[22] His appointment was announced on November 13, and on December 30 his commission was issued.

iv

From one point of view the appointment was simply a projection on to a higher plane of Hutchinson's key role in the Shirley and Pownall administrations. But in a larger perspective it was an altogether new and crucial development, for as much as any single event until his appointment to the governorship ten years later it shaped the part he would play and the responses to him in the factional and ultimately the ideological politics of the time. Not that the appointment created an immediate uproar. Though it may not have met with "the general approbation of the whole province," as Bernard claimed it did, it undoubtedly infused new energy and efficiency into the work of the superior court and helped strengthen law enforcement in general throughout the province.[23] But it also began the transformation of Hutchinson's reputation from that of an unimpeachable if conservative leader of the Anglo-American establishment to that of a sinister manipulator of secret forces. For no matter how sound, cautious, and wise Hutchinson's decisions as the leading jurist would prove to be, his appointment generated animosities on the part of those who stood to lose by the full enforcement of the law, and it bred deep suspicions in those who were especially sensitive to ideological currents.

22. Though non-lawyers were commonly appointed to the bench, Hutchinson himself remained sensitive on the subject of professional credentials, and went out of his way to describe the pains he took to train himself in the technicalities of the law. TH to ———, Dec. 31, 1765, MA, XXVI, 190.

23. FB to Lord Shelburne, Dec. 22, 1766, Bernard Papers, IV, 276; FB to Lord Egremont, Oct. 25, 1763, *ibid.*, III, 100 (and in Bernard's *Select Letters* . . . [London, 1774], letter 1), attributing his success in enforcing the navigation laws to "the steadiness of the judges of the superior court." Later Lord Hillsborough quite formally recognized Hutchinson's "ability, resolution, and integrity," as chief justice, in enforcing the law— a judgment that undoubtedly influenced his later determination to appoint Hutchinson to the governorship. Hillsborough to FB, July 30, 1768, CO5/757/244.

The general transformation of Hutchinson's reputation proceeded gradually in the months and years that followed his appointment to the chief justiceship, but John Adams and James Otis, Jr., who would ultimately shape opinion most powerfully, reached immediate conclusions. The 1760's were years in which the Massachusetts bar reached a high point of professionalization; its practitioners were exceptionally conscious of their craft and proud of their skills —and none more so than the twenty-five-year-old apprentice John Adams, struggling, as Hutchinson's appointment was being discussed, with Hale's *History of the Common Law*, Salkeld's Reports, Hawkins's *Pleas*, Fortescue, Justinian, and Coke. He was outraged by the appointment, and concluded instantly that only corrupt and sinister influences could explain it. For the law in its nature is esoteric, he wrote with indignation born of pride and of his own anxieties; its rules are numerous, complex, and difficult to extract from the deep lore of history. Mastery of the law takes "industry and genius employed from early youth":

a man whose youth and spirits and strength have been spent in husbandry, merchandise, politics, nay in science or literature, will never master so immense and involved a science; for it may be taken for a never failing maxim that youth is the only time for laying the foundation of a great improvement in any science or profession, and that an application in advanced years, after the mind is crowded, the attention divided or dissipated, and the memory in part lost, will make but a tolerable artist at best.[24]

Adams never forgot the outrage he felt at this elevation of a layman to the chief justiceship, so thwarting, insulting, and humiliating to his excruciatingly sensitive self-esteem. For years the appointment would provide him with an invaluable psychological device for handling impediments to his passionate ambitions. An appointment so unmerited, so perverse, and so unjust to those like himself who were sacrificing their lives to the law could only be the result of dangerous, secret forces whose power would no doubt otherwise be felt and that would otherwise block the aspirations of powerless but honest and able new men.

24. Adams, *Diary and Autobiography*, I, 168, On the general relationship between the rising professionalization of the practice of law and the Revolutionary movement, see Richard B. Morris, "Legalism *versus* Revolutionary Doctrine in New England," *New England Quarterly*, 4 (1931), 195–215.

Otis helped to substantiate these fears and to publicize this affront to the dignity of "old practitioners at the bar." Like Adams, Otis too registered shock that the new chief justice was "bred a merchant," but that was not the main burden of his response. Nor was it simply the rage of wounded pride at his family's humiliation, though that explains his pronouncement, when Hutchinson's name was first discussed, that neither he nor his father would ever give up their claim to the appointment, and his public threat "with oaths," as Bernard later testified, that " 'if his father was not appointed judge, he would set the whole province in a flame, though he perished in the attempt' "—a remark that circulated widely through the province. Otis was an extraordinarily perceptive intellectual, and while he tore and dove and raged in half-lunatic indignation, he was capable, as perhaps no one else of the time, of seeing the deep issues and of relating them to practical and personal politics. Crankish, unreliable if not dishonest, outlandish if not at times clinically mad, and lacking as yet a firm political base from which to operate, he not only kept up a pounding series of attacks on Hutchinson in the public prints for "engrossing places of power and profit for himself, his family and dependents," but brought the weight of these attacks to bear on what would prove to be a most sensitive constitutional point.[25]

The issue, Otis insisted, was not merely the engrossing of political offices but the relationship among these offices. Plural officeholding was nothing new—it was as common in New England as it was in old England—nor was the doctrine of the separation of powers in its modern form yet felt to impose limits on officeholding. But Otis, moving ahead of the leading ideas of his time, thinking in his curious and impressive way in terms of circularities, logical contradictions, and the inner flows of forces within institutions, tore into Hutchinson not merely for greedily accumulating a plurality of "lucrative places" but for occupying positions that were incompatible with each other. "The office of the judge of probate is incompatible

25. Waters, *Otis Family*, p. 119; James Otis, Jr., to Jasper Mauduit, Oct. 28, 1762, in *Jasper Mauduit, Agent . . . 1762–1765* (MHS *Colls.*, LXXIV, 1918) p. 77; FB to Lord Shelburne, Dec. 22, 1766, Bernard Papers, IV, 276; *Boston News-Letter*, April 7, 1763. For Otis's explanation and extenuation of the famous threat, see *Boston Gazette*, April 11, 1763. I have attempted to sketch Otis's erratic genius in dealing with the complex movement of ideas in the 1760's in *Pamphlets of the American Revolution, 1750–1776* (Cambridge, Harvard University Press, 1965——), I (1750–1765), 409–417, 546–552.

with that of chief justice, and the commission for the latter is in law a *supersedeas* of the former. . . . And all acts and decrees made below after such superior commission are illegal and void. There is no point of law clearer than this." Hutchinson, Otis pointed out, was a dominant figure in the executive by virtue of being lieutenant governor, in the legislature as a councillor ("I have long thought it . . . a great grievance that the chief justice should have a seat in the Council and consequently so great a share of influence in making those very laws he is appointed to execute upon the lives and property of the people"), and in the judiciary as chief justice. The mere plundering of the public treasury in this way by one man would be offensive, Otis said, but plural officeholding of this sort was more than that: it was unconstitutional and threatened nothing less than tyranny. He had to admit that since all of the other superior court justices also had seats on the Council, Hutchinson alone could not be blamed. But the fact that the other high court judges also held lesser judicial posts; the fact that the lieutenant governor had executive power only when the governor left the province and in any case received no salary; and the fact that all of Hutchinson's offices put together yielded less per annum than the chief justiceship of New York—all of this meant little to Otis and to those like Adams and Oxenbridge Thacher who quickly endorsed his arguments. "Mixed monarchy," Otis agreed, was, as everyone knew, the most perfect form of government, but—what everyone did not know— fundamental to it was the separation of legislative and executive powers, and without this, free government would dissolve. Montesquieu was right: "when the legislative and executive powers are united in the same person, or in the same body of magistrates (or nearly so) there can be no liberty because (just and great) apprehensions may arise lest the same monarch or senate (or junto) should enact *tyrannical* laws to execute them in a *tyrannical* manner." Within a few months of Hutchinson's appointment to the high bench Otis's attacks, cast in these terms and publicized again and again, became a blistering indictment.[26]

Otis did not at this point, however, carry the public with him. He was largely isolated in these early efforts to focus public indignation

26. *Boston Gazette,* April 4 and 11, 1763; Ellen E. Brennan, *Plural Office-Holding in Massachusetts, 1760–1780* (Chapel Hill, University of North Carolina Press, 1945), pp. 28–49.

specifically on Hutchinson, and it would be years before the modern doctrine of the separation of functioning powers, which Otis so clearly drew from the ambiguous and commonly misread pages of *The Spirit of the Laws,* would be generally accepted.[27] Hutchinson continued to preside at the Council and to perform his other public functions without effective contest. But the change in his reputation had begun. The controversy over his appointment and Otis's endless attacks created a mood of suspicion and a sense that he was in some way deeply corrupt. It would thereafter take an unusual sensitivity to public moods and great skill in handling ideologically charged situations to prevent these suspicions from growing into a general public condemnation. But such capacities were lacking in Hutchinson. Indeed, his finest qualities—respect for facts, prudence, candor, and scrupulous adherence to the spirit as well as the letter of the law—worked against him, tending to substantiate suspicions of his motives and of the charges flung against him. The nature of this self-intensifying process, which would first explode in the Stamp Act riot and ultimately climax in the disaster of his governorship, was revealed in a series of important episodes that took place between 1761 and 1765.

v

The first such episode was the famous case of the writs of assistance, which came before the superior court almost as soon as Hutchinson took his seat on the bench. The episode not only served to fuse Adams's resentment at unmerited professional advancement with Otis's fear of monopolized power, but it brought all of this into conjunction with the hostilities of a significant part of the merchant community for whom strict enforcement of trade regulations was a threatening innovation.

Hutchinson was especially well informed on the problems of these general search warrants, and he was as much concerned to limit their use to the strict letter of the law as anyone in the colony. It had been he, in fact, in 1757, who had prevented the governor from

27. Bernard Bailyn, *The Ideological Origins of the American Revolution* (Cambridge, Harvard University Press, 1967), 273ff.; Gordon S. Wood, *The Creation of the American Republic, 1776–1787* (Chapel Hill, University of North Carolina Press, 1969), pp. 150–161, 446–453, 547–553.

issuing general warrants on his own authority, and as a result the power to grant these potentially dangerous instruments in Massachusetts had been confined to the superior court acting as a court of exchequer. He knew of the warrants' unquestioned legality in England and of their common use there, and he knew too that they had been issued to eight customs officers in Massachusetts before 1760 and used by them without public controversy. He was suspicious therefore of the motives of those who questioned their legality when the death of George II made their renewal mandatory, especially since the suit brought against their use was so obviously an act of vengeance by a deeply disaffected customs official, Benjamin Barrons, in collaboration with young Otis, representing merchants seeking immunity from prosecution for customs violations.[28]

For Hutchinson there was no issue in substance in the writs case but merely the need to demonstrate what he personally knew quite certainly from his own careful examination of the questions, that such standing general search warrants were valid in English law and had commonly been issued to customs officials in England; that their use in the colonies was specified in law; and that the proper agency to issue them was the superior court, since it was authorized to act as an exchequer court, which issued such writs in England. This was the law, and the only arguments that Hutchinson could conceive of as worthy of the court's consideration were queries directed to these points. No damages were claimed, no judgment was required. He could be accused of no wrong doing in his conduct of the hearing—there was almost nothing, right or wrong, that he was called upon to do. Yet he was immensely the loser by the case. For if the positive law was clear (and such doubts as were raised were quickly settled by queries to England), the higher law of "natural equity" was not, and it was to this that Otis, who had resigned his admiralty court post and now formally represented the merchant opposition, in the end directed his plea. It was the moral basis of the law, not the literal provisions, that primarily concerned him. "This writ," he charged, in words that John Adams, an eager attendant at the trial, recorded on the spot, "is against the funda-

28. L. Kinvin Wroth and Hiller B. Zobel, eds., *Legal Papers of John Adams* (Cambridge, Harvard University Press, 1965), II, 111, 113n. This essay by Wroth and Zobel is the most complete account of the issues involved in the writs case, and it presents all the important documents. For a more recent interpretation, focusing on Otis's role and his connections with the merchant group, see Waters, *Otis Family*, pp. 120ff.

mental principles of law. The privilege of house. A man who is quiet is as secure in his house as a prince in his castle," and no act of Parliament can contravene this privilege. "An act [of Parliament] against the constitution is void, an act against natural equity is void. . . . The executive courts must pass such acts into disuse"— precedents to the contrary notwithstanding, Adams later recalled him saying, for "ALL PRECEDENTS ARE UNDER THE CONTROL OF THE PRINCIPLES OF THE LAW."[29]

The *principles* of law? Who was to say what they were? Yet it was Otis's extravagant, trans-juridical claim that entered American awareness, not Hutchinson's scrupulous regard for the law as it existed. Fifty-six years later John Adams—as romantic in old age as he had been in youth—caught the inner, quasi-mythological meaning of the event in his famous description of the scene:

near the fire were seated five judges, with Lieutenant Governor Hutchinson at their head as chief justice, all in their new fresh robes of scarlet English cloth, in their broad bands, and immense judicial wigs [and against them James Otis,] a flame of fire! With the promptitude of classical allusions, a depth of research . . . a profusion of legal authorities, a prophetic glare of his eyes into futurity, and a rapid torrent of impetuous eloquence, he hurried away all before him . . . Every man of an [immense] crowded audience appeared to me to go away, as I did, ready to take up arms against writs of assistance. . . . Then and there the child Independence was born.

Hutchinson's mere presence as the highest embodiment of positive law in the face of a passionate assertion of the claims of "natural equity"—his identification in this dramatic episode with authority, legalism, force, and resistance to the appeal of the heart and the conscience—served to deepen his alienation from what was widely felt to be the liberating, meliorating, freshening spirit of the time and strengthened suspicions of his involvement in a widespread effort apparently under way to restrict the practice of a free, familiar mode of life.[30]

For in England in these same months early in the reign of George III and in the ministry of the Earl of Bute, it was beginning to be said that secret steps were being taken to subvert the constitu-

29. Wroth and Zobel, *Adams Legal Papers*, II, 125, 127–128, 144.
30. *Ibid.*, pp. 106, 107. For Bernard's association of Hutchinson's role in the writs case with the sacking of his house in 1765, see Quincy, *Reports of Cases*, p. 416n.

tion and destroy the liberties that Englishmen enjoyed. Partly a reflection in jealous eyes of the king's deep personal attachment to his favorite, Bute, "unknown, ungracious, and a Scot"; partly the product of calculated opposition tactics; but mainly a response to the sudden change in the structure of politics at the accession of George III by which the ruling coalition of the previous reign was abruptly denied access to power—these suspicions took root and grew wild, forming a natural background and lending a distinctive coloration to suspicions of government elsewhere in the British world, and especially in Massachusetts. Again it was Otis who pointed the way. When Hutchinson, stung raw by two years of attacks published in the newspapers, week in and week out after his appointment to the superior court, turned upon his attackers and charged them with attempting "for years together to disturb the peace of the whole province . . . and to endeavor to raise animosities and civil wars among ourselves," it was Otis, responding with uncanny prescience and with an unerring sense of future lines of force, who knew the best reply. If there was trouble, he wrote, Hutchinson had only himself to blame, for the cause was his "unreasonable and unbounded desires of power and profit." Could one not guess what Hutchinson's charges of "animosities and civil wars" portended? The effect of such accusations—though "I dare say His Honor never intended [it]"—was certainly clear; it was "to make the people of England look upon us in a very bad light, forward attempts to alter our constitution, and have a tendency to procure a standing army to dragoon us into passive obedience." Misrepresentation to the highest authorities of the motives of peaceful Americans, and false or exaggerated accusations of disruptive intents insinuated into a government "at home" that was itself suspect to some—what purpose could all of this serve but to solicit from abroad reinforcements for the power of the locally over-great, flushed with profits of office and fearful that popular vengeance would dislodge them from power? Naturally, every minor episode, every trivial disturbance, would be blown up to vast proportions. Why else, Otis asked, had Hutchinson advised Bernard to offer rewards for the apprehension of those exuberant "little boys and Negroes" who broke the townhouse windows when Boston authorities denied them "bonfires, squibs, and crackers" with which to celebrate the King's accession? Was it accidental that a stranger reading the governor's declaration on that trivial occasion "would mistake us all for a parcel of Jacobites, it being impossible to find by the proclamation that loyalty misguided was the occasion of this loss of glass to the public" and that the whole thing was simply the work of "children who could not be supposed to know the difference between Jacobite and Jebusite"? There was *purpose* in such an excessive response, and somehow it had to do with representations that could be made to the authorities "at home."[31]

And indeed it was certainly true that much in politics depended on links to "home"; much depended on how the colony was portrayed, on how its interests were represented, and how its people's motivations were described. The official agent, therefore, the representative chosen and paid by the Assembly to speak for the colony in England, was inescapably a significant figure in the structure of power, and his selection by the Assembly was a constant source of disagreement. One such controversy, following closely on the writs case and still in the wake of the reaction to Hutchinson's appointment to the high court, became especially fierce; and when Hutchinson entered the dispute directly, suspicions of his motives and of his ultimate aspirations grew darker.

He need not have entered the dispute at all; but the election of the agent was crucial to the balance of political forces as it affected him personally: it was critical to the maintenance of his own subnetwork of office and influence that was tied to the greater complex centered in London. Twice—in 1757 and 1760—Hutchinson had rescued the Massachusetts agency for the incumbent, William Bollan, Shirley's son-in-law, who since 1745 had served the Shirleyan establishment as agent; but when in 1762 Bollan was finally dismissed after a campaign in which he was represented as plotting to destroy the Congregational church, there was no prospect of rescuing him. The populist, Congregationalist majority in the House favored Jasper Mauduit, a London woolen draper and leading nonconformist as his successor; Bernard put up Richard Jackson, his personal representative in London, a well-connected lawyer of ambiguous religious affiliation who was a friend of Hutchinson's but not yet clearly his political ally, and agent for Connecticut, a colony whose

31. *Boston News-Letter,* April 7, 1763; *Boston Gazette,* April 11, 1763.

interests in part conflicted with those of Massachusetts. To Hutchinson and those closest to him, neither Mauduit nor Jackson was a suitable substitute for Bollan; neither could be relied on to secure the existing arrangement of politics as Bollan had done; both might easily disrupt the existing lines of influence that reached from Whitehall to the wilderness and that reinforced the structure of community life that Hutchinson knew. How, except by intervening at such critical points as this, could stability be maintained in this world of factional politics? When Hutchinson's own name was added to the list of candidates and was supported "by the whole strength of his men" he did not attempt to resist—though there is no reason to believe he could or would have accepted the appointment if it had been offered to him. But the rival factions panicked at this intrusion, fearing that Hutchinson had just enough support to defeat both Jackson and Mauduit in a three-way vote. They therefore combined forces, dropped Jackson as the weaker of the original candidates, and so secured Mauduit's appointment.[32]

Bernard was more than just annoyed. He had hoped by Jackson's appointment to have—in Otis's phrase—"a private agent of his own invested with a public character." He needed appointments for his sons; he needed confirmation of the gift he had received of Mt. Desert Island, which he was already attempting to settle; and he had plans in motion, some of them involving Jackson, to make a killing in Maine land and to do so on a grand scale by having the lands set off into a separate colony between Massachusetts and Nova Scotia. It took two more years of careful politicking on Bernard's part to arrange for Jackson's election as assistant to Mauduit and legal counsel to the agency (by which time Jackson had become George Grenville's secretary in the exchequer and an even more influential ally than before), and an additional year beyond that before he could finally get Jackson the agency appointment he had sought for him in 1762 and that Hutchinson's intrusion had deflected.[33]

For Otis and his allies in the Assembly, Hutchinson's intervention had been more threatening still. Otis's account of the dispute, writ-

32. Waters and Schutz, "Massachusetts Colonial Politics," pp. 556–557, 564; Thomas, "Partisan Politics," pp. 65–83.

33. Otis to Mauduit, Oct. 28, 1762, in *Mauduit*, p. 78; Michael G. Kammen, *A Rope of Sand* (Ithaca, Cornell University Press, 1968), pp. 22–25.

ten to Mauduit, brought out all of his wild paranoiac fears. Hutchinson, Otis told the newly elected agent,

by the superficial arts of intrigue rather than by any solid parts, by cringing to governors and pushing arbitrary measures, has so far recommended himself to Mr. Shirley and to our present governor that by their means, though he was bred a merchant, he is now president of the Council, chief justice of the province, lieutenant general and captain of Castle William . . . [and] judge of the probate of wills for the county of Suffolk, the first county of the province. Besides this he has filled the supreme court of judicature with his friends, and the other courts with his relatives and dependents. How incompatible these offices are I need not tell you. How the subject groans under the oppression you may easily guess.

Otis believed, he said, that the lieutenant governor had made a deal with Bernard, that if he were elected agent his posts would be given only to hand-picked friends, execpt for the chief justiceship, which would lie vacant until he returned. Hutchinson's purpose was perfectly clear: "he thinks going home agent would enable him to get the government [i.e., the governorship], which event would be as terrible to the honest part of this province as a volcano or an earthquake. They have groaned under his tyranny twenty years already." Nor was the reason for his ultimate defeat unclear: he "had made himself dreaded by his enormous strides in power," and so "the lot," Otis told Mauduit, "became yours." Bernard, he said, had only reluctantly consented: "A dissenting agent is a bitter pill to an *Oxonian*, a *bigot*, a *plantation governor* whose favorite plans are filling his own pockets at all hazards, pushing the prerogative of the crown beyond all bounds, and propagating high church principles among good peaceable Christians."[34]

The appointment to the chief justiceship, the writs of assistance case, the agency fight—in all of these episodes Hutchinson had played a correct, familiar, traditional role, and in all he had been attacked for malicious intent, hidden purposes, and intolerable self-regard. By early 1763, with the newspapers suddenly carrying renewed attacks on him for having been appointed chief justice three years before, the vilification seemed so personal, so outrageous, so irrationally fierce that, though he outwardly behaved as though the

34. Otis to Mauduit, Oct. 28, 1762, in *Mauduit*, pp. 77–78.

attacks simply made him more resolute, inwardly, he confessed to friends, he grew "sometimes discouraged." He had never before met with two such men as Otis Sr. and Jr. The son was simply unaccountable: he "professes to have buried the hatchet every three or four months," but then whenever he is affronted by anyone, for any reason, "instead of returning the affront to the person from whom he received it, he wreaks all his malice and revenge upon me." Hutchinson kept hoping the father would be more sensible and introduce restraint, especially when that venerable politician initiated a conversation with Hutchinson "and mentioned that we used to think alike, etc."

I told him he could not be insensible of the injurious treatment I had received from his son and that the Monday before he had published the most virulent piece which had ever appeared, but if he would desist and only treat me with common justice and civility I would forgive and forget everything that was past. He replied it was generous; and yet his son has gone on in the same way ever since, and have no reason to think the father dislikes it.

There was no confining the passionate spirit of young Otis, nor could one account for his continuing success. Hutchinson was certain that most Bostonians thought ill of Otis, but they continued to elect him to the House. Hutchinson could only hope that the representatives of the country towns, where his own greatest strength lay, would attend the General Court and "prevent [Otis's] obtaining his ends in any matters of consequence." But the attacks went on, endlessly, blatantly, shamelessly.[35]

Yet at the same time there were continuing indications that Hutchinson was still influential and still regarded as an almost uniquely effective public servant—responsible, intelligent, and politically shrewd. When the Assembly in January 1764 voted not only to support the merchants' petition against Grenville's prospective revenue act but to send a special agent to England to present the colony's address and at the same time protect the Bay Colony from contemplated changes in its boundaries and in its constitution of government, it was Hutchinson to whom they turned once again.[36] And though he could not free himself from other obligations in

35. TH to Israel Williams, April 15, 1763, Williams Papers.
36. Thomas, "Partisan Politics," pp. 127–133.

time to accept this commission, and though in any case, weakly backed by Bernard, he failed to get official leave of absence from the home authorities, he was turned to again by the Assembly later in 1764 in the preliminaries of the Stamp Act resistance. This time his role was critical to the outcome, and this time his reputation was most profoundly and permanently affected—affected not as a result of the unaccountable agitations of Otis, nor of the merchant opposition fighting case after case in the courts in an effort to evade the customs laws, but as a consequence of his own character, of the cast of his own mind, and of the pattern of political manipulation that had grown habitual with him over the years. Nothing could illustrate the shape of his mind more clearly—nothing could better serve as a forecast of the future—nothing could so perfectly symbolize the fate of the intelligent, benevolent, pragmatic, close-calculating conservator adrift in a world of passion as the role that Hutchinson played in his colony's resistance to the Stamp Act.

vi

He had strongly disapproved of the Stamp Act from the time he first heard of it. He had said so many times—informally in conversation and in letters to his correspondents in England (letters which in later years he would insistently recall)[37] and formally in a treatise he sent to Richard Jackson in July 1764 with instructions to circulate it where it might do the most good. In this characteristically bland and densely written essay, which was well received in administration circles in England and which was probably drawn on later in the Parliamentary debates on repeal, Hutchinson had summarized his views in four forceful arguments against the projected stamp tax: first, that the crown and Parliament had long ago conceded to the colonies the power to make their own laws and to tax themselves by their own representatives; second, that Americans were in no sense represented in Parliament and hence that the justification for Parliamentary taxation based on presumptive representation was

37. William Gordon, who knew Hutchinson in Boston, recalled his "frequently show[ing] the letters he had written about the time of the Stamp Act in opposition to that measure." *History of the Rise, Progress, and Establishment of the Independence of the United States of America . . .* (N.Y., 1789), I, 357.

invalid; third, that the colonies owed no debt to the English government for their settlement and development—the colonies had been founded and sustained by private enterprise, at times in the face of state opposition; and finally, that economic arguments in favor of the act were fallacious since England's natural profit from the colonies, which would be endangered by taxation, was greater than any prospective tax yield.[38]

These were hard-headed arguments—all matters of historical fact or irrefutable logic. They contained no challenge to English authority as such and indulged in no speculative distinctions in Parliament's power. Hutchinson did not question the validity of Parliament's authority and saw through and dismissed the idea, endorsed not only by "most people" in Massachusetts but by the well-informed Jackson and by Governor Bernard as well, that there was a valid distinction between external taxation (customs duties) and internal, the latter only being prohibited to Parliament. Nevertheless, prudent pragmatist that he was, he was perfectly willing to suppress his objection to this meaningless distinction—he would even tacitly endorse it—if it would be useful to do so. If *Parliament* believed in so false a distinction, he wrote, and was willing to abide by it, and if, as he believed, it would be good for America not to have "internal" taxes imposed on it, then "I acquiesce." The distinction, he wrote to another correspondent, was a fantasy; nevertheless he thought it "imprudent to oppose it, and therefore am silent, but it is for this reason only."[39]

For him there was only one basic consideration from which all else flowed. The essential fact of life, he believed, was that the colonies could not survive in a world of warring nation-states without England's protection—without the whole of the "national" power, not merely the support of the crown. It was simply reasonable, therefore, that the colonies "should ever remain subject to the control of Britain and consequently must be bound by the determination of the supreme authority there, the British Parliament." Parliament's ultimate control, he believed, was the price of American freedom, and that control must remain paramount, he concluded—in words that a decade later would toll through the conti-

38. Edmund S. Morgan, "Thomas Hutchinson and the Stamp Act," *New England Quarterly,* 21 (1948), 461 ff. The text of Hutchinson's "Essay" appears on pp. 480–492.
39. *Ibid.,* pp. 486, 476.

nent, the death knell of his political ambition—even if it became necessary for that body to abridge "what are generally called natural rights . . . even though such rights should have been strengthened and confirmed by the most solemn sanctions and engagements. The rights of parts and individuals must be given up when the safety of the whole shall depend on it . . . it is no more than is reasonable . . . in return for the protection received against foreign enemies." It was better, he said, "to submit to some abridgment of our rights than to break off our connection." The claim to absolute rights, unassailable by Parliament or the crown, however consistent in logic and however harmonious with Hutchinson's other arguments, was to him imprudent in the extreme, and therefore irrational and insupportable.[40]

It was with these ideas and these convictions in mind that in October and November 1764 he entered into the politics of resistance.

The Massachusetts legislature undertook to prepare a petition to Parliament protesting the proposed stamp tax. The lead was taken by the "heads of the popular party" in the House, Hutchinson explained, who drafted a document that stated the colony's objections to the stamp duties in passionate and highly theoretical terms, grounded in principles of natural rights and in constitutional guarantees. The Council, over which Hutchinson as lieutenant governor presided, rejected this "informal and incautiously expressed" draft, and a joint committee of the two Houses was formed to frame an acceptable document. Hutchinson was chosen chairman of this committee, and he led it in rejecting two new versions, "both very exceptionable." "Ten days were spent in this manner," Hutchinson confided to Jackson, "which I thought time not ill spent as I had the more opportunity of showing them the imprudence of every measure which looked like opposition to the determinations of Parliament." He explained to them the folly of pressing principles merely because they seemed grand and glittering and somehow pure; he deplored the naiveté of offending constituted authority and of opposing power with theoretical distinctions; he stated the need for calm and compromise; and he expounded the value of supporting existing structures because they were the basis of civil order. But the conferees resisted, and in draft after draft

40. *Ibid.*, pp. 483, 481, 482; TH to [Jackson], Feb. 26, 1766, MA, XXVI, 198.

confronted him with demands that the *theory* of the matter, the *principles* at stake, the commitments that were involved, should be clearly stated. But Hutchinson kept control, of himself and of the situations, and waited, patiently and skillfully, for precisely the right moment to resolve the controversy. He found it when his opponents were altogether "perplexed and tired" and about to resolve wearily on yet another unacceptable proposal: he then "drew a petition to the House of Commons, not just such as I would have chosen if I had been the sole judge but such as I thought the best I could hope for being accepted," and he pressed this version through. In this way the effort of the "popular party" to draw Massachusetts into "an ample and full declaration of the exclusive right of the the people to tax themselves" had been defeated. The address as adopted, Hutchinson explained with some pride, assumed that American control of its own taxation was an indulgence which the colonists prayed the continuance of—"a matter of favor," he wrote in his *History,* "and not a claim of right."[41]

Thus Hutchinson, and prudence, prevailed—but only briefly, and for the last time, and at great cost. Two developments quickly turned his victory into a dangerous defeat. Reports from the other colonies began to come in. Their petitions—especially New York's—appeared to be "so high," Hutchinson wrote, "that the heroes of liberty among us were ashamed of their own conduct" and they would have reversed their action if it had not been too late. Second, news soon arrived that the Stamp Act had in fact passed despite all the agitation against it in America, and that in passing it Parliament had made no distinctions whatever among the various petitions filed against it; no purpose at all had been served by the prudence Hutchinson had imposed on the House; there had been no sign in fact that his moderation had even been perceived in England. The reaction in Boston was immediate and severe. It was instantly concluded, he reported, "that if all the colonies had shown . . . firmness and asserted their rights, the act would never have passed," and therefore if some one person had deliberately destroyed that unanimity—had striven for days to defeat a petition based on opposition to the *principle* of Parliament's authority, and

41. TH to Jackson, Nov. 5, 1764, MA, XXVI, 110; Morgan, *Stamp Act Crisis,* p. 35; TH to Thomas Pownall, March 8, 1766, MA, XXVI, 208–209; *History of Massachusetts-Bay,* III, 107.

by shrewd and patient handling had succeeded in this—his aim could only have been secretly to promote, not defeat, the Stamp Act, protestations to the contrary notwithstanding. And so it was that Hutchinson, as he later realized, because he had been "the promoter of the [Massachusetts petition], was charged with treachery and . . . [with] betraying his country."[42]

So the charge originated; and it stuck, as passions rose in the months between the passage of the Stamp Act and the date of its legal inception, and seemed in fact more and more persuasive. Everything served to confirm the suspicions of Hutchinson's duplicity that had first been generated by his prudent refusal to defy Parliament's power in principle. When the stamp master for Massachusetts was announced he proved to be none other than Hutchinson's brother-in-law, fellow councillor, and protégé, the colony's secretary, Andrew Oliver: by this appointment alone Hutchinson's secret motives seemed to be revealed. Vituperative squibs began to appear in the newspapers. Rumors (lies, Hutchinson said, that shocked him) circulated that he had written secretly to England to encourage the promoters of the act and that copies of those letters had been returned confidentially from London and were available in Boston to be read. Otis swore he knew for a fact that the whole idea of a stamp act had been hatched by Hutchinson and Bernard, and that he could point to the very house in Boston—indeed the very room—in which the act itself had been conceived. Hutchinson fought back. He explained his views again and again, pointing out repeatedly how serious an offense it was to oppose "by force and violence the execution of an act of Parliament, the supreme legislature of the British dominions." But the only effect this had, he confessed, was to confirm "the groundless suspicions of my having promoted the act."[43]

Everything he did to stabilize the situation seemed to make things

42. TH to Thomas Pownall, cited in previous note, p. 209. By May 1765 the House's letter to the agent, cast in very different terms from those of the General Court's petition, had left a deeper impression on people's minds than Hutchinson's carefully contrived document. FB to John Pownall, May 6, 1765, Bernard Papers, III, 289. John Adams, of course, never forgot the episode; a decade later, at the first Continental Congress, he said that Joseph Galloway and other conservative Philadelphians were then at just the stage of malevolent "dissimulation" that "the Hutchinsonian faction were in the year 1764 when we were endeavoring to obtain a repeal of the Stamp Act." *Diary and Autobiography*, II, 119.
43. TH to H. S. Conway, Oct. 1, 1765, MA, XXVI, 155–156; TH to Jackson, Sept. 1765, MA, XXVI, 150; FB to Shelburne, Dec. 22, 1766, Bernard Papers, IV, 278.

worse. In March 1765 Hutchinson delivered the first of what would prove to be eight charges to the grand jury during his ten years as chief justice; they were speeches in which he expressed some of his basic thoughts on government and law and on the challenges to both. In this first charge, he spoke in general of the need for peace and order and for public bodies like the grand juries to bring perpetrators of "riots, routs, and unlawful assemblies" to justice; and he spoke more particularly of the need for the jury to keep its own counsel and the confidences with which it would be entrusted. Too often the public had heard of juries' decisions before they were officially promulgated, and worse still, public identification had often been made of anyone who had come forward confidentially,

purely for the public good, to reveal some gross abuse of the laws and hoping he may do some good yet unwilling that he should be known to be the person. Soon after it is blazed abroad that he was the *informer,* and every circumstance aggravated to make him odious. Will he ever again hazard his reputation—nay, even his property? Will not this deter many good men from doing eminent services to the public, in consequence of which many heinous crimes will go unpunished, many wholesome laws will be broken with impunity?

This was no innovating doctrine. No one could claim to be surprised that the chief justice sought to protect public-spirited citizens who ran risks to help enforce the law. Yet the charge brought down on him a torrent of abuse. John Adams listed it first in his catalogue of accusations against Hutchinson for the year 1765. The chief justice's "constant endeavor," he wrote, has been "to discountenance the odium in which informers are held," and he had taken the occasion "in fine spun, spick and span, spruce, nice, pretty, easy warbling declamations to grand inquests to render the characters of informers honorable and respectable."[44]

By the summer of 1765 suspicious episodes throughout the entire span of Hutchinson's long public career were being recalled in public prints: his relentless, unpopular campaign to rid the colony of paper money; his endorsement of writs of assistance, which between the end of 1761 and March 1765 had been issued to eleven customs officials;[45] his apparent attempt to block the popular choice

44. Quincy, *Reports of Cases,* pp. 113, 116; Adams, *Diary and Autobiography,* I, 281.
45. Quincy, *Reports of Cases,* pp. 416–434.

for the agency; his thwarting of the will of the populist group in the drafting of the Stamp Act petition and his adroit imposition of language that did not challenge in any way the plenitude of Parliament's power; and his forthright defense of informers in the midst of the tumultuous opposition to the Stamp Act. In none of these episodes had he betrayed his country, defied the law, transcended the received wisdom, flouted decency or accepted morality, or served any interest but that of the public. He had sought, cautiously but firmly, to preserve freedom, not limit it, by stabilizing the economic and legal foundation of society upon which alone freedom could securely rest, and he had worked to the best of his ability to register, in what he considered the most effective terms, his own and his colony's opposition to the ill-conceived Stamp Act. He still commanded the respect of informed people; he was still a natural as well as a legal leader of his native society. Yet something crucial in all of his activities had been missing—some recognition that security is not all nor prudence necessarily the wisest guide to action, some understanding that in the end law to be effective must reflect human sensibilities, and authority must deserve the respect it would command. Gradually the law he represented had begun to seem arbitrary, his honors to seem undeserved, the respect he felt due him to be a form of humiliation, and the government he led to become distant, apart from the governed and insensitive to their needs.[46]

As his prominence had grown, so too had his vulnerability. In the scorching heat of the Stamp Act resistance he became a marked man, and explanations were demanded. On August 14, the night after a mob destroyed Andrew Oliver's stamp office and attacked his house, crowds directed by well-known opposition leaders turned to Hutchinson for the first time, surrounding his mansion and demanding that he "declare to them I had never wrote to England in favor of the Stamp Act." Since, the leaders said, they respected Hutchinson's private character they would accept his personal assurance that he did not favor the act. He knew he had nothing to hide, but should he concede to such intimidation? Was he responsi-

46. This sentence paraphrases, and applies to Hutchinson, Robert Palmer's general description of the essential characteristics of a revolutionary situation: *The Age of the Democratic Revolution: The Challenge* (Princeton, Princeton University Press, 1959), p. 21.

ble to a mob? Surely he was "not obliged to give an answer to all the questions that may be put me by every lawless person." Fortunately, an unnamed "grave, elderly tradesman" who was a noted town meeting speaker intervened and "challenged every one of them to say I had ever done them the least wrong [and] charged them with ingratitude in insulting a gentleman who had been serving his country all his days." Somehow the speaker convinced the crowd that Hutchinson was not likely to have done anything deliberately to hurt his country, and got them to move off. The day closed for Hutchinson with a fervent prayer for "a greater share of fortitude and discretion here than I have ever yet been master of." Twelve days later the "hellish fury" of August 26 descended on him, his family, and his property in "the most barbarous outrage which ever was committed in America."[47]

47. TH to ——, Aug. 16, 1765, MA, XXVI, 145a, 145b; Quincy, *Reports of Cases*, p. 172; TH to Bollan, [Sept. 1765], MA, XXVI, 151; TH to Lord Halifax, Aug. 30, 1765, *ibid.*, p. 299.

Chapter III

Law and Order, Liberty and Empire

So Hutchinson first glimpsed the face of revolution—a face of violence and destruction. He groped for explanations, knowing himself to be innocent of such wild charges as treason, innocent even of the milder claims of duplicity or of monopoly of office. Never, he said, in the Stamp Acts controversy or at any other time, had he done anything improper or anything against the interest of the colony; never had he "acted a double part"; he had never lied, never dissembled, never buried in private correspondence what he feared to express in public.[1] The source of the violence, he said, had nothing to do with such allegations. It involved other, dangerous forces.

There was no doubt by the summer of 1765 that the passions of the people had been aroused—aroused beyond anything Hutchinson, in his long career in public life, had ever seen before. Some great transformation had taken place. One could hardly recognize the people. "Patriots" who now would die rather than submit to the Stamp Act, he wrote in March 1766, had been angling for jobs with the stamp distributors just a few months earlier. When the inflammatory Virginia resolves were received in Boston, "a new spirit appeared at once. An act of Parliament against our natural rights was *ipso facto* void and the people were bound to unite

1. TH to H. S. Conway, Oct. 1, 1765, MA, XXVI, 155.

against the execution of it. . . . it is the universal voice of all people, that if the Stamp Act must take place we are absolute slaves. There is no reasoning with them, you are immediately pronounced an enemy to your country." They had no idea of what the threat really was, or even what the Stamp Act provided for. "There is not a family between Canada and Pensacola that has not heard the name of the Stamp Act and but very few . . . but what have some formidable apprehensions of it." He knew a country gentleman, he told Jackson, whose servant on a dark night said he was afraid to go out to the barn: "Afraid of what," asked the gentleman. "Of the Stamp Act," replied the servant. "There are many masters," Hutchinson commented, "who do not know much better what it is but notwithstanding are ready to run any hazard to oppose it." For there was a universal apprehension among the people that they were being deprived of their liberties—that there was on foot "an attempt to enslave them." The people simply "run distracted," he said; everywhere in the North and in many places in the South "the people are absolutely without the use of reason."[2]

What had set off this madness of the people? Not, Hutchinson believed, an understanding of the intrinsic impolicy of the Stamp Act, which had troubled him and other experienced public people. And not the existence of an actual threat to liberty. No such threat existed. Americans were the freest people on earth, and the acts that they said threatened them had been undertaken, however mistakenly, to strengthen the bond between them and the homeland, which was the ultimate guarantor of liberty. The ostensible motivations behind the wild opposition therefore could not possibly be the real ones. Another explanation must be sought.

It was not hard to find. For one who knew the ordinary people of Massachusetts, who had watched the Boston Town Meeting in action year after year, and who had seen street gangs sweep over the town annually on Guy Fawkes Day, and sometimes oftener, the explanation was evident. The common run of the people, lacking the necessary education, leisure, and economic independence to make an impartial assessment of public problems, were mercurial playthings of leaders who could profit by exciting their fears. Some

2. TH to Thomas Pownall, March 8, 1766, MA, XXVI, 209–210; TH to [Richard Jackson], Feb. 26, 1766. *ibid.*, p. 198; TH to Conway, Oct. 1, 1765, *ibid.*, p. 155; TH to ——, Sept. 12, 1765, *ibid.*, p. 153; TH to Jackson, Sept. 1765, *ibid.*, p. 150.

of these leaders were pure demagogues, lovers of power adept at manipulating the mob, men who "have nothing to lose and . . . will hold out, for, from public mischief and confusion they may have a chance for private advantage." But some of the leaders had only too much to lose—by certain policies. These men were impelled by a close sense of their own selfish interests as against the public good: they were "the illicit traders" whose animosity to the new administration in general and to Hutchinson and Bernard in particular had been excited by the threat of efficient enforcement of the customs laws and the renewal of writs of assistance. The two groups, the demagogues and the calculating self-interested malcontents, worked together to intimidate the moderates, forcing them by the threat of reprisals to remain silent in the face of public outrage. "The majority of the House," Hutchinson explained to Thomas Pownall, "are not disaffected or unfriendly to government, but are afraid to act their judgment, this *boutefeu* [Otis] threatening to print their names who vote against his measures." "We are in such a state that those who do not like it were afraid to oppose it."[3]

Thus the unknowing, politically naive populace had been played upon by a variety of agitators, some simply rabble-rousers seeking influence they could not otherwise command, others seeking the elimination of laws, by violence if necesssary, that worked against their private interests. To old Massachusetts hands like Thomas Pownall, Hutchinson named names, sadly and sourly: on the one hand, Mackintosh, an expert in hanging and burning effigies and pulling down houses, who led the street gangs—"a bold fellow, and as likely for a Massianello as you can well conceive," and Otis, "without dispute a madman," who "with his mobbish eloquence prevails in every motion" and so controls the Boston Town Meeting and the Massachusetts House; on the other hand, the committee of merchants who handle serious matters affecting trade—"Mr. Rowe at their head, then Molineux, Solomon Davis, etc.," and in the Council "the valiant Brigadier Royall, who has thrown up his commission, is at the head of all popular measures and become a great orator. Erving, Brattle, Gray, Otis, and Bradbury, and Sparhawk, whose characters you well know, are in the same box." Together, these demagogues and malcontents had deliberately raised

3. TH to Jackson, Sept. 1765, MA, XXVI, 150; TH to ——, Sept. 12, 1765, *ibid.*, p. 153; TH to Pownall, March 8, 1766, *ibid.*, p. 213; TH to ——, Nov. 11, 1765, *ibid.*, p. 173.

the fears of a people bred to liberty and set them against the government. Together, they had released the latent forces of anarchy, always threatening from below, and unraveled the fabric of civic order.[4]

Yet there had always been men like this, willful, irresponsible, misguided, and gifted in the ability to stimulate the people's worst instincts. Their extraordinary success in 1765 was not due to a sudden enhancement of their powers but to circumstances that peculiarly favored their efforts. The ministry in England, blinded to the realities of life in America and unable or unwilling to see the need to redefine the terms of Anglo-American relations, had blundered badly and created conditions ideal for the purposes of selfish commercial operators and ruthless demagogues. As late as 1764, Hutchinson explained to Pownall in an elaborate and confidential letter of March 1766—a letter that survives in no less than three drafts[5]—no one would have dreamt of defying Parliament; everyone would have agreed that such defiance was high treason. But the Sugar Act, which had suddenly posed the question of "how far the Parliament of right might impose taxes upon them"; the threat, immediately following, of internal taxes; and the failure of Parliament to distinguish between petitions that acknowledged its right to tax and those that did not—all of this had given the hard-core demagogues and the selfish opportunists the occasion they sought, of rallying to them the respectable, well-meaning, public-spirited part of the population. With this liberal support they had succeeded in making defiance of law and order respectable. Powerful pamphleteers[6] had habituated the people, already verging on hysteria, to question the grounds of authority and to encourage acts of violence and the nullification of law. "Authority is in the populace," Hutch-

4. TH to Pownall, March 8, 1766, MA, XXVI, 211–212, 213; TH to ——, March 26, 1776, *ibid.*, p. 216.

5. The three versions of the March 8 letter to Pownall are in MA, XXVI, 200–216. In all probability Hutchinson sent the third, and shortest, version. In it he explained to Pownall that "I dare not trust [my thoughts] to writing, for however favorable they might be, if by accident they should come to the hands of my enemies, they would infallibly be wrested and improved to my prejudice" (p. 215). In the paragraphs above where I have quoted from this letter and in the sentences that follow in this paragraph, I have used the second version, written after he had reflected on his language but before he had decided to suppress his full and frank views. He told Pownall that his son Thomas, Jr., then planning a trip to England, would explain his views more fully.

6. Hutchinson singled out John Dickinson, Daniel Dulany, "the club of political writers at New York," Stephen Hopkins in Rhode Island, and James Otis, "a meteor which has appeared since you left the province." (MA, XXVI, 215).

inson wrote, "no law can be carried into execution against their mind." No custom house officer would now dare make a seizure, and no law was safe from challenge: "I am not sure that the acts of trade will not be considered as grievous as the Stamp Act." In an astonishingly short space of months the population, essentially loyal, had lost sight of its own best interests and by 1766, only a few years after Hutchinson had confidently declared that colonists "must be stark blind if they could not see that independence [from] Great Britain must prove their ruin and therefore they would not aim at it for centuries to come," they in fact approached, he believed, "very near to independence."

What was to be done? The Stamp Act would never be peaceably accepted, and force was out of the question. If force were even attempted, "the people," Hutchinson was convinced, "will be desperate and many in their madness will run headlong to destruction rather than submit." If force in the end succeeded—if the colonists were simply overwhelmed by superior power—they would "for years to come be disaffected to such a degree as to endeavor by every way in their power, even to distressing and impoverishing themselves, to distress and impoverish Great Britain." On the other hand, if concessions were made to the organized opposition and to the mobs, Parliament would be acknowledging its loss of authority in America and indulging precisely the behavior it was hoping to suppress. Were there no alternatives, he asked Jackson, to either the use of "external force," which might create "a total lasting alienation," or humiliating concessions? "May the infinitely wise God direct you."[7]

ii

Hutchinson had no illusions about the limits of his own wisdom, but in the five years after the Stamp Act riots he undertook, in a series of guarded and partly suppressed writings, a thorough-going study of the fundamental issues at stake in the Anglo-American controversy and of the courses of action open to the administration.

7. TH to [Jackson], Feb. 26, 1766, MA, XXVI, 198; TH to same, Aug. 30, 1765, *ibid.*, p. 147. (The latter letter is quoted in full in James K. Hosmer, *The Life of Thomas Hutchinson* [Boston and N.Y., 1896], pp. 91–94.)

Like so much else he sought to accomplish during these years, his effort to grasp the inner meaning of the problems that beset the British empire and to devise a workable and consistent policy by which the government might contain the growing rebellion and create a stable Anglo-American political system came to nothing in the end; but it is no less important for that. Hutchinson's private, half-concealed, yet tenacious and at times frantic grappling with these problems in the mid and late 1760's, however personal and privately expressed, forms one of the most dramatic episodes of the Revolutionary era, and one of the most revealing. For however limited he might have been in sensibility, he was an extremely intelligent man, well read in history and law, experienced in thirty years of colonial politics, and immersed in the daily realities of the struggle. That he was defeated in the end—trapped and destroyed—was in no way the consequence of the poverty of his mind. His failure was the result of other forces which he could not control—political forces in England entirely beyond his reach and instincts within him, bred into the marrow of his personality and nourished by decades of success. And it was the consequence too of something even more fundamental: the incapacity of sheer logic, of reason, compelling in its own terms but operating within the limits of the received tradition, to control or even fully to comprehend an upsurge of ideological passion. Within his own terms of reference, within his own assumptions—which were ordinary assumptions of the age taken to a high degree of refinement—his arguments are irrefutable: which is why ultimately they became the revolutionaries' chief target. They mark the boundaries of traditional thought, and they therefore establish the point of departure for what became, to posterity, the innovative and creative thought of the time.

All of this is clear enough in the letters that poured from Hutchinson's pen, but at one point he went beyond such extemporaneous forms of expression. In 1768 he drafted a formal document which for lucidity and penetration must rank among the major writings of the Revolution. Hutchinson apparently wrote it in complete isolation and, as far as can be ascertained, showed it to no one. It has remained unpublished and unnoticed, and while it is no masterpiece of the order of the *Dialogues Concerning Natural Religion* that David Hume wrote with such care and then locked away in

75

his desk, it too raises issues that are fundamental to the great controversies of its time and reaches conclusions that transcend its immediate context to form a commentary on inescapable and permanent problems: the justification for civil disobedience and the ambiguous relation that must exist between morality and law.

Hutchinson's efforts of the 1760s to grasp the essential issues and to project solutions have another, more personal importance. Years later, in 1773, a small portion of his private correspondence of these years—an arbitrary selection from a massive body of writing—was published, and published at a time when politics was feverish and intense. In these circumstances their publication had a catastrophic effect. Not only, as we shall see, did this publication utterly destroy Hutchinson's political effectiveness but it blackened his reputation beyond any hope of recovery in the lifetime of the Revolutionary generation. Hutchinson believed at the time, and never ceased to believe, that this selective publication had falsified his motives and intentions; it gave, he claimed, a picture of his purposes and ideas of the late 1760's that was the very reverse of the truth. If the letters that were published, he insisted, were read as part of his general correspondence of those years and as part of the broad effort he had then made to explore the fundamentals of Anglo-American relations, they would be seen to be not merely innocent but constructive—part of a positive effort he had then made to preserve freedom in America, not destroy it. He was right. Study of his letters bears out this claim completely, and it illustrates thereby how savage the ironies of history can be and how tragic the complexities that beset mens lives and distort, in others' eyes, their motives and purposes.

Hutchinson was not a political theorist: he rarely wrote of politics in the abstract; his mind was inductive not deductive, political not philosophical. But his thought was nevertheless systematic, and it rested on certain underlying presumptions that must be understood if his concrete arguments and recommendations are to be reasonably assessed.

One catches a glimpse of the theoretical presumptions that underlay his conclusions and recommendations in his enthusiastic praise of Allan Ramsay's *Thoughts on the Origin and Nature of Government,* which he read at the height of the nonimportation crisis.

This pamphlet, he said, is "the best thing I have ever seen on the subject. I wonder it has not opened the eyes of the nation." It is in fact a handbook of applied Hobbesianism, cold, harsh, and disillusioned. Men are in actuality *un*equal, Ramsay had written. The idea of human equality is a dangerous fiction which, when taken up by the "very lowest class of men" at the urging of demagogues, has in the end always resulted in slaughter and the plunder of property. And society, Ramsay wrote, far from being the voluntary compact conjured up in "the idle dreams of metaphysicians" was in real life an inescapable organism created by the flight for survival of weak and solitary men to the protection of the strong. From this natural origin flowed the equally natural and inevitable division between rulers and ruled and the necessity for the ruler's ultimate power to be supreme and absolute, though never arbitrary. Taxing? It was a necessary power of any government that sought to serve society, and in fact it did not—could not—rest, in England any more than in Turkey, on the explicit consent of the governed, expressed either directly or through representatives. Taxing was simply an attribute of supreme authority, a mechanism necessary for its survival, and *"sovereignty* admits of no degrees, if it is always *supreme,* and to level it is in effect to destroy it." For Britain, Ramsay concluded, this "absolute and supreme," this "uncontrollable" authority lay in Parliament, the ultimate proof of whose authority would be found in the coercive forces it could exert, force alone being the final, uncontrollable source of all law: "those," Ramsay said, "who try to separate law from force attempt impiously to put asunder whom God has been pleased to join."[8]

Did Hutchinson approve of all of this? The answer is important. Ramsay's treatise certainly reflects Hutchinson's own essentially cold view of ordinary men as self-deluded, driven by emotion and "by their imaginations and by their expectations of imaginary good and evil,"[9] and he agreed too with Ramsay's view of sovereignty, representation, and taxation. But he was not, like Ramsay, committed to

---

8. TH to [Israel] Mauduit, MA, XXVI, 397; [Allan Ramsay], *Thoughts on the Origin and Nature of Government. Occasioned by the Late Dispute between Great Britian and Her American Colonies. Written in the Year 1766* (London, 1769), pp. 8, 9, 10, 12, 15, 29ff., 53, 55, 59.

9. Eg. MSS, 2662, p. 251v; one of a number of comments by Hutchinson on selections from various writers, esp. Melanchthon, that he copied into that notebook. Cf. *Diary and Letters,* I, 510.

basic notions systematically at variance with the liberal thought of the time. While he shared Ramsay's cold view of human nature—as did in fact most neo-Puritan intellectuals in New England—he shared too the common premise of eighteenth-century British thought: that mankind was endowed in its original, pre-social state with unlimited rights to actions of all kinds but that these rights had been restricted upon entrance into organized society. From that original abridgment of natural rights, he believed, derived the compelling authority of law and the rightful power of government.

Hutchinson's statement of these ideas, carefully recorded by Josiah Quincy, Jr., from the chief justice's charge to the grand jury in 1769, is precisely worded to convey important shades of meaning:

Now [Hutchinson explained to the jury], as the end of society is to preserve to us that security in our persons and property which we could not have in a state of nature, we are under a necessity of giving up some of our original rights in order to a full enjoyment of the remainder. And the best constitution of government must certainly be that in which we part with the fewest of our natural rights—that is, where we part with no more than is absolutely necessary to attain the very ends of society and government. All this is obvious on the first mention. The constitution of government under which we have the happiness to live is therefore the most happy because we have never yielded up more of the private rights of individuals than was needful to invest the government with power sufficient to protect us as citizens. It is, therefore, the duty of every good citizen, who is bound to preserve the laws of the state under which he lives, to apply to the legislative body for a redress of all grievances which arise from the laws. To aim at a redress in any other way is to bring everything into confusion.[10]

The conception as a whole—man in a state of nature, natural rights, the concessions that create the social and governmental contracts—is a cliché of eighteenth-century libertarianism, but the emphases reveal the degree of Hutchinson's affinity to Ramsay and more generally to the premises of establishment Whiggism that had developed during and after the ministry of Robert Walpole. Though Hutchinson spoke of the abridgment of natural rights that takes place upon entrance into society, he stressed not its voluntary and hence its reversible character (which would become the theoretical justification for the American Revolution) but its "necessity." While

10. Quincy, *Reports of Cases,* p. 307.

he agreed that government should engross no spheres of action other than those needed to secure the lives, liberties, and property of its subjects, he believed that the existing British government, at home and in its imperial capacity, was in fact safely restricted to just those limited boundaries. And he believed that if one understood the political nature of the British empire one would see how reasonable Parliament's actions really were, and that therefore, though orderly protests were proper, extralegal agitation against the government was criminal.

For like the "court" theorists under Walpole and the entire central span of respectable British opinion of the mid-eighteenth century, Hutchinson felt that Parliament fused, expressed, and protected all the liberties of Britons, and, because in its essence it was benign and freedom-enhancing, it justified its use of unlimited power. Again, his stress is important. While no one in 1765—no one indeed until Thomas Paine in *Common Sense* a decade later—was prepared to deny the structural beauties of the King-in-Parliament as a governing body, the emphasis among radicals and within the "country" tradition of opposition thought was upon Parliament's fiduciary role—its limited function as the trustee of British liberties —and not upon Parliament's limitless power. For Hutchinson as for Ramsay and the ruling Whig governments of England, the ultimate fact of all political life—which no theorist anywhere in the British world, however radical or imaginative, knew how to deny— was the logical necessity for an absolute and unitary authority to exist somewhere in every government; in its essential definition, that is what government was: a unit of absolute and indivisible authority. Absolute, supreme authority, for Hutchinson, was neither good nor bad, neither a desirable nor an undesirable thing: it simply *was*—it was an inevitable attribute of the system of power that *had* to exist in *any* organized society, and in the case of Britain that power, marvelously restricted by the balances of "mixed" government, was entrusted to Parliament in its totality: that is, to Kings, Lords, and Commons operating together as sovereign.

The necessity for some final locus of unqualified power was for Hutchinson the elemental starting point of all political thought and the basic fact of life in every political society. But though this fact was perpetually important, there were certain times when the effective use of state power was peculiarly urgent. His own time, he

79

believed, was one such moment in history. If one understood the delicate balance of power and liberty in free states and understood too the movement of history in the eighteenth century, one must conclude, Hutchinson believed, that the age he lived in was "an age of liberty." Since the time of the Glorious Revolution the thirst for liberty had become so intense as to threaten stability everywhere. If the threat of despotism had been deflected, the threat of anarchy was rising. Even on the continent of Europe people were seeking in their feeble way, Hutchinson believed, to regain their lost liberties, and in Britain the weight of the popular element had risen remarkably. He never doubted that in certain circumstances—in governments under the arbitrary rule of despots, for example—the drive to reinforce and enlarge the sphere of liberty could have a most salutary effect; but in the British colonies, "where as much freedom is enjoyed as can consist with the ends of government"—where indeed, as Jackson told him, the laxness of government was known to be so extreme as to be positively embarrassing to pro-Americans in Parliament—the heedless enthusiasm for liberty "must work anarchy and confusion unless there be some external power to restrain it." And that external power was the British government in its imperial capacity, a sense of whose glory and benevolence had affected Hutchinson so deeply during the war years when his capacities had been most fully stretched and when his successes, like Britain's, seemed to have reached their peak. If, therefore, the delicate balance of Britain's famed mixed constitution, which everyone agreed guaranteed freedom to Britons and Americans alike, was to be preserved, it was the power element, not, as was the case before 1688, the liberty element, that needed most carefully to be protected.[11]

iii

It was from these standard presumptions of eighteenth-century British political thought—inclined, though not unduly (not, for example, as in Ramsay's *Thoughts*), to favor the security of power—

11. TH to Israel Mauduit, Dec. 31, 1766, MA, XXVI, 257; TH to John Hely Hutchinson, Jan. 18, 1769, *ibid.*, p. 337; Jackson to TH, Nov. 18, 1766, MA, XXV, 104. In 1770 Hutchinson ordered a personal seal, to be inscribed with the motto "Libertatem colo, licentiam detestor." TH to William Palmer, Dec. 21, 1770, MA, XXVII, 81.

that Hutchinson developed his specific recommendations for healing the wounds inflicted by the Stamp Act and its aftermath and for nourishing the political health of the Anglo-American political world. His efforts, first to work out a program of action to deal with the immediate crisis, and then, beyond that, to sketch the terms of a rational system of imperial relations, are contained in a series of letters that begins in late 1765. What stands out most clearly in this extensive though scattered commentary is, first, his sense of indignation and disgust that such an ill-conceived enactment as the Stamp Act could ever have been passed by Parliament, and, second, a willingness to think freshly and flexibly about approaches to imperial relations that might reunite England and America into a cohesive community—something perhaps not too surprising in one who at the Albany Congress of 1754 had shared with Franklin the leadership in planning a union of American colonies under British control.

Hutchinson's program of reconstruction and reordering was conceived as a series of stages. There was no doubt in his mind of the proper way to handle the immediate crisis. The Stamp Act must be repealed, he said, promptly and resoundingly. A stupidly conceived act in the first place—"happy would it have been for us if it had not passed"—it had proved unenforceable: if allowed to remain on the books and *not* enforced it would destroy confidence in government; if attempts were made to enforce it, "there is no determining what desperate men will not attempt."[12]

Repeal, however, would only be the first step. The colonies thereafter would still be "in a deplorable state." But nothing more, he felt, should be done immediately after the repeal. There would have to be a pause, a period of inactivity, "until the minds of the people are somewhat calmed and the effect of the repeal . . . shall appear." Only then, when a suitable degree of calm and stability had been reached, could the real task of reconstruction begin. Strenuous efforts would then have to be made by the government to reach the great majority of moderate, sensible people—the "many good men among us who abhor the present anarchy"—and to rally their support for the steps that would be necessary. They must be made to see the basic fact of life, that the colonies must be subject to

12. TH to Thomas Pownall, March 8, 1766, MA, XXVI, 215; TH to Jackson, Nov. 8, 1765, *ibid.*, p. 172.

some power; if their protector were not Great Britain it could only be some other European state "which would allow them less liberty than they are sure of always enjoying whilst they remain English subjects." Once the moderates recognized this pragmatic necessity for continuing allegiance to England, then efforts could be taken to strengthen the effective power of government. And this would have to be done by measures "which shall evidently appear to be intended to preserve to [the colonies] all the rights and liberties which can consist with their connection with their mother country"—measures, in other words, which while strengthening government would be felt by Americans to be benevolent. Finally, when the government was thus strengthened and free to use its power to support the authority it claimed—then and only then an overall rethinking and reordering of imperial relations could profitably be undertaken and a coherent, rational, and mutually beneficial political reconstruction of the English-speaking world could be created.[13]

It was a rational program: first, a hard-headed, pragmatic, even cynical, alleviation of the immediate crisis; then a rallying of the support of the sensible moderates; then a strengthening of government; and finally a search for fresh approaches to the grand problems of empire. And cynical, in order to restabilize relations disturbed in the crisis, Hutchinson was prepared to be. In 1770, when Townshend's tea duty had pitched the colonies into another crisis, he began by advising the English government to ease the immediate situation by switching the actual duty collection to England and to ignore the illogicality involved. "If it be said this is a mere piece of humor, to be willing to pay it in England and refuse to pay it in America, why, it is all humor": how else but as mere humor, he asked, could one understand the colonists' willingness to submit to costly regulations of trade but not "to an insignificant duty because it is called a revenue"? If indulging this humor will "keep them quiet," why be logical to no purpose? Similarly, he believed that Lord Chatham's distinction in the powers of Parliament, between the power to tax and the power to legislate, was as specious as all the other fanciful distinctions in Parliament's power that had been suggested. But it was nevertheless true, he wrote his correspondents, that most of the colonists in fact believed in that distinction, even

13. TH to Pownall, cited in previous note, pp. 210, 211, 215; TH to Jackson, Sept., 1765, MA, XXVI, 150.

though it made no sense: therefore Pariament should act on it as if it *did* make sense; it should pass legislation on the basis of this distinction as soon as possible, before Americans became impressed with the logic of claiming that among their rights as Britishers was freedom from *all* laws, not only tax laws, to which they had not consented. Don't scruple: "possibly America for many years to come may be made easy and quiet by this distinction." Use anything reasonable that comes to hand to create the stability that is needed: exploit division within and among the colonies if doing so will help maintain authority, for though in some situations such duplicity would be criminal, when the aim is to prevent greater mischief, it may be laudable.[14]

But however narrowly pragmatic or even cynical Hutchinson was when pressed by immediate urgencies, he turned with broad imagination to the later stages of his program, in which a permanent accommodation based on clearly understood principles would be created. The question of a permanent structure of imperial relations was the most challenging problem England faced, he believed, and the worst thing that could possibly be done would be to ignore it. To meet each crisis blindly and extemporaneously, without long-term plans or digested notions for the future, would be a disaster, he warned. If necessary planning were deferred, stability would not be achieved, events would get out of hand, and the government would be forced to extemporize solutions to inescapable problems in crises that should have been prevented; and in such situations expediency not wisdom, desperation not leadership, would dictate the result. The conclusion could only be either a disastrous resort to overwhelming force or American independence, and independence would be followed first by chaos in the colonies, then by foreign conquest of the bickering American states, and finally by a severe economic upheaval in England. There must be a plan not only for strengthening the government but for stabilizing the empire, and it must be coherent, consistent, and above all enforceable. It almost did not matter what the plan was, he wrote in moments of desperation, so long as there was one. "If you would but be steady in any scheme, be it what it would," he wrote to his contacts in England in one of a hundred such exhortations, "we should come to some sort

14. TH to FB, Feb. 18, 1770, MA, XXVI, 442, 443; TH to Israel Mauduit, Dec., 1770, MA, XXVII, 69.

of settlement in the colonies." The mere existence of uncertainty and vacillation on the part of the English government was enough to stimulate disorder. "Let me beseech you," he wrote to Jackson in 1769, "not to leave us any longer than the next session [of Parliament] in this uncertain state. No people under heaven ever felt the truth of that maxim, *Ubi lex vaga,* etc., more than the colonies now do, the whole constitution being vague and uncertain. I think of the condition of England just before the Restoration. . . . Repeal as many of the laws now in force as you please, but what remain take some effectual method to carry them into execution. It is difficult to do it, I confess. But it must be done first or last or you lose the colonies. The longer you delay the more difficult it will be."[15]

Parliament *must* act, he wrote again and again; it *must* not only enforce the rule of law but articulate the principles of colonial dependency. One could already see the outlines of the future if Parliament failed in this. One could see it in the popular misreading of Lord Coke's maxim that "an act of Parliament against Magna Carta or the peculiar rights of Englishmen is ipso facto void": the opposition, taught by Otis, now took that quite traditional doctrine of judicial discretion to mean that the people had the right to say what laws they would and would not obey. When people feel justified in taking the law into their own hands—when "every individual member, or the minor parts of a community [take] upon them to judge when to obey and when not"—society will revert to the rules of the jungle; the fear of brutality will sweep across the community and terror will make savages of civilized men. It would not happen all at once. The thin membrane of law and civil discourse that constrained the natural forces of anarchy would be worn away slowly, in successive outbreaks of disorder, and reach the breaking point before men generally realized what was happening. For there was something peculiarly insidious about the cumulative effects of disorder. Riots, for some reason, Hutchinson said, do not seem to "strike the mind with so much abhorrence as some other offenses do"; yet they are self-intensifying, feeding upon themselves, and no

---

15. TH to ——, May 26, 1768, MA, XXVI, 307 (this letter, unfinished and marked "not sent," was probably a draft of a response to a letter he had recently received from Thomas Whately, and he no doubt felt that his language was too urgent in tone for so formal a correspondence); TH to ——, May 29, 1769, *ibid.,* p. 352; TH to [Jackson], Aug. 18, 1769, *ibid.,* p. 366. See also TH to Israel Mauduit, Dec. 31, 1766, *ibid.,* p. 257.

one can predict where they will end. While people's attention was fixed on the tumult and the clamor, their basic attitudes to the operation of the law would silently shift. Laws would suddenly seem "rigorous—hardly to be borne—which heretofore were never thought severe," and basic confidence in the legal process and the system of government would thereby be undermined. The more frequently disorders occurred, the less they would seem unnatural and unthinkable and the less the public at large would react with effective repulsion, though riotous disorders, he said again and again, necessarily "sap the foundation of all government."[16]

The problem could not be evaded. Those who lived in peaceful farm villages far from the tumultuous towns were equally involved, he believed, and he tried to awaken them to their stake in the growing crisis of order. Countrymen, he told the grand jury of 1768, may not yet have experienced directly the growing dissolution of law and order but unless the current trends were reversed it would only be a matter of time until they too came to panic at the rumor of a riot, disguised by the "cant word . . . rumpus," which would end in "bloodshed and murder."[17] *Of course,* he said, there were reasons for protest; *of course* some laws were offensive to some groups, others to other groups, and no doubt some actions of the government were generally offensive. But somehow people must be made to see that if the government offends, if the law is felt to be oppressive, remedies must be sought in law and not in illegality. Riotous protests would only make the problems worse by enlarging the scope of civil conflict and further eroding the power of the law, which in the end protects the strong as well as the weak.

British law and British government had created in America the freest and most humane community ever known, Hutchinson believed, and the idea that this benign, freedom-protecting Anglo-American system might collapse under the pressure of demagogues and selfish interests simply because men in authority lacked the wit or the will to correct the deficiencies that had been revealed and to

16. TH to ———, Sept. 12, 1765, MA XXVI, 153; TH to Jackson, Oct. 1769, *ibid.,* pp. 387–389 (a desperate letter, passionate in its insistence that Parliament take wise and effective action before it was too late, which Hutchinson reconsidered and did not send); TH to Thomas Pownall, Sept. 26, 1769, *ibid.,* p. 379; Quincy, *Reports of Cases,* pp. 177, 261–262, 220
17. *Ibid.,* pp. 261–262.

plan imaginatively for the future was to him maddening. The fear of the destruction of the whole system of public life that he had known impelled him to turn repeatedly to the difficult problem of reestablishing imperial order on some permanent basis. Through the middle and late sixties he groped for the terms of a new relationship that would retain the essence of the ancient association and yet accommodate in some way the changing moods and demands.

His thoughts on a new and permanent colonial policy appear in a series of letters he wrote to his closest correspondents—to Jackson above all, but also to Bollan, to both Pownalls, to Thomas Whately (the influential undersecretary of the treasury who had drafted the Stamp Act and who went out of his way to initiate a correspondence with Hutchinson), and to Sir Francis Bernard, after he returned to England in 1769. These highly placed correspondents too were seeking general resolutions of the problems of Anglo-American relations, and Hutchinson's thoughts, powerfully impelled by the course of events, were stimulated further by their ideas and were driven into a formal structure by the challenge they presented. For he disagreed with almost all of the long-term programs of reform suggested by his correspondents and with almost all of the specific recommendations they made to the government for handling the immediate crisis. The ideas of three of his correspondents—Bernard, Pownall, and Jackson—were particularly well worked out and particularly important to Hutchinson because of his personal involvement with them and because of the publicity that they received and which he feared would have adverse effects. The uniqueness of his ideas, in fact, may best be understood in contrast to theirs.

Bernard's notions were the first and most elaborately worked out, and they were the only ones, of all those circulating within Hutchinson's group of acquaintances, that were ever to any degree put into effect—catastrophically, as it turned out, in the Coercive Acts of 1774.[18] These ideas were laid out in ninety-seven numbered propositions entitled "Principles of Law and Polity" which Bernard pressed upon the ministry in 1764 as part of a campaign he conducted to have himself recalled to London for special duty as an "eye-witness" of the condition of Massachusetts and as an imperial constitution writer ("I could recomend no one for that purpose so well as my-

18. See below, pp. 189, 277–279.

self").[19] In this portentous catechism Bernard justified the absolute
sovereignty of the King-in-Parliament and its right to tax all units
of the empire whether or not they were represented, but recommended, as a possible expedient, the granting of Parliamentary representation as a special privilege to certain colonies, and suggested that
Parliament consider turning over the levying of "internal" taxes to
the colonial Assemblies, so long as they continued to provide sums
sufficient to maintain a dependable financial basis for the executive
branch of the government. But his chief ideas had to do with plans
for a permanent recasting of colonial institutions and society. The
present colonies in America, he argued, were too many in number,
too small, and too weakly structured internally. They should be
combined into a smaller number of larger units so that the financial
bases of the governments might be strengthened and the forms of
their constitutions brought closer to the pattern of England's. These
enlarged colonies should have not only financially autonomous
executive branches but also—what they had so far completely lacked
—"a real and distinct third legislative power mediating between the
King and the people, which is the peculiar excellence of the British
constitution." This independent middle order of society was to be
created by the appointment of American life peers, and the resulting
colonial nobility would not only complete the classic triad of
"mixed" government but also eliminate the need for the anomalous
and obstructive Councils that then existed, some of which, like that
of Massachusetts, Bernard said, had thrown the whole weight of the
constitution to the popular side and had paralyzed the operation of
government. The existence of colonial charters ought not to be

---

19. Francis Bernard, *Select Letters on the Trade and Government of America; and
the Principles of Law and Polity, Applied to the American Colonies*, 2d ed. (London,
1774), pp. 44, 71–85 (hereafter cited as *Select Letters*). Bernard had been convinced
within a year of his arrival in Massachusetts that a radical reorganization of the New
England governments would be necessary, and by 1763 he declared himself prepared to
return to England to unveil a plan of reform to the ministry. Receiving no response, he
wrote out his thoughts the next year and sent them to Barrington for submission to the
ministry. Still he received no response; and then in desperation in the winter of 1766–
67 he sent directly to the ministry a series of letters expounding his ideas at such great
length that he felt obliged to apologize, somewhat, for his prolixity—somewhat, but not
very much, since while such intellectual activity, he explained, was "disagreeable and
tedious" to him, he recognized that it was necessary if the problems of American government were to be solved. *Select Letters*, pp. 24, 23, 38; *The Barrington-Bernard Correspondence . . . 1760–1770*, ed. Edward Channing and A. C. Coolidge (Cambridge, 1912),
pp. 85, 93, 122. All of his ideas, which were first fully blocked out in a letter to Lord
Halifax, Nov. 9, 1764 (CO5/755/135–42), were published in his *Select Letters* of 1774.

allowed to interfere with these vital reforms since they had originally been granted only to provide government for periods of initial settlement.

From these "Principles of Law and Polity" Bernard never departed, but in the years after 1764 two points grew in importance in his mind: the need for the appointment, or election, of American members of Parliament, originally a matter of indifference to him but increasingly a move that appeared to be "a refined stroke of policy," and the need somehow to get rid of the existing Councils, especially that of Massachusetts, which was simply destroying the effectiveness of all government in the colony. All of this Bernard undoubtedly discussed at length with Hutchinson, one of the few native officials whose views he thought were at all sound, and Hutchinson commented on these ideas as they developed.[20]

At the same time Hutchinson was also considering the ideas of his former superior, Thomas Pownall who, adrift in London after a three-year sojourn in Germany, was also putting himself forward as an expert on colonial affairs. Angling for appointment as what he called a colonial "patron" (a kind of super agent), he updated and refocused his earlier ideas on government and published them in 1764 as *The Administration of the Colonies*. It was a book—originally a pamphlet—which in its six editions would prove to be a flexible vehicle for the expression of Pownall's increasingly complex, prolix, and ultimately jumbled thoughts, as he scrambled to keep up with events and attempted, to Hutchinson's increasing disdain, to insinuate himself simultaneously with the ministry and with popular leaders in the colonies. His arguments in 1764, however, and his basic proposition throughout are clear. His main point was simply that Britain must reorganize the structure of its empire into a "grand marine dominion" with efficient, forceful administrative direction at the center. A single colonial office, combining the work of the Board of Trade and the secretary of state's office, should be created. Trade, justice, law must all center in Britain and be controlled by Britain, yet the colonies were not to be victimized by this more efficient management. Quite the contrary: they were to profit by it too. For the navigation laws, he argued,

20. *Select Letters*, pp. 39, 53–63. For Bernard's comparison of his and Hutchinson's ideas, and his endorsement of Hutchinson's views, see FB to H. S. Conway, Feb. 28, 1766, Bernard Papers, IV, 202–208, only part of which appears as Letter XI of the *Select Letters*.

should be reorganized so as to bring the flow of British commerce closer to the natural harmonies of world commerce—to him the greatest desideratum of all—and such a reform would in fact favor the colonies economically. His main point, however, was that the existing administrative structure of the empire was intolerable; sweeping changes must be made which would replace the present hodgepodge of disparate offices and scattered responsibilities that had evolved through the accidents of history with a streamlined, logical, and efficiently centralized organization.[21]

All of this, with Pownall's successive afterthoughts,[22] Hutchinson studied with his usual care, but he found Richard Jackson's ideas more challenging and stimulating, though they were never developed for publication and came to him only in occasional letters. Most of what we know of Jackson's ideas, in fact, is contained in Hutchinson's comments on them, and these comments, interesting in themselves, reveal the central elements of Hutchinson's developing thought.

In November 1766 Jackson, formerly secretary to the chancellor of the exchequer and then a Member of Parliament, agent for Connecticut, Pennsylvania, and Massachusetts, and counsel to the

21. Pownall's *Administration* is discussed thoroughly, and generously, in G. H. Guttridge, "Thomas Pownall's *The Administration of the Colonies:* The Six Editions," *W.M.Q.*, 3d ser., 26 (1969), 31–46.

22. Later Pownall, like Bernard, would enlarge on particular points. He had originally sidestepped the question of Parliament's right to tax the colonies; in the 1765 edition of his book he elaborately justified it, and in 1766 he added a separate appendix on the subject to make his ideas perfectly clear. Two years later, in 1768, he argued that since Parliament could never give up its right to tax, and since Americans quite correctly claimed that property should not be alienated without consent, America must be granted direct representation in Parliament. Only in that way would the British government reflect reality and Pownall's dream of "a grand marine dominion" be realized. The alternative would be an independent American union, which could only be built on the ruins of Britain's empire and on the destruction of its great role in world affairs. Hutchinson was always severely critical of Pownall's ideas, as he was of his politics and personality. He could never take Pownall's notion of empire seriously since he could not conceive of "an empire of commerce distinct from civil government"; he and Bernard agreed that since Pownall's "grand marine dominion" would necessarily produce "that monster in politics, *imperium in imperio,* this commercial empire must be made subordinate or there is an end of the civil empire." TH to FB, Sept. 20, 1769, MA, XXVI, 377; FB to TH, Nov. 17, 1769, Bernard Papers, VIII, 23. See also TH to Pownall, March 8, 1766, MA, XXVI, 207–214; and FB to TH, Dec. 4, 1769, Bernard Papers, VIII, 26–27, for fuller discussions of the points at issue. For Hutchinson's courteous note to Pownall after reading the first edition of *The Administration* ("I think the colonies greatly obliged to you for asserting their privileges, and I do not see what they could have expected more from you consistent with that dependence which every reasonable man will allow ought to be maintained"), see TH to Pownall, July 10, 1765, MA, XXVI, 143.

South Sea Company, sought Hutchinson's opinion (which he said he valued more highly than his own) of an intricate argument he had until then dared broach only in the secrecy of an executive session of the House of Commons. Having opposed the Stamp Act, Jackson, like many Americans, was seeking to define some kind of limitation on Parliament's rightful power. Was it truly necessary, he asked Hutchinson, for governments to exercise both legislative and taxing powers? Neither, he said, was an inevitable attribute of government. Sparta after the Lycurgan laws, he pointed out, had had no legislative body at all, and innumerable perfectly stable and viable if despotic governments had raised money by simple fiat or by "plunder, rapine, or the spoils of a disgraced minister." Only free states raise money by acts of representative legislatures, but they succeed in doing so only because of the confidence of the people in the legislature. The American colonists, however, had clearly proved that they had no confidence in Parliament as a legislature for them, for the very good reason that they were not represented in it. Even if Parliament rightly had the power to tax, therefore, it "was manifestly inconsistent with policy and the principles of our constitution to exercise it until the Parliament itself was improved to the perfection the principles of the constitution required." Someday perhaps the irregular constitution of England with respect to America would be improved to the point where the necessary confidence would exist, and at that point taxation might begin. At the moment its imperfections stood out—imperfections the more difficult to change, Jackson said, because of the total ignorance in England of the nature of government in the colonies.[23]

In his lengthy reply[24] Hutchinson sketched the parameters of his own thought. Legislation, he insisted, *is* a fundamental attribute of government, notwithstanding the example of Sparta, which he elaborately refuted. And if by rectifying the inadequacies of the imperial constitution Jackson had meant introducing colonial representation into Parliament, he was—like both Bernard and Pownall —ignoring logical as well as political difficulties. Logically, colonial representation was irrelevant since the power to tax did not rest on representation; politically, it was clearly unacceptable to Americans since they quite correctly understood that it would only lend a specious approval to acts over which they would still have no

23. Jackson to TH, Nov. 18, 1766, MA, XXV, 101–107.
24. TH to Jackson, Jan. 17, 1767, MA, XXVI, 258–260.

control and of which they would still disapprove. Direct representation was one of the privileges enjoyed by some (and only some) Englishmen, and it simply could not be enjoyed by the colonists. This limitation was not a matter of will or desire or policy; it was certainly not something he personally advocated. It was, he wrote, simply a matter of evident logic and palpable fact.

For himself, he told Jackson, and with varying degrees of explicitness others in his circle, there was no mystery about the grounds for constructing a sensible colonial policy and a rational imperial constitution. Everything flowed from one simple but inescapable and undeniable fact: the American colonies were too weak to survive independently in a world of rival nation-states. Perhaps in a hundred years the colonies would be strong enough to maintain their independence, though he was glad he was "not like to live to see that time." But since they could not now strike out for themselves, they must seek protection from some power, and they did so from England, the freest state in the world. As a consequence of this necessary dependence, compounded by the colonists' remoteness, certain privileges enjoyed by Englishmen could not be held by them. It was simply a matter, he wrote in letter after letter in this period, of what was and what was not possible, not of what was theoretically good or bad. No amount of theorizing or wishful thinking could change the necessity for "an abridgment of what is called English liberty." "I doubt whether it is possible," he said (in sentences which when published in 1773 would shock the entire political population of America and utterly destroy him politically), "to project a system of government in which a colony 3,000 miles distant from the parent state shall enjoy all the liberties of the parent state. . . . I wish to see the good of the colony when I wish to see some restraint of liberty rather than [that] the connection with the parent state should be broken, for I am sure such a breach must prove the ruin of the colony."[25]

25. TH to Thomas Whately, Jan. 20, 1769, MA, XXVI, 339. This famous letter is discussed below, pp. 227–228, 243–251, 370. I have quoted these sentences exactly as they appear in TH's letter book copy as edited by Catherine Mayo and Malcolm Freiberg. The word "English" was apparently inserted in the first sentence as a correction by TH himself, and hence was probably included in the original letter that was sent to Whately. In the printed version of the letter, edited for publication by TH's enemies in 1773, the words "liberty" and "liberties" in the first two sentences quoted are interchanged, with an effect that is considered by Malcolm Freiberg in "Missing: One Hutchinson Autograph Letter," *Manuscripts*, 8 (1955–1956), 179–184. Cf. Adams, *Diary and Autobiography*, II, 80–81.

The colonists' necessary and limiting dependence did not mean, however, that they need be victims of oppression. "I am as much against arbitrary government," he wrote to a correspondent in England in 1769, "as any person living. The more favor you show the colonies in freeing them from taxes of every sort and indulging them in such forms of constitution, civil and ecclesiastical, as they have been used to, the more agreeable it will be to me, provided you do not wholly relinquish us and take away the claim we have to your protection." Not only as a matter of sensible policy should the parent state allow the colonies every possible liberty—and for the British colonies that would involve a very great deal indeed— but (and this was and had been the essence of his thought on imperial relations "ever since I have been capable of thinking upon such a subject") the parent state should compensate for the inescapable restrictions on liberty in overseas territories with extraordinary indulgences, so as to bring the condition of colonists and Englishmen into as close a general equality as possible. This would not be something new for the American colonies: it would merely formalize traditional practices. If partisans on both sides would put aside their passions, their delusions, and ambitions, they would see, he believed, that for over a century precisely such a balance had been struck and had proved workable and liberty-preserving. It had been this balance, established in many spheres, that had accounted for the prosperity, indeed the continuing existence, of the Anglo-American empire. For four generations there had been a major limitation on liberty in America in the restrictions on colonial trade, but Americans had not objected because there had been a compensating indulgence in freedom from Parliamentary taxation.[26] The same sort of balance had been struck in other ways: in the judiciary, for example. In Massachusetts the tenure of judges was held at the pleasure of the crown instead of on good behavior, as had been the case in England since the settlement after the Glorious Revolution; but at the same time the Assembly had been given the right to create and hence destroy the courts themselves, and in addition judges could not be removed without the approval of the Council.[27]

26. TH to [Jackson], Aug. 18, 1769, MA, XXVI, 365; TH to Jackson, Jan. 17, 1767, *ibid.*, pp. 258–260.
27. "This I think amounts to near the privilege of the people of England. . . . Unless you can suppose a House of Representatives who would join in erecting judicatories un-

What was needed to regain this long-successful set of balances between inescapable limitations and wise indulgences was not institutional restructuring, as Bernard, Pownall, and so many facile theoreticians claimed, but statesmanship. To Hutchinson—as to Edmund Burke, whom history would record as a friend of America— nothing seemed more delusive than blueprints for structural, constitutional change. Through all the years of controversy he, like Burke, remained constant in the belief that the world as it had been could survive and prosper with wise management, and that structural changes and sudden, constitutional innovations would cause more harm than good. Though he was careful to temper his criticism of his superior, he flatly disapproved of Bernard's idea that the boundaries of the colonies should be altered (it had been he who had so often represented Massachusetts when its boundaries had been challenged), the Councils eliminated or reconstituted, and a colonial nobility created.[28] While he had long recognized the weakness of the elective Council in Massachusetts, he thought appointed Councils would be worse; under proper management the Massachusetts Council had functioned well for generations, he believed, and he was certain that sudden changes in its constitutional character would create more problems than they solved. He openly condemned the proposal of Chief Justice William Smith of New York that a single vice-regal government be created in America, including an Ameri-

---

known to the constitution and investing them with powers inconsistent with the privileges of the people [and] the governor and Council appointing judges unworthy their station and removing them for their integrity, this people are as secure and as firmly established in their *liberties* as they are in Great Britain. I know of no difference. Certainly, if they are not up to Great Britain they are the nearest that can be." Quincy, *Reports of Cases*, p. 309 (TH's charge to the grand jury, 1768).

28. As early as 1759 Hutchinson had been critical of the Council's weakness in the face of popular pressure and acknowledged that this was largely due to its election annually by the members of the Assembly, but he was "never satisfied that the constitution of the Council in the King's governments was not liable to greater exceptions." TH to Richard Saltonstall, Aug. 22, 1759, Robert E. Moody, ed., *Saltonstall Papers*, I (MHS *Colls.*, LXXX, 1972), 429; TH to Jackson, Aug. 18, 1769, MA, XXVI, 365–366; TH to Israel Williams, May 6, 1769 ("I am not desirous of a change in the constitution"), Williams Papers, MHS. He had no illusion that mere crown appointment would create "that glorious independence which make the House of Lords the bulwark of the British constitution and which has sometimes saved the liberties of the people from threatened encroachments and at other times put a stop to advances making upon the royal prerogative." *History of Massachusetts-Bay*, II, 7. He was always extremely sensitive to charges that he was acting in any way at variance with the chartered constitution of the province, replying heatedly to the report circulating in 1768 that his commission as chief justice had been issued under English rather than provincial authority. Quincy, *Reports of Cases*, p. 304.

can parliament, not only because he thought such an arrangement would be impracticable but because it would destroy the existing structure of authority.[29] These were abstract notions that ignored the deep inner bindings of society that had developed slowly over the years; they sacrificed to theory the living complexities of community life. Even the simpler and apparently more sensible idea, rapidly gaining popularity in America, that the colonies be associated with England through the King alone and not through Parliament—what later generations would call dominion status— he felt sacrificed reality to an attractive theory. For in such an arrangement, he pointed out, there would be a withdrawal of effective governmental power from communities already beset by civil disorder, and the result would simply be chaos.[30] If order was to be restored and maintained, the ultimate power of the King-in-Parliament must remain as unitary and total over the colonies as it was over England, *imperium in imperio* (that pejorative catchword for the nascent concept of federalism) being, he was profoundly convinced, totally unworkable and a prescription for chronic disorder. What was needed was a flexible, imaginative, statesmanlike use of the powers and structures that existed.

Interesting possibilities had simply been ignored, he wrote, by an excessively rigid approach. One obviously useful, if minor, innovation would be an oath of supremacy, to be taken by every member of the colonial Assemblies, the general Declaratory Act of 1766 having proved useless in binding officeholders to the allegiance they owed the state.[31] Another possibility, which he urged in a moment

29. Hutchinson heard of Smith's proposal from Andrew Oliver (*American Historical Review*, 8 [1902–1903], 312) and wrote at least twice to Bernard criticizing it severely (Oct. 27, 1769, and Feb. 18, 1770: MA XXVI, 395, 442–444). These letters were among those later published by the Revolutionary leaders, and their appearance led to an even greater antagonism between Smith and Hutchinson than had existed before. William H. W. Sabine, ed., *Historical Memoirs [1763–1776] of William Smith . . .* (N.Y., 1956), pp. 235–236. The text of Smith's plan and an interpretation of it appears in Robert M. Calhoon, "William Smith Jr.'s Alternative to the American Revolution," *W.M.Q.*, 3d ser., 22 (1965), 105–118.

30. E.g., TH to ——, Feb. 26, 1766, MA, XXVI, 197: "When I think of this new model of our connection with England only as we are the subjects of the same princes, the nearest relation I can fancy myself to be in to you is no more than that of Hanover, a thought which strikes me with more horror than the dissolution of any natural relation which has subsisted all my life could possibly do. The confusion would be infinite from the present inclination to anarchy and the utter insufficiency of internal authority. And a prince 3,000 miles distant without aid from his other subjects could do but little towards composing it."

31. TH to [FB], Feb. 1770, MA, XXVI, 441; TH to Jackson, April 21, 1766, *ibid.*, p. 228.

of despair at England's ever understanding what was happening in the colonies, was the appointment of a royal commission to visit the colonies and to confront each Assembly separately with the question of obedience. At the least the result would be a salutary airing in England of the degree of rebelliousness that existed and of the kinds of absurd distinctions that supposedly responsible Americans were attempting to draw in England's sovereign power; it might also serve to silence opposition in Parliament to the need for taking action. And while he thoroughly disapproved of William Smith's proposal, he did admit that if such a plan were ever enacted it might at least have an interesting secondary benefit: if not one but, say, three vice-royalties were created, and if "noblemen with talents" were selected as governors-general and their term restricted, as in Spanish America, to three years, "in a short time a good part of the nobility would have a perfect acquaintance with America, and Parliament would be better able from time to time to make such provision as shall be necessary."[32]

Imagination, flexibility, political skill would alone make accommodation possible. Use whatever reasonable means are available to bring order to America, he urged. The proper course, he wrote in a remarkable letter of 1770—a discreet letter which he constructed from the pieces of a huge, disorganized, wild-swinging draft—the correct course was the most difficult and the most complicated: it was, simply, "to bear with their disorderly behavior until they have distressed themselves so as to bear their distresses no longer. Encourage the animosities already begun between the colonies, and distinguish one colony from another by favor for good behavior and frowns for the contrary. Lay aside taxation, not upon the principle that it is to be distinguished from legislation in general but because it is inexpedient. Keep up every other part of legislation and familiarize every colony to acts of Parliament. This may in time bring the colonies to their old state."[33]

Why had nothing so far been done to habituate the colonies to Parliamentary acts? The colonists "ought to have been used to acts of Parliament every session, some to respect the colonies in general,

---

32. TH to John Pownall, June 8, 1770, MA, XXVI, 503; TH to [FB], Feb., 1770, *ibid.*, p. 441.

33. The first draft of his letter to FB (#39 for 1770: Oct. 20) fills nine manuscript pages (MA, XXVII, 26–35); the final version three (40–42).

others particular colonies. . . . Perhaps it is not too late to recover what is lost by going into this practice now." Let the House of Commons appoint a permanent committee for America, and let that committee generate enactments that are manifestly to the colonists' advantage. Show Americans the *favorable* aspects of Parliament's authority; provide them with instruments and powers that they need and would welcome, and that might also have political support in England. Create, for example, he wrote in 1769, chancery courts; that jurisdiction had long been needed. A general law setting up chancery courts in the colonies would be considered, he thought, beneficial: it would secure the responsibility of executors of estates, which was badly needed, and incidentally serve the interests of English creditors. A year later, recognizing that the colonists "have been taught to have very formidable apprehensions of a court of chancery where the governor is to be chancellor," Hutchinson considered the possibility of extending to the colonies the Scottish system of granting chancery powers to common-law judges, but then withdrew that idea and gave up altogether on chancery courts. The most useful beginning, he finally decided, would be to recast all laws affecting bankruptcy, wiping out the manifestly unfair "absconding laws" that had been passed by the various Assemblies and assuring both colonial and English creditors of bankrupts an equal share of the residual property. But whatever the specific subject chosen for a beginning, let Parliament exert its authority regularly and beneficially in the colonies—and then *enforce* that authority, implacably. Only in that way would the colonists learn to respect English authority—indeed, all authority; authority as such—and see the folly of resistance. If such steps had been taken five years ago, he wrote in 1770, all the trouble would have been nipped in the bud.[34]

So Hutchinson speculated on ways of restoring civil order after the Stamp Act disaster and of securing Anglo-American relations in the future. Two points were fundamental in his thinking, and from them he never departed: the necessity for America to retain its ties to England if its liberties were to be preserved—if the colonies broke away they would become the victims of one or another of the

34. TH to [FB], Feb. 1770, MA, XXVI, 441; TH to ——, July 25, 1769, MA, XXV, 317–320; TH to Lord Hillsborough, Oct. 9 1770, *ibid.*, p. 443 (a section on chancery courts that was deleted in the final letter); TH to FB, Oct. 20, 1770, MA, XXVII, 32–34, 28.

predatory states whose subjects enjoyed none of the freedoms of Britons—and the ultimate indivisibility of sovereignty. But beyond that, in the years between the Stamp Act and his assumption of the governorship in 1770, he was imaginative and flexible in conceiving of approaches to peace within the existing constitutional framework; and he was quite capable of recognizing the sincerity of his opponents, however much he believed them to be misinformed or unconsciously biased or prejudiced in their views. Often, he wrote in 1765, both parties to a conflict see things "through a false medium and are biased, though insensibly, by one prejudice or another." The errors he saw were by no means all on one side. Nothing was clearer to him than that, while the colonists could be pitched into complete chaos by further excesses of liberty, so too could they be ruined by further innovations and impositions by Parliament or even by insensitive gestures that would alienate them further. His letters to Jackson, which are particularly far-ranging and speculative, express the mind of a political pragmatist devoted not simply to law and order as such, but to law and order within the British political system, known to be the freest and most benevolent on earth—a system far preferable to any practical alternative—and devoted too to the continuing welfare of a society in which, at least north of Maryland, property was so widely distributed that there was virtually no destitution.[35]

The conditions of American life were so favorable—liberty was so deeply rooted—that the crisis to Hutchinson was simply artificial. He was infuriated by the needlessness of it. None of the charges of the extremists had any basis in fact. He *knew* England was not preparing to jettison its hard-won liberties, at home or in the colonies; he *knew* that no one, in England or America, was plotting to rob the colonists of their freedom. And he knew that most

35. TH to Israel Williams, April 26, 1765, Williams Papers, and MA, XXVI, 136–137; TH to ——, July 21, 1768, MA, XXVI, 316; TH to Jackson, Oct. 20, 1767, MA, XXV, 207: "To restore tranquility to the colonies and at the same time to preserve a just dependance upon Great Britain *hic labor, hic opus.* Property is more equally distributed in the colonies, especially those to the northward of Maryland, than in any nation in Europe. In some towns you see scarce a man destitute of a competency to make him easy. They have as high notions of liberty as any part of the globe, but then they are as tender of their property and see the importance of enjoying their estates in quiet. I find no arguments so successful as urging to them that under the notion of obtaining their liberty they are pursuing measures which will deprive them of their property as well as liberty or render it of little value. This would infallibly be the case if Great Britain should cast them off."

Americans did not want independence from England. Yet the Stamp Act and the other clumsy actions of the British government had given rise to fears that such dangers did exist and had provided grounds for colonial malcontents and incendiaries to create upheaval for their own advantage and to stimulate desires for independence.[36] And then had come the Townshend Duties, which raised fears of still higher duties to come, of the imposition of a standing army to enforce the taxes, and ultimately of the annihilation of the local legislatures. The whole mess, he exploded uncharacteristically to an English friend and business associate of thirty years standing, was the result of gross errors in high places. "You have brought all this trouble upon yourselves and upon us by your own imprudence. You never ought to have made any concessions from your own power over the colonies, and you ought not to have attempted an exertion of power which caused such a general dissatisfaction through the colonies. God only knows when the ill effects of this mistake will cease."[37]

For himself the ill effects, through these years of examination and speculation, grew worse rather than better. His efforts to convince the sensible moderates, upon whom in the end everything would depend, of the wise course of action, grew desperate. He begged them to recognize that they were being led into measures that threatened to deprive them not only of the liberty that they were seeking above all to protect, but also of their property. He turned his charges to the juries, his speeches in Council, and his other official statements into pleas for common sense and law and order. And he reached out to the public at large through the press, by providing newspaper copy in support of the government and by publishing in the first two volumes of his *History* warnings of the evils of fanaticism illustrated in the lives of his own ancestors and demonstrations of Parliament's long-established power to regulate American trade. But it was not enough. By the spring of 1768, as the opposition press reached a new level of sophistication and effectiveness in John Dickinson's *Farmer's Letters*, Hutchinson had come to feel that some special effort on his part was called for. He must produce a conclusive demonstration of the folly of the radicals' arguments and

36. E.g., TH to General Thomas Gage, May 9, 1770, Gage Papers (microfilm), MHS.
37. TH to Robert Wilson, May 11, 1770, MA, XXVI, 480.

claims. So in the tumultuous summer of that year—as the Massachusetts House defied the ministry's order to rescind its inflammatory circular letter; as mobs assaulted the customs officers who had seized John Hancock's sloop *Liberty* and drove them to the refuge of the harbor fort; as the nonimportation committees tightened their boycott of British goods; and as plans were almost publicly made to oppose the landing of the two regiments of troops known to be en route to Boston—Thomas Hutchinson retired to the peace of his house in Milton to write what he hoped would be a definitive refutation of all the mistaken notions that had been circulating since the Stamp Act resistance had begun. The result, which he never mentioned in any of the hundreds of letters he wrote in those years and which has remained unpublished for two centuries, is one of the most revealing documents in the political literature of the Revolution.

iv

If one may infer the history of the project from the heavily corrected, interlineated, torn, and glued-together manuscript sheets that survive in the Massachusetts Archives, Hutchinson began by drafting a "letter," in fact a treatise, on the taxing power of Parliament and on the constitutional relations between parental states and their colonies. After writing fourteen pages in this form, citing and refuting Dickinson's *Farmer's Letters* (which Bernard had felt might become a veritable American Bill of Rights)[38] and meeting head-on a variety of arguments put forward by other opposition writers, he broke off and made a fresh start in a different form, though carrying over some of the same arguments and copying passages verbatim from the original piece. This time the presentation was more literary and much more likely to be popular. The effort was sustained through thirty-four tightly written and heavily amended folio pages containing several extensive marginal inserts written vertically down the page as well as four additional passages on separate slips pasted on to the pages, the whole totalling some ten thousand words. This second, more elaborate, and apparently quite finished work is entitled "A Dialogue between Europe and

38. FB to Jackson, Feb. 20, 1768, Bernard Papers, VI, 93.

America" and it is written entirely as a dramatic exchange, complete with realistic personal responses, conversational switches of topics, and rapid changes of pace.[39] It starts casually:

Europe: America is in a very different state from what it was when I saw you last in England.

America: I am sensible of it, and the worst circumstance is that there seems to be no prospect of recovering our former state.

Europe: Whose fault is that?

America: You will say it is our fault, we think it is yours. You assumed and exercised an authority over us which we thought you had no right to do. . . .

Europe: Hold, my friend, be calm. This dispute, like all other party disputes in affairs of government as well as religion, has been carried on with great zeal and warmth of temper. This temper must subside before there can be any room to hope for an accommodation.

Then the Dialogue moves into the basic problems of Anglo-American relations, with quotations from and references to Locke (all of them entirely accurate), extensive examples from ancient history, and detailed interpretations of the constitutional status of the British colonies at the time of their initial settlement. The purpose of the piece was not to set out new terms of imperial relations but to demonstrate the irrationality of the arguments of the American opposition, the impossibility of constructing a workable imperial system on the principles that the opposition had suggested, and the inescapable necessity of settling the current controversy on terms dictated by the historical tradition that Britain and America had inherited.

After the introductory exchanges there are some important preliminary skirmishes before the major battle is joined. To *America*'s claims that historically only the King, and not Parliament, had jurisdiction over newly discovered lands; that the first settlers had contracted with the King alone for their rights and privileges, and that only by their own later acquiescence were Parliament's laws

39. The remains of the Dialogue are in MA, XXVIII, 102–109; and there is in addition an unattached four-page fragment inserted at p. 109. The draft treatise in the form of a letter is in MA, XXV, 121–135. The text of the Dialogue will be published in *Perspectives in American History*, 8 (1974). I have followed Malcolm Freiberg in assigning the composition of the Dialogue to the summer of 1768: "Prelude to Purgatory: Thomas Hutchinson in Massachusetts Politics, 1760–1770" (Ph.D. diss., Brown University, 1950), pp. 215–216.

found to be acceptable by the colonists, *Europe* replies with an intricate interpretation of the nature of sovereignty and of allegiance. The land in America is not the King's private dominion but the possession of the British state, and the first settlers therefore retained all their previous allegiance to the British state when they settled there. Had that not been the case, they would have been subjects of the King in the sense that Hanoverians were now his subjects, which means that they would have been aliens with respect to British law and therefore incapable of inheriting property in Britain—which is manifestly untrue. Americans' allegiance is no more contractual than Britons': the colonial charters are either legal equivalents of municipal corporations, or trading franchises; in either case Americans' allegiance to the British state is perpetual not contractual, public not private. Only the political disruptions of early seventeenth-century England had kept Parliament from exercising its authority over America from the first years of colonization. To *America*'s claim that the American colonists are constitutionally as independent of the parent state as the ancient *coloniae* were of Rome, *Europe* replies with extended excerpts from Livy (passages which Hutchinson had first used in the identical words in the discarded treatise) documenting, with close parallels to the Anglo-American situation, the legitimacy of the Roman Senate's continuing power of taxation and coercion over even its most autonomous provinces.

But the heart of the Dialogue appears after these preliminary exchanges and goes straight to the central and universal questions of the grounds of personal obedience to the state and the limits, if any, of this obligation. The first exchange on this question is inconclusive. *America:* if there are no limits to what a government can rightfully do, the purpose of government—to protect life, liberty, and property—will be defeated since a government would thereby have unlimited authority and would be free to infringe on all areas of life. *Europe:* but if the individual is justified in defining the government's limits for himself, the purpose of government is equally defeated since the limitations set by some will surely interfere with the life, liberty, and property of others. *Impasse.* Both sides thereupon retreat to Locke for authority; both quote Locke, accurately, to support opposite conclusions, *America* to prove the need for consent to the alienation of property, *Europe* to prove that personal decisions to disobey the law cannot be permitted in a civilized society, for that would be tantamount to recreating precisely the state of nature that governments are instituted to overcome. What kind of a society, *Europe* asks, would there be if individuals were empowered to tell judges and executives when to enforce the law and when not?

Judges themselves, *America* replies, should decide not to enforce immoral laws or laws contrary to the purposes of the government. *Europe:* but if judges were to select which laws to enforce and which to ignore they would be making, not enforcing, the law, and that would violate a primary precept of free government. If judges feel that the law they have sworn to enforce is immoral, they should not violate their oath to enforce the law but resign their posts and then be prepared personally to pay the penalty for civil disobedience. For there is no agreed-on, absolute, and objective definition of morality and immorality that judges or anyone else can simply invoke. Justice and morality are relative to the circumstances and culture. Have Americans considered the plight of the Catholics in England? They are never directly represented in Parliament, yet they are not only taxed but *double* taxed, though in their religion they have long since given up seditious principles. Is that justice? Yet would an American sitting as judge in England refuse to enforce such laws if a Catholic asked him to?

Let us suppose, *Europe* says, that a person believes his government is engaged in an immoral war. (Quakers, after all, consider all wars immoral.) Is he thereby free to refuse to pay taxes in support of that war? Perhaps not, *America* replies, but the British constitution does not provide for "an umpire or judge" to determine when the government has exceeded its authority—the courts, which were in fact as well as in name "executive courts," had never been given that power—and since that is the case, "every man's own conscience must be the judge, and he must follow the evidence of truth in his own mind, and submit or not accordingly." This, *Europe* replies, would be a constitution that is no constitution at all but "a mere rope of sand." No government in the history of the world has ever survived for long on the principle that individuals may claim an exemption to the law when they decide their rights have been infringed. Nor, indeed, has the definition of fundamental rights been constant in any nation's history. The British constitution—every constitution ever known—has been in flux at all times, and it is in fact through successive alterations of the British constitution that, historically, adjustments have been made to accommodate personal or group grievances. Instead of individuals personally defying the government in order to right wrongs they claim have been committed, the supreme authority itself has modified its own actions, "and such alterations become to all intents and purposes parts of the constitution." For constitutions are not immutable blueprints of government inscribed on parchment at a particular point in time; they are living, growing, malleable arrangements of things, and it is a contradiction in terms to think that an agency of government could serve as umpire to rule the government itself out of order when it impinged on individual rights. Courts are part of the law enforcement procedure, not a check upon it. The only restraint on the action of the state is the state's *self*-restraint, and in a balanced, "mixed" constitution that is an effective limitation indeed on the abuse of power.

Well, *America* replies, you may use any argument you wish, but it is still true that the government is wrong to take my property without my consent, expressed either directly or through a personally chosen representative. Forget about contract theory and natural law if you think all of that is "merely ideal": the same immutable principles are embedded in English history and immemorial English law.

How "obstinately tenacious" you are, *Europe* replies. Let us indeed turn to the history of the English constitution. Does it justify an individual's refusal to obey the law? No—and more important, it does not contain immutable principles that might serve as the basis for such resistance. True, it is one of the glories of the English constitution that there are "certain fundamental principles, plain and intelligible," which can guide the courts in deciding difficult and uncertain cases, but these principles are far from being or having been immutable; they have always changed when circumstances changed. Magna Carta, surely, is a fundamental document in the English constitution. Yet it provides for the continuing jurisdiction of the then-existing Church, from which it follows at the very least that there should be a bishop of the Church in America. But is there one? And how have Americans in fact responded to the suggestion that there be one? If the Church really occupied the role conceded to it in Magna Carta, consider what a deplorable state we Protestants would all be in. Consider how many other provisions of that great charter of constitutional liberty have also been repealed by acts of Parliament. In fact there is only one absolutely immutable principle in the British constitution and certain to remain such: "that no act can be made or passed in any Parliament which it shall not be in the power of a subsequent Parliament to alter and repeal." No government or constitution on earth is immutable: "the power which established it may dissolve it." Yes, the British government has fundamental principles, "but if King, nobles, and people agree to make an alteration in what were before fundamentals, who is there to complain"?

The people, *America* replies, may complain, for they alone, as opposed to the other two elements of the constitution, do not personally participate in such decisions but act only through representatives. If these representatives exercise a power they were never given, they may be repudiated. Nor need this be only a majority's action: a *minor* part of the people may feel themselves free to repudiate such irresponsible actions by representatives. *Europe:* but it is an historical fact that the government was formed by representatives; surely it can be altered by representatives. *America:* I never gave my representative unlimited power; for him to give away my rights is to assume a power he never had, and any act of that sort "is void." If it is void, *Europe* replies, then there is an end to all organized government.

For the basic point, *Europe* argues, in what is surely one of the intellectual high points of the pre-Revolutionary debate in America, is that personal morality must be distinguished from law. Morality does not make law. However thoroughly you may be convinced that "merely in a moral sense" you are not bound to conform to what you consider to be an immoral law, no court will think this personal judgment sufficient reason to exempt you from the operation of the law. The courts must enforce the law as it exists; if that law and your moral judgment conflict, the law must prevail; otherwise there is no government.[40]

40. Cf. Hutchinson's charge to the grand jury in March 1769: "We, gentlemen, who are to execute the law are not to inquire into the reason and policy of it, or whether it is constitutional or not—whether one part of the community are oppressed and whether another part oppress. We and you, gentlemen, as the executive body [i.e., an executive

Yet even this, *Europe* continues, does not wholly dispose of the problem of civil disobedience. There is always the final possibility of outright revolution, and here the distinction between law and morality is fundamental:

the body of the people may rise and change the rulers or change the very form of the government, and this they may do at all times and on all occasions, just when they please. But every individual must take the consequence of a mistake if he attempts to stir up the body of a people to a revolt and should be disappointed. In a moral view he may perhaps be innocent whether his attempt succeeds or not, but consider him as a member of the political body and he must be pronounced guilty by the judiciary powers of that society if he fails of success. This is a principle essential to the nature of government and to the English constitution as well as all others.

What must be done in the present circumstances? *Europe* asks. If America is exempt from any law, it is exempt from all laws. The law as it stands must be enforced, though the supreme authority may ultimately wish to alter the law. "I would not give up the least iota of our right, but I would exercise this right with discretion, with equity, and even with a degree of partiality, but when I had once determined how far I would exercise it . . . such determination should never be departed from." If such a policy were now followed it would easily succeed, for the extremists among the colonial leaders are simply desperadoes who stand to gain by reducing everything to chaos and then starting things over again. But the generality of the people, "who are in easy circumstances," will not risk their property and security for the benefit of a few irresponsible agitators. The present popular frenzy will pass, for "you are Englishmen. . . . No people upon the globe have been oftener in a frenzy and none return sooner to their senses than Englishmen."

—— And then the manuscript of Hutchinson's Dialogue ends with *Europe*'s agreement that "laws against the *general* bent of the people" could never survive: they would be revoked by the authority that made them; "but laws against the bent of *particular parts* of

---

as opposed to a legislative court], are to inquire what is law and see that the laws are enforced. If we step over this line and judge of the propriety or impropriety, the justice or injustice, of the laws we introduce the worst sort of tyranny—the most absolute despotism being formed by a union of the legislative and executive power. I mention this, gentlemen, because from my own observation . . . I have found juries taking upon them to judge of the wholesomeness of the laws, and thereby subverting the very end of their institution." Quincy, *Reports of Cases*, pp. 307–308.

the people are and must oftentimes in every constitution be enforced by the authority of the whole."

Hutchinson's Dialogue is an extraordinary document not simply because it discusses both sides of certain controversial points skillfully and fairly and not merely because it presents a more cogent and fundamental defense of the administration's position than any other essay or pamphlet written in America, but because it goes beyond all of the immediate controversies to the outer boundaries of the issues involved, elevating the discussion to a level of universality that was unique for the time. The ordinary pros and cons of Parliament's right to tax are put aside and the discussion proceeds in terms of the nature of subjectship and allegiance. The right to defy Parliament's acts is denied in terms of the nature of constitutions as such—their mutability and conditioning by circumstance; in terms of the lack of objective criteria for moral judgments; in terms of the relation between law and morality; and in terms of what might be called an historicist understanding of public life as a process. And more than that, the Dialogue anticipates with remarkable clarity the ultimate drift of opposition thought, which to Hutchinson, so deeply committed to contemporary politics as it existed and so little impelled to transcend it, was completely unacceptable—which was indeed vague and doubtful even to the most imaginative leaders of the opposition—but which would in fact lead Americans across the frontiers of the *ancien régime* to the modern political world.

So Hutchinson concluded perhaps the central argument of the Dialogue by pointing out that there was no organ of government capable of declaring actions of the government unconstitutional, nor could there ever be such an umpiring agency since the constitution was not fixed, written, or otherwise available for unequivocal and objective reference. He was right: if the opposition continued to press claims of unconstitutionality against particular actions of the government they would indeed be led—some had already perceived the need—to think of constitutions as objective, fixed, ultimately written documents; and they would be led too to conceive of organs of government specifically empowered to rule on the constitutionality of the government's actions. So too Hutchinson saw the realistic limits of contract theory and the need to understand allegiance as perpetual and total—unless one were to move to a new conception altogether, in which allegiance would arise from desire, free migration and alienation, and the legalization of a mere commitment to a way of life. Above all, he saw more clearly than any writer of the time that persistence in the claims of a moral basis for resistance must end in revolution—a revolution that history might justify if it succeeded, but not because it was in an objective sense more moral than the establishment it overthrew. For the relationship between law and morality, he saw, was ambiguous, and only success could be a final arbiter.

So it was with remarkable perception and imagination, and with an extraordinary grasp of logical imperatives, that Hutchinson wrote out his basic thoughts on the problems of the time and put them into readable form. But the Dialogue remained buried in his papers, unpublished and unpublicized. One can only speculate on the reasons for this uncharacteristic silence: all of his instincts should have led him to use so effective a document as this to help stem the rising force of the opposition. Perhaps he felt the cogency of his own presentation of the American position more than he allowed *Europe* to admit and feared its possible usefulness to the opposition; perhaps he felt too vulnerable at the time to expose any views of his to public discussion. But there was another, more likely reason as well. His decision not to publish the Dialogue grew out of the political circumstances of the summer and early fall of 1768, and while those circumstances were to him gloomy indeed, he had reason to see in them a future prospect for himself that might make such a publication as this peculiarly inadvisable—the prospect of a major role in which he might act on his ideas as well as propound them, and serve, with greater effect than he ever had before, both his native community and the empire to which he was so deeply devoted. For among the leading figures of the imperial establishment in America he had one unique advantage. As Bernard had noted two years earlier, he and Hutchinson were essentially agreed in their ideas, but "there is this material difference between us: he, by being descended from a first settler and born and bred in this country, and having obtained the chief popular honors of it, must necessarily in some degree be prejudiced in favor of the form of its government."[41] But what to Bernard was a deficiency in Hutchinson, Hutchinson himself, seeking a decisive role as peacemaker and conciliator, knew was a major advantage, and one which the publication of the Dialogue might well destroy.

41. FB to H. S. Conway, Feb. 28, 1766, Bernard Papers, IV, 205. Bernard apparently thought twice about including this frank comparison in a letter to the secretary of state and deleted the sentence in the final version.

Chapter IV

The Furies

So Hutchinson sought to probe the sources of the spreading disorder, made urgent recommendations for alleviating the immediate crises, projected a long-term policy for stabilizing Anglo-American relations, and grappled with some of the thorniest theoretical problems created by the rising incidence of civil disobedience. But never were ideas worked out in less abstracted, less academic circumstances. Year after year as he struggled to refine his thoughts and bring them to the attention of officials in a position to affect the course of events, there were new shocks to the foundation of law and order and new erosions in the underlying stability of community life. He could scarcely believe what was happening. Despite all his warnings, and despite the self-evident dangers involved, disrespect for government and law grew steadily and by the end of the decade reached a point where ordinary people accepted violent disruptions of good order and public safety as almost normal.

He himself was subjected to continuous harassment. Though no one could produce a shred of evidence that he wished anything but liberty, security, and prosperity for his native land, he was repeatedly threatened with violence, denounced and humiliated. The annals of the late 1760's—years in which Americans, it would later be seen, came to discover their identity as a people—are a record of continuous frustration for Hutchinson and of his public denigration.

That he survived at all as a public figure is a testimony to his stamina and courage as well as to his love for public office; that he ended the decade in a more influential position than he had held at the start—as a key figure in the Anglo-American establishment—is a witness to his continuing skill in manipulating the British patronage system with which he had been involved for thirty years, and a witness too to his continuing misperception of the character of the opposition and of the ultimate sources of their political discontent.

1765 he would remember not merely for the savage destruction of his house and the threat to his life that occurred in August, but also for the intense pressure that was put on him later in the year as judge of probate in Suffolk County to ignore the Stamp Act after its effective date of November 1 and proceed in law without stamps, as if the act had never passed. "I held out, and refused," he wrote—but not for long. Like every other law officer in America he was threatened with violence if he did not openly defy the law. His resistance to such intimidation characteristically grew as the pressure mounted, but so too did the dangers he faced. "The real authority of the government is at an end," Bernard reported to the Board of Trade. "Some of the principal ringleaders in the late riots walk the streets with impunity. No officer dares attack them, no attorney general prosecute them, no witness appear against them, and no judge act upon them." In late December Hutchinson told William Bollan that he felt himself "in as precarious a state as when you advised me, after the change of the currency in '49, to retire to my house in the country." His friends, he told Judge Cushing, defined four alternatives for him to act on: "to do business without stamps; to quit the country; to resign my office; or ———." They assured him, and he agreed, that he had no time to deliberate. In the end, convinced that "further violence was just at hand," he excused himself rather unheroically on the ground that he was planning a trip to England, and, pointing out carefully to his correspondents in England that the probate judgeship had yielded him a steady £60 per annum, he resigned. "It was absolutely unsafe to hold the post any longer," he wrote; he considered himself fortunate, he explained to Benjamin Franklin, "that I was allowed to quit my post without being obliged at the same time to quit the continent." All the other courts and judges had succumbed, he wrote, and were conducting their business without stamps: "I am the only instance of non compliance." And so, at least in this negative way, he upheld the dignity of government under intense political pressure and in the face of threats of violence.[1]

It was a victory of sorts, though somewhat dimmed in the eyes of the public by the prompt interim appointment of his brother Foster to fill the vacated position—Foster, the *Boston Gazette* correctly observed, having "no scruple about the matter." ("Query," scribbled Harbottle Dorr, "whether [Thomas] was too scrupulous to share the profits? I trow not.")[2] But if this was a victory, Hutchinson had few others as time went on. Each year brought new disasters to the cause of law and stability and new humiliations to him personally.

1766, he came to believe, was one of the crucial years in the history of the Revolution, for it marked the time at which an *ad hoc* movement of political opposition became an organized conspiracy against government.

In January of that year, while secret plans were being made to

1. TH to ———, Dec. 31, 1765, MA, XXVI, 191 (a brief and succinct summary of the episode which Hutchinson apparently decided not to send); FB to Lords of Trade, Oct. 12, 1765, Bernard Papers, IV, 169; TH to William Bollan, Dec. 27, 1765, MA, XXVI, 187; TH to John Cushing, Jan. 15, 1766, William Cushing MSS, MHS; TH to Benjamin Franklin, Jan. 1, 1766, Leonard Labaree *et al.*, eds., *Papers of Benjamin Franklin*, XIII (New Haven, Yale University Press, 1969), 3–4; TH to ———, Jan. 2, 1766, MA, XXVI, 193. Bernard's official account of the pressure to do business without stamps is in letters to H. S. Conway, CO5/755/425ff.: "all real power in this town," he wrote on Dec. 19, 1765, "is in the hands of the people. . . . The time is come when even a nominal governor, though without authority or pretending to any, will not be allowed to reside here" (p. 425).

2. Leslie J. Thomas, "Partisan Politics in Massachusetts during Governor Bernard's Administration" (Ph.D. diss., University of Wisconsin, 1960), pp. 245, 278; Dorr, collection of newspapers, MHS, I, 304. Foster's appointment was not Hutchinson's idea but Bernard's. The governor told Hutchinson to appoint Foster his deputy in the probate court, but Hutchinson refused: "the thing was new, and instead of easing myself of a difficulty I was under, I should bring upon me one perhaps greater." Bernard then decided that as governor he had the authority to appoint to the post for a 12-month period, and he proceeded to do so (TH to Cushing, cited in previous note).

Bernard's behavior throughout was somewhat less than heroic. By mid-October he had concluded that while he might "stay here till my house is pulled down about my ears or I am knocked on the head . . . [he was] sure His Majesty requires no such sacrifice," and he therefore packed his valuables and prepared himself to evacuate at a moment's notice. Nothing further happening, however, and having decided to stay on, he wrote to his correspondents telling them to destroy all evidence of his having planned to leave, and began a systematic campaign to get himself recalled to England to advise the government on constitutional problems. Bernard Papers, IV, 13–15, 78–80, 198ff.; V, 23; For John Adams's response to Hutchinson's "political finesse" in keeping the superior court from proceeding without stamps, see Adams, *Diary and Autobiography*, I, 305, 310.

rescue Governor Bernard and his family in an emergency, Hutchinson's resistance to the House's demand for the opening of all official proceedings without the validation of stamps led to savage newspaper attacks on his multiple officeholding. His presidency of the Council was described as evidence of his insatiable greed for office—of his engrossment of "all the places of honor and profit in the province." This was a libelous falsehood, he knew, since he had established years before that the presidency of the Council fell automatically to the lieutenant governor by virtue of his office. Yet since timidity, he later wrote, "pervaded both legislative and executive powers," no action was taken against the libelers, and all measures designed to defy the unpopular act of Parliament succeeded.[3]

In May news of the repeal of the Stamp Act was received in Boston, but though Hutchinson himself had pleaded for it strenuously, he was alarmed at the extent to which the repeal was taken as a victory of extremism: unmistakable proof in people's eyes, Hutchinson noted, "that by union and firmness the colonies would be able to carry every point they wished for." The repeal seemed merely to stimulate the opposition and fortify its boldness. An overwhelming new power had been discovered, and since power, as everyone knew, "once acquired is seldom voluntarily parted with," it was soon again, and then repeatedly, used. Less than a fortnight later, the House, taking advantage of its unique right of nominating the members of the Council, purged that body of all executive officeholders, including Hutchinson himself, Andrew Oliver, Peter Oliver, and the attorney general, Jonathan Sewall. The typical dilemma ensued: if the administration did not do something about this disabling assault on the establishment it would in effect be surrendering a large measure of its political force as well as the dignity of government; if it tried to do something—even if it only strenuously objected—it would lay itself open to a torrent of abuse and further alienate the population. Bernard chose to protest, and seek a reversal of the vote, with grim results.

To Bernard's forthright statement that the purge of the Council could only be interpreted as a deliberate effort "to deprive [the government] of its best and most able servants whose only crime was

3. Joseph Redington and Richard A. Roberts, eds., *Calendar of Home Office Papers of the Reign of George III* . . . (London, 1878–1899), II, 2; FB to Lords of Trade, March 10, 1766, Bernard Papers, IV, 208–214; *History of Massachustts-Bay*, III, 105, 107.

their fidelity to the crown," Otis and his colleagues replied, with a cry of wounded innocence, that they had voted "according to the dictates of their consciences and the best light of their understandings," and that, just as they did not inquire into the governor's partisan motives for vetoing, as he had promptly done, six of the Council nominees who happened to be leaders of the opposition, so Bernard had no business casting aspersions on their motives. And then they added "with a sneer," Hutchinson wrote, that far from depriving the government of its best servants, they were really strengthening the government by "releas[ing] the judges from the cares and perplexities of politics and giv[ing] them opportunity to make still further advances in the knowledge of the law [and by leaving] other gentlemen more at leisure to discharge the duties and function of their important offices." They had in fact, they said, saved the government from "a dangerous union of legislative and executive powers in the same persons."[4]

The administration was helpless, and the result was not only that Hutchinson's long service on the Council came to an abrupt end but that the Council moved permanently into the orbit of the opposition, thenceforth to be directed by James Bowdoin, a highly placed merchant once favorably disposed to the government and to Hutchinson, whose opposition to the administration had an unmistakably personal coloring. And so it was that the most important institutional link between the administration and the community's leaders was destroyed.[5]

The force of this change was immediately felt, by Hutchinson more directly than by anyone else. In the same disastrous month of May 1766, the House began consideration of the administration's demand that it compensate the victims of the Stamp Act riots for their losses, chief among them of course being Thomas Hutchinson.

4. *Ibid.*, 107–108, 111–113. For a full discussion of the "purge" of the Council and its political consequences, see Francis G. Walett, "The Massachusetts Council, 1766–1774: The Transformation of a Conservative Institution," *W.M.Q.*, 3d ser., 6 (1949), 605–627.
5. In January 1767 Bowdoin's daughter married John Temple, the customs official who was locked in struggle with Bernard; but the Bowdoin-Temple affiliation in opposition to Bernard predated the marriage by several years; e.g., Temple to Thomas Whately, Sept. 10, 1764, *Bowdoin and Temple Papers* (MHS *Colls.*, 6th ser., IX, 1897), p. 27. For a contemporary interpretation of the Temple and Bowdoin opposition to Bernard, see Charles Paxton to [Lord Townshend?], Nov. 6, 1769, Misc. Bound MSS, MHS; for a careful reconstruction of one source of the conflict, see Jordan D. Fiore, "The Temple-Bernard Affair . . .," *Essex Institute Historical Collections*, 90 (1954), 58–83.

Agreeing at first with the administration that the evil-doers must by all means be brought to justice, the House proceeded to define compensation as generosity rather than justice and refused to act without specific instruction from the towns. When in October the towns indicated their support for compensation, the House incorporated that decision in a bill that combined compensation with a total amnesty for the still unapprehended rioters, and then condemned Hutchinson savagely for having approached the home government as well as Massachusetts for compensation. Since "beggars," Hutchinson wrote, "must not be choosers," he swallowed his pride and accepted, and so he received his compensation, but at the price of agreeing officially to the exoneration of the rioters and of submitting to public humiliation.[6]

And the year was not yet over. In quick succession during the final two months, the House, stampeded by that "incendiary" Otis, dismissed Hutchinson's and Bernard's friend Jackson from the colony's English agency; Bowdoin and his friends successfully appealed to common-law juries to reverse obnoxious decisions of the admiralty courts; and the radicals condemned Bernard for having a personal financial stake in the enforcement of the trade regulations.[7]

By the end of the year Hutchinson found confirmation for his darkest suspicions. The popular leaders, he was now utterly convinced, had secretly resolved, despite all their protestations to the contrary, to destroy the existing structure of government and to tear the colonies away from British control. Independence might not be attainable in their own lifetime but they had set that as their ultimate goal. They would seek relentlessly "to be continually making advances towards it, and to be prepared to accomplish it whenever it

6. *History of Massachusetts-Bay*, III, 113–115; TH to Thomas Pownall, Dec. 8, 1766, MA, XXVI, 242; TH to Lord Shelburne, CO5/755/865–868; TH to Richard Jackson, Nov. 16, 1766, MA, XXVI, 253. The Houses's request to the towns to instruct their representatives on the question of compensation struck Hutchinson as illogical and unconstitutional ("Instructions to restrain a representative from voting according to his judgment, however popular, always appeared to me to be unconstitutional and absurd"), and it mirrored in his mind the larger illogicality of the colonists' insistence on direct representation in Parliament as the legitimizing basis for tax enactments. TH to ———, Nov. 7, 1766, *ibid.*, 248. Hutchinson wrote three letters that day reviewing the debate on compensation and in each stressed the significance of the request to the towns for instructions (pp. 248ff.).

7. Bernard's extensive accounts of these events are in a series of reports to Lord Shelburne and the Lords of Trade, Oct. 10–Dec. 6, 1766, which are filed, together with accompanying documents, in vols. 755, 756, and 766 of the CO5 series. Bernard's letterbook copies of these letters are in Bernard Papers, IV, 251ff.

should be practicable." Their tactics and techniques, he believed, had been perfected. Their "extensive plan," he wrote Pownall in February 1767, was to keep creating crises and to involve the government continuously in turmoil by raising every possible objection to every move of the government no matter how necessary and just. They would vilify the establishment, pump out "swarms of contemptuous libels upon all in authority which we have not internal strength to suppress"; shamelessly lie about the government's intentions, knowing that charges against government are always popular and always difficult to refute with effect, and that false accusations, if not persisted in too long, will make "an impression upon some who never heard of the detection"; and finally, by "provok[ing] a power which they cannot resist," oblige the government to use coercion—police action by some kind of military force—that would prove to the uncritical public the accuracy of their original—and originally false—indictment.[8]

But that was not the worst of it. Hutchinson could begin to see a deeper, subtler problem, reflecting a devilish intelligence—whether conscious or instinctive he did not know—behind this concerted effort. The charges against him in these increasingly bitter personal attacks were beginning to center on one major theme that was certain to intensify the growing conflict and that was yet peculiarly difficult to refute. Increasingly the public prints (and even more the private correspondences which he knew of but did not see) claimed that it was Hutchinson who was engaged in a secret "design," that he was committed to sacrificing the general welfare to the calculated advancement of his own selfish interests, and that the crucial first step in his program was the deliberate misrepresentation to the English authorities of the truth of the situation in Massachusetts. His claim that he could see past the extremists' innocent-seeming professions into their secret motives and goals was a device, they said, to blacken the motives of anyone who opposed him. By insisting that the leadership of the opposition consisted of treasonous conspirators against the imperial government—that they were revolutionaries, or would-be revolutionaries—and that their agitations represented not a deep-lying and broadly shared sense of outrage

8. *History of Massachusetts-Bay*, III, 121, 186; TH to Thomas Pownall, Feb. 12, 1767, MA, XXVI, 265–266; TH to ——, Nov. 8, 1768, *ibid.*, p. 326; TH to ——, Feb. 23, 1768, *ibid.*, p. 293.

and frustration but only their own selfish interests, Hutchinson was hoping to rally the support—ultimately perhaps the military support—of the English government to prop up his monopoly of office and advance his corrupt plans. The subtlety of this charge was remarkable: Hutchinson could see that the very effort to reply to it might involve a self-intensifying circularity. For the more convinced he was that in fact public resentment against him was being deliberately stirred by a handful of demagogues and self-seeking merchants, and the more fervent he was in warning the English government of the danger these agitators posed and in begging for the means of resisting their threats, the more convinced the opposition would be that he was himself a willful deceiver intent on destroying the colony's free political system simply to satisfy what they took to be his lust for wealth and power.

Three years earlier, in 1763, Otis had pointed the way to this threatening impasse, though somewhat tentatively, in his public charge that, though Hutchinson may not have intended it, the effect of his warnings of demagoguery to the English authorities was "to make the people of England look upon us in a very bad light, forward attempts to alter our constitution, and have a tendency to procure a standing army to dragoon us into passive obedience." In 1766 the partial concession to Hutchinson's good intentions was gone: "There is a set of men in America," Otis wrote point blank in a Boston town committee report of that year, "who are continually transmitting to the mother country odious and false accounts of the colonies, which is a crime of the most dangerous tendency. It is probable that it has already had its ill effect in exciting a groundless jealousy in the nation, and may, if not checked, too soon prove fatal to both countries." His voice quickly found echoes. By the end of the year the same note was heard in the official statement of the speaker of the Massachusetts House to the secretary of state regretting the King's mistaken belief that the people of Massachusetts were ill-disposed to government. The colony was extremely anxious, the speaker said, "to remove from the breast of our gracious sovereign and father" the false notions that had been placed there by ill-intentioned persons. "It is unhappy for the colonists that . . . those from whom His Majesty has reason to expect the best information of the state of his colonies and the character of his subjects here, may not always be free from prejudice." No names were mentioned;

but they soon would be as the conflict implicit in these mutual suspicions worked itself out.[9]

1767 saw the conflict deepen and suspicions grow. In the first Assembly session of that year the popular leaders, Hutchinson wrote, twisted an innocent remark of the governor's into a confession that his administration had usurped the appropriation power from the House, and then proceeded to question Parliament's power to pass any acts at all "affecting the interior polity of the colonies"—a move so fundamentally subversive of authority that Hutchinson in later years said that "the revolt of the colonies ought to be dated from this time rather than from the Declaration of Independence." Then they turned to Hutchinson, discovering that he was still attending meetings of the Council, though without claiming the right to vote, in the *ex officio* capacity of lieutenant governor. This, they said, "affords a new and additional instance of ambition and lust of power to what we have heretofore observed," and, ignoring all the historical precedents that Hutchinson quickly assembled, they insisted, with the somewhat embarrassed concurrence of the Council itself, that his conduct was unconstitutional and inexcusable. His voluntary withdrawal from the Council without prejudice to the issue, on the grounds that he did not wish to be a center of controversy, was taken by the House to be an insult, and he was forthwith condemned in a formal resolution censuring his conduct. In the House speaker's ten-page summary of the arguments against Hutchinson's claim, not only was the lieutenant governor accused of parading bad logic and worse history and of lacking gratitude for the Assembly's generosity to him in compensating him for his losses, but he was accused as well of accumulating offices and functions totally incompatible with each other. "The office of chief justice," the speaker wrote for the edification of the ministry in England (most of whom served in different branches of government simultaneously)

is most certainly incompatible with that of a politician. The cool and impartial administration of common justice can never harmonize with the meanders and windings of a modern politician. The integrity of the judge

9. *Boston Gazette,* April 11, 1763; Boston Town Committee to [Dennys De Berdt], Oct. 20, 1766, Arthur Lee Papers, box 1, #25, Houghton Library, Harvard University, and printed without date in [*Sixteenth*] *Report of the Record Commissioners of . . . Boston . . .* (Boston, 1886), p. 194; Thomas Cushing to Lord Shelburne, Dec. 4, 1766, CO5/756/1–2.

may sometimes embarrass the politician, but there is infinitely more danger in the long run of the politician's spoiling the good and upright judge. This has often been the case, and the course of things may be expected again.

Then in May, after the failure of private efforts to work out a deal by which Hutchinson and the other excluded officials would be returned to the Council, he was again defeated in the Assembly's election of councillors, this time by only three votes.[10]

And below these surface events, the deeper suspicions of Hutchinson's motives that Otis had first expressed continued to grow and were more and more explicitly discussed. A Charlestown merchant, Edward Sheaffe, reporting to the Assembly's agent in England on the "present state of the times," conceded that there may have been faults on both sides in the political disputes of 1765, but for their continuation into the present year he blamed only the governor and his party. They had been deliberately provocative, and not accidentally. He could guess at the devious long-term plan that lay behind these provocations: "a trap's being laid to take [the Assembly] in," he wrote, " a scheme in some persons to drive this people into some extraordinary measures in order to furnish a ministry less favorable to the province than the present with materials to deprive [them of] their invaluable liberty and privileges, both [civil] and religious." All sorts of rumors were circulating "of what is to be done to us": a court of customs commissioners, or perhaps a court of exchequer, was to be established; more important, it was commonly said, he reported, that the colony's executive officers, who had always been paid by the Assembly, were in the future to be paid out of revenue raised from new import duties. If that rumor proved to be true and the executive officers were in fact paid in this way by the crown, which already controlled them by the power of appointment, the

10. *History of Massachusetts-Bay*, III, 123–128; Thomas Cushing to De Berdt, March 16, 1767, Arthur Lee Papers, box 1, #33–35. In 1757 Thomas Pownall reported that Hutchinson himself thought his appointment to the lieutenant governorship "would take him out of the Council" (Pownall to Lord Halifax, Sept. 4, 1757, Peter Force Papers, ser. 9, box 7, Library of Congress); but there is no other evidence for this. His controversy with William Pepperrell over precedence in the Council when he became lieutenant governor presumed his right to active membership in the Council. Cf. Eg. MSS, 2664, p. 64 from end, where Hutchinson discusses the precedence issue in detail. He was extremely cautious in reporting to his correspondents in England about the struggle with the Council in early 1767. His letterbook contains at least six letters on the subject (MA, XXVI, 265ff.), in which he insists on the confidentiality of what he is writing: two of the letters—the most detailed and informative—he decided not to send.

balance of forces within the colony's constitution would be completely thrown off, popular affection for government would be alienated, and mutual confidence between the governors and the governed utterly destroyed. How wretched, he wrote, was a situation in which "some persons from hence have so much influence as to deceive those who I am persuaded wish well to the colonies." He could take comfort only in the belief "that Jehovah rules in the hearts of kings and great men, into whose hands I commit the cause of this province."[11]

Others were less confident of divine benevolence. The speaker of the Massachusetts House too warned the Assembly's agent of "people on this side of the water that represent the province in a bad light" and who endeavor "by false representations" to destroy the harmony between England and America. Being better informed than Sheaffe he could see their effort in a broader perspective.

. . . there are some people on both sides the water that are on the one hand representing the colonies as setting up for independency, as turbulent, factious, and disloyal, and on the other are insinuating to the people here as if the government at home were disposed to treat the colonies with severity and to deprive them of the most invaluable privileges. The designs of such people must be very pernicious, and have a fatal tendency; and it is difficult to name a punishment adequate to the offense.

His hopes for the future lay not so much in Jehovah's benevolence as in the English government's political wisdom and sense of justice. He instructed the agent to insist that the colony be allowed to correct any falsehoods and misrepresentations that might be sent to England by self-seeking colonial officials before action of any kind was undertaken.[12]

1768 was to Hutchinson a continuous series of crises and disasters in which popular resentment against him, stirred, he believed, by a handful of malcontents, reached an explosive pitch.

News of Secretary of State Shelburne's condemnation of the Massachusetts Assembly for its dismissal of Hutchinson from the Council and for its conduct in general led to an attack on the governor that Bernard said was "so wild, unreasonable, and out-

11. Edward Sheaffe to De Berdt, July 1, 1767, Arthur Lee Papers, box 1, #38.
12. Cushing to De Berdt, June 24, 1767, *ibid.*, #36–37.

rageous that it exceeds all bounds of discretion and common prudence and outdoes even Otis's outdoings." It had been Bernard's "obstinate perseverance in the path of malice," the House alleged, his "diabolical thirst for mischief," and his "jesuitical insinuations" that had led Shelburne to praise Hutchinson as a man of character, learning, ability, and public service, and "to form a most unfavorable opinion of the province in general and some of the most respectable inhabitants in particular." Even the now normally supine Council felt it necessary to cite this savage publication as a "scandalous and impudent libel . . . an insolent and licentious attack on the chief magistrate" and to pledge its undying support for "the honor and dignity of the King's governor." But Hutchinson's elaborate speech to the grand jury on the corrosive effects of the public defamation of officers of state and his careful discrimination between culpable libel and the legitimate boundaries of a free press, culminating in a plea to the jury to bring charges against the publisher—all of this was simply ignored.[13]

The House had meanwhile released its famous circular letter condemning the rumored payment of executive officers and judges from crown income and calling for resistance to the Townshend Duties. In March Hutchinson reported that mobs celebrating the anniversary of the repeal of the Stamp Act were terrorizing the town of Boston and publicly abusing the governor. Gangs of thugs, he wrote, "armed with bludgeons," defied the new American Board of Customs Commissioners—who were by then almost totally ostracized in Boston—and carted smuggled goods openly through the town. Rumors of the pending crown salaries, the lack of which Bernard insisted had caused an "imbecility of government in Massachusetts" and which he begged the ministry to supply, swelled into cries of outrage that echoed beyond the boundaries of the colony. When word reached John Dickinson in Pennsylvania that Hutchinson had been granted "a pension . . . out of American revenue," he wrote immediately to Otis to inquire if it was true, and if it was, to ask that he be sent the exact wording of the grant as soon as possible. The same rumors accounted for the final, most bizarre episode in the long drama of Hutchinson's exclusion from the Council. In

13. FB to Jackson, Feb. 20, 1768, Bernard Papers, VI, 93; Quincy, *Reports of Cases,* pp. 271, 273, 262–268; *History of Massachusetts-Bay,* III, 134–135.

May a final and almost successful effort to elect Hutchinson to the upper chamber ended in a nightmare scene in which Otis, fearful that his enemy would at last succeed, created bedlam just before the final vote was taken by running through the House chamber—whose newly built spectators' gallery was crowded with his partisans—like "an enraged demon," Hutchinson reported, crying that the choice was between "pensioner or no pensioner."[14]

In June the seizure of Hancock's sloop *Liberty* on a charge of smuggling brought chaos. Hutchinson reported riots in the streets, physical assaults on the customs officers, the burning of patrol boats, Town Meeting resolutions of the wildest kind, and the harassment of the customs commissioners (except for Bowdoin's son-in-law John Temple) to the point that they were forced to hide for safety in Castle William. And even that stronghold, three miles off the coast, was not safe: rumors spread that a mob would somehow storm it. Bernard became fearful "of such a convulsion as would render it unsafe for him to remain in the province"; formally applied for leave to return home while contemplating an emergency refuge in Nova Scotia; and ordered Hutchinson to stand by for the worst. Then on June 30, after frenzied speeches in which the King's ministers were called, among other things, ignorant, ill-educated, francophiliac despots, came the famous House vote, 92–17, defying Lord Hillsborough's order to rescind the circular letter. The public vilification of the seventeen-man minority was savage and almost universal, despite the fact, Hutchinson noted, that they were all "men of very reputable general characters and most of them distinguished for their good sense as well as integrity." It takes courage, he noted in

14. *Ibid.*, p. 136; FB to Lord Barrington, Oct. 20, 1768, *The Barrington-Bernard Correspondence . . . 1760–1770*, ed. Edward Channing and A. C. Coolidge (Cambridge, 1912), p. 178; John Dickinson to James Otis, [July 1768], *Warren-Adams Letters*, I (MHS *Colls.*, LXXII, 1917), 7; William Gordon, *History of the Rise, Progress, and Establishment of the Independence of the United States of America . . .* (N.Y., 1789), I, 155; TH to Nathaniel Rogers, May 31, 1768, MA, XXV, 258; TH to Thomas Pownall, June 7, 1768, *ibid.*, p. 262. The popular clamor against Hutchinson's rumored crown salary, based on the conviction that it would throw off the balance of the constitution by making the executive independent of the representative assembly (but which Bernard insisted was necessary to *restore* the balance of the constitution which had been destroyed by the overwhelming power of the House) had been heard at least since the end of 1767 (Cushing to De Berdt, Oct. 15, 1767, Arthur Lee Papers, box 1, #39). In Aug. 1768 the *Boston Gazette* published five articles on the subject. Since these rumored salaries were understood to be drawn from the Townshend Duties, those duties—thus seen to be the basis of a new civil list—became especially obnoxious.

his *History,* "to stand against a popular torrent when it runs with violence."[15]

Such courage was increasingly needed in 1768, and increasingly rare. There seemed to be no end to the disorder. By July, Hutchinson said, Boston was in the grip of a plebiscitarian tyranny—a *"dominatio plebis"*—worse than any autocracy Massachusetts had ever known before "even under Dudley and Andros in the reign of King James." "The people," he wrote, "seem to me in a state of absolute dementation." They had lost all sense of proportion and responded almost insanely to the slightest suggestion of affront. At the Harvard College commencement in July Governor Bernard made the mistake of remarking jokingly to the Council leader James Bowdoin that he agreed with the Council's recent petition to keep funds raised by the Townshend Duties in the colony, since he hoped to avail himself of a good part of that revenue. He was instantly attacked, first for having misrepresented the Council's petition, which had been primarily directed against the *raising* of the revenue not against its distribution; and second for seeking an unconstitutional supplement to his salary. Bowdoin had no doubt at all that the governor had already sent this misconstruction of the Council's petition to the ministry. Explanations were demanded; Bernard was obliged to read his recent letters to Lord Hillsborough aloud to a delegation of councillors (who concluded that his remark had been "entirely in joke"); there were debates in the Council; attacks in the newspapers; and two explanatory petitions were sent off to England, lest any possible misrepresentation by the governor be taken seriously by the authorities there. Nine months after Bernard's pleasantry had been uttered in Cambridge, Bowdoin was still warning the secretary of state that the governor had probably falsified the Council's intent.[16]

When ordinarily sensible men like Bowdoin acted so madly there was little hope, as far as Hutchinson could see, that stability could be achieved by normal means. The law was not merely ignored and

15. TH to Richard Jackson, June 16, 1768, MA, XXVI, 310–312; Thomas, "Partisan Politics," pp. 505ff.; Gipson, *British Empire,* XI, 152–156; FB to Lord Hillsborough, June 25, 1768 and letters following, CO5/757/509ff.; TH to Jackson, July 14, 1768, MA, XXVI, 313–314; *History of Massachusetts-Bay,* III, 143–145.

16. TH to ——, July 21, 1768, MA, XXVI, 315; FB to Hillsborough, Nov. 30, 1768, CO5/758/23; Bowdoin to Hillsborough, April 15, 1769, *ibid.,* 86.

deliberately defied, but gratuitously, even playfully, flouted. In August the anniversary of the destruction of Oliver's stamp office was publicly celebrated, and among the most active revelers was the leader of the gang that had sacked Hutchinson's house in 1765, one Will Moore, who had been jailed for that exploit but "rescued since by a number of people in the night. That man is now at liberty," Bernard wrote Hillsborough, "to celebrate those exploits by which he legally incurred the penalty of death."[17]

We cannot long continue this way, Hutchinson wrote grimly, "Government must be aided from without or else it must entirely subside and suffer anarchy to rise in its place." But the help, when it arrived on October 1 in the form of two regiments of troops, only compounded the trouble. For weeks after Bernard had carefully leaked the news of the troops' imminent arrival (if they had arrived without warning he was sure there would have been an open insurrection), the radical leaders kept the town in a turmoil of emergency protest meetings, frantic preparation of arms, and endless denunciations ("ravings," Bernard called them) of those presumed to be responsible for the outrage. Their worst fears, they said, had been realized. Hutchinson and Bernard had achieved the means they had long sought of creating a veritable autocracy in Massachusetts and of destroying the constitution—a triumph they had managed by deliberately misrepresenting the true state of affairs in Massachusetts to the authorities at home. The mere rumor, weeks before, of the possible arrival of troops had led the Boston Town Meeting to order its inhabitants to arm and to call for the convening of an extralegal convention of representatives of all the towns. The convention when it met on September 22 represented to Hutchinson "a greater tendency towards a revolution in government than any preceding measures in any of the colonies," though its leaders, aware that it was being described to Whitehall in those terms, denied that it had been convened "upon the precedent of 1688" and insisted that its proceedings were "legal, innocent, and even meritorious." As Hutchinson expected it would, the convention condemned the calling of the troops, denounced Hutchinson and Bernard for having summoned them (though they had in fact scrupulously avoided doing

17. FB to Hillsborough, Aug. 29, 1768, Bernard Papers, VII, 26. In 1778 TH was told that Moore also led the "Indians" in the tea party. *Diary and Letters,* II, 228.

so), and demanded that the governor call an official Assembly so that grievances could be formally expressed.[18]

Once the troops were settled in Boston, Hutchinson told Jackson that he slept better than he had for years, but he had to admit that the town soon trembled on the edge of a bloody upheaval. The citizenry defied every effort of Hutchinson and others to house and maintain the troops and were provocative to the soldiers in every way. In their newly founded and widely distributed *Journal of the Times* the radical leaders painted a picture of a community in the grip of an iron-fisted military dictatorship, its inhabitants cowering in terror, its legal constitution abandoned. Yet informed people knew perfectly well, Hutchinson wrote, that the troops could do nothing without civilian direction, and they must have known too that prior to the arrival of the troops "we were upon the brink of ruin, and their arrival prevented some most extravagant measures"—what measures precisely, he confessed he did not know, except that they were "dark," that the first step had obviously been the convening of the convention, and that they were "something more extravagant than had ever been attempted before." Of course, he added wearily, once the troops had arrived, the radicals suddenly declared that they had never been "in earnest and that it was all a

18. TH to —— Grant, July 27, 1768, MA, XXVI, 317; FB to Hillsborough, Sept. 16, 1768, *Papers Relating to Public Events in Massachusetts Preceding the American Revolution* (Philadelphia, 1856), pp. 101–105 (hereafter cited as *Mass. Papers*); *History of Massachusetts-Bay*, III, 149; Samuel Cooper to Thomas Pownall, Feb. 18, 1769, "Letters of Samuel Cooper to Thomas Pownall, 1769–1777," *American Historical Review*, 8 (1902–1903), 304 (hereafter: "Cooper-Pownall Letters"). The belief that Bernard and Hutchinson had called for the troops would never be effectively discounted and became a standard refrain in the revolutionaries' charges against them. It is certainly false with respect to Hutchinson, and it is ambiguous with respect to Bernard. For Bernard was extremely careful to explain to his correspondents that he was *not* asking for troop support and that he could not do so without the concurrence of the Council ("I no more dare apply for troops than the Council dare advise me to it" [to Barrington, March 4 and July 30, 1768, *Barrington-Bernard Corr.*, pp. 148, 170]), and in Sept. 1765 he had refused an offer of troops and had asked that if troops were sent he be removed from the colony first. Bernard Papers, IV, 162; V, 9. But he had already intimated that troops would eventually be needed (*ibid.*, IV, 12–13, 19) and when in July 1768 he was certain that they were on their way, he said that if they had been sent three years earlier all the trouble would have been avoided. The formal request for troops came from the customs commissioners after the *Liberty* riot (Thomas, "Partisan Politics," p. 519), but Hillsborough's order to General Gage to send the troops (June 8, 1768) cited Bernard's recent letters as well as the request he had received from the customs commissioners. *Mass. Papers*, p. 61.

The latest and most thorough investigation of the convention of Sept. 1768 supports Hutchinson's view of it: Richard D. Brown, "The Massachusetts Convention of Towns, 1768," *W.M.Q.*, 3d ser., 26 (1969), 102.

puff" and consequently that the summoning of troops could only be part of a plan to terrify a liberty-loving population into submission.[19]

Nothing was too wild for the radical leaders—"one half dozen of the most wicked fellows . . . of any upon the globe. They stick at nothing." No libel against the government was too vicious or too seditious for them, no lie or slander against individuals too outrageous. At the end of 1768, Hutchinson told his English friends, he had received for sale a trunkful of ordinary cloth bandannas, only to discover that the rumor was being spread "that it was a trunk of rich silks, a present from Lord Clive of £500 value"—an outrageous lie, heavy with political implications, which no amount of denial would effectively refute. The boldness of these "deceivers," these "pretended patriots," was growing all the time. They did not hesitate to publish in the *Gazette* what Hutchinson described as nothing less than their step-by-step plan for attaining independence, and they continued brazenly to hoodwink the mass of the people into believing "there was a design to subject them to heavy taxes of which the late acts only gave them a small specimen." They were less and less careful as time went on in hiding their motives. It was perfectly clear that "a particular family of large property and high resentment" was responsible for much of the tumult. For by 1768 the Council was simply a junta of the in-laws of John Temple— the board included Temple's wife's father, Bowdoin; her grandfather, Erving; and her uncle, Pitts—and their politics was simply an expression of Temple's anger at having been demoted from surveyor general of customs to one of the Board of Customs Commissioners: "the Board must therefore be dissolved and Temple restored." The people in general, however, remained innocent: Hutchinson continued to believe that if they were left "to act their free judgment, the major part of them would [n]ever consent to the schemes of this party."[20]

19. TH to Jackson, n.d. [Jan. 1769], MA, XXVI, 337; *Boston under Military Rule (1768–1769) as Revealed in "A Journal of the Times,"* ed. Oliver M. Dickerson (Boston, 1936); Bernard Bailyn, *Ideological Origins of the American Revolution* (Cambridge, Harvard University Press, 1967), pp. 113–115; *History of Massachusetts-Bay*, III, 162; TH to Bollan, Nov. 1768, MA, XXVI, 328; TH to ——, [Nov. 1768], *ibid.*, p. 328.
20. TH to Israel Mauduit, Dec. 5, 1768, MA, XXVI, 332; TH to William Palmer, Dec. 24, 1768, *ibid.*, p. 334 (six years later Hutchinson was still trying to sell the bandannas: TH to TH, Jr., Dec. 9, 1774, Eg. MSS, 2661, p. 88); TH to ——, Nov. 14, 1768, MA, XXVI, 327; TH to ——, Feb. 16, 1769, *ibid.*, p. 346 (this description of the Temple-

How powerful the subversive party, how lethal their threat, Hutchinson fully realized, according to his own record, only in the course of 1768 when he suddenly noted the importance of the encouragement they were receiving from the very seat of power in England. Not, he was sure, that they had convinced by their arguments any significant group of people in England, or tapped sympathetic sources of true conviction there. It was simply that their attacks on the government and their more and more audible declarations that the administration was malevolent in its purpose played into the hands of party politicians in England seeking leverage—any leverage—against the ministry. Even some of the great men of England—revered and honorable men like Chatham and Camden—backed the colonial radicals as a way of attacking the administration; and with such encouragement, lesser men like Barré and Conway, to say nothing of the Wilkesites, embraced the radicals' cause with abandon. In Parliament the opposition, Hutchinson knew, was still small, but their influence, he believed, was sufficient to enable them to paralyze the government's will to put down the insurgents. They were able to convince people that the majority of the House of Commons, which could outvote them on any issue, had been corrupted by a ministry intent on oppressing the colonies, quite against the wishes of "the mind of the Kingdom." So the ministry had been prevented from acting, except for the desperate move of sending troops in a crisis.[21]

The result of this effective English reinforcement of the radical cause in America, Hutchinson wrote in his annals of 1768, was catastrophic. For once the people of Massachusetts realized that Parliament was not able or willing to act to assert its authority, "lenity was construed into timidity," the long-feared statute of treason "became a subject of contempt and ridicule," and crown officers, despairing of support, "grew very cautious lest they should incur the resentment of the people." It was a particularly tragic

---

Bowdoin domination of the Council, which was common knowledge, Hutchinson decided not to send); TH to Thomas Whately, Aug. 24, 1769, *ibid.*, p. 367.

21. *History of Massachusetts-Bay*, III, 160–161, 190. As early as 1763 the contagion of English "licentiousness" had been evident to Hutchinson (TH to Jackson, Aug. 3, 1763, MA, XXVI, 65: "Our *boutefeus* take the advantage of the licentiousness in England, and their partisans vindicate them by saying they do not go the lengths Wilkes does"). But it was not until 1768 that he was confident that the two opposition groups were operating within a single political design.

development, Hutchinson thought, because it was based upon so profound a misunderstanding. For though the junta in the colonies believed the party opposition in England to be its counterpart, sponsor, and protector at the seat of government, the two opposition groups were in fact fundamentally different, and everything would depend upon the English government's understanding the difference: "the combinations in England are for removing particular persons from the places they are in; the combinations in America are against government itself, the authority of which is in express words denied by the combinations themselves. . . . If both are criminal, yet they greatly differ in degree."[22]

Thus reinforced, stimulated, and legitimized, the agitations of the colonial extremists continued into 1769 and reached heights of excess that Hutchinson confessed he could scarcely have imagined only a few years earlier. The year had barely begun when Hutchinson found explicit documentary evidence of the hidden purposes he had long believed lay behind the opposition's extravagant behavior. On January 23 an innkeeper, one Richard Silvester, made a formal deposition before Hutchinson, as chief justice, which was immediately dispatched to London. Silvester swore that on various occasions he had heard Sam Adams, "trembling and in great agitation," cry, " 'Let us take up arms immediately and be free, and seize all the King's officers,' " and such remarks as " 'The times were never better in Rome than when they had no king and were a free state, and as this is a great empire we shall soon have it in our power to give laws to England,' " and " 'we will destroy every soldier that dare put his foot on shore; His Majesty has no right to send troops here to invade the country, and I look upon them as foreign enemies.' " But Dr. Benjamin Church's inflammatory words, which Silvester also reported, were undoubtedly more interesting to Hutchinson. Silvester had heard Church say publicly not only that the people of Boston would resist the King's troops and that England's empire, now at its zenith, must soon fall, but that he had certain knowledge that Hutchinson and Bernard " 'wrote home against the people. It will be necessary to seize them and their papers to come at the truth, and send them home in irons.' " In fact, as things

22. *History of Massachusetts-Bay*, III, 161; TH to John Pownall, May 6, 1770, MA, XXVI, 478; TH to Robert Wilson, May 11, 1770, *ibid.*, pp. 479–480.

turned out, Silvester remarked, once the troops had arrived it was Church himself who was mainly concerned about being sent home in irons; he had been seen scrambling through the town searching for the originals of treasonous letters he had sent to the press. But Church's threat had not been idle. Hutchinson knew that the plan against him and Bernard that Church had revealed was serious, far more serious and important in the end than such wild ravings as the innkeeper also reported having heard from one of the radicals, to the effect that " 'the King is a fool and a rascal and ought to have his head cut off, and the Lords and Commons are rogues and scoundrels.' "[23]

The seriousness of Church's threat was only too soon made clear. Week after week in February and March the Boston Town Meeting in a series of official addresses blasted the misrepresentations that, they were convinced, had been sent to the ministry by "artful and mischievous men." These "partial or false representations" of the recent disorders, in which Boston was alleged to be "in a state of disobedience to law and ready to resist the constitutional authority of the nation," had been the cause of England's sending "ships of war and military troops even in a time of peace, quartered in its very bowels, exercising a discipline with all the severity which is used in a garrison and in a state of actual war." Only outright lies, the Boston selectmen charged, could have convinced the nation that peace and good order and the safety of civil magistrates required a naval and military force.[24]

The tone of the attacks grew more and more shrill, more and more personal, and more and more likely to lead to an explosion. At the end of January a satirical pamphlet appeared reporting a dialogue between an English traveler and an independent-minded New Englander ("neither placed nor pensioned") who explained the error of believing that "only a small *faction*" opposed the government's measures, and identified the loyal *"prerogative* men" as

23. CO5/758/54–55. Silvester's testimony was one result of a concerted effort that Bernard made in Jan. and Feb. to uncover evidence of the treasonous nature of the "faction's" purposes, especially in calling the convention of 1768. He created a "cabinet council" consisting of Hutchinson, Andrew Oliver, and the admiralty judge Robert Auchmuty to take depositions that might be used as evidence in court trials for treason. *Ibid.*, 50; CO5/767/209; Bernard Papers, VII, 124. And since the regular j.p.'s were too weak-willed or disloyal to be relied on, he added the same three and also Thomas Flucker (who would succeed Oliver as the province secretary) to the commission of the peace.

24. *Mass. Papers,* pp. 115ff.; Arthur Lee Papers, box 1, #42ff.

Jacobites, smugglers, peculating revenue officers, and penniless placeholders. These government men were described physically and biographically as they were encountered "upon . . . the north side of the 'change" in Boston. At the center of the group stood Hutchinson, "that *meager tall-man*," as he was referred to throughout the pamphlet:

now a provincial state officer with a *pension;* was once an unsuccessful *smuggler* and merchant in this town; he is the idol of that group and some few more in the country, but has lost the confidence and esteem of the people, which was once his glory. He has two passions that prevail with great strength, *ambition* and *avarice,* all others being totally absorbed. These are in great force indeed and frequently cannot determine which most predominates. They are alternately uppermost, and having none of the common passions of life to disturb him, he remains a man of assiduity and application. In whatever he undertakes he is thoroughly accomplished in every art both to make a friend or take off the enemy as he may have occasion, and is the masterpiece of human nature for *dissimulation* and *disguise.*

The rest of the government group—Oliver, Sewall, Auchmuty, Flucker: sixteen in all—were similarly caricatured and all of them shown to be tied in some corrupt way to Hutchinson, who had "every art of dissimulation and hypocrisy; but when these *few* find him out (as they certainly will) he then will be as much despised by them as he now is by the rest of the people."[25]

The pamphlet is no masterpiece of wit, but it was an effective polemic, which gave notice that anyone loyal to Hutchinson and the administration would be the object of blistering public abuse. At the same time more formal and direct attacks were made. On February 25 the selectmen wrote openly and fully to the Assembly's London agent (with copies to Pownall, Franklin, Bollan, and the presumably sympathetic agent and M.P., Barlow Trecothick) describing and condemning "enemies of the town . . . who are seeking its ruin . . . in the daily practices of secret art and machination." It

25. *A Dialogue between Sir George Cornwall, a Gentleman Lately Arrived from England . . . and Mr. Flint . . .* ("printed in London and reprinted in Boston," 1769), pp. 4, 5, 14. Flucker accused Temple of having written the pamphlet, and they "had a sort of fight about it upon 'change." TH to Thomas Pownall, July 24, 1769, MA, XXVI, 357. "The tall man" became a standard polemical reference to Hutchinson (e.g., *Boston Gazette,* April 9, 1770, quoted below, Chap. V, note 15). For the role of the pamphlet in Jonathan Sayward's refusal of office, see below, pp. 181–182.

had been these men, the selectmen had "best grounds to believe," whose "stations and connections gave them great weight and influence," who had induced the ministry, "by a partial if not a false account of facts sent from hence," to surround the port with warships and quarter troops on the peaceful population. The town was utterly convinced "that His Majesty's ministers had greatly misapprehended the public transactions of the town," and they proceeded to review the recent events in exhaustive detail, refuting in page after page what they described as Bernard's and Hutchinson's deliberate misrepresentations of the facts.[26]

The explosive climax was soon reached. In April, through the efforts of Bollan, then unemployed and seeking appointment as agent to the Council, the opposition leaders got hold of letters that Bernard, the military commanders in Boston, and the customs commissioners had written confidentially the year before to the secretary of state describing the breakdown of government in Boston and the threat they felt of an approaching insurrection, and urging that the Council be changed in its constitution, from an Assembly-elected to a crown-appointed body, and that a review be undertaken of the loyalty of all incumbents of crown offices in America. The letters were exactly what the opposition had been looking for; it made it possible for them, Hutchinson wrote, to succeed in their "professed design," which, he explained to Jackson, was "to wear [Bernard] out and cause him to resign his government and to induce the ministry to remove him because [he was] disagreeable to the people." No further proof seemed to be needed of the governor's evil intentions and of the existence of an Anglo-American plan to reduce the constituted liberties of the colonies. In the uproar that followed the publication of the letters, Bernard was charged by the Council in a twenty-eight-page letter, and subsequently by the town of Boston and by the House, and once again by the Council in a follow-up letter, with willful misrepresentation of the truth, intent to destroy the constitution of the colony, character assassination, and a lust for

26. Boston selectmen to Dennys De Berdt, Feb. 25, 1769, Arthur Lee Papers, box 1, #43–45. Samuel Cooper's comment to Thomas Pownall (Feb. 18. 1769) is revealing: the people of Massachusetts, he wrote, are at a great disadvantage in that "living so distant from the great fountain of government they know not what has been alleged against them nor in what light their conduct has been placed, and consequently it is out of their power to vindicate themselves till the misrepresentation has had its effect." "Cooper-Pownall Letters," p. 303.

"exorbitant and uncontrollable power." His immediate and permanent dismissal from office was demanded.[27] The House's resolutions reduced the accusations to formal articles which Admiral Hood, the commanding military officer in Boston, believed were so ferocious that some Bostonians would take them "as an alarm bell to revolt," and he hesitated before completing the scheduled removal of the troops. Six months after the publication of the letters the public response was summarized in a pamphlet drafted for the town of Boston by Samuel Adams, in which every statement of the famous letters was scrutinized, every charge refuted, and the representations of events lampooned as "slanderous *chit chat*."[28]

Bernard had in fact long since wearied of his post. For five years he had been asking for a leave of absence, and he had already received permission to return to England, together with word of the reward of a baronetcy for his labors, before his letters were published. But his actual departure on August 1, 1769, following a totally chaotic and aborted session of the Assembly, was taken to be yet another proof, Hutchinson believed, that absolute ruthlessness—even so criminal an action as publishing letters stolen from official files—paid off.[29]

For Hutchinson, Bernard's last months in America and his own first experiences as acting head of the government formed as dark a period as any he had known and provided a bitter foretaste of the ordeal that would follow. Though he was, as Admiral Hood predicted he would be, "quite sensible of the temper of the times and . . . very cautious to do nothing to irritate," and though, as Rogers noted, the opposition was "much disappointed that not a line of his

27. CO5/767/247–298, 302ff., 341–352; 768/22ff. Samuel Cooper's letters to Thomas Pownall, May-Sept. 1769, reflect vividly the fears induced by the publication of Bernard's letters ("Cooper-Pownall Letters," pp. 306–310). For Bollan's account of his obtaining the letters, which had been requested by the Council, see his letters to Boston, June 21 and 23, 1769, in MHS *Colls.*, 6th ser., IX (1897), 144–148; for his later censure in England, see pp. 180–181. On this definitive switch in Bollan's loyalty, see Malcolm Freiberg, "William Bollan, Agent of Massachusetts," *More Books*, 23 (1948), 179–180. On the episode in general, and for details of the publication of the letters, see Francis G. Walett, "Governor Bernard's Undoing . . . ,"*New England Quarterly*, 38 (1965), 217–226.

28. Gipson, *British Empire*, XII, 40; Hood to the Admiralty, CO5/758/170; [Samuel Adams, *An Appeal to the World; Or, a Vindication of the Town of Boston* . . . (Boston, 1769), p. 32.

29. Letters to Hillsborough and John Pownall, May 15, 1769, *et seq.*, Bernard Papers, VII, 163ff.; *History of Massachusetts-Bay*, III, 163–183.

appears in the copies [of the letters] lately transmitted here" and could "find no flaw in his conduct," he could not stop the harassments and outbreaks of violence.[30]

In September, after less than a month as acting governor, Hutchinson was attacked in vicious squibs in successive issues of the *Boston Gazette*. In October a mob of several thousands set upon a sailor falsely accused of informing on the smugglers, tarred him and feathered him, and dragged him through the town, threatening to break every window in Boston that was not illuminated as a sign of sympathy. Nothing could be done: the justices of the peace were helpless before such force, and the Council refused to concur in Hutchinson's request that the troops be called to restore order. So it was discovered, as Hutchinson had predicted it would be, that the feared and hated regiments were in fact ineffective, indeed worse than useless: they were too powerful and too numerous to be politically safe to use as a constabulary in controlling street riots, and too weak to put down a widespread armed rebellion—yet their presence was provocative. The mobs, sensing this, became bolder, became invincible, in intimidating those who challenged in any way the developing nonimportation movement.[31]

The nonimportation movement, organized in 1769 in opposition to the Townshend Duties, was the most seditious development, Hutchinson believed, that had yet been seen in America, for it had been organized by otherwise respectable merchants who by the use of boycotts and manipulated public opinion had forced all traders to join them and then gained the backing of "the three professions, lawyers, physicians, and clergy, depending entirely on the people for their support and who must comply with popular humors." With this intimidating force behind it, the movement had snowballed, even without the use of strong-arm methods, into a massive conspiracy, or "combination," against the operation of law. The nonimportation movement was to Hutchinson "more dangerous

30. Hood to Admiralty, July 10, 1769, CO5/758/171; Nathaniel Rogers to ——, Oct. 25, 1769, New England Papers (Sparks MSS 10), III, 44, Houghton Library, Harvard University.
31. *History of Massachusetts-Bay*, III, 187, 189–190; TH to Gage, Oct. 29, 1769, MA, XXVI, 398. Two years earlier Hutchinson had written that if the people felt that submission to government was in their own interest, a mere 300–400 troops "would be sufficient to prevent accidental riots and tumults in any colony, but when they are fixed in the contrary opinion it is difficult to determine what number would be necessary to enforce obedience." TH to Jackson, Oct. 20, 1767, MA, XXV, 206.

than the riots and tumults which have been so justly condemned,"
for unlike outright rioting this kind of intimidation was believed
by many to be constitutional since its coercion was tacit and indirect
and it did not depend on seditious publications and "illiberal resolutions." The leaders acted as if they were engaged in legitimate
political activity, assembling quite openly in Faneuil Hall; yet what
they were engaged in, Hutchinson believed, was not simply illegal
but "utterly incompatible with a state of government. . . . For
particular persons to forbear importing cannot be deemed criminal,
but it is quite another thing for numbers to confederate together
and compel others to join them, and all with an avowed design
to force the legislature to repeal their acts." Parliament must step
in, he wrote desperately to England, and put a stop to a combination
that had overwhelmed the feeble internal powers that existed in
America. It had done so before, he recalled, in 1741 when it had
suppressed the Land Bank by subjecting those who persisted in the
scheme to the penalties of the statute of *praemunire*. Some such
action must now be taken—perhaps the action recommended by
one of the leading victims of the boycott, that the ringleaders be
barred from bringing an action in any of the King's courts. But the
particular form of Parliament's action was less important than its
existence, for time was running out. "If something is not done [in]
the next session of Parliament to suppress the combinations against
their acts," he wrote in August 1769, "all other measures will be to
no purpose."[32]

But the intimidation of the populace by the nonimportation
conspiracy grew worse: less and less tacit, more and more savage, in
the end simply insupportable. Certain episodes were particularly
brutal, and proved especially galling to Hutchinson as he watched
effective authority slip through his fingers. John Mein, a printer
who had not only refused to obey the radicals' order to boycott
English goods but also ridiculed their leadership in his newspaper,
was beaten up on a public thoroughfare in broad daylight when he
drew a pistol against a threatening mob and was then further set

32. TH to FB, Aug. 8 and 26, 1769, MA, XXVI, 361, 362, 368; TH to Thomas Whately,
Aug. 24, 1769, *ibid.* p. 368. For a particularly emotional explanation of his inability to
prevent or control an "illiberal, puerile, and very dishonorary" meeting of merchants
and other substantial Bostonians in support of the nonimportation movement, see TH to
Hillsborough, Jan. 24, 1770, New England Papers, III, 64 (also CO5/768/71, no. 3). On
the nonimportation movement in general, see Gipson, *British Empire*, XI, 181ff., 286ff.

upon by a crowd that collected when a shot was fired in the scuffle. He had fled to the main guard of the town and placed Hutchinson in a dilemma by begging him to order the troops to protect him. Hutchinson knew that nothing had made Bernard "more obnoxious to the inhabitants than the opinion, fixed in them, that he had been the cause of sending troops among them," and he knew that if he now used the troops in what was essentially a police action, the populace would overwhelmingly rally to the extremists in horror at such a use of physical force, and credence would at once be given to the radicals' charges that the troops had originally been sent to serve the purposes of political repression. On the other hand, if he failed to use the only power available, he would be chargeable before his superiors in England with failing to maintain order while the means of doing so lay at hand and with having deserted a defender of the government. He chose the conciliatory path. Considering, he wrote, that Boston was not Ireland where the people were used to military force; considering too that Mein had probably been provocative on his side and that he had certainly been foolish ("I think it not well judged to attack so many of the heads of the populace when they have all the power in their hands"); and considering finally that a show of force in a single episode would do more harm than good until general sanctions and support arrived from England, Hutchinson chose to risk the reprimand and contented himself with ordering the powerless justices of the peace to do their duty, and then watched with dismay as Mein, in fear of his life, set sail for England carrying with him a list of charges against Hutchinson for failing to maintain order.[33]

No one was safe. His own sons, with whose business affairs he had continued to be silently involved, had been forced to deposit their English goods with the merchant radicals during the life of the original nonimportation agreement, but refused to abide by a further extension of it after January 1, 1770. A mob rose against them, delegations waited on Hutchinson with menace in their voices, and his own closest friends advised him to force his sons to comply with

33. *History of Massachusetts-Bay,* III, 186–187, 180; TH to Hillsborough, Nov. 11, 1769, MA, XXVI, 403 (also CO5/758/222, which includes a supplementary note stressing the seriousness of the problem); TH to Hood, Nov. 11, 1769, *ibid.*, 404. Mein's four letters of appeal to TH are in MA, XXV, 455–459. See in general John E. Alden, "John Mein: Scourge of Patriots," *Publications of the Colonial Society of Massachusetts,* XXXIV (*Transactions,* 1937–1942), 571–599.

the demands in order to prevent violence to themselves and to property generally in Boston. He agonized, and then, in order to free himself from any taint of personal interest in the outcome, consented to urge his sons to give in, but when they did, he immediately regretted the concession. For though he had forsaken his public trust in forcing his sons to concede, the peace of the town had not been secured and the proscribed merchants continued to suffer. To make matters worse, the very friends who had urged him to make his sons concede soon reproached him for having done so.[34]

One of the most savagely victimized merchants was his nephew, Nathaniel Rogers, who had grown up in the Hutchinson family and been favored politically by Hutchinson's influence. Sickly, the victim of a stroke that had partly impaired his faculties, he was known to have advocated caution in opposing the Townshend Duties, and stubbornly resisted the nonimportation pressures. For over a year the enforcers of the boycott sought to intimidate him—threatened him physically, smashed the windows of his house, terrorized his wife until she refused to stay at home, dumped "tubs of ordure at his door," and twice smeared his house with "the vilest filth" ("Hillsborough paint," it was called: a mixture of urine and feces). Though soldiers were billeted in his house, he was too worn out and frightened to remain in Boston, and fled to New York. But the Boston Sons of Liberty sent word to their colleagues to the south, so he was hounded there too and "obliged to fly in the night," first to a suburban New York retreat, then to Hutchinson's house in Milton. In August 1770, no longer capable of resisting and known to be ready to concede, he suffered a seizure that killed him. Technically his death was "natural" but Hutchinson never doubted that it was the result, if only indirect, of the unbearable assaults to which he had been subjected.[35]

Violent death in more direct form, in this situation of constant

34. *History of Massachusetts-Bay*, III, 192; TH to Hood, Aug. 14 and 23, 1769, MA, XXVI, 364, 378; TH to FB, Oct. 4, 1769, *ibid.*, p. 383. For his later (1778) recollection of his dilemma in "yielding to the demands of the people when my sons were in danger," see *Diary and Letters*, II, 203.

35. FB to TH, Oct. 9, 1770, Bernard Papers, VIII, 134; *Boston Gazette*, Nov. 21, 1768; Rogers to ——, Oct. 25, 1769, New England Papers, III, 44; G. B. Warden, *Boston, 1689–1776* (Boston, Little, Brown, 1970), p. 220; TH to FB, Feb. 28 and Aug. 12, 1770, MA, XXVI, 450, 534; TH to Gage, Aug. 19, 1770, *ibid.*, pp. 537–538; TH to Hillsborough, May 21, 1770, CO5/759/201.

intimidation and explosive hostility, was inevitable, though its first appearance took an unpredictable form. A shopkeeper and former customs informer named Ebenezer Richardson, "peculiarly obnoxious to the people," attempted to defend a merchant picketed and mobbed for holding out against the nonimportation boycott. In retaliation, Richardson's own house was surrounded and assaulted, and in his effort to defend himself he fired a charge of birdshot that killed an eleven-year-old boy named Snider. Richardson was instantly seized and would have been lynched on the spot if it had not been for the quick action of the mob's leaders, who threw him into jail where he lingered for three years before he was convicted of murder and then granted a royal reprieve. Here again Hutchinson had been helpless. The sheriff he had ordered to stop the mob simply refused to obey him: "he did not think it safe to attempt it, nor is there a j.p. in the town who will appear upon such an occasion." Several days later he was forced to stand by in silent rage while the grandest funeral in Boston's history was put on for the boy—though, Hutchinson noted, he was only "the son of a poor German"—in an effort, Hutchinson believed, to duplicate if not the historic funeral of Sir Edmund Berry Godfrey, which everyone knew had been staged in 1678 to give credence to the so-called Popish Plot, then the spectacular burial of the boy Allen, killed in London in 1766 in the guardsmen's "massacre" of a Wilkesite mob. Like those two famous funerals, the burial of young Snider "was designed to raise the passions of the people" and to advance the radical cause.[36]

36. *History of Massachusetts-Bay*, III, 193–194; TH to Gage, Feb. 25, 1770, MA, XXVI, 445, 448. For an exhaustive account of the episode and its legal aftermath, see L. Kinvin Wroth and Hiller B. Zobel, eds., *Legal Papers of John Adams* (Cambridge, Harvard University Press, 1965), II, 396ff. Forty-six years later John Adams recalled Richardson as "the most abandoned wretch in America. Adultery, incest, perjury were reputed to be his ordinary crimes" (*ibid.*, p. 397). In his almanac diary for 1770 Hutchinson commented on the uniformity of human nature: "I don't think one of the sons of liberty ever thought of the effect which the public burial of Sir Edmondsbury Godfrey had upon the people of England when his body, with the sword through it, was exposed for two days together, and at this funeral the bier preceded by 72 clergymen, near 1,000 persons of condition following through the city, besides an innumerable crowd in silent order. This was worthy Lord Shaftsbury, the great conductor if not contriver of the Popish Plot. Just so, when the boy was killed by Richardson, the sons of liberty in Boston, if it had been in their power to have brought him to life again, would not have done it but would have chosen the grand funeral, which brought many thousands together; and the solemn procession from Liberty Tree, near which the boy's father lived, to the Town House and back to the burying ground made an inconceivable impression, [of] which the faction was so sensible that when those persons who were killed in the street [in the Massacre] were

Anarchy, riot, violence everywhere, and everywhere a threat to the structure of society as well as to the order of government. Mob rule, Hutchinson wrote in one of scores of such pronouncements he made in these years, "has given the lower sort of people such a sense of their importance that a gentleman does not meet with what used to be called common civility, and we are sinking into perfect barbarism." Even the College was affected. In 1768, Harvard undergraduates, Hutchinson recorded in his *History,* assembled at what they chose to call their liberty tree and, convinced that their tutors' rules on attendance at College exercises were "unconstitutional," proceeded to break windows; they were thereupon interrogated, and responded by charging brutality in these inquisitions ("confine[ment] without victuals or drink in order to compel . . . a confession"), and rioted; then three of their number were expelled. Whereupon the entire freshman, sophomore, and junior classes resigned in a body from the College, while the prudent seniors, three months before their commencement, applied for transfer to Yale. Only "a vigorous execution" of the powers of the overseers in strengthening the president's hand stopped the revolt.[37]

There was no end to the public disturbance. Shortly after Bernard left Boston more stolen letters arrived from England, and some of them, written to home authorities by the customs commissioners, were said to reflect adversely on Otis by name and, as Otis put it, on "all true North Americans in a manner that is not to be endured, by . . . representing them as traitors and rebels and in a general combination to revolt from Great Britain." Otis replied with provocative insults to two of the commissioners. One of them Hutchinson managed to keep from challenging Otis to a duel, which would have ended that officer's usefulness in Massachusetts; but the other met Otis in a coffee-house and gave him a brutal thrashing with a cane—a beating, it was believed, that left his mind impaired ever after. The customs official was forthwith sued for £3,000 damages and charged with "very unfair play"; and it was soon given out, as Hutchinson knew it would be—and it was generally believed, as he predicted it would be even "if there were

---

buried, pains was [*sic*] taken to draw the whole body of the people together." Eg. MSS, 2666, p. 77.

37. TH to John Pownall, March 21, 1770, MA, XXVI, 464; *History of Massachusetts-Bay,* III, 135–136.

a thousand witnesses to the contrary"—that the beating had been the calculated result of "a confederacy to destroy Otis."[38]

No indignity, no insult, was too trivial to be inflicted upon the government. So, to Hutchinson's amazement, three otherwise quite sensible merchants in the Council suddenly declared that the portraits of Charles I and James II must be removed forthwith from the Council walls. Hutchinson's arguments to the effect that this was an official chamber in which it was appropriate to recall the memory of all English kings simply because they had in fact been kings were ignored, and the portraits were banished. Such behavior was to him fantastic, incomprehensible. You are right, he wrote his old friend William Parker, to think the people of Boston mad—they were more mad than they had ever been in their history: "The frenzy was not higher when they banished my pious great grandmother," when they hanged innocent Quakers and witches, or when they went berserk with a passion for the Land Bank or were transported by the ecstasies of New Light religion.[39]

No one could say where all of this would end, but to Hutchinson the signs, by the time of Bernard's departure, could scarcely have been worse. A deepening alienation of the population from its government and laws—an alienation that had been created artificially, he believed, and continued to be fostered by self-seeking malcontents supported, for purely partisan purposes, by the political opposition in England; the constant vilification, even physical abuse, of those who exercised legal power and who embodied the dignity of the state; a progressive incapacity of government to preserve public order despite the presence of troops; riots in the streets; property casually destroyed; intimidation, fear, disorder everywhere. The English government seemed infinitely reluctant to review its policies and take effective action, and nothing in Hutchinson's own power seemed likely to turn the tide back from the inundated shore. Little wonder that he despaired of the future, suffered fits of depression, and longed for escape and for the peace of private life where he might recover the respect he had so unaccountably lost.

38. *Boston Gazette,* Sept. 4, 1769; TH to General Mackay, Sept. 11, 1769, MA, XXVI, 375.

39. TH to FB, Oct. 23, 1769, MA, XXVI, 393; TH to William Parker, Aug. 26, 1770, *ibid.,* p. 540 (Hutchinson prudently deleted this sentence from the letter).

As early as 1764, contemplating the gloomy prospect for the colonies, he had written to Jackson, as he did again to Thomas Pownall two years later, that if he had been younger, he would have been glad to spend the remainder of his life "in the country in England, perhaps in Alford, where my ancestors lived, though with a small fortune; but it's too late." Partly, no doubt, this bucolic note, which occurs frequently in the correspondence of these years, was a fashionable pose, but the pressure of events must have made the sentiment real. He felt the new acerbity of politics deeply, suffered each disturbance inwardly, fumed, raged at the relentless, cold-eyed malevolence of the radicals, and worried endlessly over how to conduct himself and what the future might bring. His nerves, he admitted, like his father's, "were always weak," and soon after the Stamp Act troubles they had begun to give way. Forcing himself to overcome a chronic fatigue, he had pushed himself on until by mid-1767 he could stand no more. In the spring and early summer of 1767 Hutchinson had suffered the breakdown which shadowed his life thereafter. He had dismissed it publicly as the consequence of an illness caused by exposure on a sea voyage. But privately he had admitted that it was a "nervous disorder" and that it had kept him "paralytic" for five or six weeks. He had recovered only slowly, on a regimen prescribed by physicians: total avoidance of work, deliberate efforts to divert his mind from the concerns that created the pressure, and long horseback rides, both for exercise and a change of scenery. As he had regained his strength and composure he had spoken more feelingly of a desire for retreat. At least one of his friends had feared that he would suddenly retire. But though he had carried on, he admitted that he grew "every day more and more weary of my political life."[40]

It was at this point—soon to be isolated by Bernard's departure, with insupportable pressure building up against him, fearful of his own inner weakness as well as of the external events that might occur, and yet hopeful that somehow he might be able to reconcile the warring forces and cap his career by reestablishing good will and

40. TH to Jackson, Nov. 1764, MA, XXVI, 119; TH to Pownall, Dec. 8, 1766, *ibid.*, p. 242; for references to his breakdown, see above, Chap. I, note 46; TH to Jackson, Jan. 24, 1769, MA, XXVI, 340. For Jackson's concern about Hutchinson's health after receiving his letter of June 2, and his plea to TH to remain active in politics, see Jackson to TH, July 15, 1767, MA, XXV, 186.

law and order—that he considered breaking with the existing policies, disavowing Bernard's administration, and striking out, to some degree at least, on a course of his own. The precipitating issue was Bernard's insistence, just before leaving the province, that the Assembly comply with crown instructions to continue paying him half his regular salary *in absentia* and to pay the other half to the lieutenant governor acting in his place. Hutchinson urged him not to make this demand, arguing that the Assembly would never comply and that the result would be only "new affront and indignity." When Bernard went ahead despite this plea and the Assembly replied in even more bitter terms than Hutchinson had predicted, he found himself, by his tacit endorsement of Bernard's demand, in an acutely embarrassing position from which to assume the executive responsibility when Bernard left. He appealed to Bernard once again, and then apparently threatened a public disavowal of the governor's policy on this issue and perhaps on others too. How far he meant to go we do not know—he probably did not know himself—but it seems clear that he hoped in some measure to disengage himself publicly from Bernard's administration, which he knew well enough had been "very obnoxious to the people." For the governor replied sharply that "your disavowal of the measures which I have thought fit to pursue . . . must weaken your administration as well as reflect upon mine"; if Hutchinson thought "that a contrast of your administration with mine will be for the best, I shall sincerely wish you success in it." Word of the rift got out; rumors circulated that there had been "a great misunderstanding between his excellency and the lieutenant governor, that Your Honor [Hutchinson] has said his conduct deserves the severest punishment"; it was held on good authority that Bernard was "nettled" at the behavior of certain "considerable persons" [i.e., Hutchinson] who could have helped keep things quiet but did not.

As soon as these rumors reached Hutchinson he wrote to his friends to deny that there was any misunderstanding between Bernard and himself and to assure them of the "perfect harmony" that existed in the administration. But even in these denials he dwelt on the contrast between Bernard and himself—"It is natural to suppose I have attachments to old modes and customs, civil and religious, which are not to be expected in him"—and he emphasized his loyalty to the colony's ancient constitution, his great personal "inclination and desire to assuage and extinguish" the controversy, and his confidence in his special ability to calm the people's minds and induce a better spirit. If he could create this reconciliation, he said, "I shall think it the happiest circumstance in my whole life."[41]

But if he attempted a public disavowal of complicity in Bernard's disastrous administration, it was at most a genteel, an ambiguous and subtle, disavowal. For Hutchinson was a captive of the administration as well as a member of it, and no one knew this better than Bernard, who pointed out in his response to Hutchinson's objections that not only had he assumed that Hutchinson agreed with him, but he had informed the secretary of state, Lord Hillsborough, of Hutchinson's concurrence; if now the lieutenant governor insisted on repudiating him and on striking out on a new political course, he would have to let the secretary know that he was reversing himself.[42] And that, he knew, was a potent threat. For Hillsborough was no stranger to Hutchinson's thoughts, though he did not presume to correspond directly with the minister until after he had officially taken over the government of Massachusetts. Hutchinson had been indirectly involved with Hillsborough, as he had been with the earlier secretaries of state, from the very beginning of the decade. The fate of what mattered greatly to him lay, he knew, in the secretary's hands.

ii

For none of the vicissitudes of office, none of the harassments of almost ten years of upheaval, had extinguished Hutchinson's desire for influence, authority, profit, and position, nor had the recent events led him to understand the essence of the opposition's aspirations or correctly to gauge the grip of the evolving revolu-

41. *History of Massachusetts-Bay*, III, 172; FB to TH, June 19, 1769, Bernard Papers, VII, 228–229; Israel Williams to TH, May 3, 1769, MA, XXV, 308; TH to Williams, May 6, 1769, Israel Williams Papers, MHS; TH to ——, Oct. 9, 1771, MA, XXVII, 243. Two days after Bernard accused Hutchinson of *intending* to demonstrate a contrast between their administrations, he apologized, saying he had written in haste and meant only to say that that would be the likely *consequence* of Hutchinson's actions. June 21, 1769, Bernard Papers, VII, 229.
42. FB to TH, June 19, 1769, Bernard Papers, VII, 228.

tionary ideology on the minds of his fellow New Englanders and hence the dimensions of the problems he faced. Through the hundreds of letters on constitutional questions, on Anglo-American relations, on the existing plight and future prospects of the colonies, on politics and confrontations, there runs a dark thread, not so much of crude avarice as of the acquisitiveness of the provincial bourgeois playing the hard-headed politics of Walpole in an age of ideology. The effect, as one reads through the correspondence, is at times startling; the public consequences were profound.

Hutchinson had always been careful to seek influential political allies in England, but such contacts, in the rapidly churning politics of the early years of George III, were increasingly difficult to secure, especially when one was obliged to maneuver largely through such secondary figures as Jackson, Bollan, the Pownalls, and the Mauduits. By the summer of 1764 Hutchinson was beginning to feel dangerously isolated from the sources of influence in London, and, amid his comments about the new trade regulations and the impending Stamp Act, he wrote nervously and with an edge of bitterness of his neglect by the authorities at home and of his almost total lack of "interest"—support and influential connections —in England despite his thirty years of public service. He was shocked at the difficulty he had experienced in renewing his commission as lieutenant governor after the death of George II, though that non-paying job, he said, was only a headache and made him the butt of malicious party politics among his own people. His anxieties at his insecurity in the remote and all-powerful world of Westminster turned into suspicions of duplicity when specific problems arose. It had been Thomas Pownall, he decided in 1764, who had blocked his appointment as colony agent (though he was never sure he wanted the job). So he bent over backwards to be solicitous to the influential former governor, who, he recalled with unending bitterness, had attempted to reduce him to "a mere machine" as lieutenant governor. At the same time he kept Jackson apprized of his suspicions of Pownall and informed of his strong desire to offer a defense against whatever secret complaints Pownall might be nursing against him.[43]

43. TH to ——, July 11, 1764, MA, XXVI 87; TH to Jackson, Nov. 5, 1764, *ibid.*, p. 111; TH to Thomas Pownall, July 10, 1765, *ibid.*, p. 143; TH to Jackson, Jan. 25, 1765, *ibid.*, p. 128.

It was a year later, in his effort to extract repayment from the English government for his losses in the Stamp Act riot, that he realized fully how much he was in need of a reconstitution of his position if he was to survive politically. In the late summer and fall of 1765 he wrote to everyone he knew, on however slight a basis, who might conceivably help him get repayment in England. But the results were meager, and his efforts in some cases must have been embarrassing. His two letters to Benjamin Franklin on the neglect of his claim could at least draw on shared experiences ("when you and I were at Albany ten years ago"), and his chatty, confidential denigration of the Bay Colony's fickle politics probably did not seem misplaced at the time, however curious they may appear in retrospect. Even his approach to Lord Adam Gordon, admittedly on a very slight acquaintance, was not altogether far-fetched since Gordon had been in Boston during the recent disturbances and must have known first hand of Hutchinson's troubles. But his appeal to the Earl of Kinnoul, who twenty years earlier as a member of the Board of Trade had approved Hutchinson's efforts to maintain a stable currency in Massachusetts, was so unlikely as to require the explanation that "I have few or no friends at court and my very name perhaps is obscure." Kinnoul in fact, as he eventually informed Hutchinson, had retired in 1762 and lived removed from all affairs on his estates in the Scottish highlands. The connection with Lord Edgcumbe was even more remote, consisting as it did entirely of a passing recommendation by Pownall.[44]

It is not surprising in view of the obvious ineffectiveness of these appeals that Hutchinson decided in March of 1766 to reach directly into English politics for support in his campaign for compensation and at the same time reestablish his position in the new patronage world of Rockingham, Grenville, Hillsborough, and Grafton. What he knew from his most hard-headed advisers to be the most effective method—to go to England himself and serve a "long-attendance" on the great—he would not do: he felt it to be "extremely dissonant from my natural temper and disposition," and

44. Hutchinson's letters to Franklin, Loudoun, Bollan, Kinnoul, Gordon, Jackson, Thomas Pownall, and several unidentified correspondents, soliciting support for his compensation claim, were written in Oct., Nov., and Dec., 1765; MA, XXVI, 157–176; Kinnoul's reply, Feb. 5, 1766, is in MA, XXV, 57.

furthermore his absence from home might cost him more in the end than the trip would yield. Instead, he sent in his place his twenty-five-year-old son, Thomas, Jr., writing in advance nostalgic letters to the friends he had known in England twenty-five years earlier asking them to look after the boy, together with requests to his current political contacts to help guide Thomas through the channels of power. He wrote, too, injunctions to Thomas himself to preserve virtue and religion no matter what the temptations of London; to turn a profit on new investments and collect certain old debts; and above all to gain the favor of everyone he could reach in politics. Specific instructions were issued on the correct attitudes to assume in talking with each of the main figures he was to contact, and he was particularly ordered to treat any Americans he happened to run into with the greatest care, "as many of them may happen to have connections which you know nothing of."[45]

Young Thomas did well on almost all counts. He threaded his way through a fight between Jackson and Bollan and managed through the latter to gain access to the Marquess of Rockingham, who "took me by the hand," he reported, "in a very friendly manner and asked me to set down," grilled him on the situation in Massachusetts, and complimented him on his father's conduct in office. But though this and perhaps other new and valuable contacts were made, and though Thomas managed to calm Bollan's rage at discovering that Hutchinson thought he was not exerting himself sufficiently on his behalf, and though Thomas succeeded, too, in putting at rest rumors going around that Hutchinson was writing secret denunciations of leading Massachusetts politicians to the ministry—despite all of this, the assurances he was given of compensation by the English government were guarded, and soon proved empty. The most he could produce to satisfy his father was a hint he heard that the ministry would in the end respond not by monetary repayment but by the eventual gift of the governorship.[46]

It was quite enough. Though Hutchinson professed to "have known courts too long to place any dependence upon favor there,"

45. TH to ——, Nov. 7, 1766, MA, XXVI, 248; TH to Franklin, [Jackson], Charlton Palmer, Jonathan Barnard, Arthur Haywood, Robert Wilson, and Peter Leitch, March 20–29, 1766, MA, XXVI, 219–222; TH to TH, Jr., n.d. and April 14, 1766, *ibid.*, pp. 223–226.

46. TH, Jr., to TH, May 29, June 14, July 1, 2, 3, 11, 26, and Aug. 1, 1766, MA, XXV, 74–75, 80, 84–90.

the prospect of capturing the governorship was never absent from his mind and crops up repeatedly in his letters to his English friends and sponsors—in the same letters, at times in the same paragraphs and sentences, in which he expresses imaginative and farsighted views of imperial relations—gradually becoming the dominant note. How early and in what form he had begun to send out feelers cannot be established from the correspondence, but in May 1767 (around the time of his "nervous disorder") he was drafting letters to Jackson to say more plainly than he had dared to do before that Bernard's request for leave of absence to visit England should be granted: "a short absence would be the means of removing the unreasonable prejudices against him and . . . his future administration would be rendered more easy and peaceable." That would also have had the effect, he later explained, of making him "commander in chief for a year or two, and I flatter myself my natural interest is such that it would have been of service in composing the minds of the people and introducing a better spirit." He would then have been in an excellent position to succeed to the chair if the rumors he had received proved to be true and Bernard were given "a better government or . . . otherwise provided for." But whether because his "interest" had falsified his perception or because Bernard changed his mind about a leave of absence, it soon developed that the governor was not particularly eager to leave Massachusetts at that point, and furthermore was not especially keen on Hutchinson advancing at his expense. Hutchinson promptly backpedaled, professing despondently that he now saw "no prospect for rising," and turned, for the time, to two or three other irons he had in the fire.[47]

One was membership in, or chairmanship of, the new American Board of Customs Commissioners, a body which was under discussion when young Thomas was in London and which was formally constituted in the summer of 1767. Hutchinson had not sought the job, and though it was expected to be highly lucrative (it would pay three times, he believed, what he received as chief justice); though it was said to be a boost toward the governorship if the

47. TH to [Jackson], June 2, May 2, 1767, MA, XXVI, 276, 267–268; TH to Samuel Touchet, n.d. [June/July 1767], *ibid.*, p. 277; TH to thomas Pownall, Dec. 14, 1767, MA, XXV, 225; TH to Jackson, July 18, 1767, MA, XXVI, 280; TH to Touchet, July 18, 1767, *ibid.*, p. 275. For details of Jackson's maneuverings on Hutchinson's behalf, see his letter of July 15, 1767, MA, XXV, 186–188.

Commission's work proved successful; and though he was backed for it by a remarkable array of powerful supporters, he believed the post would be a political dead-end. Any customs post he might take, he wrote, would lessen his "weight and influence" with the people of Massachusetts and weaken his capacity to help maintain stability and order in the empire; he would have tried to evade the appointment if it had actually been offered to him. Fortunately, Townshend decided the post was incompatible with Hutchinson's other positions, and he was free to wait for better opportunities to mingle profit with effective public service.[48]

And indeed profit and public service were naturally related in his mind. For while he wanted "no greater salary than is adequate to the service," he was convinced that "the stipends to my present places" were inadequate. He and Secretary Oliver, he wrote, were chagrined to see new crown officers arriving in the colony "with salaries sufficient to support equipages and elegant tables whilst others of not inferior rank, and who, it is expected, should live with them," were less well provided for than high-level clerks. Furthermore he had his children to worry about: "If I had no children I should be very little concerned about the emoluments of any post further than the income of my present fortune added to it would afford me a decent support."[49] He could not maintain the dignity of his office without some special provision. His friends and agents were soon at work seeking to satisfy his desires, but by the time they succeeded the world had clearly changed, and Hutchinson had begun to see, not, to be sure, the fundamental incongruity between all such sources of profit and power and the aspirations and convictions of the rebellious opposition (that he was destined never to understand) but the political embarrassment of such rewards.

The special crown salary that Bernard and his English contacts sought to obtain for Hutchinson materialized in agonizingly slow stages. In July and then again in September 1767 Jackson was optimistic about getting Hutchinson a salary out of the income

48. TH to Duke of Grafton, Feb. 3, 1768, MA, XXVI, 287. TH to Touchet, July 18, 1767, *ibid.*, p. 275; TH to Jackson, Oct. 20, 1767, MA, XXV, 205; TH to Bollan, Oct. 31, 1767, *ibid.*, p. 209. For Thomas Pownall's support for Hutchinson's appointment to the customs office and for the crown salary discussed below, see Pownall to TH, Sept. 9, 1767, MHS *Colls.* 3d ser., I (1825), 148–149.

49. TH to Bollan, Oct. 31, 1767, MA, XXV, 209; TH to [Jackson], Feb. 4, 1768, MA, XXVI, 288.

from the new Townshend Duties, though he did not know whether it would be attached to the chief justiceship or the lieutenant governorship. Pownall on September 9 assured him that the Duke of Grafton intended him to have "a handsome salary fixed as chief justice, as soon as the American revenue shall create a fund." By November Hutchinson was confident enough that "first or last something will be done for me" and shrewd enough politically to disapprove strongly of efforts being made to get him one of the unpopular admiralty judgeships and to insist that Bernard, having suffered more, should be rewarded first. Rumors of the source and assignment of his new salary were still vague, however, until in December Lord North, the chancellor of the exchequer, was quoted directly to the effect that Hutchinson's salary would definitely be drawn from the Townshend fund and rank second in priority on that list to the customs commissioners themselves. But it was only six months later, in June 1768—a month after the rumor of this special salary had inspired the "pensioner . . . pensioner" cry that had defeated Hutchinson's final bid for election to the Council—it was only then that Jackson could write from London that the grant was official, though probably not as a salary attached to a specific position and not at the level he had hoped for. It was to be paid, he understood, as a "general proof" of the ministry's recognition of his merit, and the sum was to be £200 a year—a figure so low that Jackson apologized for his "ill-success." By then Hutchinson had already begun to doubt the wisdom of having such a singular grant and to wish that it had been included in a general civil list where it would not have been so conspicuous and would have been less likely to generate envy. And he soon saw deeper problems in accepting this unexpected "pension"—as he now found himself obliged to call it. If he had thought, he wrote Jackson in January 1769, that his "enemies would have considered it in that light [as a pension] I should have chose to have been without it, though it had been double what it is. It has incapacitated me from doing some service which I should have been capable of without it, particularly in the Council." Furthermore, it had led the House to decline to grant him his usual salary as chief justice. And the worst of it was that now, after two years of maneuvers and promises, not a penny of the politically dangerous grant had in fact been received, though when fully paid it would

The Ordeal of Thomas Hutchinson

hardly cover the additional expenses he had been forced to incur to keep face with the crown officers in Boston. The net result at the moment was that he was receiving no payment whatever from any source for his work as chief justice. When in September 1769 he still had not received payment, he wrote to Bernard that he now doubted that it would be wise for him to receive any of this money at all—in Boston, that is; could it be credited to him in London?[50]

But the salary grant was a side issue next to the engrossing problem of assuring himself of the governorship. Month after month he threw out hints to his friends and solicited assurances that they were doing everything they could to support him, and month after month he sought to assess his chances, steeled himself against disappointment, and prepared attitudes with which to face all possible eventualities. All of this was habitual, all of it the almost automatic reaction to stimuli to which he had been accustomed to respond from his earliest years.

The prospects of success appeared dim in 1767, but they brightened somewhat in the following year when it became known that Bernard had definitely decided to seek a more lucrative and more peaceful post elsewhere and in any case to request a leave of absence from his post in Massachusetts from the new secretary of state, Lord Hillsborough, a close friend of his patron, Viscount Barrington. But then disturbing rumors arose. Bernard, it was said, had been passed over for the governments of Barbados, Carolina, and Nova Scotia—perhaps New York as well. He had been offered Virginia, Hutchinson was told, which was no Barbados, to be sure, but worth £1000 a year more than Massachusetts and it was a place where the people would not be so easily convinced that he wished them ill. The rank there, unfortunately, was only that of lieutenant governor, but a baronetcy might make up for it. Yes,

50. Jackson to TH, July 15, Sept. 7,-1767, MA, XXV, 187, 194; Pownall to TH, Sept. 9. 1767, *Warren-Adams Letters*, I, 7n; TH to Jackson, Nov. 19, 1767, MA, XXV, 227; Israel Mauduit to TH, Dec. 10, 1767, MA, XXV, 237; Jackson to TH, June 3, 1768, *ibid.*, p. 260; TH to —— Grant, July 27, 1768, MA, XXVI, 317; TH to Jackson, Jan. 24, 1769, *ibid.*, p. 340; TH to FB, Sept. 11, 1769, *ibid.*, p. 375. "Nobody," Hutchinson wrote Jackson, "Less deserves to be called a pensioner than I do. I never desire to receive more wages than is equivalent to my work" (Jan. 28, 1769, MA, XXVI, 349). It is interesting to note that Jackson, who worked hard to get Hutchinson his supplementary crown salary, was understood to be "principled against governors being independent of their people." Bernard hoped that some day Jackson would realize how necessary it was for the maintainance of good order for governors to have financial security as well as firm tenures in office. FB to Jackson, Jan. 13, 1767, Bernard Papers, V, 282.

148

Hutchinson "should like well enough" to take over the governor-ship of Massachusetts; it would give him the chance he sought to reconcile the divided population. Still, though he knew he had many more loyal friends in the local population than Bernard ever had, he was beginning to wonder whether even he could possibly succeed. One thing was certain: if anyone else were appointed governor he would never serve as his lieutenant. No lieutenant governor in Massachusetts's history had suffered as he had; all had had greater satisfactions in the post than he had had: every lieutenant governor but one "was a great part of his time commander in chief. In eleven years I have had a run of only two months."[51]

Jackson continued to encourage him. In June 1768 he was sure his plan to get Hutchinson the governor's chair was working, though he had hoped for a better place than Virginia for Bernard. In July, Rogers, then in London, confirmed the encouraging rumors, adding that Hutchinson might have his choice of controlling the government either as governor or as lieutenant governor. Then in August it seemed that a climax had been reached. Late that month Bernard told Hutchinson, not the whole truth, which was that three months earlier Hillsborough had decided to appoint Hutchinson the next governor of Massachusetts (for Bernard had been told that in the strictest confidence), but only that it was his hope and expectation that the lieutenant governor would succeed him. Bernard had told Hillsborough he thoroughly approved of Hutchinson's appointment, and for very particular reasons; it will be a blow to the opposition, he said, who hate the native son more than the English-born governor, "and it will afford another great instance of rewarding faithful servants of the crown." But by October it had become clear that Bernard would not be able to leave Massachusetts that winter (he had in fact been ordered by Lord Barrington, in view of the recent events in the colony, "not [to] stir from thence on any account though you have leave of absence"), and Hutchinson was beginning to worry still more about the difficulties of the task that he was assured on all sides would soon be his; he suddenly

51. FB to Barrington, Feb. 7, 1768, *Barrington-Bernard Corr.*, pp. 141–145; TH to [Jackson], Feb. 14, 1768, MA, XXVI, 288; Nathaniel Rogers to TH, July 2, 1768, MA, XXV, 265; TH to Rogers, May 31, 1768, *ibid.*, p. 259. Bernard's baronetcy, offered to him by Hillsborough in May 1768, was sent out to him together with the orders for his return to England, and "thus timed to prevent any triumph from insinuation that I was removed in disgrace." *Barrington-Bernard Corr.*, pp. 154, 204.

began talking about the pressure being put on him to accept. Nevertheless, he took the necessary steps to assure his succession: he arranged for the province secretary, Andrew Oliver, to succeed him as lieutenant governor, and authorized his London banker to pay the heavy fees, upon Jackson's request, for passing the commission.[52]

Still, everything hung fire. Six months later, in May 1769, with Bernard's leave of absence definitely arranged, rumors reached Hutchinson that it would not be he but the obnoxious Pownall who would succeed to the post—a particularly wounding slight, he felt, after "the repeated intimations" he had received that he would have the job; if the rumor turned out to be true he would resign the lieutenant governorship forthwith. In June he was again gloomily contemplating the difficulties of the governorship, and while in August, with Bernard finally away on his leave, he was beginning to line up political support all over New England, word was received that, though he was sure to get *a* governorship, it might not be that of Massachusetts. Again he was mortified, and wrote that though the offer of a governorship elsewhere was better than no mark of royal favor at all, at his age and with his involvements in Massachusetts he would never willingly leave the province "unless it be for some special service and a short time only." If it came to that, he would resign all his offices but the chief justiceship.[53]

So resentment at the possibility of not receiving the appointment mingled with growing anxieties at having to face the heavy burdens that the post would impose. He did everything he could to conciliate the opposition and to avoid further antagonism. He opened his *pro tempore* administration, Samuel Cooper reported to Pownall, with "a soft complaisant speech to the Council," avoided

52. Rogers to TH, July 2, 1768, MA, XXV, 265–266; Barrington to FB, May 9 and Aug. 11, 1768, *Barrington-Bernard Corr.*, pp. 154, 164; FB to Barrington, Aug. 27 and Oct. 20. 1768, *ibid.*, pp. 174, 180; TH to ——, Nov. 14, 1768, MA, XXVI, 327; TH to Jackson and to William Parker, Nov. 23, 1768, *ibid.*, pp. 329, 330.

53. TH to Bollan, May 5, 1769, MA, XXVI, 352; Cooper to Pownall, May 11, 1769, "Cooper-Pownall Letters," p. 308; TH to FB, Aug. 26, 1769, MA, XXVI, 369. For Bowdoin's encouragement to Pownall to succeed Bernard as governor, see his letter of May 10, 1769, MHS *Colls.*, 6th ser., IX (1897), 143. Later, Pownall disavowed any interest in the position—up to a point: "I would not accept any post whatever in America under the present system of government; in the next place, ministry are too well informed of my sentiments and too angry with me ever to make me any offer or proposal." Pownall to Cooper, July 11, 1770, in Frederick Griffin, *Junius Discovered* (Boston, 1854), p. 277.

convening that body as much as possible, and sought in every way he could to encourage the idea that he had never been "closely connected with Sir Francis, etc." But it was uphill work. His friends, whose help he desperately needed, had been friends of Bernard and had no desire to repudiate that association. As the disorders of the nonimportation movement spread and grew more violent, he discovered how little ground for maneuver he really had. He considered, but then rejected, the dramatic proposal that he appoint John Adams his attorney general: how could he appoint any man to that post, "let his talents otherwise be ever so great," "who avows principles inconsistent with a state of government"? He could make only small gestures of conciliation, it seemed; nothing substantial could be done, as Cooper recognized, "without a change of measures at home," and of that there was still no sign.[54]

As the personal attacks on him increased in number and intensity in the fall of 1769, he tried more deliberately to brush them off, writing bravely to one of his closest political allies that his only goal was "to save this poor province from ruin; for if I can be instrumental in that, I don't care what they say of hypocrisy and cant and a hundred more such aspersions. . . . They can charge me with no fact which is culpable." But in fact he did care. His anxieties grew, and began to overcome him. "I tremble for my country," he wrote his boyhood friend and political associate Charles Paxton; "I wished to leave its constitution at my death in the same state it was in at my birth," but he could see only trouble ahead, and he began to hedge, at first hesitantly, on the responsibility he would be assuming. If in fact he became governor, he said, his aim would be only "to keep the ship in her course until a better helmsman comes and takes charge of her."[55] But then his nerve gave way altogether, and in confidence and utter candor he wrote Bernard an extraordinary letter which purported to announce a major decision but which in fact expressed the very essence of the struggle within him—a struggle shaped by his deepest instincts: acquisitiveness, public concern, prudence, honesty, and a deferential acceptance of constituted authority.[56]

54. Cooper to Pownall, Sept. 8, 1769, "Cooper-Pownall Letters," p. 311; TH to FB, Sept. 10, 1769, MA, XXVI, 378.

55. TH to Israel Williams, Sept. 18, 1769, Williams Papers; TH to [Paxton], Sept. 1, 1769, MA, XXVI, 370, 371.

56. TH to FB, Sept. 8, 1769, MA, XXVI, 374.

He had decided, he wrote, that he could be of more service as chief justice than as governor, and he therefore wished to withdraw from the competition for that post. The change of plan, however, would have to be handled with great care. For the opposition in Massachusetts, he explained, was counting on being vindicated by the ministry's rejecting Bernard's replies to the colony's charges and by Hutchinson's being passed over for the governorship. Therefore he could say quite objectively—quite aside from any selfish views he might have of the matter—that if he were not *offered* the governorship "the cause of government will be much disserved." Yet his qualifications for the chief justiceship, he believed, made him unique among those who might accept appointment to that ill-paid and burdensome post, while circumstances, he had come to believe, would soon require the appointment of governors "of a different education from mine"—military men, he implied—and so if he were appointed governor he would soon be superseded. If therefore, as he still hoped, he were finally offered the position, he proposed to decline it publicly (the very act of refusal "would give me a very great additional weight with the people"), then resign the lieutenant governorship in favor of Oliver, and confine himself to the bench. He was quite prepared, he explained in somewhat nervous detail, to suffer the serious financial loss involved: "it would make a great odds to me in pecuniary matters, and I should be less able to provide for my children, but . . . it does not signify whether I leave a few thousand pounds more or less behind me when I die." He would be content with the chief justiceship, he said, even "if no further provision be made [for it] than the present pitiful allowance."

A bold decision, a decisive step—but not quite. He did not know, he said, how such a plan would go down with the ministry. Would they approve? He had no way of knowing, and so "I must leave the affair entirely with you," he told Bernard, and he asked him either to suppress the letter or bring it forward to Hillsborough, according to what he, Bernard, expected the reaction to it to be. In case the ministry proved sympathetic to this sudden reversal and Bernard decided to withdraw the application for the governorship, Hutchinson enclosed a letter to be delivered to Jackson revoking all orders for payments toward the commission until further notice.

Four months later he had his answer. Bernard, having received a pension of £600 and having decided not to return to America, had taken up Hutchinson's case in earnest. Ignoring the anxieties that lay behind Hutchinson's letter, he had argued, along with Hutchinson's other supporters, that Hutchinson, being "well acquainted with the humors of the people and the constitution of the government," was as well able to control the demagogues in Massachusetts as anyone who was likely to accept the poorly-paid governorship, and in any case Hillsborough's predecessor Shelburne had already pledged the position to Hutchinson. And to Hutchinson privately, after chiding him for setting his terms too low, Bernard reported that the ministry thought most highly of him, and held out the prospect of his retaining the judicial post in abeyance for his own later occupancy while he served as governor. Though rumors kept reaching Hutchinson that the whole project had fallen through (which would now not only be mortifying, he wrote in November 1769, but physically dangerous since it would be less criminal for popular leaders to abuse him as a private person than as an official), he continued to put his trust in Bernard, who had in effect become his personal emissary to the ministry. Greatly flattered by Bernard's report of Hillsborough's good opinion of him, in February 1770 he formally concurred in the decision that Bernard had already made in his behalf, to accept the governorship if offered it.[57]

iii

But his anxieties had not been stilled nor his insecurities overcome nor his vulnerability lessened. He continued almost mechanically to mend his political fences—to remind the Duke of Grafton in 1768 of the respect he had paid his naval-officer father thirty-five years before when that young man had visited Boston, and to assure him that had the father lived he would have kept "an interest with him to this day"; and to write Soame Jenyns in December 1769, solely on the basis of a rumor received from a distant relative in Dublin to the effect that Mrs. Jenyns might be re-

---

57. FB to TH, Jan. 13, 1770, Bernard Papers, VIII, 44–47; TH to FB, Jan. 10, 1770, MA, XXVI, 429; FB to TH, Nov. 4, 1769, Bernard Papers, VIII, 14–16; TH to FB, Nov. 14, 1769, MA, XXVI, 405; TH to FB, n.d. [early Feb. 1770], *ibid.*, p. 439.

lated to the Hutchinsons, an explanation of his policy in governing Massachusetts, including certain historical touches that might
appeal to that litterateur.

And he continued too, despite assurances to his commercial correspondents that "I have done with all [business] schemes, and all my
ambition is to be easy," to engage in a line of business, politically
the most dangerous possible, that greatly increased his vulnerability
to attack.[58]

He was deeply engaged in the tea trade. As early as 1764 his
correspondence establishes his interest in that lucrative commerce.
By 1768 his investments, some in partnership with his sons and
some in joint undertakings with London merchants, especially with
his old friend William Palmer, were averaging £1,000 a year; and
his sons, who before the trade boycott of 1769 had been underselling
the tea smugglers and still making a profit, took the occasion of
nonimportation to stockpile that politically controversial commodity
against the eventual release of sales. In 1769 with nonimportation
at its most severe and threats abounding (at least one of which was
acted on) that any tea imported would be destroyed, Hutchinson
continued to invest, though with deepening secrecy. On October 5
he wrote Palmer, in the semi-secret cipher of vowelless script, "to
keep to yourself my being concerned with you, for . . . the malignant party here make a clamor often when there is no reason for
it. . . . Mention nothing of your correspondence with me. Alter the
mark, and do it frequently." And then on October 24 he added:
"fill the tea order, but use blank endorsements on the bills of lad-
ing and invoices"; and finally: "say nothing to my sons of your
having shipped, nor let the master know whether it is the property
of anybody here or of Rhode Island."[59]

So engaged in trade and politics—still acquisitive, still ambitious,
but increasingly fearful of what the future might bring; longing for
peace but doubtful of his ability to create it; sincerely concerned
for America's rights and well-being but insensitive still to the

58. TH to Grafton, Feb. 3, 1768, MA, XXVI, 288 (for the "gay company" in Boston
that had included Grafton's father, Lord Augustus Fitzroy, *Diary and Letters*, I, 47); TH
to Jenyns, Dec. 4, 1769, MA, XXVI, 412; TH to Robert Wilson, Feb. 24, 1764, *ibid.*, p. 81.
59. TH to Palmer, Dec. 24, 1768, MA, XXVI, 334; TH to FB, Oct. 5, 1769, *ibid.*, p.
384; TH to Palmer, Oct. 5, 1769, *ibid.*, pp. 386–387; TH to FB, Aug. 8, 1769, *ibid.*, p.
361; TH to Palmer, Oct. 24, 1769, *ibid.*, p. 395.

sources of the passions sweeping across the land, and incapable of conceiving of sustained opposition to government save as the work of demagogues and vicious self-servers—so poised, so involved, he entered upon the governorship.

Chapter V

The Captive

Seventeen-seventy was a decisive year. Everything that happened before was prologue to the crisis Hutchinson then faced; everything that happened after flowed from the decision he made—or drifted into—in June of that year. The consequences that followed inescapably from it were predictable even by him as he moved from one dark encounter to another.

i

When the year opened he did not yet know whether Bernard had endorsed his desire to withdraw his candidacy for the governorship, and so he could not know whether the crisis he saw developing would become his responsibility or not. But he was convinced that an explosion between the soldiers in Boston and the populace was likely. Though he had himself welcomed the troops to Boston as the only means of maintaining order in a province "disposed to tumults and disorders upon the slightest pretenses," he knew the dangers of their presence, and was reminded of these dangers again and again—by the many individual complaints he heard of the soldiers' incivilities and by the public accusations of their brutality printed in "The Journal of the Times." He was determined to take no chances. Just as in October 1769 he had refused to call on the troops to protect the Tory printer Mein, so in January 1770 he refused to accede to the customs commissioners' demand that troops be used to put an end to the nonimportation boycotts and to the intimidation of law-abiding merchants—a decision on which the secretary of state for the colonies, Lord Hillsborough, complimented him. The atmosphere was too highly charged; the slightest accident could produce a tragedy, and "anything tragical," Hutchinson wrote on January 29, 1770, "would have set the whole province in a flame, and maybe spread farther." Yet, for all his caution, the danger kept mounting, and week by week in early 1770 he became increasingly fearful of an explosive encounter between the soldiers and the townsmen and increasingly insistent that the greatest care be taken to prevent it. The danger of a clash, he predicted in February, would be particularly great in mid-March, when the General Court was scheduled to meet in Boston, and he therefore wrote to General Gage with the request that the main guard be withdrawn from the town before the fourteenth of that month.[1]

No amount of foreknowledge, however, and no degree of certainty that he had done everything in his power to prevent it, could soften the blow of the Boston Massacre when it fell, on March 5, almost on the schedule he had predicted. The killing of five townsmen by the soldiers, in a scene of great confusion, was without doubt, he wrote, the most catastrophic thing that could have happened. Boston was pitched into a perfect frenzy, he reported to Hillsborough, and the province as a whole was on the edge of civil war.[2] If, as was threatened, the populace rose against the soldiers,

1. TH to Robert Wilson, May 11, 1772, MA, XXVII, 334; TH to Lord Hillsborough, Jan. 24, 1770, and Hillsborough to TH, March 24, 1770, CO5/759/36–37, 53; TH to Thomas Hood, Jan. 29, 1770, MA, XXVI, 436. There are many accounts of the violent intimidation of merchants like Nathaniel Rogers who resisted the nonimportation pressures; see, e.g., Hutchinson's summary of the brutal treatment of James, Patrick, and John McMaster in his letter to John Pownall, Aug. 29, 1770, and also the two petitions from the McMasters that are enclosed: CO5/759/269, 271, 273; TH to General Gage, Feb. 25, 1770, MA, XXVI, 445. Hillsborough, hearing from Gage that the troops in Boston, despite their "decent and exemplary behavior . . . have been exposed to very great insult and indignity from the populace," also feared a violent clash. CO5/759/22. For apprehensions of the popular leaders, see Samuel Cooper to Thomas Pownall, Jan. 1, 1770, "Cooper-Pownall Letters," p. 314.

2. Hutchinson's official account of the events leading up to the Massacre, and of the event itself, was written to Hillsborough on March 12, 1770, and includes a copy of his preliminary report to Gage, March 6 (the original of which is in the Gage Papers, micro-

the consequences would be terrible and irreversible. "Whether 10,000 of them," he later said, "could have drove out 600 regulars is another question, but an attempt to do it would have been like passing the Rubicon." The troops must somehow be removed from the town. But how? By whose order? The decision, by force of circumstance, fell to him, and he quailed before it. Not from cowardice. He had shown great personal courage on the night of the Massacre itself, responding instantly to the plea "For God's sake . . . go to King Street" or "the town would be all in blood." He had plunged into the great press and confusion of the mob in King Street, "some brandishing their bludgeons and some their cutlasses"; had been thrown up against the soldiers' bayonets; in the tumult had shouted at Captain Preston, "How came you to fire without orders from a civil magistrate!"; and had been forced up by the crowd into the Council chamber. From the balcony he had somehow managed to control the mob, promising them a full and impartial inquiry ("The law shall have its course! I will live and die by the law!"), and had convinced them to disperse, after which he had conducted an immediate investigation that lasted until 4 A.M. Yet he faltered before the less spontaneous, and more calculated, legal, and formal, decision to evacuate the troops before an even greater catastrophe took place.[3]

The issue quickly came into sharp focus. At eleven o'clock on the morning after the Massacre, the Boston selectmen confronted Hutchinson in an emergency meeting. If Hutchinson, they declared, did not order the removal of the troops from the town there would be "blood and carnage" and "the most terrible consequences were to be expected." Hutchinson informed them that he had no authority to dispose of the King's troops and so could not give the

---

film, MHS). The emendations in TH's letterbook draft of the March 12 letter (MA, XXVI, 452–455) show the great care he took to explain his decision of March 6 to order the troops out of Boston. The recipient's copy, which arrived in London on April 21, is CO5/759/59ff., and transcribed in CO5/768/85ff. For a detailed account of the Massacre and references to the entire documentary literature, see Hiller B. Zobel, *The Boston Massacre* (N.Y., W. W. Norton, 1970), chap. xvi.

3. TH to ——, n.d. [mid-March 1770], MA, XXVI, 458; *History of Massachusetts-Bay*, III, 196; Eg. MSS, 2666, p. 70; CO5/759/367–368 (TH's testimony at Capt. Preston's trial); Zobel, *Massacre*, p. 203. The account of the Massacre and its aftermath that Hutchinson wrote in his *History* (pp. 195–201) is based on—at certain points directly copied from—the almanac diary he kept at the time (Eg. MSS, 2666). Hutchinson omitted revealing passages of these MS notes when he composed his history, and I have drawn on them, as well as on his official accounts, in the paragraphs that follow.

order they demanded. They alone, he said, had the power to calm the people, despite the insistence of one of them that they could not hold back the mob even if they got down on their knees before them. If there were further violence, Hutchinson said, and an attempt were made to drive the troops out, "everyone abetting and advising would be guilty of high treason." Colonel Dalrymple attempted a compromise, and in so doing inadvertently trapped Hutchinson into making the controversial decision. The colonel said he would *voluntarily* dispatch the hated 29th regiment to the harbor fort and, while leaving the 14th regiment in the town, would do everything possible to minimize the possibility of future clashes with the townsmen. To this the aldermen immediately replied that if he had the authority to remove one regiment, he had the authority to remove two, and then they easily edged him into agreeing to remove the 14th if Hutchinson merely expressed the *"desire"* that he do so. This effectively reduced the options available to Hutchinson to the point where it seemed that the entire destiny of Anglo-American relations and the lives of hundreds of innocent people rested on his willingness, not to issue an illegal order but merely to express a personal wish—but a wish that in the circumstances everyone knew would have the force of the order he sought to avoid giving. So the terms were set for the intense struggle that took place at the afternoon session of the Council meeting on March 6.[4]

The proceedings of that afternoon session would be disputed for months in the public prints of England and America.[5] The threat of violence had escalated by mid-day. The selectmen now stated flatly that if the troops did not leave, the people of Boston would drive them out, with the help of the men from the surrounding towns if need be, and they added, Hutchinson told Hillsborough, that if that happened, "all the blood would be charged to me alone." He was faced, he believed, with nothing less than a "general insurrection," and it was furthermore made clear to him that if he refused he would himself be seized unless he fled to the safety of the station ship or the Castle.[6]

4. *History of Massachusetts-Bay*, III, 197–198; Eg. MSS, 2666, p. 59; TH to Hillsborough, March 12, 1770, MA, XXVI, 453.
5. *History of Massachusetts-Bay*, III, 198, 230–232. Hutchinson's fullest account is in Eg. MSS, 2666, pp. 58–59.
6. TH to Hillsborough, March 12, 1770, MA, XXVI, 453; TH to Jackson, March 26, 1770, *ibid.*, p. 465 (a valuable summary of the Massacre and the March 6 Council meeting).

He polled the Council, constitutionally charged with advising the chief executive, and found that though in the morning it had divided in its judgment it now voted unanimously, "under duress," Hutchinson believed, "and terror of 3 or 4,000 of the enraged multitude and threats of 10,000 more," that Hutchinson could not justify a refusal. The regimental commanders themselves agreed with this, as did the captain of the station ship. Even Hutchinson's loyal kinsman, the province secretary Andrew Oliver, urged him to concede. But through the long afternoon, despite the most intense pressure, he could not bring himself to agree.[7] He held out alone against the public clamor and the unanimous judgment of every public official he consulted. It was, Andrew Oliver later wrote, in sympathy for "the distress I saw the lieutenant governor in for so many hours together" and in an effort to support the "very being of the man I loved," that he drew up that night for the record and for the immediate information of Governor Bernard in London (who to Oliver's horror later allowed it to be published) a complete and precise account of what happened at that afternoon meeting.[8]

Hutchinson believed that a decisive turning point had been reached. What was at stake in retaining these troops was nothing less than the possibility of the British government maintaining its authority in America. Removing the troops to the Castle was no mere technical relocation: there they would be too remote from

7. Eg. MSS, 2666, p. 60. Gage too felt it was impossible to make a correct decision in the situation: "The governor could neither order it nor dissent from it," he later recalled. Responses to George Chalmer's Queries, MHS *Colls.*, 4th ser., IV (1858), 370–371.

8. Andrew Oliver to William Bollan and to Thomas Pownall, Nov. 3, 1770, and Oct. 25, 1771, Eg. MSS, 2670 (Andrew Oliver's Letterbook), pp. 40, 57 ("The political existence of my friend, the then lieutenant governor, depended upon a just representation of his conduct; it was the interest of one gentleman . . . to represent it so as to shift the blame . . . from himself . . . upon the lieutenant governor, and there appeared an utter indifference in others how it might affect him, so that they could but maintain their own popularity"). Oliver's notarized account of the Council meeting is in CO5/759/114ff.; it was published by Bernard, as an Appendix to *A Fair Account of the Late Unhappy Disturbance at Boston in New England* . . . (London, 1770), in an effort to counter the effect of Boston's *Short Narrative of the Horrid Massacre in Boston* . . . (Boston, 1770). Hutchinson later recalled that the morning after the crucial Council meeting he had asked Oliver to commit to writing an exact account of what had transpired but had found that Oliver, "of his own mere motion, and for his private satisfaction . . . had done it the evening before, while the debates were fresh in his mind." *History of Massachusetts-Bay*, III, 229. Hutchinson believed that the publication of Oliver's deposition had in fact "destroyed the credit of [Boston's] *Narrative*, which indeed never deserved any credit," but he reported that Bowdoin and other councillors were enraged by Oliver's account and were making him suffer for having written it. TH to FB, Oct. 30, 1770, MA, XXVII, 48.

the town to perform the police duties they had been assigned. More important—to him all-important—was his conviction that the entire crisis had been deliberately manufactured—the so-called Massacre itself deliberately incited—to bring about precisely the result that his concession would create. For the evidences of the brutality of the troops, he recorded in his unpublished journal notes for 1770, were fabrications; the aggressors throughout had been the townsmen not the soldiers, and they had acted in response to a secret plan which had been inadvertently revealed in the heat of the afternoon's Council debate. In a passage of Oliver's confidential minutes of that meeting (which when published by Bernard would lead to criminal charges against the secretary, newspaper claims in England and America that he was a "perjured traitor," and accusations, testimonies, and counter-testimonies that fill the Council records of October 1770) Oliver recorded verbatim the open declaration of one influential councillor that,

"it was not such people as had formerly pulled down the lieutenant governor's house which conducted the present measures, but people of the best character among us—men of estates and men of religion; that they had formed their plan and that this was a part of it, to remove the troops out of town and after that the [customs] commissioners; that it was impossible the troops should remain in town; that the people would come in from the neighboring towns, and that there would be 10,000 men to effect the removal of the troops; and that they would probably be destroyed by the people—should it be called rebellion, should it incur the loss of our charter, or be the consequence what it would."

Though the technical accuracy of Oliver's transcription of this outburst was assailed, Hutchinson never doubted that the whole affair had been preconcerted, the so-called Massacre itself deliberately incited, precisely for the purpose of driving out the troops and with them the authority of the British government.[9]

Yet in the end, Hutchinson wrote Hillsborough in a painstaking letter of explanation, weighing all the elements—noting particularly the unlikelihood that any civil magistrate would thereafter ever

9. *History of Massachusetts-Bay*, III, 230; *Fair Account*, p. 26. The "perjured traitor" charge was made by "Junius Americanus" [Arthur Lee] in *Bingley's Journal* (London), June 29, 1771, reprinted in *Boston Gazette*, Oct. 21, 1771. Records of the elaborate Council hearings on charges growing out of the publication of Oliver's minutes of the March 6 meeting are among the Misc. Bound MSS, MHS. The episode is summarized in Clifford K. Shipton, *Sibley's Harvard Graduates*, VII (Boston, MHS, 1945), 402–406.

dare order the use of troops even if they were immediately available; noting too that the spirit of the town was "as high . . . as it was at the time of the [Glorious] Revolution and the people four times as numerous"; and noting that if he refused to give in "I could have done no act of government after my refusal"—considering all of this in his total isolation, and recalling the disastrous consequences of Bernard's inflexible adherence to the letter of the law—he finally, and wearily, "under duress," conceded. Five days later the last of the royal troops, ignominiously patrolled by the town's militia, left Boston.[10]

The episode left Hutchinson exhausted, humiliated, and defeated, and it led him directly back to the personal decision he had approached but failed to make six months earlier. The future, he felt, could only bring more grinding harassments and more humiliations for anyone who attempted to uphold law and order and the authority of legitimate government.[11] The success of the extremists in getting rid of the troops had proved to them that by sheer brutal assertiveness they could intimidate the moderates and succeed in anything they tried. Boston, he wrote John Pownall, was the key to the political situation, and it was simply ungovernable. The town meetings were mob scenes with 3–4,000 people crammed into the hall, though there were not more than 1,500 legal voters. "You would be amazed," he wrote Bernard at the end of March, "to see the alteration since you were here in the people." They are infatuated; there is no hope of reasoning with them; and in this situation the friends of government are helpless, and will remain helpless until there are firm assurances of strong, steady support from England.[12]

10. TH to Hillsborough, March 12, 1770, MA, XXVI, 454; Oliver to Bollan, Nov. 3, 1770, Eg. MSS, 2670, p. 40; *History of Massachusetts-Bay*, III, 208. A copy of Hutchinson's note to Col. Dalrymple "desiring" him to remove the troops "in consequence of [the] unanimous advice of the Council" and acknowledging his own lack of authority to order the troops out, is among the Gage Papers. Hutchinson insisted, in a lengthy and agonized letter to Gage on March 18 (Gage Papers) that a close examination of the precise terminology used in the transaction would show that, despite appearances, he had not exceeded his authority; but he never doubted that he, and through him the government, had been coerced and defeated.
11. For Hillsborough's continuing orders to Hutchinson, written after news of the Massacre had been received in London, to use "the powers placed in your hands for the due execution of justice and for the support of the dignity of government," see his letter of April 26, 1770, CO5/759/133.
12. TH to John Pownall and to FB, March 21 and 30, 1770, MA, XXVI, 464, 467.

For himself, he concluded as soon as the immediate shock of the Massacre passed, there was little to hope for. Despite all his circumspection in using the troops and despite all his warnings of possible bloodshed and his efforts to prevent it, the Massacre, he knew, would be used by the opposition to brand him a bloodthirsty tyrant whose misrepresentations, rather than the opposition's own belligerence, had brought on the killings. The town of Boston's official account of the episode, which was dispatched as a pamphlet to London by the end of the month, was in fact deliberately written "to frustrate the designs of certain men who, as they have heretofore been plotting the ruin of our constitution and liberties by their letters, memorials, and representations, are now said to have procured depositions . . . to bring an odium upon the town as the aggressors in that affair." The pamphlet, written chiefly by Bowdoin, completely falsified what had happened; even the "legal" depositions it included, Hutchinson said, were false, and "all connected in this wickedness" should be punished. In April the *Gentleman's Magazine* in London published a letter written by a committee of the town to Thomas Pownall blaming the deaths on "the intrigues of wicked and designing men to bring us into a state of bondage and ruin." Hutchinson knew all such charges were nonsense—wicked, slanderous nonsense, calculated to make a bad situation worse; and in his manuscript almanac he refuted the letter line by line, at certain points word for word. But there was no way of making such refutations stick. Nothing would alter the convictions of people like John Adams, writing privately in the persona of the dead Crispus Attucks, that Hutchinson was "chargeable before God and man with our blood. The soldiers were but passive instruments, were machines, neither moral nor voluntary agents in our destruction. . . . You was a free agent. You acted coolly, deliberately, with all that premeditated malice, not against us in particular but against the people in general, which in the sight of the law is an ingredient in the composition of murder. You will hear further from us hereafter."[13]

Hutchinson's confidence that, as a native with forty years of ex-

13. James Bowdoin *et al.* to ——, March 23, 1770, in *Mass. Papers*, pp. 135–136 (the pamphlet is the *Short Narrative* referred to in note 8 above). Hutchinson's refutation of the letter to Pownall, passages of which he carried over verbatim into his *History of Massachusetts-Bay* (almost all of the detailed narrative on III, 197, for example), is in Eg. MSS, 2666, pp. 55–64. Adams, *Diary and Autobiography*, II, 84–85.

perience in local politics, he could keep control of the situation was fading. He had found himself "absolutely alone" in attempting to support law and order after the Massacre, and he was more convinced than ever of "the designs of particular persons to bring about a revolution and to attain to independency." He felt his grip steadily slipping, his capacity to act effectively eroding, and his always infirm confidence trembling. He began to fear another physical and psychological collapse despite his periodic retreats into the country and the program of light exercise that he maintained.[14] The burdens of the governorship under these conditions, he felt, were too great for him to bear, and within a fortnight of the Massacre he had made up his mind to withdraw his nomination for the appointment that he had so relentlessly sought. All of his essential humility and his respect for—his awe before—the constituted authority came out in the series of soul-baring letters he wrote at the end of the month.

He knew he was not without talent, he wrote Bernard two weeks after the Massacre, but "if I had more talents than I have, yet I have not strength of constitution to grapple with burdens which, everybody tells me, exceed beyond comparison what you met with." He felt he lacked the dignity, the rank, the personal authority for the task: a "person of much greater weight than I"—of "superior weight and rank"—was needed. "I must beg you," he therefore concluded to Bernard, "to make my most humble excuse or resignation from a sense of my utter inability to discharge the trust." And on March 27, in a carefully worded letter of resignation to Hillsborough, he made it official: "I have not strength of constitution to withstand the whole force of the other branches of government as well as the body of the people united against the governor . . . and must humbly pray that a person of superior powers of body and mind may be appointed to the administration of the government of the province." He requested that he be allowed to resume the chief justiceship, a position "in which I thought I had done good, and had been very little abused for it."[15]

14. *History of Massachusetts-Bay*, III, 208. His health was a constant concern in these months: e.g., TH to FB, March 1 and May [6–10], 1770, MA, XXVI, 450, 479.
15. TH to FB, March 18 and 22, 1770, MA, XXVI, 456, 459; TH to John Pownall, March 21, 1770, *ibid.*, p. 464; TH to Hillsborough, March 27, *ibid.*, p. 461; *Diary and Letters*, II, 192; *History of Massachusetts-Bay*, III, 208.
Within two weeks Hutchinson's decision had found its way into the opposition press,

So Hutchinson, convinced that "the state of the times is such . . . that a governor must be deprived of that tranquillity of mind without which life itself is scarce desirable," threw off the oppressive burden and freed himself to assume what he considered to be his natural role, that of a provincial leader capable of seeing issues clearly and acting freely for the public good. But he was not to be so cleanly and conveniently released. His fate, in fact—and indeed the fate of Anglo-American relations—turned on the timing of those letters of resignation and the circumstances that existed in England when they were received. Two months passed after he sent off his resignation before he heard anything from London, and then the news from the capital was disconcerting. Apparently his letters had not yet arrived. Worse than that, in April Bernard wrote enthusiastically that he was not only advancing his protégé's appointment with all his force but had locked into it his own prospects for preferment. An irritating confusion about paying the fees for Hutchinson's commission, he reported, had been neatly overcome and the interlocking set of appointments he had so carefully contrived was going forward splendidly. Then, late in April, with Hutchinson's letters of resignation still at sea, his commission as governor was approved by George III. Two weeks later his resignation arrived in London.[16]

The shock was instantaneous. Bernard, deeply embarrassed by what he called Hutchinson's irresolution, reported that Hillsbor-

---

where it was wildly lampooned, "The TALL MAN," the *Boston Gazette* wrote on April 9, 1770, "(through some of his little tools) has lately given out that he has wrote home desiring he *may not* be appointed governor-in-chief in the room of his recalled friend. *If this be true,* he really might have saved himself the trouble. For, from the best intelligence, there never was the least chance or prospect of his ever having such an appointment, even though he has sacrificed many *valuable* considerations to obtain it! His principles and abilities for that station are *now* better known at home, as well as here. And, whatever his givings out may now be, *shooting over the heads of his little tools,* it is certain and very well known on both sides the water that no person ever adored the sun with more fervency than he, for years past [he] has worshipped that object, *the chair!* And indeed (taking a review of the past five years conduct) if wading through thick and thin, right and wrong, at all events! give the best pretentions, no man in America has a better claim to such a reward—it is doubtful whether ever Sir Francis himself has more merit in that way."

16. TH to Thomas Hood, May 21, 1770, MA, XXVI, 487; Bernard's reports to Hutchinson on the progress of his efforts in his behalf began in early Nov. 1769 and ran continuously until May 13, 1770. Bernard Papers, VIII, 14–93. The arrangement was for Andrew Oliver to succeed Hutchinson as lieutenant governor, taking over the £200 supplementary salary that Hutchinson had had, and for Hutchinson's nephew Nathaniel Rogers to succeed Oliver as province secretary. Hillsborough's official notification to Hutchinson of all of these appointments is dated April 14, 1770: Co5/759/55.

ough too was chagrined. American affairs were just then under discussion in Parliament, and this was no time to cancel a gubernatorial appointment that had just been made, nor would it be possible at this time, he added rather brutally, to generate the new constitutional powers and the financing necessary to attract a more eminent and capable person to the post. There was no need for Hutchinson to be concerned about his reputation in London, Bernard told him; his conduct after the Massacre had been approved by the administration, though of course he had been attacked in the London press. He would do what he could to help relocate Hutchinson in his former, or perhaps other, positions if he insisted, but he made it clear that for the moment nothing could be done except to suspend the force of the new commission, which would only have the effect of leaving Hutchinson still in charge in Massachusetts, but as lieutenant governor rather than as governor.[17]

Then Hillsborough joined in. Through Bernard, His Lordship told Hutchinson that despite his resignation he remained the ministry's choice for the governorship, and that he himself had no one else in mind for it. He had complete confidence in him, and would take no action until Hutchinson explicitly confirmed his determination to resign. Did Hutchinson know that the governorship would now carry a crown salary, freeing the incumbent from reliance upon the Assembly? When Bernard replied for Hutchinson that the problem was less that of money than of "the impracticality of the government in its present state," Hillsborough instructed him to solicit Hutchinson's recommendations for constitutional reforms that might strengthen the power of the Massachusetts government. And directly, in a private letter that would mean much to Hutchinson, the secretary of state told the weary Bostonian that no one had ever given more general satisfaction to the government than he, and assured him, in a phrase Hutchinson would recall in later years with the deepest bitterness, that, if he agreed to be thus

17. FB to TH, May 13, 1770, Bernard Papers, VIII, 93–94. If Hutchinson persisted in his withdrawal, Bernard said he was prepared to arrange for his reappointment as chief justice, with a salary of £500 a year, and also as lieutenant governor, if Hutchinson wished to hold both posts again. *Ibid.*, p. 97 (June 8). Hutchinson replied in some heat to "what you [Bernard] call my irresolution," explaining that it was not irresolution that had led him to withdraw from the governorship but "a justifiable diffidence of my sufficiency for affairs." TH to FB, July 24, 1770, MA, XXVI, 519 and 521 (the earlier, more angry-sounding version of the letter was not sent).

drawn into the governorship, he would never as a consequence "be left to suffer."[18]

So it was in early June 1770 that an exhausted and dispirited Hutchinson found that what he had assumed had been an irreversible decision was in fact still an open question. The governorship would lie vacant until he confirmed his resignation. He had no choice but to reconsider. And indeed, circumstances, he had to admit, had changed in the months since the Massacre. Not only, in the aftermath of the bloodshed, had there appeared what he later described as an "abatement of the tumultuous, violent spirit which had prevailed," but there suddenly seemed also to be the prospect, slight but palpable, in his momentary success in transferring the seat of the Assembly from the inflamed center of Boston to the more placid Cambridge, that shrewd management, a subtle blend of firmness and conciliation, might yet stabilize the political situation. And then his friends, "hurt at the news of my having declined the post," closed in on him. Fearful of the arrival of yet another insensitive hand like Bernard's, fearful too of the loss of the direct influence that Hutchinson's governorship would have created for them, and convinced that, while no one in the governor's chair could alone restabilize the situation, Hutchinson was as likely as anyone to keep it from deteriorating still further, they pledged him their complete support and begged him to change his mind. It was his duty to his native land to accept, they said; it was his duty to them; and it was his obligation as a servant of the crown.[19]

But none of this weighed as heavily in Hutchinson's mind as the solicitude he felt had been shown him by the great men in London and the embarrassment he felt at having upset a whole network of their appointments. Lord Hillsborough's "condescension," as he termed it, touched the deepest springs of his being and elicited the most profound responses. The respect the secretary of state had paid him, the care His Lordship had taken to endorse his conduct

18. FB to TH, June 20 and Aug. 20, 1770, Bernard Papers, VIII, 99–101, 119. Hillsborough's private letter to Hutchinson was not copied into the official file of letters sent out from the secretary of state's office, and since Hutchinson apparently kept the letter itself with him for the rest of his life, referring to it again and again, it is not among the papers that ended up in the Massachusetts Archives. Hutchinson paraphrased the letter in his diary in 1778 (*Diary and Letters*, II 192) and I have quoted from that paraphrase.

19. *History of Massachusetts-Bay*, III, 239; TH to Josias Lyndon, David Cheeseborough, and Richard Jackson, March 17 and Feb. 11, 1771, and Oct. 15, 1770, MA, XXVII, 131–132, 119, 23–24; Eg. MSS, 2666, pp. 61–63.

and request his judgment on important questions, his refusal to take political advantage of the vacancy Hutchinson's resignation had created—all of this moved Hutchinson deeply. It warmed him; it gave him heart; it reached through his isolation and made his suffering and the sacrifice of his reputation among his own country-men seem worth while; it gave him back his self-respect. In the face of "so unexpected a mark of favor" from this near-ultimate author-ity, and in view of what appeared to be at least a ray of hope for political peace, Hutchinson's desperate determination to withdraw from the conflict weakened. He was never in doubt, he would later insist, about his personal inclination: to resign and "spend the re-mainder of my life in ease and quiet" on his decent country home-stead in Milton. But Hillsborough's response had given him what he termed a new "political existence," and had stirred such deep de-sires in one admittedly never "destitute of ambition" that, combined with the pleadings of his friends and the momentarily favorable prospects of politics, it overcame his fears—overcame his better judg-ment—overcame, as it proved, his instinct for survival.[20]

So in June 1770 he drifted, "with fear and trembling," back into the maelstrom. Clumsily he explained away his resignation: it had merely been a gesture, he told Hillsborough, to give the govern-ment the opportunity of appointing someone of greater strength and superior abilities; in the Massacre crisis his health and doubt-less his judgment had been impaired by overwork, lack of exercise, and the expectation of still further troubles. He had morbidly feared that his death or incapacitation in office would have created even more trouble for the government than already existed, and he had wished to spare the authorities that. And of course it had never occurred to him that his resignation would arrive at an embarrassing time for His Lordship. But happily, he said, his health had now im-proved, and he was relieved to know that the ministry understood the difficulties anyone in his position faced in Massachusetts: that, given the adamant opposition of almost every person and body con-stitutionally obliged to assist the governor, he would only have a "choice of evils." Hutchinson therefore apologized for the trouble he had caused. Then reluctantly, and tremulously—prudently re-

20. TH to FB, July 24, 1770, MA, XXVI, 521; *History of Massachusetts-Bay,* III, 239; TH to Cheeseborough and to ——, Feb. 11, 1771, and Dec. 13, 1772, MA, XXVII, 119, 429; *Diary and Letters,* I, 80, 291, II, 79.

questing the right to appoint his replacement as chief justice on a temporary basis only, in case later he himself might have to fall back on that post—he agreed to continue as chief executive. Six months later, on December 7, Hillsborough sent off to him his commission as governor, and ordered the Treasury to provide him thereafter with an annual crown salary of £1500 sterling to be paid out of the income from the tea duties. On March 14, 1771, Hutchinson publicly took the oath of office in Boston. That same month he was issued special instructions which, while ostensibly strenthening the legal authority of his administration, limited his capacity to maneuver politically and in themselves created new sources of controversy.[21]

ii

The events of the eight months between his agreement and his investiture in office, and those of the year that followed, seemed to prove the wisdom of his decision, but in fact his finest successes of those months nourished the seeds of his destruction. By the end of 1770 the trauma of the Massacre had begun to fade, and there seemed to be "a surprising change in the temper of the people." "The crests of our late incendiaries are much fallen," he proudly wrote Jackson on December 27, and the politics of Massachusetts was calmer than it had been for four or five years, a turn of events, he said, that gave him "more pleasure than I could have received

21. TH to ——, Oct. 9, 1771, MA, XXVI, 243; *Diary and Letters*, II, 79; TH to Hillsborough, June 8, June 29, and Oct. 9, 1770, MA, XXVI, 501, 512–513, XXV, 446; Hillsborough to TH and to Treasury, Dec. 7, 1770, CO5/759/296, 298. Huchinson's "Additional Instructions," March 28, 1771, is in British Papers Relating to the American Revolution (Sparks MSS 43), IV, 35, Houghton Library, Harvard University. The new clauses forbade the Council to meet without the governor's approval; restricted the appointment of colonial agents to those elected by both Houses and endorsed by the governor; forbade local taxing of the customs commissioners' salaries; and affirmed the crown's right to command the garrison in Castle William in Boston Harbor. For Samuel Adams' furious denunciation of these instructions, which, he said, if not resisted, would lead to a complete substitution of tyranny for the free constitution, see *Boston Gazette*, Oct. 14, 1771 (reprinted in H. A. Cushing, ed., *Writings of Samuel Adams* [N.Y., 1904–1908], II, 250–254). For the magnificent reception held for the new governor at Harvard College on April 3, in the course of which Hutchinson responded to the "handsome gratulatory oration in Latin" with "an elegant reply in the same language," see Samuel Eliot Morison, *Three Centuries of Harvard, 1636–1936* (Cambridge, Harvard University Press, 1936), pp. 141–144.

from any addition to my private fortune."[22] Of course, confrontations with authority, some ridiculous, some threatening, continued, but Hutchinson's apparent success in enforcing the power of government was striking and appeared to vindicate Hillsborough's confidence in him. It was true that the break-up of the nonimportation movement resulted not from anything Hutchinson did but from the repeal of most of the Townshend Duties and from the rivalries among the merchants that resulted.[23] It was true also that Hutchinson could claim to have contributed relatively little to the reasonable jury decision in the trial of the soldiers accused of the Massacre killings, though his deliberate postponement of the trial had been important in giving time for tempers to cool and for a proper defense to be prepared.[24] But his success in effecting the transfer of the General Court from Boston to Cambridge and his management of the substitution of crown troops for provincial levies in the harbor garrison seemed clearly to be personal achievements. He was proud of them both, and bragged of them both (the latter remained his accomplishment as governor of which he was most proud), yet in fact both helped to destroy him. For his acceptance of high office led him inescapably into a deepening self-delusion. He could proceed thereafter only by exaggerating every favorable trend and by developing programs that in other circumstances he would have known could not succeed. While what he most needed was an increasing sensitivity to the deepening difficulties of his position and a broadening responsiveness to the inner meanings of the opposition voices, he became more and more tone deaf, more and more locked into a narrowing set of responses—less imaginative, less flexible, less perceptive—courageous, concerned, striving, but ever more dangerously vulnerable.

In handling the two problems that immediately faced him when his ordeal of decision was concluded he was the victim of his finest instincts: rationality, prudence, a decent regard for the opinions of others. It was not enough for him simply to follow his instructions from Hillsborough and shift the General Court from the

22. *Diary and Letters*, I, 24; TH to Jackson and to ——, Dec. 27, 1770, and Jan. 7, 1771, MA, XXVII, 88–89, 91.

23. *History of Massachusetts-Bay*, III, 238; *Diary and Letters*, I, 24.

24. L. Kinvin Wroth and Hiller B. Zobel, eds., *Legal Papers of John Adams* (Cambridge, Harvard University Press, 1965), III, 3–4, 12.

tumult of Boston to the relative calm of Cambridge and to do it in such a way that the opposition would be obliged to transact business there. He must convince the opposition that the move was right, he must justify his actions and his authority, he must overcome his opponents by sheer force of logic and draw them to his side. When first the Boston Town Meeting and then the House claimed that in relocating the Assembly by executive order Hutchinson was not only violating the Massachusetts charter and the fundamental rights of Englishmen but palpably advancing the autocratic designs known to be lurking in the English court, he leapt to the challenge, justifying himself in writing with references to historical precedent, practical necessity, and the clear stipulations of the charter. When the Council replied to his reply, Hutchinson not only undertook a comprehensive rebuttal but, on July 25, delivered a formal speech to both houses reviewing all the arguments *in extenso* and once again justified himself with what seemed to him unanswerable logic. But that merely stimulated the House to greater exertions (a paper of some five thousand words), which obliged Hutchinson once again to respond. A year later the Assembly was still protesting and Hutchinson was still replying point by point. In all, during the two years of the controversy over the relocation of the Assembly, ten papers were exchanged.[25]

His handling of the relocation was generally approved in London, but cautionary notes were sounded by men more sophisticated than he. Bernard, who wrote that he thought Hutchinson had conducted the affair "in a masterly manner, and [had] fairly routed" the opposition, denied Hutchinson's request that he publish the exchanges together as a pamphlet: they were too voluminous for anyone to read, he said, and, more important, publicizing the Assembly's "flagitious" arguments, even if only to refute them, might lead to a dangerous reaction on the part of Parliament. And in the same letter he turned down Hutchinson's suggestion of a Parliamentary commission of inquiry into the claims of the colonial Assemblies, again on the ground that it could only lead to arguments on first principles and hence would bring into open contention the founda-

25. The documents are reprinted in *History of Massachusetts-Bay*, III, 370–404. Hutchinson's formal history of the episode is on pp. 216ff., especially p. 220. For a detailed analysis of the controversy, see Donald C. Lord and Robert M. Calhoon, "The Removal of the Massachusetts General Court from Boston, 1769–1772," *Journal of American History*, 55 (1969), 735–755.

tions of Parliament's authority. Hillsborough too was sympathetic but cautious, commending Hutchinson's conduct in general and praising in particular the "candor and moderation" of his speech of July 25 and the "prudence and spirit" of his reply to the Assembly's reply. But he too explicitly warned him against ever again involving himself in arguments with the legislature over their pretentious and subversive theoretical claims.[26]

But there was a still more dangerous potential in Hutchinson's handling of the Court removal. His actions were such as to misrepresent his personal feelings and project an image of deceit. It was unclear to the public just what authority he was acting under. Hillsborough had issued not a flat instruction to move the legislature to Cambridge but a discretionary and advisory order effective unless Hutchinson had "more weighty reasons" for declining to act. Characteristically, Hutchinson had himself been against the move, just as he had been against the Stamp Act and the Townshend Duties; indeed, a year earlier he had advised Bernard to ignore a more explicit command to move the Assembly. Left to himself he would never have transferred the Assembly, and in fact, when he had first received Hillsborough's order, he had drafted a reply stating that, in view of the likely consequences, he would not act unless he had an outright royal command: the resentment and animosity the move would generate would outweigh any possible advantages. But then, prudently, he had checked himself, weighed both sides, and decided to move more cautiously. It was, he had confessed to Bernard, a "delicate situation . . . I shall be charged [either] with want of resolution or . . . want of discretion." In the circumstance, resolution, he had finally decided, was a higher virtue than discretion, especially since, with Bernard calling the shots in London, he ran the risk of losing support there if he refused the secretary's recommendation. He had therefore reversed himself, changed his letter to Hillsborough before the ship that was to carry it sailed, and substituted a new version agreeing to the removal. So resolution—or a higher prudence—had prevailed; but the result was that he entered the controversy with the Assembly both against his own better judgment and without the support of an outright royal command. Since he could produce no crown orders upon the

26. Hillsborough to Hutchinson, July 6, Aug. 4, Oct. 3, Oct. 31, Nov. 15, 1770, CO5/759/206ff.; FB to TH, Oct. 7, 1770, Bernard Papers, VIII, 129–131.

opposition's demand, they concluded that he was acting out of his own desire to advance the cause of prerogative power, and that his claim that he had had no choice in the matter was deceitful. But in his own mind Hutchinson was satisfied that though he had never had direct crown orders to relocate the Assembly, political necessity had transformed Hillsborough's recommendation into an order as binding on him "as if I had received the most positive instruction." And so, he concluded, "there is no reason to pretend I deceived them."[27]

It was a devious logic, born of a desire to please both sides and an instinct for manipulation; and while Hutchinson and his sponsors were satisfied that he had effectively defended the crown's right to fulfill its traditional constitutional role, others could see that by doing so he had forced the opposition to challenge more profoundly than ever before the whole structure of traditional constitutional thought that justified the right of "prerogative" to act independently of the people's will.[28]

His reputation for deceit was further enlarged, and his challenge to the opposition to probe the boundaries of tradional thought was intensified, by his handling of the second immediate problem he confronted after his agreement to serve as governor: the substitution of royal troops for the provincial levies in the harbor garrison in Castle William that took place in September 1770. This time he did have direct crown orders. He was instructed by Hillsborough, who was determined to strengthen the crown's presence in the Boston area, to remove the provincial troops in the garrison and substitute a company of regulars so that the harbor could be controlled by British authorities and the harassed customs commissioners given firm support. The charter, however, gave command over forts and garrisons in Massachusetts to the governor, and it was a real ques-

27. *Diary and Letters*, I, 526; FB to Hillsborough, June 10, 1769, Bernard Papers, VII, 170; TH to Hillsborough, April 19, 1770, MA, XXVI, 462; TH to Hillsborough, Feb. 28, 1770, *ibid.*, p. 448 (not sent), p. 446 (sent, but showing the deleted passage in which Hutchinson originally declined to relocate the Assembly; the letter in its final form is CO5/759/57); TH to FB, March 1, 1770, MA, XXVI, 451. Hillsborough's deliberately ambiguous order to Hutchinson (Dec. 9, 1769) is quoted in Lord and Calhoon, "Removal of the General Court," p. 737. The issue remained so much alive in public awareness and was felt to be so substantial a grievance that Jefferson included it among the charges against the King in the Declaration of Independence. Hutchinson replied to that charge, as he did to the others in the Declaration, in his *Strictures upon the Declaration . . .* (London, 1776). Lord and Calhoon, "Removal of the General Court," p. 752.
28. *Ibid.*, p. 754.

tion in Hutchinson's mind whether he had the legal right to sur-render that command to another officer, even at the order of their common superior, the King. The whole idea of such a transfer troubled him, but he could not evade his direct orders, and so, putting aside all doubts of his own in the face of a fact of life, he decided to act immediately, before the inevitable opposition could organize itself, and to do so ostensibly not because he had been *ordered* to do so but because he chose to do so in his independent authority as governor. Throughout, he maintained the stance—the "appearance," as he explained it to Bernard—of acting as the independent commander of the fort who had the right to assign any soldiers he chose to stand duty there. In this way he submerged the dangerous political question of *why* he made the change into sub-jective considerations that were not susceptible to criticism. "What my motive was," he later explained, "whether by the King's order or my own judgment, was not a matter of inquiry." And he was careful to preserve that ambiguity in his detailed handling of the change so that he retained the appearance of control and could continue to claim that the transfer had been made without the slightest violation of the charter.[29]

It was clever, and it worked, in that the forces of the opposition petered out. Hutchinson exulted in his success: "as I have steered it, they are nonplussed"; and he never ceased thinking of this piece of management as an ideal combination of firmness and tact.[30] But in fact it added one more increment to the growing belief that he was a dissembler, hiding his true purposes beneath disarming ap-pearances. For his subtle and ambiguous position convinced the Assembly not of the propriety of his actions or the innocence of his intent but of his skill in covering himself legally. The Assembly was in fact so suspicious of him that it conducted a public hearing on the transfer, and though it was true, as Hutchinson claimed,

29. *Diary and Letters*, I, 27–29; Hillsborough to TH, July 6, 1770, CO5/759/207; *History of Massachusetts-Bay*, III, 222, 223; TH to FB, Oct. 20, 1770, MA, XXVII, 27. Hutchinson explained his doubts about the legality of the transfer quite freely to Gage, but concluded that by his deliberate use of the ambiguity of his role—as governor under the Massachusetts charter and as a servant of the crown—he had managed to evade the problem. TH to Gage, Sept. 9 and 12, 1770, Gage Papers.

30. TH to FB, Oct. 20, 1770, MA, XXVII, 28; TH to Hillsborough, Oct. 9, 1770, MA, XXV, 442 ("a sudden stroke which when done the people [did] not have it in their power to undo"). Hutchinson's most detailed account of the actual transfer (Sept. 9) is in TH to FB, Sept. 15, 1770, MA, XXVII, 1–3 ("the whole garrison was in tears").

that they "don't know what exception to make," they resolved nevertheless that he had violated the charter. Both Houses proclaimed a day of prayer to mark their concern, and defiantly requested Hutchinson himself to designate another such day out of respect for the colonies' grievances—a demand, Hutchinson thought, portentously reminiscent of the politics of 1641.[31]

Yet he continued to believe that the transfer of troops had been a success, and an important one, for not only had he demonstrated his ability to maintain the authority of government without touching off an explosion, but the resulting control of the harbor fortress, together with the simultaneous relocation of the headquarters of the British navy in American waters to Boston harbor, marked the beginning, he believed, of a process certain to bring the province "to a due sense of the subjection to the supreme authority."[32] The supporters of government, he believed, were now confident that hereafter the King's force would not desert them, and he was sure that the confidence of the opposition had been shaken. He was not surprised to hear that certain leaders of the "faction" were understood to be ready to break with the opposition.[33]

iii

Yet these encounters were only preliminary skirmishes in what he knew would be an extended campaign that he must somehow win. Though in the fall of 1771 he could look back upon a successful year, he acknowledged that he had much to do before he could overcome the "peculiar disadvantage" he had started with, "that my predecessor was very obnoxious to the people and I was known

31. *History of Massachusetts-Bay*, III, 224; TH to John Pownall, Sept. 30, 1770, MA, XXVII, 10. Later, in small but significant ways the Assembly's doubts about the transfer seemed to be confirmed: when Thomas Pownall in London, uninformed of the ambiguities that Hutchinson had cultivated, wrote Bowdoin forthrightly that he thought the transfer illegal (TH to ——, Oct. 20, 1770, MA, XXVII, 36); when the new fort captain blandly ordered repairs without the slightest acknowledgment of Hutchinson's command (TH to John Pownall, Feb. 4, 1771, *ibid.*, p. 114); and when the commander in chief of British forces insisted on commissioning all the fort officers himself (TH to ——, Nov. 30, 1772, *ibid.*, p. 421).

32. TH to Hillsborough, Oct. 9, 1770, MA, XXV, 445. The Privy Council had assigned the fleet headquarters to Boston at the same time as it had ordered the garrison transfer (July 6, 1770).

33. TH to FB, Oct. 20, 1770, MA, XXVII, 27; TH to Jackson, Feb. 3, 1771, *ibid.*, p. 111.

to have approved of his administration in general." He had, he knew, "still a great way to go before I reach the mark and attain to a state of order and tranquillity," and if that state were ever to be achieved, deep changes would have to be made.[34] In the five years in which he exercised the executive command in Massachusetts—1770–1774—it was the prospect of somehow shifting the basis, or the structure, of the situation that engrossed his attention. He did not know precisely how to proceed; he had no program, no guidelines, no deliberated strategy for a campaign; he merely followed his instincts, and they led him, not to the heart of the matter, which he would never understand, but to those elements of influence, power, and calculated self-interest which a lifetime of Anglo-American politics had taught him to respect. Wound in among the details of his governorship, spread out through hundreds of letters, memoranda, and speeches, lies the evidence of the efforts Hutchinson made as governor to contain the growing rebellion in Massachusetts and help stabilize Anglo-American relations. It was his failure in these efforts—to him a baffling personal failure but to the historian a failure that brilliantly illuminates the origins of the Revolution—that assured his political, and psychological, defeat.

Of his first long-term obligation he was never in doubt: it was the essence of the politics he knew. It was necessary above all else for the administration in Massachusetts to impose its political control over the whole of the governmental process, to discipline the dissident elements politically, and through that discipline to bring them into accord with British policy. Indeed, there was a peculiar necessity to form such a political grouping in Massachusetts—to create an effective "interest" or "party" that could stand firm for law and the needs of government—because the government as set out in the charter was poorly balanced. Instead of an equilibrium between the necessary elements of power and liberty—between the state and the people—mediated by an independent aristocracy, the charter had created a government all branches of which "depended more or less upon the voice of the people." The capacity of government to act depended, therefore, to an unusual degree, upon the ability of crown officers to knit together informally a political group that could be relied on when, once again, as inevitably they would,

34. TH to ——, Oct. 9, 1771, MA, XXVII, 243.

all other elements panicked and ran before the facile demagoguery of a small group of fanatical agitators.[35] Every available device must be used in a Walpolean build-up of influence, every technique of political coercion carefully deployed, and for this work Hutchinson, one of the most experienced politicians in America, seemed ideally suited. He began on the task even before his commission as governor was officially received.

Patronage, traditionally, was the key, and it became Hutchinson's engrossing concern. In letter after letter to friends, clients, patrons, and potential supporters he cast out the lines of a projected network of influence by which he hoped to control the political system and confine the radicals' power. At the lowest level it was a matter of manipulating choices for the militia offices, lesser judgeships, and other local offices. The names of the faithful and of susceptible influentials were solicited and duly recorded. Only one of Hutchinson's annual almanac journals survives, but it is fortunately of the year 1770, when he was forming his administration. The end papers of this notebook are covered with the names of candidates for office and of those who recommended them—"Dudley Carlton, a justice for Lincoln County . . . recommended by Mr. Goldthwait. Thomas Robie, Esq., Marblehead, recommended by the secretary . . . Samuel Todd, [see] Woodbridge letter."[36]

There were all sorts of possibilities. **Rewards could be given** (an office for the loyal victim of a Cape Ann mob who had the fortitude to prosecute his tormenters) **or denied** (to the author of an "insolent, incendiary" letter nominated in England for a probate post).[37] **Economic pressure could be brought to bear:** laborers' jobs at the Castle could be restricted to those free of suspicion of participation in public agitation; printers of proven loyalty to the government could continue to receive official patronage despite the superior qualifications of others.[38] **Appointments could be juggled to produce the maximum reinforcement for government:** let the politically controversial customs commissioner Robinson be replaced by the valuable Putnam and appointed to the Halifax vice-admiralty court in place of the loyal Jonathan Sewall so that Sewall could serve full

35. TH to Hillsborough, June 29, 1770, MA, XXVI, 513.
36. Eg. MSS, 2666.
37. TH to FB, Nov. 30, 1770, MA, XXVII, 61; TH to ——, Feb. 25, 1773, *ibid.,* p. 459.
38. TH to FB, Sept., Feb. 3, 1771, March 31, 1772, MA, XXVII, 229, 110–111, 309.

time in his other office, that of the attorney general of Massachusetts; Sewall's skill as a pamphleteer would make him doubly valuable in Boston.[39] **Writers could be bought off:** the famous Dr. Church, for example, whose treasonous words and subsequent panic Silvester had reported, could be secretly retained to write anonymous blurbs for the government and to report on the radicals' plans. **Key opposition figures might be turned by subtler means:** John Hancock, for example, eager to enter the Council, a power in the opposition because of his wealth, and resentful of the overbearing Samuel Adams—let various deals be tried with him; offer him the Council seat in exchange for the House's nomination of Secretary Oliver to that body; if that did not work, take in exchange a motion in acceptable terms that the Assembly be returned to Boston, which would surely reinforce the Adams-Hancock split and also make it possible for Hutchinson to "have the members [of the General Court] every day at my table and provide an antidote," he wrote Bernard in a letter which he wisely did not send, "for the poison of that white-livered fellow that you used so much to detest."[40]

Such social projects were very much part of the game. "For the sake of peace" Hutchinson even endorsed plans of the Sons of Liberty for a regular soiree guaranteed to be nonpolitical, though it meant he would have to "quit my study for the card room one evening in a fortnight." ("Don't suspect me of any concessions out of character," he hastily assured Bernard; "I shall give up nothing.") All of this was useful, all of it necessary, because like patronage it would in the end influence the voting of the House and help bring the branches of government into harmony with the administration.[41]

Nothing was more vital than that the proper people be elected to that mercurial body, and that once elected, they attend, for the radicals were always there. Letter after letter went out to the

39. Mary Beth Norton, ed., "A Recently Discovered Thomas Hutchinson Letter," MHS *Procs.*, 82 (1970), 105–109.

40. TH to FB, Jan. 29, 1772, MA, XXVII, 286–287; TH to ——, June 5, 1771, *ibid.*, pp. 180–181; TH to John Pownall, May 30, 1771, *ibid.*, p. 174; TH to ——, April 1772, *ibid.*, p. 314; TH to FB, May 29, 1772, *ibid.*, pp. 340–341. Oliver reported on Hancock's defection to James Gambier, May 8, 1772, Eg. MSS, 2670, p. 65.

41. TH to FB, Jan. 8, 1771, MA, XXVII, 93. For Hutchinson's dining with members of the Charitable Society just after his official installation as governor, see Anne R. Cunningham, ed., *Letters and Diary of John Rowe . . .* (Boston, 1903), p. 214.

stalwarts: to Colonel John Worthington, for example, and Colonel Israel Williams, pillars of government in Hampshire County. Take no offense, Hutchinson begged the latter in one of a dozen such political exhortations, at the official endorsement of a measure proposed by the obnoxious Major Hawley, for "government has but few supporters, and . . . when there is a disposition in any who have formerly been otherwise minded to promote a measure favorable to government, shall a governor refuse to use their aid in support of government because they do not esteem him personally? By no means." In any case, he wrote Williams, "come down to election, and bring Partridge with you. I wish every good town would send two." Above all, "remember," he wrote, "you don't live in the Commonwealth of Plato but in the dregs of Romulus. Cato himself would make a poor figure in our days."[42]

But it was steeply uphill work, and in the end, despite the most elaborate efforts, it did not succeed. Everything seemed prejudiced against the political success of the government. Some of these invidious conditions were only too familiar: they were part of the structure of colonial politics. But some were consequences of the immediate situation, strange and difficult to comprehend.

The mere fact that there were annual elections, Hutchinson recorded in his almanac notebook for 1770, had led in the years after the Stamp Act not only to the progressive elimination from the Assembly of the friends of government but also to an exaggeration of dissent, for once assembled the representatives "find business whether necessary or not . . . maybe to redress imaginary grievances." But nothing, he knew, could be done about this constitutional limitation on the political power of the administration, so crippling in comparison with the power available to the ministry in England, nor would he ever have the ministry's capacity to extend the life of a compliant House, if ever one appeared during his tenure.[43] More fundamental, and more debilitating, was the

42. TH to Worthington, March 19, 1772, MA, XXVII, 306; TH to Israel Williams, May 9, 1771, Williams Papers, MHS.
43. Eg. MSS, 2666, p. 79; TH to [John Pownall?], draft of letter of July 21, 1772, MA, XXVII, 361; TH to Hillsborough, May [1], 1771, *ibid.*, p. 157: "In conformity to the uninterrupted usage from the first year of the present charter, I have dissolved the Assembly and issued writs for a new election. I can find no clause in the charter which makes a new house of representatives necessary every year, and I think if the practice had been otherwise it would have been well warranted; and it would have strengthened government if the governor could have continued a house of representatives that should

insufficiency of patronage in a world assumed to be dominated less by public opinion than by the manipulation of "interests." Bernard had put the point succinctly: "If punishments and rewards are the two hinges of government, as politicians say," he had written Barrington in 1768, "this government is off its hinges, for it can neither punish nor reward."[44] Hutchinson too knew, at least as well as Bernard, that "honors and posts of profit are the chief weights in the royal scale which keep the balance of political power in equilibration, and it is not too much to say that to this influence Great Britain at present owes its very being." And he too sought to use these proven techniques to balance the forces of politics in Massachusetts. Knowing the colony and its politicians far better than Bernard ever had, proud now that outsiders like Bernard thought his "regard for [Boston] made me too tender of its interests, to the damage of the public interest: I cannot help an attachment to the place of my birth," and proud too to be able to point out his personal financial stake in the community, he strove to succeed where Bernard had failed. But he could not overcome the limitations that had helped defeat Bernard. "There are very few places in this government, except such as are elective, worth anything," he wrote Hillsborough. The Assembly prevents anyone they decide is a "tory" from receiving an elective office, and those who are given appointive offices, professing at first their loyalty to government, quickly buckle under to the popular pressures, join the opposition, and then deny the governor the right to remove them. In addition, in some areas the practice had grown up for sons to replace fathers in local offices, which had led either to a reduction of the governor's influence in the locality or an alienating struggle with the resident powers. And the governor's patronage suffered from inroads made upon it from abroad. For there was always the chance that one's

---

be well disposed, but an usage of fourscore years has rendered such continuance as impractable [*sic*] as if the charter had been expressly in favor of it."

44. FB to Barrington, Oct. 20, 1768, *The Barrington-Bernard Correspondence . . . 1760–1770,* ed. Edward Channing and A. C. Coolidge (Cambridge, 1912), p. 179. Later that year Bernard had complained at length to Hillsborough about the weakness of the governor's patronage powers, and had recommended the creation of a new "standing council" consisting of the attorney general, the solicitor general, and the advocate general, all to have special salaries paid by the crown. This, he claimed, would at least guarantee that the legal establishment would adhere to the government and not to the opposition, and it would significantly increase the governor's patronage powers. Dec. 12, 1768, Bernard Papers, VII, 116–117.

personal patrons—a Hillsborough, a Bernard—to say nothing of politicians of altogether alien interest, would have need of a colonial office or two to handle an immediate problem and would make their desires effective.[45]

These were critical problems for a politician, but they were at least familiar problems, that had crippled the political power of the governors for three quarters of a century.[46] And they forced Hutchinson, as they had so many of his predecessors, to fall back on just those controversial executive powers that in England after the Glorious Revolution had been eliminated as excessive: to veto a bill, to dismiss a difficult Assembly, to block the election of an opposition councillor. But there were other, less familiar forces at work even more potent in reducing Hutchinson's political influence than such traditional inhibitions, and these he understood less well. One of them leaps from the pages of a letter written to Hutchinson from York, Maine, in August 1769 by one of the seventeen "rescinders" who had supported the government under the most intense pressure the year before. It is a short letter, so compact and curiously idiomatic in expression that it deserves to be quoted in full:

> Honored and Dear Sir:
> When you were here on your circuit in this county, you intimated an honor you intended for me when you should take the [governor's] chair. As I have since heard of a pamphlet entitled, *A Dialogue,* I am convinced that those sons of violence that composed that, wait only for some others that are obnoxious to them to be called into view that they may be a more public mark to shoot at (and they shoot bitter arrows). The effects of this I have not conquered as yet, and reluct to have the clouds return so soon after the rain.
> This therefore with submission, I desire not to be named as a candidate for the office you proposed.
> No business suffers for want of that being filled, and possibly such a

45. FB to Lord Halifax, Nov. 9, 1764, CO5/755/139–140; TH to FB, March 25, 1770, MA, XXVI, 471; TH to Hillsborough, June 25, 1772, MA, XXVII, 349; TH to FB, April 28, 1770, MA, XXV, 396; *History of Massachusetts-Bay,* III, 70. For Hillsborough's personal reappointment of the Indian truckmaster at Fort Pownall, Me., whose dismissal Hutchinson had felt was politically necessary, see FB to TH, June 23, 1770, Bernard Papers, VIII, 101; for Bernard's imposing his own candidate (his son) over Hutchinson's (his brother-in-law) for a vice-admiralty post, see FB to TH, Oct. 8, 1770, *ibid.,* p. 131–132.

46. Bernard Bailyn, *The Origins of American Politics* (New York, Knopf, 1968), chap. ii.

spirit may be checked (I am sure it is high time), the way and means to do it are above my comprehension.

While many are watching for your halting, I sincerely say I wish you an easy and happy administration, and am with the greatest respect,

Your Honor's

Most

Obedient and

Most Humble

Servant,

Jonathan Sayward[47]

Others declined less poetically: the stolid Colonel Worthington, for example, who, convinced his support of government had alienated him from the people and lessened his personal influence, refused executive office and preferred not to attend the House. Other known supporters of the government also refused to help: "The government is deserted," Hutchinson wrote in despair after crucial Assembly sessions in 1773; "ten or a dozen" of the best men simply were not there when they could have swung the vote or at least kept sheer "absurdities" from passing through unanimously.[48]

There was nothing new, of course, in the weakness of ordinary men who chose to remain silent in the face of intimidation. Nor was there anything new in the demagoguery of the time—what Hutchinson called "the crafty design of a few wretched men who make no scruple of sacrificing the country if they can but keep up their importance among the people."[49] What *was* new, and what puzzled Hutchinson beyond all else, was the refusal of good and sensible men to recognize demagoguery when they were faced with it, and their willingness, indeed their apparent eagerness, to follow it politically. This was the most baffling, the most elusive, the most intractable force working against his success in politics, and try as

47. Sayward to TH, Aug. 22, 1769, MA, XXV, 328. The pamphlet referred to is *A Dialogue*, discussed above, pp. 128–129. A year later Sayward, whom John Adams had thought the most courageous of the "rescinders" (*Diary and Autobiography*, I, 356). was working closely with Hutchinson in lining up a slate of reliable j.p.'s (Sayward to TH. Oct. 6, 1770, MA, XXV, 440; and TH to Sayward, March 5, 1771, MA, XXVII, 125). In 1772 Sayward himself accepted appointment as county judge of probate and "special judge of the inferior court"; upon receipt of his appointment he congratulated Hutchinson on his "new and further alliances, by the spread of your family," and advised him at length on other possibilities for appointment. Sayward to TH, July 6, 1772, MA, XXV, 521–522.

48. TH to Worthington, Jan. 16, 1772, MA, XXVII, 282; Worthington to TH, Sept. 15, 1770, MA, XXV, 427–428; TH to Israel Williams, Jan. 8 and April 7, 1773, MA, XXVII, 435, 476.

49. TH to [John Pownall], July 21, 1772, MA, XXVII, 365.

he might he could never understand it or come to terms with it. But he never doubted its importance and never left off asking, probing, searching for some explanation he could use. In July 1772, in one of the most poignant scenes recorded in his letters, he drew aside members of the House whom he knew to be well-meaning and asked them directly—one sensible, realistic man to another —"what good can come from such rash, intemperate measures?" They told him he was wrong if he thought they were merely trying to make trouble for him; they had no quarrel at all with him: "but they suppose," Hutchinson recorded, "a design is formed to enslave them by degrees," and they promised him that they would continue to "make a stand against the measures which the ministry are taking to enslave them" even if there were no hope of their ever carrying their point.[50] But Hutchinson *knew* the ministry intended Americans no harm; he *knew* all such talk of enslavement was hysterical. The ministry, he told these otherwise sensible men again and again, was as well disposed to America as Americans could possibly wish, if only they had a true sense of their interest; but that they evidently lacked.

Yet there was no turning back. If he could not wholly succeed in directing the political system to the needs of government, he would at least try, using all the persuasion of which he was capable and squeezing every possible advantage from what patronage there was. But the yields were not only meager but at times perverse: his very efforts seemed to damage the prospects of success. In the context of the time his political maneuvers fed suspicions that his professions were not sincere, and that his real and hidden purposes threatened the public good. And indeed, in the narrowing circle of those reliably committed to maintaining law and order, the role of Hutchinson's family and personal associates grew so great that in itself it created the deepest suspicions. The coincidence of his rise to the highest authority and the multiplication of offices within his extended family could not, it was said, be accidental: Andrew Oliver, lieutenant governor; Peter Oliver and Foster Hutchinson, chief justice and associate justice of the superior court, respectively; a nephew, Nathaniel Rogers, nominated province secretary in succession to Andrew Oliver—all of this within the same years in which

50. Draft of letter to Pownall cited in previous note, *ibid.*, p. 358 (the language in this preliminary version is closer to the direct discourse of the conversation reported).

three intermarriages took place between the Oliver and Hutchinson families. Could this be accidental?[51] And then there were minor nepotistic nominations (a customs clerkship for his nephew Mather, a vice-admiralty court job for his brother-in-law Cotton, an inferior court seat for his son); and in addition, a controversial customs post for Hutchinson's boyhood friend Charles Paxton. Could one doubt that what was visible was but evidence of more as yet unseen, and that all of Hutchinson's denials were dissembled? Everything fitted the pattern suggested by this evident monopoly of office. Even Hutchinson's religion, it suddenly appeared, served the goals of his politics. It was observed in 1771 and blazoned in the papers that this born-Congregationalist, this son of a family whose Puritanism had been undefiled for five generations, had stood godfather in the Church of England for the son of his friend Commodore Gambier, that he had been a witness to the christening of an Apthorp child, scion of the Anglican church in Cambridge; and that he himself had been seen worshipping, with brazen unconcern, at King's Chapel, Boston. It was a flagrant, an almost deliberate, offense against the community's social and political sensibilities, but was this "late defection to the Church of England" surprising? It was well known, the *Boston Gazette* explained "that a sober dissenter, on the receipt of a [crown] commission, like *Bunyan's Pliable*, will *kneel at church*, and that the prospect of another will make him *turn godfather*." It was only later, in 1775, that the radicals found and published Hutchinson's confidential letter of 1772 explaining not only the Lockean catholicity of his religious views and his natural sympathy for the Church of England but his pragmatic reasons for continuing at all in the church of his birth, and his hatred of the bigotry of all clerics, particularly New England's, and of the latent intolerance of the New England mind. In 1772 none of this was positively known, but of all of it there were suspicions, broadcast in the press with matching evidence from other spheres, suggesting an underlying betrayal of ancestral faith and motives of *machtpolitik*.[52]

51. The relationships among the officeholders were explained in detail in the *Boston Gazette*, April 22, 1771, but the names were omitted; Harbottle Dorr, in his personal file of newspapers (III, 454), happily filled them in.

52. *Boston Gazette*, March 11, 25, 1771 (with details supplied by Dorr, III, 429). The letter on his religious views, which the revolutionaries would later publish (originally in the *Boston Gazette*, June 26, 1775, quickly reprinted in the *New-England Chronicle* and

iv

Thus political control eluded Hutchinson, and this failure, he knew, threatened the long-term prospect of that "state or order and tranquillity" he so desperately sought. But local political control was not the only, or even the most essential, resource available. In the same years in which he attempted to discipline the factional politics of Massachusetts, he turned instinctively to another, more powerful source of control. It was to England, through these years —its power and its benevolence; its capacity to persuade, to attract, and to coerce; its desire to placate and conciliate—that Hutchinson looked increasingly for relief, for justification, and for rescue, as the difficulties grew. Its power, its sympathy, and its capacity to act in its own interest he never doubted, and so he assumed that ultimately justice would be done, law-breakers punished, insults repaid, loyalty rewarded.

England had of course always been the ultimate resource, and in the troubles of the sixties Hutchinson had become practiced in appealing to its aid. But even then his confidence had been troubled. The Stamp Act had been repealed, it was true, but he had always been convinced that it should never have been passed in the first place, and it had been followed by the only slightly less obnoxious Townshend Duties, which too reflected to Hutchinson not so much ill will as insensitivity, indifference, and misinformation. The same deficiences must surely have accounted for his own personal neglect by the English government after the Stamp Act riots: its failure to compensate him for his great losses, its failure even to acknowledge his sacrifice, though others who had suffered less had received not only compensation but honors as well.[53] Indeed, in May 1766, during the critical Council election in which he had been

---

the *Massachusetts Spy*, and in 1776 in the London *Remembrancer*) was written to Bernard, Aug. 27, 1772 (MA, XXVII, 377–380). Curiously, however, what would have seemed one of the most damning sentences in the letter was *not* published: "I have no objection to [an Episcopal] bishop upon the proposed plan in America. I think the inhabitants of the Episcopal persuasion have a right to it. It's a degree of intolerance to oppose it." (The proposed plan was to limit the bishop's jurisdiction to "spirituals" and to voluntary professors.) Nor did the revolutionaries later publish his letter to Bernard of Dec. 24, 1771 (MA, XXVII, 265), in which he goes into all of this in greater detail ("Had I been born and bred [in the Episcopal church] I would never have left it for any other communion"). On these later publications, see below, pp. 335ff.

53. TH to ——, Dec. 31, 1765, MA, XXVI, 190.

defeated despite his majority vote, it had been not he—lieutenant governor, chief justice, and victim of the mob—who had received a personal letter from the secretary of state, but, unaccountably, the chief trouble-maker, Otis, who in the midst of the electoral proceedings had read out the letter to the assembled House with devastating political effect.[54] Nor, after the Stamp Act and Townshend Duties debacles, had there been evidence that the government had learned to listen, and was beginning to evolve a coherent colonial policy. Not only were his own suggestions ignored in England, and the elaborate discussions of colonial policy that he held with his friends conducted in the air, as it were, without the slightest relation to the thinking and planning of the government—but more important, there was no evidence that the government was thinking or planning at all. It almost didn't matter, he wrote to a correspondent in England two months before he took over the government, what the policy was: "If you would but be steady in any scheme be it what it would, we should come to some sort of settlement in the colonies." It was the heedlessness, the insensitivity, of England's response to the American question that seemed to him most threatening. For us in the colonies, he told Jackson shortly after Bernard left America, every session of Parliament is critical, for a crisis "cannot be far off" and action of some sort must be taken. His own views, he insisted, were altogether liberal: he was against Parliamentary taxation and in favor of continuing the loose constitutional ways of former years, but almost any policy would do so long as it was coherent, enforceable, and enforced. "Let me beseech you," he wrote Jackson, "not to leave us any longer than the next sessions in this uncertain state. No people under heaven ever felt the truth of that maxim, *Ubi lex vaga*, etc. more than the colonies now do, the whole constitution being vague and uncertain. I think," he said in an ingenious historical parallel, "of the condition of England just before the Restoration." Repeal as many of the laws as you please, he repeated again and again, but *execute* the ones that remain. "It is difficult to do it, I confess. But it must be done, first or last, or you will lose the colonies. The longer you delay the more difficult it will be."[55]

54. TH to TH, Jr., May 29, 1766, *ibid.*, p. 231.
55. TH to ——, May 29, 1769, MA, XXVI, 352; TH to Jackson, Aug. 18, 1769, *ibid.*, pp. 365–366.

But the delays continued, and so too did Hutchinson's Cassandran letters, written most freely to Jackson, Bernard, and the Pownalls, but written too, though with greater delicacy, to Hillsborough. Almost every letter he sent abroad in the early seventies contains some reference to both the necessity and the imminent prospect of Parliament's acting in a decisive and comprehensive way—by repealing the revenue acts, by passing new penal legislation, by reconsidering the imperial constitution. The need was so urgent, so obvious, so inescapable, that any vessel, Hutchinson felt, might be the bearer of the long-awaited news of Parliamentary action; any moment would see the situation transformed.[56] But instead of action there was silence, month after month. He hung on every rumor— that Wilkes was said to be confident that the government would finally go along with him and not his enemies; that John Pownall believed England would soon decisively reject the radicals' false ideas. By February 1770 he was forced to conclude that Parliament had decided to do nothing for the moment, though it was clear to him that if such inaction continued nothing but brute force would bring Massachusetts to its senses.[57]

That spring it seemed that the most ordinary functions of imperial government had come to a halt. The simplest executive instructions were not regularly forthcoming. Nine months—ten months—a year—after he had informed the home government of the Assembly's seditious belligerence at its summer session of 1769 he still had received no answer to his plea for orders, and this silence, he begged his superiors to realize, was the greatest possible encouragement to the wilder elements within the opposition. "The longer we are neglected the harder our cure will be," he wrote in various forms again and again.[58] The merest sign from England, the least recognition that thought was being taken, would keep the friends of government from seeking safety in withdrawal. Still there was no word. Four months after the Massacre he still had not received an official response to his report on the event—with the

56. One reason he had declined to order military protection for the harassed John Mein in 1769 was to keep from irritating the people just before the impending change. TH to Hillsborough, Nov. 11, 1769, MA, XXVI, 403.

57. TH to FB, Nov. [27], 1769, MA, XXVI, 409; TH to John Pownall, Dec. 6, 1769, *ibid.*, p. 413; TH to FB, Feb. 18, 1770, *ibid.*, p. 442.

58. TH to Gage, April 13, 1770, MA, XXVI, 462; TH to Hillsborough, May 13, 1770, *ibid.*, p. 482; TH to FB, March 25, 1770, *ibid.*, p. 472.

result, he believed, that the opposition had become progressively bolder.[59] Perhaps, he thought in June 1770, he would have some word in August, but in August all he found out was that a year had passed before the Treasury had even bothered to open a packet of the greatest consequence that he had sent, and then it had done so only at the request of a visiting official from Massachusetts. Finally, instructions came, but to his infinite frustration they were exhortatory and discretionary, and gave no indication that general solutions were being considered.[60]

Bernard, at least, was reassuring, up to a point, and informative in conveying messages from Hillsborough that failed somehow to get through the official channels. Not that Bernard was able to extract from the government any clearer or firmer directions for Hutchinson than he had been able to get for himself when he had been governor. But at least he passed on reports of all the relevant debates and the gossip of Parliament; gave plausible explanations of the delays; and held out hope that strong measures were in preparation. "If administration fails in this session," he concluded in a letter of October 1770 that must have given Hutchinson heart, "I will never ask you to expect relief again."[61]

The failure, when shortly it came, was the more painful because Bernard could plausibly blame it on Hutchinson himself. And again it was Hutchinson's moderation, his refusal to fly in the face of long-established usages and time-honored institutions, his prudence, his instinct to conserve, and his continuing desire to be identified with local interests while serving the needs of the empire, that created trouble. For not only had the ministry in the wake of the Massacre assigned the fleet's rendezvous to Boston harbor and transferred control of the harbor fort to the regular army, but it had set in motion preliminaries of Parliamentary legislation that would alter the chartered constitution of Massachusetts. Not that the British government was eager to move in so controversial a matter as imposing new controls on the colonies, but the Massacre had

59. TH to Gage, April 29, 1770, MA, XXV, 398; TH to FB, July 2, 1770, MA, XXVI, 515. Silence on the part of the home government, he wrote Thomas Pownall on May 11, was leading the colonies to independence faster than he could imagine. *Ibid.*, p. 481.
60. TH to Hillsborough, June 8, 1770, MA, XXVI, 500; TH to William Parker, Aug. 26, 1770, *ibid.*, p. 540.
61. FB to TH, Feb. 20, Jan. 10, May 13, Oct. 7, 1770, Bernard Papers, VIIII, 65ff., 42, 94–95, 131.

made action of some sort unavoidable. After hectic debates in the
Commons touched off by that event, and after hearings before the
Privy Council on the "disorders, confusion, and misgovernment
which have lately prevailed" in Massachusetts, John Pownall, the
undersecretary of state, had prepared an extensively documented
narrative of events in Massachusetts from the Stamp Act to 1770,
and the Privy Council had advised the King "to recommend the
consideration of the state of the province of Massachusetts Bay to
Parliament."[62] Hillsborough had thereupon convened a small group
to consider possible lines of action. Besides Hillsborough himself, it
included only the two undersecretaries, Pownall and William Knox,
and Governor Bernard, who since his arrival in London had undertaken a veritable campaign of vengeance against those who had so
harassed him in Massachusetts; he was determined to recast the
constitution of the colony in ways he had been talking and writing
about since 1764.[63] He proposed to the group no less than ten
articles of drastic change, of which two were understood to be the
most urgent and the most likely to be enacted: changes in the manner
of selecting councillors and jurymen, both alterations calculated to
bolster the force of executive government in the face of popular opposition. Documents were assembled to support these proposals. A
selection of letters that had been written to England by officials in
Massachusetts—including, fatefully, several by Hutchinson—especially letters that had been channeled to Grenville through his secretary, Thomas Whately, were brought together into a dossier that
supported Bernard's, and Hillsborough's, conviction that constitutional changes were necessary. And in August both John Pownall and
Hillsborough himself wrote Hutchinson privately soliciting his
current opinion of all of the contemplated changes.[64]

62. FB to TH, June 8, 1770, Bernard Papers, VIII, 98–99; Thomas Pownall to Boston
Town Committee, June 1770, *Bowdoin and Temple Papers* (MHS *Colls.*, 6th ser., IX,
1897), 191–192; CO5/759/166–191; CO5/765/176. For the Massachusetts Council's replies
to the Privy Council's charges against Massachusetts, see *Bowdoin-Temple Papers*, pp.
224–232.

63. His hope, he wrote Hutchinson, was to "make the managers of those unnatural
confederacies tremble." FB to TH, Dec. 4, 1769, Bernard Papers, VIII, 26. For an extremely detailed presentation of his ideas on the revision of the Council, see his letter to
Hillsborough, Feb. 4, 1769, *ibid.*, VII, 132–140.

64. William Knox recalled the committee meeting of 1770 in his recollections of the
background of the drafting of the Coercive Acts of 1774 (which finally enacted Bernard's
proposals in full): Historical Manuscripts Commission, *Report on Manuscripts in Various
Collections*, VI (Dublin, 1909), 257. The only charter revision that Knox would agree to,

Pownall's letter arrived first, and Hutchinson was in the midst of writing a discursive response to it when, on October 7, he received Hillsborough's letter requesting an immediate reply to specific queries about the composition of Councils and juries in other colonies and an opinion on the proposed revisions of the Massachusetts charter. The man-of-war *Romney* was about to leave Boston harbor for England, and since Hillsborough's letter had been long delayed in delivery, Hutchinson felt he could not afford to wait for another conveyance after the *Romney* sailed, and so he put together hastily what he called a "rough, incorrect letter" for Hillsborough and included with it the "loose, unconnected, and unfinished" thoughts he had jotted down for Pownall "just as they occurred to my thoughts and as the pressure of public business would permit." He sent off this reply on the *Romney* on October 9. It arrived in London on November 7.[65]

It is a perplexed and perplexing letter, reflecting Hutchinson's agonized response to the idea of disciplining the politics of his

---

he recalled, was the change in the Council. "The others were for all, and for my dissent in this case, I was ever after excluded by Lord Hillsborough from all consultations whilst he stayed in office." On June 12, 1770, Hillsborough had written Hutchinson that the aftermath of the Massacre had convinced him that the Massachusetts constitution would have to be changed, but to what extent and precisely how he did not say. CO5/759/156. Bernard's account of the committee's discussion is in FB to TH, Nov. 10, 1770, Bernard Papers, VIII, 138–142. The assembling of the dossier is discussed in connection with the affair of the Whately letters, below, Chap. VII.

65. The recipient's copy of the letter has not been located. Two drafts of it remain in Hutchinson's letterbook, however. MA, XXV, 441–447, is a pastiche of segments, some of them crossed out, others pasted in, in which Hutchinson discusses not only the proposed legislation but the terms of his appointment to the governorship, his desire to keep the chief justiceship open for his eventual return to it, and the splits that were opening up in the nonimportation movement. MA, XXVII, 13–14, is a succinct, though unfinished, revision of that earlier draft using the same ideas in more careful language and restricting the subject matter to Hillsborough's queries. The follow-up letter (Oct. 1770: *ibid.*, pp. 22–23), referred to below, in which Hutchinson continues his general discussion and refines his own proposals, was written ostensibly to enclose a list of former councillors who had been defeated for reelection because of their loyalty to the government, together with advice on which of them would be likely to serve in a newly constituted Council.

All of these letters were found by the Revolutionaries among Hutchinson's other papers in 1775 and published by them. The whole of the long first draft, faithfully transcribed under the title "Further accounts of Thom. Hutchinson's assiduity in rooting up our *once* happy constitution," was printed in the *Boston Gazette,* Aug. 7, 1775, and reprinted in the *Massachusetts Spy;* the follow-up letter appeared a week later in the *Boston Gazette,* was also reprinted in the *Spy,* and in addition was reprinted in *The Remembrancer . . . Part I, For the Year 1776* (London, 1776), pp. 158–159. For John Pownall's use of these letters in 1774 in an effort, according to his own account, to stop the passage of the Coercive Acts, see below, pp. 279, 284.

native colony through altering its constitutional forms. Though he was firmly convinced that intervention of some sort by England was necessary if order was to be restored in the colonies, he knew too that the existing constitution of Massachusetts had worked successfully for several generations, and he believed that structural changes introduced in the present heated atmosphere could do more harm than good. It was no new problem for him. Three years earlier he had written, "I dread, with you, any alterations of constitutions, and I think the appointment of the Council in the same manner with the Councils of the royal governments would cause, just at this time, a terrible convulsion. . . . It seems as if we could neither bear our malady nor the cure of it."[66] In the long, rambling, disjointed letter to Hillsborough of October 9, and in a more carefully worded sequel he wrote soon after, he furnished the factual data that Hillsborough had requested but talked all around the various proposals he had been asked to consider without explicitly endorsing them. His emphasis throughout was on caution. He warned that there would be "violent opposition" to the proposed change in the constitutional character of the Council. The new crown-appointed Council would be as obnoxious to the opposition in Massachusetts as the Board of Customs Commissioners, and it might well encourage the "more factious people," who had long felt that respect for the charter had impeded the "free assertion of their natural and constitutional rights," to ignore constitutional restraints altogether. Furthermore, it seemed doubtful to him that a new crown Council, facing open opposition, would be able to function effectively. The House would probably refuse to work with such a body, and the government might as a consequence be paralyzed for a period of years before the new arrangement was finally accepted. And he pointed out the need to confirm, in the contemplated charter revision, all existing appointments that had been legalized by the old Council, "as there will be less danger of interruption in all judicial proceedings which would increase the confusion and bring on a general anarchy."

In the end he offered his own quite different proposals. Rather

---

66. TH to ——, Feb. 14, 1767, MA, XXVI, 266. So too he had written Israel Williams, May 6, 1769, "I am not desirous of a change in the constitution. . . . If we could be prudent—I think I may say only silent—we might save the country and retain the rights we contend for." Williams Papers.

than amending the ancient constitution of Massachusetts, he suggested scrapping it altogether and then substituting a new charter to be worked out in collaboration with the colony itself. If revisions of the existing charter *had* to be made, he urged that action be postponed for another year until the colony could be officially warned and perhaps have a chance to defend itself. If ultimately the revisions were still to be undertaken he advised leaving intact the existing system of Assembly nomination of councillors but extending their terms of office from one to three years and transferring their executive powers to a new privy council made up of a group of the elected councillors selected by the governor. And he indicated that he was not only against changes in the structure of the court system and in the tenure of civil officers, but also against attempting to restrict the unconstitutionally broad range of activities that the town meetings had assumed.

Bernard was horrified by this ill-timed prudence. The letter Hutchinson had written on October 9, Bernard wrote him a month later, had struck Hillsborough "like a lawyer's opinion, in which doubts and difficulties are stated but no conclusion drawn." Bernard strove to overcome the impact of Hutchinson's response by directing Hillsborough's attention to those "former letters" of Hutchinson's that had been collected; they clearly documented, he said, the fact that Hutchinson had "expected, not without impatience, such an alteration." And he added to that collection some more recent letters from Hutchinson and Oliver that *plainly* showed, he argued, "that the supporters of government rested all their hopes of a restoration of government upon the intervention of Parliament, which must certainly emancipate the Council, whatever else they might do." He knew for a fact, he assured the minister, that Hutchinson would bitterly regret it if his spasm of caution kept the proposed legislation from advancing.[67]

But his assurances were futile. The impetus had been lost, and nothing Bernard could do would restore it. On November 15, he reported to Hutchinson that "the intention has cooled since the receipt of your letter." And then he added acidly and with great penetration—in a sentence that might have been taken as an

67. FB to TH, Nov. 10, 1770, Bernard Papers, VIII, 138–142.

epitaph to all of Hutchinson's hopes for support, understanding, relief, even rescue, from England—that there lay at the heart of the English government such a propensity to avoid troublesome business that any excuse to do so "is laid hold of." By April 1771, after a passing war scare killed the immediate prospects of enacting the Massachusetts government bill, all hopes of reviving it had died— the result, Bernard insisted, of Hutchinson's failure to speak out decisively for change at the one fleeting moment when circumstances had made action possible.[68]

That it was thought that Hutchinson himself had been responsible for keeping the English government from acting was maddening to him, and it heightened his despair of seeing the undeniable, the inscrutable, power of England at last stir itself, cast down the impertinent and uphold the loyal. It will be an outright disaster, he wrote, if Parliament continues to suffer the opposition's defiance silently; it was "shocking" what impudence England put up with; "sooner or later," he warned the Massachusetts House, your be-

68. FB to TH, Nov. 15, Dec. 22, 1770, and Feb. 11, 1771, Bernard Papers, VIII, 150–151, 153-154, 159-63. "I am mistaken," Bernard wrote in the last of these letters, "if the time will not come when you will be obliged to speak out, which if you had done some time ago much trouble might have been saved which will fall chiefly upon yourself." In late 1770 and early 1771 rumors had circulated wildly in pro-American circles in London and among the patriot leaders in the colonies that drastic constitutional changes were being planned, though Thomas Pownall had assured Bostonians that the ministry was not likely to follow through with such plans (to Samuel Cooper, March 22, 1769, in Frederick Griffin, ed., *Junius Discovered* [Boston, 1854], p. 221.) The more agitated and fearful among the opponents of the government never believed that the ministry would completely relent. Arthur Lee, in what is perhaps the most paranoid letter in the entire literature of the American Revolution, wrote Samuel Adams from London on June 10, 1771, that the mere fact that Hillsborough was known to be giving assurances that he would make no further efforts to alter the Massachusetts charter proved that he was doing precisely the opposite. Since he was treacherous by nature and was being acted upon by "the implacable hatred of Bernard," Hillsborough could not conceivably "abandon a favorite system of tyranny and revenge without any apparent reason . . . the fire still subsists, though covered with deceitful ashes." The fact too that Franklin, who Lee believed was a tool of Hillsborough's (actually they hated each other), was offering the same assurances merely compounded the danger. And in the midst of all of this treachery, Lee saw the figure of Thomas Hutchinson. Having risen to the same heights of evil that Bernard had achieved but "by sacrificing every sacred tie and every duty due his country and to the community of which he was born a member," Hutchinson, Lee wrote, was doubly guilty. People like Hutchinson, Lee said, "with plausibility to conceal their want of principle and ambitious views, and knowledge to conduct them successfully to their pernicious ends . . . become the most dangerous instruments of oppression. I will therefore venture to foretell that Mr. Hutchinson will prove one of the most abject tools of administration that ever disgraced the dignity of human nature or trampled on the rights of mankind." Richard H. Lee, *Life of Arthur Lee, LL.D.* (Boston, 1829), I, 215–219.

havior will "bring the wrath and indignation of Parliament in its full force upon [your] heads."[69]

But when that would be, he was no closer to knowing when 1771 ended than when it had begun. He wrote for orders—he pleaded for action—in July; he wrote, he pleaded again, in August; and again and again through the autumn, but by January 1772 all he had heard was that Parliament was due to meet that month and that there was a rumor that Hillsborough had been seen in London as late as December and so he still might hear something from him soon. He heard in fact in March when the December packet arrived, by which time he had dissolved the Assembly for fear of facing it uninstructed; but the secretary's letters did not help him much, nor did others in February's mail, which, to compound confusion, arrived before January's.[70] And then disasters fell in quick succession. Bernard, he heard, his goad and sponsor, his one sure pipeline to authority, had had a "paralytic fit"; Hutchinson, deeply distressed and morbidly reminded of the time he himself had been "unstrung, my nerves relaxed, and lost my sleep," could only send a recommendation for a program of exercise and diversion and pray that he would still have Bernard to assist him with the authorities in England.[71] Then came the news of the burning of the customs schooner *Gaspee* in Rhode Island—so flagrant an insult to the state, he wrote, that if it were ignored all friends of government will despair, for the participants in the burning were not the rabble of the port but respectable men of property whom the local courts would never touch: this must, this *will* "certainly arouse the British lion which has been asleep these four or five years," and he recommended, in rising indignation, that if, as he fervently hoped, Parliament took up American matters at its next session, it would nullify all acts of "the Lilliputian Assemblies of America" that defy its sovereign authority.[72] But still there was silence. He could not

69. TH to John Pownall, Jan. 24, 1771, MA, XXVII, 108; TH to FB, April 23, 1771, *ibid.*, p. 154; TH to ——, July 1771, *ibid.*, p. 201; in Jan. 1771, to underscore his belief that England must act, he quoted the rustic phrase of Col. Chandler, the former sheriff of Worcester County, that "if Parliament don't give us a flogging, we shall be as rampant as ever." TH to FB, Jan. 23, 1771, *ibid.*, p. 104.

70. TH to Hillsborough and to FB, March 12, 14, 1772, MA, XXVII, 301, 302; TH to ——, April 5, 1772, *ibid.*, p. 311.

71. TH to FB, March 30, 1770, MA, XXVII, 307.

72. TH to [John Pownall], Aug. 29, 1772, MA, XXVII, 381–382; TH to Samuel Hood, Sept. 2, 1772, *ibid.*, p. 385a.

fathom its meaning. He was bewildered and desperate; and in that mood of abjection and desperation he turned increasingly to the only other source of control by which the rebellion might be contained: the appeal of reason, the capacity of self-interested minds to reach balanced, prudently self-interested conclusions.

Chapter VI

The Failure of Reason

Rational appeal to principles of self-interest had always seemed to Hutchinson a vital mode of persuasion: he had always acted on the assumption that in the end self-interested reason would prevail. It had prevailed in his first great political struggle, a quarter of a century earlier, when he had fought to maintain a hard-money policy in Massachusetts; and it had prevailed, though barely and after a costly denial, in the Stamp Act crisis. In the years that followed he had drawn again and again on the same few central ideas—liberal, commonsense ideas, he believed—which had been the basis of British liberty for a century. How could any independent person doubt their validity? And after 1770 how could he as governor fail to speak out to defend them when they were called into question, or, despite all the political dangers involved, neglect to fling them back as challenges to those who defied them?

i

He was embroiled in argument with the opposition from almost the first day of his acting governorship. His lengthy exchanges with the Assembly in 1770 over the relocation of the meeting place of the General Court had been an effort to argue his opponents into compliance, but when in the months that followed he was attacked in the press in snarling, furious squibs more savage than any he had been subjected to before, he found it increasingly difficult to respond with reasoned discourse. Stimulated by pieces published in London by Arthur Lee ("Junius Americanus") furiously denouncing officials who accepted crown salaries as *"absolute creatures of the crown"* and *"tools of an unjust government"* bent on introducing "a judicial system which *the ministers of Charles,* however abandoned, were yet *ashamed to support,"* the Boston press exceeded all earlier bounds of viciousness. Perhaps Hutchinson had not originally planned to free himself from constitutional dependence on the Assembly for his salary, the *Boston Gazette* declared, but the fact was that he had done exactly that, and "a governor independent of the people for his *support,* as well as his *political being,* is in fact a MASTER and . . . soon will be a TYRANT."

It will be recorded by the faithful historian for the information of posterity that the first *American pensioner*—the first *independent governor* of this province—was not a stranger but one *"born and educated"* in it—not an ANDROS or a RANDOLPH, but that *cordial friend* to our civil constitution, that *main pillar* of the religion and the learning of this country, the man upon whom she has (I will not say wantonly) heaped all the *honors* she had to bestow—HUTCHINSON!!

Is it possible, the *Gazette* asked, "to form an idea of *slavery* more complete, more miserable, more *disgraceful* than that of a people where justice is administered, government exercised, and a standing army maintained at the expense of the people and yet without the least dependence upon them? . . . If this be not a state of despotism, what is?" Hutchinson was a Caesar, a *"smooth* and *subtle* tyrant," who, like that ancient despot, would lead his people *"gently* into slavery." He was a falsifier of history, who would lull the people into compliance by allegations of ancestral obedience to the absolute power of Parliament. And he was, by virtue of his crown salary that made him "independent of the people," said "Mucius Scaevola," quite simply "a monster in government . . . a USURPER," and "any act of Assembly consented to by him in his pretended capacity of governor is *ipso facto* null and void and consequently not binding upon us."[1]

1. Articles by "Junius Americanus" [Arthur Lee] (reprinted from London newspapers) and "Candidus" and "Valerius Poplicola" [both Samuel Adams] in *Boston Gazette,* Oct.

It was this piece by "Mucius Scaevola" (Joseph Greenleaf) that finally broke the back of Hutchinson's patience. It was published on November 14, 1771, in the *Massachusetts Spy*, a journal that had been founded a year earlier by Isaiah Thomas and had quickly become, in the writings of Thomas Young, Samuel Adams, and Greenleaf, the chief outlet for extremist views. Hutchinson had attempted, in articles that he, Andrew Oliver, and Jonathan Sewall had written or sponsored in the *Massachusetts Gazette,* to respond in some measure to the *Spy's* as well as the *Boston Gazette's* vituperation.[2] But "Mucius's" furious attack, touched off by Hutchinson's remark in a thanksgiving proclamation that thanks should be given for the continuance of the privileges Massachusetts enjoyed,[3] could not be treated so casually. If action could not be taken against so outrageous a libel—a straightforward repudiation of the government's, and his own, right to rule—then the government was scarcely worth the respect he sought to restore to it. It was not enough to strike Greenleaf's name from the list of justices of the peace. His vicious attack was actionable: "the attorney general thought it so plain a case that no grand jury could, upon their oaths, refuse to find a bill," Hutchinson later wrote. The government presented the case to the jury. But that body was

7, 14, and 28, 1771; and by "Mucius Scaevola" [Joseph Greenleaf] in *Massachusetts Spy,* Nov. 14, 1771. The charge of falsifying history referred to a passage in vol. I of Hutchinson's *History of Massachusetts-Bay* (pp. 272–273) in which he explained the error of the seventeenth-century New Englanders in thinking that the laws of Parliament did not reach beyond the boundaries of the British Isles. Adams and others scoured Hutchinson's *History* for passages like this and made them subjects of extended public discussion.

2. For a listing of these artcles, see Timothy M. Barnes, "Loyalist Newspapers of the American Revolution, 1763–1783: A Bibliography" (unpublished pamphlet, n.d., n.p.), pp. 4–5 (based on the same author's study, "The Loyalist Press in the American Revolution, 1756–1781" [Ph.D. diss., University of New Mexico, 1970]).

3. "This was deemed by the people an open insult upon them and a profane mockery of heaven. The general cry was, we have lost our most essential rights and shall be commanded to give thanks for what does not exist. Our congregations applied to the several ministers in town praying it might not be read as usual, and declaring if we offered to do it they would rise up and leave the church. And though no little pains were taken by the governor's friends . . . to explain away the sense of the clause by saying all were agreed we had some privileges left and that no more was meant by the public act than such privileges as we in fact enjoyed, all would not avail. . . . It was read only in Dr. Pemberton's church, of which the governor is a member. He did it with confusion, and numbers turned their backs upon him and left the church in great indignation. . . . It has been said that the governor's intention . . . was to convey an idea to your side of the water . . . that the people were become sensible that they were really free and happy. If this was his intention . . . I believe [he] wishes from his heart he had never made the experiment." Samuel Cooper to Thomas Pownall, Aug. 23, 7771, "Cooper-Pownall Letters," pp. 325–326.

packed, Hutchinson recorded, with the "most active persons in encouraging the opposition to government," and they declared, after the foreman had portentously inquired if the cited writing had to be false in order to qualify as a libel and after the *Boston Gazette* had predicted a repeat of the Zenger case, that there was insufficient evidence to warrant a trial.[4]

Something, nevertheless, would have to be done, especially since "Mucius's" piece stimulated a seemingly endless flow of supplementary articles—elaborations, encomiums, documentation—that exceeded in violence even what Greenleaf had originally written. Hutchinson, whom "Hyperion" (Dr. Thomas Young) referred to as "The Man Whom Conscience Forbids to Style My Governor," was now portrayed not only as a Julius Caesar but as a power-mad Oliver Cromwell, and his salary was analogized to that of a puppet of the Pope and repeatedly cited as marking the end of the constituted liberties of the people.[5] All of this was infuriating to Hutchinson, not so much because it caricatured the executive head of the government in the most vicious way but because it falsified the facts in order to intensify a political polemic. Replies would have to be given—sustained and deliberate replies—that would once again tell the truth of the constitution and make it impossible to peddle falsehoods as if they were basic principles of freedom. On November 23, 1771, therefore, Hutchinson and Andrew Oliver founded a new journal, *The Censor,* for the specific purpose of refuting these slanders and of explaining the truth of the constitution, especially as it related to the issue of crown salaries.[6]

Through most of its existence *The Censor* made no pretense of being a regular newspaper, with casual news, announcements, and advertisements. Though it was a typical newssheet of the time in

4. Catherine Barton Mayo, ed., "Additions to Thomas Hutchinson's *History of Massachusetts-Bay,*" AAS *Procs.,* n.s., 59 (1949), 46–47. *Boston Gazette,* Nov. 25, 1771.

5. *Boston Gazette,* Nov. 25 and 18, 1771.

6. At the end of 1771 and in early 1772 Hutchinson regularly sent Lord Hillsborough copies of the *Censor* and the *Massachusetts Gazette* (filed in CO5/761/53ff.). He had high hopes for the political effectiveness of these publications, to which he and Andrew Oliver devoted much effort. "The strange notion of independence," he wrote, "was so generally favored that I thought it necessary people should have a just view of the constitution, and gave the facts and the groundwork of the piece signed A.Z. in the paper of the 5 March; but the chief part is of the lieutenant governor's composure, and I think it has silenced the writers of the other side, and I am informed has opened the eyes of great part of the country where it has been spread." TH to ——, March 23, 1772, MA, XXVII, 306.

that it was full of snarling vituperation, furiously snapping at every insinuation and allegation of the opposition, fierce, petty, and wearying to read, it was more than that. Each of the twenty-five issues, which appeared weekly until May 2, 1772, contained an essay on the British constitution and an attack on the intellectual foundations of the arguments that had been published by "Mucius," "Leonidas," "Candidus," and the other *"state-desperadoes."* The opening number reprinted "Mucius's" piece verbatim and branded it the work of "the *brawler* FACTION" which, unchecked, becomes in time "that *destroying fiend,* rank, rank REBELLION." Other issues too challenged specific attackers of Hutchinson and the government, but all contributed in some way to the general explanation of the constitutional position that Hutchinson was attempting to make clear. The centerpiece was the seventh issue (January 4, 1772), which stated in unequivocal terms the principles of Britain's "mixed monarchy," a constitution so nearly perfect that Tacitus, *The Censor* said, thought it capable of existing only "in idea." What was its essence? It was easily misunderstood: of course it consisted of three branches, *"King, Lords, and Commons,"* which together created a dynamic balance of counterpoised forces. But how was this balance created? *Not* by one branch interposing into the affairs of either of the others so as to restrict their freedom to act in their assigned spheres: any branch that so interfered with another, *The Censor* wrote in a key passage, would *ipso facto* "cease to be a part of the supreme power." The very heart of the free British constitution lay in the freedom of each branch to act independently in the area reserved for it, the liberty-preserving balance being created by the need for all three branches to concur, after deliberating independently, in order to create lawful enactments. Whenever this independence had been interfered with—as it had been in opposite ways under Cromwell and James II— autocracy of one sort or another had resulted. And this was precisely the threat now in Massachusetts, *The Censor* insisted. The independence of the second, aristocratical, branch, the Council, had already been destroyed; it had simply been torn to pieces between the Assembly's power to nominate members and the governor's power to veto them, as the history of the purge of 1766 had proved. Only the third, popular, branch "can be said to be free upon the plan of the British constitution," and if it were to have no check from another power free of its influence—the executive power, representing government itself—there could be no doubt of the outcome. Massachusetts would sink into a "dominatio plebis—the *rule of the multitude*," a system, *The Censor* pointed out, that had led, in the case of Rome, to such anarchy that "the greatest happiness which the Romans could look for was the despotic power of the CAESARS." How could one doubt that this was the tendency of the present situation and that if it were not checked Massachusetts too would simply collapse into anarchy? History, political theory, the wisdom of the culture—all proved that chaos would result if things continued in their present course. It was simply undeniable that what stood between Massachusetts and the anarchy of mob rule was the executive element of the first branch, which was sustained, and could only be sustained, from abroad. If the third branch, the democracy, deprived the governor of his independence of action by controlling his salary and then prevented him from accepting a crown salary, the freedom-preserving balance of the constitution would simply be destroyed.

It was all tied together: the bond with England was the guarantor of the independence of the first branch of the constitution in America; without the independence of the first branch the constitution would be overwhelmed by the democracy, and freedom would vanish into first a plebiscitarian, and then a military, dictatorship. Behind the whole system lay the necessity for England's sovereignty to remain unimpaired—total and integral; if that ultimate power failed or was reduced or somehow crippled, all else failed with it.

ii

So Hutchinson and his co-authors of *The Censor* sought to convince an apparently deluded public of the inescapable facts of life and of the reasonable—the liberal—conclusions to be drawn from them. But these publications had no more effect than his private admonitions. The attacks in *The Spy* and the *Boston Gazette* continued uninterrupted, and they were supplemented in March 1772 by the appearance in installments of the first of Mercy Otis Warren's closet melodramas, *The Adulateur. a Tragedy,* which casts Hutchinson as Rapatio, the bloodthirsty dictator of Servia, who gloats to find,

> My gayest wishes crown'd. Brundo [Bernard] retir'd,
> The stage is clear. Whatever gilded prospects
> E'er swam before me—Honor, places, pensions—
> All at command—Oh! my full heart! 'twill burst!
> Now patriots think, think on the past and tremble.
> . . . all the posts of honor
> Are filled with beings wholly at my service.
> The b[enc]h what are they? *Creatures* of my own;
> Who if I spoke, would mangle law and reason,
> And nobly trample on the highest ties.
> And hence the soldier, whose *security*
> Is the *prime basis* of my government,
> May scoff, insult, nay, in the face of day,
> Abuse the citizens, yet go unpunish'd
>
>   . . .
>
> I'll make the scoundrels know who sways the sceptre;
> Before I'll suffer [ridicule], I'll throw the state
> In dire confusion, nay I'll hurl it down,
> And bury all things in one common ruin.
>   O'er fields of death, with hasting step I'll speed,
>   And smile at length to see my country bleed;
>   From my tame heart the pang of virtue fling,
>   And 'mid the general flame, like Nero sing.[7]

Such was the response to his appeals to reason, his efforts to explain the constitutional necessity for stabilizing the power of government. The opposition seemed impervious to argument, to logic, to the demands of self-interest. Nothing he could say or write seemed to help ease the grinding controversy. It grew worse, the more he tried, rather than better. An eruption was inevitable. It took place not in a single outburst but in an extended confrontation that began in July 1772, when the long-circulating rumors were finally confirmed that Hutchinson had been granted a special crown salary as governor, and it ended eight months later in a crushing rebuke by the highest authorities in England.

7. Mercy Otis Warren, *The Adulateur, a Tragedy, As It is Now Acted in Upper Servia* (Boston, 1773), reprinted in *Magazine of History,* 16, extra no. 63 (1918); for its original appearance in the *Massachusetts Spy,* see Maud M. Hutcheson, "Mercy Warren, 1728–1814," *W.M.Q.,* 3d ser. 10 (1953), 383–384.

When definite news of Hutchinson's gubernatorial salary arrived, a hastily formed House committee met instantly to denounce the grant, and charged, with the concurrence of the whole House, that since the Assembly had always paid the governor's salary the move was "a dangerous innovation which renders him a governor not dependent on the people, as the charter has prescribed. . . . It destroys that mutual check and dependence which each branch of the legislature ought to have upon the others, and the balance of power which is essential to all free governments." Such an unconstitutional change, they charged, could only have been inspired by falsified information and sheer malevolence; if Hutchinson wished to prove his innocence and good faith he must forthwith petition the crown to reverse its decision and allow his salary to be paid by the Assembly "according to ancient and invariable usage."[8]

Hutchinson's first response was, yet again, to appeal to England for support against such defiance, and to warn the ministry for the hundredth time that to do nothing would be to invite the faction to ignore every decision of the crown or Parliament that happened to displease it. He begged Lord Hillsborough to send him instructions before His Lordship left on a rumored trip to Ireland.[9] But this time his patron's silence was permanent. Hillsborough resigned his office in August, leaving Hutchinson to start all over again with his successor, Lord Dartmouth.[10] But the urgency now was too great and Hutchinson's mood too desperate for merely hoping, praying,

8. Report of Committee of the Assembly, July 1772, in *History of Massachusetts-Bay*, III, 405; Hutchinson's account of the vote on the report is in *ibid.*, p. 257. Word of the crown salaries had been received at the end of 1770, but official confirmation had been delayed. *Boston Evening-Post*, Dec. 31, 1770.

9. TH to ——, July 21, 1772, MA, XXVII, 365–366; TH to FB, Aug. 23, 1772, *ibid.*, pp. 373–374.

10. Hutchinson learned of the likelihood of Hillsborough's resignation from a letter of Bernard's written Aug. 5, which apparently did not arrive until mid-September. TH to Gage, Sept. 24, 1772, MA, XXVII, 389. By early November he knew of Dartmouth's appointment and was writing that "a state of government and order" would be restored when the sons of liberty and "such of the sons of Levi as abet them" find that Dartmouth would pursue the same policies that Hillsborough had followed "and that no countenance can be shown to their principles of anarchy." TH to John Wenthworth, Nov. 7, 1772, *ibid.*, p. 404. By Dec. Arthur Lee was already at work preparing Dartmouth for "representations" he would be receiving from Samuel Adams, and was "giving him a proper idea of Mr. Hutchinson." He counted on Adams being able to undermine the secretary's confidence in Hutchinson. "The removal of Mr. H. would I think be a very great mortification and check to those among you who are selling their country for plunder and preferment. I do not despair of this being effected." Lee to Samuel Adams, Dec. 24, 1772, Richard H. Lee, *Life of Arthur Lee, LL.D.* (Boston, 1829), I, 225.

and writing abject entreaties to the implacable and inscrutable sovereign. If no reply was quickly given to the House's Resolves, their claims, whose errors he had labored to explain in *The Censor*, would be taken for the truth, and that, he believed, was exactly what the extremists were hoping for. Perhaps, he argued in his endless effort to impute rationality to the impenetrable silence of the deities that ruled his political existence, perhaps to the politically sophisticated in England silence was a proper expression of the contempt that was felt for such petty defiance, but it was not interpreted that way in Massachusetts. The false arguments must once again be exposed and the truth explained, and if the English government would not do it, he would, this time not in an anonymous newspaper polemic but directly and in his official capacity. And so, overcoming what he described as a personal aversion to making "argumentative speeches," he pitched himself into formal conflict with the opposition and wrote out an official reply to the House's charges against him that probed, in some twenty-five hundred words, the fundamental issues involved in the attack on the governor's salary.[11]

The main point was simple and clear enough; he had been arguing essentially the same case for years; but it was now important to stress certain implications. The basic fact, which he had developed so fully in the unpublished Dialogue of 1768, was that the Massachusetts charter was not a treaty between two independent states but a crown gift of limited powers granted to a group of petitioners, and that document in no way restrained the crown from supporting its own agencies financially if it felt impelled to do so. The Assembly had grotesquely—and how else but deliberately?—misrepresented the principle of checks and balances, which Hutchinson once again, and in detail, explained in this state paper. The basic check, he once more explained, "consists in the necessity of the concurrence of all the branches, in order to [create] a valid act," and it was in no way a limitation on the full power of any *one* branch to

11. TH to ——, July 21, 1772, MA, XXVII, 365–368. Hutchinson's motivation for involving himself in an open controversy with the House was candidly revealed in a passage of this letter (probably written to John Pownall) which he deleted from a preliminary draft: "If this foolish proceeding [the Resolves] should be despised in England, yet it seems necessary for some way to be found by which the people here may know the contempt with which it is received and that *this* is the reason why no further notice is taken of it." *Ibid.*, p. 359 (emphasis added). The text of his reply is in *History of Massachusetts-Bay*, III, 406–410.

Hutchinson's house in Boston, built by his grandfather, John Foster, between 1689 and 1692 and almost completely destroyed in the Stamp Act riot of August 26, 1765.

Two nineteenth-century views of Hutchinson's house in Milton—his "Monticello i Massachusetts"—which he built in 1743, lived in weekends and almost every summer unt: he left America thirty years later, and longed to return to from his exile in England.

Lord Gage's estate, Firle, Sussex, which Hutchinson and his children visited in 1774 and 1775. One of several "noble seats" that Hutchinson came to know well, he found there an example of the "high life: but I would not have parted with my humble cottage at Milton for the sake of it."

The wicked Statesman, or the Traitor to his Country, at the Hour of DEATH.

BOSTON: Printed by ISAIAH THOMAS. Sold at his Printing
Office near the Market, and at his shop near the Mill Bridge
[Price 7 coppers single, and 20 s in tenor the dozen]

"... how wretched, how intolerable are the last moments of one who has made it
his business to sacrifice mankind to accumulate a little pelf! Look at the engraving
... and endeavor to form some faint idea of the horrors that man must endure who
owes his greatness to his country's ruin, when he is about taking leave of this world
to receive a just and proper punishment for his crimes. Let the destroyers of mankind behold and tremble!" Comment on the print, *Almanack*, p. 2.

"America in Distress," an engraving by Paul Revere, 1775, adapted from an English cartoon of 1770, "Britannia in Distress." Hutchinson appears at the upper left.

Boston 20 July 1773

Dear Sir

I mislaid the list of Officers you
gave me at Springfield which is the only reason
the Commissions were not sent & I must desire you
to send another list.   Bowdoin at the Council
and Adams in the House have certainly shown
themselves very adroit, but it will be a reproach
upon the body of the People to the latest posterity
that they have suffered themselves to be made such
dupes, especially after a publick declaration
in the House that all that was intended was to
raise a general clamour against the G & L G and
then they should be sure of their removal.
    The deception can't last longer than it did
in the time of the witchcraft. Truth, at worst,
will finally prevail. As for the Resolves they
are every one false, most of them are villanous.
I would have declared them to be so in the most
open manner, if it had been in character, &
would in the same manner have vindicated
every part of the Letters. In so plain a case,
if but a few persons only remain undeceived,
                                                        a few

Colonel Williams

Letter from Hutchinson to Israel Williams, July 20, 1773, commenting on the publication of Hutchinson's letters to Thomas Whately and on the Assembly's Resolves
that followed.

a free upon testimony against the delusion will soon undeceive the rest.

I pitied the poor Members more than one half of them being forced to vote in verba Magistri either directly against their judgment or without understanding what they voted.

I have no great doubt that sooner or later this proceeding will reflect more infamy upon all concerned in it than any publick transaction since the Country was settled, for it was founded upon such baseness as no civilized people have ever countenanced, and has been conducted through every part of its progress with falshood and deception, which although for a short time they have their intended effect yet as soon as they are discovered prove ignominious to the Authors of them.

I am

Your Assured friend

Your most humble Servant

Tho Hutchinson

20. I advanced to Guineas to the Coachmaker. Judge Oliver afterward, Paston called and dined. Peggy scarce able to lye upon the Sopha after 10 drops of Laudanum sat in an easy chair ~~about~~ at the head of the table but it was rather grievous than pleasing to me as it brought to my mind her sitting there when in health. She was glad to return to her couch.

It is said they are satisfied at Court by comparing the several accounts that Burgoyne was at Albany, and that the Howes and all their force were gone to New England

21. I was dressed going to a little Chapel near us when I saw my daughter so ill that I did not care to leave her sister alone with her. She continued in much the same state until dinner time, wishing among other things to try the Sea. I told her I would go round the world to help her — her sister asked if she thought she could bear it she said yes. When we sat down to dinner she would be carried from the Sopha & sit up with pillows in her former place at the head of the table. About 6 .. o'clock she started up on the couch & said I am dying I thought it a fright, but her sister called

Peggy's death.

Hutchinson's Diary, September 20–23, 1777, recording the death of his daughter Peggy. Pagination and headings inserted by Peter Orlando Hutchinson, editor of Thomas Hutchinson's *Diary and Letters*.

called for the maid & she was carried to her bed in the next room. After some time Doctor Obrien my daughters husband said to me she could not live long. I had not fortitude to go in until she called for me and then I could not stay. She asked me if I thought she was dying. I could not tell but expressed my self so as that she supposed I believed she was, however to her sister & desired her to burn all her papers & I promised it should be done She said must I die — I am not fit to die — I encouraged her to put her trust in the mercy of God thro' Jesus Christ her Saviour — she repeatedly said Lord Jesus save me — When I went again into the other room, her sister asked her if I should pray with her which when she desired I told her it was not in my power to collect in my mind proper expressions for a prayer — Instead several ejaculations pertinent to her case in which she joined with the greatest devotion — Mrs Saunders where we lodge said to me she wished to see some clergyman. I knew of none near her or I had never seen. She Saunders proposed a Brewer a man of fortune a methodist who of late

preaches

preaches to his own family." Whereat I
I gave no answer, but desired that
my daughter to attend to the prayer
in the Church Service to a person when
there is but small hope of recovery
which I read kneeling at her bed side
the people in the room joining and
she most devoutly in every petition

This was as much as I could
support my self under. Her breath
grew shorter the last words she said
were to Dr Oliver — I am dying, and
continued speechless but little if at all
sensible until about half after ten
when she expired. My distress I cannot
describe — A tender parent losing a
most affectionate child with every
desirable accomplishment of body
and mind is the only person who can
conceive of it.

~~But with all the ... ...~~
~~... ... ...~~
~~... ... ...~~
~~... ... ...~~
~~... ... ...~~
~~... ... ...~~
~~... ... ...~~
~~... ... ...~~
No distress since the death of her
dear mother has equalled this.
But thy will O God it is my duty
to submit to without murmuring.

22? Scarce a night for more than 12 months have I slept without hearing more or less of a cough which filled me with anxiety. Deep silence all night is now still more distressing. My dear dear daughter lies dead in the next room to me. I desired my two eldest sons to go to Croydon and provide a grave for her near Miss Katy Hutchinson lately buried there

General Haldimand set out yesterday from town for Quebec — I sent a card to him to wish a happy arrival and recommended Jnº & Edwd Clarke as two Consignees of E. India Tea & Shelburne & J Woolds to Mauduit at Wherwell

Sep. 1777.

23? A solitary morning my daughter leaving me to go to London to her children but returning to dinner. Mr Tucker only looked in a few minutes. I kept the air in the garden &c. by advice for the distress of mind weighs upon the body —

Sir Francis Bernard, by John Singleton Copley.

The Earl of Hillsborough, by John Downman.

The Earl of Dartmouth, by Thomas Gainsborough.

Thomas Pownall, by Daniel Gardner.

General Thomas Gage, by John Singleton Copley.

Commodore James Gambier, by John Singleton Copley.

Andrew Oliver, by John Singleton Copley.

Peter Oliver, artist unknown.

Charles Paxton, by Edward Truman.

James Bowdoin, by Robert Feke.

Samuel Adams, by John Singleton Copley.

James Otis, by Joseph Blackburn.

John Temple, by John Singleton Copley.

Mercy Otis Warren, by John Singleton Copley.

act independently *in its own area:* it is *that*—namely, the lack of compulsion on any one branch to act against its own judgment within its own sphere—that is "the glory of the English constitution." If he as governor were to interfere with the freedom of the Council or House to deliberate and conclude, he would himself be severely culpable. "Is it not reasonable," he asked, "that the governor should be entitled to the like share of freedom and independence in the exercise of his judgment with the other branches?" True despotism is an executive's freedom to impose his personal will and whim on the community without the restraint of law; but that could not happen in Massachusetts whether the governor received his salary from the crown or from the Assembly, since in either case the concurrence of the other branches was necessary to create a valid and effective public enactment. The only question was whether the executive would or would not be free to exercise his rightful power within the balance of powers in the constitution: if he was under the financial coercion of the Assembly, he would not be free; if he was financially independent of the Assembly, he would be free. What could be plainer or more undeniable? To deny so palpable, so obvious, a principle of English constitutionalism could only be "an artifice," an artifice, he wrote, that unfortunately was not unfamiliar in the colony: it had "often been made use of by writers in newspapers, with design to give false notions of government and to stir up discontent and disorder." He could only hope it would not now be endorsed by the general membership of the House of Representatives.

It was a forceful reply to the House's attack on his crown salary; Hutchinson was confident that it would blunt the effect of the Resolves. But whether in fact it would have done that would never be clearly known. Shortly after Hutchinson had issued this reply to the Resolves, word was received in Boston that the Massachusetts judges too would receive crown salaries. Indignation, fear, and rage roared like a sheet of flame across the troubled community, leaving Hutchinson's careful reply to the Resolves far behind. The Boston Town Meeting took the initiative in this escalating crisis by demanding that Hutchinson tell them officially whether the information they had of this effort "to complete the system of their slavery" was accurate, and upon his refusal to discuss such matters of state with them, they seized the occasion to issue, on November 20, 1772, not a protest on the immediate question of crown salaries, but a comprehensive statement of the rights of the colonists "as men, as Christians, and as subjects," publishing it in a pamphlet entitled *Votes and Proceedings of the Freeholders . . . of . . . Boston.* And more than that—they circulated the pamphlet to all the towns and districts of the colony with a request for supporting statements.[12]

To Hutchinson, already actively involved in an attempt to refute erroneous and seditious claims of the House, Boston's *Votes and Proceedings,* written largely by Samuel Adams, was a wildly inflammatory document. Not only, Hutchinson believed, did it deny in principle the authority of Parliament, and not only did it cry to the housetops that "the plan of *despotism* . . . is rapidly hastening to a completion . . . under a constant, unremitted, uniform aim to enslave us," but it laid the basis for nothing less than a continent-wide declaration of independence from Britain. For he saw at once that it was part of a political scheme whose first aim was "to bring the several towns and districts [of Massachusetts] into an avowal of independency, and then to bring this avowal . . . into the Assembly"; once the Massachusetts Assembly endorsed Boston's position, "the other Assemblies throughout the continent were to be desired by a circular letter to join with the House of Massachusetts Bay." A local controversy was thus being used to instigate a general revolt, and, quite on the schedule Hutchinson anticipated, "the plot," in Andrew Oliver's words, quickly "began to thicken." Town after town wrote to endorse the inflammatory *Proceedings,* committing themselves to a position from which it would be extremely difficult for them to withdraw. When over one third of the 260 towns had done so, Hutchinson panicked. The momentum was becoming irresistible; not a single town would be able to stand firm against the pressure; the Assembly would be swept up in the storm, and the

12. Hutchinson's exchange of messages with the Boston Town Meeting is printed in the *Boston Gazette,* Nov. 2, 1772; he immediately reported to Dartmouth on this development: CO5/761/247. The background and passage of Boston's *Votes and Proceedings* and its subsequent history in Massachusetts politics are traced in Richard D. Brown, *Revolutionary Politics in Massachusetts: The Boston Committee of Correspondence and the Towns, 1772–1774* (Cambridge, Harvard University Press, 1970), pp. 48ff., 68ff. James Warren, prominent in the radical leadership, rejoiced at this new initiative of the Boston Town Meeting; it will not only strengthen the force of the entire opposition, he wrote Samuel Adams, but it will display Hutchinson "in his proper colors." Warren to Adams, Nov. 8, 1772, *Warren-Adams Letters,* II (MHS *Colls.,* LXXIII, 1925), 399.

same thing would be repeated all over America. The "dangerous plot" must somehow be stopped; but never, Hutchinson wrote, had he had "more difficulty to determine what was my most prudent step."[13]

The central point was not in doubt. Boston's *Votes and Proceedings* was blatantly seditious as well as fallacious in argument, and of this fact the great sensible majority must be informed. Once again he reviewed with himself the dangers of moving into argumentative conflicts with the Assembly, and once again he recalled the clear warnings he had received in 1770 against precipitating, in this way, seditious opinions. But he recalled too the endless, maddening frustrations he had endured in "begging for measures to maintain the supremacy of Parliament"; he considered the magnitude of the pending catastrophe; and he pondered the danger of letting false doctrines go unchallenged. His duty, he decided, was clear, no matter how inscrutable the powers in England might be; and therefore, amid a flurry of letters to his superiors begging their understanding and indulgence, he threw all caution to the wind, summoned the Assembly together for an emergency session, and when it met on January 6, 1773, presented it with a direct challenge in the form of a speech on the fundamental principles of Anglo-American constitutionalism.[14]

He was immediately enveloped in controversy. The Council responded in writing on January 25, and the House, in a document of twenty-five printed pages, followed a day later. To both of these on February 16, Hutchinson replied in another twenty-five-page essay, only to receive by March 2 two additional responses, to which he again responded, on March 6, in another speech, after which he abruptly adjourned the session. The entire debate was published in a pamphlet of 126 pages, which revealed for all to see, Hutchinson was convinced, the irrationality of the extremists' claims, the compelling logic of maintaining the independence of the constitutional orders, and the full extent of the revolutionary spirit that drove on

13. Brown, *Revolutionary Politics*, pp. 85ff.; *Votes and Proceedings* . . . (Boston, [1772]), p. 30; Hutchinson, "Account and Defense of Conduct," (unpublished MS [1775], Chapin Library, Williams College), p. 6; TH to James Gambier, Israel Mauduit, Thomas Gage, and ——, Feb. 19, 20, March 7, and Jan. 7, 1773, MA, XXVII, 448, 450–451, 461–462, 438; Andrew Oliver to Edward Montague, Jan. 20, 1773, Eg. MSS, 2670, p. 71.

14. TH to John Pownall, Jan., 1773, MA, XXVII, 439.

the radical leaders and hence "the reasonableness and necessity of coercion" if Britain's empire was to remain intact.[15]

There had been many exchanges before between governors and Assemblies, in Massachusetts as well as in other colonies, but never so dramatic a confrontation, never one so deliberately aimed at probing the most sensitive issues of Anglo-American relations, and never one so carefully staged for maximum publicity. The utmost effort was put into the drafting and presentation of the papers. Hutchinson, according to John Adams, worked feverishly and "reduced himself to a most ridiculous state of distress. He is closetted and soliciting Mr. Bowdoin, Mr. Dennie, Dr. Church, etc., etc., and seems in the utmost agony." The House, no less feverishly engaged, sent an express messenger five hundred miles, to Maryland, to enlist the services of Daniel Dulany as draftsman, and when he declined, turned first to John Dickinson in Philadelphia before settling on Samuel Adams and Joseph Hawley assisted by John Adams, who furnished "the law authorities and the legal and constitutional reasonings." Newspapers all over America carried word of this debate upon what John Adams called "the greatest question ever yet agitated," and people from Maine to the Carolinas studied and judged the arguments. Hutchinson himself was convinced at the time that he had done the right thing in launching the debate, but John Adams knew better: "He will not be thanked for this," Adams wrote in his diary when the debate ended, "his ruin and destruction must spring out of it, either from the ministry and Parliament on one hand, or from his countrymen on the other."[16]

15. The documents appeared in part first in the Boston newspapers, then together in *Speeches of His Excellency Governor Hutchinson, to the General Assembly of the Massachusetts-Bay . . . with the Answers . . .* (Boston, 1773), and finally in [Alden Bradford, ed.,] *Speeches of the Governors of Massachusetts from 1765 to 1775 . . .* (Boston, 1818), pp. 336–396. Hutchinson sent Dartmouth copies of all of the exchanges as they appeared in print: CO5/762/54–107.

16. Adams, *Diary and Autobiography*, II, 77; *History of Massachusetts-Bay*, III, 268–269n (information about the approach to Dulany, which Hutchinson heard twice from Jonathan Boucher in London in 1776: *Diary and Letters*, II, 93, 163–164); Gipson, *British Empire*, XII, 53n. For John Adams's romantic recollection of his role in reducing the House committee's initial draft of its reply, "full of those elementary principles of liberty, equality, and fraternity . . . which are founded in nature and eternal, unchangeable truth but which must be well understood and cautiously applied" to hard-headed, legal and constitutional arguments, and for his memory of trapping Hutchinson in the technicalities of the legal doctrine of sovereignty, see Adams to William Tudor, March 8, 1817, in Charles F. Adams, ed., *Works of John Adams* (Boston, 1850–1856), II, 311–313.

In fact, he was struck down by both. To his countrymen Hutchinson was doubly the loser in the debate, first, because he came before them in the unnatural role of a native justifying the imposition of an external power; and second, because the case he presented seemed both rigid and weak. There was nothing new in what he said. He had been arguing in the same terms since the Stamp Act crisis: that in the nature of things it was impossible for Englishmen overseas to enjoy all the liberties of Englishmen at home; that the sovereignty of the King-in-Parliament was—had to be—unitary and total: to divide, limit, or contract it in any way was to destroy it; that the Massachusetts charter, while it created "subordinate powers with legislative and executive authority," in no way limited England's sovereignty; that natural rights never can be, and never have been, absolute in the real world; and that the alternative to Parliament's supremacy was subjection to some foreign power to whom English liberties were completely alien. "I hope it will never be our misfortune," he wrote, "to know by experience the difference between the liberties of an English colonist and those of the Spanish, French, or Dutch." Familiar doctrines—but now they were stark and rigid, stripped of all the imaginative and constructive applications that had surrounded them in his earlier correspondence and private discussions, and altogether unresponsive to the opposition's more humane aspirations. And not only hard, narrow, and coldly insistent: they were vulnerable, too, for Hutchinson was confident that the received wisdom was essentially unanswerable and only opposed by a stubborn faction blinded by fanaticism to the obvious truth and devilishly successful in propagating its views. He was convinced that by evoking what could only be intellectually absurd replies he could isolate this core opposition and force it by public embarrassment into compliance. "If I am wrong in my principles of government," he boldly concluded, "or in the inferences which I have drawn from them, I wish to be convinced of my error. Independence I may not allow myself to think that you can possibly have in contemplation."[17]

It was a dare, a challenge, to the opposition to face up to what they were doing; to admit that their arguments and actions led directly to high treason. If his challenge was accepted, the opposition, by their own confession, would be declaring themselves in open

17. *Speeches of His Excellency,* quotations at pp. 5, 11, 13.

rebellion and the crown would be justified before the world in taking the final step of coercion; if, as Hutchinson expected, they did not accept the challenge, they would expose the essential incoherence of their claims and strategically weaken, if not destroy, their political position. Above all, the Boston Town Meeting's plan of rallying the colonies to its seditious protest would be headed off.

The responses, when they came, were shocking. It must have been difficult for Hutchinson to decide which of the two replies was the more irrational and the more self-destructive. Both the Council and the House remained defiant, but in different ways. The councillors in their reply ("lost," Oliver said, "in a mist of words") disclaimed a blanket approval of Boston's *Votes and Proceedings,* but they explained that when people feel violated, "despairing of redress in a constitutional way," they understandably express themselves in extremes. For their part they refused to accept any human agency as a supreme and unlimited authority; Parliament's power "must be limited." But they admitted that fixing those limits was an extremely difficult task, and they were not equipped to undertake it. So they were obliged to settle for illogicality: they refused to "adopt your 'principles of government' or acquiesce in all the inferences you have drawn from them," but they did not attempt to produce more satisfactory doctrines themselves. And that was that.[18]

The House was shrewder, bolder, and more logical. Though they argued over every point in Hutchinson's paper, in the end they conceded his ultimate claim. If he insisted that it was logically impossible to find a workable line between Parliamentary supremacy and the total independence of the colonies, they would be obliged to agree, but they would draw a different conclusion. If it had to be all or nothing, they would choose nothing. "Notwithstanding all the terrors which Your Excellency has pictured to us as the effects of a total independence," they wrote, "there is more reason to dread the consequences of absolute uncontrolled supreme power, whether of a nation or a monarch, than those of a total independence." No doubt it would be a terrible misfortune to have to live under Spanish or French or Dutch rule, but in what essential way would British rule be preferable if it too were, as they believed it

18. Andrew Oliver to Peter Oliver, Feb. 26, 1773, Eg. MSS, 2670, p. 73; *Speeches of His Excellency,* pp. 18, 19–20.

now was, absolute and arbitrary? And they twisted the knife by documenting their reply with quotations from Hutchinson's own historical writings.[19]

By the end of March American reactions to the debate began to take definite form. Hutchinson was shocked to find that the opposition leaders, far from being embarrassed or routed or refuted, were jubilant; they seemed to think they had won a great victory. Ordinary partisans, like Harbottle Dorr, exulted in the proof they found in Hutchinson's speeches of what they had known all along, that Hutchinson had been supporting "endeavors to enslave us," and proof too of his unbounded "ambition and avarice." Samuel Cooper wrote Franklin that Hutchinson's challenge had united the Assembly in opposition to him: "Opposed, as he now stands, to both Houses and the body of the people, an undisguised and zealous advocate for everything we account a grievance, how far his situation resembles that of his predecessor I leave you to judge." All over America, Cooper said, people were reading the Assembly's replies with approval and were finding reinforcement for their opposition to England. For all his "connections and abilities," the governor had failed to change anyone's mind, "and the more openly and strenuously he exerts himself, his influence and ability to promote such a purpose becomes the less." Reflective men like Charles Carroll of Maryland pointed out that though "the controversy has been well handled on both sides," the House had been able only to hint at the ultimate conclusions of its arguments and at the action that followed logically from them. And some of the most loyal supporters of the government were dismayed. William Smith of New York had never been a friend of Hutchinson's, but he was objective in concluding that Hutchinson had forced the majority of the moderates, who had wished to avoid taking a final position, to support the most committed leaders of the opposition; and he correctly pointed out that the effect of the debate in England had been catastrophic.[20]

19. *Ibid.,* pp. 57, 48–55.
20. Cooper to Franklin, March 15, 1773, *Works of Benjamin Franklin* . . . , ed. Jared Sparks (Boston, 1836–1840), VIII, 38; Cooper to Thomas Pownall, March 25, 1773, "Cooper-Pownall Letters," p. 327 ("Whether the governor will be thanked by administration for his speech . . . you can best tell. It is certain he has gained nothing by it here"); Charles Carroll of Carrollton to Charles Carroll, Sr., April 3, 1773, *Maryland Historical Magazine,* 15 (1920), 63; William H. W. Sabine, ed., *Historical Memoirs [1763–1776] of William Smith* . . . (New York, 1956), p. 207.

iii

For it was not so much that in London American radicals like Arthur Lee were free to condemn Hutchinson for rekindling the controversy and to claim, with some reason, that public opinion universally supported them;[21] nor was it simply that they could now declare with assurance that Hutchinson had refuted his own claim that the opposition was plotting independence, since it was obvious that it had been *he* who had precipitated this struggle. More than that—and more than the necessity conservative supporters of the government suddenly felt to clear up the "mist of ambiguity" they detected in certain difficult passages of Hutchinson's messages[22]— beyond all of this agitation in extreme radical and extreme conservative circles in London was the effect that Hutchinson's debate with the Assembly had on the essentially conciliatory colonial secretary, Lord Dartmouth.

Dartmouth, encouraged by Franklin and cool heads at the center of the government, had taken the view at the start of his tenure of office that the solution of the Anglo-American conflict must lie in the healing effect of time, stimulated by small gestures of conciliation. In the early months of 1773 he had felt that the policy of restraint and the refusal of the government to engage in direct controversy with the more belligerent elements in America was working, and he was encouraged enough, apparently, to consider moving for the repeal of the tea duty. Rumors of Hutchinson's debate disturbed him; the texts of the Assembly's replies to the governor, which Franklin published the minute they were available, shocked him deeply.[23]

21. For Arthur Lee's "infinite contempt" for the "shameless prostitution of character" and the "turpitude of mind" that he found revealed in Hutchinson's speech and replies, see Lee to Samuel Adams, June 11, 1773, Lee, *Arthur Lee*, I, 228–231.

22. On April 21, 1773, one John Gray, in London, submitted to Lord Dartmouth for approval the manuscript of a pamphlet he had written to clear up the ambiguities he had detected in Hutchinson's response to the House's "bold manifesto of rebellion." He did not question Hutchinson's "honest, well-meant zeal" but he felt a "proper supplement" to his writing was needed in order "to pull up the seditious doctrines of the colonists by the roots in such a manner as to prevent them from sprouting again" (Dartmouth Papers, Staffordshire County Record Office, Stafford, England). The resulting pamphlet is *The Right of the British Legislature To Tax the American Colonies Vindicated* ... (London, 1774).

23. Dartmouth to John Thornton, Feb. 12, 1774, *Manuscripts of the Earl of Dartmouth*, II (Historical Manuscripts Commission, *Fourteenth Report*, Appendix, Part X,

Franklin hastened to discuss Hutchinson's debate with the minister, and cheerfully summarized the reaction he found in high government circles:

If [Hutchinson] intended, by reviving that dispute, to recommend himself here, he has greatly missed his aim; for the administration are chagrined with his officiousness, their intention having been to let all contention subside, and by degrees suffer matters to return to the old channel. They are now embarrassed by his proceedings; for, if they lay the governor's dispatches, containing the declaration of the General Court, before Parliament, they apprehend measures may be taken that will widen the breach. ... On the other hand, if they do not lay them before Parliament they give advantage to opposition against themselves on some future occasion in a charge of criminal neglect. Some say [Hutchinson] must be a fool; others, that through some misinformation he certainly supposed [the more conservative] Lord Hillsborough to be again in office.

But the details of Franklin's interview with Dartmouth were not nearly so bland and logical as this summary might indicate. Dartmouth had in fact been beside himself with frustration when Franklin talked with him on May 5. "What difficulties," Franklin reported him exclaiming, "that gentlemen has brought us all into by his imprudence!—though I suppose he meant well. Yet what can now be done? It is impossible that Parliament can suffer such a declaration of the General Assembly, asserting its independency, to pass unnoticed." The only thing to do, Franklin said, is to ignore the House's statement: "It is *words* only. Acts of Parliament are still submitted to there. No force is used to obstruct their execution, and while that is the case Parliament would do well to turn a deaf ear and seem not to know that such declarations had ever been made. Violent measures against the province will not change the opinion of the people," he added prophetically; "force could do no good." He was not thinking of force, Dartmouth replied, but rather of some kind of "inconveniences, till they rescind that declaration." What he really wanted, the colonial secretary told the Massachusetts agent, was to have the Massachusetts House reconsider its statement "and do it of themselves, voluntarily, and thus leave things between us on the old footing, the points undiscussed." Did Franklin think that was a possibility? "No, My Lord, I think it impossible," Frank-

London, 1895), 197; Franklin to Thomas Cushing, May 6, 1773, *Writings of Benjamin Franklin* ..., ed. A. H. Smyth (New York, 1905–1907), VI, 48.

lin said. It was not conceivable, he explained, that they would re-consider their reply until Hutchinson withdrew his statement of principles, and that would be awkward indeed. As for "inconveni-ences," Massachusetts would surely retaliate until such acts were repealed—had they not done just that before?——"and so we shall go on injuring and provoking each other instead of cultivating that good will and harmony so necessary to the general welfare." Yes, Dartmouth agreed, that might well be the result, but "we are yet *one empire*" despite the Massachusetts Assembly, and something had to be done. What would Franklin do if *he* were colonial secre-tary? Would he really attempt to ignore the whole thing and run the risk that Parliament would call him to task for suppressing vital information? The only thing to do, Franklin repeated, was nothing. There was absolutely nothing that Parliament could do in an effort to increase its authority in America that would not in fact diminish it, "and after abundance of mischief they must finally lose it."[24]

But Dartmouth would not be persuaded. Again he turned to Franklin: if the agent wished to be of service, let him prevail upon the Massachusetts Assembly to withdraw its answers to the gover-nor's speech. Again Franklin explained the futility of any such effort; and this time, to support his opinion more fully, he took the occasion to dispute firmly the impression Hutchinson had undoubt-edly given the ministry that the Assembly's replies expressed the views of one small clique only—an impression which the ex-gover-nor, Bernard, who by chance had preceded Franklin that day in the secretary's reception room, had attempted to reinforce. There had not been a single dissenting voice in the votes taken on these belligerent messages, Franklin pointed out. Partisan leaders always tend to exaggerate the numbers of those who support their opinions; surely His Lordship had observed that in English politics.[25]

24. Franklin to Cushing, May 6, 1773, Smyth, *Writings,* VI, 48–50. Franklin had anticipated the drift of opinion in England as soon as he had read Hutchinson's initial speech, and wrote an anonymous piece in the *Public Advertiser,* March 16, 1773, con-demning Hutchinson for "needlessly [reviving] a dispute that can end in nothing but mischief. I am sure he could not expect to convince an individual there by such known false facts and sophistical reasoning. . . . and therefore I think it written to recommend himself here, and not to do service there." Verner W. Crane, ed., *Benjamin Franklin's Letters to the Press, 1758–1775* (Chapel Hill, Universty of North Carolina Press, 1950), p. 229.
25. Franklin to Cushing, May 6, 1773, Smyth, *Writings,* VI, 50–51.

He had; but still Dartmouth felt that an effort must be made somehow to reverse the train of events that Hutchinson had set in motion. And so, swallowing his pride, he undertook on his own, surreptitiously, the task that Franklin had said was impossible to accomplish.

On June 19 he drafted, and carefully revised before sending, a "private and confidential" letter addressed to the speaker of the Massachusetts House, which he dispatched to Boston not by one of the many official conveyances available to him but by the private hand of a young Bostonian who happened to call on him seeking employment.[26] He was writing, the King's secretary for colonial affairs declared, "as a private member of the community and a hearty friend and well-wisher to every part of the British dominions" to express his great concern at "that unhappy spirit of disunion and dissatisfaction" that prevailed in Massachusetts. He knew, he said, that the ultimate cause of the trouble was the recent acts of Parliament taxing the American colonies to support civil government. But he knew far too well, he said (in what could only be construed as a direct slap at Hutchinson), how delicate the questions of principle were "to take upon me to enter into a disquisition" on the subject. He had no hesitation in declaring, however—writing as he was, not "as a minister of the crown and servant of the public, but only as a simple individual according to the dictates of my own private judgment and opinion"—that if his personal wishes could prevail, Parliament's undoubted right to tax its dominions "should be suspended and lie dormant" until there were an occasion ("if any such can be") when the necessity of such exercise would be obvious "to every considerate man in every part of the dominions of Great Britain"—which was to say, never.

Having made so frank a declaration of a remarkably conciliatory position—having, indeed, thus personally repudiated the official policy of the government he represented—he turned to the Assembly, to "lament the wild and extravagant doctrines" contained in

26. The letter is reproduced in full in B. F. Stevens, comp., *Facsimiles of Manuscripts in European Archives Relating to America, 1773–1783* . . . (London, 1889–1895), #2025; the revised draft showing Dartmouth's corrections is in the Dartmouth Papers. The courier was Thomas Danforth, who apparently gave his recollection of the event to George Chalmers, July 15, 1783: New England Papers (Sparks MSS 10), IV, 33, Houghton Library, Harvard University. For Danforth's trip to England in 1773 and his search for employment, see Clifford K. Shipton, *Sibley's Harvard Graduates*, XV (Boston, MHS, 1970), 218–219.

their answers to the governor. Their declaration, he said, in effect repudiated the connection with Britain from which the very privileges and advantages they wished to preserve flowed. But what troubled him most was not so much the doctrines in themselves as the fact that the Assembly's affirmation of them in itself created a bar to the tranquillity that he wished so much to restore. "Till that unhappy bar shall be removed out of the way by the same hands that laid it there" it will be impossible to eliminate the causes of the problems they complained of, "to some of which," he added significantly, "I flatter myself an easy remedy might otherwise have been applied."

Was it so difficult for the Assembly to reconsider its position and retract? "All human councils are liable to err, and . . . I shall always consider it as a mark of the truest wisdom and soundest judgment to rescind, revoke, amend, or alter as occasion may require." He fervently hoped that the General Court of Massachusetts would find a way to remove this new obstruction to reconciliation "before the opening of the next session of Parliament" so that that body would have reason to "overlook the mistakes of a well-intentioned, though perhaps not well-informed, part of His Majesty's subjects." He could never give up the *principle* of the supreme authority of Parliament over all the dominions of the empire, but he pledged to the people of Massachusetts that if they reconsidered their replies to Hutchinson he would labor to the fullest extent of his powers to remedy "every real or imaginary evil of which the province may think she has reason to complain." He closed by repeating what he had said at the start, that he was writing to them privately and confidentially, trusting that they would not make the letter public in any way.

And, indeed, they did not. But otherwise the reaction to Dartmouth's letter in Massachusetts was scarcely what he had hoped for. A decade later Dartmouth's private courier, Thomas Danforth, would recall that Speaker Cushing passed the secretary's letter around the "junto," "who laughed at it most heartily." Supporters of the government, however, and friends of the governor, when word of the letter leaked out, found nothing at all to laugh at. "They think it beneath the dignity of a secretary of state," the Reverend William Gordon wrote Dartmouth, "to correspond with the speaker of a petty provincial assembly." And the customs comptroller Benjamin Hallowell, who had suffered much from the resentment of the opposition, told Undersecretary Pownall that Hutchinson's administration, the most difficult of any in recent memory, had been seriously injured by the secretary's letter. Coming as it did "otherwise than through the hands of the governor," it had given the opposition great satisfaction, making it appear "that His Lordship has given the governor the go-by, a circumstance, they say, not unfavorable to their intentions of getting rid of Mr. Hutchinson."[27]

But it was the speaker's formal reply that measured the full futility of Dartmouth's gesture. Cushing thanked His Lordship for his frankness, complimented him on his virtue and disinterested devotion to the public good in general and the welfare of the colonies in particular, and then proceeded to place the entire blame for the Assembly's statements on Hutchinson. His speech had been "little short of a challenge"; he had driven the House "to the unhappy alternative either of appearing by their silence to acquiesce in His Excellency's sentiments or of thus freely discussing this point." They themselves had not had the slightest desire to meddle with such controversial questions, but they had to do their duty "to God, to their country, and to their own consciences." Even so, they had been cautious and temperate: they had carefully avoided an effort, Cushing pointed out, to "draw a line of distinction between the supreme authority of Parliament and the total independency of the colonies." They had in fact resented the necessity Hutchinson had imposed on them to enter into the discussion of these matters. "Nothing," Cushing repeated, "but a sense of duty, nothing but a due attention to the trust committed to them by their constituents, could have prevailed with them to enter into [such] a disquisition."

As to His Lordship's specific question, Cushing, insisting that he too wrote not as a public official but only as "a simple individual," explained that, considering the great pains that the Assembly had taken in writing its replies to Hutchinson, considering too "the interest which every part of America takes in this important question, and that the eyes of the whole continent . . . are turned upon

27. Danforth's recollection, cited in the previous note; Gordon to Dartmouth, Sept. 18, 1773, in *Dartmouth Manuscripts*, II, 173; Hallowell to John Pownall, Sept. 29, 1773, Stevens, *Facsimiles*, #2029.

this province"—considering all of this, he was obliged to say that the Assembly "never will be brought to rescind or revoke what they have advanced." Indeed, any leader who so much as attempted to persuade the Assembly to do so would be destroyed politically—unless, that is, all the grievances that the Assembly had enumerated on recent occasions had been previously redressed and "things brought to the general state in which they stood at the conclusion of the late war." Only in that way, hereafter, could "the entangling question of the right of Parliament (which I humbly think, for the happiness of both countries, ought never to have been agitated) . . . be kept out of sight."[28]

How much Hutchinson knew of Lord Dartmouth's humiliating effort to turn back the movement of politics that his speech of January 6 had begun, and whether he was told of the Assembly's refusal even to consider the secretary's request, cannot be established from Hutchinson's surviving papers. But by the time the secret exchange between Dartmouth and Cushing was concluded Hutchinson was miserable enough without knowing of his superior's embarrassment. For when word of the debate had reached London, the ministry, suddenly recovering from the torpor from which Hutchinson had struggled to rouse it, had leapt into action, but not so much to condemn the House for having issued a treasonous statement as to rebuke Hutchinson for having provoked it.

Your speech and papers, Lord Dartmouth informed Hutchinson curtly, may have halted the spread of support for the Boston resolutions, but in doing so they have evoked doctrines "of the most dangerous nature . . . subversive of every principle of the constitutional dependence of the colonies upon this kingdom." Had Hutchinson not realized that his invitation to the Assembly to challenge his view of the constitution would result in a series of irreversible policy statements of the most extreme kind? Did he not know that a public body that issued such pronouncements could never, by any conceivable argument or mode of persuasion, be made to yield obedience thereafter to the power they opposed? Avoid, Dartmouth commanded the governor, all further discussion of these questions "the agitating of which has already produced such disagreeable consequences," and do not "press either the Council or House of Representatives to a declaration of their

28. Thomas Cushing to Dartmouth, Aug. 22, 1773, Stevens, *Facsimiles*, #2028.

sentiments upon points that cannot be kept too much out of sight."[29]

This brutal reaction from a minister known for his gentleness and consideration was a fearful blow to Hutchinson, and his apologies began as soon as he received the first indications. He had long believed, he wrote Dartmouth abjectly but with an edge of bitterness, that if absurd notions of government had beeen effectively refuted when they had first been broached, they would never have gained their present popularity, and so how could he have remained silent in the face of Boston's outright denial of Parliament's authority? For almost four years, he pointed out with rising emotion, he had had no guidance from England—no advice, no signal, no sign. He had been left to guess the ministry's intent, and if he had guessed wrong, he apologized, but he knew his intentions had been good, and the results had not all been bad. At the very least he felt he had smoked the radicals out; they had shown how far they intended to go, and been forced to shift the basis of their claims from charters and constitutions to the universal rights of man.[30]

But nothing he could say would make any difference. He was, he knew, "almost worn out with four years of hard service" and now in the spring of 1773 for the first time in his life began to doubt whether, if Parliament's authority were adequately explained and reasonably and firmly enforced, the people would ultimately support it. He was simply incapable, he knew, of standing up to another series of direct conflicts. His longing to escape somehow from this "most perverse set of men upon earth" became overpowering, and in May he decided to request leave officially to go to England in the summer and exert all his influence to exchange

29. Dartmouth to TH, April 10 and June 2, 1773, New England Papers, IV, 29 (also CO5/762/108, 164, and CO5/765/255).
30. TH to Dartmouth, June 1, 1773 (responding to the first indication of Dartmouth's displeasure, March 3), MA, XXVII, 486, 488. Dartmouth's letter of April 10 arrived on June 13 or 14, and Hutchinson immediately told Dartmouth of his pain upon reading it (TH to Dartmouth, June 12/14, *ibid.*, p. 494). He then wrote a letter of great length (*ibid.*, pp. 489–492) reviewing the history of his views on government and of his controversies with the Assembly, concluding that "the principles of independency" had been so universally accepted in Massachusetts that he could not see how Parliament would ever be able to exert its authority there again, and offering to resign. But he did not send that letter, and wrote his extended justifications to [Jackson], June 21; Bernard, June 29; and John Pownall, Aug. 16 and 23 (*ibid.*, pp. 498–499, 503, 528, 532). Five years earlier Bernard had written an almost identically bitter response to the same kind of criticism that he had received from the government. Bernard Papers, VIII, 146–148 (*Select Letters*, pp. 61–62).

the governorship for some other position—he did not know exactly what: deputy postmaster general occurred to him, or surveyor general of the woods—anything that provided some refreshing travel, "little anxiety," and the £500 or £600 a year he had enjoyed from his offices before he had taken the governorship. But it was not to be.[31]

Anyone who observed him at all sympathetically in that spring and early summer of 1773 could reasonably have thought he was hounded by avengers of some filial crime. All his conscientious plans for the governorship had failed: his effort to mobilize the political system to support the government; his strenuous, at times frantic, appeals to England to devise, in its own self-interest, a judicious and comprehensive colonial policy, sensitive both to the fears and desires of the people and to the needs of government, and to enforce law and order before it took a massive military effort to do so; and finally, his struggle to persuade the great moderate majority of the population of the sheer irrationality and self-destructive nihilism of the extremists' claims and demands. And not only had he failed in all of this, but, in his effort to inject rationality into an increasingly irrational situation, he—*he, and not the enemies of order*—had been rebuked by the government itself.

Politically weak to the point of debility, supported only by a dwindling band of stubborn loyalists less thoughtful, less liberal than he, hated, feared, condemned throughout the land, he yet continued to believe that somehow the great British ship of state would right itself and he would end his life in peace. And then the furies struck once more, the most savage blow of all, which meant for him world's end.

31. TH to Dartmouth, n.d. [June, 1773: not sent], MA, XXVII, 490–492; TH to FB, June 29, 1773, *ibid.*, pp. 502–503.

Chapter VII

The "Scape-Goat"

Behind all of Thomas Hutchinson's anxieties and apprehensions in the years of his governorship there lay the fear that his enemies would attempt to destroy him by some revelation of his private thoughts, some dramatic unmasking, and prove to all the world that his innocent appearance hid an evil intent. It was no vague, neurotic fear. Like so much of his thought it was based on an accurate assessment of the dangers through which he had passed and a pessimistic view of the persistence of evil in human nature; and while he was neither detached enough nor analytic enough to see that the need to find hidden malevolence was part of the very structure of opposition thought, he was acutely aware of the political importance any such revelation would have. Nor was he in doubt as to the form such an attack was likely to take. After his house had been gutted in 1765 he had been shocked to find the story spreading "that intercepted letters have occasioned this rage."[1]

1. TH to Jackson, Sept. 1765, MA, XXVI, 150. There seems never to have been a time when Hutchinson did not fear that his confidential letters, or those written to him, would be stolen or intercepted and used against him. As early as 1758, fearing Gov. Thomas Pownall's connivance with the anti-Shirleyan opposition, he had warned his friend Col. Williams "to clothe your sentiments with such a dress that nobody besides you and I can understand them. Letters are liable to miscarry. Sometimes they are opened before they come where they are directed. . . . By and by you will be found guilty of treason or misprision of treason, and neither of us will be able to do much service afterwards." TH to Williams, Aug. 11, 1758, J. Davis Papers, MHS.

No evidence of anything of the sort had been forthcoming, but the rumors of a clandestine correspondence had persisted. So he wrote more guardedly than ever, rewrote sensitive phrases, threw out drafts that might be misconstrued, took to cipher, used vowelless script, and month after month in the late sixties warned his correspondents to protect the confidentiality of his letters, let none of them circulate, and write nothing to him from which an echo might be caught of anything prejudicial he might have said.

But the dangers increased, and were vividly dramatized in 1769 by the publication of Governor Bernard's confidential letters to the ministry. Though, to the opposition's disappointment, none of Hutchinson's letters were then disclosed, he had been scorched by the episode, which had ended Bernard's usefulness as governor.[2] But what had brought his premonitions to the edge of paranoia was the departure for England in November 1770 of the disaffected customs official John Temple, Bernard's implacable enemy and a key figure in the Massachusetts opposition. The fiercely hostile Temple, described by his brother-in-law James Bowdoin, Jr., as "a man of delicate passions [who] I am afraid can't bear adversity," was allied not only by marriage to the clique that dominated the Massachusetts Council but also by birth to the powerful Grenville-Temple connection that had operated for years at the summit of English politics. Convinced that Bernard and Hutchinson had connived against his interest and were in some way responsible for the

2. On the opposition's disappointment, see Nathaniel Rogers to ——, Oct. 25, 1769, New England Papers (Sparks MSS 10), III, 44, Houghton Library, Harvard University. One of Hutchinson's first duties as acting governor was to send Hillsborough documentary evidence of the political havoc that had resulted from the publication of Bernard's letters. TH to Hillsborough, Sept. 11, 1769, CO5/758/196. When in Dec. 1769 a second bundle of Bernard's confidential dispatches arrived back in Boston, he could only repeat anxiously to Hillsborough that "it destroys the confidence which is necessary to be placed in the servants of the crown if their letters to the ministry are suffered to be sent back to the colonies and they are made amenable to judicatories there." He begged His Lordship to protect him (Dec. 11, 1769, MA, XXVI, 416). In response, a year later, he was given assurances—of sorts. Hillsborough told him that no copies of any of Hutchinson's letters that were in the colonial office and whose disclosure could in any way inconvenience him had been, or would be, released. In addition, Bernard, then in London, quoted the secretary, and the undersecretary John Pownall as well, to the same effect, and advised the nervous Bostonian not to worry. For, Bernard said, despite the fact that "copies of such papers as were laid before Parliament are as easily obtained as ever," "the impropriety of exposing governors' letters is now well understood, and last session [of Parliament] it was admitted on both sides, and copies of letters were not desired by the opposition." Hillsborough to TH, Nov. 15, 1770, CO5/759/292; FB to TH, Nov. 15, 1770, Bernard Papers, VIII, 150.

relative demotion in the customs service that he had suffered, he was capable, Hutchinson believed, of inflicting infinite harm on the administration in Massachusetts. He was never in doubt as to the main direction that Temple's "malignity" would take. Temple, he believed, was "continually furnishing [his] correspondents here with intelligence of everything [he] can collect of my letters, public or private, in order to distress government and to prejudice the minds of the people against me in particular."[3]

So he cast about for some means of convincing the British government to maintain security over its official correspondence, or at least keep the House of Commons' confidential reports from America from being divulged in the press. He warned of the dangers ("if copies of private letters can be obtained we are never safe"), pleaded for cooperation, and begged for understanding; but he sensed the storm growing in the darkening rumors circulating early in 1773 of "a story of something that would amaze everybody" and the announcement just after the May election, 1773, that a revelation would be made of "something" which if handled properly would restore the colony to the condition it had enjoyed in 1760. One June 2 the "something" was revealed to a closed session of the Assembly: "letters of an extraordinary nature . . . greatly to the prejudice of the province" that had been sent back secretly to Massachusetts where they had originated. Two weeks later thirteen letters written principally to Thomas Whately at the end of the 1760's by Hutchinson and four of his relatives and friends were published as a pamphlet—a pamphlet in which, its readers were told on the title page, would be found "the fatal source of the confusion and bloodshed in which this province especially has been involved and which threatened total destruction to the liberties of all *America*."[4]

3. Bowdoin, Jr., to Mrs. John Temple, March 29, 1774, Bowdoin-Temple MSS, MHS; TH to FB, Jan. 29, 1772, MA, XXVIII, 287; TH to General Mackay, Feb. 23, 1773, *ibid.*, p. 455.

4. TH to [FB], Aug. 25, 1772, MA, XXVIII, 375; TH to FB, June 29, 1773, MA, XXVII, 502; Gipson, *British Empire*, XII, 57. The first printing of the pamphlet is entitled *Copy of Letters Sent to Great-Britain, by His Excellency Thomas Hutchinson, the Hon. Andrew Oliver, and Several Other Persons, Born and Educated among Us in Which (Notwithstanding His Excellency's Declaration to the House, That the Tendency and Design of Them Was Not To Subvert the Constitution, But Rather To Preserve It Entire) the Judicious Reader Will Discover the Fatal Source of the Confusion and Bloodshed in Which This Province Especially Has Been Involved, and Which Threatned Total Destruction to the Liberties of All America* (Boston, printed by Edes and Gill, 1773). It

ii

Hutchinson said at once, and to the end of his life never doubted, that the publication of these letters was the result of a carefully laid plot to destroy him—"a conspiracy," he said, "managed with infinite art," that succeeded "beyond their own expectations."[5] But though in later years in England he would seek to retrace the winding trail of the intrigue that had led to the publication of his letters, for all of his efforts, which became obsessive as he bitterly contemplated the wreckage of his career, he was never able to follow the story back to its ultimate origins. From the start he knew that Franklin was involved. As agent of the Massachusetts House it had undoubtedly been he who had sent the letters back to the speaker of the House; and by the end of 1773 Franklin, shocked to discover that a duel had been fought, and might be refought, over an erroneous identification of the culprit, had confessed to that much in print.[6] But Franklin said also—and Hutchinson knew that too from the start—that he had not been given the letters by their addressee, Thomas Whately (who had died in June 1772); nor could he have taken them—stolen them—unassisted. Someone else, whose designs must have been even darker than those of Franklin, had also been involved. Who it was who had managed to get hold of Hutchinson's letters in the first place despite all of Hutchinson's precautions, and had made them available to Franklin, was an unsolved mystery at the time (Franklin identified this inner plotter only as "a gentleman of character and distinction," and it appears likely that he was a Member of Parliament). It has remained something of a mystery to this day, and not surprisingly. For the true origins of this intrigue—which resulted

_____

contains six letters from Hutchinson, four from Oliver, and one each from Charles Paxton and Nathaniel Rogers, all to the same unstated recipient, Thomas Whately, and in addition one from Robert Auchmuty to Hutchinson. A later printing of the pamphlet (Charles Evans, comp., *American Bibliography* . . . [Chicago, 1903–1934], #12818) included five more letters, one from George Rome and four from Thomas Moffat. The printing history of the pamphlet in its various forms and the prior appearance of the letters in the newspapers are traced in Thomas R. Adams, *American Independence . . . a Bibliographical Study* . . . (Providence, Brown University Press, 1965), #96.

5. TH to FB, June 29, 1773, MA, XXVII, 502.

6. Franklin's letter to the *Public Advertiser*, Dec. 25, 1775, is reprinted in his "Tract Relative to the Affair of Hutchinson's Letters," A. H. Smyth, ed., *Writings of Benjamin Franklin* (N.Y., 1905–1907), VI, 284.

not only in the final destruction of Hutchinson's public career and the commitment of Franklin to the cause of American independence but also in the conviction on the part of untold thousands of Americans that all the rumors of plots against their liberties were true and that hopes for reconciliation were unrealistic—the origins of this remarkable event are not simple: they are not merely the consequence of one man's or a few men's manipulations, but grew out of a complex set of circumstances and motivations. There are two distinct clusters of events that lay back of the disclosure, one centering on the original gathering of the bundle of letters that was published, the other on the motives of those who used them. And while the actions of three individulas were crucial—Bernard, Franklin, and in all likelihood Thomas Pownall—many others were involved too, knowingly or not, and first among them of course was Hutchinson himself.[7]

He had responded willingly to the invitation he had received in 1765 to open a correspondence with Thomas Whately, a former secretary to the Treasury under George Grenville and a key figure in the drafting of the Stamp Act. Whately, whose involvement in American affairs went back to the mid-fifties, had written in 1765 to his old friend John Temple, newly returned to Boston as surveyor general of customs in the northern colonies, that he had heard much of "a Mr. Hutchinson," who was known to be planning a trip to England, and he told Temple that he would like to make the Bostonian's acquaintance.[8] When exactly the correspondence between them began is not known; what is known is that between 1768 and the end of 1771 Hutchinson and Whately exchanged at

7. The reconstruction of the background of the "letters" affair that follows is based on an examination of the published correspondences of Franklin and Thomas Pownall, all of the Hutchinson and Colonial Office MSS, and the Grenville Papers (Add. MSS 42,083–8) and the two volumes of Thomas Whately correspondence (Dropmore, or George Grenville, Papers, acquired 1972 from John Murray, Ltd.) in the British Museum. The identification of the person who gave Franklin the letters—who I believe was Thomas Pownall—remains conjectural, however, though in ways that I have indicated Pownall's complicity is powerfully supported by the circumstantial evidence. I wish to thank Mr. G. B. Warden, assistant editor of the *Papers of Benjamin Franklin*, for allowing me to see his progress report (1972) on the search being conducted by the Franklin editors for the identity of Franklin's colleague in this intrigue. For a brief summary of the writing on the subject, see Gipson, *British Empire*, XII, 59n.

8. Whately to Temple, May 10, 1765, *Bowdoin and Temple Papers* (MHS *Colls.*, 6th ser., IX, 1897), p. 55.

least seventeen letters, thirteen of them written by Hutchinson, nine of those in 1768 and 1769.[9] At the same time Whately had begun a correspondence with Andrew Oliver, who was, Whately said, "a sort of family acquaintance" of whom he had heard all his life; for two generation the Olivers had been managers of lands in Rhode Island owned or claimed by the Whately family. Oliver's appointment as stamp master in 1764 had pleased Whately, and on that occasion they had undertaken a correspondence, which also climaxed in 1768.[10]

Temple, Hutchinson, and Oliver were not Whately's only American correspondents. Both Hutchinson's old friend and protégé, the customs officer Charles Paxton, and Hutchinson's unfortunate nephew Nathaniel Rogers were also in touch with Whately, as were George Rome in Rhode Island and Dr. Thomas Moffat in Connecticut, formerly members of the royalist clique in Newport that in 1764 and 1765 had sought the revocation of the Rhode Island charter and that had supported the Stamp Act and had been savagely attacked by the mobs as a consequence.[11] By the end of the decade, when Whately and his patron Grenville were both out of office, Whately was the center of a small network of correspondents in New England.[12] But though an occasional letter of Whately's that had some special interest was passed around among the Bostonians, the various correspondents did not know what the others were writing. For they wrote for no agreed-on purpose but only, in their various ways, to gain the influential Englishman's support and to express their feelings on the state of politics in the

9. In addition to the six published letters, Hutchinson wrote Whately on Oct. 17, 1768 (MA, XXV, 283); July 29 and Aug. 24, 1769 (MA, XXVI, 359, 367–368); April 30 and Oct. 3, 1770 (MA, XXV, 399–400; MA, XXVII, 11–12, 21); and Jan. 25 and May 14, 1771 (MA, XXVII, 106–107, 166). In addition, the unaddressed and undated letter Hutchinson wrote in Sept. or Oct. 1770 (MA, XXV, 433–436) was also probably written to Whately.

10. Whately to Temple, May 10, 1765, *Bowdoin-Temple Papers,* p. 55. There are references to or surviving copies of fourteen letters between Oliver and Whately. The history of the relationship between the two families and the involvement in Rhode Island lands is explained in a letter from Oliver to Whately, May 15, 1771, Eg. MSS, 2670, p. 49.

11. Edmund S. Morgan and Helen M. Morgan, *The Stamp Act Crisis* (Chapel Hill, University of North Carolina Press, 1953), pp. 47–52, 145–148; David S. Lovejoy, *Rhode Island Politics and the American Revolution, 1760–1776* (Providence, Brown University Press, 1958), pp. 49, 174–176.

12. At least 46 letters were exchanged between Whately and the Bostonians before 1770.

colonies. At the very least Whately was an excellent source of information and gossip, and an occasion might well arise when his support would be invaluable.

So they wrote—freely, often pungently, and very differently. Paxton and Rogers kept mainly to questions of patronage and jobs. Oliver surveyed politics in general and detailed an entire program of constitutional reform in Massachusetts aimed at strengthening the executive force of government, while Moffat and Rome wrote savage indictments of the populist forces in Rhode Island and Massachusetts, pleaded for direct crown intervention in appointments and governance, and complained bitterly of their inability to collect compensation for their losses in the Stamp Act riots. Hutchinson's letters were the most restrained and discreet. The nine letters that he wrote to Whately in 1768 and 1769—from which would be drawn the six which when published in 1773 would set in motion an almost unstoppable landslide of public opinion—were quite mixed in their purport, and they contained no sentiment that he had not elsewhere, and publicly, expressed. His despair at the failure of the Council to support the executive authority in general and the governor in particular was nothing new—he had expressed it often before, both in personal letters and in public statements. Equally familiar was his warning that in the end Parliament would surely show its "marks of resentment" against those who were weakening the effectiveness of government, and would reward, as he believed it should, "those who have been most steady in preserving the constitution and opposing the licentiousness of such as call themselves Sons of Liberty." No less familiar to those who had followed his pronouncements of those years was his insistence that the empire would simply dissolve if no steps were taken to secure the colonies' dependence on England, and that it was literally impossible for "a colony 3,000 miles distant from the parent state [to] enjoy all the liberty of the parent state." Whatever one's wishes might be, it was simply a matter of fact, he wrote, that if the tie to England were to be maintained there would have to be "an abridgment of what are called English liberties." He had said all this before: explicitly, in the essay of 1764 which Secretary Conway had used in arguing for the repeal of the Stamp Act, and subsequently in correspondence; implicitly in all of his formal expositions of the imperial constitution. It was perfectly obvious to him that America's well-being depended on the maintenance of an effective bond to the mother country, and if, inevitably, given the existing conditions of life, some kind of restraint of privileges was necessary in order to secure this overriding and undeniable good, then he would wish to see that restraint imposed—for "the good of the colony" and for no other reason. The strategy of all of his constitutional arguments had been to recognize this fact of life and then to suggest balancing compensations.[13]

Hutchinson's wording in these informal letters to Whately was loose and, for him, somewhat rhetorical; in later letters to Whately he would use quite graphic language.[14] But the viewpoint was not new, nor was it being conveyed to Whately for some special or secret purpose. He was writing generally, and not, like Oliver, to consider or propose a program of constitutional reform, or like Moffat and Rome to vilify the opposition. Indeed, the most revealing letters that Hutchinson wrote Whately were not the six that would become so famous, but two others that he wrote in the summer of 1769. In them he said that the difficulties he anticipated as head of the government would lead him to act with even greater caution and circumspection than he had used before; that he still believed most Americans were loyal to Britain and wished to remain so; that military force, which should always be under the control of the civil authorities, could never be used effectively in the colonies and *should* never be used except in the last extremity, and then not for one second longer than was necessary; and that, though he was convinced that some kind of new plan would have to be conceived to secure the ties to England, he had to confess he did not know what to recommend: "I can think of nothing but what will produce as great an evil as that which it may remove or will be of a very uncertain event."[15]

13. Edmund S. Morgan, "Thomas Hutchinson and the Stamp Act," *New England Quarterly*, 21 (1948), 483; TH to [Jackson?], Feb. 26, 1766, MA, XXVI, 198. On Hutchinson's constitutional arguments as they relate to the idea of "abridgment," see above, pp. 91–92.
14. E.g.: "the wound may be skinned over but can never be healed until it be laid open to the bone. Parliament must give up its claim to a supreme authority over the colonies or the colonies must cease from asserting a supreme legislative within themselves." TH to Whately, Oct. 3, 1770, MA, XXVII, 21.
15. Letters of July 29 and Aug. 24, 1769, cited in note 9 above.

Hutchinson wrote these cautionary and perplexed thoughts to Whately late in August 1769. Two weeks later Governor Bernard, now Sir Francis Bernard, had arrived in London and had begun his campaign of vengeance against those who had harassed him in Massachusetts, and he had launched his effort to reform the colony's constitution. He was slow, however, in making contact with the leading politicians. It took him two weeks to get ten minutes of the time of the prime minister, the Duke of Grafton, and Grafton spent most of that interview urging Bernard to take a fortnight's holiday in the country since the colonial secretary, Lord Hillsborough, was in Ireland. Six weeks went by before Bernard managed to confer at all seriously with a single minister of state about the urgent problems of Massachusetts, and as a result Bernard's main political contact during these early weeks and months of his return to England was, willy-nilly, Whately, who at least was himself in constant touch with Grenville. It was therefore to Whately that Bernard first expressed his conviction that acts alone, not resolves or statements of principles, would have any effect in America and to whom he confided his doubts whether, since "none but Americans" now headed the executive in Massachusetts, the resistance of the government to popular pressures would be as firm as when he was governor—a remark that led Whately, in reporting the conversation to Grenville, to comment coolly on Bernard's self-importance and to explain to his chief that he himself had "great reliance on the temper and the steadiness of Hutchinson."[16]

Overfull of his own importance, Bernard steadily pursued his object and eagerly took the leadership of the group that Hillsborough convened in the summer to draw up Parliamentary legislation amending the charter of Massachusetts. It was in all probability he who assembled the documentation needed by the committee. From his recent close contact with Whately, as well as from his earlier discussions with Hutchinson and Oliver, he knew of the letters that had been sent to Whately by members of his own administration in Massachusetts, and he probably knew too that those letters had been passed on to Grenville, who was then, in

16. William Knox to George Grenville, Oct. 18, 1769, *Grenville Papers . . .*, ed. W. J. Smith (London, 1852–53), IV, 470; Whately to Grenville, Sept. 22, 1769, *ibid.*, pp. 459–460.

Franklin's phrase, "the center to which flowed all the correspondence inimical to America."[17] He, or someone else in the Hillsborough group, borrowed the letters and selected those that would best support the proposed charter changes. Oliver's letters were particularly useful, especially that of February 13, 1769, in which he commented at great length on Whately's observation that the two main defects in the Massachusetts constitution were "the popular election of the Council and the return of juries by the towns."[18] But Hutchinson's letters too were valuable—certain of them, at least. For Bernard, or whoever it was who selected the correspondence, removed the letters in which Hutchinson had expressed his opposition to precipitous action, his extreme reluctance to recommend the use of military force of any kind at any time, and his frankly admitted uncertainty as to what course of action would be best to follow. What remained of Hutchinson's in the collection were six letters that could be taken as expressing a firm and clear if general conviction that constitutional changes, especially those affecting the Council, would have to be made, and that he favored abridging British liberties in America. A few letters by others that generally supported Bernard's position were also included, the whole group being presentable as evidence from the highest authorities in Massachusetts that the changes under discussion were necessary.

When, as a result of Hutchinson's letter to Hillsborough of October 9, and as a consequence too of the war scare of 1770–71, the committee's work was abandoned, the letters were not destroyed, nor in all probability were they returned to their original recipients. They probably remained in the colonial office, and were there when Grenville died in November 1770, their presence known of course to Whately and to those who had participated in the discussions, and particularly well known to John Pownall, who was the chief subministerial authority on North American affairs.

Two years went by before these letters of the late sixties were turned to again, and by then circumstances had changed significantly. Bernard had been pensioned off with a sinecure in the Irish

17. Franklin to Cushing, July 7, 1773, Smyth, ed., *Writings*, VI, 82. The Hillsborough committee and its demise are discussed above, pp. 189–193.
18. *Copy of Letters*, pp. 28–32.

customs establishment; Thomas Whately, the original recipient of the letters, had died (June 1772); Dartmouth had replaced Hills-borough in the colonial office; Franklin had become the London agent for the Massachusetts House; and Hutchinson's ancient enemy, the former governor Thomas Pownall, now a Member of Parliament and in close touch with the Massachusetts radicals as well as with the Massachusetts administration, was attempting to play a central role in reconciling the differences between England and America.

Pownall's position in Anglo-American affairs, which lies in the background of the "letters" affair, was a direct projection of the position that he had taken as governor of Massachusetts many years before and that had then so stimulated Hutchinson's resentment and anger. In principle he did not disagree with the administration's, or Hutchinson's, insistence that Parliament's sovereignty must remain undivided and that its theoretical right to tax the colonies was beyond challenge; but in speeches in the House in 1769 and 1770 and in the successive revisions of his *Administration of the Colonies* he had opposed the administration's policies strongly and had continued to advocate the theory—which the colonists had long since rejected—that colonial representation in Parliament could be the basis of an overall reconciliation.[19] Close to major administration figures in England through his brother as well as through his own contacts, and a regular if cautious correspondent of both Hutchinson and Oliver—who knew how valuable an ally and how dangerous a foe he could be—he was in close touch too with the extreme pro-Americans in London and also, through his correspondence with Samuel Cooper and James Bowdoin in Boston, with the radical opposition in the colony as well. He had become, in fact, an important counsellor to the Massachusetts radicals; from time to time he was their goad, even their leader, and he responded sensitively to their promptings.[20] The reports of the Massacre that

19. For an early effort of Pownall to clarify his ambiguous position; for his joining with Franklin to propose a paper currency for the colonies; and for his explanation of his dedicating the second edition of his *Administration of the Colonies* to Grenville, see Pownall to TH, Dec. 3, 1766, MA, XXV, 112–113a. Cf. George H. Guttridge, "Thomas Pownall's *The Administration of the Colonies:* The Six Editions," *W.M.Q.*, 3d ser., 26 (1969), 36–37.

20. E.g., Pownall to Cooper, July 14, 1770, in Frederick Griffin, *Junius Discovered* (Boston, 1854), pp. 277–286. Pownall's speech to the Commons against the tea duty was read aloud to the Massachusetts House and "heard with great avidity and pleasure";

had been sent home by officials in Massachusetts, Cooper told Pownall in a passionate and portentous letter, were grotesque misrepresentations, and the men responsible for such misrepresentations "ought to be exposed." A year earlier James Bowdoin had told him that the ministry's false notions of colonial wealth, which he believed had started all the trouble, had probably been "encouraged by persons here who expected to share in the revenue by an increase of salary or appointment to office." Pownall welcomed this information, which did not surprise him. He himself warned Bowdoin that the Bostonians had among them "some false friends who keep up correspondencies here with people that you little suspect," and he advised him "to form a circle of a few that can be trusted with confidential communication."[21]

Pownall's aim, however, was not to stimulate opposition to the British government for its own sake or to encourage a movement to American independence. His purpose was to reestablish the empire on a foundation that would last, for he had a profound emotional commitment to the idea of an "empire of commerce," dreading "that period when America shall be left to itself," and he had substantial material interests in America as well. But he believed the possibility of reconciliation was dwindling. Attempting to "form some line of reconciliation and reunion," he encountered stiffening

---

the representatives could only marvel, Cooper reported, that such splendid reasoning and force of expression apparently had so little effect in Parliament. Cooper to Pownall, July 2, 1770, "Letters of Samuel Cooper to Thomas Pownall, 1769–1777," *American Historical Review*, 8 (1902–03), 318. The speech (T. C. Hansard, *The Parliamentary History of England* . . . [London, 1806–1820], XVI, cols. 855–870) was reprinted in Boston as an untitled pamphlet (Evans, *Bibliography*, #42157), as was an earlier speech of his (*ibid.*, #11424: 1769).

21. Cooper to Pownall, July 2, 1770, "Cooper-Pownall Letters," p. 319 ("What chance have we," Cooper wrote, "if men disaffected to the country in general may accuse us and give a malevolent turn to every incident while we can neither know the authors nor the matter of the accusation?"); Bowdoin to Pownall, May 10, 1769, and Pownall to Bowdoin, July 21, 1770, *Bowdoin-Temple Papers*, pp. 139, 205. On one occasion the Cooper-Pownall association became notorious. A letter written by Pownall to Cooper was credited by Hutchinson with having turned the scale among the radicals in favor of continuing the nonimportation movement when the likelihood had been that it would be dropped. "Good God," Hutchinson had then exclaimed in an extremely confidential letter to Bernard (which Bernard promptly showed to John Pownall and which every politician in London, including the prime minister, soon knew about), "can the people of America ever return to a due subordination to Great Britain whilst members of the House of Commons there publicly and privately justify them in their revolt?" TH to FB, May 19, 1770, MA, XXVI, 485; FB to TH, June 20, 1770, Bernard Papers, VIII, 101.

resistance on both sides. "The great men here despise my advice," he wrote from London in June 1770; but at the same time he felt that the colonists were wrong in failing to keep the peace and were abusing the privileges they had been given. He was caught in an uncomfortable middle position, which no amount of proud insistence that he stood above party and only spoke for the general good could make attractive or effective. By 1772 he was a committed opponent of the North-Hillsborough administration, but at the same time he had been declared by Samuel Adams to be "a doubtful friend of the province"—a charge to which he replied with the enigmatic words, "Judge not of the tree by the coloring of the blossoms; wait the bearing time, and judge by the fruits."[22]

Pownall was not alone in the increasingly weak and difficult position of opposing, on the one hand, a crown policy that appeared to be robbing the colonies of its rights and privileges and, on the other, extremism in America that defied the duty to maintain law and order. Benjamin Franklin's sympathies were similarly divided. Coolly pragmatic in all things, identified, for all his international fame in science, philosophy, and letters, as an American, Franklin was never so happy as when he was circulating in the intellectual and social *haut monde* of England. Made wary by his near misfortune of having supported the Stamp Act in 1764, he was careful to keep in step with colonial opinion, as far as he could,[23] and as a result he was, like Pownall, distrusted by extremists of both sides. Arthur Lee, Franklin's second in the Massachusetts agency in London, denounced Franklin to Samuel Adams as a hireling of the British ministry, bought by the lure of office; at the same time Hillsborough refused even to see Franklin, being convinced, as was Hutchinson, that Franklin was stirring up sedition.[24]

But Franklin's ambivalence in the growing conflict, his disin-

22. Pownall to Committee of the Town of Boston, June 1770, *Bowdoin-Temple Papers*, p. 191; Pownall to Samuel Adams, April 10, 1772, in Griffin, *Junius Discovered*, p. 298; John A. Schutz, *Thomas Pownall, British Defender of American Liberty* (Glendale, Calif., Arthur H. Clark, 1951), pp. 226, 234.

23. Bernard reported confidently from London in 1769 that Franklin's "principle seems to be to have no fixed principles at all" for the very good reason that he knew that any position he staked out would soon be transcended by his constituents. FB to TH, Nov. 17, 1769, Bernard Papers, VIII, 21.

24. Arthur Lee to Samuel Adams, June 10, 1771 in Richard H. Lee, *Life of Arthur Lee, LL.D.* (Boston, 1829), I, 216–217. Franklin to William Franklin, Aug. 19, 1772, Smyth, ed., *Writings*, V, 413.

clination to take a final and decisive position, had a deeper source than any of his critics could see, and it was this that led him into the "letters" affair. Franklin was convinced that a conflict between Britain and America was unnecessary even if the ministry was quite as malevolent as the American radicals said it was. For the future lay with America, no matter what the ministry did. As a consequence of its natural and inevitable growth in tranquil circumstances, America's developing strength would eventually make its claims undeniable. The main objective of rational policy, therefore, was peace—the rest would take care of itself. His greatest hope, he wrote the speaker of the Massachusetts House in March 1773, was "that great care will be taken to keep our people quiet; since nothing is more wished for by our enemies than, by insurrections, we should give a good pretense for increasing the military among us and putting us under more severe restraints." Britain, he pointed out, was deeply in debt, and when another war came the financial situation would be desperate. *Then,* he wrote his American constituents, "then is the time to say, '*Redress our grievances.* You take money from us by force, and now you ask it of voluntary grant. You cannot have it both ways. If you choose to have it without our consent you must go on taking it that way, and be content with what little you can so obtain. If you would have our free gifts, desist from your compulsive methods, and acknowledge our rights and secure our future enjoyment of them.' Our claims will then be attended to and our complaints regarded." Cling fast, he urged the colonists, to every right, privilege, and just claim, but avoid violence; avoid open conflict of any kind; and cultivate harmony. Keep in mind not only the inevitable growth of America and its destined domination of the English-speaking world, but the condition of Europe and England's fate in a universe of warring nations. Remember, he urged, "that this Protestant country (our mother, though lately an unkind one) is worth preserving, and that her weight in the scale of Europe, and her safety in a great degree, may depend on our union with her."[25]

25. Franklin to Cushing, March 9 and July 7, 1773, Smyth, ed., *Writings*, VI, 22, 73–78 ("by our rapidly increasing strength we shall soon become of so much importance that none of our just claims of privilege will be, as heretofore, unattended to, nor any security we can wish for our rights be denied us"); Franklin to John Winthrop, July 25, 1773, *ibid.*, pp. 273–274 ("there seem to be among us some violent spirits who are

It was with this complex, imaginative, and indeed ambiguous attitude to the growing conflict—with a firm desire to avoid final commitments and to find some means of diverting and cooling the flow of passion that was running so high—that Franklin entered into the many discussions of Anglo-American affairs that took place in his, and Thomas Pownall's, circles in London in 1772. It was inevitable that Franklin and Pownall should come together in that year in some significant way, and not only because of their political sympathies. In 1772 both were much involved in promoting the Grand Ohio Company, that grandiose land speculation and settlement scheme so strongly opposed by Hillsborough, and both were active in the Royal Society, to which Pownall had just been elected. The two men met no doubt on many occasions, most often in gatherings of political reformers and American sympathizers. It was in all probability on one such occasion, in the summer or early fall of 1772—after Dartmouth had replaced Hillsborough in the colonial office and hence when the prospects of new approaches to the American problem were better than they had been for several years—that the conversation took an unusual turn. Someone— Pownall, probably; in any case "a gentleman of character and distinction" who was also a Member of Parliament—assured Franklin that his anger at the ministry for having sent troops to Boston was misplaced. For not only that unfortunate act but "all the other grievances we complained of . . . were projected, proposed to administration, solicited, and obtained by some of the most respectable among the Americans themselves as necessary measures for the welfare of that country." Franklin, according to his later statement, refused to believe such a thing; the gentleman therefore undertook to convince him and through him to convince other unsuspecting Americans and Britishers as well. And so a few days later he called on Franklin and produced, as evidence of what he had earlier argued, the letters that Hutchinson and Oliver had written in 1768

---

for an immediate rupture. But I trust the general prudence of our countrymen will see that by our growing strength we advance fast to a situation in which our claims must be allowed; that by a premature struggle we may be crippled and kept down another age; that as between friends every affront is not worth a duel, between nations every injury not worth a war, so between the governed and the governing every mistake in government, every encroachment on rights, is not worth a rebellion").

and 1769 and that had been gathered for the discussions with Hillsborough in 1770. The addressee's name had been erased from all the letters.[26]

Franklin was astonished to read the letters (at least he later said he was) and—so he said—he was instantly convinced of the truth of the gentleman's argument. He proposed now to convince his constituents of this truth as well. He felt, indeed, that he had no choice but to send the letters to Boston.

. . . it appeared . . . my duty to give my constituents intelligence of such importance to their affairs, but there was some difficulty, as the gentleman would not permit copies to be taken of the letters, and that if that could have been done the authenticity of those copies might have been doubted and disputed. My simple account of them as papers I had seen would have been still less certain; I therefore wished to have the use of the originals for that purpose, which I at length obtained, on these express conditions: that they should not be printed, that no copies should be taken of them, that they should be shown only to a few of the leading people of the government, and that they should be carefully returned.

Such were the terms on which Franklin obtained the letters.[27]

As he would repeat again and again in later months, his purpose in returning the letters to Boston was simply and solely to clear the ministry, and with them the English nation, of the blame that the colonists had wrongly heaped on them and to place the responsibility for all the trouble where it belonged, on the heads of the few "very mischievous men" who could now be seen to have "laid the foundations," in these letters, "of most if not all our present grievances." For "perhaps the only chance America has for obtaining *soon* the redress she aims at" lay in somehow, "by some painstaking and proper management," removing "the wrong impressions" of the colonies that the King and his ministers had received—impressions of a community in continuous turmoil, defiant of all law, order, and decency, and whose grievances and protests were not matters of general concern but the work of a few vicious demagogues. Somehow the opposite picture must be conveyed, the more

26. Franklin, "Tract," pp. 262–263, 287; for another version, Franklin to Joseph Galloway, Feb. 18, 1774, Smyth, ed., *Writings,* 195–196.
27. Franklin, "Tract," p. 263.

graphically and dramatically the better, and by that means a new departure in Anglo-American relations begun.[28]

As for the letter writers themselves when thus exposed, it is possible, Franklin said (in words which, since they could not have been meant ironically, must be either the most naive or the most cynical that Franklin ever uttered) they

> may not like such an exposal of their conduct, however tenderly and privately it may be managed. But if they are good men, or pretend to be such, and agree that *all good men wish a good understanding and harmony to subsist between the colonies and their mother country,* they ought the less to regret that, at the small expense of their reputation for sincerity and public spirit among their compatriots, *so desirable an event may in some degree be forwarded.*

In other words, the writers should rejoice if this exposure of their private correspondence ruined them since the greater good of Anglo-American reconciliation would thereby be effectively served. But in fact Franklin did not care if they did *not* see it this way, for he explained that he had little sympathy for such people as these. It might perhaps be the part of charity to excuse these letter writers as sincere but deluded—to concede that having been "educated in prepossessions of the unbounded authority of Parliament," they simply could not have known better than to have construed opposition to unconstitutional measures as sedition that must instantly be suppressed. But he confessed that he could not himself extend such charity to them; he could not believe that they really *were* sincere. For,

> when I find them bartering away the liberties of their native country for posts and negotiating for salaries and pensions extorted from the people,

28. *Ibid.,* pp. 282, 262; Franklin to William Franklin, July 14, 1773, Smyth, ed., *Writings,* VI, 98. Franklin's purpose in the "letters" affair and the underlying presumption of his thought are particularly well expressed in his ironic pseudo-Machiavellian piece, "Rules by Which a Great Empire May Be Reduced to a Small One," supposedly written for presentation to Hillsborough upon his accession to the ministry (1768), which Franklin published on Sept. 11, 1773. Rule XVI: ". . . Take all your informations of the state of the colonies from your governors and officers in enmity with them. Encourage and reward these *leasing-makers;* secrete their lying accusations lest they should be confuted, but act upon them as the clearest evidence; and believe nothing you hear from the friends of the people; suppose all *their* complaints to be invented and promoted by a few factious demagogues whom if you could catch and hang all would be quiet. Catch and hang a few of them accordingly, and the *blood of the martyrs* shall work miracles in favor of your purpose." Smyth, ed., *Writings,* VI, 135–136.

and, conscious of the odium these might be attended with, calling for troops to protect and secure the enjoyment of them; when I see them exciting jealousies in the crown and provoking it to wrath against so great a part of its most faithful subjects, creating enmities between the different countries of which the empire consists, occasioning a great expense to the *old* country for suppressing or preventing imaginary rebellions in the *new* and to the new country for the payment of needless gratifications to useless officers and enemies—I cannot but doubt their sincerity even in the political principles they profess, and deem them mere timeservers, seeking their own private emolument through any quantity of public mischief, betrayers of the interest not of their native country only but of the government they pretend to serve, and of the whole English empire.

Their ruin in any case was incidental. If the colonists could be convinced, as he had been, that the cause of all the troubles was nothing but the machinations of those squalid careerists—"those caitiffs," as he called them—who had written the letters, a unique opportunity would be put into the hands of the ministry of restoring the lost harmony with America. Exonerated, by this exposure, of all the charges that had been made against them, the ministers, no longer under any pressure of pride or loss of face, could proceed to punish the authors of these "misrepresentations and calumnies" and restore imperial relations to what they had been at the close of the Seven Years War. The guilty parties could charitably be "placed or pensioned elsewhere" and thus, "like the scape-goats of old . . . [carry] away into the wilderness all the offenses which have arisen between the two countries."[29]

iii

Such, Franklin said, were his expectations. But if in fact they were, he soon discovered that once again he had misjudged the passions that gripped the minds of men less rational, more committed, more ideological, than he.

The letters were sent off to the speaker of the Massachusetts House, Thomas Cushing, on December 2, 1772, with instructions not to allow them to be copied, and to show them only to the Com-

29. "Tract," pp. 266, 267, 276, 282–283.

mittee of Correspondence, to five specified individuals, and to "a few such other gentlemen as you may think fit to show them to." The package arrived in Boston at the end of March 1773, just as Hutchinson was concluding his debate with the two Houses of the Assembly on constitutional principles. The letters were shown around to the limited group Franklin had designated, and pressure immediately built up against the restrictions that had been imposed. Everyone agreed, Cushing wrote Franklin, that if the letters were to serve the purpose he had intended them to they must either be copied or retained for more general circulation. Would Franklin not release them? He could not say; he must consult the person from whom he had obtained them. On June 4 he replied: no copies and no publication of the letters would be permitted, but they might be kept as long as they proved useful, and be shown to anyone at all. The prohibition on publication, he explained, was not unreasonable, for if the letters were published all possessors of such correspondence would be on their guard and "so prevent the obtaining more of it"; and in any case, the limited circulation should do the main job, of "spread[ing] through the province so just an estimation of the writers as to strip them of all their deluded friends, and demolish effectually their interest and influence. The letters might be shown even to some of the governor's and lieutenant governor's partisans and spoken of to everybody, for there was no restraint proposed to talking of them but only to copying."[30]

But the pressure for publication could not be contained. For weeks the letters circulated widely. John Adams took them with him on the circuit of the superior court to show them to selected non-Bostonians. By the time the Assembly met on May 26 everyone was talking about the letters, and on June 2 Samuel Adams, "perceiv-[ing] the minds of the people to be greatly agitated with a prevail-

---

30. "Tract," pp. 266–267, 268–269, 270; Franklin to Cooper, July 7, 1773, in Jared Sparks, ed., *Works of Benjamin Franklin* . . . (Boston, 1836–1840), IV, 419n. Several years later Hutchinson obtained a copy of the letter to Cooper of July 7, 1773, and transcribed into his diary the passage quoted above justifying the prohibition on publishing Hutchinson's letters. But in the version that Hutchinson copied, the letter continues with sentences that do not appear in the later publications of Franklin's correspondence: "And possibly, as distant objects seen only through a mist appear larger, the same may happen from the mystery in this case. However this may be, the terms given with them could only be those with which they were received. There is still some chance of procuring more, and some still more abominable." *Diary and Letters*, II, 337–338.

ing report that letters of an extraordinary nature had been written and sent to England greatly to the prejudice of this province," had them read aloud to the House, though still with the increasingly meaningless restriction that they be neither printed nor copied. The House immediately voted, 101–5, that "the tendency and design of the letters . . . was to overthrow the constitution of this government and to introduce arbitrary power," and a committee was appointed to draw up detailed resolutions. By then the stories circulating of what the letters contained had grown so wild—so many people believed that "there is something in them treasonable against the state"—that even Andrew Oliver felt they should be published, and on June 3 the *Massachusetts Spy* further stimulated public excitement by declaring that the "amazing discoveries" recently made would reveal the infamy of certain well-known public figures, and would bring "many *dark* things to *light*—gain many proselytes to the cause of freedom—make tyrannical rulers tremble."[31] When on June 10 Samuel Adams reported that copies of the letters had been received from a source in England independent of the original one and were circulating in Boston, Cushing and the other original recipients decided that the restrictions on publication were frustrating the sender's original purpose.[32] On June 15 the signal was given to the printers, who must already have set the letters in type, to produce copies for members of the Assembly. At the same time the House committee submitted its report, which was overwhelmingly adopted the next day in the form of a set of resolves.

Even in the context of eighteenth-century polemics, these resolves are remarkable for their searing vituperation. Quickly establishing

31. Adams to David Hosack, Jan. 28, 1820, quoted in Franklin, *Works*, ed. Sparks, IV, 443 (Adams feared that the secrecy surrounding "the grand discovery of the complete evidence of the whole mystery of iniquity" would defeat "the friends of liberty" in the May 26th election, and favored disclosure for that reason particularly: Adams, *Diary and Autobiography*, II, 82); *Journal of the Honorable House of Representatives of . . . Massachusetts-Bay . . . Begun . . . the Twenty-sixth Day of May . . . 1773* [–June 29] (Boston, 1773), pp. 26, 27 (for Hutchinson's immediate replies to the accusations, see pp. 29, 40–41); Andrew Oliver to William Whately, June 1, 1773, Eg. MSS, 2670, p. 75; Arthur M. Schlesinger, *Prelude to Independence* (N.Y., Knopf, 1958), pp. 150–151.
32. *House Journal, May 26–June 29, 1773,* p. 44; Cooper to Franklin, June 14, 1773, Smyth, ed., *Writings*, VI, 58. Franklin declared immediately that it was impossible for copies of the letters to have come from an independent source in England. Such a claim he said was simply "an expedient to disengage the House" from the responsibility of having broken its pledge to him. Franklin to Cushing, July 25, 1773, *ibid.*, p. 109.

the authenticity of the letters and dismissing the defense of them that Hutchinson had issued, the House declared that Hutchinson's letters

had a natural and *efficacious* tendency to interrupt and alienate the affections of our most gracious sovereign King George the Third from this his loyal and affectionate province, to destroy that harmony and good will between Great Britain and this colony which every friend to either would wish to establish, to excite the resentment of the British administration against this province, to defeat the endeavors of our agents and friends to serve us by a fair representation of our state of grievances, to prevent our humble and repeated petitions from reaching the royal ear of our common sovereign, and *to produce the severe and destructive measures* which have been taken against this province, and others still more so, which have been threatened.

Furthermore, Hutchinson's and Oliver's letters, the House resolved, expressed their "desire and endeavor" to see Parliament's revenue acts put into effect "*by military force* and, by introducing a fleet and army into this His Majesty's loyal province, to intimidate the minds of his subjects here and . . . suppress the very spirit of freedom." The letter writers—"*a set of men born and educated among us*"— had formed a conspiratorial cabal "to raise their own fortunes and advance themselves to posts of honor and profit, not only to the destruction of the charter and constitution of this province but at the expense of the rights and liberties of the American colonies." They were "*justly chargeable* with the great corruption of morals and *all that confusion, misery, and bloodshed which have been the natural effects of the introduction of troops.*" Therefore, for these and lesser reasons that it enumerated, the House humbly prayed that His Majesty remove forever from the government of Massachusetts His Excellency, Thomas Hutchinson, governor, and the Honorable Andrew Oliver, lieutenant governor. A formal petition to the crown requesting the immediate dismissal of the two men, "justly obnoxious to your loving subjects," was passed at the same time. In London six weeks later Franklin, his "scape-goat" plan now come to fruition, submitted the petition to Lord Dartmouth with a covering letter assuring the minister that the colony had "a sincere disposition . . . to be on good terms with the mother country," for, "having lately discovered, as they think, the authors of their grievances to be some of their own people, their resentment against Britain is thence much abated."[33]

He was wrong. As he soon came to realize to his own great inconvenience, the "scape-goat" theory that the circulation of the letters would improve Anglo-American relations proved false in every respect but one, and that one was that the colonists would find the letters conclusive evidence of a conspiracy against American liberty; that they would assign the blame primarily to Hutchinson; and that they would vilify him and drive him into exile. As John Adams later recalled, for many people there was no surprise in the letters except "the miracle of their acquisition": long before there had been any such evidence as the letters, the leaders of the opposition had been convinced that the writers were guilty of "malignant representations" and that they had suggested to the ministry the "nefarious projects" that had been launched against America. Such was the readiness and susceptibility of many people's minds to such "proof" as the letters that the mere suggestion that such a revelation might be forthcoming made the New England countryside seethe with indignation. "Nothing," Cooper wrote Franklin on the eve of the publication of the letters,

could have been more seasonable than the arrival of these letters. They have had great effect; they make deep impressions wherever they are known; they strip the mask from the writers who, under the professions of friendship to their country, now plainly appear to have been endeavoring to build up themselves and their families upon its ruins. They and their adherents are shocked and dismayed; the confidence reposed in them by many is annihilated; and administration must soon see the necessity of putting the provincial power of the crown into other hands . . .[34]

Once the revelation became official and public, copies of the letters poured from the presses, and a sense of outrage swept through the provincial towns. The pamphlet containing the letters, together with varying amounts of accompanying documentation, went through ten printings on both sides of the Atlantic before a year was out. In Massachusetts the letters were serialized in the *Spy,* the

33. *House Journal,* [*May 26–June 29, 1773*], pp. 55–56, 58–61. The resolves are published also in Franklin, *Works,* ed. Sparks, IV, 426–429; the petition and Franklin's covering letter are on pp. 430–432. On the early release of the letters to the printers, see Adams, *Bibliographical Study,* #96a (p. 73).
34. Adams to Hosack, Jan. 28, 1820, in Franklin, *Works,* ed. Sparks, IV, 443; Cooper to Franklin, June 14, 1773, Smyth, ed., *Writings,* VI, 59.

Boston Gazette, the *Boston Evening-Post,* and the *Essex Gazette* with editorial comments likening the letters themselves to "footsteps *stained with blood"* and the writers to "vipers whose poison has already destroyed the health of your province and spilt the blood of your people." They were picked up and presented similarly by newspapers in almost every colony in America, and everywhere the opposition press, scrutinizing every word and every conceivable implication of every word, of Hutchinson's letters, boiled with anger and roared with outrage. Hutchinson, said "Lucius" (William Phillips, whose election to the Council Hutchinson had vetoed) in one of a dozen such tirades in the *Boston Gazette,* was "a shining example of the corrupt traffic of the times," a "pack horse of tyranny," a "political Pilate" vainly attempting to wash himself clean of the "guilt of parricide," a "skillful gambler" who had filled places of rank and profit with rascals snatched from the dunghill, the better "to abet the designs of a traitor."

You insist, *there must be an abridgment of what are called English liberties: you wish to see a further restraint of liberty in the colony.* For what reason, Sir! Because your misrepresentations would fail of their designed effect without the total ruin of the colony! Let me challenge you in the face of Heaven. . . . You have intended the colonies an irreparable mischief by inculcating that narrow and diabolical maxim, that *a colony distant from the parent state cannot possibly enjoy all the liberty of the parent state.* You refer probably to the colonies of Rome, the fruits of conquest; do not the circumstances of these colonies differ from those? . . . Those colonies were harassed by other Bernards and other Hutchinsons; they finally revolted; and after tearing the empire to pieces by intestine broils, *Rome,* the mistress of the universe, gave up the ghost, and bequeaths a wiser lesson to *Britain* than that of the sage *Mr. Hutchinson* quoted above.[35]

Hutchinson was burned in effigy in Philadelphia and Princeton, and compared in verse to Catiline, Caligula, and Nero. John Adams's outrage at this "vile serpent"—"bone of our bone, born and educated among us!"—spilled over into his "Novanglus" papers, which treat Hutchinson's letter of January 20, 1769, containing the fatal phrase, "there must be an abridgement of what are called English liberties," as so outrageous and so flagrant a revelation of

35. Schlesinger, *Prelude to Independence,* p. 152; *Boston Gazette,* June 21, 1773, and *Supplement to the Boston Gazette,* June 28, 1773.

"Machiavellian dissimulation" that it bore, Adams wrote, the "evident marks of *madness*. It was written in such a transport of passions, *ambition*, and *revenge* . . . that his reason was manifestly overpowered." Harbottle Dorr tore into his copy of the pamphlet with a frantic pen, scribbling curses all over the margins (*"traitor!" "a vile lie!" "oh, the villian!"*), interleaving the text with refutations, and directing the reader to the truth through an infinitely complex series of cross-references to other documents in his monumental collection. His index contains no les than thirty references under the entry "Hutchinson, Governor, his original traitorous letters," the last of them being: ". . . an insinuation, that he and [Lieutenant] Governor Oliver ought to have been immediately put to death on the receipt of their letters."[36] Lampooning ballads were written to "Tommy Skin and Bones," and Mercy Otis Warren rose to new heights of poetic passion. "Self-love," she wrote to John Adams,

> . . . that stimulus to noblest aims,
> Bids Nero light the capital in flames,
> Or bids H——— sell his native land
> And his vile brother lend his perjured hand
> While freedom weeps and heav'n delays to shed
> Its awful vengeance on the guilty head.

And in "The Defeat," selections from which were published in two installments in the *Boston Gazette,* she continued her theatrical jingle-jangle about Rapatio (Hutchinson), whom she had introduced in her *Adulateur* the year before as the bloodthirsty Bashaw of Servia triumphantly stamping out the last embers of freedom in his native land. Even Hutchinson's lifelong friend the Reverend Andrew Eliot began to doubt the governor's motives, and less well-informed New Englanders, stirred by remarks such as Franklin's that the letter writers were like "Judases ready to betray their country for a few paltry pieces of silver," swung over to the opposition.[37]

36. Clifford K. Shipton, *Sibley's Harvard Graduates*, VIII (Boston, MHS, 1951), p. 203; *Boston Gazette*, July 19, 26, Aug. 2, 9; Adams, *Diary and Autobiography*, II, 81, 119; *Works of John Adams*, ed. Charles F. Adams (Boston, 1850–1856), IV, 120. Dorr's copy of the pamphlet is bound into vol. IV of his newspaper collection, at pp. 1144–1181; his index references are on p. 24.

37. Mercy Warren to John Adams, *Warren-Adams Letters*, II (MHS *Colls.*, LXXIII, 1925), 403; *Boston Gazette*, May 24, July 19, 1773; Franklin to Samuel Mather, July 7, 1773, Smyth, ed., *Writings*, VI, 88.

It was widely felt that a turning point had been reached; that the revelation of the Whately letters, in manifesting what had previously only been feared, hinted at, suspected, and inferred, had elevated the controversy to a new level of explicit enmity, and an explosion seemed now to be a more likely outcome than it had before. The Reverend William Gordon had an accurate sense of the trends of events. He quickly decided that the Whately letters had entirely destroyed the province's confidence in Hutchinson, and he forthwith wrote to Lord Dartmouth suggesting a successor. Later, in his history of the Revolution, he put the event in a fuller context. Before the letters episode, Gordon wrote in his curious present-tense style, Hutchinson had been an unexceptionable if partisan leader: his judgments as chief justice had generally been fair, his appointments sensible, and his attachment to the colony and his opposition to the Stamp Act well publicized.

He [had] ingratiated himself by the free, familiar, and condescending intercourse with the common people, whom he would join, walk and converse with, in his way from the meeting to his seat [home]. On these accounts he had a number of friends and advocates who thought highly of him: but since the discovery of his letters they begin to own that they were deceived in the man and woefully mistaken in the good opinion they entertained of him. He will be execrated in America if not in Great Britain.[38]

By the end of June the execration was so torrential and so damaging politically that a formal effort had to be made to stem the flood. The task was undertaken by the attorney general and admiralty court judge, Jonathan Sewall, who as "Philanthrop" three years earlier had written to defend Bernard after his letters had been published. Now as "Philalethes," Sewall published in the course of the summer seven substantial essays which are the fullest defense of Hutchinson's letters that appeared in print. They are calm, careful, lawyer-like responses to the accusations; they seek to measure the value of each of the specific charges against Hutchinson by the actual clauses in question and then to assess the overall allegation, that "the design and tendency" of the letters were to subvert the

38. Gordon to Dartmouth, June 16, 1773, *Manuscripts of the Earl of Dartmouth*, II (Historical Manuscripts Commission, *Fourteenth Report*, Appendix, Part X, London, 1895), 156; Gordon, *History of the Rise, Progress, and Establishment of the Independence of the United States of America* . . . (N.Y., 1789), I, 357.

constitution. But they begin with an attack on the prejudicial editing of the letters by those who had prepared them for the printer. The title, Sewall pointed out, was a polemic in itself, and a peculiarly vicious one, not only because its design was to prejudice the reader against the letters but, more insidiously, because it led the reader to assume that Hutchinson himself had acknowledged that the entire group of letters "must *all* stand or fall together—than which nothing can be more directly opposite to the truth." What Hutchinson had written, Sewall explained, had nothing at all to do with what the others had written; their judgments and efforts formed no pattern with his; their sentiments could in no way be assumed to be shared by him. And beyond the editorial mischief of conflating all of the letters so that they appeared to be aspects of a single communication, the punctuation of the original letters had been altered to reinforce the editors' arguments and prejudices, and italics had been added that contributed substantially to the same overall falsification.[39]

All of this, however, was incidental to the main distortions, which lay in the twisted meanings that had been attributed to particular passages that were taken out of context. Hutchinson's purpose in writing the letters, Sewall explained, had only been to describe the situation as he had seen it in 1768 and 1769, and nothing else, and if they expressed a horror of civil disorder, a belief that an innocent people were being victimized by an ambitious party manipulating the mobs, there was nothing criminal, unconstitutional, or treasonable in that. When Hutchinson had quoted himself to Whately as telling the Council that its action *"must be resented in England,"* he had been expressing a prediction, a warning, and perhaps an expectation, not a desire. He had been similarly factual in the most famous passage of all (to which Sewall devoted most of his sixth essay), in which Hutchinson had written "there must be an abridgment of what are called English liberties." These sentences, which were being quoted all over America, Sewall pointed out, are essentially descriptive and predictive statements; they express an observation, not a possible innovation; facts not desires; expectations not hopes; regrets not joys. The understanding behind these remarks might be penetrating or dull, right or wrong, but it could only be a matter of amazement that anyone could rationally claim that they

39. *Massachusetts Gazette, and the Boston Weekly News-Letter,* June 24, July 1, 1773.

express a desire and plan to destroy the constitution and substitute a military dictatorship for a free British constitution. Read in context the letters in fact express just that warm attachment for his native land and that lifelong desire to see the colony stable, orderly, free, and prosperous that Sewall said he had found in Hutchinson all his life, and at no time more so than during the years in which he had served as chief justice, lieutenant governor, and governor. Let those who now accuse him, Sewall concluded, throw off party prejudice and testify to the great good that Hutchinson had done in public office.

Who is there that will not recognize the patient attention, the unremitted assiduity, and the penetrating perspicuity by which he searched out the matters which came before him, and adorned and rendered amiable the seat of justice? And I may ask, whose ox hath he taken? Or whom has he defrauded? Whom has he oppressed? Or of whose hands has he received any bribe to blind his eyes therewith? . . . Judge for ourselves—this is all I desire. The letters *we* have been considering are the only *pretended* evidence of his being, in his true character, the *reverse* of what *long experience* has taught us to believe—*we* must have been *fools,* or *he* must have been a *prodigy in nature* thus, and for such a length of time, and in such a variety of characters, to dupe and deceive us. . . . History will furnish us with innumerable instances of similar impositions and infatuations—instances of the best of men and patriots being sunk in the esteem of a people by the insidious wiles of a discontented party. . . . Peruse his letters without prejudice and with attention, and if you do not find every offensive passage pointed solely at riotous mobs and unlawful combinations tending inevitably, if persisted in, to your utter ruin—and if you do not, on the other hand, discover the most tender concern for your interests uniformly prevailing throughout the whole, a warm zeal to prevent those very evils which you have been made to believe him in part the author of, and an invariable disposition to preserve your constitution entire, just as you received it, against all internal or external violence—I say, if upon such a candid inquiry you do not find this to be the temper and tendency of all the governor's letters, I must be contented to wait till time, that sure discoverer of all truth, shall remove the films from your eyes and set in its true light the now oppressed character of your much injured patron, friend, and governor.[40]

Sewall's essays—eloquent, exhaustive, closely argued, and effectively documented—immediately brought down on him the same

40. *Ibid.,* Aug. 5, 12, 1773.

wild attacks that he was seeking to protect Hutchinson from. Mercy Otis Warren, in the second installment of "The Defeat," devoted some forty lines to savaging "Philalethes": "Long hackney'd in venality's low walks/ . . . a fit minion for the vilest deeds/ . . . Distorting truth to hide the leopard's spots/ . . . And rashly strive to wash an Ethiop white"; while advertisements appeared in the *Boston Gazette* for "WHITE-WASHING & BLANCHING GRATIS" by "PHILALETHES," offering "to make black, white, and the grossest falsehoods appear as truth . . . he will remove all spots and blemishes, and . . . *treason* against a country he can prove to be designs of benevolence."[41]

There were some, Hutchinson among them for a while, who believed that Sewall's efforts had turned the tide of public opinion. When Sewall's series was concluded, the Reverend Eli Forbes, an admirer of Hutchinson's in the town of Brookfield whom Hutchinson scarcely knew, wrote him a long letter so touching in its respect and admiration, so sincere in its desire "in some measure to alleviate the burden with which a spirit like yours must be oppressed," and so convinced that Sewall's "cool, judicious, and candid remarks" had "silenced the clamorous" and that reason had overcome passion and prejudice, that Hutchinson sent the letter to Lord Dartmouth, among whose papers this moving and idiosyncratic document from the heartland of provincial New England remains to this day.[42]

Yet there seemed in fact to be little reason for optimism. Samuel Cooper also exaggerated, but he was probably closer to the truth than Forbes when he wrote to Franklin that Sewall's essays "made but a feeble impression and, except among a few, rather provoked than pacified." "Philalethes" continued to be vilified, and Hutchin-

41. *Boston Gazette*, July 12, 1773.

42. All was peaceful in the small circle of his parish, Forbes wrote; "Your Excellency rises fast in the esteem and veneration of my good people." He begged the governor not to resign under the fierce pressure, promising him that the present madness would soon pass. "Human nature," he wrote, "is incident to partial madness," but it had restorative powers as well. The people's sanity would return, he assured Hutchinson, and with it their affection for their native governor. Forbes to TH, Sept. 26, 1773, Dartmouth Papers, Staffordshire County Record Office, Stafford, England. On Oct. 16 Hutchinson replied, suggesting that, since the wild resolves were so little substantiated by the letters themselves, the "faction" probably never intended to publish them, but had been forced to do so by the popular interest they themselves had stimulated, and concluding with a brief statement of his basic position, which was simply—he explained to Forbes—that he had always wished America to have every liberty that could consist with the single undeniable fact of political life, that "there must be one supreme legislature in every state." MA, XXVII, 556–557.

son's letters came under even more extended attack than they had before in a series of seven slashing articles written by Josiah Quincy, Jr., entitled "Nedham's Remembrancer" (after the seventeenth-century radical republican Marchamont Nedham) which appeared in the *Boston Gazette* weekly between December 20, 1773, and February 7, 1774. Quincy, who a decade earlier had been deeply moved by Hutchinson's plight after the destruction of his house and had served as defense lawyer for Captain Preston after the Massacre, raked over every innuendo of the "letters" affair, probing every phrase in the letters themselves and the defenses of them that had been made, and concluded as he had begun, with the conviction that Hutchinson is "the first, the most malignant and *insatiable* enemy of my country; that he is the chief author and supporter of the severest calamities under which this people labor; . . . that he has done more general mischiefs and committed greater public crimes than his *life* can repair or his *death* satisfy; and that *he is the man* against whom the blood of my slaughtered brethren cries from the ground." The same savagery was later rendered even more effective by John Adams, who in his "Novanglus" papers (January-April 1775) built the conclusions that Quincy, his friend and colleague at the bar, had reached concerning the conspiratorial intent of Hutchinson's letters into a sophisticated legal and constitutional argument, and so gave all these allegations a final respectability in the context of expert knowledge.[43]

Hutchinson himself was less shocked by the evident aim of the opposition to use the letters to discredit him and force his removal than by their easy and overwhelming success in doing so. He marveled at the "infinite art" they had used to ensnare him. "The first artifice and the foundation of all the fraudulent reports, insinuations, and resolves which followed," he later explained in the first, full draft of the account he wrote for his *History,*

was the collecting together the letters of persons none of whom had any knowledge of the correspondence of the rest, and making the whole correspondence a conspiracy, and the act of any one of the letter writers the act of the whole. Some of the letters speak with great freedom of the necessity of alteration in the constitution of Massachusetts Bay, others of vacating the charter of Rhode Island, others of sending troops to Boston;

43. Cooper to Franklin, Nov. 10, 1773, Franklin, *Works,* ed. Sparks, VIII, 99–100; *Boston Gazette,* Feb. 7, 1774; *Works,* IV, 119–120.

but there is not a word upon either of those subjects in any one of Mr. Hutchinson's letters.

He had known from the start that the opposition would attempt to use the Assembly as the main instrument of his condemnation, but he had been helpless to stop them. Since the letters were not only innocent but private, the Assembly should have had nothing to do with them, but "if I had put an end to the session the construction would have been that I was conscious of my guilt." And once in motion the avalanche could not be stopped no matter how false the allegations were, no matter how grotesque the overall picture, no matter how unjust the likely outcome.[44]

He scarcely knew how to describe the preposterousness of the charges placed against him, though he tried to make that clear by every means at his disposal—in an initial message to the House and in a stream of letters: to Dartmouth, Bernard, Jackson, Thomas Pownall, John Pownall, General Gage, Commodore Gambier, Colonel Dalrymple, at one point even to his former patron Lord Hillsborough, long since free of such broils as these. To all of these correspondents and in all of the various accounts of the letters he wrote, he said again and again that he could not possibly have been responsible, as charged, for summoning the troops since, first, he had had no executive authority when the letters were written; second, Whately, the addressee, had at the time been not in the ministry but in the active opposition; and third, the dates were wrong: the troop movement had already been under way when the letters had been written. But the worst falsehood had been the result of the vicious misconstruction that had been placed on his words "there must be an abridgment of English liberties." The distortion that had been made of that passage infuriated and profoundly saddened him; it would come to obsess him, and he would struggle for the rest of his life to explain it to others and to find some consolation himself for the misery it caused him. To the public he could reach, and to himself, he was far more eloquent than Sewall had been. In writing these words he had never meant to say that he hoped the freedom that existed in America would be restricted. "They might just as well," he wrote, "have charged David with

44. TH to FB, June 29, MA, XXVII, 502; Catherine Barton Mayo, ed., "Additions to Thomas Hutchinson's *History of Massachusetts-Bay*," AAS *Procs.*, n.s. 59 (1949), 62; TH to Dartmouth, June 26, 1773, MA, XXVII, 500.

having said, 'There is no God.' " He had meant only what he had often, publicly, said, that circumstances in fact had made such an abridgment inevitable—"must" in the predictive sense; that it was a fact of life that could not be otherwise, not that he *wished* it to be so. "It gave me great pain to think the colonies could not enjoy every liberty which the Kingdom could, but I did not see how it could be helped." This had been the substance of the speech he had given to the Assembly only the year before: then he had used almost precisely the same words ("it is impossible the rights of English subjects should be the same, in every respect, in all parts of the dominions") and no one had read treason into them. Englishmen had the right to share in the election of those who make the laws that govern them, he had then pointed out, as he had so many times before, but if they lived in the colonies that right could not be exercised, or if exercised would not have the same effect. Does it not follow from that fact that "by this their voluntary removal they have relinquished, for a time at least, one of the rights of English subjects which they might if they pleased have continued to enjoy and may again enjoy whenever they will return to the place where it can be exercised?" Except for those determined to distort his meaning, the issue could scarcely be clearer. "To a candid mind," he wrote in his *History,* the tragically distorted passage meant only this: " 'I am sorry the people cannot be gratified with the enjoyment of all that they call English liberties, but in their sense of them it is not possible for a colony at 3,000 miles distance from the parent state to enjoy them as they might do if they had not removed.' "[45]

But none of this—reiterated again and again by Hutchinson himself as well as by his friends and colleagues in the government —qualified in the slightest the willingness, apparently the eagerness, of the populace to impute to Hutchinson the most malign and sordid motives. Despite almost half a century of devoted public service during which "he had never been charged with a single arbitrary, tyrannical act," his enemies, by a long series of deceptions and frauds, had succeeded in fixing upon him, he wrote, "arbitrary and tyrannical principles in government which he detests and abhors." How could their success be explained? The accusations

45. TH to ——, Oct. 27, 1773, MA, XXVII, 565; Mayo, "Additions," p. 64; *History of Massachusetts-Bay,* III, 294n.

were outrageous: falsehoods "more completely . . . cooked up, without any support except from assertions altogether arbitrary and [from] forced and unnatural constructions, [are] nowhere to be met with." And yet they had succeeded. Why? How? He thought he had an explanation of the *leaders'* intensified hatred of him. In the course of his governorship he believed he had fought the leaders to a standstill, and furthermore he had enraged them in the debates of the previous January and February by convincing "the sensible part of the province" of the folly of their arguments; therefore "to revenge themselves upon me" they had invented "a conspiracy of persons of the first character, with others, to overthrow the constitution." But still, this did not explain the willingness of the people in general to be duped, their eagerness to find him guilty as charged. No doubt carefully planted and cultivated rumors had prepared people's minds to receive anything: "if they had brought [the song] 'Chevy Chase' into the House and proved it had been sent to England by the governor, they would have found some latent treasonable meaning against the constitution, and a vote would have passed accordingly"; but that predisposition did not explain the public reception of his letters to Hutchinson. Nor did his despondent observation that "bodies of men collectively are capable of acts which no one of them would do separately," for he knew that so glaring an instance of injustice, so baseless and fatal an accusation, had seldom appeared in the entire course of history. No fact, or concept, or instinct he could command could explain to him that he was disposed by the shape of his career, the temper of his mind, the nature of his political sensibilities to fall victim to the passions of the age. All he knew was that somehow, in some way he did not understand, he had misjudged the people, misconceived the capacity of the moderate, sensible, middle stratum of the population to arrive at moderate, prudent judgments.[46]

What, in the end, could he say? To the faithful Israel Williams he wrote late in July that, quite aside from the condemnation due the leaders of this conspiracy, "it will be a reproach upon the body of the people to the latest posterity that they have suffered themselves to be made such dupes." Yet the deception could not last: it

46. "Account and Defense of Conduct" [1775] (MS in Chapin Library, Williams College), p. 16; "Additions," p. 64; TH to James Gambier, Aug. 2, 1773, MA, XXVII, 526–527; TH to Richard Jackson, Aug. 12, 1773, *ibid.*, p. 527; TH to Rev. —— Lyman, July 16, 1773, *ibid.*, p. 514.

would not last "longer than it did in the time of the witchcraft. Truth, at worst, will finally prevail. . . . In so plain a case, if but a few persons only remain undeceived, a free, open testimony against the delusion will soon undeceive the rest. . . . I have no great doubt that sooner or later this proceeding will reflect more infamy upon all concerned in it than any public transaction since the country was settled, for it was founded upon such baseness as no civilized people have ever countenanced and has been conducted through every part of its progress with falsehood and deception which, although for a short time they have their intended effect, yet as soon as they are discovered, prove ignominious to the authors of them." Long ago his father had warned him of such a reward for a lifetime of public service as he had now received. When he had first considered accepting a public office, Hutchinson told Williams, he had asked his father for advice. " 'My son,' says he, 'if you can be content with country pay, accept—otherwise not.' I desired him to explain himself. 'Depend upon it,' says he, 'if you serve your country faithfully you will be reproached and reviled for doing it.' "[47]

It was clear he had come to the end. Whatever had remained of his original hope, that as a native governor of liberal views with decades of experience in provincial politics he might bring peace to the tumultuous colony, had now vanished, and his thoughts turned to escape and to the rescue of his honor and of the £500–£600 per year that was needed to sustain it. Before the end of June he had written to Lord Dartmouth requesting an honorable and swift acquittal by the King's government of all the charges that had been placed against him. He hoped it would come automatically and without trouble, but if he had to petition for it personally in England he would do so: "I had rather even make a voyage to England at my advanced time of life than [that] my reputation and character should suffer." He requested leave for six or nine months, either for that reason or for more personal reasons, presumably a need for rest, diversion, and recuperation, and then he wrote once again to Dartmouth defending himself against the Assembly's charges and begging His Lordship to certify to the colony, on the basis of the letters on file in the secretary of state's office, that he

47. TH to Williams, July 20, 1773, MA, XXVII, 516; TH to Williams, Oct. 30, 1773, Williams Papers, MHS.

had never, at any time, suggested to the ministry that the constitution of Massachusetts be changed in the slightest degree, nor "endeavored that [the colonists] should be deprived of any of their privileges, nor exaggerated any of their irregularities."[48]

His official exoneration came quickly enough, and more dramatically than he could have expected. Though the extreme radicals in London may have echoed Arthur Lee's wild denunciation of Hutchinson when the letters were published there,[49] opinion in governmental circles ran in the opposite direction. By the end of October, when the contents of the House Resolutions were known in London, Hutchinson had received a letter from Dartmouth "more favorable to me than I could venture to hope for," and he had seen a letter that Franklin had written to Cushing explaining that "the great men about the court . . . were all of opinion the letters were not sufficient foundation for the Resolves, and that it was not likely Mr. Hutchinson would be removed, but that he had desired leave to come to England and would be at liberty to resign and would be provided for in England." Franklin's central role in the "letters" affair was not yet publicly known, and London was buzzing with speculation about the identity of the transmitter of the letters, when Hutchinson, in a mild counter-attack, sent back to Lord Dartmouth a copy of the letter that Franklin had written to Cushing on July 7 outlining the ideas of growing American strength and present British weakness that underlay his "scape-goat" strategy, and recommending the convening of a colonial congress in which the colonies would state their common grievances and beliefs. This was proof, Hutchinson wrote, that Franklin was working to "bring the dispute *to a crisis*" and to eliminate whatever hope for reconciliation there might still be.[50]

48. TH to Dartmouth, June 26, 1773, MA, XXVII, 500–501; TH to Dartmouth, July 2, 1773, CO5/762/352–353. His official request to the ministry, Hutchinson was always careful to point out, was for permission to take a short leave of absence, not to resign. When later he resigned it was to "acquiesce in the King's pleasure, depending upon the assurances given me that I should be no sufferer by the discontinuance of the King's commission." TH to ——, July 1776, *Diary and Letters*, II, 80.

49. Lee, *Arthur Lee*, I, 232ff.; *Boston Gazette*, Sept. 27, 1773. He would not have been surprised, "Junius Americanus" wrote, if "the just indignation of the people had put the authors of [the letters] to instant DEATH."

50. TH to Williams, Oct. 1773, Williams Papers; TH to Dartmouth, Oct. 19, 1773, MA, XXVII, 558; TH to John Pownall, Oct. 18, 1773 (not sent), *ibid.*, p. 557. A year later Dartmouth asked Gage to get the original or a certified copy of Franklin's letter, and to search for others like it as evidence to support possible indictments for treason. The

But the ministry did not need such evidence as this to be convinced that Franklin was stirring up discontent. By December 25, when the duel between William Whately and John Temple led Franklin to publish an account of his role in the "letters" affairs, his official respectability had been substantially undermined, and the disastrous failure of his "scape-goat" strategy had become fully evident. By the time, a month later (January 29, 1774), the Privy Council held its official hearing on the petition of the Massachusetts House requesting the removal of Hutchinson and Oliver, Franklin had become the subject of official displeasure. The ferocious tongue-lashing that Franklin received that day from Solicitor General Wedderburn as he stood silent and impassive before the Lords of the Privy Council and the brilliant crowd of witnesses was only a rhetorical exaggeration of the conclusion the government had already reached. Hutchinson, Wedderburn declared to this extraordinary gathering of notables, was an honorable, able, conscientious public servant; a man of tried integrity whose actions during four years in the governorship had never been faulted; an experienced jurist whose wisdom was widely acknowledged; a distinguished scholar of his province's history and of its constitution; and he had now fallen victim to a conspiracy set on foot by thieves of his private and personal correspondence who were determined to bring about his ruin. And why? Because, Wedderburn said, by his successful challenge to the Assembly a year earlier, he had "stopped the train which Dr. Franklin's constituents had laid to blow up the province into a flame, which from thence was to have spread over the other provinces. This was the real provocation, and for this they have been seeking for some ground of accusation against him." It was Franklin (standing motionless before him in the dress suit of Manchester velvet that he would wear once again when he signed the treaties with France)—it was Franklin who was the criminal. It was he, not Hutchinson, who should be dismissed from office and denied the favor of the crown. Not even a properly accredited colonial agent, he was apparently, Wedderburn declared, "so pos-

letter, in an abbreviated and much doctored form, had been published by the radicals in the *Boston Gazette*, Sept. 27, 1773. Verner Crane, ed., *Benjamin Franklin's Letters to the Press, 1758–1775* (Chapel Hill, University of North Carolina Press, 1950), pp. 229–231. For Franklin's calm response to Hutchinson's effort at a reverse disclosure, see his letters to William Franklin and Thomas Cushing, Oct. 6, 1773, and Jan. 5, 1774, in Smyth, ed., *Writings*, VI, 144, 173.

sessed with the idea of a Great American Republic that he may easily slide into the language of the minister of a foreign independent state." His counsel to his constituents had been seditious, his purposes malign, his methods ruthless; and the petition he had brought to the Lords Committee of His Majesty's Privy Council was unworthy of that body's serious consideration.

And so it was concluded. The Privy Council reported to the King

their astonishment that a charge of so serious and extensive a nature . . . should have no other evidence to support it but inflammatory and precipitate resolutions founded only on certain letters written . . . before [Hutchinson and Oliver] were appointed to the posts they now hold . . . to a gentlemen then in no office under the government, in the course of familiar correspondence and in the confidence of private friendship . . . which letters appear to us to contain nothing reprehensible or unworthy of the situation they were in . . . the said petition is founded upon resolutions formed upon false and erroneous allegations . . . groundless, vexatious, and scandalous, and calculated only for the seditious purpose of keeping up a spirit of clamor and discontent . . . nothing has been laid before [the Privy Council] which does or can . . . in any manner or in any degree impeach the honor, integrity, or conduct of the said governor or lieutenant governor, and their lordships are humbly of opinion that the said petition ought to be dismissed.[51]

Everyone, it seemed, had lost. Franklin was immediately dismissed from his post of deputy postmaster general of the American colonies; and while his status as an American patriot and quasi-republican hero had been suddenly and sensationally elevated, his strategy for reconciliation, which had been the cause of the entire furor, lay about him in ruins. If the ministry had really been interested in reconciliation, as they professed to be, Franklin wrote Galloway soon after the Privy Council hearing, they should have thanked him for the opportunity he had given them; "but they chose rather to abuse me."

You can have no conception [Franklin wrote Cooper] of the rage the ministerial people have been in with me on account of my transmitting

51. Wedderburn's speech and the Privy Council's report are reproduced in [Israel Mauduit], *Proceedings of His Majesty's Privy Council, upon an Address of the Assembly of Massachusetts Bay, To Remove Governor Hutchinson and Lieutenant Governor Oliver* . . . [1774], in *A Collection of Scarce and Interesting Tracts* . . . (London, 1787–1788), IV, 229–263. For a detailed account of the scene in the cockpit, see Carl Van Doren, *Benjamin Franklin* (New York, 1938), pp. 467–475.

those letters. It is quite incomprehensible. If they had been wise, they might have made a good use of the discovery by agreeing to lay the blame of our differences on those from whom, by those letters, it appeared to have arisen, and by a change of measures, which would have then appeared natural, and restored the harmony between the two countries.

Even Lord Dartmouth, from whom Franklin had expected so much, personally agreed with the Privy Council's conclusion, and condemned Franklin for his involvement in the whole affair. And in addition to all of this, Franklin was faced with a chancery suit brought by William Whately to ascertain the means by which Franklin had obtained the letters, to extract from him an accounting of the number of copies printed and the profits made from them, and to recover the letters as his property. The Philadelphian, after responding laconically to Whately's interrogatories, proposed to reply to Wedderburn's attack, and then "give this court my farewell."[52]

Hutchinson, on the other hand, looked forward to an arrival, not a departure. But it was long delayed. It was not until April 1774 that he heard of his dramatic vindication by the Privy Council, for which he humbly thanked Wedderburn and Dartmouth.[53] He had hoped long since to have been in England, but the delays had been endless. It must have seemed, indeed, that he would never be released from duties that became ever more burdensome and hopeless. Three times in the year that intervened between his request for leave and his final departure for England in June 1774 he felt his duty done, his freedom earned, his path to repose opening before him. But each time something intervened and he felt obliged to

52. Franklin to Galloway and Cooper, Feb. 18 and 25, 1774, Smyth, ed., *Writings*, VI, 196, 204; Dartmouth to Joseph Reed, [ca. June 1774], *Manuscripts of the Earl of Dartmouth*, I (Historical Manuscripts Commission, *Eleventh Report*, Appendix, Part V, London, 1887), 355. On Franklin's "Tract Relative to the Affair of Hutchinson's Letters," written as a general explanation of his role in the affair but not published until after his death, see Crane, *Franklin's Letters to the Press*, pp. 253–254. A year later Hutchinson wrote that Franklin had left England (March 1775) just in time, as his answers to William Whately's interrogatories were deemed insufficient and he would have been faced with arrest. TH to Jonathan Sewall, April 9, 1775, Eg. MSS, 2661, p. 137.

53. Not only, TH wrote on April 23, had Wedderburn rescued his and Oliver's reputations, but he had also done "a great deal towards saving a whole province from ruin, for truth enforced with so much eloquence must prevail with many, notwithstanding the prejudices they have been under by the wicked arts of their pretended friends." Eg. MSS, 2661, pp. 22, 23.

postpone his trip and to struggle on with the forces he knew he would never defeat.

At first it was his self-respect, his honor and reputation, that created the restraint. He could not afford to have the disruptive forces of the opposition that he had sought so long to contain "triumph in my resignation, until there should be an honorable acquittal." Nor was a quick withdrawal prudent in a practical sense: he needed help, he knew, to regain those lesser posts, with their salaries, perquisites, and fees, that he had given up when, as he reminded his former patron Hillsborough in a letter of appeal, "by Your Lordship's favor I was advanced to the government." If he gave in to his instinct and desire to resign and retire precipitously into private life he would sacrifice not only his self-respect but the official favor he was still counting on for part of his own security and for the future prospects of his family. So he waited—for official leave, for the rescue of his honor, for the restoration of the patronage that would keep him from being "wholly without employment and support in advanced life" and from having to "sink below the moderate living I had always been used to before I came to the chair." And as he waited anxiously for word of his deliverance through the summer and fall of 1773 rumors of all sorts reached him—that Thomas Pownall had been created a baronet and reappointed governor of Massachusetts, that Lord Dartmouth would resign over the question of removing Hutchinson from the governorship, that a "grand reconciler" would be sent to America to work out a settlement—and he eased his mind in long reports to Lord Dartmouth stressing the conspiratorial roots of all the disturbances, their origins in the ability of a few designing men to manipulate the fears of an innocent people, and in a stream of bitter letters to friends and allies denouncing "such baseness as no civilized people ever countenanced"—denouncing the falsehood, deception, and unprecedented villainy he had had to endure.[54]

His recall—"at his own request"—had in fact been granted, on August 12, and the notification had been dispatched five days later. Had it arrived in the normal time, he would have boarded one of the two men-of-war then riding at anchor in Boston harbor, for

54. TH to FB, June 29, 1773, MA, XXVII, 503; TH to Hillsborough, n.d. [June 1773], *ibid.*, p. 506; TH to Dartmouth, Oct. 9, 1773, *ibid.*, pp. 549–551. Hutchinson's letterbook includes copies or drafts of no fewer than eleven letters to Dartmouth during October, eight of them personal or "secret," or "separate" from the official correspondence.

"the state of the province was such," he wrote after the disastrous results of the delay had become clear, "that I might well enough have justified by leaving." But the notice was three months at sea: it did not reach Boston until November 14, and by that time not only had all ocean-going vessels left Boston except those "so small that I should have been afraid of the fatigue of a winter's passage, being constantly sea-sick," but, more important, he had once again become embroiled in a major crisis—the third major crisis he had had to face that year—"and I should have feared the King's displeasure if I had left my government."[55]

iv

The origin of the tea crisis, which was clearly building up in November 1773, was in no way Hutchinson's devising. It developed from conjunctions of forces far above him, in spheres he did not know. But the tea trade itself he knew as well as any man in America. He knew its management, legal and illegal; he knew its risks and profits; and he knew enough of its political dangers to have opposed the tea duty in the first place and to have pleaded repeatedly for its repeal.[56] He knew enough too of the political sensitivity of that trade to have hidden in deepest secrecy his personal involvement in the actual merchandising of tea; while he handed over much of that business to his sons, he continued to be personally involved in the fortunes of the trade. Most of his liquid capital—nearly £4000—was invested in East India Company stock, and in addition his crown salary of £1500 sterling per annum was drawn from the income of the tea duty in America. In addition to all of this, two of his sons, and relatives of theirs, the Clarkes, had become—though not, he swore, at his solicitation—principal consignees of the East India Company's new monopoly of American sales. Nor could he evade the responsibility for handling the approaching crisis: he knew the burden was his from the start, and he faced up to it boldly. Putting his leave aside and refusing to join the tea consignees in their flight to the safety of the harbor

55. *Dartmouth Manuscripts*, I, 338; TH to ——, Jan. 24 1774, *Diary and Letters*, I, 107–108; TH to Dartmouth, Nov. 15, 1773.

56. TH to Thomas Whately, Oct. 3, 1770, MA, XXVII, 12; "Account and Defense of Conduct," p. 9.

fort as the threat of physical violence mounted, he considered the situation carefully, blocked out the lines of action he thought best, and braced himself to stand his ground.[57]

The position he took in November and December was correct, honorable, courageous, and fatal. Later he would come to believe that the radicals had deliberately created the crisis, intending from the first to force him to defy the tea duty or take the responsibility for the destruction of the cargoes. For he would later record that he had advised the tea consignees (his sons included) not to permit the vessels bearing the Company's tea to enter the harbor knowing that once there they would not be able to leave again until the duty had been paid. The radicals—so it would later seem to him—had forced the owner and captain of the main tea ship, the *Dartmouth,* by threat of violence, to enter the harbor and register the cargo, thus leaving it to Hutchinson to choose between, on the one hand, issuing an illegal exit permit, which would in effect make him an agent of the radicals, and on the other, suffering violence to take place yet again within his jurisdiction.[58] In fact, the immediate crisis was as much Hutchinson's devising as it was the opposition's. For after the deep frustration of his confrontation with the Assembly in the early months of the year, and after the fearful trauma of the disclosure of his letters that had made the summer months the most agonizing he had known, he seems to have welcomed the black-and-white simplicity of the issues in the tea controversy, and he knew that for once he could fight from a position of strength. The law was unambiguous, and the British navy was there to support him.

Whatever the legal niceties of what constituted a legal "entry" of a vessel, and however complicated Hutchinson's later memory of the precise sequence of events might have been, it was an undeniable fact that Joseph Rotch's *Dartmouth,* bearing 114 casks of tea, entered Boston harbor on November 28, rode at anchor on November 29 while customs officers boarded her and while the Boston leaders demanded that the consignees order the vessel to return to England (which they knew was illegal), and on November

57. TH to ——, April 25, 1774, Eg. MSS, 2661, p. 24; Benjamin W. Labaree, *Boston Tea Party* (New York, Oxford University Press, 1964), pp. 76, 104; Andrew Oliver to John Pownall, Dec. 11, 1773, CO5/763/19; TH to Dartmouth, Dec. 2, 1773, MA, XXVII, 577–578.

58. "Account and Defense of Conduct," p. 17.

30 the vessel was formally entered in customs and docked at Griffin's wharf. There, all its cargo but the tea was unloaded and a militia guard, under John Hancock, began to patrol it to prevent the tea from being unloaded surreptitiously.[59]

The opposition knew, and Hutchinson knew, that the *Dartmouth* (later joined by the *Eleanor* and the *Beaver*, both similarly loaded) could not legally leave the harbor without a customs clearance, and that duties on taxable goods must be paid within twenty days of the date of arrival or the goods would be subject to confiscation. The twenty days would be over on December 17. With the harbor blocked by British naval vessels, Hutchinson would enforce this altogether unambiguous law despite the wild mobs that were menacing the town, and despite the Boston mass meetings' rising crescendo of demands, threats, denunciations, and personal vilification. ("He? He?" Samuel Adams had cried in a speech on November 30 defying the governor's proclamation ordering the mass meeting to disperse; "Is he that shadow of a man, scarce able to support his withered carcass or his hoary head! Is he a *representation* of *Majesty?*") It would be, Hutchinson felt, a final test, in a situation in which, for once, he had effective force on his side. For two years, he told himself, no one had objected to the tea tax (though he himself, characteristically, had warned of its dangers), and if now the radicals, supported no doubt by smugglers fearful of new competition from the East India Company, deliberately chose to elevate the issue into one of constitutional principle in the hope of keeping up the flagging resistance of the populace to Parliament's legal authority, he would face them down. "Surely, My Lord," he wrote Dartmouth on December 14, "it is time this anarchy was restrained and corrected by some authority or other." The issue was absolutely clear—uncomplicated even by possible action elsewhere in the colonies since all the other tea consignees had resigned their commissions. There was no room for equivocation, compromise, or even discussion, and he attempted none in the late afternoon of December 16 when the harassed owner of the *Dartmouth*, trapped between the mass meeting and the mobs on the one hand and Hutchinson and harbor guns on the other, rode out to the governor's house in Milton to make a final plea to Hutchinson to relent and let the vessel leave the harbor with the tea un-

59. Labaree, *Tea Party*, pp. 126–132.

loaded and without a customs clearance. It was hardly with a sense of a decision being made, still less of setting in motion an irreversible chain of events whose end would be war and revolution, that Hutchinson—confident, exultant, that now at last the law would be enforced no matter what efforts might be made to defy it, and that Parliament's legitimate authority would finally prevail—refused the request. Three hours later the tea in the vessels—340 chests, worth about £9000—was thrown into the harbor.[60]

Hutchinson was stunned by this sacrifice of property and by the utter ruthlessness of the radical leaders. It seemed so unreasonable to him that men of property should prefer to pay for the destroyed tea (as he at once assumed they would do) rather than pay the far cheaper duty on the tea. But for himself, he said at the time, he had had no choice. The only alternative to refusing the permit would have been to concede "to a lawless and highly criminal assembly," and thus flagrantly to encourage violation of the law. He had fulfilled his oath of office and maintained the law and if the immediate result was less, rather than more, law and order in the province, at least the determination of the opposition to precipitate a rupture between England and America had once and for all been revealed, and with it the necessity for England to act.[61]

Yet, in the aftermath of the event it developed that there *were* ambiguities. He had to recognize that he had been involved, however blamelessly, in the destruction of a great deal of property for the protection of which he had had as much responsibility as he had had for the enforcement of the revenue laws. Having implemented the law in one sphere, he had shared, in an indirect way, in violating it in another—or so, at least, it might be said. Indeed, some of his more severe critics felt that it would have been so easy for him to protect the Company's property and still maintain his own principles that his failure to do so could only be explained by a secret hope on his part that he would be handsomely rewarded "for being persecuted for righteousness' sake." There was no other explanation, James Bowdoin wrote, for his refusal to let the ships return to England. For when Hutchinson and the tea consignees "saw a determination in the people that the tea should not be

60. L. F. S. Upton, "Proceedings of Ye Body Respecting the Tea," *W.M.Q.*, 3d ser., 22 (1965), 293; TH to Dartmouth, Dec. 14, 1773, MA, XXVII, 588; Labaree, *Tea Party*, pp. 125, 141; MHS *Procs.*, 13 (1873–1875), 169ff.
61. TH to Israel Mauduit, Dec. 1773, MA, XXVII, 606.

landed and that it was impossible for them to execute their commission, they might have made a virtue of necessity and declared
they would have nothing to do with the tea any further than to
send it back to the India Company." But Hutchinson had not seen
it that way: his duty to enforce the revenue acts rather than to concede to the pressure of a lawless mass meeting had been clear. Still,
he was troubled. He hoped such criticism would not carry weight
with the ministry, and, anticipating that possibility, he explained
in great detail to Lord Dartmouth exactly what had happened, what
his role had been, and why he had acted as he did. Yet his apprehensions remained, and rose significantly when he received word
that the tea ships sent to New York and Philadelphia had been
returned to England with their tea cargoes intact. Should he not
have conceded to that degree? Had he been too rigid, too severe?
"Upon reflection," he wrote Lord Dartmouth on January 4, "I am
not sensible that I have shown any greater marks of disapprobation
of the proceedings here than my duty to the King and the support
of the honor of the government required from me, nor do I know
of anything omitted which has been in my power and would have
consisted with my duty to His Majesty to have prevented the destruction of the teas." He was relieved to hear in mid-January that
at least in South Carolina tea had been successfully landed; but he
continued to send home documents that would justify his conduct,
and he began to consider ways of arranging for some group, public
or private, to pay for the destroyed tea. If in the end the tea was
paid for, the wisdom of his decision would surely be clear. Only
later, in London, would he discover that others criticized him, not
for having been too rigid and taking too many risks in enforcing the
law, but for having been too lenient: they felt, as had Colonel Leslie
in Boston at the time, that he should simply have sent in the troops
to seize the tea and hold it until the situation cleared. But this he
had never considered doing.[62]

Slowly the tumult died down and the pressure in Boston eased.
Once again Hutchinson's thoughts turned to relief, an honorable

62. Bowdoin to John Temple, Dec. 13, 1773, *Bowdoin-Temple Papers*, p. 328; TH to
Dartmouth, Jan. 4, 6, 1774, and to William Tryon, Jan. 15, 1774, Eg. MSS, 2661, pp. 6–7;
TH to ——, July 20, 1774, *Diary and Letters*, I, 190; Lt. Col. Alexander Leslie to
Viscount Barrington, Dec. 16, 1773, Gage Papers, microfilm in MHS; TH to Thomas
Flucker, July 25, 1774, Eg. MSS, 2661, p. 38.

escape, and the restoration of his family's fortunes. True, in January he was obliged to send discouraging reports back to Lord Dartmouth: that John Malcom, a customs officer notorious for his temper and erratic zeal, had been tarred and feathered by an uncontrollable mob, then beaten with clubs and rope until he agreed to curse the governor as an enemy to his country, and finally carted half naked through the snow for four hours before being released, so frozen he "rolled out of the cart like a log," the flesh hanging off his back "in steaks"; that other mobs had menaced the town at the mere rumor that Richardson, the customs officer who had shot the Snider boy in 1770, was back in town; and that the tea consignees were still in Castle William, fearful of their safety if they set foot in Boston. "There is no spirit left in those who used to be friends of government," Hutchinson wrote, or in any others who oppose "the prevailing power." Still, the tea riots were over, and the chronic disorder was nothing his presence was likely to remedy. So he resumed preparations for his long-postponed departure. He took precautions to secure his extensive correspondence from prying eyes. At some point during the tea riots he had his voluminous letterbooks taken from Boston and hidden in a place in the attic of his house in Milton "where I thought no persons would look for them." And plans for the future were made with his children.[63]

His close-knit, affectionate family would have to be broken up, temporarily. His own voyage to England, he explained carefully to Elisha (who with his wife had twice been driven out of Plymouth by an angry mob), was being undertaken for their sakes only. If he had no children he would not attempt such a voyage at the age of sixty-two; he would simply retire and try to get along by gradually consuming such property as he had accumulated; but he hoped to leave that property to them, and so he was seeking a provision for himself in England that would keep their inheritance intact. Elisha and Thomas, Jr., should stay behind, both because "the appearance of going away and carrying so great a part of my family may be a disadvantage to me here and in England" and because their leaving might be politically and financially imprudent for them. If, for

63. Frank W. C. Hersey, "Tar and Feathers: The Adventures of Captain John Malcom," *Publications of the Colonial Society of Massachusetts*, XXXIV (*Transactions*, 1937–1942), 429–473, especially pp. 441, 447, 445, 451; TH to Dartmouth, Jan. 8, 1774, Gage Papers; *Diary and Letters*, I, 502.

example, Tommy, as a tea consignee, were in England when public hearings were held on the background of the destruction of the tea, he might find himself forced, in explaining his conduct, to make enemies among his countrymen who would harass him forever after. And he explained to Elisha that he could see no business advantage for them at all in the voyage, the cost of which he estimated at between £200 and £300; nor was he being partial in denying Elisha the trip abroad which Tommy had had eight years earlier and which the feckless Billy was still enjoying; the patrimony would be equally divided in all respects. The most difficult problem was the twenty-one-year-old Peggy, his favorite child, the namesake and surrogate of his wife, whose memory continued to be vivid and fresh to Hutchinson. He was worried about her health. She was frail, and he opposed her joining him, fearing that on the long voyage and in England's damp climate she might develop consumption. But, as she explained to her sister-in-law, she had been "running from a mob ever since the year '65"; she and her father had argued about the wisdom of her traveling, "but you know, the women always gain their point." So on February 2 Hutchinson sent word to the governor of New York to reserve berths for himself, his daughter, and two servants on one of the large comfortable vessels he understood were about to leave that port for England.[64]

Yet, though he continued to plan for his departure, he was forced to admit that the situation was worsening again in February. The new Assembly, which had convened on January 26, had resumed with a new intensity the question of the judges' crown salaries. Now it focused its attention on the stubborn, outspoken, and indiscreet chief justice, Peter Oliver, Hutchinson's kinsman and the younger brother of the lieutenant governor, Andrew Oliver. The chief justice, who had been a member of the high court for eighteen years and its presiding officer for two, alone among the members of the bench refused to renounce his crown salary. The House, on February 11, resolved that the governor should forthwith remove him from office, and Oliver himself was given to understand that he would be physically assaulted—perhaps murdered—if he attempted

64. Clifford K. Shipton, *Sibley's Harvard Graduates*, XV (Boston, MHS, 1970), 265–266; TH to Elisha and to TH, Jr., Jan. 27, Feb. 6, 1774; Peggy to Mary Watson Hutchinson ("Polly"), Jan. 25, 1774; TH to Tryon, Feb. 2, 1774, *Diary and Letters*, I, 107–111.

to resume his seat on the bench. When Hutchinson refused the request (it was "a most explicit declaration against the just authority, as I conceive, of the King as well as the Parliament"), the House on February 24 formally impeached the chief justice. While the governor could block all such proceedings (which he described as "*outré* even for a House of Representatives") simply by refusing to cooperate, he could not, even at this near-final moment of his tenure, ignore the misinterpretation of the constitution that underlay the action of the House.[65] So once again—now, surely, for the last time—he expounded the constitution to them: explained their errors in supposing they could force a governor to act contrary to his own determination, in thinking that he was *obliged* to convene the Council when the Assembly told him to and when he knew their business was illegal or contrary to the public interest, or in thinking that a governor did not have a final and absolute veto. Patiently, once again, he went back to first principles and explained the inner theory of British constitutionalism, summarizing briskly his earlier state papers on the subject: that mixed government, with its freedom-saving balances of power, succeeds not because there is a conformity of sentiment through all its parts or because one part can dictate to another (that would create just that totality of power which the British constitution was designed to eliminate), but because each part has the right to exercise its own independent judgment within its own sphere, thus limiting actions of the government as a whole to matters of general assent. Perhaps, he once again concluded, he was wrong in this—perhaps he had always been wrong about the British constitution (though he knew he was not)—but if so, he told the House, the crown in its wisdom would recognize that fact, and "you may be sure of redress; but until I am convinced of my error I may not voluntarily depart from my own judgment or discretion and govern myself by the discretion of the House of Representatives, for I shall then be justly chargeable with subverting a material part of the constitution."[66]

His public voice was still firm and clear and, as always, consistent. But his private despair had reached a new depth, and on February 17, in the midst of this latest contest with the Assembly, he wrote

65. Clifford K. Shipton, *Sibley's Harvard Graduates*, VIII (Boston, MHS, 1951), 749–751; *Diary and Letters*, I, 137–140; *Mass. Papers*, pp. 177ff.
66. *Mass. Papers*, pp. 182–186.

the fullest and most despondent of all of his letters to Lord Dartmouth—a letter so remorseless in its cold-eyed description of a
world collapsing that it must have served in some way as an unconscious act of revenge, by this least vengeful of men, upon those
who had so long bedeviled him. In any case the letter was extraordinarily vivid and persuasive, and it had a remarkable effect not only
on its recipient, Lord Dartmouth, but on the King, to whom the
colonial secretary immediately referred it.[67]

The objective news it contained was not new in kind. Hutchinson
had often before reported having received such furious, malicious,
and illiberal messages from the two Houses as he now described,
and while the almost completely successful intimidation of the
high court judges had not happened before, the difference between
that and the earlier intimidation of so many others who had tried
to support law and order was almost incidental. Nor was the impossibility of prosecuting those guilty of stirring up disorder and
destroying property something new in his reports: he had been
commenting on that kind of thing ever since the memorable summer of 1765. What was new, and what so penetrated the awareness
of the King when he read the letter, was Hutchinson's description
of what all of this was finally adding up to.

Those who disapproved of this lawlessness, he reported, too terrified to speak their minds unless given far more physical support
than the governor could offer them, now believed that things had
reached the point where either the British government intervened
in force to restore order and the operation of law, or they must
assume that the home authorities had decided to abandon the
American colonies. It would soon be clear which alternative had
been chosen, and if for whatever reason—or neglect of reasons—
His Majesty's government failed to intervene in force, those like
Hutchinson who had struggled for so long to preserve the empire
would know how to respond. They would have no choice: "we must
join with those from whom we have hitherto kept separate, and
submit to them on the best terms they will grant us."

Everything, Hutchinson wrote, now depended on the willingness
of the British government to intervene. Every informed person

67. Eg. MSS, 2661, pp. 10–12, printed in full in *Diary and Letters,* I, 112–117; *Dartmouth Manuscripts,* I, 348–349. The letter was taken to London for Hutchinson by
Richard Clarke.

could now see the "regular plan" that the opposition had in mind: once revenue duties were removed, the customs commissioners would be forced out; and once they and their apparatus were gone, trade would be thrown wide open. As soon as they carried one point, they would move on to another until finally they would feel strong enough "to cast off subjection of every kind." To some degree this might be prevented if the King seized or secured fortresses in every colony and stationed a ship of the line in every principal seaport. But such measures would not restore interior order, for "the people, My Lord, in every colony, more or less, have been made to believe that by firmly adhering to their demands they may obtain a compliance with every one of them." As a consequence the very structure of government and the fragile integument of respect and toleration that separates barbarism from civilization was being destroyed. He believed "the anarchy will continually increase until the whole province is in confusion." The successful opposition to the power of Parliament had become a model that was being imitated at every level: "the subjects of subordinate powers . . . conclude they may also shake off subjection whensoever they are dissatisfied with them." In the hills of Berkshire County, for example, armed gangs had formed to stop all payments of lawyers' and sheriffs' fees, since some people had decided that the rates set by law were too high. If the dissolution of civil order were to be checked and coherence restored to the local communities, the process would have to start at the top. For, he repeated, all the present disorder in the colonies was the result of allowing "that sense of the supreme authority of Parliament" to be neglected "until it is entirely lost." Only seven years before, he pointed out, it was universally believed to be treason to oppose the authority of Parliament by force and violence: now such radical opposition was commonplace. Only a firm imposition of Parliament's authority could make a difference at this point, but how that could be successfully managed he could not say. All he could be sure of was that leaving all taxation to the colonial legislatures "would greatly tend—if it is not absolutely necessary— to conciliate the affections of the colonies to the parent state."

For Hutchinson personally there was an even deeper note of anxiety in this final report of February 17, 1773. He was obliged to inform Lord Dartmouth that the lieutenant governor—his closest friend, brother-in-law, and staunch ally in a hundred encounters

—had had a recurrence of a "bilious disorder" that had almost killed him once before. He had been young and strong then; and now he was suffering from the demoralizing effects of the disclosure of his letters to Whately. Oliver's letters had been far more outspoken, indiscreet, and politically vulnerable than Hutchinson's, and he had striven desperately to recover face and to gain satisfaction where none had been possible. He had been brutalized by that event, and his subsequent illness seemed as tragic as it was portentous to Hutchinson. Quite aside from the personal grief Oliver's death would cause Hutchinson, the governor knew that if Oliver died he would have to cancel or at least postpone his long-delayed departure until his successor arrived, since he could not leave the province without a chief executive.[68]

Two weeks later, on March 3, Andrew Oliver died, and his death, Hutchinson wrote, "put a stop to my intended voyage." He dare not, he acknowledged to Dartmouth, "without His Majesty's express order, leave the province until some person shall succeed." It was a bitter disappointment to him, but "my private views must terminate whenever the King's service comes in the way," he wrote in canceling his ship reservations.[69] So he would have to wait—for three months, as it turned out—until his successor, General Gage, arrived in Boston. And they were among the worst months he had known. Stripped of all effective authority even after he had prorogued the Assembly on March 9, he was subjected to seemingly endless humiliation. The personal vilification was beyond his powers to describe. It came from everywhere: from other colonies (Philadelphia, for example, where he and Wedderburn were hanged and burned in effigy), and from every hamlet of his native Massachusetts. The town of Gorham denounced Hutchinson in a letter to the Boston Committee of Correspondence as "the most restless, secret, plotting enemy to our free and happy constitution," breaking first into Biblical paraphrase in its fervor ("my own familiar friend in whom I trusted, which did eat of my bread, has lift up his heel against me") and finally into verse:

68. Oliver's comments on the publication of his letters are in his letterbook, Eg. MSS, 2670, pp. 76ff.; for his plea to John Pownall, June 28, 1773, to allow him the privilege of answering the Assembly's charges, see Joseph Redington and Richard A. Roberts, eds., *Calendar of Home Office Papers of the Reign of George III* (London, 1876–1899), IV, #213.

69. TH to FB and to Samuel Hood, March 9, 13, 1774, *Diary and Letters*, I, 130, 133; TH to Tryon, March 21, 1774, Eg. MSS, 2661, p. 19.

O hated name continued for a curse,
Were it remov'd we could not have a worse
If all the powers of darkness were combin'd
To make a fury seven times refin'd—
He is the darling of his smutty sire
His best belov'd because the greatest liar.

The Gorhamites concluded that only the means that had served their rustic hands so well in battling "with savage bears and other beasts of the wilderness . . . would be the most proper and suitable to make impressions on a Hutchinson, a Hillsborough, or a Bute."[70]

What more could Hutchinson say, or do? Never, he wrote Bernard on the day he adjourned the Assembly, had anyone met with "such a mixture of improper, unnatural sentiments and reasoning, rude and indecent language, sophistical and fallacious reasonings and evasions, oblique allusions . . . below the dignity of the Robin Hood, or even a schoolboys', Parliament." He was utterly exhausted: "five years constant scene of anxiety would weary a firmer mind than mine." His family was scattered—none of them dared appear in Boston—ostracized and threatened wherever they went. He himself had left Boston and was living in his country house in Milton, returning to the town only occasionally for business. On March 7 a new and unexpected cargo of tea that had arrived in Boston the day before was dumped into the harbor when a stubborn customs officer assumed the position that Hutchinson had taken in December and to which he still adhered. This time the whole procedure was undisputed, almost casual, so far had the government lost control of the colony. Andrew Oliver's funeral took place the next day, and it was a nightmare for his family; the first of kin, Andrew's brother Peter, the chief justice of the colony, had not dared attend, and the pitiful train had been followed by a hooting mob. "If we have not passed the Rubicon this winter, we never shall," Hutchinson wrote at the end of March, and while the English newspapers carried notices that he would be rewarded by a peerage or otherwise honored upon his arrival "home," there was nothing he could do until his release.

70. *Gentleman's Magazine, and Historical Chronicle* (London), 44 (1774), 285. Samuel Adams *et al.* to Franklin, March 31, 1774, *Mass. Papers,* pp. 186–192; Gorham Committee of Correspondence to Boston Committee, Feb. 18, 1774, in papers of the Boston Committee, microfilm, reel 2, Charles Warren Center, Harvard University (I owe this reference to Mr. Jack Rakove).

That long-postponed event drew near on May 13, when Gage arrived in Boston—close on the heels of the news of the Boston Port Act, the first of the "coercive acts" which embodied the proposals that had first been advanced by Bernard four years before and from the mildest of which Hutchinson had so egregiously dissented, but for which he would now be generally blamed.[71]

To Gage, armed with greater powers than Hutchinson had ever had,[72] Hutchinson handed over the authority he bore so wearily, and from him he received the most heartening reward he had received. Almost five weeks earlier, on April 9, King George had read Hutchinson's despondent letter of February 17, and had immediately requested Lord Dartmouth to reply to the governor with "some comfortable expressions that may make his mind easy that he is not discarded and will receive marks of favor." Dartmouth had complied immediately, writing Hutchinson a "private" letter in addition to the regular public communication he had already sent him that day, and he drafted it with care. It is His Majesty's royal intention, Dartmouth informed Hutchinson,

to testify his gracious approbation of your services to all mankind by an early mark of his favor. This expectation will contribute much to alleviate the anxiety of your mind and to support you under any difficulties you may have yet to encounter; but you will allow me to say that, to a mind like yours, there are secret sources of tranquillity that are superior to such great and encouraging considerations. The conscious sense that you possess of an upright and uniform regard to the duty of your situation, joined to a dispassionate and real concern for the welfare of the people over whom you preside, . . . do at this moment, if I am not deceived in my opinion of you, supply you with that steadiness and fortitude which discover themselves in your firm and temperate conduct, and which, under such support, it is not in the power of the most unreasonable prejudice, or even of the most inveterate malice, to shake or intimidate.

The King, he wrote, understood the state of the province, and he knew too that all would depend on the ability of "wise and tempe-

71. TH to FB, to Dartmouth, and to Israel Mauduit, March 9 and 31, 1774, *Diary and Letters*, I, 131, 139, 133, 147, 165; Labaree, *Tea Party*, pp. 165–167; English newspaper reports of Hutchinson's elevation, Eg. MSS, 2670, p. 83; Gage to Dartmouth, May 19, 1774, CO5/763/180.

72. Gage was commander in chief as well as governor, and his instructions were carefully devised to enhance his authority: Dartmouth to Gage, April 9, 1774, CO5/763/77ff.; CO5/765/294.

rate men" like Hutchinson to undeceive the multitude from the delusive ideas they had come to believe. Once the basic balance of life had been restored, he felt sure that Parliament would grant the colonists the indulgences that Hutchinson had requested on their behalf; for just as Parliament now claimed the obedience a sensible parent requires of "an obstinate and refractory child," so it would concede the indulgences an obedient child deserved.[73]

Hutchinson's response overflowed with gratitude. He had feared, he told Dartmouth, that in all the recent controversies "some impressions had been made to my disadvantage." He was greatly relieved that that was not the case. The approbation he had now received, "together with Your Lordship's declared sense of my regard to the duty of my station and of my concern for the welfare of the people over whom I presided, prepared me to resign the chair without the least reluctance." He could now fortify himself against his present unpopularity with this extraordinary mark of approbation "without despairing of the return of the favor of the people, which I have found by experience uncertain and fluctuating." And the letter helped him make his farewells, to those who mattered to him, with grace. When, the day after he received this heart-warming letter, he wrote a farewell letter to Israel Williams, his college classmate and loyal friend and political supporter for over thirty years, it was to explain that the King had replaced him as governor not "to slight but to oblige me," and that he had been discharged not only with the strongest official testimonials of the government's approval and continuing favor, but with· something much more valuable to him, a private letter of high commendation from "so upright and good a man as Lord Dartmouth," which he quoted at length.

I go with great reluctance [he continued], but I think it will be more for my quiet as well as more for my honor and reputation to be absent for some time than to remain here, for every step which Gage shall take will be laid upon me, though I should come and live with you in Hatfield; and I shall be less able to avoid abuse now [that] I am in a private station. There will be no need of evidence; it's enough not to be absolutely impossible. I am now charged with advising to the late act for shutting up

73. George III to Dartmouth, April 9, 1774, *Dartmouth Manuscripts*, I, 439. Dartmouth's letter was published by Hutchinson's grandson in the Preface to the third volume of the governor's *History of Massachusetts-Bay* (London, 1828), and it is reprinted in MHS *Procs.*, 13 (1873–1875), 175–176.

Boston, although I never suggested to the ministry any measure whatsoever, and if I had been called upon to do it, I never could have brought myself to one so severe and distressing.

Whether I shall live to return, or if I do return shall find you alive, God only knows. Be that as it may, let both of us, living and dying, more and more put our trust and confidence in Him.

There was a final satisfaction, of sorts. On May 30 three groups in Boston—merchants and traders, Episcopal clergymen, and lawyers —and a group of Hutchinson's neighbors in Milton presented him with warm farewell testimonials, noting his long and faithful public service and the "calumnies, trials, and sufferings" he had endured, wishing him well on his voyage and good fortune for the future. The 123 merchant subscribers went beyond that, to express their regret that his success had not been equal to his endeavors in his "wise, zealous, and faithful administration," and requesting him to represent them to the home authorities and help them obtain quick relief from the Port Act since they were prepared to pay for the destroyed tea. But the same newspapers that printed the Boston testimonials carried blistering indictments of "sycophants in cassocks" and others bent on misrepresenting the people's view by such favorable gestures to "the disgraced and execrated TRAITOR."[74]

When on the morning of June 1, he, Peggy, and the insistent Elisha (but not Elisha's pregnant wife) boarded the *Minerva* for England, Hutchinson left behind a province in open rebellion, facing a military governor backed by four regiments of troops. On that day the first of the Coercive Acts, paralyzing the economic life of the colony, went into effect, and the church bells tolled in mourning.

74. TH to Dartmouth, May 17, 1774, CO5/763/178; TH to Williams, May 14, 1774, Williams Papers; *Boston Gazette,* May 30, June 6, 1774; *Boston Evening-Post,* May 30, 1774; A. K. Teele, *History of Milton, Massachusetts, 1640 to 1887* (n.p., 1887), pp. 421–422; *Diary and Letters,* I 158–159. For an enumeration and classification of the signers of the addresses to Hutchinson, see James H. Stark, *The Loyalists of Massachusetts . . .* (Boston, 1910), pp. 123–130.

Chapter VIII

Exile

The final act of Thomas Hutchinson's ordeal was played out in England, and, like the other phases of his career, it proceeded from high hopes and eager expectations to disillusionment, a search for understanding, bewilderment, and finally despair. But now the scale is grander, the conclusions final, and the public failure embittered by private tragedy.

The voyage to England had been short—twenty-eight days—but Hutchinson and his daughter Peggy had been seasick much of the time and were weak when they landed at Dover on June 29. The next day Billy, who had been in England for two years, met the party on the road to London and brought them to the lodgings he had reserved for them in Parliament Street, the first of six residences Hutchinson and his family would occupy in London during the next six years. Hutchinson immediately sent a note to Lord Dartmouth informing him of his arrival, and the next morning, July 1, he received in return a request to call on His Lordship at 1:00 P.M. Well in advance of that time, Hutchinson appeared at the secretary of state's residence, and after appropriate greetings plunged directly into the thickets of Anglo-American relations and ministerial politics. There was much, of course, that he did not know about the current state of affairs—he had heard only of the first of the Coercive Acts, closing the port of Boston, when he had left America—but in what must have been an intense hour's conversation he went to the heart of the central problem as he saw it, probing Dartmouth's views of the terms on which the Port Act might be withdrawn and the normal life of the town permitted to resume. The merchants' address that had been presented to him on his departure he took to be a commission to solicit the relief of the town, and he inquired immediately of the colonial secretary whether a formal acknowledgment of Parliament's authority would be required (that, he knew, would never be forthcoming) or whether a *de facto* submission, the terms of which he was already formulating, would be sufficient.[1]

At the end of the interview Dartmouth proposed to introduce Hutchinson immediately to the King, and though the Bostonian was still weak from the sea voyage and not properly dressed for the occasion, and though Dartmouth's own toilette took so long to complete that the King's regular levée was over when they arrived, they nevertheless proceeded and were received by the King in his private chambers. For two hours on that memorable first day in London Thomas Hutchinson stood talking with King George III. That night he recorded in his diary as much of their conversation as he could recall, verbatim—in direct, dramatic dialogue, "*K.*" talking with "*H.*" with occasional interjections from the witness, "*Lord D.*,"—noting as accurately as he could not only every word the monarch uttered in the long interview but his facial expressions and the movements of his body as well; noting too the pauses and pacing of the discussion, and recording above all, at great length and in precise detail, the responses he gave to the King's remarkable series of questions.[2]

For not only did the King prove to have an extraordinary knowledge of Massachusetts but he seemed determined to inform himself on everything he did not know about every person, event, and circumstance of possible interest in the embattled colony. No one knew Massachusetts in all its aspects as well as Hutchinson; no one —before or after—has ever known as much of the colony's seven-

1. *Diary and Letters,* I, 157.
2. Hutchinson's account of the interview, accurately transcribed from Eg. MSS, 2662, is in *Diary and Letters,* I, 157–174.

teenth- and eighteenth-century history. Yet his knowledge was pressed to the limit by the King's inquiries, and beyond it at a few embarrassing points. The subject they discussed the longest was the divulgence of Hutchinson's letters to Whately. "Nothing could be more cruel" than this betrayal of private correspondence, the King said in sympathizing with the "abuse and injury" Hutchinson had suffered in his administration. Who were the men to whom Franklin had originally intended the letters to be shown? Of the six Hutchinson listed, the King said he knew four by reputation. But who were the other two, James Pitts and Dr. John Winthrop? And who was John Adams? "*K.* – I have heard of one Mr. Adams, but who is the other? *H.* – He is a lawyer, Sir. *K.* – Brother to the other? *H.* – No, Sir, a relation."

K.–In such abuse, Mr. Hutchinson, as you met with, I suppose there must have been personal malevolence as well as party rage?

H.–It has been my good fortune, Sir, to escape any charge against me in my private character. The attacks have been upon my public conduct, and for such things as my duty to Your Majesty required me to do, and which you have been pleased to approve of. . . .

K.–I see they threatened to pitch and feather you.

H.–Tar and feather, may it please Your Majesty; but I don't remember that ever I was threatened with it.

What guard had Hutchinson had in all these turmoils? "I depended, Sir, on the protection of Heaven. I had no other guard. I was not conscious of having done anything of which they could justly complain. . . . By discovering that I was afraid, I should encourage them to go on." Did Hutchinson not generally live in the country? Yes, "seven or eight miles from the town, a pleasant situation, and most gentlemen from abroad say it has the finest prospect from it they ever saw." What was the state of Hancock's finances? What accounted for Sam Adams's importance? How was it possible for upright clergymen, in the name of "liberty or the public good," to preach immorality or the toleration of evil, and why did Massachusetts ministers join with the people against the government? ("They are, Sir, dependent upon the people. They are elected by the people, and when they are dissatisfied with them . . . they get rid of them.") Why were Congregationalists not Presbyterians? Of what denomination were Hutchinson's ancestors? What church did he regularly attend? What was the Episcopal form of service? At what rate was the population of Massachusetts growing? Why did not foreigners immigrate to Massachusetts? (". . . our long cold winters discourage them.") Why did the colony raise no wheat? (It blasts.) Why did it blast? For what was the climate of Massachusetts best adapted? (Grazing.) Did maize make good bread? How would Hutchinson compare the constitutions of Connecticut and Rhode Island? Was the newly appointed lieutenant governor of Massachusetts, Thomas Oliver, a relation of the previous lieutenant governor, Andrew Oliver? (No.) But the present chief justice was the former lieutenant governor's brother, was he not? (Yes.) How was *that* Oliver related to Hutchinson? ("One of his sons, Sir, married one of my daughters.") How many Indians were there in Massachusetts? Why were they dying out? What part of his family had Hutchinson brought with him to England? How was their health? In the end, the King advised the sixty-two-year-old former governor, who must by then have been thoroughly exhausted, to stay at home for a few days until he had recovered from the effects of his voyage.

But the crucial questions had been raised at the very start of the interview. The first substantive question the King had asked Hutchinson was by far the most important, and the ambiguities of Hutchinson's responses reveal as much of the Bostonian's political personality as they do of the issue itself. The King asked: as of the time that Hutchinson had left Massachusetts "how did the people receive the news of the late measures in Parliament?" How, in other words, did Hutchinson judge the impact and prospects of the Coercive Acts? All Hutchinson could speak of was the Port Act, since news of the other acts had not been received by June 1; and that enactment, he said (according to the diary entry), "was extremely alarming to the people"—"extremely severe," but no more than that, for it was not for him, he wrote Gage, to presume to say, or even to think, that an act of King and Parliament was *unnecessarily* severe, however much distress it might create in the life of the town.[3] As to the King's question about the effect of the Massachusetts Government Act—which transformed the Council at long last from an elective to an appointive body, limited the range of action of the town meetings, and redefined the manner of re-

3. TH to General Gage, July 4, 1774, *Diary and Letters*, I, 175.

cruiting juries—Hutchinson recorded himself as failing to give any direct answer at all, since he had no first-hand or even second-hand information on the subject; all he allowed himself to say was that the actual choices of the first councillors under the new system would greatly affect the outcome. But if these cautious, noncommittal remarks were what Hutchinson actually uttered in answering these crucial political questions, they were not what the King believed he said. From what must have been phrases of great ambiguity, spoken in an attitude of extreme deference to an overpowering authority who knew what he wanted to hear, the King derived a quite different impression. The late governor of Massachusetts, King George informed his first minister, Lord North, at nine o'clock that night, had told him that "the Boston Port Bill was the only wise effectual method that could have been suggested for bringing them to a speedy submission, and that the change in the legislature will be a means of establishing some government in that province which till now has been a scene of anarchy." As a result, the King concluded, he was "now well convinced they will soon submit."[4]

Hutchinson himself felt no such assurance, and his activities over the next days and weeks were largely devoted to an intensive effort to set up the machinery for relieving Boston of its punishment for the destruction of the tea, and thereby to take the first steps in the complex process of reconciling England and the colonies. This Hutchinson took to be his special mission in England, for he was convinced that he, and he alone, knew enough of the politics and people of Massachusetts, had influence enough in the right places both in England and the colony, and had the proper balance of concern for both liberty and law, the rights of the people and the powers of government, to manage the alleviation of the conflict.

On July 7 he had a long conference with Lord North, and again he pursued the question of the terms required for the withdrawal of the Port Act. He was able to establish with the prime minister what he took to be the basic, life-saving point, that the government was not interested in "words and declarations" but, as Hutchinson had hoped, would consider repayment for the destroyed tea as "strong evidence of a return to duty" and implicitly, but suffi-

4. King to North, July 1, 1774, John Fortescue, ed., *Correspondence of King George the Third from 1760 to December 1783* ... (London, 1927–1928), III, 116.

ciently, an acknowledgment of Parliament's authority. By then Hutchinson knew the details of the Massachusetts Government Act, which shocked him, and he discussed it rather boldly with North. He was not surprised, he had to admit, that something like this had finally been passed; he had feared the necessity of it and had been struggling to deflect it for at least four years. When such a measure had first been proposed to him, he told the prime minister—proudly recalling, as he would on every possible occasion during the remaining years of his life, the letter he had written Hillsborough in 1770 discouraging exactly these constitutional changes—he had advised at the very least that the colony be permitted to be heard in its own defense before any action be taken against it. The mere apprehension that such an act would be passed might have led to changes of conduct that would have made the act itself unnecessary, and in any case the ultimate legislation would have been felt to be less of a grievance. Lord North replied that in general he agreed with Hutchinson that an opportunity for self-defense should be given before punitive action was undertaken, but in the present case it was much too late for that. Action had already been delayed far too long; it should have been taken at least a full year earlier, when the Massachusetts House and Council had issued what North called their "Declaration of Independence" in response to Hutchinson's speech of January 6. Now "all parties [are] united in the necessity of a change in order to prevent the colony from entirely throwing off their dependence," and he could only hope that the people of Massachusetts would not be so bemused as to try to obstruct the enforcement of the Government Act, for they would now find no such support in England as they had received in 1765 and 1766. Circumstances, political and economic, had entirely changed since then, and, as Hutchinson himself could already personally testify, the entire kingdom was determined to follow through on the actions that Parliament had taken. Even those who had originally questioned the wisdom of the Government Act—some of whom, Hutchinson now knew, like Lord Dartmouth and Undersecretary John Pownall, had cited Hutchinson's correspondence of 1770 in a hopeless effort to defeat all clauses save that pertaining to the Council—even these sympathetic and reasonable men "say now there is no going back."[5]

5. TH to ——, July 8, 1774, in *Diary and Letters*, I, 181–182.

To Hutchinson the crucial problem was still the management of a quick relief of Boston from the Port Act, which was destroying the colony's commercial life, including, as he would later point out, the value of his own extensive investments in Boston real estate.[6] From his interviews with the King and Lord North and from his almost daily discussions with Lord Dartmouth he had enough information to perfect the plans that he had apparently blocked out while still in America, and he incorporated them in three letters, two (July 4 and 8) to Governor Gage, and one (July 20) to George Erving, a councillor and a reliable leader of the merchant community.

In the letters to Gage, which Hutchinson read aloud to Dartmouth for his approval before sending, he recounted his interviews, emphasizing the King's and Lord North's explicit disavowals of any intention to extract a formal declaration of submission from the colony and their willingness to accept as evidence of submission "such orderly behavior in the inhabitants" as would indicate a willingness to obey the laws, including the laws of trade, and an abstention by the Assembly and the towns from passing any further votes and resolves that might stimulate civil disorder or that defied the authority of Parliament. Actions, he quoted the King as saying, speak louder than words, and if His Majesty really meant that homily to apply to the present situation, as Hutchinson believed he did, it was a fact of the greatest importance. If the people of Massachusetts were willing simply to refrain from future belligerence, letting bygones be bygones, and merely proceeded from then on to obey the law and maintain order, the problem would largely be solved. Once the governor could testify that the people's behavior conformed to this minimum standard, he wrote Gage, he should so inform the secretary of state, and the first step in reconciliation would thereby have been taken. For the second step, he asked Gage to pass his letters on to Erving, who would then take the lead.[7]

To Erving, Hutchinson explained, now with outspoken pride, that because of his intervention with the ministry, demands for a humiliating formal submission by Massachusetts had been avoided, and so now if Erving could arrange for a private group to repay the

6. TH to Lord Dartmouth, May 3, 1775, *Diary and Letters*, I, 437.
7. TH to Gage, July 4, 8, 1774, *Diary and Letters*, I, 176–177, 181–182.

East India Company for the loss of its tea, a second major step would have been taken; for repayment, Hutchinson wrote Erving, was in itself necessary if the Port Act was to be withdrawn, and would moreover be considered palpable evidence of a general submission to government and an earnest of future order. Once repayment had been made, Hutchinson said, he was confident that he would be able to move quickly to obtain the desired relief. But he thought it also advisable for Erving to produce, in addition to the repayment, a humble petition to the King in Council

from as many of the principal inhabitants and proprietors of estates in the town of Boston as can be obtained; and I think it would be best to confine it to the inhabitants and proprietors, setting forth your distress, disapproving of all the late violent measures in opposition to government, declaring your desire always to remain part of the empire and domain of Great Britain, humbly hoping for the enjoyment of every of [*sic*] the liberties and privileges of English subjects which can consist with your local situation, and signifying your resolution to do everything in your power to maintain government and order, or which would be better if it can be obtained, using the words . . . to do everything requisite on your part that *the terms of the act may be complied with.*

With the repayment of the tea and with convincing evidence of a general disposition on the part of the leading inhabitants to obey the law in the future Hutchinson felt the immediate impasse would be cleared and the road to an ultimate reconciliation would lie open.[8]

His confidence, he believed, was well founded. For by the time he wrote the letter to Erving—three weeks after his arrival in England —he had had an extraordinary opportunity to gauge the condition of politics in England, to savor once again, after thirty-three years, the quality of English life, and to make his own direct judgments of the leading public figures. He had left England after his trip in 1741 a provincial nonentity, he had returned a national celebrity. His career, he discovered, was a matter of interest to some of the most luminous figures in Britain. Everyone in politics seemed to know of his exchanges with the Assembly in 1773 and of Franklin's divulgence of his letters to Whately, and everyone seemed to have

8. TH to Erving, July 20, 1774, *Diary and Letters,* I, 189–191.

heard too of his vindication and Franklin's condemnation in the sensational scene at the Privy Council. He was sought after, lionized, and consulted by everyone who had the slightest interest in Anglo-American affairs, save the extreme radicals and the leaders of the opposition to the ministry. "My reception here exceeded everything I could imagine," he wrote Tommy on July 4, and he enjoyed it as much as it was in him to do.[9]

Within a month of his arrival he had been visited by or received cordial invitations from the solicitor general, Wedderburn; Undersecretary John Pownall (whom, with his colleague William Knox and with Lord Dartmouth, Hutchinson saw almost daily in his visits to the colonial office); Lord Gage, the general's brother, and Lady Gage, the sister of the banker Sampson Gideon; the Earl of Suffolk, secretary of state for the southern department; the Earl of Hillsborough, his former patron in the governorship, who sought Hutchinson out "and made the strongest professions of affection and esteem, and has charged me, whenever anything does not go to my wish, to let him know in Ireland, intimating an interest in the King which should be employed to my benefit"; Charles Jenkinson, once Lord Bute's "man of business" and still powerful in Parliament and in his several offices; the Earl of Hardwicke, a privy councillor affiliated with the Rockingham Whigs who had refused executive office but played a considerable role as a senior political figure; the lord chief justice, Lord Mansfield; Lord Apsley, the lord chancellor; Welbore Ellis, a prolific officeholder who had kept up with affairs in Massachusetts at least since 1760, formerly secretary at war and presently vice treasurer of Ireland—and half a dozen more of the leading politicians affiliated with the government. At the same time the ex-governor fell in quickly with the group of lesser figures who had been especially involved in Massachusetts affairs and with his own recent career: Sir Francis Bernard, "much more impaired in body than I expected, having the countenance of a sickly man of 70 and emaciated in all parts" but still mentally alert, though "his natural peevishness is increased";[10] Richard Jackson, his faithful correspondent and adviser for over a

9. TH to TH, Jr., July 4, 6, 1774, *ibid.,* pp. 179, 180, 184.
10. TH to Thomas Flucker, July 25, 1774, Eg. MSS, 2661, p. 38. For a somewhat less dramatic description of Bernard's condition, see *Diary and Letters,* I, 195. A year later Hutchinson noted that Bernard was suffering from epilepsy: *ibid.,* p. 488.

decade; Israel Mauduit, the former colony agent who had remained loyal to Hutchinson through all the turmoils of his governorship; Robert Thompson, who now agreed to confer the agency of his Rhode Island lands, vacated by Andrew Oliver's death, on Hutchinson's eldest son; and the various customs commissioners, bankers, and merchants with whom Hutchinson had dealt at long distance over the years.

There was a rush of formal introductions and initial encounters in high society, and the beginning of what would come to seem an endless series of levées, dinner parties, country house visits, and miscellaneous social outings. Hutchinson and his daughter were formally presented to the Queen and the court on July 14 (". . . it is next to being married," Peggy wrote; "I thought I should not mind it, but there is something that strikes an awe when you enter the royal presence"). The King and Queen both inquired after Hutchinson's health, he noted in his diary, and the whole court, it seemed—the lord chancellor, the lord chief justice, the attorney general, the solicitor general, together with a galaxy of noblemen and notables—took that occasion to welcome him publicly to England. He was later proud to hear that the Queen had declared Peggy to be "very genteel" and with "much the appearance of a woman of fashion."[11] Some of the dinners that followed were glittering affairs held in sumptuous settings. Lord Suffolk entertained him at Bushy Park, near Hampton Court; Lord Mansfield at Kenwood, in Hampstead; Welbore Ellis at Alexander Pope's famous villa in Twickenham, which he had recently acquired, and whose house, gardens, and grotto Hutchinson, like so many other visitors before and after him, attempted to describe in his diary; and on August 18 he and Peggy visited Lord Gage and his family at Firle, in Sussex, where they remained, on this first of many visits to that magnificent "country seat," for the better part of a week.[12]

There was so much in these early encounters for him to learn, so much of the background of events for him to discover. The American question was uppermost in people's awareness, and he entered enthusiastically into discussions of this subject, which he knew so

11. Peggy Hutchinson to Mary Watson Hutchinson, Oct. 27, 1775, *Diary and Letters*, I, 275, 191–192.

12. For this first visit to Firle, whose appearance today (see the illustrations following p. 204) is much as it was when Hutchinson visited it, see *Diary and Letters*, I, 223–225, 229.

well and had thought about so long and so deeply. His conversation, as always, was discreet—too discreet at times, it developed, as in discussing the sensitive question of the severity appropriate for America, a question on which his true feelings were in deep conflict; in such situations discretion became ambiguity and his ambiguous statements would soon be cited against him by partisans at both extremes. But for the moment everything absorbed and fascinated him. The chief topics were vital, the level of conversation at times extremely high, and the people and situations new to him and exciting. He felt that what he said and did was important; he was at the center of the world where, he thought, the future would be shaped—to some degree by him, he hoped.

So with Wedderburn he discussed the doubts he had had about whether he or anyone else as governor had the authority to order the King's troops to fire on riotous mobs. It was a nice and important legal question on which their views differed and which one way or another would have to be resolved. From John Pownall first, and then from Lord Mansfield himself, he heard with fascination an inside story of the origin of the Coercive Acts—how Pownall and others had used Hutchinson's letters to Hillsborough in an effort to block the proposed changes in the Massachusetts constitution but how stronger voices had advocated harsh measures, including a proposal "to send over Adams, Molineux, and other principal incendiaries, try them, and if found guilty, put them to death," and how, Pownall told him, "the lords of the Privy Council actually had their pens in their hands in order to sign the warrant to apprehend them— . . . I say literally, they had their pens in their hands prepared to sign the warrant" when they hesitated—because of doubts of whether the evidence would be sufficient to convict, according to Mansfield—and turned to what became the coercive measures. It was a story that altered his point of view. For the Coercive Acts were extraordinarily difficult for him either to accept or reject. While he was proud of having dissuaded the ministry from passing such measures earlier, he knew that decisive action of some kind was now necessary if England was to retain the colonies; and while at times he was convinced that if he had arrived in England six weeks earlier he might have prevented the passage of these severly punitive acts, he was greatly relieved to think that he had not in fact been forced to take a stand that might have shaped the outcome either way. Now Pownall's story made a difference. Given the actual situation that had existed when that legislation was written, the Coercive Acts could be seen as lesser evils and one could reconcile himself to them more easily.[13]

Mansfield himself, he discovered, and others too, had a special interest in his career. The great jurist found it surprising that Hutchinson had "persevered so long, seeing I was without any assurance of support from administration, there being no dependence upon measures." To him, and later to Sir William De Grey, chief justice of the common pleas, Hutchinson explained the way in which, once he had committed himself, one thing had led to another and "I could not well help going forward without dishonoring myself. I came forward one step after another, until I came to the chief command." Lord Hardwicke was particularly forthcoming. He reviewed with Hutchinson his own political career, particularly his long involvement with American questions, his opposition to the Stamp Act and Townshend Duties (including the tea tax), and then his conversion to the belief that coercion was now the only way of dealing with the colonies. Together the two men discussed the pros and cons of Parliamentary taxation, and Hutchinson dissuaded the privy councillor from demanding that Massachusetts be required to issue an explicit declaration of submission. And everyone, it seemed, had something to say on the background of the "letters" affair, which, according to Jenkinson, had finally convinced the ministry to act against the colonial rebellion. The "revelations" and sheer gossip about Hutchinson's letters, especially on the question of the identity of the person who had stolen them and given them to Franklin, were bewildering in their number and complexity.[14]

Lord Suffolk, who seemed to take a special interest in the matter, told Hutchinson flatly that Franklin had lied when he had said in his public statement that the letters had never been stolen from William Whately but rather had been loaned by Thomas Whately himself in his lifetime and hence that no crime had been involved. The ministry, Suffolk said, had positive evidence that that declara-

13. *Diary and Letters,* I, 183, 219, 245; TH to Erving, July 20, 1774, *ibid.,* pp. 190–191; TH to David Cheeseborough, June 1, 1775, Eg. MSS, 2661, p. 155; TH to Foster Hutchinson, Aug. 1774, *ibid.,* pp. 43–44.
14. *Diary and Letters,* I, 193, 290–291, 185–186. For Welbore Ellis's and Lord Dartmouth's exceedingly confusing tidbits, see *ibid.,* pp. 203–204, 221, 222, 232.

tion of Franklin's was false; they knew for certain the manner in which Franklin had obtained the letters. John Pownall filled in the details. Lord North, he revealed to Hutchinson, had been told by an eyewitness that after Whately's death the letters had been in the possession of John Temple in a package addressed to Franklin, and therefore, just as William Whately had claimed, Temple had been, if not the thief himself at least a co-conspirator, and on that supposition he had been dismissed from his post in the customs administration and the informer suitably rewarded.[15] That seemed clear enough, though Hutchinson doubted the accuracy of the story as soon as he heard it. Then Temple himself appeared in London, and after several days of delicate fencing and feinting through intermediaries, he suddenly appeared at Hutchinson's house "alone and unexpectedly," and the two men—enemies at long distance for several years—talked at length. They reviewed the entire history of their relations and antagonisms, beginning in the early 1760's. Hutchinson convinced Temple that he had had nothing to do with the struggle between Bernard and him—he had in fact supported Temple indirectly—and that he had never wished to have him dismissed from office. Temple on his side easily convinced Hutchinson, and Hutchinson later convinced Suffolk, that the ministry's information was wrong; Temple was in fact innocent in the "letters" affair. Yes, he had vilified Hutchinson, both in Boston and London, for he had been convinced—wrongly he now confessed—that Hutchinson had sought to destroy him; and while he had published nothing himself, he had supplied Arthur Lee with choice (and largely false) bits of information to use in his savage attacks on Hutchinson in the London newspapers. But he insisted—in terms that were entirely convincing to Hutchinson—that he had never stolen the letters and had never conspired with Franklin to reveal them. He could not deny, though, that Franklin had told him who his co-conspirator had been; but he had been sworn to secrecy, since the revelation would prove the ruin of the guilty party.[16]

Once Temple had been exonerated, there could be little doubt in Hutchinson's mind who the most likely candidate was. In all his elaborate, almost compulsive, writing on the subject of the Whately letters Hutchinson never once mentioned the name of the person

15. *Diary and Letters,* I, 192, 309.
16. *Diary and Letters,* I, 199, 205ff., 209–211.

he suspected, and indeed after some further efforts to fit together pieces of the puzzle that kept coming his way, he decided that it would be "prudent to discourage any further inquiry," which could only increase the number and venom of his enemies.[17] But all the indirect evidence indicates that he believed that it was Thomas Pownall who had given Franklin the means of betraying him.

His inevitable meeting with the former governor was delayed as long as politeness allowed. Thomas Pownall, so different in his politics from his consistent and reliable brother John, the under-secretary of state for the colonies,[18] was still attempting to play both sides of the Anglo-American struggle, conniving with the American radicals but at the same time supporting the government's strong line, and still seeking to emerge somehow through the miasma of his increasingly incomprehensible ideas of empire as the grand reconciliator. His first encounter with Hutchinson—their first meeting in fourteen years—was brief: he stopped by on July 15 long enough to tell Hutchinson that only "an explicit submission from Massachusetts province" would be satisfactory. Then, four days later, Hutchinson and his daughter dined with the Pownalls, and the two men talked seriously. Their conversation on that occasion is the only thoroughly nasty exchange that Hutchinson recorded in his diary. In a characteristic gesture, Pownall produced a copy of a speech that he said was *falsely,* though not illogically or inappropriately, attributed to him (Hutchinson knew at once from both style and substance that it had indeed been written by Pownall) in which he was quoted as saying that when *he* had been governor of Massachusetts he had not hesitated to act without the Council. The implied accusation was clear, and Hutchinson's usually slow-burning anger shot up. What Pownall in this duplicitous way was saying was that the entire Anglo-American crisis was Hutchinson's fault, for if he had acted on his own and called out the troops to save the tea and to control the tea mobs when the Council had refused to support him, he could have prevented the tea party and made the coercive measures, and hence the present impasse, unnecessary. It was a galling accusation—annoying enough when made by others who did not know the political realities in America (to them Hutch-

17. *History of Massachusetts-Bay,* III, 299n.

18. All the evidence supports John Pownall's statement to Hutchinson that "his brother and he seldom thought alike." *Diary and Letters,* I, 251.

inson was always able to give a convincing explanation of his failure to act), but maddening coming from someone who knew as much about Massachusetts as Pownall did and who as governor had himself taken a populist line in order to ingratiate himself with precisely those legislative forces which he now blamed Hutchinson for not defying. Hutchinson, who understood the constitutional relation between the governor and the Council in Massachusetts far better than Pownall did, challenged him to cite one example, one single instance, in which he, Pownall, when governor, had acted independently of the Council in civil affairs. A single instance? "In every instance," was the evasive reply. Hutchinson refused to be put off. "Mention one." "In all," Pownall repeated. "But recollect one," Hutchinson insisted. The only answer he could get was, "All; and there," Hutchinson recorded in his diary, "it ended, his own house being an unfit place to carry the dispute any further."[19]

But Pownall's belligerence, which by the end of the year would turn into an intensive campaign of vilification, was altogether exceptional in these early weeks. Hutchinson's encounters were otherwise almost entirely agreeable and absorbing. He continued to be flattered by the attention shown him and by the access he had to the ministry—not only to Lord Dartmouth, "the most amiable man I ever saw," and to Lord Suffolk, whose extraordinary kindness to him he could not explain but deeply appreciated, but to the prime minister himself, with whom he found he could speak "with great freedom and plainness." As the summer passed into fall his circle of acquaintances widened, and he made contact with even more of the interesting men of the time, some whose politics differed considerably from his: the Marquess of Rockingham, who did not seem to realize, in their cautious conversation, how similar their views really were; Lord Camden; Edmund Burke; Pasquale Paoli, the Corsican liberator in exile who was the hero of patriots and libertarians everywhere; and Edward Gibbon, then diligently at work on the first volume of his great history while serving as a neophyte member of Parliament.

19. *Diary and Letters*, I, 192, 194–195. For another version of the interview, see TH to Thomas Flucker, July 25, 1774, Eg. MSS, 2661, p. 38. Five years later Pownall was still raising the same issue, at that time with Hutchinson's patron Lord Hardwicke, to whom Hutchinson was obliged once again to explain the constitutional relation between governor and Council. TH to Hardwicke, Nov. 19, 1779, Add. MSS, 34527, p. 199.

Gibbon and Hutchinson met accidentally and then saw each other frequently. They must have made a curious pair: the one short, fat and corseted, fashionable, clever, and sophisticated—a powdered *homme du monde,* confident and at peace with himself in a secular, cynical society of style and gossip; the other tall, thin, gray, gaunt, provincial, instinctively parsimonious, spare in speech and manner, absorbed in political questions that pressed the boundaries of received knowledge, and committed to principles he knew were right but that alienated him from the world he knew best. Hutchinson, however, was useful to Gibbon, who was searching for positions on the main questions of the day. He pumped the former governor for news, quoted his opinions as facts, and not only included him in those "prettiest little dinners in the world" that he gave with such pleasure and pride but drew from him a view of the American crisis which he exaggerated into a story that fitted nicely with what he was then thinking about Rome. It was a story of the forces of reason and order in an agreeable, stylish world beset by a handful of barbarians and venal *banditti* determined to incite an idiot rabble to deeds of mad destruction.[20]

There was scarcely a disappointment in these early weeks as Hutchinson awaited the results of his proposals and the American response to the Coercive Acts. Peggy, with whom he was so deeply involved, was slowly recovering from the debilitating effects of the sea voyage, and though the July weather seemed as cold to her as November's would have been in New England, and though she seemed to suffer intensely from the damp and had a racking cough through the entire summer, there seemed no special reason for Hutchinson to doubt that she would recover her health. And she was excited by London and England—by the endless comings and goings of that extraordinarily sociable community: by the dinners, the teas, the levées, and the ingenious entertainments, public and private; even the stiff formalities of the court were exciting. The evenings, she wrote back from this sophisticated world to her sister-in-law in Plymouth, Massachusetts, only began at ten o'clock. She would not, of course, want to live in such a style and such a place for very long: "London, my dear, is a world in itself. You ask me how I like it. Very well for a little while: it will do to see once in

20. Solomon Lutnick, "Edward Gibbon and the Decline of the First British Empire: The Historian as Politician," *Studies in Burke and His Time,* 10 (1968–1969), 1100–1103.

one's life, and to talk of ever after; but I would not wish to fix my abode here. In the country, methinks, had I my friends with me, I could not but be happy. For seventy miles around it is a perfect garden, and exceeds all that the most romantic fancy could paint.[21]

Nor, for the time at least, were there financial difficulties. Hutchinson's prudence—his instinct for squirreling away small advantages until they became substantial benefits—was vindicated in the security of the investments, primarily in East India Company stock, that he had carefully made over the years, and this capital, which totaled around £5,500 when he arrived in England, plus the pension he received of £1,000 per annum, payable from the expiration of his salary as governor, made him the most secure of the loyalist refugees, as he was the most influential.[22]

He was offered even greater rewards. Before he had left home Dartmouth had indicated the King's intention to bestow on him a "mark of honor" for his services, losses, and sacrifices. The promise was acted on soon after his arrival. By early August the terms were settled: he would be offered a baronetcy, an altogether appropriate distinction, Dartmouth advised him, in the dignity of its rank and its permanence in his family. But it was also an expensive honor. Bernard had been advised, when the same honor had been given to him, that the mere formalization of the title would cost £300–£400 in fees. And for Hutchinson, cautious and unostentatious, there was the more basic consideration that he did not have "an estate to support a title." For he was deeply concerned about the need to provide equally for all his children; and with the economic basis of the family's life so disrupted by events, with Peggy unmarried and Billy still without employment, he could not bring himself to divert the family's substance to the maintenance of this honor for himself or in this way to favor his eldest son so unequally above the others. So on this ground, ostensibly, he declined the "mark of honor" the King had wished to bestow—after obtaining permission to discuss the offer publicly if he chose to.[23]

21. Peggy Hutchinson to Mary Watson Hutchinson ("Polly"), Aug. 2, 1774, *Diary and Letters,* I, 200.

22. TH to William Palmer, March 22, April 25, 1774, Eg. MSS, 2661, pp. 19, 23–24; *Diary and Letters,* I, 312, 487. At his death Hutchinson had over £6,000 in investments. *Ibid.,* II, 361.

23. TH to [TH, Jr.] and to ——, Aug., Nov. 4, 1774, Eg. MSS, 2661, pp. 51, 76; TH to Foster Hutchinson, Nov. 1, 1774, *Diary and Letters,* I, 283; Viscount Barrington to

But there were other, subtler considerations in this important decision, and these he never openly discussed. If he accepted the title he knew that whatever obligation the government felt it owed him would thereby be fully liquidated. Any benefits he might thereafter receive from the government would be, if not gratuitous favors, then acts of generosity, neither of which, in the savagely venal political world he knew, he could reasonably expect to receive. Yet benefits he might well need, not for himself but for Billy, whose only hope for security, he had long known, lay in obtaining some kind of public office or sinecure. If he could translate the hereditary honor the government proposed for him—as intangible as it was impressive—into the concrete favor of an office that would sustain his youngest son when he himself could no longer do so, the exchange would be altogether advantageous.[24]

Yet even that consideration did not exhaust his reasons for declining the baronetcy. Hutchinson had left Massachusetts intending to return quickly; he did not even rule out a resumption of his governorship.[25] After two months in England he still considered himself "only upon an excursion from home," and he had by no means "give[n] up the hope of laying my bones in New England." But by the end of August he was beginning to worry about the developing course of events and the effect it might have on the prospects of his return. He became more than ever determined to avoid doing anything that might make his return more difficult. As far back as 1770, shortly after Bernard had been knighted, the opposition press in Boston had suggested, by way of condemnation, the appropriateness of a similar honor for him—"Possibly you may become a BARONET too!—*Sir Thomas* sounds well"—and when it was known in the spring of 1774 that he would take leave in England, the Boston papers had republished with relish notices that had appeared in the London press to the effect that he would be

---

Francis Bernard, May 9, 1768, March 21, 1769, *The Barrington-Bernard Correspondence . . .*, ed. Edward Channing and A. C. Coolidge (Cambridge, 1912), pp. 154, 187. The refusal was not easy to handle properly. Hutchinson feared that it might be misinterpreted, perhaps as unseemly arrogance, and so he suggested to Dartmouth that "there might be some advantage from considering . . . it rather as a doubt than a peremptory refusal." TH to TH, Jr., Nov. 11, 1774, Eg. MSS, 2661, p. 80.

24. TH to ——, July 1776, *Diary and Letters*, II, 79.

25. "I have been told by the highest authority I may return to my government whenever it is agreeable and I have bona verba from all under this authority as far as concerns me." TH to Colonel Abercromby, July 29, 1774, Eg. MSS, 2661, p. 40.

made a peer and be "promoted to a considerable post in administration." He was still, he knew, as deeply devoted to the welfare of his native land as any of those who opposed him, but if accepting honors, gifts, or posts in England tended to cast doubt on that fact, he would decline them, for that reason alone. So he scarcely considered the possibility of a lucrative governorship elsewhere when that was proposed shortly after his arrival, and dismissed even more brusquely a proposal that he accept one of the government's seats in the House of Commons in the election of 1774. He knew what the long-term stakes were for him in these beguiling offers, though only once—and then in a letter he did not send—did he speak to the point directly: "I have been offered titles of honor, and it has been intimated to me that I may have a much better government than I have had. I have hitherto made the insufficiency of my private fortune an excuse for not accepting the one, and my time of life will be for the other. I hope to leave my bones where I found them, and that before I part with them I shall convince my countrymen I have ever sincerely aimed at their true interest."[26]

ii

So, splendidly welcomed into this world at the center of the world, honored and apparently drawn into its councils, he awaited word of America's response to the ministry's enactments. While he was careful in his private correspondence to make clear that he had had nothing to do with the drafting of this legislation, and that on earlier occasions he had refused to support such draconian measures and in all probability would have taken the same position this time if he had been consulted, he hoped they would have the good effect the ministry expected them to, which, he believed, he had significantly facilitated.

The responses came to him in stages in the months that followed—a series of clustered revelations of decisions long since taken and actions long since concluded, hence events utterly beyond control, that shook him profoundly, each more savagely than its predeces-

26. TH to Isaac Winslow, [Aug. 1774], *Diary and Letters*, I, 231; *Boston Gazette*, March 26, 1770; [*London*] *Morning Chronicle*, April 6, 8, 1774 (excerpts in Eg. MSS, 2670, p. 83); TH to ——, [Feb. 1775], *Diary and Letters*, I, 389; TH to Mr. Lee, Sept. 1774 (not sent), Eg. MSS, 2661, p. 58.

sors, wrenching him and racking him unendurably, gradually killing all hope for a peaceful end to his ordeal, and marking the destruction of the world he had known.

He had intimations as early as mid-July that trouble was brewing in Massachusetts when he received word of proposals for a continental-wide embargo of British vessels. He brushed such rumors aside. He was confident that "the men of character" in Boston, with whom he was in contact, favored measures quite different from this, and in any case neither he nor Governor Gage thought it at all likely that the colonies would go along with such extravagant belligerence; and in all of this Lord Dartmouth concurred. Two weeks later, on August 2, the first full and accurate revelation of what had happened reached him; and as he read that packet of letters from home, which he promptly sent on to Lord Dartmouth, he knew—despite the brave words he would speak and write in the weeks that followed and the ingenious ways he would continue to imagine that the world might still right itself—that a tide was in motion that might wipe out all efforts at reconciliation and that would require all of England's most resolute efforts to control.[27]

Instead of a search for reconciliation in Massachusetts, there was outright defiance. The embargoed colony was seeking and receiving supplies from elsewhere in America—not only from nearby Rhode Island and Connecticut but also from Pennsylvania, even South Carolina. And the town of Boston had again seized the initiative and had reinvoked the nonimportation scheme of 1769–1770, this time with a vengeance, circulating for individual signatures in every town in the colony a "Solemn League and Covenant" pledging the signatories to support a total boycott of British goods until all grievances were redressed. Worse than that, the Assembly in its first meeting with Gage, held in Salem in June, had once again turned to passing "criminal resolves" and insulting and unacceptable addresses to the governor charging that Hutchinson's administration had attempted to introduce tyranny by sending false accusations to England and deliberately misinforming the King and his

27. TH to ——, July 14, 1774, *Diary and Letters,* I, 188; Gage to Dartmouth, May 31, 1774, CO5/763/184; *Diary and Letters,* I, 199. In July Dartmouth told Knox that Hutchinson's reports "do not shake the hopes I have begun to conceive." Historical Manuscripts Commission, *Reports on Manuscripts in Various Collections,* VI (Dublin, 1909), 113.

ministers about the truth of the situation in Massachusetts; and they had proceeded, moreover, to invite the other colonies to a "grand congress at Philadelphia." All of this was exactly the reverse of what Hutchinson, and the ministry, had wished for, and in itself it led Hutchinson to conclude that there was little hope for the immediate relief he had sought and for which he had made such detailed plans. The colony and town must be mad, he wrote back to Boston, if they thought defiance could bring "a future, or even a very distant, relief to the town of Boston. Providence, I hope, will avert its total ruin, and I should have thought it the happiest event of my life if I might have been the instrument. The prospect of it was very favorable when I first arrived."[28]

Yet even this reckless defiance was not the worst of the news. Something more decisive and transforming had taken place, he learned from the letters he read on August 2. The governor, faced with the prospect of these illegal actions, had dissolved the Assembly; but the two Houses had refused to disband, and Gage had been obliged to read the proclamation of dissolution to them through the locked doors behind which they continued to sit "until they had finished their inflammatory resolves," Hutchinson reported to Hillsborough, "and appointed their committee consisting of three of the most guilty of their own members and two of the negatived councillors." They seemed to have no doubt about the legality, or at least the general validity, of their enactments, and were thus somehow drawing sanction for their actions from sources beyond the realm of existing law and the existing constitution. It was the moment, brief but decisive, in which a revolutionary government was born. While Hutchinson did not perceive the event in quite these terms, he understood that something of a new dimension had developed. He saw it reflected in the fears he found, in this first batch of letters, of what might happen next. No one he knew who was on the scene was able to predict how long it would be "before the people come to their senses"; some people, he told Hillsborough, "are apprehensive of bloodshed and a general convulsion."[29]

Subsequent events, which came to him in successive, smaller

28. TH to Hillsborough, Aug. 4, 1774, Eg. MSS, 2661, pp. 42–43; to Mr. Cotton, Aug. 29, 1774, *Diary and Letters*, I, 231.
29. TH to Hillsborough, Aug. 4, 1774, Eg. MSS, 2661, pp. 42–43. For Gage's account, also received in London on Aug. 2, see Gage to Dartmouth, June 26, 1774, CO5/763/195.

revelations through the month of August, strengthened the impression of a drastic transformation of public affairs. While Hutchinson had been busy commenting with great delicacy on the choice of the first appointive ("mandamus") councillors and advising his friends on how to adjust the rank-list within the Council so as to accommodate the new members, in fact most of the mandamus councillors—including his own son and his old political ally Israel Williams—had resigned their commissions in the face of the threat of violence, Tommy explaining to Gage that his special responsibilities as acting head of the family had made the step particularly advisable for him. Hutchinson could not blame them, though he was sure that he himself would have stood fast even if the radicals had tarred and feathered him; for most of the new councillors lived in the countryside, he knew, and they would have had to have fled from their families and businesses to the protection of the troops in Boston to have continued to defy the mobs. Not to have resigned, he commented with uncharacteristic self-righteousness, would have required "too great virtues . . . for the present age." Nor could he blame his neighbors in Milton and the Boston merchants who had signed the commendatory address to him for recanting and confessing their guilt for having committed so grievous a crime. They too had to survive and protect their families from violence. But it was all adding up to a fearful destruction of the very structure of political society, and in the end it could not possibly benefit anyone.[30]

For England, he now knew, would never back down. The ministry was absolutely adamant, he informed his correspondents, in its determination to see the struggle through. Even the amiable Lord Dartmouth, so well disposed to the colonies, so hopeful for reconciliation, had been enraged by the news. He had personally returned Hutchinson's letters to him the day after he had received them (they had merely confirmed what he had heard from Gage officially) and had vented his feelings "with great emotion." He was not, he reminded Hutchinson, "one who thirsted for blood, but he could not help saying that he wished to see Hancock and Adams brought to the punishment they deserved"; peace, he declared,

---

30. TH, Jr., to Gage, Aug. 30, 1774, CO5/763/279; TH to Lord Hardwicke, Nov. 2, 1774, Eg. MSS, 2661, p. 76; A. K. Teele, *History of Milton, Mass., 1640 to 1887* (n.p., 1887), pp. 422–423.

would never be restored "until some examples were made which would deter others."[31] If these were Dartmouth's feelings, who would there be to recommend that the government concede? The American radicals, Hutchinson believed, had been grotesquely misled, primarily by Franklin but by others as well, into thinking that a sizable segment of the British political population supported them and that therefore in the end the government would back down and once again, as in 1766 and 1769, allow the American opposition to prevail. Nothing could be less likely, Hutchinson knew, and if he could only make that unmistakably clear—if he could only convince his countrymen of that single fact—he might prevent a holocaust.

So again and again, in letter after desperate letter in August and then in September and early October, he wrote to everyone in Massachusetts who would conceivably listen to him, that the British nation was utterly united behind the ministry. Everyone—"flaming patriots as well as fawning courtiers"—supported the government's implacable determination to impose the rule of law: no one of any importance—not even the great hero of the "patriotic" opposition, Lord Chatham, to say nothing of such sunshine radicals as Thomas Pownall (now firm as granite for Lord North)—supported the American resistance. All the American opposition was accomplishing by its belligerence was to confirm the ministry and the nation in their determination to force the issue to its obvious conclusion.[32]

What was the opposition contending for? The central issue was as crystal clear to everyone Hutchinson met in England as it had been to him for years; and as the implications of the August 2 dispatches settled in his mind he reviewed, as he would at every turning point in the mounting crisis, the issues and principles that were at stake in the conflict, reassuring himself, if not his listeners and correspondents, of the unassailable logic, the transparent and compelling reasonableness, of the position he had maintained for so long and which now had become the overwhelming conviction of the British people.

31. *Diary and Letters,* I, 203.
32. TH to ——, Aug. 8, 1774, *Diary and Letters,* I, 213; TH to Harrison Gray, Aug. 9, 1774, Eg. MSS, 2661, p. 40.

The issue was not taxation; essentially, it never had been that. No one of importance in the government—and certainly not Hutchinson himself—wished Parliament to tax America, directly or indirectly. The problem was simply and solely the right of the British state to preserve its integrity, and that meant its right to impose its law, promulgated by legitimate procedures, within the territories that were British. That was what a territory's being British meant: being subject to British law. For a community to be British and *not* admit the validity of British law was a contradiction in terms—a solecism. That and that alone was the issue, and not a single person Hutchinson had met in England—not Chatham, nor Rockingham, nor Burke, nor Camden—would admit that any part of the kingdom or its dominions could "be exempt from the authority of Parliament" and still remain British. This had always been Hutchinson's fundamental position: on the one hand, that the authority of Parliament must reach into a given segment of the British polity or it would have no authority there at all, but on the other hand that Parliament should never use that authority to tax the colonies, which were not, and could not be, represented in it. To contend—as the resisting groups in Massachusetts were now doing; as the Council in its fumbling response to his speech of January 6, 1773, had done; and as innumerable colonial pamphleteers led by John Dickinson had attempted to do—that somehow one could select some areas of activity which sovereignty might reach and others where it could not, "is contending for a phantom," Hutchinson wrote in a passionate epistolary tract he drafted on August 8, "which has no existence but in the fancy." He hoped and prayed that Parliament would never again attempt to tax America, but to claim that it had no such *right* "I must utterly deny." Denial of part of Parliament's authority but not other parts involved a tangle of logical absurdities, which he quickly sketched. Once the hopeless quest "for a phantom . . . a mere shadow which it is impossible you should ever grasp" is given up, the path to peace "is plain and easy." All of this was clear; to all of this the British nation was so totally committed that the mere discussion of the subject was threatening to become a bore in the highest circles.[33]

33. TH to ——, Aug. 8, 1774, *Diary and* Letters, I, 213–217. "Your Lordship remarks very rightly on the supineness of the public," Edmund Burke wrote Rockingham on

So he wrote, as the summer faded into fall, reviewing once again the ideas he had developed in the sixties, and discussing freely, on every likely occasion, his lectures to the Assembly in 1773, which he now found relevant, prophetic, and universally approved.[34] And as he wrote and considered the difficulties that appeared to lie ahead, his emotions became increasingly divided. Responsible people were returning to the idea of bringing the leaders of the rebellion to England for trial; Lord Dartmouth had already asked Gage to send him copies of letters that might incriminate Franklin and Arthur Lee, the two ringleaders within easy reach.[35] But though Hutchinson was as furious with the opposition in America as anyone in the government, the idea of trying Americans for treason repelled him. The Americans were not *primarily* to blame. It was the encouragement they had received from the political opposition in England, he believed, that had made resistance possible in the first place, and, therefore, if examples were to be made, he told Mansfield, let them be made first of the more fundamentally guilty English politicians. Despite all the abuse he had received at home and despite all the honor and recognition he had been accorded in England, he wrote his brother, he was deeply moved by "the affection I still feel for my native country, and shall do as long as I live." He was tempted from time to time simply to forget that he was an American, and settle down for what remained of his life in England; "but the passion for my native country returns." Surely Americans were no more basically inclined to violence and

Feb. 2, 1774. "Any remarkable highway robbery at Hounslow Heath would make more conversation than all the disturbances of America." *Correspondence of Edmund Burke,* II, ed. Lucy Sutherland (Cambridge, Eng., and Chicago, 1960), 524. Hutchinson dwelt upon the logical absurdities he continued to find in the opposition's claims. "If Parliament has a constitutional authority over the colonies," he wrote in the Aug. 8 letter, "a declaration that they have not, will have no force whenever another declaration is made to the contrary"; on the other hand, if Parliament does not have such authority, a declaration proclaiming that fact is unnecessary since it adds nothing to what already exists.

34. On Oct. 20 he wrote Tommy to pick up some copies of the pamphlet containing his speeches and messages to the Assembly. He thought there were still some lying around "in the Council lobby or in the lobby of the House"; but if not he told his son to buy ten copies from the printer, "as cheap as you can." Eg. MSS, 2661, p. 70.

35. On Sept. 25 Gage replied to Dartmouth's request for "either the originals or some regular attested copies" of letters of Franklin and Arthur Lee (June 3, 1774: CO5/763/174) by explaining that such letters were written to the speaker of the House personally, whose practice it was to declare them to be private letters and who put them in his own pocket once he had read them to the House. Aug. 25: CO5/763/242.

disorder than Englishmen were, or than they would be "under like inducements and temptations." In any case, the New England countryside was a part of him, and he would never reject it in favor of England. "I can't help thinking that nature alone has done as much in some parts of America as nature and art together have done in England, and I should prefer even my humble cottage upon Milton Hill to the lofty palaces upon Richmond Hill, so that upon the whole I am more of a New England man than ever, and I will not despair of seeing my country and friends again, though I fear the time for it is farther off than I imagined when I left you."[36]

Everything, it had become clear by the early fall, would depend on the reasonableness of the Continental Congress, and that, he felt, was a frail reed to have to rely on. That the Congress could do great damage to the cause of peace he did not doubt. It might attempt to deny Parliament all authority whatsoever in America, in which case "persons guilty of such offense shall certainly be brought to punishment." Or it could deny Parliament's authority in some cases only: "This will cause a general laugh and render the members of the Congress contemptible in the eyes of every man in the kingdom" just as the Council had been ridiculed for its response to him in 1773. The best thing the Congress could do, he wrote, would be to follow the program he had set out with such care so long ago: avoid any argument in favor of insupportable distinctions in the sovereignty of the state but claim an exemption from Parliamentary taxation on the basis of the ancient and pragmatic balance of advantages (tax exemption) and disadvantages (trade restrictions) which had so richly benefited England and the empire since the earliest days, but which had so unfortunately been destroyed by recent events. If the Congress would petition England in those terms—for the restoration of privileges so ancient and so deeply woven into the texture of Anglo-American life as to be almost indistinguishable from practices based on constitutional principles—"peace may soon be restored to America," not all at once, perhaps, but gradually and surely. If pronouncements of illogical or treasonous principles were made, "I dread the conse-

---

36. *Diary and Letters*, I, 219–220, and letter of Aug. 8, to ——, *ibid.*, p. 215; TH to Foster Hutchinson and to William Pepperrell, Aug. and Aug. 15, 1774, Eg. MSS, 2661, pp. 43, 48.

quences both to the persons who constitute the Congress and to the colonies in general."[37]

Having written and talked to everyone whose ear he could reach urging moderation, accommodation, and an avoidance of declarations of principle, he could do no more than await the outcome, which he did with increasing anxiety and foreboding. He passed the time in August and September largely in travel: to the south, for the week at Lord Gage's estate in Firle; then northeast to Norwich via Cambridge for seventeen days to visit the Murray family (a daughter, Polly, had traveled from Boston to England with the Hutchinsons); then west to Buckinghamshire, to visit Sir Francis Bernard and his family at Aylesbury—all with extensive side trips for sightseeing and for short visits with more casual acquaintances. And in the intervening times in London he was endlessly engaged in minor social activities, often with old friends from home, at the New England Coffee House and elsewhere. But through all of this his ear was sensitively tuned to every whisper of news from home that might indicate the way the world would turn, and he continued to stimulate his hopes by rehearsing and refining the program of reconciliation he had worked out soon after he had arrived and that he had entrusted to Gage and Erving. As late as September 24, on his visit to Aylesbury, he reworked the entire schedule in a letter to Erving, observing that recent events made no difference to what he had earlier written. For no matter what the Congress did "it will be necessary as soon as possible to effect the payment for the tea"; and as for the petition that Erving was to produce, he had now decided that the mere number of signers was more important than the purity of their credentials, and therefore he urged Erving to let two hundred, three hundred, or even more people sign if they wished to, excluding of course people "of doubtful character—I mean moral character, or desperate circumstances as to estate, but if any good men who have been of a different way of thinking are now willing to join you, so much the better." And to make sure that Erving would handle things correctly, he drafted the actual text of the petition for him, and explained the timing he considered best for presenting it to the King.[38]

37. TH to ——, Aug. 8, 1774, *Diary and Letters*, I, 215–217.
38. TH to [George Erving], Sept. 24, 1774, Eg. MSS, 2661, p. 59.

Yet none of this could relieve his anxiety. He haunted the colonial office and chatted at every opportunity with anyone in authority who might know more than he did of the portents and prospects of the Congress and of the consequences that might result from its deliberations. And as he waited and traveled and listened, his longing to return to America grew stronger and his professions of loyalty to his native colony became more insistent. Then news from home began to arrive.

He was at Norwich on October 5 when letters from Boston that had been sent on the *Scarborough* early in September caught up with him and brought him the first bits of the "very alarming and distressing news" that would in the end overwhelm him. Five days later, having vented his feelings in conversation on American affairs with the notables of Norfolk (spiking in the process an idea that Thomas Pownall had planted there, that a simple requisition scheme would have avoided all the fuss about taxation), he was back in London, and though the reports of the Congress were not yet in, he knew the worst.[39]

Massachusetts was in open rebellion. The entire Mandamus Council had been forced to resign, Lieutenant Governor Oliver having been besieged by a mob of four thousand Middlesex farmers in "Elmwood," his elegant Cambridge mansion, and, having been forced to choose, as he explained in agonized letters to Hutchinson and Dartmouth, between resignation from the Council and death, had chosen to live, and had capitulated completely.[40] Gage's dispatches were ominous and also somewhat mysterious. "The state not of this province only but of the rest is greatly changed since Mr. Hutchinson left America," he wrote Dartmouth on September 2.

39. *Diary and Letters,* I, 256, 258–259
40. Gage to Dartmouth, Sept. 2, 3, 12, 20, 1774, CO5/763/763ff. For Oliver's panic-stricken, remorseful, and dramatic accounts of his confrontation with the mob at "Elmwood" (now the residence of the presidents of Harvard), see his letters to Dartmouth, Sept. 3 and 10, 1774, CO5/769/98ff. and CO5/763/309. These extraordinary documents—which form perhaps the most vivid personal account of an official's confrontation with a mob of enraged townsmen and farmers in the literature of the Revolution—are not referred to in either of the two published narratives of the affair, Clifford K. Shipton, *Sibley's Harvard Graduates,* XIII (Boston, MHS, 1965), 338–341, and Oliver Elton, "Lieutenant Governor Thomas Oliver, 1734–1815," *Publications of the Colonial Society of Massachusetts,* XXVIII (*Transactions,* 1930–1933) 47–59. Hutchinson condemned Oliver for his weakness in this encounter: Nov. 24, 1774, *Diary and Letters,* I, 321 (also printed in Elton, "Oliver," p. 56).

Civil government is near its end, the courts of justice expiring one after another. . . . I mean, My Lord, to secure all I can by degrees, to avoid any bloody crisis as long as possible, unless forced into it by themselves, which may happen. . . . Conciliating, moderation, reasoning is over; nothing can be done but by forcible means. Though the people are not held in high estimation by the troops, yet they are numerous, worked up to a fury, and not a Boston rabble but the freeholders and farmers of the country. A check anywhere would be fatal, and the first stroke will decide a great deal. We should therefore be strong and proceed on a good foundation before anything decisive is tried, which it's to be presumed will prove successful.[41]

What did this mean? Not only, it quickly became clear, was Gage completely inactive, claiming the forces he had—which were far more powerful than any Hutchinson had ever had—were too weak, but he was developing an interpretation of events quite different from any that Hutchinson had suggested to the ministry. He appeared to be arguing that the rebellion was not simply the work of a few ruthless demagogues deluding and inflaming an otherwise well-disposed but inert population; he was faced, he claimed, with a general, popular, widely- and deeply-shared movement of resistance, and he did not think it could be suppressed with less than twenty thousand troops. By the end of the month the development he had seen in process had been completed. The still loyal members of the new Assembly, he then reported, had been forced to leave Salem and take refuge in Boston, which had become a fortified enclave in a hostile land. The old House and Council had taken the place of the official government, and the writ of crown law could now no longer cross the Charles River, and would no longer do so until the whole of New England was conquered by military force. The extremity of the situation, Gage wrote, was beyond the conception of most people, and had been foreseen by none. Perhaps in Hutchinson's time the virus of rebellion had been confined to Boston, "but now it's so universal there is no knowing where to apply the remedy."[42]

41. Gage to Dartmouth, Sept. 2, 1774, CO5/763/263.
42. Gage to Dartmouth, Sept. 20 and 25, 1774, CO5/763/313, 333. These dispatches, which arrived in London on Nov. 18, were completely at variance with the official expectation in London and were therefore discounted in the colonial office. They brought Gage's credibility into question almost immediately. By Dec. 18 John Pownall was telling

Bad as this news from Boston was, what was soon reported from Philadelphia was worse, and proved to be critical. That the Congress would declare an embargo on British goods had been anticipated, and in view of the outcome of earlier efforts at nonimportation that threat had not been taken very seriously. Even when supported by the Congress's Association, which created enforcement procedures that would reach into every community in America and that would remain in force until all the American grievances were redressed, the nonimportation, nonconsumption, and nonexportation program was not thought to be a hopeless or irreversible development; nor was the Congress's "Appeal to the British Nation," with its ringing reminder of Britain's past defense of liberty and its prayer to the British people to cast off their "wicked ministers and evil councillors" and repudiate the enslaving enactments that were leading to war. What seemed to Hutchinson and those he saw most frequently to be the ultimate and irreversible defiance was the Suffolk Resolves, which had been produced at a county convention held in Hutchinson's own town of Milton, and adopted by the Congress on September 17. This, it was felt, was a truly revolutionary document, an explicit declaration of independence. After its fervent, inflammatory preamble, the document declared that since the recent acts of Parliament were "the attempts of a wicked adminstration to enslave America," they were infractions of the rights for which the colonists' ancestors had died and therefore need not be obeyed; that judges whose tenure and salary derived from the crown were unconstitutional officers and their courts and rulings should be ignored; that mandamus councillors who refused to resign were enemies of their country and should be dealt with as such; that town militias should be organized and ordered to seize anyone who served "the present tyrannical and unconstitutional government"; that the governing bodies in Massachusetts would hereafter be the new Provincial Congress, soon to meet in Concord, and the Continental Congress; and that the colonies should join together

Dartmouth of his "alarm and astonishment at the manner in which Gages writes, and the inactivity and irresolution of his conduct." He was "at a loss to account for the strange conduct of General Gage, which seems devoid of sense and spirit," and suggested steps to be taken to overcome this embarrassment. *Manuscripts of the Earl of Dartmouth,* II (Historical Manuscripts Commission, *Fourteenth Report,* Appendix, Part X, London, 1895), 240.

in mutual support in their resistance to the unconstitutional and tyrannical forces of the ministry and the crown.[43]

The world had been transformed. Hutchinson hardly knew what to say or what to propose. The plan for reconciliation he had worked out with such precision and delicate care was now totally irrelevant: its reality had simply dissolved with the first news from the *Scarborough*—blown aside like a leaf in a gale. And not only that particular plan. The Suffolk Resolves, he wrote, "are enough to put it out of my power to contribute to any accommodation." He had become a spectator overnight, and a spectator to a development that until then had been almost beyond his imagining. The future had become indeterminate. Anything could happen. The responses in England to what seemed to be an uncontrollable madness at home were overwhelming. Both Dartmouth and John Pownall were "thunderstruck with American news; at present [they] seem to suppose it impossible to give way." "Why, Mr. Hutchinson," Lord Dartmouth declared, "if these [Suffolk] Resolves of your people are to be depended on, they have declared war against us: they will not suffer any kind of treaty." What could he reply? "I cannot help it, My Lord. Your Lordship knows I have done everything in my power to close the breach between the kingdom and the colonies, and it distresses me greatly that there is so little prospect of success." Calm words—they masked the turmoil that grew in him as he made the rounds of officials and social acquaintances at all levels.

William Knox, whose attitude had never been severe, had become a different man: "he supposes now that all treaty is over. The first thing, he says, will be to let America know that Britain will support its authority, and then concede what shall be thought fit." The entire ministry concurred in the King's view that "the New England governments are in a state of rebellion; blows must decide whether they are to be subject to this country or independent." And not only the ministry. It was a matter of the greatest importance to Hutchinson that the crisis, as he wrote his brother on November 1, was

43. On the First Continental Congress and the Suffolk Resolves, see Gipson, *British Empire*, XII, chap. ix, esp. pp. 244–246. As soon as Hutchinson read the Suffolk Resolves, which were published in the London newspapers at the end of October, he declared them to be "more alarming than anything which has yet been done." It would not surprise him to hear, he wrote his brother on Nov. 1, that Massachusetts would now resume its seventeenth-century charter; and then he added the remarkable comment that "if I should be chosen governor, I am determined not to serve." *Diary and Letters,* I, 272, 282.

"not a ministerial but a national concern," and the measures that would emerge to deal with it, he felt certain, would not be party measures but national measures; they could as well be prepared by Edmund Burke as by Lord North. For the old, immensely difficult, and divisive problem of finding a balance between American claims and English authority no longer existed. The only question left—which would be dealt with by the Parliament newly elected in November for the specific purpose of responding to the American crisis—was, "How shall an entire separation of the colonies from the kingdom be prevented?" It was a transcendently important issue: "The general voice is, that so important an affair has not come before Parliament since the [Glorious] Revolution. Indeed, I do not think that affair was of so great importance." He could not believe the colonies would be so mad as to risk actual warfare with a country "so disproportioned in power." But with the controversy so inflamed, nothing was certain. He put his trust in God—and Parliament—to "open the eyes of the blind before it comes to that."[44]

iii

So, now a spectator, beginning to doubt that he would himself ever be able to shape events, a somewhat marginal figure though still well known and welcome in government circles, and very much the center of a growing group of American refugees, Hutchinson focused his attention on Parliament, which convened on November 29. He looked forward to an overwhelming effort on the part of the government, backed as it was by a fresh mandate in the election that had just been held, to rally the unanimous support of both Houses, project its plan, mobilize the forces needed to put it into effect, and begin the necessary if harsh process of reconstituting the sundered empire. But he was bitterly disappointed—he was bewildered—by what happened.

He thought the opening speech by the King was splendid: a forthright statement that rebellion existed in Massachusetts and was

44. TH to Foster Hutchinson and to ——, Nov. 1, 1774, *Diary and Letters*, I, 284, 282; *ibid.*, pp. 272–273; King George III to Lord North, Nov. 18, 1774, *The Correspondence of King George the Third with Lord North from 1768 to 1783*, ed. W. Bodham Donne (London, 1867), I, 215.

supported elsewhere in America, coupled with a firm and dignified restatement of Parliament's authority and an appeal to both Houses to act unanimously in exemplifying and asserting "a due reverence for the laws and a just sense of the blessing of our excellent constitution." The opening ceremony, too, impressed Hutchinson, even thrilled him: he received from this pageantry, he recorded, "greater pleasure than I have done from any other public scene since I have been in England." But on the very next day, the first day of business, the trouble started. There was a sour note for Hutchinson even in the opening address in support of the King's speech. It was delivered by his old patron, Lord Hillsborough, who in the course of his remarks quoted a letter of Hutchinson's, and though he did not mention the letter writer by name, the letter was well known to both North and Dartmouth and probably also to others; in itself, Hutchinson feared, it would inject him willy-nilly into Parliamentary politics. But the real business, which followed Hillsborough's speech, reduced this personal concern to triviality.

The Duke of Richmond moved an amendment to Hillsborough's motion, challenging the ministry to lay all of its information on the state of affairs in America before Parliament, and in his peroration made declarations so strongly in favor of the colonies that Hutchinson thought it must be inferred "he was in favor of the claims of independency of the Americans." And Richmond was supported in this view by Lords Camden and Shelburne. In the end, thirteen members of the Lords voted for Richmond's amendment, and in a similar challenge to the government that followed Richmond's effort, nine peers of the realm not only voted in opposition to the administration but issued formal protest against the government, a protest that in Hutchinson's view "plainly exempts the Americans from Parliamentary authority in some cases." Hutchinson was astonished, and as the meaning of these preliminary skirmishes became clear to him his confidence in Parliament, which alone, he believed, had the power to save the empire, began to crumble. What had happened to Parliament's concern for the public interest and for the integrity of the British empire, to preserve which he himself had made such costly personal sacrifices? If men of such exalted position lacked the honor and sense of responsibility that he had struggled so long to maintain, could they not be expected at least to be consistent? Lord Rockingham was one of the supporters of the protest; but it had been Rockingham and his party in 1766 who had fathered the Declaratory Act which had stated unequivocally that the colonies were "subject in all cases whatsoever." It had been this principle, supported by logic, history, and common sense, on which Hutchinson had staked his career, yet its original sponsors seemed now to be repudiating it. "Strange," he wrote in his diary, "to what length party spirit carries men. Here is an instance of nine lords who had rather give up the colonies to a foreign power and run the risk of making the kingdom a province of the same power than not indulge a spirit of opposition to the measures of [the] administration." And in the Commons the situation was worse. A similar challenge to the government was supported by the votes of no fewer than seventy-three members and by speeches by a formidable array of orators led by Burke, Fox, and Barré.[45]

And what of the government? Where was its program, its energy, its capacity to command? By virtue of the "interest" that the ministry controlled and the uncomplicated patriotism of the independent country gentlemen, the administration could be sure of a majority in the Commons. But it did not seem inclined to use this power to any purpose that Hutchinson could see. Lord North and his supporters fenced with the opposition, not always effectively, and made promises for the future, but aside from this, and aside from defending itself from attacks, the government did little else. Hutchinson knew that the ministry was now fully informed of the outcome of the Continental Congress—its official proceedings had been transmitted—and he knew that the reports that were coming in from Gage and from himself were increasingly pessimistic. Such powerful figures as Lord Mansfield were certain that the convening of the Provincial Congress in Concord was flagrant treason. Yet the government was allowing a critical period of time to slip away in inactivity. "There's a strange silence upon American affairs," Hutchinson wrote just before Parliament recessed for the Christmas holidays; and it was to him simply unaccountable, considering the importance of these problems. Perhaps "it proceeds from amazement," he said; perhaps the government did not wish to tip its hand before the holidays for fear that the opposition would use the break to its advantage; perhaps there was something in "the nature of the

45. Gipson, *British Empire*, XII, 272–273; *Diary and Letters*, I, 310, 308–309, 311, 315–316.

English constitution" or "some other cause" that he did not understand to account for the continuing inaction. But whatever the
reason the cabinet was silent and apparently inert. There were
rumors of differences of opinion. He heard that it was Lord North
himself who was dragging his feet; Dartmouth, it was said, was
attempting to stir him into action. Perhaps there would soon be
some activity—not panic or brutal repression, he hoped, but firm,
consistent, and intelligent action—when Parliament reconvened
on January 19.[46]

Until then there was not much he could do, or even witness, and
with London almost deserted he decided to travel some with Billy
and Elisha: to Bath, via Reading and Maidenhead, hoping there
"to keep up my spirits" in visiting old friends and acquaintances
and in relaxing at the famous resort; then to Bristol, where he
found, among many other acquaintances, the ubiquitous Temple,
who informed him that Chatham, at least, wholly approved of the
work of the Continental Congress. But though the company was on
the whole good and his curiosity to see the countryside and meet
the west-country notables strong, he could not abstract himself
from the anxieties that beset him nor shake off the impression of
inertia, corruption, and impending disaster that he had received
as he had watched Parliament in action. The more he thought
about what he had witnessed the worse it seemed. "I never met
with anything," he wrote from Bath,

which set the depravity of human nature in a more striking light than the
conduct of the noblemen at the heads of the past administration. Lord
Rockingham, who was the father of the Declaratory Act for the undivided
authority of Parliament but against the exercise of it in taxation; Lord
Temple, who protested against the repeal of the Stamp Act and [yet] has
been uniform upon all subsequent occasions with Lord Chatham; Lord[s]
Camden and Shelburne, who have all, at different times, declared that
Parliament has no authority to tax the colonies, have their meetings . . .
and are laying their heads together to distress the present administration,
though they know it must be at the expense of, if not fatal to, both kingdom
and colonies. Their plan is to propose nothing themselves but to enflame
the minds of the people against everything proposed by administration,
and they have lowered themselves so far as to consult *Junius* Lee, and

46. *Diary and Letters*, I, 330, 320, 329, 331, 337, 333; TH to Gage, Dec. 19, and to
Jonathan Sewall, Dec. 30, 1774, Eg. MSS, 2661, pp. 94, 97.

some of them even [Josiah] Quincy [Jr.]. . . . Franklin is stirring up a meeting of the merchants in London. . . .

Again he reminded himself that the entire opposition, drawn from no matter how many previous administrations, could not outvote the government; but he could take little satisfaction from that if the government itself continued to be silent. Nothing could distract him from this central concern, and when word reached Bristol that letters from home had arrived for him in London, he left precipitously and was back in good time for the reconvening of Parliament.[47]

The letters he found waiting for him, some from distressed members of his own family, described in greater detail than he had had before what had happened to Boston as a consequence of the Port Act and convinced him more deeply than ever that that enactment had been a disaster, personal as well as public. He was determined once again to try in some way to convince the government at least to modify that Act, and perhaps the Government Act as well, and in the process to sound out the ministry's plans for the future. He rushed about to see those in authority he could easily reach—Suffolk, Wedderburn, Dartmouth, and the two colonial undersecretaries. But the interviews were bleakly discouraging. Suffolk, a reasonable man, refused even to consider anything that might sound like a concession. Talking with Wedderburn was a particularly chilling experience. On the one hand, the solicitor general gave him the impression either that the cabinet had still not thought through the issues to a conclusion and prepared plans, or that he himself, unaccountably, was uninformed. On the other hand, he rejected outright Hutchinson's plea for the repeal of the Port Act, which, Hutchinson pointed out from certain knowledge, was inflicting burdens not on its presumed victims, who were being supported in idleness by the charity of the neighboring colonies, but on the friends of the government, who were not. Webberburn's own proposals Hutchinson thought were fearful: a test oath to allow a selective exemption from the Port Act ("I told him that would make a great convulsion"), the capture and incarceration of the leaders of Congress ("the people in Scotland," Wedderburn said, "were better humored ever since the bloodshed in the rebellion

47. *Diary and Letters*, I, 343, 345, 349; TH to TH, Jr., Jan. 9, and to Mr. Green, Jan. 10, 1775, *ibid.*, pp. 352, 355.

[of 1745]"), and the punishment of the entire membership of the Congress by declaring them to be legal aliens.[48]

Once again frustrated in his efforts to relieve Massachusetts of its punishment and feeling utterly helpless to influence the actions of the government, Hutchinson turned his attention to Parliament and found, in the weeks and months that followed, that his hopes had been misplaced and his earlier apprehensions more than justified. Attention centered first not on the government's program at all but on Chatham's sweeping proposal for reconciliation, based on the withdrawal of troops; the restriction of Parliament's authority to matters "touching the general weal of the whole dominion of the imperial crown" (hence not taxation); the recognition of the legality of the forthcoming Second Continental Congress, which would be asked to enact a requisition scheme for colonial support of general expenses; and the eventual repeal of all the protested enactments of Parliament dating back to 1763. This to Hutchinson was scarcely serious legislation at all—a "strange bill," he called it, correctly described, he said, as "more like a newspaper or declamatory speech . . . than like a bill"; it was so extravagant in its "absurdities," he believed, that the reasonable if naive people who earlier had thought it possible for Parliament to bind itself never to tax America were now convinced of the logical fallacy of that view. Yet though Chatham's bill was defeated on the first preliminary test, thirty-two members of the upper House voted to consider it, and this opposition, paralleled in the lower House, continued unabated. When the government's program finally emerged in the course of February, the opposition tore into it from every angle, and though they could not defeat it, they subjected it to every sort of punishment short of defeat.[49]

Hutchinson's feelings as he watched these proceedings and tried desperately, and in the end ineffectively, to participate constructively, behind the scenes, were doubly drawn. While the opposition's assaults on the government seemed to him to be inexcusable, almost treasonous in their unprincipled opportunism, and utterly

48. TH to George Erving, Jan. 19, 1775, *Diary and Letters*, I, 357; *ibid.*, pp. 360, 353–354.

49. Gipson, *British Empire*, XII, 379–382; *Diary and Letters*, I, 358, 366, 367; TH to Daniel Leonard, Feb. 14, 1775, Eg. MSS, 2661, p. 120.

illogical in their presumption that sovereignty could in some way be made divisible, he found the government's program inadequate, unimaginative, and at the same time provocative. He agreed with Lord Hardwicke that while the opposition was "daring, resolute, and determined," capable of any degree of ruthlessness to carry its points, the administration was "tender, doubting, and undetermined." Fiercely harassed by the opposition and faced with problems of great complexity, the government seemed to Hutchinson to be almost paralyzed by a fear of failure, and its consequent caution, he wrote, in itself contributed to the very failure it feared, for "it tends to give spirit to the Americans." So the ministry decided to send more troops to America, but not an overwhelming number, scoffing at what it took to be Gage's timidity and false interpretation of the forces at work. At the same time it declared Massachusetts to be in a state of rebellion. (Had *Scotland,* Hutchinson asked, been declared to be in rebellion in '45? No, it was then only said that there was a rebellion in Scotland; "and the most that can be said now is, that there is a rebellion in Massachusetts Bay." Was it just to proscribe a whole people, the innocent together with the guilty?) And the government imposed just the test oath that Hutchinson had objected to. Then, to Hutchinson's great distress and acute personal embarrassment, it brought in a bill that became the New England Restraining Act, aimed at countering the Congress's boycott of British trade by confining all of New England's commerce to British ports, and further, in a provision that Lord Dartmouth told Hutchinson had been developed from a suggestion that Hutchinson himself had once made, New England vessels were barred from the Atlantic fisheries. Finally, a plan for conciliation was announced that Hutchinson felt was badly worded and incapable of having the slightest effect in America; the government did not seem to realize, he wrote, that a decade earlier a similar plan had been throughly ridiculed by Otis. The measure, naive and rigid in its stark simplicity, stated that when a colony agreed to provide sums voluntarily for the general support of civil government and to put those sums at Parliament's disposal, Parliament would refrain from taxing it. The best that could be said for this bill, Hutchinson thought, was that it conceded no essential point and would silence those in the opposition who had mistakenly thought such a device would settle everything and had therefore withheld their support for more forceful measures.[50]

It was a hopelessly inadequate program. Every imaginative touch that might have cut through the rigidities and complexities of the Anglo-American impasse (the sending to America of special commissioners to open negotiations, for example, which Dartmouth as well as Hutchinson had favored, or some effort to straighten out the colonists' crucial misunderstanding of Parliament's and the ministry's motivations)—all of this had been eliminated in an effort to concede nothing that might be thought by the majority of patriotic and impatient Members of Parliament to be essential.[51] But the worst aspect of the whole program to Hutchinson was that New England had been singled out for special and extreme punishment— the Restraining Act, he knew, would vastly increase the economic havoc wrought by the Port Act—and that Hutchinson himself was implicated in its authorship.

He had been disheartened by what had happened in Parliament before the government had come forward; he was agonized by what happened thereafter, especially by the passage of the Restraining Bill. He undertook a feverish campaign to modify that bill to prevent its ruining law-abiding merchants loyal to the government, or at least to generalize it in order to remove its special condemnation of New England. He mobilized all of his political acquaintances and buttonholed a group of sympathetic M.P.'s, pleading with them to recognize the bitter truth (which he did not need his own son to tell him) that the act would punish the innocent as much as it would the guilty, perhaps even more so, and begging them to approve his plan to provide exemptions to the force of the act for those who disavowed the boycott of Britain. But the key figure was Wedderburn, who had written the bill in its final form and who took responsibility for its passage, and he would not even consider Hutchinson's proposal, though he said he personally approved of

50. *Diary and Letters*, I, 375, 374, 363, 306, 365; TH to George Erving, Feb. 22, 1775, Eg. MSS, 2661, p. 123. Hutchinson believed Lord North's conciliation plan originated "when I read to him," he wrote an unnamed correspondent (Jonathan Sewall, probably), "the latter part of your last letter. He said with a start, I like that proposal. I am told he has pressed ever since in the cabinet until it was consented to." TH to ——, Feb. 21, 1775, *ibid.*, p. 123.

51. *Diary and Letters*, I, 363, 364 ("At Lord Dartmouth's who informed me that divers forms had been proposed to satisfy the colonists of the intentions of Parliament, but all had been excepted to as tending to encourage them in their claim of independency . . .").

it. Such a concession, he said, would disgust a significant segment of the Commons "and weaken, if not break to pieces, the whole system of America." And for similar reasons he refused to discuss Hutchinson's proposal that the port of Boston be opened *automatically* when and if the tea was paid for. The only appeal possible was to Lord North, but the case was hopeless. The entire country seemed so enraged with America, Hutchinson wrote back to Massachusetts, "that they will hear nothing in your favor. . . . they say neither words nor oaths will bind you and that you will renounce one thing today and resume it tomorrow. It hurts me to think that the [trade] of a whole country should be lost through the wretchedness of a very few men, for though the multitude are misled, it is but a few who have been concerned in those false representations which have destroyed all confidence in us." All he could do was to seek a postponement of the effective date of the commencement of the act, but even in this he failed, and he saw the bill, later extended to include all but three colonies, become law on March 30.[52]

By then it was difficult for him to know where to turn or how to react to the politics in which he was so bewilderingly entangled. The whole spectacle of the most powerful and freest nation on earth struggling ineffectively for seven months to deal with a crisis that threatened its very existence had been bitterly disillusioning. Instead of a rallying of leaders to save the nation, as had happened, he recalled, in 1588, there was savage divisiveness and a heedless pursuit of selfish interests that weakened every halting, indecisive step the King's ministry took to save the situation. The ministry, Hutchinson believed, was altogether right-minded but half-paralyzed with indecision and insecurity, and it had lost the art of making imaginative adjustments that retained essential principles while accommodating the pressures of circumstance. The opposition had will, decisiveness, and oratorical brilliance, but lacked principles, logic, consistency, and above all a concern for the general good: it would destroy the nation, as it was destroying the empire, in the hope of gaining power.

Hutchinson was of course a government man, but he was no less fervently opposed to the Coercive Acts and the Restraining Act

52. TH to Peter Oliver, Feb. 13 (an addition to a letter of Feb. 9) and March 1, 1775, Eg. MSS, 2661, pp. 119–120, 126; TH to ——Clarke, March 4, 1775, *ibid.*, p. 128; TH to Foster Hutchinson, March 5, 1775, *ibid.*, p. 131; *Diary and Letters*, I, 393. On the history of the Restraining Act, see Gipson, *British Empire*, XII, 294, 297–300, 307.

than the most outspoken members of the opposition (though his reasons were different from theirs), and his condemnation of those acts became increasingly intense as he saw their consequences unfold. Similarly, though deeply loyal to the government, he held no one in greater contempt than Thomas Pownall, who, having lost his seat in the recent election, had accepted a Treasury seat simply to stay in the House, and was now prepared to die fighting gloriously to retain the last syllable of the government's most unbending formulation. Lord Camden was a much more important case in point. Hutchinson heard his brilliant speech in the Lords attacking the Restraining Bill, and he must have left the House in a tumult of conflicting emotions. Never had he heard such a flow of words; it would have been hard to imagine a more eloquent attack on the bill that he was himself struggling to deflect or amend. But he was appalled not only by the great lawyer's savage vilification of the King's ministry and his uncritical support of Chatham's ideas, but by his brutal disregard of truth. The speech was crawling with errors of fact. Hutchinson had no trouble filling three pages of his diary with an enumeration of the falsehoods he could recall, not the least of which he was involved in directly himself. Camden, in a dramatic moment in his speech, had charged that Hutchinson, whom he named, had so packed the inland town of Marshfield, Massachusetts, with justices of the peace of his own choosing that the town had given a false impression to Gage and the ministry that the population in the interior of the colony welcomed the support of crown troops. "Upon mentioning my name most of the bishops and many lords who sat with their backs to me turned about and looked in my face." "But alas!" Hutchinson wrote in his diary, Marshfield "appears by the map to be a town upon the sea coast . . . [and] it happened that I never made a justice in that town whilst I was in the government." "Attending two or three debates in the House of Lords," he wrote in a careful understatement to his old colleague Jonathan Sewall, "has lessened the high opinion I had formed of the dignity of it when I was in England before."[53]

53. *Diary and Letters*, I, 303; TH to Mr. Green, Jan. 10, 1775, *ibid.*, p. 355. For Pownall's defense of the Restraining Act, see Gipson, *British Empire*, XII, 298 (cf. p. 295); for Camden's speech, see *ibid.*, p. 299, and for Hutchinson's reaction to it, see *Diary and Letters*, I, 409, 410. Hutchinson, who reported with grim satisfaction on Pownall's adherence to the administration, had earlier recorded in detail what he had heard about financial irregularities attributed to Pownall when he was in Germany. *Ibid.*, p. 313.

A craven opposition, a weak administration, a riotous conflict of selfish interests; savagery, falsehoods, and greed—English politics was far more squalid than he had imagined or could recall. He could not leave off recording in his diary and in his letters the debauchery and corruption of the general election he had witnessed and the more ordinary spectacle of noblemen who feasted with unembarrassed gusto at the public trough and who, like Bernard's patron, Lord Barrington, thought of the state as "a great plum pudding which he was so fond of that he would never quarrel with it but should be for taking a slice as long as there was any left."[54] Yet if this was the underside of politics, it was the underside of a political world that was still essentially his. He accepted its presuppositions, structure, and processes, and he continued through all these months and years of anxiety to struggle within its interstices, seeking security, recognition, vindication—less and less for himself, more and more for his children, and to set the record straight. His letters and diary record an unending succession of dutiful visits to the offices and levées of the great; whispered suggestions, at a hundred interviews, of candidates for offices that had been vacated by disgrace, intrigue, death, or the rumor or prospect of death; and the most subtle manipulation of recommendations to protect the future of his own family by keeping his noble patrons from feeling that his appeals for others were personal and hence that support for his candidates for jobs would once and for all settle their obligations to him.[55] For he had become, in the year or so after his arrival, the chief broker for jobs in the increasingly meaningless royal administration in New England, consulting—always humbly, always deferentially—with men of influence on whom to appoint to the Mandamus Council, the crown courts, the customs administration; and seeking posts, pensions, unpaid salaries, benefits of any kind for his old friends and colleagues—Sewall, Burch, Flucker, Paxton—who were cast adrift by the rising tide of revolution and turned to him for help.[56] Threading his modest, undramatic way successfully

54. *Diary and Letters,* I, 309.

55. "If I had asked as a personal favor it would have given some pretense for retarding the fulfillment of a promise made me for my youngest son who has no other prospects than from a place under government. This I hope will excuse me to all my friends who have desired my interest." TH to Samuel Quincy, April 6, 1775, Eg. MSS. 2661, p. 140.

56. On the intricate politics of filling the lieutenant governorship and the seats on the Mandamus Council, see TH to Dartmouth, March 9, 29, Sept. 20, 21, 1774, CO5/763/148,

through the brilliant, crowded corridors of power would in any case have been difficult for him to do, especially since he had had no direct contact with this grueling process for over thirty years and since he had made it a point of pride at home never to affiliate himself overtly with any English faction but to treat all servants of the crown as if they were as impartial and non-partisan as he assumed the crown to be.[57] But the task was made particularly difficult by the peculiar structure of power under George III. The present administration, he wrote Sewall (whose overlapping appointments in the colonies were still matters of controversy and were still unsettled), was not an integrated, disciplined, and stable political group from which one might extract a reliable quantum of protection and security. It was, rather, a coalition of groups "which have been engaged in very different measures" and the result was that "blocks and bars are thrown in the way, sometimes from one quarter and sometimes from another, quite unexpected. Under such circumstances, solicitations of any sort is very unpleasant, for it's 10 to 1 but somebody or other considers you as thwarting their designs and conceives a dislike to you."[58] But however difficult it might be to manage, patronage politics in a deferential society was the essence of the public life he knew, and it was as natural for him to continue to search and strive and ferret within it as it was for him to breathe. He knew no other form of public life, and he had neither the independence, nor the practical need, nor the imaginative instincts to seek to transcend its rigid confinements.

The deference suitable for this political world was so powerful an instinct in him that it shaped the very boundaries of his im-

---

160; *Dartmouth Manuscripts*, II, 226–227; TH to Gage, Aug. 16, 1774, Eg. MSS, 2661, p. 51; TH to William Burch, July 9 and Dec. 4 (where Hutchinson advises Burch generally on possiblities for future employment), 1774, *ibid.*, pp. 33, 86. Descriptions of Hutchinson's efforts to assist his old colleagues and his advice to them on possibilities and procedures fill the pages of his letterbook in late 1774 and in 1775. A comprehensive tracing of these recommendations would reveal in detail the intimate workings of patronage politics at an ordinary level in the government of George III.

57. "We in America who are servants of the crown consider the ministers of state as the mesne between us and the Lord Paramount. We are always alike attached to ministers without any sort of concern in your party disputes." TH to Thomas Whately, Jan. 25, 1771, MA, XXVII, 106.

58. TH to Jonathan Sewall, April 9, 1775, Eg. MSS, 2661, p. 139. On Hutchinson's efforts to straighten out Sewall's complicated appointment problems, see TH to Gage, April 10, 1775, *ibid.*, p. 144.

agination. He could only be grateful to find that the Archbishop of Canterbury treated him "more like a person upon a level with him than one who is so much inferior" and to be allowed to visit the royal nursery and to report that "a little prince not above three years old held out his hand to Peggy and she had the honor of kissing it." Lord Mansfield—seventy years old, massive in learning, presence, and reputation—overwhelmed him when he met him soon after his arrival. Though Hutchinson disliked romantic daydreams, he confided to his old friend Paxton, after a visit with the great lawyer, that he wished he were young again and that he might "rise in the world under his protection."[59]

Protection was the key to it all—protection of the weak by the powerful, of the obscure by the famous and influential, protection sought after, intrigued for, and earned. It colored the world in all its aspects, as he discovered anew when he was rebuffed by both the Bishop of London and Lord Sandwich in his effort to place the son of a friend's friend in the school of his choice (Charterhouse).[60] He knew the urgencies, sanctions, and opportunities of the system. He knew the importance of maintaining old ties of reciprocal loyalty and protection ("Lord Dartmouth is my chief patron") and of opening new affiliations when the opportunity arose. In November 1774 he responded willingly to an invitation from Lord Hardwicke to undertake a regular correspondence with him on political, particularly American, affairs; and he supplied that concerned but uncommitted nobleman with a flow of news and comment from London to His Lordship's country house, or wherever he might be, that ran continuously to within six months of Hutchinson's death —a string of almost two hundred letters that served the same purpose for Hardwicke that Burke's correspondence did for *his* patron Rockingham, Whately's for Grenville, Jenkinson's for Bute.[61]

He could survive in this world, but its pressures were great, and his personal situation grew ever more complicated and ever more

59. TH to "Sally" (Sarah Hutchinson Oliver), Nov. 1, 1774, Eg. MSS, 2661, pp. 71, 72; TH to Paxton, Sept. 19, 1774, *ibid.*, p. 57.

60. Eg. MSS, 2664, pp. 36–37.

61. The entire correspondence is in the British Museum, Add. MSS, 34527. Hutchinson may also have served Hillsborough, less regularly, in something of the same capacity. TH to Hillsborough, Oct. 17, 1778 (Public Record Office of Northern Ireland, Belfast), filling in the gaps in the official accounts of the American war from Aug. 11 to Sept. 1 with "my own and other private letters," is a model of such correspondences.

embattled as time went on. There seemed to be some inner per-versity of events that forced him into corners to defend what were self-evidently sensible positions and actions of impeccable propriety. Thus, he was proud of his association with high officialdom, not only because it flattered him but because it showed to all the world, and especially to his enemies at home, that his career had been approved, that he had been right and they wrong. Yet he was obliged from the start to dissociate himself, as well as he could, from the ministry's chief response to the rebellion, the Coercive Acts: to explain that he had had nothing whatever to do with their passage, just as he had never approved of the Stamp Act or the Townshend Duties. It was a difficult position to maintain, however. The opposition in Massachusetts, which had for so long been blaming the entire Anglo-American struggle on his misrepresenta-tions to the ministry, now triumphantly cited his visible association with the leaders of the English government, not as proof of his vindication but as proof of his guilt. He felt obliged to redouble his efforts to make his innocence clear, but nothing he could do seemed to make any difference. His apparently close and harmoni-ous associations with the ministry seemed irrefutable evidence, to those who wished to see it that way, not only that he was guilty as charged of earlier crimes against America but that he had been compounding his guilt more recently in England. And it was in large part to nullify what they took to be Hutchinson's increasingly menacing role in England that the opposition leaders in Massachu-setts sent over to London the young lawyer Josiah Quincy, Jr., who, as "Marchamont Nedham," had so savagely vilified Hutchinson for writing the Whately letters and who, since then, as the author of a pamphlet attacking the Port Act with extraordinary passion and learning, had become a torchbearer of the radical cause.[62]

Quincy arrived in London on November 17, 1774, on a vessel that also bore a letter from Gage warning the ministry that there was "something mysterious concerning the object of his voyage." The young Bostonian remained in England for three and a half months, and in that time he made his purpose perfectly clear. His

---

62. Josiah Quincy, *Observations on the Act of Parliament Commonly Called the Boston Port-Bill; with Thoughts on Civil Society and Standing Armies* . . . (Boston, 1774). For an excellent account of Quincy's career, including his important trip to England at the end of 1774, see George H. Nash, III, "From Radicalism to Revolution: The Political Career of Josiah Quincy, Jr.," AAS *Procs.,* 79 (1969), 253–290.

aim, Lord North easily deduced, was "to present the colonies in the most formidable view" and convince the world that the recent measures of the British government, misconceived and counter-productive as he believed they were, had resulted from the mis-representations fed the ministry by ruthless colonial officials, notably Thomas Hutchinson.[63]

Quincy called on Franklin almost immediately, and at once fell into congenial company. Within twenty-four hours of his arrival in the capital he was told, by the absentee Massachusetts customs inspector John Williams, "that Governor Hutchinson had repeatedly assured the ministry that a union of the colonies was utterly impracticable, that the people were greatly divided among themselves in every colony, and that there could be no doubt that all America would *submit,* and that they *must,* and moreover would, *soon.*" Franklin promptly confirmed the story, or at least said that he had heard the same information from "several of the nobility and ministry." These were but reinforcements for the conviction Quincy had brought with him and of which, on the second day of his stay, he attempted to convince Lord North himself. The causes of most of our political evils, he blandly informed the prime minister in an interview on November 19, were "gross misrepresentation and falsehood," and they were the result not, as Lord North attempted indulgently to suggest, of error or unintended biases, but of "worse motives." But if, as Hutchinson heard from the colonial undersecre-taries, Lord North refused to take the suggestion seriously and informed Quincy that the government's measures were responses to documented actions and published statements, not to mere rumors or representations, and that in view of that evidence any minister who had done less than he had done to contain the rebellion "should expect to have his head brought to the block . . . and he should deserve it," there were others in England who were only too eager to agree with the young radical, to stimulate him and to be stimulated by him further.[64] Thomas Pownall, who had by then

63. Gage to Dartmouth, Sept. 25, 1774, CO5/763/341; *Diary and Letters,* I, 302. For Hutchinson's warnings of Quincy's intentions, see *ibid.,* p. 269; TH to Gage, Nov. 19, 1774, Eg. MSS, 2661, p. 81.

64. "Journal of Josiah Quincy, Jun., during his Voyage and Residence in England from September 28th, to March 3d, 1775," MHS *Procs.,* 50 (1916–1917), 438, 439, 440; *Diary and Letters,* I, 299–300, 302, 304–305; TH to ——, Nov. 24. 1774, Eg. MSS, 2661, p. 84.

already sold his independence to the government in exchange for a seat in the House, was always eager to attack his old enemy and always ready to ingratiate himself, privately at least, with the radicals. "Mr. Quincy," he told the young American (in the only words Quincy recorded of a three-hour conversation with the former governor), "I do assure [you] all the measures against America were planned and pushed on by Bernard and Hutchinson. They were incessant in their application to administration and gave the most positive assurances of success; and I do assure [you] America has not a more determined, insidious, and inveterate enemy than Governor Hutchinson. He is now doing and will continue to do all he can against you." Corbin Morris, another customs official, concurred: "Governors Hutchinson and Bernard were principally attended to in the late measures against the colonies," Quincy recorded him saying; "but he added that government had found that many things had turned out different from Mr. Hutchinson's representation, and that things had not been at all conformable to what he foretold." Even men of the highest station agreed—Lord Shelburne, for one, who added that he knew for a fact that all of Lord Mansfield's belligerence against the colonies "was grounded on Governor Hutchinson's information." There was no end to it: Williams extended his attack on December 23; Colonel Barré joined the chorus on January 2. By the time, three weeks after his arrival, Quincy came to summarize his impressions in a circular letter addressed to his wife, the theme had become obsessive:

Will you believe me when I tell you that your letting a certain character escape from your justice is imputed to you on all hands as a fault? Your enemies impute it to your cowardice, your friends to your want of political sagacity. Certain it is that from one man—from one man, I say, and he neither a Bute, a Mansfield, a North, or a Bernard—are all your miseries supposed to flow. This supposition is not made by those alone who are sanguine in your common cause; it is the general sentiment of all parties, and were I to show you my journal . . . you would find unexpected characters intimating or speaking out the same idea.[65]

Quincy's conviction was passionate, and his influence grew as he circulated energetically among pro-Americans and neutrals in Lon-

---

65. "Quincy's London Journal," pp. 444, 446, 447, 450, 452; Quincy to Mrs. Quincy, Dec. 7, 1774, in Josiah Quincy, *Memoir of the Life of Josiah Quincy,* [Jr.] (Boston, 1825), pp. 256–257.

don, fed ideas for speeches to such sympathetic M.P.'s as David Hartley,[66] and filled his correspondence and conversation with the charges that he heard repeated day after day. By March 4, when he left England—fatally ill but determined to carry home personally the impressions he had formed and the suggestions for action that had been confided to him by the leading strategists of the English opposition—he had made Hutchinson's position in London far more difficult than it would otherwise have been. For he had renewed and brought to a high level of specificity not only the ancient charge that Hutchinson had conspired against freedom in America in order to establish himself in power, but a view of affairs in America and England entirely at variance with Hutchinson's and one that events were apparently beginning to justify: that the colonies were united, or soon would be; that the resistance to England had massive public support; that the colonists, convinced that their cause was right, would never relent and were economically and militarily capable of sustaining a war to support their claims; and that open warfare was unlikely in view of the broad support for the colonies and the broad opposition to the ministry that existed at all levels in England itself.[67]

Was Hutchinson to be challenged on everything he had predicted? Were all his expectations to be proved wrong? Increasingly he felt thrown back into defensive positions, despite the formal credit he seemed to have with the ministry, and forced to explain himself, excuse himself, make clear why his predictions and expectations had gone wrong—or why so many people seemed to think they had. While Quincy was working so diligently against him on the broad issues of the struggle, others were noting an apparently more limited error, in Hutchinson's estimate of the military forces that would be required to handle the rebellious colonies. Had he not— consistent with his view that the root of the troubles lay not in deep-lying, almost universal, fears of absolutist government, but rather in the ruthless ambitions of demagogic politicians and their merchant allies—had he not indicated that no massive army was needed but simply a few smart regiments smartly commanded?

66. *Diary and Letters,* I, 317.
67. Thus Hutchinson himself summarized the interpretation of events that Quincy was effectively promoting: TH to Robert Auchmuty, Dec. 9, 1774, *Diary and Letters,* I, 318.

And was he not as perplexed as Dartmouth and his undersecretaries by Gage's pleas for far greater forces, the general's refusal to budge until he had them, and his suggestion to Hutchinson, which was immediately passed on to a horrified ministry, that the Coercive Acts be suspended until an overwhelming force was at hand?[68]

It was true that Hutchinson had not originally thought that a huge continental army would be needed to control the troubles in America, but then neither did he think—or have any reason to think—that Gage and the ministry would be so dilatory and indecisive. He knew perfectly well that the longer the controversy dragged on, the greater the force would have to be to control it. This was not a fire that would burn itself out if let alone, for, as he explained again and again, the rebels were continuously broadening the base of their support by well-practiced arts of intimidation and propaganda. He had seen it all happen before, and now could see it developing again before his own eyes. There was Franklin, he noted with dismay, in the gallery of the House of Commons, "staring with his spectacles" as he listened to an "unguarded" speech by Lord Clare calling for instant and ruthless action against the colonists "or they will finally conquer . . .—if they are able to hold out, we know that we are not"; within twenty-four hours, Hutchinson knew, "the relation of this speech is on its way to America."[69]

Fanned by such encouragement, by the irresponsible agitations of the English opposition, and by the near paralysis of the ministry, the rebellion would not easily die down. But that he could not have known at the start. Strong measures would have to be taken, he knew by the fall of 1774, but not because of any misjudgment of his. He had always thought, and had made very clear in his letters of 1769–70 when he himself had shared responsibility for the deployment of troops in Boston, that too few troops were worse than none since they could only provoke and not control a difficult

68. King George III to Lord North, Nov. 19, 1774, Donne, ed., *Correspondence of George III to Lord North*, p. 216.

69. *Diary and Letters*, I, 404. "The ministry say, let the fire alone and it will burn out in America as it has done in England, for it is agreed that the opposition here has not at any time been at so low an ebb as it is at present. But I tell them that there is more fuel in proportion than there is in England." TH to Israel Williams, Sept. 29, 1774, Eg. MSS, 2661, 62.

situation. Yet he found himself blamed now, by some, for the ministry's failure to send an overwhelming force in the first place.

All of these embarrassments and frustrations were disturbing in themselves; but they took on added meaning and became increasingly portentous as the news from home grew worse. And not merely the public news—that the New England countryside was completely in the hands of the rebels; that a militia army was being successfully raised (for which he would eventually be blamed since he had encouraged the forming of town militias in 1771);[70] that the Second Continental Congress threatened to be more belligerent than the First; and that, with America forming into two armed camps, the slightest spark could touch off an explosion that would make the situation almost irrecoverable. What deepened the effect of all of this on Hutchinson was the fact that his own family was so seriously and directly involved. Three of his children were with him, but not Tommy and not Sally and not Elisha's wife and infant child. They, and the rest of his more extended family, were in danger; they faced dangers, indeed, that he would not even hear about for weeks or even months after they had been confronted. He tried to piece together, from the long-delayed letters he received, the tragic history of the intimate community he had known. His in-laws, the Olivers in Middleborough and the Watsons in Plymouth, and his oldest friends and former colleagues were fleeing properties they and their kin had possessed and cultivated for generations, and were crowding into Boston to seek refuge with Gage and his troops. From Tommy, now the acting head of the family, on whom he relied to keep things in hand until he could return, he heard very little in the winter of 1774–75—a letter of September 15 reached him only on January 4—but what he did hear from him was similarly discouraging: wild mobs unaccountably encouraged by sober, sensible, respectable men; economic paralysis, panic, fear everywhere. At least, though, his son indicated that he still had

70. "For my credulity in [believing that most Americans did not want independence] and for not encouraging proposals for altering the constitution when made to me, I have been blamed here, and the encouragement I gave to military discipline in the several parts of the province is considered as a great oversight. I have been blamed particularly for forming the artillery and cadet companies." TH to ——, July 28, 1775, Eg. MSS, 2661, p. 161

control of the precious Milton property, the simple but beautiful hill-top "cottage in the country" that he had built with such affection and care thirty years earlier, that had been an ultimate refuge to him ever since, and that continued to represent peace and stability in a world that had been mad with violence for over a decade.[71] And it was to this still and ordered center of his now wildly disordered world that his thoughts turned increasingly as the weeks of his absence from home became months and as he came to see the reality of English life in sharper and sharper focus.

iv

For his deepening gloom, in the spring of 1775, was not only the result of the threatening course of public affairs; it was the consequence too of a culture shock. It was the compounding of the two—the political and the cultural, the public and the private— that created the desperation he felt by the time Parliament concluded its disheartening session late in May.

He continued to be impressed with London—official London, the law courts, the palaces, the houses of the great—but he could not bend back the stiff nonconformist provincialism that had bound him all his life, to enjoy the city's pleasures and relax in its sophisticated ambience. It was a "strange world," he concluded, and a cruel world, of women so callous they could ignore a child killed by their carriage; and a dissolute world, of statesmen, drunk through the night, still asleep when he called at 11:00 A.M. He tried to adjust. He followed advice: to wait on the great; to visit the theaters, "deceptions," and "routs"; to pass from one to another salon so as never "to leave the room quite empty until it is so late as to be proper . . . to quit"; above all, to remain in circulation and never lose contact with those who might support him.[72]

But he could not conform. The "punctilios" and protocol wearied him. The mores shocked him ("The vitiated, detestable taste of the present age"); the gossip depressed him ("Dined at Mr. Ellis's . . . Not a word of English politics. Routs, concerts, operas, etc., in

71. TH to TH, Jr., Jan. 9, 1775, *Diary and Letters,* I, 352.
72. *Diary and Letters,* I, 477 ("The coach full of ladies drove on as if nothing had happened"), 379, 307; II, 57.

which I took no part"); and the theater—even Garrick—bored him, though he was intrigued by the great actor's wealth and even more by his fabulous dissipation and the diseases that so appropriately followed ("disorders in his kidneys and bladder," Hutchinson recorded, "a stone being found in the neck of the latter and one of the former having wholly perished"). During their first four months in London he and Peggy saw only one play, "and I think one or two more will content us, maybe we shall add an opera." "I never go into gay company from any pleasure I can take from it," he wrote when the initial excitement of his arrival had worn off. He found the continuous movement, "from one town and place to another, walking, riding, receiving and returning visits, going to court, etc.," so burdensome that he had no energy left for the chief pleasures of his former life, "my pen and my book." But as far as possible he kept to his old habits, regulating his diet carefully, exercising regularly, and keeping his social and political visiting to the daytime hours. "I am very seldom out of my house on an evening," he wrote, exceptions being made for the weekly "conversations" he attended "where are commonly half a dozen bishops and as many dignified clergymen of inferior rank, several members of Parliament, and gentlemen of distinguished characters in different branches of science." And if once "to avoid being singular" he joined a fashionable throng in Lord Loudoun's private gardens to see a "trifling, puerile, insipid regatta," he would no more return to another such scene than he would to the Pantheon's "magnificent show," which he saw as a guest of Lord Hardwicke. Never, he concluded, had there been a time "when so great a part of the people spend so great a portion of their time and estates in amusements and dissipation."[73]

It was not his world, and he longed for the one that was. His comments on London, the people he met, and the country houses he saw became comparative judgments in which he measured this unfamiliar world against his own. Lord Dartmouth he liked best

73. *Diary and Letters*, I, 273, 307, 476; II, 327, 192, 240, 36, 24; TH to Sally Oliver, Mr. Foster, and ——, Nov. 1, Oct. 10, Nov. 4, 1774, Eg. MSS, 2661, pp. 71, 64, 76; TH to Mr. Walter, April 11, 1775, *Diary and Letters*, I, 434. Hutchinson's disgust at the regatta was heightened by the fact that it coincided with receipt of news of the first battles of the Revolutionary War and of the siege of Boston. The expense of the regatta, he wrote Hardwicke, "would have supported half a dozen battalions one campaign at least." TH to Hardwicke, June 24, 1775, Add. MSS, 34527, p. 23.

of all the people he met: "amiable," he called him, "a man of literature [and] good natural sense . . . he would pass in New England for an orthodox good Christian." Lord Gage and his lady he also respected for their sense and sobriety, especially after seeing them read the evening service "with great propriety" to their thirty servants and the company of thirteen in the great hall at Firle, "the whole family joining in the responses." But most of what he saw suffered sadly by comparison. Bath, for example, that center of fashionable entertainment, had nothing, he reported, "so agreeable to me as what I could find at home": he preferred staying in his room writing letters to joining the throngs at the concert and ball; the town of Milton: "not so pleasing as my own Milton would have been"; Bristol: "taken in all circumstances I should prefer living there to any place in England. The manners and customs of the people are very like those of the people of New England, and you might pick out a set of Boston selectmen from any of their churches." He tried to ease the shock, to minimize the differences by living "as much in the New England way as ever we can, and I have not missed either Church or Meeting any Sunday since I have been in England except one, when bad weather and a cold kept me home." With a few possible exceptions—Lord Dartmouth, whom Hillsborough condemned for having "too much humanity—too much religion"; Welbore Ellis, who apparently shared Hutchinson's interest in the general problems of politics and constitutionalism; and the scholarly, somewhat withdrawn Lord Hardwicke—his closest friends remained his oldest: his children, Mauduit, Jackson, the debilitated, quiescent Bernard, and, increasingly, his former companions and associates from home who joined him in exile abroad. And of all the hundreds of dinners he recorded himself attending the ones he most enjoyed were those most like his father's codfish suppers in Boston fifty years before—small, intimate, relaxed, unpretentious affairs where the conversation was serious and opinions sincere.[74]

But politics remained at the center of his awareness. Old world corruption in itself he thought he understood: like so many of his countrymen (like Jefferson, for example) he had long been used to

74. TH to ——, to TH, Jr., and to Sally Oliver, Nov. 1774, Jan. 9, 1775, and Nov. 1, 1774, *Diary and Letters*, I, 285, 352, 281; *ibid.*, I, 224, 444; II, 105, 148; TH to Paxton, Jan. 11, 1775, Eg. MSS, 2661, p. 110.

warning the young of its dangers. But what he was not prepared for, and what shocked him beyond all else, was the insidious effect the social corruption of England seemed to be having on its political behavior. It was this that explained to him the almost total indifference of the English political public to the crisis at hand, its incapacity to see the issues and problems and to sense the temper of the American people and hence to judge the consequences of actions that were taken. Years before, he had warned that the worst mistake England could possibly make would be to do nothing until a massive punitive assault was necessary, and then to act so harshly that the colonists would have no choice but to fight or surrender abjectly. And that, he believed, was precisely what was happening —and not simply because of the sloth or corruption or stupidity of the politicians, but because the public had lost its sense of values.

The more he saw of England the more certain he was that the basic trouble lay deep within society and not on its political surface. No one seemed aware of the stakes. There seemed to be no way to cut through the indifference. What could one say to a Member of Parliament (brother-in-law of Lord Dartmouth) who "asked whether it was not better to give up the Americans than to be at the expense . . . to reduce and afterwards secure them"? What could one say to the delightful Edward Gibbon, who within a few months of his entering the House had become bored by America and its problems and recommended clapping the Massachusetts leaders in prison and sending over Russian mercenaries to deal with the rest? And these were presumably responsible public men. The population at large, it seemed, was simply frozen in a complacency so deep, an indifference so glacial as to be impenetrable by the appeals of reason, sensibility, or even enlightened self-interest.[75]

As all of this became clear to Hutchinson in the weeks and months in which the political prospects grew darker, his longing for home—for an escape from this alien land to the peace of New England and the simple beauty of Milton—grew into a commanding passion. By the spring of 1775 it had come to color almost every page of his diary and almost every letter he wrote to intimates at home.

75. *Diary and Letters*, I, 329, 364 (for Gibbon's proposal "to attaint 14 or 15 of the Provincial Congress"); Lutnick, "Gibbon and the Decline of the First British Empire," p. 1100.

He hoped, he wrote in September 1774, to leave his bones where he found them and to be received again by the country in which he had been born, for despite all the "cruel persecution" he had suffered there, "it is the nearest to my heart." Nobility and royalty were impressive, but "I had rather live at Milton than at Kew," and he had rather see his grandchildren playing about him than the Princess Charlotte or Prince Augustus. He tried to assure himself that his removal from office had been entirely honorable and his exile not something for which he could blame himself. New England, he wrote on November 1, "is wrote upon my heart in as strong characters as Calais was upon Queen Mary's, but there is this difference: she lost the one by her own folly; I am not sensible I could have kept the other except in a way which would have caused more pain from reflection than I now feel from the loss of it." He bore his neighbors at Milton no ill-will for any share they had taken in causing the upheaval; he had no case to prove against them: all he hoped for was yet to "live and die among them, and I trust recover their esteem." It was suggested by old friends that he remain in England. "I am like the old Athenians; I can't bear the thought of laying my bones anywhere but with my ancestors and friends in my native land. And I hope to return and convince my countrymen that I have ever aimed at their real interest and that I am like some good wives who, the more their husbands beat them, the more they love them." He hated to hear New England condemned, especially by his own countrymen. When his immediate family, joined by his old friend Richard Clarke, the tea consignee, discussed one evening "which was the best country, New England or Old," Hutchinson, Peggy reported to her sister-in-law, could not keep from expressing his partiality for his homeland "in very strong terms." "How happy should I be," she concluded, "to see that country restored to a state of peace and quiet! Not so much for my own sake as Papa's."[76]

He could not take his mind from Milton. He yearned for its order and quiet. In the midst of the worst turmoils of his first year abroad he planned for its future and for the peaceful conclusion of

76. TH to Mr. Lee, Israel Williams, and Henry Caner, Sept. (not sent), Sept. 29, Nov. 10, 1774, Eg. MSS, 2661, pp. 58, 62, 80; TH to Sally Oliver, Foster Hutchinson, and ——, Nov. 1, 2, 1774, *Diary and Letters*, I, 281, 283, 284; Peggy Hutchinson to Mary Watson Hutchinson, Oct. 29, 1774, *ibid.*, pp. 276–277.

his own life in its decent, simple surroundings. Could Tommy send him the measurements of the bedroom door? he wrote in December 1774; he had some improvements in mind. Would Tommy please plant the fine gooseberry cuttings he sent early in March 1775 as soon as possible, to catch the early spring growing season? "I hope those heads of the pear trees which were grafted in the garden last year and failed, you either have grafted or will graft again from some of the heads which did not fail; and the trees will bear to have some of the old boughs taken off." He was swept away by the power of his own longing and imagining. Put the grounds in order, he told Tommy in an elaborately detailed letter of instruction in April; see that the grass is mowed, the tillage marketed, the wagons repaired for the spring and summer work, and be careful in loading and transporting the manure from one field to another, he wrote—then he caught himself. "This is a strange letter from London, but I write it more for my own sake than for yours, as it affords me some amusement."[77]

But he was not amused. He was frightened, hearing very little from home and perhaps half suspecting the truth—which was that Tommy had abandoned Milton in the fall, informing only Elisha, so as not to worry his father. Hutchinson's fears and anxiety could not be controlled through these long tense months of waiting. He thought of death continuously, dreamed of dying at home in Milton.[78] In February he planned, in the most meticulous detail, the construction of a new tomb in the family burying ground in Milton and wrote to Tommy to have it built as soon as possible; "on one side or other of the gate would be the best place." On some quiet evening, he instructed Tommy, he should have the sexton of the Old North burying ground in Boston enter the old tomb there and have

your mother's bones removed to the new tomb at Milton, where I hope you will be able to place mine with them. . . . It is not probable more than the bones can remain, but it will be better to make a narrow and rather thinner common box, that they may be kept as whole as may be. If the old

77. TH to TH, Jr., Dec. 9, 1774, and [April 1775], Eg. MSS, 2661, pp. 88, 142; March 2, 1775, *Diary and Letters,* I, 399.

78. TH, Jr., to Elisha Hutchinson, Nov. 20, 1774, *Diary and Letters,* I, 314; TH to [Col. Phips?], Dec. 30, 1774, Eg. MSS, 2661, p. 96; TH to ———, Jan. 11, 1775, *Diary and Letters,* I, 356.

coffin is not perished I could wish it might be removed even without open-ing. Let it be done at once without suffering people to go into the tomb or to handle or view the coffin.

And then he added:

I am sensible this fond fancy will not bear examining upon mere rational grounds, but it is not criminal, and I am countenanced by the like sort of fondness in the old patriarchs.

And then he stopped abruptly:

I cannot write upon any other subject after writing upon this.[79]

His fears and anxieties, his sense of dissociation and alienation, as he awaited news through the winter and early spring of 1774–75, took, at one point, a strange form. In January he recorded a bizarre but meaningful "reverie." On his way back from Bristol to London he had stopped off in Whitechurch where he had had a tooth ex-tracted, and, continuing the ride back to the capital, he had found himself imagining the removal of other parts of his body too: a finger, a hand, an arm—all parts, finally, leaving only his con-sciousness while the rest took on some other, better form altogether. The idea had transfixed him "the more easily," he wrote in his diary, "from my situation at this time of life, so unexpected to me, three thousand miles from my country and friends, so that every scene has the appearance of a dream rather than a reality."[80]

Then suddenly, in late May and June, the suspense was ended, and the dream became a nightmare.

79. TH to TH, Jr., Feb. 22, 1775, Eg. MSS, 2661, p. 123, printed in full in Malcolm Freiberg, *Thomas Hutchinson of Milton* (Milton, Mass., 1971), p. 13.
80. *Diary and Letters*, I, 351.

Chapter IX

World's End

April 1775 had been full of warnings and anticipations of an open clash of arms, but Hutchinson had refused to believe that war would be the outcome of the contest of wills that had begun when he had stood his ground in the tea crisis. Not that he doubted his countrymen's physical courage, as so many in England apparently did; but he had never been able to believe that the colonists would be so irrational as to fight the King's troops, for they must, he reasoned, see as clearly as he did that if by chance they were successful at first, every last shred of support they had in Britain would vanish at once, and their friends in the opposition would be instantly silenced. And so, believing that an open war between England and America would be "the most unnatural, the most unnecessary" war in history, a war that no one in the end could really win no matter whose arms prevailed, he discounted the first reports of Lexington and Concord that arrived on May 28, explaining that they had been sent by the "faction" and that therefore the whole affair had undoubtedly been exaggerated.[1] But by the tenth of June the official reports were in, and it was clear that the origi-

1. TH to the Earl of Hardwicke, Thomas Oliver, TH, Jr., and Jonathan Sewall, Nov. 21, 1774, April 8, 10, 1775, *Diary and Letters*, I, 305, 427, 428; TH to Samuel Quincy and to Sewall, April 6, 9, 1775, Eg. MSS, 2661, pp. 140, 139; TH to Hardwicke, May 29, 1775, Add. MSS, 34527, pp. 11–12. On May 29 Hutchinson sent a similar interpretation of Lexington and Concord to Dartmouth: *Manuscripts of the Earl of Dartmouth*, II (Historical Manuscripts Commission, *Fourteenth Report*, Appendix, Part X, London, 1895), 304.

nal information was essentially correct; and furthermore that Gage's army was under siege in Boston, which had become a fortified city crammed not only with an army and its equipment but with a host of refugees; that war had indeed come—*"bella, horrida bella,"* as Hutchinson kept repeating; and that his own family was in mortal peril.[2]

Overcome with shock and worry, and also with guilt for what might be thought to have been his own role in this catastrophic development, he wrote letter after letter—commiserating with Tommy, begging for news, considering with him whether it would not be best for him to stay in Boston, or, if he had to evacuate, whether he would be better off in Halifax or Quebec rather than in England; assuring all his correspondents that the weakness of the British force in Massachusetts was in no way his fault since he had always believed that "the more force, the less danger of the provincials taking up arms"; asking friends and relatives to look after his children; and rearranging his plans so that he would be at hand to receive the latest dispatches the minute they arrived in London.[3]

But the more news there was, the worse it became, until by June 19 Hutchinson could hardly bear to hear any more. For by then he knew that food, especially meat, was running out in Boston—Tommy, now attempting to provide for a household of eighteen, had been able to find only one small joint of meat since the siege began—and that the family was subsisting on bread and maize pudding. He knew too that Gage would be obliged to stop the regular processes of government and rule by martial law. And though the besieged loyalists among his correspondents cried out for a massive assault to stifle the uprising before there was an overwhelming disaster, he could see no sign that Gage, or indeed his superiors in London, were thinking in aggressive terms at all. Surely, he wrote Hardwicke, this was "the strangest war that was ever heard of. . . . It seems as if, until they are attacked, nothing is to be done lest it should be deemed offensive."[4]

2. Dartmouth to Gage, July 1, 1775, CO5/765/407; TH to Hardwicke, June 10, 12, 1775, Add. MSS, 34527, pp. 15–18; TH to ——, June 3, 1775, Eg. MSS, 2661, p. 156.
3. TH to Hardwicke, June 14, 17, 1775, Add. MSS, 34527, pp. 19–21; TH to TH, Jr., and to ——, May 31, June 19, 27, July 28, 1775, *Diary and Letters,* I, 456, 473, 478–479, 505; Elisha Hutchinson to Mary Watson Hutchinson, Aug. 1, 1775, Eg. MSS, 2668, p. 88.
4. TH to Hardwicke, June 27, July 7, 17, 24, 26, Add. MSS, 34527, pp. 24–32. Hutchinson himself had drafted a proclamation of martial law and had discussed the technicalities with Sewall: TH to Sewall, April 9, 1775, Eg. MSS, 2661, p. 137.

But it was the effect of all this on his family that was the hardest for Hutchinson to endure. Tommy's letters were bad enough, though they were, everything considered, business-like in tone. But those of Dr. Peter Oliver, Sally's husband, were not. The Olivers had been threatened, humiliated, and harassed by mobs through the whole of the previous summer and fall, and had finally fled from the family property in Middleborough to Boston, seeking, Peter had then written, an asylum "out of the reach of threats and insults . . . , confusion and uproar . . . some blessed place of refuge." On June 1 Peter wrote his brother-in-law Elisha, whose wife and child were still in Boston, a searing, demoralizing letter, warning him and everyone else that though England would in the end conquer America, it would do so only after such "a horrid, bloody scene . . . as never was in New England before. What comfort and satisfaction do you think we take now or can take when the dreadful scene opens? . . . Good God, do thou avert the impending calamity that threatens this former happy land and turn the hearts of those deluded brethren from the power of sin and satan to thy unerring precepts. . . . By the time this reaches you, havoc will begin, and whether we shall ever see one another in this world I am not clear in."[5]

But Elisha was distraught enough simply thinking of his own wife in Massachusetts and the child he had never seen. He had struggled unsuccessfully with his father, he had written Mary, to be allowed to return to his family and lead them out to safety, but having been forced, as he saw it, to remain a prisoner in England "with my heart and affections in New England" he was now utterly sunk in despair. He could only write his wife that he blessed heaven "for making you mine for the two years that I was happy, my dear, in having you near me; for the last dear little baby; for the one I am longing to see; and for innumerable other favors which we have experienced. Let us still trust in the same kind providence, that he will bring us together and make us again happy in each other. However that may be, let it be our chief concern that we meet together in a world where is no trouble, no separation."[6]

5. Dr. Peter Oliver to ——, Aug. 11–Sept. 23, 1774, *Diary and Letters,* I, 246–248; same to Elisha Hutchinson, June 1, 1775, Eg. MSS, 2659, pp. 151–153.
6. Elisha Hutchinson to Mary Watson Hutchinson, April 9, 13, June 5, 1775, Eg. MSS, 2668, pp. 72, 73, 79.

Such hopelessness, such a splintering of Hutchinson's deeply affectionate, tightly bound family, drove him, he wrote Tommy, into "such a state that I know not how to apply myself to anything." Then, on the morning of June 26 a friend arrived from Boston with letters from Tommy which made all of this seem secondary; that day, Hutchinson recorded in his diary, was "the most distressing . . . I have had since I have been in England."[7] For it was only then, with the receipt of that packet of letters, that Hutchinson heard the essentials of what had happened in Milton.

After Tommy had abandoned the house, late in November, it had remained unoccupied, and its contents were partly looted. After the battle of Lexington the house had fallen within the provincial army lines, then drawn tightly around Boston, and the Milton town committee of safety had removed all the furniture, "to save it from being totally ruined" before turning it into an army barracks. The only thing they had left in the house was an old trunk in a dark garret, which was said to contain nothing but useless papers. Sometime late in April a curious neighbor, "desirous of seeing how the house looked when stripped of all the furniture," had inspected the famous mansion, had found the trunk, and had discovered that it contained the entire collection of Hutchinson's personal papers, including copies of all the hundreds of letters, personal and official, that he had written since the early 1760's and that he had hidden in the house during the tea crisis and then forgotten about. The trunk had been quickly brought to army headquarters, where it apparently remained open for general inspection for some time while interested parties helped themselves to portions of the contents and while samples were sent out to such experts on Hutchinson as John Adams.[8]

By early May the Provincial Congress had decided to reassemble

7. *Diary and Letters,* I, 477.

8. William Gordon, *History of the Rise, Progress, and Establishment of the Independence of the United States of America* . . . (N.Y., 1789), I, 356; MHS *Procs.,* 13 (1873–1875), 223ff.; TH to Richard Clarke, July 24, 1775, *Diary and Letters,* I, 502; Abigail Adams to John Adams, May 4, 1775, L. H. Butterfield *et al.,* eds., *Adams Family Correspondence* (Cambridge, Harvard University Press, 1963——), I, 193. There were various versions of where and how, precisely, the letters had been hidden and found. A letter from New York printed in the London *Remembrancer* in 1775 (Part I, p. 182) stated that the letterbooks had been "sealed up with brick and mortar in a little arch on one side of a chimney." But Gordon had spoken directly with the person who had found the letters (Samuel Henshaw) and was immediately thereafter involved in the affair himself; there is no reason to question his account.

the contents of the trunk and appoint a committee to supervise publication of extracts. Later that month the Reverend William Gordon of Roxbury—something of a busybody recently arrived from England and already contemplating the history of the Revolution he would eventually write—had intruded himself into the situation, had got permission to take over the editorial work, and had begun sorting out the mass of papers. It had not taken him long since he had had no need to spend time pondering the details of the correspondence as evidence: he had known before he had seen the letters that they "discovered the diabolical plans that have been laid to enslave this country" and showed the world "what an indefatigable slave [Hutchinson] has been to his masters, the ministry, and their grand master, the devil." Publication had commenced in the June 5 issue of the *Boston Gazette,* and it would continue in installments in the *Gazette,* the *New England Chronicle,* and the *Massachusetts Spy,* with reprints in the newspapers of other colonies and in the *London Chronicle* and *The Remembrancer,* until, by mid-September 1776, the whole or parts of fifty-five letters had appeared, most of them written during the years of Hutchinson's governorship. The first installment was there for Hutchinson to read on June 26, and with it the Introduction that Gordon had written for the whole series. Anyone, Gordon had written—and Hutchinson now read—still unpersuaded that the former governor "was an enemy to the rights of Americans" would find in these publications all the proof he could conceivably want. And in case there were any doubt about the interpretation that should be put upon any of these letters, Gordon promised his readers that he would help them out by inserting comments from time to time "in order the more effectually to develop [Hutchinson's] character."[9]

He was as good as his word. At quite a number of points in this serial publication of what was intended to be, in effect, a documentary history of Hutchinson's tyranny, Gordon correctly felt that his readers might need help in reaching the right conclusions. For it was not self-evident why he printed a letter from Bollan to prove that Hutchinson had argued for the summoning of troops; why letters about Massachusetts should be taken as proof that Hutchin-

9. MHS *Procs.,* 13, (1873–1875), 223–225; *ibid.,* 63 (1929–1930), 313, 314; *Boston Gazette,* June 5, 1775. For details of the conflict of jurisdiction over the letterbooks that developed between Gordon and Samuel Dexter, see the latter's letter to John Temple, [Sept. 1782], *Bowdoin and Temple Papers* (MHS *Colls.,* 6th ser., IX, 1897), pp. 482–484.

son had been "busily and unswervingly" plotting tyranny over the whole of America; why Hutchinson's writing to Undersecretary Pownall and to Bernard proved that he had had a regular team of "under-advisers and go-betweens at home to direct and influence and ripen every measure that might be concerted by him and his adherents"; and why the letter he had written to Hillsborough which had stopped the efforts to alter the Massachusetts constitution was really evidence of his "assiduity" in destroying it.[10]

Gordon did his work well. The publication of the edited letters created a sensation in the colonies, though not so great a one as the publication of the Whately letters had created, and the reprints in London were widely noticed. These letters, it is true, appeared too late and were by then too familiar a kind of revelation to transform public opinion dramatically, but they had a significant effect nevertheless on the opinion of a public that still retained a residual respect for Hutchinson's integrity and honesty, if not for his political opinions, and still assumed that he was deeply influential in shaping the ministry's programs. Nothing these letters contained, of course, was news to Abigail Adams, who now merely renewed her familiar denunciations of "that forlorn wretch" Hutchinson; but even she, and those of her intense persuasion, could hear in these passages of a correspondence that stretched back over more than a decade a more elaborate orchestration of the forces they had committed themselves to oppose than they had heard before, and to that degree they were more confident of their cause than they had been before. And those, like Chief Justice William Smith of New York, who in general agreed with Hutchinson's politics but who had personal grievances against him, found in the letters exciting new evidence to justify their antagonisms. But beyond all of that, the publication of the letters threatened to prove the Reverend Charles Chauncy right when he wrote to Richard Price that the letters "make such a discovery of the perfidy, treachery, and villainy of the man that his once best friends now give him up as a traitor to his country."[11]

10. *Boston Gazette*, July 10, June 19, 12, Aug. 7, 1775.
11. James Warren to Samuel Adams, May 7, 1775, *Warren-Adams Letters*, I (MHS *Colls.*, LXXII, 1917), 49; William H. W. Sabine, ed., *Historical Memoirs [1763–1776] of William Smith* . . . (N.Y., 1956), pp. 235–236; Charles Chauncy to Richard Price, July 18, 1775, MHS *Procs.*, 2d ser., 17 (1903), 301; Abigail Adams to John Adams, May 4, 1775, cited in n. 8 above.

That was the worst threat that Hutchinson found in the letters as he read the successive installments; and it was this danger—that his reputation and status among his own followers, defenders, colleagues, and sponsors, both in England and America, would now be brought into question—that led him to cry out in an agony of spirit when he discovered, not merely the obvious bias of Gordon's melodramatic editorial comments but the subtle mischief of the selections Gordon had made, the emphases he had added to the original letters, and the silent alterations in the text that he had introduced. Hutchinson knew there was nothing he could do to stop the rebels from believing all sorts of distorted "revelations" of his presumed villainy; but these publications were something different. They seemed to condemn him out of his own mouth and in such a way as most effectively to undermine his reputation among those at home and in Britain who had followed his lead or had approved and defended his conduct, and who had endorsed the soundness of his views. He seemed to be accusing himself of having plotted against the welfare of his own people.

"I have suffered more the last 24 hours," he wrote Tommy the day after he had read his letter and the enclosures, "than I have done since I have been in England." No falsehoods, he assured his son, would be revealed in any letters they chose to publish, nor anything "which my duty to the King, in the station I was in, did not require of me, though to have everything of the most private nature maliciously exposed to public view is a cruelty hard to bear." He tried to ease the pain by assuring himself that there was nothing he could have done to prevent all this from happening. How could he have known that within a year of his departure the Milton house would become an army barracks? His removing the letters from Boston and securing them in Milton had in itself been a caution against precisely such uses of them as were now being made. "Human foresight," he wrote his brother, "will not secure us against all adverse events."[12] All he could do was to try to make sure that his closest allies—those who had sacrificed the most for him and had placed the greatest confidence in him—were in no way led into prejudices against him.

12. TH to TH, Jr., and to Foster Hutchinson, June 27 and July 28, 1775, *Diary and Letters,* I, 478–479, 505. Hutchinson believed that only the use of the house as a barracks could explain the discovery of the letters; a mob searching for them would probably not have found them, he told Foster.

So he wrote to his immediate family and to his in-laws assuring them that there was nothing in this whole vast correspondence but evidence of his "upright aim and endeavor" to save Massachusetts from the miseries that a few men had threatened to impose on them (and had now succeeded in doing). If only the publishers of his letters would not distort them but would "take the whole of them," they would reveal to the world not tyranny but simply repeated expressions of the two basic propositions that had governed his conduct through all the turmoils of the past decade: that there was no way, in logic or in political reality, to escape the fact that affiliation with England meant accepting the principle of Parliamentary authority; but that Parliament should indulge the colonies "in every point in which the people imagined they were aggrieved." But to his old associates who might still be expected to influence others and whose confidence in him was most necessary for his self-respect, he wrote in greater detail and to the specific points he thought might threaten his reputation most seriously.

To Jonathan Sewall, who had so eloquently, patiently, and, he thought, so effectively defended him after the publication of the Whately letters, he wrote most fully and on a particularly tender point. After reviewing at great length the innocence of the principles of government he had always professed and had always acted on, and after explaining that, though his letters undoubtedly contained passages presenting the pros as well as the cons of altering the charter, in the end he had always felt that the evils of constitutional change outweighed the benefits and had always advised against it, he turned to the subject of religion. He had seen a snippet of a letter to Bernard that had been published in which he appeared to have been saying that he had attended the Congregational church only out of family tradition and for political reasons and not out of conviction—a charge, he knew, that would damage him profoundly among devout New Englanders whose good will he would need if he were ever to return to his home. But what was the true context of the letter? In fact, he explained to Sewall, the letter had been a reply to one from Bernard, who had been urging him as governor to forsake the church of his ancestors and worship only at the Anglican church, for political reasons and not for reasons of faith. The purpose of his reply, now so dramatically published for the whole world to read, had been to refuse that suggestion and to give reasons for refusing that were effective *politically*. His aim in writing to Bernard had been to tell him that going over to the Anglican church would decrease his political effectiveness and the effectiveness of the crown executive in Massachusetts, not increase it. Out of context, as printed in the newspapers, the letter sounded like a cynical repudiation of the religion of his people; in context, it was an effective defense of the governor's remaining faithful to the Congregational way. So too, later, Hutchinson discovered, and attempted to explain, the significance of the change of the words "pious ancestors" to "poor ancestors": changing those few letters had eliminated the respect he had meant to pay to the sincerity of the founders' belief, in the course of a factual account he had written of their intolerance in religion and their fanaticism—both of which were, surely, matters of simple historical fact. The tone of his intended meaning had lain in the balance of the respect and the criticism; the change of the single word had destroyed that balance.

Hutchinson heard by late July that a "gentleman of reputation" had read the whole of his correspondence. He was gratified by this, for then there was one person, at least, who knew that he had in fact never charged that the people of New England in general were plotting secretly to break away from England, but only that there were a few fanatics who were driving all the rest in that direction—one person, at least, who knew that he had never wanted the American people to be taxed by England and had never wanted the colonial constitutions to be altered—who knew that he had never allowed selfish, private goals to determine his conduct of public business—and that his aim had always been to prevent precisely the distress and misery that the American people were now suffering. Knowing that at least one person understood this helped keep the installments of the edited letters from crushing him altogether.[13]

Gradually, but only very gradually, he became used to the regular appearance of these passages of letters he had long ago written, with their occasional guides to "correct" interpretation. He had done what he could to defend himself. Having written to his most im-

13. TH to Sewall, July 8, 1775, *Diary and Letters,* I, 500–501, and the unpublished portions of that letter, Eg. MSS, 2661, p. 159; TH to TH, Jr., and to ——, Aug. 23, July 28, 1775, *ibid.,* pp. 163, 161.

portant correspondents warning them of the distortions they would find in the published letters and reviewing his conduct in the episodes the rebels were deliberately reviving in these publications, and having heard with relief that sensible people in London were surprised that the letters had been published in America at all, since they seemed to be so favorable to the American people, he became almost reconciled to these continuous attacks and "revelations." They still hurt him, as they appeared, and he continued to relieve his feelings in letters to his friends when he found his meanings and intentions distorted in particularly vicious ways. But by September his more general concerns—for the welfare of his family, for the progress of British arms, and for the prospects of his quick return to America—were again dominant.[14]

There was little change in the kinds of news he heard that summer and fall—all of it threatened still further the safety of his family and the likelihood of his return. The American invasion of Canada, the battle of Bunker Hill ("a few such victories," he wrote Hardwicke, "would ruin us"), and the decision to evacuate Boston all made the frightening situation more fearful still and the future even more uncertain than it had seemed when the first reports of fighting had been received. He continued to do what little he could in ways that had become familiar to him. He kept up his visits to the offices and levées of the major political figures, taking comfort in the observation he heard that all of England's most successful wars had started disastrously, but passing on in any case his own well-informed and favorable estimation of the military skill of the Americans and his conviction that the sooner and more massively the British army responded to the American challenge the better would be the eventual outcome. To his family, trapped in Boston, he wrote continuously, though his advice must have been difficult to interpret. For while he feared for their safety and prayed that they might be spared any further misfortunes, he knew that if they once left Massachusetts the prospect of his and their eventual return would be greatly diminished.[15]

Lord Dartmouth, he wrote Tommy, had assured him that a large

14. TH to Daniel Leonard and to ——, Sept. 2, and Dec. 8, 1775, *Diary and Letters*, I, 526, II, 9; TH to Abijah Williams, Sept. 7, 1775, Eg. MSS, 2661, p. 165.
15. TH to Hardwicke, July 26, 31, 1775, Add. MSS, 34527, p. 32, 33–34; TH to TH, Jr., July 26, 1775, *Diary and Letters*, I, 503; TH to Sewall, July 8, 1775, Eg. MSS, 2661, p. 158.

land force was being sent, certain to arrive the next spring, and all sorts of food supplies were on their way, together with a plan (though of this he was less sure) for extracting fresh provisions from the New England countryside. In a year the vast new army, to be deployed against the colonists as if they were French or Spanish enemies, would be on the scene and the likelihood of a final reversal of the situation would no doubt then be excellent. "I therefore think there is a strong probability that you and your sister and both your children may be reinstated there." Would it not, consequently, be advisable for Tommy to hold out through another year? Perhaps not. But then, if it really became too difficult for him to stay in Boston, perhaps he would want to move only a short distance away, to Rhode Island, where he could reside on family property and be close enough to Boston to keep some kind of supervision of the situation there and be in a position to return quickly if and when the opportunity arose. "Or could you bear the cold winter of Quebec?" In any case if he had to leave Boston and so cut the family's last ties to their native province, he should be sure to "secure, as far as you are able, what plate, furniture, books, papers, and other property was left, and still remains. I now wish I had brought great part of [it] with me, as it would have saved me considerable [expenses] which I now pay extraordinarily in rent for having a house furnished."[16]

By late September such hesitations and hopes were over. Hutchinson had heard that Boston would be abandoned by the army and that the loyalists would be evacuated. There was no real alternative to Tommy's joining the rest of the family in England. Hutchinson wrote to General Howe, Gage's successor, and to others in authority begging for protection for his family and for help in transporting them to England together with as many of their possessions as might be moved. He told Tommy to be bold in requesting this protection. He should apply, Hutchinson instructed him, to the governor and his brother, Admiral Lord Richard Howe, "for favor in bringing your and my effects of every kind, as I may claim every right to be distinguished on account of my service and sufferings. . . . If you can bring all the furniture of the several familes, your brother's included, we can take one large house in the country if

16. TH to TH, Jr., and to Daniel Leonard, July 26 and Sept. 2, 1775, *Diary and Letters*, I, 503–504, 525. He suggested Rhode Island as a refuge to Peter Oliver also: *ibid.*, p. 532.

not in town and be able to furnish it; but I know not what to expect or what to fancy in so uncertain a state of things, and must rely upon you that you will do the best you can."

He panicked repeatedly as flashes of news—some of it accurate, most of it false—reached him during those months of continuing acute anxiety. Late in September he heard that the British troops would burn Boston to the ground when they left, an idea that struck him as fearful and altogether senseless. It might deprive the rebels of the use of the city for the winter, but they could not hold Boston as it stood against the British navy for any length of time, and in any case destroying the city would only have the effect of making the rebels more obstinate. For they had very little stake in the property of the town, and destroying the property of others would make no difference to them. The only thing that would affect their conduct was "what is called by the army a good drubbing." But he confessed he might be prejudiced on this question, for "besides ten or twelve houses and large well-built wharves, I have an exceedingly good house there in which I dwelt, which, exclusive of the land, cost my ancestors two thousand pounds sterling."[17]

On November 14, General Gage arrived in London, and from him and a new group of refugees Hutchinson heard that his Milton property had been sold at auction and the estate leased out. He wrote Tommy immediately to compile a complete inventory— "by the help of nurse's memory" if necessary—of all the stock and equipment that had been left at the farm and of every piece of furniture and all the goods in the house, room by room, and to have the document "sworn to before the lieutenant governor" and sent over to him as soon as possible. He had no idea whether he would be able to obtain compensation for these losses from the government, but "if I was possessed of such an inventory, I would try what could be done." And he added that he particularly hoped Tommy would be able to ship over "the epergne, the mahogany case of knives, and the tea kettle and stand," which would be of great use "whilst we are here." But he seemed to be writing into a void. He did not know what more to write "or what to think or

17. TH to William Howe and to TH, Jr., Sept. 11, 24, 14, 1775, *Diary and Letters*, I, 532, 538–539, 534.

where to find my children or any of my friends. God Almighty I trust will be their protector and friend wherever they are."[18]

It all seemed the same nightmare, extended—of hopes continously deferred; of uncertainty and fear for the future of his family; of a superficial immersion in an alien world from which he could derive very little satisfaction and in which he felt constantly called upon to defend himself and his career; and of an endless longing for peace and for home. And yet it was not all the same. For in the fall and winter months of 1775–76 a subtle but profound change took place in Hutchinson's life that brought him to the threshold of his last and most bitter years.

ii

He had become a permanent refugee in a foreign land. He still spoke longingly of home—he would never give up his dream of returning—and he continued to scour the incoming reports—any reports he could find: written to him from home, tipped to him by government officials, found in occasional newspapers, heard from stray ship captains and merchants—for signs of an ebb in the tide of revolt. But he knew by early 1776 the prospects were dim for his ever returning and ever recovering the respect of his countrymen which he had so unaccountably lost. At the same time he realized too that his political position in England had suddenly changed. The novelty of his presence in London had worn off, the relevance of his views had paled, the usefulness of his connections had melted in the heat of English politics. The great issues of public concern had been transformed. They were no longer the theoretical problems of sovereignty and taxation; of imperial constitutions and colonial charters; of liberty and power; of the maintenance of the rule of law in the face of civil disorder—problems to which Hutchinson had devoted the previous decade of his life. The great issues had become the immediate and practical problems of conducting a land war three thousand miles from Europe and in the face both of a military foe that fought tenaciously in unorthodox ways and of a

18. TH to TH, Jr., Nov. 17, 1775, *Diary and Letters*, I, 558–559; TH to TH, Jr., Oct. 10, 1775, Eg. MSS, 2661. p. 169. The total volume of the property inventoried (I, 559–564) is £1,092 18s.

political opposition at home that was tireless, brilliantly articulate, and convinced that the war was an abomination being poorly fought against a people whose worst crime was to have struggled for the rights of men.

No longer useful to the government—indeed, something of an embarrassment to a ministry still vaguely hopeful of reconciliation —and an easy target for the opposition, Hutchinson found his public role increasingly marginal and increasingly difficult to make meaningful at all. As early as February 1775 he complained that though he kept busy he was no longer consulted by the ministry and felt idle and purposeless. In May he had to confess to Hillsborough that he no longer saw Lord North, and saw Dartmouth only when he attended his levées. In September he told Hardwicke he would be happy to execute any orders he happened to have for him since he was now "a man of leisure, which I never was in my life before," and he explained that he was never consulted on American questions. And in January he said he scarcely ever concerned himself about public affairs, accepting what he could discover from the best informed people he knew. He learned of Dartmouth's replacement in office by George Germain only from the newspaper accounts, and his first interview with the new colonial secretary, in which he discussed modifications of the Coercive Acts, was formal and stiff; it was quite clear that he would never thereafter be able to stop by casually and chat with the officials closest to the American problems as he had done only a few months before.[19]

But the meaning of his new status ran deeper than politics. The swift elimination of the royal government in Massachusetts, the spread of the fighting throughout the continent, and the forming of committees of safety and new governments all over America had set in motion an exodus that so flooded London in the course of the winter of 1775–76 that the newcomers became, not curiosities and admired fighters in a notable cause, but public burdens, social embarrassments, and, in the end, bores. "We Americans," Hutchinson wrote in February 1776, "are plenty here, and very cheap.

19. *Diary and Letters,* I, 445, 556; TH to Hardwicke, Sept. 6, 1775, Add. MSS, 34527, p. 42; TH to ——, Jan. 27, 1776, Eg. MSS, 2661, p. 171; TH to ——, Nov. 18, 1775, *Diary and Letters,* I, 568. Hutchinson reported in the letter of Jan. 27 that Germain "has the character of a great man, and I verily believe is a true friend of both countries."

Some of us at first coming are apt to think ourselves of importance, but other people do not think so, and few if any of us are much consulted or inquired after." He was not saved from the common fate by having served as governor. He had discovered, he wrote Hardwicke, that nothing was "so like an old almanac as an old governor," and by February 1776 he was asking his correspondents to leave off *"His Excellency"* in the addresses of letters they wrote him, for "everybody laughs at such things here." From Knox at the colonial office he obtained a list of 938 persons known to have emigrated from Boston alone; among them were some of his closest friends—Paxton, Sewall, Flucker. They met together, often with loyalists from other colonies, in an unending series of teas, dinners, coffees, walks, and journeys in the course of which they talked over the latest news from home and the prospects of the war as it developed, organized to seek jobs, pensions, and compensation for their losses, and, above all, found mutual support for the decisions they gradually came to make by which they adjusted themselves to continuing their lives permanently in England.[20]

But this Hutchinson could not do. The contrast with some of his closest associates of earlier years is striking. Some, like Peter Oliver, the chief justice, enjoyed England hugely, found it a bigger, more exciting, more vital and exuberant world than the one they had left behind and rejoiced in the contrast.[21] Most were more cautious than Oliver and more regretful of what had been lost. But they too involved themselves mainly in the everyday business of resettlement, and they learned to live with the new condition of their lives. Hutchinson was unique in his stubborn refusal to accept in any degree the twists of fate that had led him to this point of isolation, rejection, and alienation. He seemed to experience life on a different plane. He simply could not chatter on about the palpable surface of life. "If I could bear the storms in the moral and political

20. TH to Charles Paxton, Feb. 16, and to ——, Feb. 27, 1776, *Diary and Letters,* II, 40, 17–18; TH to Hardwicke, Aug. 4, Sept. 22, 1775, Add. MSS, 34527, pp. 36, 44–45; *Diary and Letters,* II, 61. On the arrival and settlement of Hutchinson's friends in London, see Mary Beth Norton, *The British-Americans: The Loyalist Exiles in England, 1774–1789* (Boston and Toronto: Little, Brown, 1972), esp. chap. iii.

21. Peter Oliver's journal, 1776–1780, is preserved in two volumes, Eg. MSS, 2672, 2673; his spirited letters to his granddaughter are in the Hutchinson-Watson Papers, MHS. The contrast between Oliver's spontaneous exuberance and almost childlike enthusiasm and Hutchinson's brooding concern could hardly be greater.

world," he told Hardwicke, "as well as I do the natural, I should be very happy."[22] He had never lived at the tactile, sensuous surface of life; he had always sought deeper meanings and a greater coherence than passing events and immediate circumstances would give him, and indeed he had attempted in his *History,* which would become the engrossing concern of his last years, to draw together the experience of his own people into a single integrated whole and thereby extend the meaning of his own life to the farthest boundaries of verifiable knowledge. But what meaning could be imputed to these latest events? Had the revolt in Massachusetts, and hence throughout all of America, been his fault, as his enemies claimed? Were the propositions he had defended at such drastic cost to be proved in the end false? Again and again he returned to these questions, reviewed his ideas and his recollections of events, verifying again and again the accuracy and logic of his views and the rectitude if not the grace of his behavior.

He had heard, he recalled, "more than an hundred times in New England . . . the ministry spoken of as a set of men combining to deprive the colonies of their liberties and to introduce an arbitrary and despotic government, and sometimes it has been said popery." He had known at the time that all such talk, which had so stirred the fears of ordinary people, was simply nonsense; the longer he lived in England the more ridiculous it seemed to charge that the throne had been seized by a desperate cabal bent on destroying liberty in America and England. He was now himself at the seat of power, and what he saw was not a vicious, efficient cabal, but a government paralyzed by inefficiency, consumed with self-doubt, almost totally innocent of purpose good or bad, and barely capable of surviving the conflicts within it. The claims of the colonial agitators were not simply wrong but grotesque, and the imputation that he had himself been at the root of the conspiracy—that, as he had been told the Connecticut preachers had proclaimed from their pulpits, he had joined with Lord Bute, Lord North, and General Gage to introduce "popery etc." into New England—was more fantastic still. How could the radical leaders continue to condemn as insupportable his central doctrine, that in point of theory "there can be no line between absolute authority and absolute independ-

22. TH to Hardwicke, Sept. 11, 1775, Add. MSS, 34527, p. 43.

ency," when that very idea had become the intellectual basis of the rebellion they led? Their most respected spokesman and his great detractor, Franklin, now said exactly the same thing "in the most express terms. . . . He infers the colonies are therefore independent. I draw no inference, but—*utrum mavis elige?* I lay the stress on prudence only."[23]

He could not let the issues rest. He felt driven to point out the destructive folly of the American radicals and to demonstrate, despite what his enemies said of him, the constant advocacy of American rights that he had maintained over the years. In June 1775, with the British world suspended in expectation of news of warfare in New England, and with the newspapers at home charging him with secretly shaping Britain's aggressive policies, he recalled the essay he had written in 1764 arguing against the Stamp Act. He had sent the manuscript to Jackson, who in turn had passed it on to the then secretary of state, General Conway, and Conway had used it effectively in the debate on repeal. Could he recover the document now? It might be useful to produce at this point, perhaps to publish. He applied to Jackson, who said that Conway had probably lost it;[24] but before Hutchinson could pursue the question further, Gordon's publication of his letters began to appear, and Hutchinson was faced with a mass of more up-to-date issues to explain. Then in October an occasion arose for a more general reconsideration of the Anglo-American controversy and of his role in its development. He leapt at the opportunity.

The occasion was typical of the situations Hutchinson seemed increasingly to find himself in as he drifted into the margins of politics and into the limbo of the easily condemned and the disregarded. On October 26, 1775, he attended the autumn opening of the House of Commons and heard a long and eloquent attack on the ministry's policies delivered by George Johnstone, the former governor of West Florida, a fiery ex-sailor passionately opposed to Lord North and his policies, though opposed too to the independence of the colonies. How, Johnstone asked, could one account for the ministry's disregard of the colonists' determination to oppose force with force, its "total ignorance of the force, character, and

---

23. TH to —— and to Samuel Quincy, Nov. 2, 1774, and Feb. 9, 1775, *Diary and Letters*, I, 284–285, 390–391; *ibid.*, p. 333.

24. *Diary and Letters*, I, 473. On the writing of the essay, see above, pp. 62–63.

dispositions of the people in America," and its more general ignorance of the effect that cruelty and oppression had "on high-minded
men acting under the spirit of freedom"? The answers to all these
questions, he declared, lay in the activities of Thomas Hutchinson.

All [the ministry's] knowledge seems to have been drawn from one source,
that of Governor Hutchinson. The civil war now raging in America seems,
step by step, to have been carried on by his advice. Whoever reads his
letters, lately published in America, sees every measure pursued by administration to have been antecedently pointed out by this gentleman in his
confidential correspondence, until his sentiments seem dictated at last
more by revenge and disappointment than any other principle. What
confidence should be placed in the advice of a man who has declared, in
the cool moments of committing his reflections to paper, that every
Machiavellian policy is now to be vindicated towards the people in America? . . . I must avow my sentiments as freely as Governor Hutchinson has
communicated his, that any officer in government, much less the supreme
magistrate entrusted with the preservation of the rights of every individual in his province, who could entertain such sentiments is unfit to be
employed in any office, civil or military. . . . I am confident our ancestors,
instead of giving such a man an enormous pension, would have inflicted
the punishment he deserved, which I think should have been an address
to the crown that he might never more have been employed in the service
of the public.

Johnstone also attacked Lord Lyttleton, the former governor of
Jamaica, but Lyttleton, "being a Member," Hutchinson wrote in
his diary, "exculpated himself and vindicated his conduct. I sat
below and wished I had been allowed to speak." But if he could
not speak in his own defense he could write. He would write a
general vindication of his career, an *apologia* specifically directed to
charges that had been made against him, not only by Johnstone and
others in England but by the opposition at home, and he would
explain, briefly, the forces that had in fact created the present
crisis. Six weeks later the essay was finished: a nineteen-page manuscript, which he submitted to Israel Mauduit for an opinion and
then had printed. On January 19, 1776, he presented the paper to
Lord Dartmouth, who promised to show it to the King.[25]

25. T. C. Hansard, *The Parliamentary History of England* . . . (London, 1806–1820),
XVIII, cols. 744–745; *Diary and Letters,* I, 548, 575; II, 7. The manuscript of the *apologia*,
entitled "Account and Defense of Conduct," is in the Chapin Library, Williams College;
a typed transcription of that MS, including Mauduit's emendations, is in the MHS. I

Normally, he wrote in this "Account and Defense of Conduct," it is best for public persons to ignore abuse, but when one is vilified by malicious falsehoods passed on "to persons of the first rank"; when abuse is propagated in the highest public forums; and when private papers are seized "by acts of fraud and violence" and published in "detached parcels . . . with comments and remarks torturing . . . words to an unnatural sense and meaning totally different from what they were intended to convey"—then a public response is called for. There was little need for him to dwell on events before 1772; they were quickly summarized. He had opposed the Stamp Act, though agitators had misconstrued his opposition to all law-breaking as support for the act; he had transferred the General Court to Cambridge only because he had been instructed to do so "unless he would make himself chargeable with all the consequences of not doing it"; he had substituted crown troops for the provincial levies in Castle William because the King had ordered him to do so, but he had managed the transfer so as "to reserve to the governor all that power which the charter gives him"; he had not wanted the governorship, he had in fact declined it, but then he had relented and accepted because there was a promise of tranquillity and because his fellow countrymen had pleaded with him to keep the position from falling into "hands more disagreeable."

All of that, together with quick summaries of the other notable events of the sixties, was preliminary, though all of it was important for the overall record. The real trouble had started in 1772 when the opposition had projected a scheme to lead, first the Massachusetts towns, then the Massachusetts Assembly, and then the Assemblies of all the colonies "into an avowal of independency." Until then, Hutchinson explained, he had scrupulously avoided getting into controversies over the theoretical question of Parliament's authority, but this plot had compelled him to debate the issue even though he knew perfectly well that those who had trapped him into doing so would claim that they themselves wished

have quoted from the typescript in the paragraphs that follow. I am grateful to the director of the Chapin Library for permission to quote from the document. The printed version of the document that Hutchinson presented to Dartmouth is apparently not among the Dartmouth Papers in the Staffordshire County Record Office; Dartmouth was probably faithful to his word and sent the document on to the King.

to avoid such debates and that *he* had pushed *them* into it. The exchange that he had initiated by his speech of January 6, 1773, had had no ill effects in America; it had in fact stopped the snowballing support for the independence movement, and for some months thereafter there had been peace. But then had come the great rupture. The publication of his letters to Whately had been the result of a conspiracy to create a general belief that a conspiracy to destroy the liberties of Americans existed and that it was led by him. This plot of his enemies, not dissimilar to the conspiracy denounced by Cicero in his second Philippic (which Hutchinson quoted at length), had been "contrived and executed with great, great success. This flame which had been extinguished was rekindled and raised to a greater heighth than ever." When later in the year it threatened to fade out again, it was restimulated by the resistance to the Tea Act, whose passage he had disapproved of and whose consequences he had struggled to confine in all ways compatible with his oath of office.

Such had been the main events of his career, and in connection with them Hutchinson retold, with similar emphases, the history of a range of secondary episodes that had marked the course of his administration. But what were the general issues and the general forces behind the issues? Basically shaping events through all these years had been his faithfulness to his legal and constitutional duty to oppose the "<attempts> <designs> <endeavors> [he groped for the exact word] of those who during the whole time of his government and many years before secretly were at work to bring about the overthrow of the constitution and to form a new one entirely independent of the authority of Parliament." Because he had been faithful to his oath of office, the opposition had had to get rid of him, and they knew they could do this simply by embroiling him in one public controversy after another (the merits of the issues were irrelevant) and then claiming that he was unacceptable to the people because he engaged in controversies with them. But no one had ever succeeded in blackening his private reputation. The chief accusations were that he had misrepresented Massachusetts to the King's government and that he had sought to abridge English liberties in America. But these charges, growing out of the publication of the Whately letters, were "groundless and injurious . . . contrary to the tenor of his whole life." Never had he wished to deprive Americans of any liberties that "they were capable of enjoying, compatible with their constitutions." If Americans *could* have been regularly elected to Parliament, he would have favored their being elected; if Americans *could* have voted regularly for Members of Parliament, he would have favored their doing so. Since as a matter of fact neither had been possible, he had favored the maximum legislative autonomy for the separate colonies consistent with the minimum supervisory authority of Parliament—the authority, that is, to protect the integrity of its own jurisdiction and to preserve peace and order throughout British territories.

These had ever been his views; this is what he had said again and again and again. And yet, by the malicious and perverse misuse of a single sentence in a single letter, the opposite idea had been drummed into the minds of a people whose fears of Parliament's authority had been excited to the point of hysteria by talk of continuous tax enactments that in the end would make property worthless in the colonies. (*Property:* how clever the opposition had been; they had taught people first to think of property as equal to life and liberty, which it was not, and then to ask why property should be imposed on while life and liberty were not!) Not only had he never intended to abridge any liberties that Americans had been capable of enjoying, but he had said so clearly in the very letter that had so often been cited against him. He had told Whately, with reference to the inescapable limitations of political life in America, "that he wished it could be otherwise." But this phrase had simply been ignored by the opposition, and so "by a long series of deception, fraud, and falsity, endeavors have been used to fix upon the governor arbitrary and tyrannical principles in government which he detests and abhors, an accusation which must be considered as utterly improbable seeing in a course of public business for nearly forty years he had never been charged with a single arbitrary, tyrannical act."

Hutchinson's "Account and Defense" is a rambling piece. The manuscript is covered with corrections, interlineations, and alternative phrases, signs of a desperate search for words that might somehow do what words had never done for him before: establish his innocence of the charges that continued to pursue him, and make clear that he was essentially at one with his own people, differing only in having seen more clearly than they the fallacies of the arguments that ambitious men had propounded, and in having had the courage to oppose these arguments publicly, in accordance with the demands of the offices he had held. Though he touched on many episodes in the essay, swinging back and forth in time, the heart of his defense was the effort, yet once again, to explain the Whately letters, whose publication had come to seem the critical moment of his career. He ended on a weary note. " '*Gubernatorum vituperatio populo placet,*' " he said, was an ancient phrase, the truth of which the governors of Massachusetts had known for a century. But that reproaches similar to what governors had been used to receiving from ruthless politicians at home should be cast upon him "by any members of that most respectable body, the authority of which he had supported," was something altogether new, and he hoped it would justify his unusual *apologia*. It had been written, he said, by one who had been injured without ever having injured "by indecency or disrespect . . . any other person or character."

So he wrote, for he could not let the questions rest. But his writing made no difference. There is no evidence that his "Account" was ever formally acknowledged, let alone read, by Dartmouth or the King. The winter of 1775–76 was bitterly cold—the worst since 1740, he wrote Tommy: snow, temperatures between ten and twenty degrees, and an east wind that had "all the feeling of NNW in America. . . . With this degree of cold I think that Cambridge river, as low as Boston Neck, would be froze over." The whole family came down with "a most malignant disorder, called the influenza. . . . I have not had so much of a fever for 35 years past." He remained ill, on and off, for six months, in January suffering "a vertiginous turn," brooding through the long, dark, wet, freezing days on the future of his country (as he now regularly referred to America), on the unknown fate of his friends and the remnants of his family in America, and on the savage twists of his personal fortunes. Occasionally he lashed out at his countrymen—"the most infatuated people upon the globe"—and considered ingenious schemes for dealing with them (if they succeeded in taking Canada, he wrote Hardwicke, England might wish to reverse the decision of 1763 and hand that province back to the French in exchange for Guadeloupe). From time to time too he made the rounds of the senior officials, to lend his support for bold and decisive military action, to pick up some news, or respectfully to offer his advice on particular points of policy, usually points in which he was personally involved. But mainly he was at home, as Samuel Curwen found him in April 1776, "alone, reading a new pamphlet entitled, 'An Enquiry Whether Great Britain or America is Most in Fault' "; writing in distress to his relatives and friends, encouraging them to hold out until the summer when the "vast armament" under the Howe brothers would certainly suppress the rebellion, and telling them how much he hoped they would all live through the winter and soon be united again; filling his diary with the gossip and news that reached him; and—always—reviewing his career and assuring himself that it was he who had been right and not his enemies, no matter how successful they appeared to be. "I count the days," he wrote in January 1776, "and, absurd as it is, so near the close of life, I can hardly help wishing to sleep away the time between this and the spring, that I might escape the succession of unfortunate events which I am always in fear of."[26]

Four months later, on May 2, the suspense which had begun when he had first heard of his family's fleeing to Boston ended. Late that afternoon a friend from Boston appeared suddenly at his house with the news (not otherwise known in London) that Howe had evacuated Boston on March 26, and that on April 31 Tommy, Sally (with a new-born child), Grizell Sanford (Hutchinson's sister-in-law), the Olivers, and all their children and servants had arrived safely at Falmouth, and that Hutchinson's immediate family, a party of fifteen, was on its way overland to London. Letters followed from Tommy, first from Falmouth, then Exeter, and then Salisbury, and finally, on May 11, Hutchinson's carriage picked them up at Hounslow and brought them to his house on St. James's Street.[27]

The house had five "lodging rooms" in addition to servant quarters on the top floor, but the household consisted of twenty-five people, and it was a very tight squeeze. But whatever the temporary discomfort Hutchinson rejoiced as never before in the

26. TH to TH, Jr., Jan. 28, 1776, Nov. 17, 1775, to Charles Paxton, Feb. 16, 1776, and to ——, Jan. 27, 1776, *Diary and Letters*, II, 12, 18, 11, 6; I, 558–559; II, 13; TH to Hardwicke, Oct. 21, 1775, Add. MSS, 34527, p. 51; Andrew Oliver, ed., *The Journal of Samuel Curwen, Loyalist* (Cambridge, 1972), I, 132 (cf. pp. 155, 161).

27. *Diary and Letters*, II, 41, 42, 46. Elisha's wife did not arrive until Sept. 1777.

company of his family, whom he found "in tolerable good health." They prayed together the next day, and began the process of settling into a London now swarming with American refugees.[28]

He revived the idea he had written Tommy about, that they all take a house together somewhere in the country to cut down expenses, but Welbore Ellis, whom he consulted on the question, warned him against doing so: " 'Remain *in oculis civium*,' " he said, " 'if you have anything to hope for yourself or family. You will be forgot in the country.' " The warning must have carried great weight, not merely because it came from so experienced a politician as Ellis but because Hutchinson had already tasted the practical meaning of neglect. Despite his most assiduous efforts, he had not been able to get the government to liquidate its long-standing obligation to him by giving a government post to Billy—a prospect he had nursed with infinite care. The target had narrowed down to the receiver generalship of Canada, which in February 1775 Lord North, in a conversation at a levée, had promised Hutchinson he would give to Billy as soon as the incumbent could be provided for in England. In May Hutchinson had had word that this preliminary problem had been disposed of, and he therefore had written Dartmouth requesting the Canadian post for Billy. He faced great difficulty, he had explained, in providing for his children in England, and if one of them could be settled in this fashion it would be a great relief to him. He had no "avaricious or accumulating views" in mind; all he wanted was a decent provision for his family. And he had reminded his patron that he would never have come to England if it had been a matter of his own free choice. He had, in fact, been quite prepared to remain in Massachusetts after Andrew Oliver's death even if no further military aid had been forthcoming, but public duty had required the voyage to England. It might already be too late, he feared, for the commission to be processed in time for Billy to get one of the last vessels of the season to Quebec; if so, he hoped things would be in order for Billy's departure early the next spring.[29]

But nothing had happened in 1775. The appointment was obviously delayed a season. This was not too surprising, and so Hutchin-

28. *Diary and Letters*, II, 54, 46. For Hutchinson's letter of thanks to General Howe for having assisted the family, see *ibid.*, p. 43.
29. *Diary and Letters*, II, 57; I, 375; TH to Dartmouth, May 3, 1775, *ibid.*, pp. 437–438.

son prepared himself to see his youngest son, who seemed always to be in poor health and needed a good deal of looking after, leave for Canada early in 1776. But there was no word of the appointment. Perhaps, he thought, the change in the colonial secretaryship accounted for the delay. So he called on Germain, "mention[ing] the neglect of performing the promises made to me. [Germain] condemned it; attributed it to Lord North's indolence; said Lord Dartmouth could prevail on him if he would; he should dine with him; promised to speak to him, and would let me know how it stands." Still nothing happened. He kept in touch, but got nowhere, and finally in July he wrote a humble, beseeching letter reviewing the history of the application, his present heavily encumbered financial situation, and the nature of the government's obligation to him. Of course he was grateful for the generous provision he had been given by the government, but he pointed out that he now had seventeen children and grandchildren in England to provide for besides other relatives in America, and he was so straitened that he had had to give up a trip to the continent that he badly needed for his health. He was so close to falling into debt that he was thinking of trying to do without a carriage, though he had never in his life been without one. He had had no need to take on the responsibilities that had led to his present reduced condition. He had lived very well in New England and had been able to provide nicely for his children. He had desired nothing more, and he had taken the governorship only at Lord Hillsborough's desire. It had been that decision that had led to the "loss of my own and my children's fortunes." He had no doubt that if he had followed his own inclination he would still be living quietly on "one or other of my estates in the country without engaging on the side of rebellion and perhaps might have interfered so far as to stop or retard the progress of it." Indeed, he recalled, he had so far succeeded in the governorship that for the first three years of his administration the revolutionary movement had receded, "and if it had not been for the plot laid by Franklin and others here in England, and the sending over my private letters, and the false representations made of them, I doubt whether there would have been a rebellion to this day." Furthermore, he had not been rejected from the governorship but had voluntarily given up that valuable official property, relying on the assurances he had received "that I should be no sufferer by the discontinuance of the King's commission, and that some distinguishing mark should be shown of His Majesty's approbation of my conduct. The former part I gratefully acknowledge has been complied with—the latter remains."[30]

And it would continue to remain, never to be redeemed—a source of the deepest frustration and bitterness to Hutchinson as he worried about the future of his frail and feckless son and brooded on his own failure to obtain in this practical form the respect he was sure he had earned from the government he had sacrificed himself to support. There were occasional rewards that brightened his life, besides the presence of his children, for which he was profoundly grateful. He was immensely pleased to hear in May 1776 that General Conway, perhaps reminded by the request for the return of Hutchinson's paper of 1764, had mentioned him favorably in the House of Commons and had represented his views with perfect accuracy. No one, the former secretary of state declared in urging that the colonies be assured that England would never tax them—no one, surely—would suspect Governor Hutchinson of being unfriendly to government, but he had seen a manuscript paper of Hutchinson's a decade before containing "very sensible and unanswerable arguments against passing the Stamp Act, and which showed to his honor that he was a friend to his country as well as to government." And it was on July 4 of that year that he and Chief Justice Peter Oliver were honored at Oxford by the award of honorary doctorates of civil laws.[31]

But nothing could rebalance the agonizing disequilibrium of his life except a return to his homeland and some kind of overwhelming vindication of his innocence of the accusations against him that had become commonplace on both sides of the Atlantic. For the former there was nothing he could do but follow the news of the military campaigns and analyze their meaning in conversations with his friends and in letters to Lord Hardwicke. But for the latter he

30. Elisha Hutchinson to Mary Watson Hutchinson, April 9, 1775, Eg. MSS, 2668, p. 72; *Diary and Letters*, II, 22; TH to ——, July 17, 1776, Eg. MSS, 2661, pp. 176–177 (the last part of the letter is printed in *Diary and Letters*, II, 79–80). Two years later he was still drafting similar appeals, most of which he apparently did not send. There are drafts of such a letter dated May 23, 1778, Eg. MSS, 2661, pp. 180–183.

31. TH to James Murray, March 3, 1777, MHS *Procs.*, 5 (1860–1862), 363; *Diary and Letters*, II, 58, 75. The text of Conway's Speech, May 22, 1776, is in Hansard, *Parliamentary History*, XVIII, col. 1358.

continued to think that he could convince the world of the truth. If his "Account and Defense" had had no visible results, he would try again, at the next opportunity. It came in August 1776 when he read a copy of the Declaration of Independence. This, he told Hardwicke, was "a most infamous paper reciting a great number of pretended tyrannical deeds of the King." The facts cited in the "long train of abuses and usurpations" were simply wrong, and if the truth were known this whole justification for the rebellion and independence would appear to the world to be "to the last degree frivolous." So he would make the truth known, and not merely as a public duty.[32]

The Declaration of Independence was for Hutchinson a document of great personal importance. Not only were a number of charges in it directed specifically at him, but more important, it was the final, full formal statement of those allegations of conspiracy that had been threaded through all of the radical agitations since the Stamp Act crisis and that had culminated in the publication of his letters to Whately. If his personal reputation and that of his administration were ever to be vindicated, these charges would have to be refuted; and so he wrote for Lord Hardwicke and published anonymously in November 1776 a pamphlet entitled *Strictures upon the Declaration of the Congress at Philadelphia, in a Letter to a Noble Lord.* He sent copies to the appropriate people, explaining to Hardwicke that it would have been conceit in him to have dedicated such a "bagatelle" to him, and inscribing the copy for the King with elaborate and extravagant humility.[33]

The pamphlet itself, however, is far from humble. Its substantive section begins with a dismissal of the ringing prefatory paragraph of the Declaration, but not because Hutchinson did not think it worth debating "in what sense all men are created equal, or how far life, liberty, and the *pursuit of happiness* may be said to be unalienable" (though he could not refrain from asking the dele-

32. TH to Hardwicke, Aug. 10, 16, 1776, Add. MSS, 34527, pp. 94, 98.
33. Malcolm Freiberg, ed., *Thomas Hutchinson's "Strictures upon the Declaration . . ."* (*London, 1776*) (Boston, 1958: Old South Leaflets, no. 227), p. 3. The inscription to the King, written with the advice of Welbore Ellis, reads: "Governor Hutchinson, being prompted by zeal for your Majesty's service and a desire to expose, and as far as may be to frustrate, the very criminal designs of the leaders of your Majesty's deluded, unhappy American subjects, has wrote and caused to be printed a small pamphlet, which he begs leave to lay at your Majesty's feet, humbly entreating your Majesty's forgiveness of this presumption." *Diary and Letters,* II, 112.

gates of the southern colonies "how their constituents justify the depriving more than an hundred thousand Africans of their rights to liberty and *the pursuit of happiness,* and in some degree to their lives, if these rights are so absolutely unalienable"). He did not discuss the opening peroration because it was based on a false premise, namely, that the colonies were "one *distinct people* and the kingdom another, connected by *political* bands." Everything rested on that "hypothesis," which was not, Hutchinson said, and never had been, true. Therefore the invocation of the principle of natural rights and the contract theory to justify the dissolution of this "*political* band" was irrelevant. The "long train of abuses and usurpations" interested Hutchinson more, since on their truth or falsehood any justification of rebellion would have to depend. He took up the charges against the King in order, as they appear in the Declaration, citing and discussing every incident he could think of to which they might have been meant to apply, and showing, with particular emphasis on the episodes in Massachusetts which he knew especially well, that they were either altogether inapplicable or inaccurately stated or falsely interpreted.[34]

This extended analysis of the enumerated charges against the King forms the central substance of the pamphlet, but Hutchinson's main assertion—his own declaration of belief—appears in the introductory and concluding paragraphs, and it is free-flowing and impassioned. The underlying cause of the entire struggle, he wrote, lay not in the "abuses and usurpations" attributed with such inaccuracy to the King but in the agitations of the "men in each of the principal colonies who had independence in view before any of those taxes were laid or proposed which have since been the ostensible cause of resisting the execution of acts of Parliament." He had himself always opposed Parliament's taxing the colonies, but "if no taxes or duties had been laid upon the colonies, other pretenses would have been found for exception to the authority of Parliament." Not, he conceded, that these agitators had had a "regular plan . . . for attaining to independence"; their idea had simply been to capitalize on "every fresh incident which could be made to serve the purpose [of independence] by alienating the affections of the colonies from the kingdom." The hopes of compromise they had repeatedly tossed out had been used simply, "to

34. Freiberg, *Hutchinson's "Strictures,"* pp. 11, 10, 11–29.

amuse the authority in England. . . . No precise, unequivocal terms of submission to the authority of Parliament in any case have ever been offered by any Assembly. A concession has only produced a further demand, and I verily believe if every thing had been granted short of absolute independence they would not have been contented, for this was the object from the beginning." And so it had gone, he explained: the threat of taxation grotesquely exaggerated; groundless fears of tyranny stimulated to provide evidence of a plot that never existed; false letters and stolen letters published; connivance with the ruthless opposition in England happy to support anything that could make trouble for the ministry. "The tumults, riots, contempt and defiance of law in England were urged to encourage and justify the like disorders in the colonies and to annihilate the powers of government there. Many thousands of people who were before good and loyal subjects have been deluded and by degrees induced to rebel against the best of princes and the mildest of governments." But why publish a declaration of independence? It certainly was needed, not, as was claimed, to show a decent respect to the opinions of mankind, but to serve a very real and immediate political purpose. Hitherto the claim of the agitators intent upon independence had been that they were not seeking independence at all; now at the edge of attaining their goal, they needed somehow "to reconcile the people of America to that Independence which always before they had been made to believe was not intended. This design has too well succeeded."[35]

The pamphlet was duly acknowledged. Hardwicke told Hutchinson he thought well of it; Lord North, inquiring if it had indeed been written by Hutchinson, declared it to be "very good"; and John Almon republished it in his annual *The Remembrancer,* which was then carrying reprints of Hutchinson's letters.[36] But such passing interest as it aroused quickly faded, and it was clear that if writing the *Strictures* had helped Hutchinson relieve his need to defend himself and to explain yet again to a public he seemed never able to penetrate that the true motivations of the leaders of the Revolution were not the ostensible ones, that the whole Revolutionary movement had a deeper, darker origin than any-

35. *Ibid.,* pp. 5–6, 6–7, 9, 30.
36. *Ibid.,* p. 3; *Diary and Letters,* II, 112.

thing that was publicly acknowledged, the pamphlet had little other effect. He turned increasingly to other, more private forms of expression and relief. It was in the summer and early fall of 1776, when he had more leisure than he had ever had before, when his political correspondence, save for the continuing contact with Lord Hardwicke, had so far fallen off that he ceased keeping copies of his own letters for the first time in his life,[37] that he turned his attention seriously to completing the third volume of his *History of Massachusetts-Bay*.

This last volume would cover the years of his administration, and it would be a final, and posthumous, *apologia*. He had all the sources he needed. His own copies of his correspondence of course were gone—except for the scraps that turned up in more or less garbled form in the newspapers. But he had two other excellent sources, besides his own memory, to aid him, and in the course of the next two years he used them extensively in working out the history of those critical years. First, he had with him at least one, and probably several, of the annual almanacs that he had used as political diaries, and in which he had entered not merely notices of events but well-composed passages of description and analysis, some of which he could now simply transcribe directly into his *History*. He had entered in these almanacs also short polemical dialogues in which he had refuted in detail various published allegations of the opposition; and though these passages were too argumentative to use directly in the *History*, they must have served to recall past controversies to him with extraordinary vividness as he wrote about them almost a decade later. The other, and main, source he had available to him was the archive of the colonial office, in which he could find the official records of the General Court of Massachusetts and copies of his own official letters and reports and the documentary enclosures he had sent with them.[38]

He worked at the *History* steadily, though at first slowly, having resumed it, he said, "from want of better employment." He had been encouraged, however, by the interest of the Hardwicke family

37. Memo, Dec. 17, 1776, Eg. MSS, 2661, p. 178.
38. Eg. MS, 2666, is the annotated almanac for 1770. A number of its pages were copied directly into Hutchinson's account of that year in the *History*; almost all of the almanac entered into the book at least indirectly. *Diary and Letters*, II, 78 ("spend some time in continuing my *History of Massachusetts-Bay*, having the advantage of the books of the General Court from the secretary's office").

in the earlier volumes of his *History*, which he told them apologetically had been intended only for the "Yankees." "It is too uninteresting to the rest of the world. But as His Lordship condescends so far, I will go on more cheerfully in continuing the story and taking into it the rise and progress of the present rebellion, which I hope Lord Polwarth [Hardwicke's son-in-law], and Your Lordship also, will read after I am dead."[39]

Writing the *History* came to take on increasing interest for him as his other involvements fell away, but still the days were long and the periods of isolated reading, thinking, and brooding on the fortunes of his life and his country grew longer. The news continued to shock him and to strip away still further the remnants of optimism he still clung to. The beautiful Cambridge estates, so wonderfully built and cultivated by their owners—Thomas Oliver's "Elmwood," the great Vassall property, and others of what was already being called "Tory Row"—were being sold off to the highest bidders ("this is tyranny beyond any instance in time of the rebellion in England"). He did not know what had happened to his own Milton house, but he heard that his and Tommy's Boston property had been divided between two radical preachers, one of whom was said to be living in his house.[40]

Still, he did not completely give up hope, and hung on each incoming report for the signs he so desperately desired that the tide was turning in the fortunes of the war. Good news might come any time, especially since it was clear in late 1776 that a vast new military campaign was building up, which would in the end determine the outcome altogether. In September, as he followed the latest news of the war, he refused to leave London, though the town was almost entirely deserted of people he knew, for fear of missing word of a decisive turn. He was never completely alone, however, for his family, though now set up in separate establishments, was still in London, and they all came together frequently. "This," Hutchinson wrote, "is some alleviation—to have my children and grandchildren; but we are all in a state of exile from a country which of all others is most dear to me, notwithstanding the

39. *Diary and Letters,* II, 78; Eg. MSS, 2664, 38; TH to Hardwicke, [Sept. 1776], Add. MSS, 34527, p. 113.
40. *Diary and Letters,* II, 66, 67, 85.

unjust, cruel treatment I have received from it."[41] Without his children, and especially without Peggy, around whom his emotional life had been intimately woven from the day she was born, there would not be much left to him.

It was that fear—that even his family, or at least the part of it that meant the most to him, would be taken from him—that suddenly, at the end of 1776, rose to grip his heart as nothing that had happened to him before had ever done.

Peggy had never been strong. She had almost died of measles in 1772, and though she had finally thrown off the chills and infection that she had complained of in midsummer after their arrival in England, she had never been wholly well again, and she had been stricken with influenza along with the rest of the family in the winter of 1775–76. On November 9, 1776, Hutchinson recorded that she contracted a serious cold, and it seemed to settle quickly in her lungs. By the end of the year she was in the care of doctors. Hutchinson himself attended her constantly, took her carefully on rides in the fresh air, walked her as much as he dared, but the medical reports turned pessimistic. She was consumptive, and the disease was advanced. By early 1777 she was a permanent invalid, and Hutchinson's diary becomes a series of agonized reports on every nuance of her health, week by week, then day by day, and finally hour by hour. He was racked—frozen—with fear. He took her on frantic trips to therapeutic baths—two months at the Hot Wells in Bristol —which were exhausting, and probably worsened her condition, as most certainly did the extensive bleedings prescribed by the doctors and the frightful gashing of her foot and arms by a blundering apothecary groping for a vein to open (Hutchinson could not bear the sight and stopped him). By August she was fading quickly, and Hutchinson, in constant attendance, was drained and almost stricken dumb with hopelessness. The days and nights of her illness, he wrote, swept on with incredible speed toward her death; it all appeared "like the dream of a night."[42] The diary entries, most of them omitted in the later publication of his papers, are almost too agonizing to read:

41. *Diary and Letters*, II, 95.
42. *Diary and Letters*, II, 147–148, 152, 156.

August 1: Six months of my short remains of life have passed in a different manner from any six months preceding, my attention fixed upon one object, the recovery of my daughter, and in almost every day . . . ready to despair of it, but sensible that while life remains the care of it ought not to be neglected.

August 2: An emetic last night occasioned great distress . . . Still, she [keeps] the air and sits on a horse, but more feeble and more emaciated from week to week.

August 6: . . . great soreness at her breast upon any considerable motion, and lost her eyesight for a short time on coming into her chamber.

August 18: No relief but while the effect of laudanum remains.

August 19: It is wonderful that with such evacuations she has continued so long.

August 31: . . . scarce able to walk a few steps without help . . . . So much as a glimmering of hope is now hardly left.

September 4: Symptoms from diarrhea . . . the last stage threatening.

September 13: . . . the death countenance.[43]

On September 21 Peggy was so ill that Hutchinson refused to leave the house even for his usual walk to a nearby chapel. Propped up with pillows at dinner time, she talked briefly, Hutchinson recorded in his diary, "wishing among other things to try the sea. I told her I would go around the world to help her." But then she collapsed, and she was carried to bed. The family gathered.

I had not fortitude to go in [Hutchinson continued in his diary] until she called for me, and then I could not stay. She asked me if I thought she was dying. I could not tell, but expressed myself so as that she supposed I believed she was; turned to her sister and desired her to burn all her papers, and I promised it should be done. She said, "Must I die? I am not fit to die." I encouraged her to put her trust in the mercy of God through Jesus Christ her Saviour. She [said] repeatedly, "Lord Jesus save me." When I went again into the other room her sister asked her if I should pray with her, which, when she desired, I told her it was not in my power to collect in my mind proper expressions for a prayer. I uttered several ejaculations pertinent to her case, in which she joined with the greatest devotion. . . . [I] desired my daughter to attend to the prayer in the Church service for a person when there is but small hope of recovery, which I read kneeling at her bedside, the people in the room joining, and she most devoutly, in every petition.

43. Eg. MSS, 2664, pp. 4ff.

This was as much as I could support myself under. Her breath grew shorter. The last words she said were to Dr. Oliver—"I am dying," and continued speechless, and but little if at all sensible, until about half after ten, when she expired.

"My distress," Hutchinson wrote, "I cannot describe. A tender parent losing a most affectionate child with every desirable accomplishment of body and mind is the only person who can conceive of it." And then he wrote ten lines in his diary, which he, or a respectful descendant, later scored through so heavily that they will never be read by anyone else. Only his conclusion survives, that "no distress since the death of her dear mother has equalled this. But thy will, O God, it is my duty to submit to without murmuring."[44]

Nothing could ease the loss of this twenty-three-year-old child, the namesake and constant reminder of the wife he had lost a quarter-century earlier. Peggy's death was even worse for him than his wife's had been, he wrote to Israel Mauduit the next day. For when his wife had died there had at least been the possibility that Pliny the Younger's remedies for extreme grief—the sheer necessity to recover, the passage of time, and the surfeit of the grief itself—might be effective. At that earlier time he had had all three "in prospect"; now he had none, and least of all the second. He brooded over her death constantly, morbidly; revisited not only her grave but the room she had died in, and mourned not only the anniversary of her death but the day on which she had contracted her fatal illness. Tommy tried to distract him by taking him on trips into the city, but they did no good. He moved his lodgings, for the house in which Peggy had died was "too affecting, every part bringing my daughter constantly before my eyes"; but that did not help either. He sought comfort in seeing his own grief reflected in greater minds than his—in Grotius, whose biography he was then reading, and whose political career seemed to resemble his own to an uncanny degree, and who also had lost a precious daughter. He tried to think like Grotius, who had written, in words Hutchinson copied into his diary, that one should be glad the beloved daughter had died so young, before she had seen the evil of the world; unlike her mother she would never have to see "judges incensed against her husband because he is innocent. She will never be obliged to

44. Eg. MSS, 2664, pp. 14–15.

shut herself up in a prison for her husband's sake. She will never lead a wandering life for the sake of his company." But he found it almost impossible to regain his equilibrium. He was, he said, "like a ship loaded to her bearings—a small additional weight must sink her."[45]

iii

There seems never to have been a moment in the remaining years of Hutchinson's life when the wound of Peggy's death was not open in his mind and a source of unending pain. For months thereafter he could do very little but follow passively the news of the progress of the great military campaign that he knew was intended to cut the American states into two segments and break the rebellion once and for all. All sorts of rumors came to him, but the burden of the news was favorable: Burgoyne, he heard as Peggy lay dying, had captured Ticonderoga, was marching south, and would take and destroy Boston. So the war might yet be won—but at what cost! "What have those men to answer for who have brought on this destructive war!" But as the autumn progressed, the news worsened, and then early in December the results of the great campaign burst upon London like a bomb. Howe, far from making a juncture with Burgoyne on the Hudson, had gone south to Philadelphia, had met "obstinate . . . astonishing" resistance on the Delaware, and had suffered severe losses; and in the north, Burgoyne and his entire army had surrendered at Saratoga.[46]

Wild rumors flew through the city, and experienced men like Hutchinson's friend Welbore Ellis cried that "the kingdom must subdue the colonies or the colonies must subdue the kingdom." There was "universal dejection," Hutchinson recorded. He knew what the news meant for him even before its international repercussions were felt. "Everybody in a gloom," he wrote on December 12, 1777; "most of us expect to lay our bones here." The government's response seemed to him to make things worse. Lord North's

45. Eg. MSS, 2661, p. 179 (see above, Chap. I, note 49); Eg. MSS, 2664, pp. 16–17, 38; *Diary and Letters*, II, 179, 197, 257, 293. Hutchinson found the peculiarly apt words of Grotius in a biography he was then reading, *The Life of . . . Hugo Grotius . . . Written Originally in French*, by Jean Lévesque de Burigny (London, 1754), p. 357.

46. *Diary and Letters*, II, 140, 145, 147, 148, 156, 157, 169.

attempt at a compromise with the colonies—the instructions to the Carlisle Commission—seemed to Hutchinson to be ridiculous; it surrendered the main principles for which England—and he—had been struggling from the beginning, but not in a way that would settle the conflict peaceably. The ministry did not seem to know what the struggle was all about—that America, for its sake as well as for England's, must be retained on terms that alone could guarantee a viable connection. But then, he thought, it was not the ministry that was at fault so much as the powerful opposition in the House. The majority in Parliament, and the ministry, *must* know better, but they were again being led by the ruthless minority. Perhaps here at last, it suddenly occurred to him as he tried to make sense of the latest political events, he was witnessing the truth of Montesquieu's famous remark, which he had never before understood, that the English constitution would perish when the legislature became more corrupt than the executive.[47]

But concession, it became clear, was in everyone's mind, and the mood turned to panic in February and March 1778 when France's treaties with America were announced and its entry into the war was confirmed. "Everybody is struck dumb!" Hutchinson wrote. There was little thereafter that he could reasonably expect would ever restore the fortunes of the war. Faced now with a world conflict and without an ally in support, deeply engaged in a land campaign against a tenacious guerrilla army three thousand miles away, the whole London world that Hutchinson knew—even such faithful colleagues as Mauduit—spoke hysterically, it seemed to him, of abandoning America immediately in order to save the nation.[48] Hutchinson was trapped. Caught between his own passionate desire for England to retain the colonies—a desire for which he had sacrificed his career and the fortunes of his family—and England's rising determination to fight once again victoriously against its ancient enemy France at whatever cost to the deeply divisive war in the colonies, Hutchinson was reduced to silence. What could he say? If he were to discuss publicly his view that the ministry's concessions to end the war surrendered the principle of

47. *Diary and Letters*, II, 170, 174, 185–186, 189.
48. *Diary and Letters*, II, 192–193. On Hutchinson's struggle to keep Mauduit from making a fool of himself by expressing his panic in a pamphlet, see *ibid.*, pp. 196, 197, 203, 204.

the war without hope of benefits, it would not only make the ministry's work more difficult but would appear to be unpatriotic as well, and it would harm him both socially and politically. So he decided to "keep more at home than usual, to be out of the way of giving offense," a decision heartily concurred in by his friend Ellis, who once had advised him to "remain *in oculis civium* if you have anything to hope for yourself and your family." Now he told him: "Keep as much out of sight as you can. There is scarce a day but somebody or other has a fling at you in the House. Don't offend the ministry, who are friendly to you."[49]

So he worked at his *History,* put in whole days of reading and writing, and became increasingly absorbed in the world of the past as his own world slipped away from him. "Stayed all day at home," he recorded on January 14, 1778,

Wrote five or six folio pages of the history of my own administration. This has been my diversion at times ever since I came from the Hot Wells. Sometimes for a week together I write more or less every day, and then neglect it some days together, and fill the time with reading. If I had not found such employment for my thoughts, my troubles would have preyed upon me much more than they have, and I believe been too powerful. I thank God I have never quited books, and so I have not lost the relish for them.

History, he told the King (when "the drawing room [was] very thin [and he] said more to me than usual"), was the most entertaining and instructive thing he knew in these present wicked times, and his own history—the story, as he told it in his undramatic, factual narrative, of a judicious administration overthrown by a junta of ambitious fanatics determined to lead the colonies to independence —was the most absorbing story of all. It was with great satisfaction that he recorded finishing the work on October 22, 1778, and "laid it by." A year later he sent the manuscript to Lord Hardwicke, apologizing for the many erasures and for the local character of the story, which ended with his departure for England. No doubt Hardwicke would find a fuller account of the progress of the re- bellion and of the war itself more entertaining.[50]

But completing the *History* was only part of Hutchinson's deep-

49. *Diary and Letters,* II, 187, 188.
50. *Diary and Letters,* II, 178, 216–217, 218; TH to Hardwicke, Dec. 23, 1779, Add. MSS, 34527, p. 205.

ening involvement in the past. At the same time as he completed the third volume, working into it details from his current reading and using stray data from other sources as well as the basic documentary sources he had at his disposal, he wrote out also, in the back pages of the volume of his diary that begins with Peggy's last illness (August 1777), a memoir of the Hutchinson family in America. This family history, "intended for my own children and no part to be published to the world," was the most personal piece that Hutchinson ever wrote, and it is unquestionably the most deeply felt.[51] For in it he was able to show the deep transpersonal roots of his involvement with America and his blood relationship to the people and the land from which he had been expelled. It is the only portion of his writing in which he seems to have broken through all of his usual prudential restraints, and it is as a result colorfully opinionated, as opposed to the constrained and austere *History*, gossipy, intimate, and aggressive. For the early part of the family history he relied in large part on what he had written of the seventeenth century in volume I of the *History*, elaborating on the personal role of his ancestors in the well known public events. Half way through the 105-page manuscript, the memoir turns into an autobiography, in which Hutchinson for the last time, and now more freely than ever before, recounted the main public events in which he had been involved. His views are essentially the same as those he had always expressed, but the language is strikingly different: "The Assembly, finding that the chief justice [Oliver] did not go to Boston to have his brains beat out by their rabble, they attacked him in a new quarter, where he happened to be invulnerable. . . . Never did cannibals thirst stronger for human blood than the adherents to this faction. Humanity seemed to be abhorrent to their nature . . . ."[52] But it is not only a difference of style that distinguishes the memoir from the *History*. The family history contains information on the struggle with Thomas Pownall in the late 1750's not mentioned in anything else Hutchinson wrote and that constitutes what seems to be not only an explanation of the origins of his controversy with Pownall but also, by indirection and analogy, his private understanding of where the guilt lay for the publication

51. Eg. MSS, 2664, p. 1 from end.
52. *Diary and Letters*, I, 146, 147.

of his letters to Whately. For after explaining, in slashing terms, Pownall's ruthless opportunism as governor, his apparently deliberate sacrifice of the general good to his greed and lust for command, he told the story of an "unpardonable" act. Abercromby, the commander in chief in 1759, had sent letters to General Amherst through Governor Pownall, and Pownall, "there is no doubt . . . opened the letters and then destroyed them." When Abercromby asked Pownall what had happened to them, he lied in replying, though Abercromby as well as Hutchinson knew the truth. Amherst too, who succeeded Abercromby, knew of "the affair of the letters," which was, Hutchinson wrote, "the most wicked breach of trust that ever came within my observation."[53]

But neither this private, indeed secret, history nor any other effort to set the historical record straight and to demonstrate the authenticity and profundity of his attachment to the land of his birth could wholly relieve the tension that racked him. Alone, brooding, he read extensively, in history and biography, and everything he read seemed to form a commentary on his personal problems. The volume of his diary that contains the account of Peggy's death and the history of the Hutchinson family contains also, in the pages proper and especially in the end papers, clusters of apposite quotations from his reading, in Latin, French, and English, that reflect an almost compulsive self-absorption.[54] Thus Hutchinson read, in French, a lengthy biography of Erasmus, who also, he discovered, had been trapped between two powerful forces in a revolutionary movement and had ended his life in the shadows, and he copied into the diary a passage from one of Erasmus's letters that must have leapt out at him as he read: "Suppose [Erasmus had written in reference to the Catholic purists who questioned his orthodoxy at the time of the Reformation] that in the large number of books I have written I did somewhere say that it is not necessary to put the heretics to death; was it humane to report this without noting what preceded it, what followed it, what could make it less odious and closer to my true feelings?" Below the quotation

53. The passages on Pownall in the 1750's (Eg. MSS, 2664, pp. 63ff. from end, especially pp. 68 and 70 from end) are omitted from the transcription of the memoir that appears in *Diary and Letters*, I, 60ff. The editor of those volumes explained that these comments were "personal remarks which are not material in a historical point of view" (I, 60).

54. Eg. MSS, 2664, *passim*. Selections from these miscellaneous quotations and musings appear in *Diary and Letters*, I, 509ff.

Hutchinson wrote: "How applicable is this to the case of my letters to Whately and the expression, *There must be an abridgement of what are called English liberties!* Everything which preceded and followed which could have given the real sentiments and taken away all the odium was left out."[55]

He mused on what he had lived through, and reflected on the ironies of his life. How often and how preposterously had he been accused of seeking to introduce tyranny and *"popery"* into free, Protestant New England; yet now it was his accusers who were governing with barely a nod to the representative institutions he was charged with ignoring and who confiscated property without the slightest regard for the processes of law. And it was they, moreover, who had unashamedly allied themselves to the most powerful Roman Catholic state in Europe and who now welcomed the worship of the papal mass in Puritan Boston. What could one say to this? Or to the strange relevance of Joseph Galloway's career to his own? All his life Hutchinson had been prudent, circumspect, and restrained in everything he had written and everything he had said publicly, while Galloway, who had finally joined the loyalist colony in London after discovering that no compromise was possible with the radicals, had written and talked freely, aggressively, and acrimoniously. Had it made the slightest difference? Had Galloway suffered a worse fate than he? "I don't see that they who strive to avoid giving offense fare better than those who give it freely."[56]

He still sought relief in the company of old friends and, more out of habit than hope of recognition, he resumed attending the levées of the great. At the royal receptions he was still spoken to kindly by the King and Queen when they happened to recognize him in the line of attendants, but he cut an increasingly poor figure, especially when accompanied by the crippled Sir Francis Bernard. Gray, gaunt, unsophisticated, and silently beseeching, Hutchinson was an easy target for the bitter sarcasm of his rivals among the loyalists and for the malice of his enemies from home who watched him in these final years. Hutchinson, the ever-present and slippery

55. Eg. MSS, 2664, p. 2 verso, from end. Hutchinson found the passage in another biography by Jean Lévesque de Burigny, *Vie d'Erasme* . . . (Paris, 1757), where the words quoted, copied in French with minor errors by Hutchinson, appear on II, 310.

56. TH to Hardwicke, Oct. 30, 1778, and Aug. 23, 1779, Add. MSS, 34527, pp. 151, 194. For Hutchinson's encounters with Galloway, whose career is an interesting counterpoint to Hutchinson's, see *Diary and Letters*, II, 227, 229, 237–238.

John Temple later recalled, was "constant in his attendance at court—Sunday, Wednesday, and Thursday—a way never to rise; made communications to the King that he did not to the ministers; raised North's jealousy. Once showed what he got from his brother Foster Hutchinson, and next, when the King asked him the news, he fumbled for a letter. The King said, 'I suppose from Brother Foster,' and passed him before it could be produced." Hutchinson knew he was clumsy, and suffered from such slights, recording in detail a humiliating snub by the King when his conversation was especially "disordered."[57]

Some luminaries sought to comfort him and treated him with courtesy and respect, but there was always a bitter aftertaste in his experience of their kindness. Lord Hillsborough called on him frequently, and on one occasion confessed, Hutchinson recorded in his diary, that "when he persuaded me to take the government he thought he was doing public service, and serving me; now [that] he saw what I suffered, he wished, for my sake, he had not urged me."[58] Lord Hardwicke was especially kind and insisted that Hutchinson visit him at Wimpole Hall. Staying at that noble establishment was an even more memorable event than visiting the Gages at Firle, but he was not comfortable there; the contrast with the simpler, more natural, less privileged world he had lost was painful to him. It accounts for one of the finest passages of the diary, a vivid and effortless description that is almost interchangeable with those that record John Adams's response to wealth and elegance.

Nothing can be more polite than my entertainment [at Wimpole Hall] has been. The economy is too steady, or has too much sameness, to please for a long time together. The library is always open to everybody. The first appearance of My Lord and Lady is in the breakfast room exactly at ten. Breakfast is over about eleven. Everyone takes care of himself and does just what he pleases until half after three, when all meet at dinner. Between five and six the ladies withdraw; the gentlemen generally go into the library—some chat, others take up books. At eight a call to one of the

---

57. L. F. S. Upton, ed., *The Diary and Selected Papers of Chief Justice William Smith, 1784–1793* (Toronto: The Champlain Society, 1963–1965), I, 263. "I never was more disordered in speaking to the King than today; and by his sudden turning and speaking to the next person I think he discovered it." *Diary and Letters*, II, 247 (March 21, 1779).

58. *Diary and Letters*, II, 186. For Hutchinson's records of other rather intimate encounters with Hillsborough, whose private letter urging him to accept the governorship in 1770 Hutchinson continued to show to his friends (*ibid.*, p. 192), see *ibid.*, pp. 201, 205

drawing rooms to tea or coffee, which over, if there is company disposed to cards, any who don't like them converse or take their books. Exact at ten the sideboard is laid with a few light things upon it, that anybody disposed to supper may take it; and exact at eleven, as many servants as there are of gentlemen and ladies, come in with each of them two wax candles, and in procession we follow to the gallery at the head of the great staircase, and file off to different rooms. This is high life: but I would not have parted with my humble cottage at Milton for the sake of it.[59]

Milton remained the unattainable goal, to which he returned in all his reveries; but he began to give the appearance, at least, of being reconciled to some degree to ending his life in exile. He had done what he could. The record was complete—publicly, in the meticulously edited, factual, documented, irrefutable pages of the third volume of his *History;* privately, in the personal memoir he had written for his family. He had only one wish, which he put most succinctly in a letter to his cousin Edward: "I wish it may be in my power to convince my countrymen of one truth (which I feel the force of to my own great comfort every day) that I never, in my public character, took any one step in which I did not mean to serve their true interest, and to preserve to them every liberty consistent with it, or with their connection with the kingdom. Whether they, or I, mistook their true interest, time will discover." Enclosed in an almost entirely private world, preferring now to sit home and read the Parliamentary speeches of the seventeenth century rather than go out to hear those of his own time, he looked forward, bleakly but with composure, to a quiet and dignified retirement.[60] But there was no peace. He was beaten down at the end by a series of blows that was beyond his capacity to survive.

In July 1779 he received a copy of the Massachusetts act of banishment formally listing him the first of the "conspirators against the liberties of the people" who were barred from ever returning to Massachusetts, and confiscating all his property for the benefit of the state. And soon thereafter he heard that the Milton estate had been put up for public sale. So the property of the state of Massachusetts would be enhanced by the seizure of property of his. His bitterness could hardly be expressed. Had it not been he in 1773

59. *Diary and Letters,* II, 290.
60. TH to Edward Hutchinson, Aug. 5, 1777, Collection of Mark Bortman, Newton Centre, Mass., photocopy in MHS; *Diary and Letters,* II, 495.

who alone had negotiated the agreement with New York that had guaranteed to Massachusetts all the territory specified in the original charter? Without his intervention, which had been requested by the General Court, the state would now be vastly poorer. "I hope the ingratitude," he wrote, "as well as the extravagant cruelty of this act will appear hereafter for the benefit of my posterity."[61]

But his bitter brooding on the banishment act was cut off by a far greater, and more immediate, disaster. On September 9 he noted in his diary that Billy "spat blood, which alarms us all and him exceedingly, he having long been troubled with a cough which threatens his lungs." The same wasting disease that had killed his sister consumed him with even greater speed, and in five months, marked again by a series of desperate entries in his father's diary, Billy died, "struggling for life."[62]

Death was everywhere. In January, while Billy's illness was entering its last stage, Hutchinson heard that Bernard had died, not peacefully and with dignity, but in the agony of an epileptic seizure, constrained by the arms of his children. And his own Sally was ill too, how ill he would never know.[63] For by then the burden had become too great. He was himself in pain. A deep cough, constrictions in his chest, and dizziness were symptoms, he knew, of what no amount of rest, careful regulation of diet, and light exercise could prevent. He died, of a stroke, on June 3, 1780, the month that John Adams's constitution for the Commonwealth of Massachusetts went into effect.[64]

Soon thereafter James and Mercy Otis Warren bought the Milton estate, and wrote of the pleasure they took in "the shady walks, the pleasant groves that adorn this little villa," and the wonderful scenery they could now enjoy: there was a striking view from the east portico and from the parlor windows they could see "the warm influences and beautiful aspect of the western sky."[65] Arthur Lee wrote to congratulate them:[66]

61. TH to Hardwicke, July 31, 1779, Add. MSS, 34527, p. 190; *Diary and Letters*, II, 271.
62. *Diary and Letters*, II, 281, 341.
63. *Diary and Letters*, II, 319. Sally died June 28, 1780.
64. *Diary and Letters*, II, 353–355.
65. Mercy Warren to Sally Sever, Dec. 1781, Mercy Warren Letterbooks, MHS.
66. Arthur Lee to James Warren, April 8, 1782, *Warren-Adams Letters*, II (MHS,*Colls.*, LXXIII, 1925), 171.

It gave me great pleasure to hear that you and Mrs. Warren were settled so near Boston and at so beautiful a seat as that of the late Governor Hutchinson. It has not always happened in like manner that the forfeited seats of the wicked have been filled with men of virtue. But in this corrupt world it is sufficient that we have some examples of it for our consolation.

Epilogue

"Governor Hutchinson is dead," the Boston *Independent Chronicle* wrote in January 1781.

He was born to be the cause and the victim of popular fury, outrage, and conflagration. Descended from an ancient and honorable family; born and educated in America; professing all the zeal of the Congregational religion; affecting to honor the reputation of the first planters of the New World and to vindicate the character of America, especially of New England; early initiated into public business; industrious and indefatigable in it; beloved and esteemed by the people; elected and entrusted by them and their representatives; his views opened and extended by repeated travels in Europe; minutely informed in the history of his own country; author himself of an history of it which was extensively read in Europe; engaged in very large correspondences there as well as in America; favored by the crown of Great Britain, and possessed of its honors and emoluments—with all these advantages, and surrounded with all these circumstances, he was, perhaps, the only man in the world who could have brought on the controversy between Great Britain and America, in the manner and at the time it was done, and who could have involved the two countries in an enmity which must end in their everlasting separation. Yet this was the character of the man, and these his memorable actions. An unextinguishable ambition and avarice that were ever seen among his other qualities and which grew with his growth and strengthened with his age and experience and at last predominated over every other passion of his heart and principle of his mind, rendered him credulous to a childish degree of everything that favored his ruling passion, and blind and deaf to everything that thwarted it, to such a degree that his representations with those of his fellow laborer Bernard drew on the King, ministry, Parliament, and nation to concert measures which will end in their reduction and [in the] exaltation of America. . . .¹

This was the common view, muted somewhat and dignified by an effort at balance and a presumption of objectivity. It was the view that would soon thereafter, in more virulent form, enter the first, heroic histories of the Revolution, by William Gordon, David Ramsay, and Mercy Otis Warren. But these interpretations are themselves part of the struggle in which Hutchinson was involved, and they document not the actuality of Hutchinson's character or the nature of his motivations so much as the persona that made sense to those who had defeated him. His qualities were in fact more impressive than those allowed him by even the most generous of his enemies, and the sources of his ordeal more revealing of the history of the time than their chronicles could possibly make clear.

For besides being honorable to a fault, sincere, industrious, and profoundly loyal to the community of his birth, he was also more tolerant and more reasonable than those who attacked him and drove him into exile. "I doubt not," he wrote in a letter of 1775, "that there are [men] of both parties who sincerely wish to promote the interest of the country, though one or the other must have mistaken the way to it. I wish such as differ from me would only allow me the same freedom which I am willing to allow them." Is it not extraordinary, he asked in 1767, to find people "contending for an unlimited freedom of thought and action which they would confine wholly to themselves? We find one side hardly allowed to contradict what the other advances and not permitted even to reason without being treated in the most abusive manner, and vilified beyond all bounds. Nothing can be more unjust than this."² He never sought to suppress contrary opinions, and would never

---

1. [*Boston*] *Independent Chronicle & The Universal Advertiser*, Jan. 4, 1781. The author of this "*anatomizing* [of] Governor Hutchinson" was John Adams, then American representative in the Netherlands, who included these comments in a letter to the president of the Continental Congress. Abigail Adams, who received a copy of the letter, sent on the extract to the editor of the *Independent Chronicle*. L. H. Butterfield and Marc Friedlaender, eds., *Adams Family Correspondence*, IV (Cambridge, Harvard University Press, 1973), 22, 58–59.

2. TH to [Samuel] Quincy, Feb. 9, 1775, Eg. MSS, 2661, p. 124; Quincy, *Reports of Cases*, p. 244. Hutchinson was against prior restraint of the press, insisting only that people take full responsibility for what they said or published: "When [prior] restraint was taken off, then was the true liberty of the press. Every man who prints, prints at his peril, as every man who speaks, speaks at his peril." *Ibid.*, p. 266.

allow anyone "to be punished for his principles in government." Nor did he seek revenge against those who injured him—not even against Franklin, who he believed had deliberately destroyed his career.[3] He wished for stability and peace on the only terms he could conceive of their being firmly established. In his understanding of government he was of course conservative, but no more so than John Adams, who despised him and feared him and attacked him publicly and privately on every possible occasion but whose constitution for the Commonwealth of Massachusetts, which went into effect the month that Hutchinson died, exhibited to perfection the ideal of balance achieved through the independence and separation of powers which, in an older context, Hutchinson had struggled to retain. Hutchinson, no less than his enemies, had feared concentrations of power, though they differed in their understanding of where the danger lay: Hutchinson feared the anarchic force of mass public opinion and popular demagoguery unchecked by law and the power of the state; his enemies feared the state itself and the monopolization of its authority by officeholders like him. Hutchinson believed that sovereign power in the nature of things could only be absolute and indivisible, that a government that did not in the end have a monopoly of the legitimate use of coercive power was no government at all—an idea which even the cleverest of the Revolutionary leaders, after years of groping for compromises, were ultimately obliged to admit. The widespread notion that he was in some special sense corrupt and that he had plotted to deprive Americans of liberty was even less true than his own converse conviction that his enemies had been determined from the start, and had plotted from the start, to destroy the connection with England and to overthrow the established form of government and those who legitimately controlled it even if the cost of doing so was anarchy.

Yet he failed, and the forces he fought swept over him. More intelligent, tolerant, experienced, and perceptive—and less sanctimonious and self-righteous by far—than most of those who opposed him, he was yet overwhelmingly the loser.

3. TH to ——, Dec. 20, 1770, MA, XXVII, 80. "I thank God I feel no pleasure from revenge. If the same purposes might be answered by [Franklin and Temple] being in place as by their being out, I could wish them both restored." TH to ——, May 2, 1774, Eg. MSS, 2661, p. 26.

A multitude of circumstances, events, and personalities shaped this defeat; but ultimately Hutchinson failed, and died in exile grieving for the world he had lost, because, for all his intelligence, he did not comprehend the nature of the forces that confronted him and that at a critical point he might have controlled, or if not controlled then at least evaded. He was never able to understand the moral basis of the protests that arose against the existing order. Committed to small, prudential gains through an intricate, closely calibrated world of status, deference, and degree—the Anglo- American political world of privilege and patronage and of limited, arbitrary access—he could not respond to the aroused moral passion and the optimistic and idealist impulses that gripped the minds of the Revolutionaries and that led them to condemn as corrupt and oppressive the whole system by which their world was governed. He knew the general trends of the time better than most of his enemies; he knew, as he wrote in 1775, "that a dissatisfaction with government was not confined to America nor the English dominions, but [was] rather the general temper of the age . . . in Europe as well as in America."[4] But he did not sense the burdens of the system within which he lived so deeply, nor the frustration it engendered in those who lived outside or at the margins of its boundaries, nor the moral indignation it could provoke.

So in 1771 he vetoed a bill prohibiting the importation of Negro slaves into Massachusetts in part because he doubted the sincerity of its sponsors' professed belief that slavery, "so great a restraint of liberty," was unlawful "in a merely moral respect." What, Hutchinson asked, was the moral issue? In Massachusetts, he pointed out, slaves could not be legally executed by their masters; strictly speaking a slave was in no worse a position than "a servant would be who had bound himself for a term of years exceeding the ordinary term of human life"; indeed, it might even be possible, Hutchinson thought—though the point had not yet been determined—for slaves to own property in Massachusetts. What was the moral issue?[5]

So too, though Hutchinson himself had always opposed Parliament's taxing of the colonies, he could not understand why anyone

4. *Diary and Letters,* I, 447.
5. TH to Hillsborough, May 1, 1771, MA, XXVII, 159. On the history of the bill, and its renewal in 1774, see George H. Moore, *Notes on the History of Slavery in Massachusetts* (N.Y., 1866), pp. 130–140.

would want Parliament to pledge itself formally never to tax. Since it was perfectly obvious in law and logic that no one session of a sovereign body could legally bind its successors, what possible force could such a declaration have? What counted was that Parliament was not in fact taxing America, and that it was not in its interest to do so; the most explicit renunciation of taxation by Parliament, he said, would be trivial next to this simple matter of fact.[6]

So too he recognized the corruption of the English political system, and he was as profoundly shocked as other sensitive American visitors—John Dickinson, Charles Carroll, Josiah Quincy—by the dissoluteness and irresponsibility of the English ruling class and by their disregard of the general good. But he did not translate this recognition and shock into general conclusions, or into guides for his own conduct, or even into an understanding of the motivations of those who opposed him—at least until it was too late. For one can only wonder what went through Hutchinson's mind when he heard from Galloway in January 1779 a detailed account of Franklin's return to America in 1775: of how that acute politician had evaded Galloway's plea that they join forces "to promote a reconciliation"; how Franklin had kept silent for five or six weeks while people puzzled about the role he would play in the developing revolution; and how finally late one night, in conversation with Galloway, Franklin had "opened himself, and declared in favor of measures for attaining independence—exclaimed against the corruption and dissipation of the kingdom, and signified his opinion that from the strength of opposition, the want of union in the ministry, the great resources of the colonies, they would finally prevail."[7]

Franklin too had once been surprised and caught short by the passions of more spontaneous, more naive, and less calculating people than himself and by the profundity of the colonists' indignation. But he never forgot the lesson; and when in 1773 Hutchinson was puzzling over why rational people would rather pay £10,000 for the destroyed tea than a few pennies for duty, Franklin denounced Parliament for believing that the only force that could motivate people was "interest" and that reducing the price of tea 3d. per

---

6. TH to ——, Feb. 1775, Eg. MSS, 2661, pp. 117–118.
7. *Diary and Letters*, II, 237–238.

pound "is sufficient to overcome all the patriotism of an American."[8]

Failing to respond to the moral indignation and the meliorist aspirations that lay behind the protests of the Revolutionary leaders, Hutchinson could find only persistent irrationality in their arguments, and he wrote off their agitations as politically pathological. And in a limited, logical sense he was right. The Revolutionary leaders were not striving to act reasonably or logically. Demanding a responsiveness in government that exceeded the traditional expectations of the time, groping toward goals and impelled by aspirations that were no recognized part of the world as it was, they drew on convictions more powerful than logic and mobilized sources of political and social energy that burst the boundaries of received political wisdom. Hutchinson could not govern an aroused populace led by politicians manipulating deep-felt ideological symbols. He could not assimilate these new forces into the old world he knew so well, and, attempting uncomprehendingly to do so, lost the advantage of his greatest assets: a deserved reputation for candor, honesty, and a tireless and impartial devotion to the general good. Failing to carry the new politics with him by arguments that were accredited and tactics that were familiar, he was obliged to become devious; inevitably he appeared hypocritical, ultimately conspiratorial, though in fact he was neither. As the pressure mounted, his responses narrowed, his ideas became progressively more rigid, his imagination more limited, until in the end he could only plead for civil order as an absolute end in itself, which not only ignored the explosive issues but appeared, unavoidably, to be self-serving.

There is no better testimony to the character of the forces that were shaping the Revolutionary movement and that would determine the nature of American politics in the early national period than the failure of so prudent, experienced, and intelligent a man as Thomas Hutchinson to control them.

8. Franklin to Thomas Cushing, June 4, 1773, A. H. Smyth, ed., *Writings of Benjamin Franklin* ... (N.Y., 1905–1907), VI, 57.

Hutchinson Genealogy

*Appendix. The Losers: Notes on
the Historiography of Loyalism*

Note on the Hutchinson Manuscripts

Index

Hutchinson Genealogy

simplified to show stem-line American ancestry of Governor Thomas Hutchinson and the marriages of his children

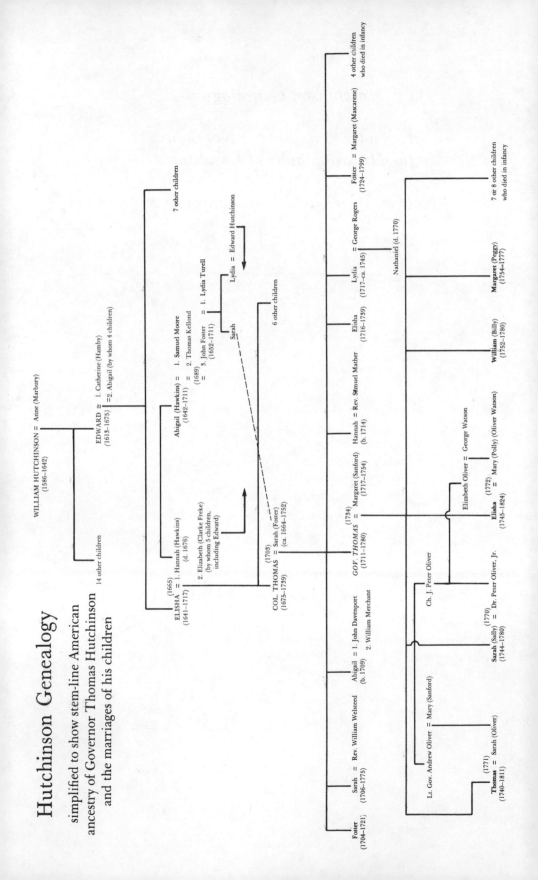

Appendix

The Losers: Notes on the
Historiography of Loyalism

The history of historians' writings on loyalism and the loyalists is a bizarre story, unnaturally vivid and exaggerated. There is even something exaggerated in the first, heroic phase of interpretation, dominated by participants in the Revolution or their immediate successors, which in any case one would expect to have been sharply polemical. In the first flush of victory the American patriots saw the loyalists as the worst of all enemies—betrayers of their homeland, unnatural sons, traitors. Furthermore, any impulse that might have been felt to explain the popularity and the logic of the loyalist opposition, if only in order to enhance the magnitude of the patriots' ultimate victory, was constrained by a logical embarrassment. The central object of the first American chroniclers of the Revolution was to prove that the Revolution was not just a party victory but a spontaneous uprising of the entire population. National dignity was involved, and there was no desire whatever to make human sense of the Americans who had opposed the creation of the nation, or even to notice their existence. And when the very survival of the country seemed to be at stake during the first party battles of the post-Revolutionary period, what purpose could be served by proving that the birth of the United States had been fiercely opposed by a sizable and highly placed segment of the American population and that the Revolution's aims had been despised by important American leaders? So American heroics of this earliest, myth-making period were grotesquely exaggerated: the founding fathers were portrayed as flawless paragons, commanding the almost universal allegiance of the population, and those loyalists who could not be totally ignored were simply blasted into oblivion as craven sycophants of a vicious oligarchy, parasites typical of the worst corruptions of the *ancien régime*.[1]

None of this is particularly surprising. What is surprising is that these wildly patriotic heroics so completely engrossed the field. There were no *counter*-heroics at all; there was scarcely a shred of contemporary writing that presented the opposite view in equally polemical terms. The explanation for this important fact leads directly to the loyalists themselves. For it would surely have been from them that one would have expected such a heroic counter-interpretation to come. And indeed one such slashing vilification of the victors was written—by the last royal chief justice of Massachusetts, Peter Oliver, who composed it between 1777 and 1781 in "the quiet of a small cottage in suburban London." It is a wild polemic comparable in its unqualified heroics to Parson Weems's *Life of Washington;* but it lay in manuscript for almost two hundred years, and when it was finally published, in 1961, it proved to be so antique and bizarre in its partisanship that its scholarly editors felt obliged to introduce it with a careful explanation of its value as an account of the Revolution.[2] A few other, less vituperative loyalist histories were published earlier, but none was issued as direct challenges to the patriotic histories of Mercy Otis Warren, William Gordon, David Ramsay, or the ineffable Weems; and none attempted to dislodge the structure of the narrative built into the essential documentation by Edmund Burke in the pages of the *Annual Register*.[3] By far the best of the loyalist histories was Thomas

1. E.g., Mercy Otis Warren, *History of the Rise, Progress and Termination of the American Revolution* . . . (Boston, 1805), I, 79, 85; Mason L. Weems, *The Life of Washington* [1800] (ed. Marcus Cunliffe, Cambridge, 1962).

2. Douglass Adair and John A. Schutz, eds., *Peter Oliver's Origin & Progress of the American Rebellion* (San Marino, Henry E. Huntington Library, 1961), p. xii.

3. Peter Oliver's New York equivalent, the supreme court justice Thomas Jones, wrote in his Hertfordshire exile a history that parallels Oliver's for events in New York, but it emerged into print only in 1879 and then in a somewhat watered-down version prepared by a judicious descendant. (Thomas Jones, *History of New York during the*

Hutchinson's carefully documented chronicle of the Revolutionary movement in Massachusetts, but he pruned it, as we have seen, of all polemics and forbade its publication until both he and his enemies had passed from the scene. Even the loyalists' private journals and letters, which might have served something of the same purpose as their chronicles of events, were withheld from publication until after they could have affected the initial historiographical tradition.[4]

What lay behind this remarkable reticence? The loyalists faced a paralyzing dilemma in attempting to adjust to their fate. The most distressing element in their lot, G. O. Trevelyan wrote in a deeply sympathetic passage, "was that they had always been animated, and now were tortured, by a double patriotism; for they were condemned to stand by, idle and powerless, while the two nations, which they equally loved, were tearing at each other's vitals."

Revolutionary War . . . , ed. Edward F. de Lancey, 2 vols., N.Y., 1879). The hundred-page introduction the exiled Maryland preacher Jonathan Boucher composed in 1797 for an edition of his collected sermons does constitute a contemporary counter-interpretation of sorts, but it was written to capitalize on the public interest in the French not the American Revolution, and its point is therefore diffused and it did not block out a useful counter-interpretation (Boucher, *A View of the Causes and Consequences of the American Revolution . . .*, London, 1797). And Joseph Galloway's *Historical and Political Reflections on the Rise and Progress of the American Rebellion . . .* (London, 1780), though it is in part an historical interpretation of the origins of the Revolution, is mainly a polemical pamphlet "written in great haste, amidst a multiplicity of other engagements." It is one of four pamphlets Galloway published in 1779 and 1780 in which he continued to promote the plan of union he had first proposed in 1774 and carried forward his condemnation of General William Howe and Admiral Lord Richard Howe for having blundered inexcusably in the military campaigns of 1775 and 1776. The pamphlet was lost among the polemical writings of the time and had no impact on the development of historical ideas. Julian P. Boyd, *Anglo-American Union: Joseph Galloway's Plans to Preserve the British Empire, 1774–1788* (Philadelphia, University of Pennsylvania Press, 1941), p. 102.

4. An unreliable epitome of Samuel Curwen's *Journal and Letters* was published by his great-grandnephew George A. Ward in London in 1842 (the later editions of this book—1844, 1845, 1864–did not improve the text); the whole of Curwen's voluminous and revealing journal reached print only in 1972 in a meticulous edition prepared by Andrew Oliver (2 vols., Harvard University Press). William Smith's important journals and papers are still not fully published. One segment of the manuscripts in the New York Public Library has appeared as a two-volume mimeographed typescript, edited by William H. W. Sabine, privately distributed, the first volume (1956) covering the period March 16, 1763, to July 9, 1776, the second (1958) covering July 12, 1776, to July 25, 1778; a later segment has been better served: L. F. S. Upton, ed., *The Diary and Selected Papers of Chief Justice William Smith, 1784–1793*, 2 vols. (Toronto: The Champlain Society, 1963–1965). Jonathan Boucher's *Reminiscences of an American Loyalist, 1738–1789* appeared only in 1925 in an edition prepared by his grandson, Jonathan Bouchier, and his letters were printed only in 1912 and 1913 in various issues of the *Maryland Historical Magazine*.

Exiled for the most part in England, they found the English upper classes utterly disdainful of refugee provincials who, George Selwyn explained with what must have been unbearable hauteur, "when people of fashion were mentioned, did not know to what country they belonged, or with what families they were connected; who had never in their lives amused themselves on a Sunday, and not much on any day of the week; who were easily shocked, and whose purses were slender." And they found the common people of England to be even worse. For they so abused, to the faces of these exiles who had sacrificed their lives for England, the character and motives of what they called those "damned American rebels" that the loyalists were forced, Trevelyan correctly wrote, "to assume the cudgels against defamers of their nation." The exiled Judge Samuel Curwen, of Salem, Massachusetts, wrote bitterly in his journal in London in 1776 that a returning soldier he met

speaks of the Yankees (as he is pleased to call them) in the most contemptuous terms, as cowards and poltroons, or as having as bad quality the depraved heart can be cursed with. . . . It is my earnest wish [that] the despised American may convince these conceited islanders that without regular, standing armies our continent can furnish brave soldiers, judicious, active and expert commanders, [and will do so] by some knockdown, irrefragable argument; . . . not till then may we expect generous treatment. It piques my pride (I confess it) to hear us called, *our colonies and our plantations* as if our property and persons were absolutely theirs, like the villeins and their cottages in the old feudal system.[5]

Curwen and most of the other articulate, informed exiles hoped for nothing so much as a quick end to the hostilities and a settlement that would allow them to return to their homes. Proud of their American identity and fearful of still further antagonizing their countrymen who had banished them, they had no desire to refute the patriot histories publicly. They wrote; but they kept their writing private, and left it to posterity to vindicate the choice they had so fatally made.

Who else was there to bear their banner, to make sense of their lives, to show the reason and humanity that had lain with them in the days when the outcome had still been uncertain, when men of

5. George Otto Trevelyan, *The American Revolution, Part II* (London, 1903), II, 241, 239, 240 (pronouns in the Selwyn quotation made consistently plural); Curwen, *Journal*, I, 284.

equal virtue and wisdom could differ on the path most proper to take? The English Whig opposition? Their influence on historiography, if not on history, was great, and had they found use for the loyalists' cause, the course of historiography would have been very different from what in fact it has been. But the loyalists bore living witness against everything the English opposition of the Revolutionary era sought to establish in their writing. Stripped of all embellishments, the Whig opposition's song had but a single theme: Americans loved their British homeland; they wanted nothing better than to remain British until the end of time; and given a modicum of just and sympathetic governance they would have clung to England forever; instead, they had in effect been driven out of the empire by the ignorance, folly, venality, and blindness of a vicious gang of ministers who took over the reins of government from the weak hands of George III and drove England back toward that state of autocracy from which it had emerged barely a century before. The loss of the colonies was the unfortunate result of misdeeds in high places, and not something generated in the hearts of Americans themselves or born of the inevitable resentments, the humiliations, of colonial dependence.

Now what good were the loyalists for such a story as this? For years they had claimed the exact opposite. The loyalists had warned again and again, in the years of open controversy in America, that the true source of the struggle did not lie primarily in the policies of a reactionary ministry (though many of the loyalists themselves had opposed the Stamp Act and Townshend Duties); the ministry's enactments had merely agitated, they said, the deep and essential source of trouble, which was the implacable determination of certain discontented and power-hungry Americans to throw off the tie to England as the first step in revolutionizing both government and society. There was nothing accidental in this, the loyalists had explained; the whole effort had been planned, and no policy of the English government that in any way preserved the empire would have made the slightest difference. But the Whig opposition kept up its cry—half sincere, half opportunistic—that Americans wanted nothing more than an appropriate place in the empire and were being driven out by the ministry. The loyalists were therefore liars or self-seeking hirelings of a ministry whose corrupting influence they were not at all surprised to discover seeping even into these provincial interstices.

But it was not in any case the English opposition, for all its brilliance, that set the first important historiographical tradition for the reign of George III, but the Tory historians of the early nineteenth century: particularly John Adolphus and, later, Viscount Mahon. For them sympathy with the loyalists would seem to have been irresistible, for in interpreting the causes of the American Revolution they would seem to have taken over the loyalist line quite directly. The Revolutionary leaders, Adolphus insisted, were simply "resolute republicans" and their complaints about taxation were flimsy pretenses. They "would not have been satisfied with a total abolition of the claim to taxation"; their aim was revolution and independence from the start; nothing England did would have made any essential difference. The Declaration of Independence, Adolphus declared, was a party screed, abounding in "low and intemperate scurrility," unworthy of an official reply by any agency of the British government, and he recommended to his readers one of the line-by-line refutations of the Declaration that had been published in England "in which every fallacy in argument, every false assumption in principle, every misstatement in fact, was exposed and refuted with so much clearness, perspicuity, and irrefragable force as to render it surprising that a public body should found their defence of an important measure on pretences so fallacious and so extremely open to detection."[6]

Now had not the loyalists said the same thing? Had they not in fact written the very replies to the Declaration of Independence that Adolphus found so convincing? Were they not, then, his heroes, and did he not therefore portray their struggles sympathetically and justify them to the world? He did not. He mentions them only to note the embarrassment they caused the British army by the excess of their zeal and to illustrate in their fate the cruelty of their republican enemies. For Adolphus's purpose was to defend George III and his ministry against the charges of the opposition and to show that they acted wisely and humanely throughout. To have justified the loyalists and told their story in full would necessarily have been to see in their warnings early and accurate perceptions of just those secret, conspiratorial causes of the trouble which he as historian was now revealing, and hence to convict King and

6. John Adolphus, *History of England from the Accession of King George the Third to the Conclusion of the Peace* . . . (London, 1802), II, 66, 172, 176, 406, 408.

ministry either of inexcusable deafness to the cries of their most faithful subjects or stupidity in not acting on their warnings before it was too late.[7]

It was not for Adolphus, or for Mahon (who managed to imply that the responsibility for the whole mess lay with the loyalists for not having made their warnings effective),[8] or for any other early nineteenth-century Tory historian to make sense of the loyalists' opposition to the Revolution, or to show the events through their eyes.[9] Much less was it the appropriate work of the later, great Whig historians.

What is in fact remarkable in the treatment of the loyalists in G. O. Trevelyan's superb narratives of the Revolution and the Revolutionary era is not that he failed to make sense of the loyalists' opposition to the Revolution, but that, given his central point

7. Cf. Herbert Butterfield, *George III and the Historians* (London, 1957), pp. 62–63.

8. Mahon's interpretation is more complex than Adolphus's. Again and again he moderated Adolphus's charges against the American leadership; but though his materials led him ever closer to what would become the central line of the Whig interpretation, and though he asked, in a remarkably emotional seven-page peroration on the causes and meaning of the Revolution, that justice be done on both sides, he never joined with the Whigs on the critical point of the King's, and the ministry's, guilt. The King had done his duty. Surely he could not be blamed for resisting the dismemberment of his empire or for refusing to concede to a popular insurrection. But then if the American leadership was not wholly to be condemned, who was to blame? The finger of suspicion pointed close to the loyalists and the officials with whom they were associated. For if the King was guilty of anything, it was of a willingness to lend "too ready an ear," Mahon wrote, "to the glozing reports of his Governors and Deputies—the Hutchinsons or Olivers—assuring him that the discontents were confined to a factious few, and that measures of rigour and repression alone were needed." And if among the "main causes" of the Revolution was the tendency in England "to undervalue and contemn the people of the Colonies," particularly to minimize their courage and pertinacity in fighting for their liberties, who was responsible for propagating such fatally erroneous views but "such men as Hutchinson and Gage, who, having the best means of information, and being Americans by birth or kindred, might well be trusted and believed"? Mahon, *History of England from the Peace of Utrecht to the Peace of Versailles, 1713–1783* [1836–1854] (3rd ed., Boston, 1854), VI, 99–106, 7.

9. It was not until 1911 that an English historian, Henry Belcher (Fellow of King's College, London, and Rector at Lewes, Sussex, with access to the Gage Papers there) set out to defend the crown from the "high lights and dark shadows invented by Whig disciples of Clio on either shore of the Atlantic," and in doing so wrote an account almost entirely from the loyalists' point of view. But his two-volume work, significantly entitled *The First American Civil War*, is poorly composed, covers only the years 1775–1778, and is tangled in an over-ambitious effort to combine social, political, and military history; it was nothing to put against the lucidity of the great works of G. O. Trevelyan and W. E. H. Lecky, which by then had set the major lines of interpretation for this whole era of British history in terms that would survive in England without effective challenge until Lewis B. Namier published his epochal volumes, part mystical and part statistical, of 1929 and 1930: *The Structure of Politics at the Accession of George III* and *England in the Age of the American Revolution.*

of view, he devoted as much sympathetic attention to them as he did.[10] At certain points he depicted their dilemmas sensitively and analyzed skillfully the paralysis these tensions induced. But in the end the loyalists had to be wrong—indeed, stupidly wrong—in choosing to side with the corrupt and reactionary ministry. Naive, provincial dupes of an insentive and venal government—dupes too of a romantic belief which in England the crown itself had shattered for every knowledgeable Englishman—Trevelyan's loyalists are a pathetic lot, and their lives, as he portrays them, for all their poignancy, make it less rather than more understandable that so foul a regime as that of George III could ever have endured or that anyone but a fool would have supported it.

So, for a century, the main lines of interpretation either ignored the loyalists or noticed them accusingly in passing to prove a point in what was essentially a political argument of the writer's own time. Then suddenly at the end of the nineteenth century the situation was apparently transformed. An entirely new phase of interpretation began. Books and articles appeared in a rush on both sides of the Atlantic between 1880 and 1910, apparently devoted to telling the loyalists' story. Their writings took on an importance they had never had before and entered increasingly into the standard accounts of the Revolution. It must have seemed as if the whole balance of the story was shifting and a new structure of interpretation was emerging in which the loyalists would be crucial. But this effort was no less partisan than what had gone before. It was simply partisan in a different way: it reflected a sense of "relevance" at least as distorting as that of the previous generation, but rooted in different interests, different needs, different problems.

It was an extraordinary development, this late nineteenth-century revisionism. It is a vividly revealing example—I know of no better—of the intricate way in which American self-identity has been shaped by an awareness of England. It involves some of the most celebrated and accomplished historians ever produced by the two countries and

10. Trevelyan published seven volumes on the Revolutionary period: *The Early History of Charles James Fox* (London, 1880); *The American Revolution* (3 Parts in 4 vols., London and N.Y., 1899–1907); and *George III and Charles James Fox* (2 vols., London and N.Y., 1912–1914). For his treatment of the loyalists, see *American Revolution, Part II,* II, 231ff.; *Part III,* 347ff.

some of the most obscure and strange. It starts with the magisterial figure of W. E. H. Lecky.

Why Lecky, in his *History of England in the Eighteenth Century*,[11] should have broken out of the existing orthodoxies to reach a breadth of view and a balance of judgment on the American Revolution unknown before is not apparent from his published letters or from the *History* itself. It was not simply that he was a thorough and judicious scholar and responded open-mindedly to the wealth of the documentation that had become available: the structure of the story, we know, was essentially clear in his mind before he saw the hundreds of volumes that are cited in his footnotes. Perhaps his being Irish—in his youth a fervent Irish patriot yet against home rule—helped broaden his view of colonial questions. But for whatever reason, it is a fact that his third and fourth volumes (1882), which cover the Revolution, presented the most carefully balanced assessment of the causes of the Revolution that had yet been seen, and flatly challenged the prevailing pieties.

For Lecky agreed with the Tory view that "the American Revolution, like most others, was the work of an energetic minority, who succeeded in committing an undecided and fluctuating majority to courses for which they had little love, and leading them step by step to a position from which it was impossible to recede." The American people did not want independence; they wanted a redress of grievances, and "it was only very slowly and reluctantly that they became familiarized with the idea of a complete separation from England." And then he wrote, in a passage that is central to his view of the Revolution and that would evoke the most fervent responses in America:

There were brave and honest men in America who were proud of the great and free Empire to which they belonged, who had no desire to shrink from the burden of maintaining it, who remembered with gratitude all the English blood that had been shed around Quebec and Montreal, and who, with nothing to hope for from the Crown, were prepared to face the most brutal mob violence and the invectives of a scurrilous Press, to risk their

11. Lecky's *History* was published in eight volumes, London, 1878–1890. The sections on the American Revolution, in the third and fourth volumes, were extended, edited, and published as a separate book by James A. Woodburn: *The American Revolution 1763–1783, Being the Chapters and Passages Relating to America from [Lecky's] History of England in the Eighteenth Century* (N.Y. and London, 1898).

fortunes, their reputations, and sometimes even their lives, in order to avert civil war and ultimate separation. Most of them ended their days in poverty and exile, and as the supporters of a beaten cause history has paid but a scanty tribute to their memory, but they comprised some of the best and ablest men America has ever produced, and they were contending for an ideal which was at least as worthy as that for which Washington fought. The maintenance of one free, industrial, and pacific empire, comprising the whole English race, holding the richest plains of Asia in subjection, blending all that was most venerable in an ancient civilization with the redundant energies of a youthful society, and destined in a few generations to outstrip every competitor and acquire an indisputable ascendancy on the globe, may have been a dream, but it was at least a noble one, and there were Americans who were prepared to make any personal sacrifices rather than assist in destroying it.

Yet, despite all the loyalists' idealism, vision, and courage Lecky believed that it was their enemies, the Revolutionary leaders, few in number, anti-majoritarian, who in the end had in fact been right. The colonies, he said, were justified in resisting the encroachments of the English state and in refusing to pay taxes that their Assemblies had not approved. The example of Ireland, with its "hereditary revenue, the scandalous pension list, the monstrous abuses of patronage," was always before their eyes, "and they were quite resolved not to suffer similar abuses in America." In such men as Samuel Adams, Lecky wrote in a brilliant passage, perfect embodiments of "the fierce and sober type of the seventeenth-century Covenanter . . . poor, simple, ostentatiously austere and indomitably courageous . . . hating with a fierce hatred, monarchy and the English Church, and all privileged classes and all who were invested with dignity and rank"—in such men as these, Lecky wrote, "permeated and indurated" with "the blended influence of Calvinistic theology and of republican principles," the government's impositions could only stir the most explosive reactions.

So it was Adams—fierce, narrow, unbending, ungenerous, intolerant—who had been right. Who then had been wrong? Like Trevelyan, Lecky blamed an insensitive and blundering ministry; but otherwise the breadth of his sympathy seemed limitless. There had been as many heroes and villains on one side of the water, he made clear, as on the other; and if he labored to convince his readers that the victorious Adams contained within his fierce personality the elemental virtues of strength, courage, and an unending devotion to a righteous cause, he declared with equal insistence that the defeated loyalists had had the same virtues, together with perhaps greater vision, and in addition had paid for their convictions with suffering that the triumphant patriots never knew.[12]

This is a remarkably well-balanced judgment; it marks a great advance in interpretation, and it approaches, within the limitations of the knowledge of the time, a rounded perception of the whole. But its great impact on the developing lines of historical understanding in the United States had less to do with the comprehensiveness of Lecky's sympathy than with the essentially pessimistic message that could be derived from his writing. For while those who persisted in thinking of American origins as a unanimous uprising of virtue found little comfort in what he wrote, there were others who discovered in his *History* and in his later essays—which were increasingly fearful, alienated, conservative, and anti-democratic— a revelation and an inspiration. Before the 1880's were out Lecky was being cited again and again by a new group of American writers developing a dark view of the American past that spoke directly and relevantly to overwhelming problems of contemporary American life. For them, Lecky, and through Lecky the loyalists, took on a new and unique importance.

The first of these problems was the question of the ethnic character of American society, a question that obsessed American thinkers at the end of the nineteenth century. Who were the American people? In the course of the 1880's and 1890's nine million immigrants entered the United States. Of the total population of seventy-six million in 1900, over ten million had been born abroad, and almost half of them had come from central, eastern, and southern Europe—peasants in large part, almost totally ignorant of Anglo-American culture. Were all of these people in more than a technical sense equally American? Some—Jeffersonian humanists—never doubted that they were, since they shared the passion for freedom that had motivated the founding fathers. Others, anticipating the results of a still-emerging process of ethnic mixing, were equally optimistic. But for yet others, of British ancestry and inherited status if not wealth, the immigrant hordes, the frightful slums they seemed to create, the crudeness, violence, and corruption of a new

12. Lecky, *History*, III, 443, 414, 418, 354, 361.

boss-run political system that seemed to violate every principle of a proper democracy—all of this was a threat and a challenge. It evoked elaborate responses and seemed to demand a rethinking of the past.

For as they looked about them at the condition of industrial mass society in America they could only think the patriotic historians' optimism romantic and childish. What struck these writers—amateur historians for the most part, leading figures in the many patriotic, genealogical, and historical societies that were then reaching the height of their importance in the eastern states—what struck them most forcibly was not the relentless march of progress and the broadening amplitudes of freedom but the opposite: the loss of essential qualities that had once created a more agreeable, better ordered, freer, more comprehensible way of life. Some basic source of integrity must have been destroyed; at some point in the past a profound retrogression must have been set in motion. When and how had it happened? Some men of cosmic vision, broad learning, and imagination—Henry Adams—reached beyond the whole of the modern world and located the source of the decline in such vague and distant events as the destruction of the unity of medieval culture in the twelfth century. But more ordinary American historians turned to their own recent past and found a new meaning in the earliest years of American history and in the Revolution.

What a strange, anxious lot they were, these now obscure but then widely read antiquarian scholars, and what romantically "relevant" things they wrote. Sydney George Fisher, of Philadelphia, for example, a wealthy lawyer and sportsman descended on one side from an original Quaker founder of Pennsylvania and on the other from a Connecticut loyalist: he was obsessed with the menace of the immigrants and wrote article after article with such titles as "Alien Degradation of American Character," "Immigration and Crime," "Has Immigration Dried up Our Literature?" "Has Immigration Increased Population?"—until at the age of forty he discovered history and found in a peculiar reading of the past an effective leverage over the unpleasantness of his own time which he employed relentlessly through eleven volumes, many of which have *"True"* in their titles (*The True Benjamin Franklin, The True History of the American Revolution*), as if everything that had been written before was false and it had been left to him to reveal for the first time the unmythologized, unvarnished, quite miserable truth about where the American people had gone wrong.[13]

Or the more judicious and scholarly land conveyancer, lawyer, and judge, Mellen Chamberlain of Chelsea, Massachusetts, who became a prince, a Borgia, among American autograph collectors, and whose antiquarian and bibliographical interests led eventually to the directorship of the Boston Public Library and to innumerable small, disconnected publications in the *Proceedings* of the Massachusetts Historical Society in which he verified signatures, dated and edited documents, traced ancient land titles, argued about the origins of the New England towns, and memorialized such neglected notables as the loyalist Daniel Leonard.[14]

Or, best of all, the Reverend George E. Ellis, son of a rich Boston merchant and grandson of a loyalist, who quit his Unitarian parish in Charlestown, Massachusetts, in disgust at developments in both church and society and retired to a house on Marlborough Street, Boston, and to the insulating book stacks of the Massachusetts Historical Society, which he served as president for ten years. A dour man (his candid Yankee colleagues in that venerable body said in implacably honest tributes to him after his death), who talked in soliloquies or not at all, he had been, they correctly recorded, a "melancholy failure" as Professor of Theology at the Harvard Divinity School and had repaid Harvard for its lack of response by publicly striking it from the list of beneficiaries in his will. Never known to have uttered a single good word for any reforming cause, never having evinced the slightest interest in art, poetry, fiction, or music, and, on the one occasion in his entire eighty years when he was known to have quoted a phrase from Shakespeare, having quoted it wrong, he "lived in the past," despaired of the future, and worked like a beaver on his antiquarian research and his writing—though he wrote, his relentlessly candid associates confessed, in a most "cumbrous, clumsy, diffuse" style. The most that could be said for Ellis, it was firmly recorded, was that he was "sober, peaceable,

13. For the articles cited, see *Forum*, 14 (Jan. 1893), 608–615; *Popular Science*, 49 (Sept. 1896), 625–630; *Forum*, 16 (Jan. 1894), 560–567; *Popular Science*, 48 (Dec. 1895–Jan. 1896), 244–255; [Lawrence H. Gipson], "Sydney George Fisher," *Dictionary of American Biography*, VI, 411–412.

14. Henry W. Haynes, "Memoir of Mellen Chamberlain," MHS *Procs.*, 2d ser., 20 (1906–1907), 119–146.

morally clean . . . sensible, and dutiful." And also that he "belonged to the ancient order . . . of privilege."[15]

And that is the essential fact. The history that Ellis, Chamberlain, and Fisher wrote remains significant as an expression of opinion within a group of the highest social status and as a reflection of the challenges they felt. Their writings differ, of course, in quality and emphasis, but they share the same underlying concern, and they agreed that the Revolution, and the role of the loyalists, had been misunderstood.

Fisher hammered away most directly and colorfully at the idea that the Revolution had broken the progressive thread of American history. The pre-Revolutionary period had in truth, he said, been full of arcadian gaiety and bucolic virtue; the people had lived "a glorious life of enjoyment." "It was merry England transported across the Atlantic, and more merry, light, and joyous than England had ever thought of being." Then came the Revolution, which ushered in the money-grubbing culture of a "sullen and depressed" polyglot populace that had no notion of how to amuse itself and furthermore was dominated by elements of the lower classes which in the colonial period had been firmly controlled by the aristocracy. The Revolution, naturally, far from having been the "spontaneous, unanimous uprising, all righteousness, perfection, and infallibility" that Americans had been taught to think true, had actually been an unpleasant affair, as full of atrocities, mistakes, and absurdities as any other such upheaval, and the history of the loyalists proved it. The terror they had been forced to endure at the hands of the Revolutionary mobs was doubly revealing, Fisher claimed in detailing their sufferings. It illustrated, first, the essential violence and brutality of the Revolutionary movement, and it marked "the rise of the ignorant classes into power and the steady deterioration in the character and manners of public men."[16]

Conceptually, the loyalists were essential to Fisher's story, and it is not surprising that his finest piece of writing is an essay in which

15. O. B. Frothingham, "Memoir of George Edward Ellis, D.D., LL.D.," MHS *Procs.*, 2d ser., 10 (1895–1896), 207–255; and remarks of C. F. Adams *et al.*, *ibid.*, 9 (1894–1895), 244ff. (esp. 253).

16. Sydney George Fisher, *Men, Women & Manners in Colonial Times*, 2d ed. (Philadelphia and London, 1898), I, 72, 75–77, 97; *True History of the American Revolution* (Philadelphia, 1902), chap. viii, p. 165; *Struggle for American Independence* (Philadelphia and London, 1908), I, chaps. xxi, xxii.

he reviewed the role of the loyalists in the historiography of the Revolution.[17] It was with them that his sympathies lay. Their plight offered him intellectual control over the social dislocations of his own time, for in his identification with them he found a means of removing himself from the present and associating himself with an original, authentic American tradition from which the present had departed.

So too Ellis, an inner émigré, felt a deep kinship with the loyalists. They had simply been conservatives, and none the worse for that. For the Revolutionary movement, Ellis made clear, had been born in the lawlessness of the radicals and the destructiveness and terrorism of the mobs. As leading conservatives, the loyalists had been "intelligent and excellent persons, who dearly loved their country"; they had been subjected to the worst kinds of abuse simply because they hesitated to join a rebellion. Of what had the loyalists in fact been guilty? Ellis's ingenious answer—which allowed him to rejoice in his patriotism and exonerate the loyalists at the same time—first appeared in 1884 in a review essay on the first volume of Thomas Hutchinson's *Diary and Letters*. The question, he said, is not one of justice or guilt, but of something quite different: "the fitting time," he wrote in a characteristically meandering metaphor, "had *nearly* come for the colonies to drop away from the mother country by a natural, unaided, unimpeded ripening, as mature fruit drops from the tree. . . . the question left now is whether the process, a little premature, was violently hurried by one party, by pounding and shaking the tree, to anticipate the fruit before it was ripe; or whether the process was blindly and perversely, and also violently, resisted by the other party, in an obstinate refusal to allow the natural and the inevitable." That central and fiercely vilified figure, Hutchinson, he said, was "a man of high integrity, of good judgment, and of noble magnanimity. . . . in heart and purpose a true friend of what he believed to be safest and best for his native country." But he had misjudged the ripeness of the fruit. As a native New Englander he should have known, Ellis said, in another of his collapsing agricultural metaphors, "that civil as

17. "The Legendary and Myth-Making Process in Histories of the American Revolution," *Proceedings of the American Philosophical Society*, 51 (April–June 1912), 53–75. In revising the essay for a second edition, Fisher added a paragraph praising Lecky and contrasting his *History* with "the ridiculous limitations of the school of Bancroft and Fiske."

well as religious independence of the mother country germinated in the first field-planting of the colony, and had been bearing and resowing its own crops, strengthening on their stalks through the generations." In other words, Hutchinson should have known that independence was inevitable and he should have anticipated that as governor "his official duty would require him to dam a current that had already become dangerously swollen."[18]

Four years later Ellis amplified this interpretation of the loyalists. He was now certain that, in the civil war that was called the Revolution, the vast majority of the people had been conservative and loyal until intimidation, or possibly honest conversion, gave the advantage to the patriot leaders. Until crown authority had been destroyed and until the only source of law and order had become Congress or the new state governments, loyalism had been utterly justified, for in essence it was simply "allegiance to established authority as a safeguard against anarchy," and it was heroic in the face of the brutality with which it was met. When the legitimate sources of law changed, the loyalists should have switched sides or silently conformed since by then the only alternative to Congress was anarchy. "They had but to extend the meaning of the term loyalty from its limited reference to the British king to the recognition of Congress, which had established a government."[19]

So the amateurs—Fisher, Chamberlain,[20] Ellis—responded to the tensions of the late nineteenth century by following Lecky and devising an interpretation of the American Revolution that was as much social therapeutics as history and in which the loyalists were respected and important—though still utterly unreal—figures. They wrote at a time when modern professional scholarship was evolving rapidly, however, and the purest amalgam of their fervent philanglicism was the work of one who linked their antiquarianism to the creative lines of force developing within the universities.

18. George E. Ellis, "Governor Thomas Hutchinson," *Atlantic Monthly*, 53 (1884), 665, 675, 676, 667, 669.
19. George E. Ellis, "The Loyalists and Their Fortunes," in Justin Winsor, ed., *Narrative and Critical History of America* (Boston and N.Y., 1884–1889), VII, 192–193.
20. For Chamberlain's views of the loyalists and for his understanding of the role of the Revolution in American History, see his "The Revolution Impending," in Winsor, *Narrative and Critical History*, VI, chap. i, and his "Address," in *John Adams . . . with Other Essays . . .* (Boston and N.Y., 1898), pp. 429ff.

James K. Hosmer was far more of a professional historian than his colleagues in the Massachusetts Historical Society, yet he was still a generalist and wide-ranging historical thinker in the manner of Lecky, to whom he acknowledged his deep indebtedness. A Harvard-educated Unitarian minister turned scholar and university teacher, Hosmer sought to present an integrated world view in which history bore directly on the problems of his age. He had the time for such a task (he lived to be ninety-three) and he had the range of interests and skills. Professor at one time or another of History, English Literature, German Literature, and Rhetoric, Hosmer produced a history of the Jews, a history of German literature, four volumes on the American Civil War, a biography of Sir Henry Vane, a *Short History of Anglo-Saxon Freedom,* a biography of Samuel Adams, and a biography (the only one that has existed) of Thomas Hutchinson.

Disparate as they were, these books together compose a general statement—as history, as ideology, and as social commentary. The key work is the *History of Anglo-Saxon Freedom,* which is subtitled "The Polity of the English Speaking Race." Hosmer wrote it to illustrate "the substantial identity of the great English-speaking nations . . . and the expediency that these nations should, in John Bright's phrase, become one people." Is is a fascinating book. The first part flows easily, disposing of everything between 100 B.C. and the settlement of British America in a hundred pages. For the seventeenth and eighteenth centuries the pace slows somewhat, as Hosmer felt it necessary to explain in some detail the ups and downs of freedom under the Stuarts, the Commonwealth, and Walpole's Parliamentary system. The great explanatory challenge lay in the American Revolution, since it had sundered the English and American people, and he faced it with a bold fusion of the thought of Lecky and the American antiquarians. Americans, he wrote, did not fight England in the Revolution; Americans and Englishmen were both fighting "the Hanoverian George III and his Germanized Court," or more generally, English and American liberals were both fighting conservatives—in England "the struggle was to recover what was lost . . . [in America] to preserve what had been retained." Indeed, the two peoples, he declared in a fine flight of imagination, were interchangeable: if all the people of England had been transported to America after the Seven Years War and all the Americans to England, exactly the same history would have resulted—to prove which he quoted Lecky for several pages on the political history of England under George III and got into a fearful muddle trying to keep party views of the American question consistent.[21] But the main point is never obscured: America was fighting to preserve the same liberties for which England had fought over the centuries. Americans were loyal and never wished to throw off allegiance to England, and the loyalists above all were, he said, striving to maintain the unity of the English-speaking peoples. The loyalists were in fact the superior people "as regards intelligence, substantial good purpose, and piety." Their one mistake was to have conceded supremacy to "distant arbitrary masters," a mistake which "a population nurtured under the influence of the revived folkmoot ought by no means to have made." This was a cunning formulation, for it let Hosmer have the argument both ways: both the loyalists and their enemies were seeking to fortify Anglo-Saxonism; the loyalists, however, failed to see the Anglo-Saxonism of the popular assemblies (the "folkmoots") that opposed them. But that was the loyalists' only error. Otherwise every human virtue had been theirs in abundance: grace, chivalry, courage, poetic spirit, and a generous and dignified style of life understandably offensive to the coarse democracy of the town meetings. The strife therefore was "not of countries but of parties . . . carried on in each arena for the preservation of the same priceless treasure,—Anglo-Saxon freedom. . . . What a noble community is this,—common striving so heroic for a common cause of such supreme moment! How mean the nursing of petty prejudice between lands so linked; how powerful the motive to join hand with hand and heart with heart!"[22]

Hosmer's two biographies exemplify this theme. The book on Sir Henry Vane's dual career in England and Puritan Massachusetts seeks to show the essential unity of the struggle for freedom among English-speaking peoples in the seventeenth century, and the biog-

---

21. [Solon J. Buck], "James Kendall Hosmer," *Dictionary of American Biography*, IX, 244–245; James K. Hosmer, *A Short History of Anglo-Saxon Freedom* (N.Y., 1890), pp. ix-x, 219–221, 225–230, 222. Apparently Hosmer drew the attractive idea that the Revolution had really been a war between Englishmen and Germans, rather than between Englishmen and Americans, from an article by O. J. Casey, "Anglophobia in the United States," *Westminster Review*, 131 (1889), 328, itself a reply to a belligerently anti-American article of the same title that had appeared in the *Review* the year before (vol. 130, pp. 736–756).

22. Hosmer, *Anglo-Saxon Freedom*, pp. 225, 228, 229, 230–231.

raphy of Hutchinson contains the same message in somewhat different form. It follows perfectly the theme laid out in *Anglo-Saxon Freedom,* and it follows too the favorable scenario of Hutchinson's life that Hosmer had sketched a decade earlier in his unenthusiastic biography of Samuel Adams. From the opening pages, which quote in full Lecky's view of the loyalists, to Hutchinson's death 350 pages later, the exoneration of this key loyalist from all blame save a single honest error, "disloyalty to the folk-moot," proceeds in heavily documented detail. Hutchinson had been "a sleepless, able captain who went down at last with his ship"; how sad, Hosmer felt, that he did not live to sense if not to witness the recovery that England would make, the strength that America would gain, and the vindication that would be found in both countries for precisely the values that this sensible, destroyed man had held most dear.[23]

The reception of the book is revealing. The reviewer in the *American Historical Review* was a patriot of an earlier vintage, and he filled seven pages with abuse. His attack was aimed partly at Hutchinson for having favored the subjection of the colonies "as mere tributaries of the realm," partly at Hosmer for having attempted to exonerate Hutchinson, with whom, he correctly pointed out, Hosmer had revealed himself to be decidedly more in sympathy than he was with his earlier biographical subject, Adams; and this, he charged, "is a necessary consequence of his concurrence in the new-school views from which we dissent." But one reviewer, Moses Coit Tyler, praised the book enthusiastically: it was "wise, kindly, and patriotic" of Hosmer to have written it, he declared in *The Nation*—words which, Hosmer wrote in a letter of thanks, coming from "the one scholar in America who was best equipped to sit in judgment on such a book as mine, . . . let me know I have succeeded: I really need nothing more."[24]

23. Hosmer, *The Life of Young Sir Henry Vane* . . . (Boston and N.Y., 1888); *The Life of Thomas Hutchinson* . . . (Boston and N.Y., 1896), pp. [xiii], 349; *Samuel Adams* (Boston and N.Y., 1885), p. 281.

24. Abner C. Goodell, Jr., in *American Historical Review*, 2 (1896–1897), 163–170 (on Goodell—"in matters historical, he lacked all sense of proportion. . . . his [death] now causes in us no sense of immediate loss"—see MHS *Procs.*, 48 [1914–1915], 5, 6); [Tyler], *Nation*, 62 (March 26, 1896), 258–259; Howard Mumford Jones, *Life of Moses Coit Tyler* (Ann Arbor, University of Michigan Press, 1933), p. 266. Hosmer sent a copy of the book to Peter Orlando Hutchinson, Hutchinson's great-grandson, the editor of his *Diary and Letters,* who was then in his eighty-sixth year. Hutchinson responded, March 18, 1896 (Misc. Bound MSS, MHS), in a warm letter of thanks, describing his long years of work preserving and editing the papers that were in the governor's possession when he died

For Tyler, whose career brings us a step closer to the world of modern professional scholarship, was then emerging as a major figure among American academic historians and one of the leading protagonists of the loyalists. A Connecticut-born descendant of seventeenth-century settlers in New England and a Yale graduate who had become a Calvinist minister, he had spent the Civil War years in Boston doing gymnastics to music under the tutelage of a crusading homeopathic physician, and had taken his muscular Christianity to England, where he had remained as a lecturer on homeopathy and other subjects for three formative years. He had been transfixed by the London of John Bright and Gladstone, of Lord John Russell and Disraeli, and had soaked up what he could of its cultural life. By the time he left, in 1866, he had developed a permanent interest in American history; had referred to the Revolution in his public lectures as "that unlucky quarrel" which would never have happened if the ministry had been well enough informed; and had been accustomed to use experiences of the loyalists to illustrate what he called in a lecture title "English Hallucinations Touching America." By the time Lecky's *History of England* appeared, Tyler was Professor of American history at Cornell University and the noted author of a two-volume history of American literature covering the years 1607–1765. Lecky's chapters on America gave Tyler immense pleasure. They were, he said, "by their perfect judicial fairness one of the very best means of getting the coming generation of American students out of the old manner of thinking upon and treating American history, which has led to so much Chauvinism among our people." He had long since decided to work to the same goal in a *magnum opus* on the Revolution that would help overcome the deplorable "race-feud" he believed existed between the two countries as a result of the disruption of the "English-speaking race" at the end of the eighteenth century. A particularly sympathetic treatment of the loyalists was essential to his purpose in what became *The Literary History of the American Revolution;* and it was not artificially contrived. Tyler loved England; he regretted the Revolution; and he instinctively favored all those who sought the unity of the English-speaking peoples, in the past as in

and his final sale of the fourteen volumes to the British Museum for £100. See Note on the Hutchinson Manuscripts.

the present. He could only have been deeply grateful to the president of Cornell, a historian himself, who in writing to congratulate him on his book, praised him in almost the same terms in which Tyler had praised Lecky—"a marvellous balance"; "marvellous impartiality"—and declared that "the most successful part, . . . the most striking part, is your dealing with the Loyalists. . . . you have done the Loyalists full justice," he added, "without going over to their side, as I feared you would do."[25]

But he had not seen the loyalists as people, nor had he grasped the peculiar mental and psychological dispositions of the late eighteenth-century world which alone makes sense of their experience and allows one to explain their conduct and the responses of others to them. His book is a series of summaries with occasional interpretations of the contents of their major writings; and while it was a significant step forward for him to present the loyalists' writings along with those of the Revolutionary leaders, he had neither the documentation, nor the conceptual grasp, nor the understanding of the context that would allow him to explain their side of the origins of the conflict.

Nor indeed did those far more magisterial scholars, the so-called imperialist historians, who were young when Tyler was at his height and who carried forward into our own time the philanglicism of the nineteenth-century antiquarians and infused that spirit into some of the most impressive monuments of twentieth-century scholarship.

The distance between the romantic amateurs like Fisher and Ellis, deeply concerned with questions of ethnic identity, and such scholars as George Louis Beer, Herbert L. Osgood, Charles M. Andrews, and the late Lawrence H. Gipson is vast, but in their original cultural orientation the two groups were in fact close. They were bred in the same culture and shared the same ultimate sources of ideas and attitudes; they all sought to express in historical terms

25. Tyler, "On Certain English Hallucinations Touching America," in *Glimpses of England* (N.Y. and London, 1898), pp. 279, 283–285; Andrew D. White to W. E. H. Lecky, July 30, 1890, in [Elisabeth Lecky], *A Memoir of . . . Lecky . . .* (N.Y. and London, Longmans Green, 1909), p. 186; Jones, *Tyler*, p. 258; Tyler, *Literary History of the American Revolution, 1763–1783* (N.Y. and London, 1897), I, chaps. xiii–xvii; II, chaps. xxvii–xxix; Charles Kendall Adams to Tyler, July 30, 1897, in Jessica T. Austen, ed., *Moses Coit Tyler, 1835–1900: Selections from His Letters and Diaries* (Garden City, N.Y., Doubleday, Page and Co., 1911), pp. 295–296. For Lecky's appreciation of Tyler's book, see *ibid.*, pp. 300–301.

their belief in the kinship of the British and the American peoples; and like Lecky, whom they all admired and quoted, they viewed the Revolution in some degree as unfortunate and the continuing unity of the English-speaking peoples as necessary for survival in a world that was tending, as Lecky wrote at the end of his life, more and more toward "great political agglomerations based upon an affinity of race, language and creed, which has produced the Pan-Slavonic movement and the Pan-Germanic movement, and which chiefly made the unity of Italy."[26] In this sense, as intense partisans of the unity of the English-speaking peoples, they were all, emotionally, loyalists. But there were great differences. These modern historians were more concerned with international relations than with domestic social problems, and they were obliged to express their views through the documentary constraints of a large and growing body of historical knowledge and in expositions that satisfied the most demanding technical requirements of their profession. Andrews wrote twenty volumes, most of them devoted in one way or another to depicting the bonds that had unified England and America before the Revolution. His is an imposing historical *oeuvre,* and it remains fundamental to any understanding of early American history. But, like Osgood, who opened his prolific career in the 1890's by urging historians of America not only to work in the British archives but in imagination to station themselves in London in order to "view colonial affairs in their proper perspective," Andrews avoided a detailed commentary on the Revolution that destroyed the eighteenth-century Anglo-American empire, an event he came increasingly to regret. Beer too confined his scholarly writing to the pre-Revolutionary period, but his implicit sympathy with the loyalists came out in striking comments in these books and in political essays, which illustrate dramatically the political relevance of the loyalists for those of a "Pan-Anglian state of mind" in the early years of the twentieth century. He concluded a study in 1907 with the statement that the American Revolution, "in so far as it led to the political disintegration of the Anglo-Saxon race," ran counter to the deepest tendencies of history and that in the future it may well "lose the great significance that is now attached to it and will appear merely as the temporary separation of two kindred peoples." Ten years

26. Lecky, *Historical and Political Essays* (London, 1908; reprinted, Freeport, N.Y., 1970), p. 64.

later, in a book written during World War I to explain the necessity for "a co-operative democratic alliance of all the English-speaking peoples," Beer repeated the forecast of an ultimate reunion of the two nations though he warned against any "premature forcing of the pace."[27]

But it was left to Lawrence Gipson, in his fifteen-volume *British Empire before the American Revolution* (1936–1970), to work out most fully a view of the loyalists consistent with the vast world of technical scholarship that had been created by the "imperialist" historians. The goal of his enormous work was to justify the old British empire against the "terrible indictment" of the Declaration of Independence, and to do so by presenting "a detached, unbiased view of [it] under normal, peace-time conditions." It is a favorable and defensive view, full of nostalgia. The trade acts were not offensive; they were made to seem so by colonial smugglers. The Declaratory Act declaring Parliament's supremacy "in all cases whatsoever" was nothing new; it was modeled on the Irish Act of 1719 and had been effectively operative at least since 1696. Responsible people in the colonies did not object to the presence of British troops; such objections were generated by the Sons of Liberty, "these zealots," who deliberately raised in an otherwise inert populace "an ineradicable hatred of the British government," apparently to serve private purposes, which are not described. Gipson's warmest sympathies are reserved for the loyalists. His first publication, in fact, which appeared sixteen years before volume I of *The British Empire,* was a sympathetic biography of a loyalist, Jared Ingersoll, of Connecticut; and in the last volumes of the *Empire* series he continued to adjust the balance of interpretation more in the loyalists' favor: their plural officeholding is indulgently explained, their opinions defended, and their responsibility for the outcome discounted.[28]

Yet in the end Gipson could hardly say that they had been right and the Revolution wrong, nor was he able to formulate the issue in any other terms. It was not possible for him, given his basically

27. Herbert L. Osgood, "The Study of American Colonial History," *Annual Report of the American Historical Association for the Year 1898* (Washington, D.C., 1899), p. 72; A. S. Eisenstadt, *Charles McLean Andrews* (N.Y., 1956), chap. v; George Louis Beer, *British Colonial Policy, 1754–1765* (N.Y., 1907), pp. 315–316; Beer, *The English-Speaking Peoples* (N.Y., 1917), pp. x, ix.

28. Gipson, *British Empire*, I, vii; Gipson, *Jared Ingersoll: A Study of American Loyalism in Relation to British Colonial Government* (New Haven, 1920).

institutional explanation of historical development, to penetrate into the mental, psychological, or ideological world of either side in order to portray the human reality. He wrote of events but not of motivations, of what happened but not of why things happened or of what people understood was happening. Despite all the massive detail in his huge book, the basic forces at work prove to be entirely abstract and impersonal. The cause of the Revolution as it emerges from his volumes has very little to do with anyone's specific decisions or actions. The basic pressure toward what became a revolutionary change came from the development of institutions. The Revolution, as Gipson saw it, was the result chiefly of the desire of the lower Houses of Assembly, which in England were still thought of as provincial councils possessed of limited and inferior powers, to gain the autonomy and powers of full legislative bodies. This difference in viewpoint, he believed, was irreconcilable, and when the issue was squarely posed in the 1760's a fundamental conflict was inescapable. Gipson expressed this most often in the metaphorical terms of children nourished and fostered by an indulgent and somewhat neglectful parent; they grew to political maturity, and in the vigor of early manhood cast off their dependent state.

Gipson's *British Empire* is an immensely learned work; its interpretation is woven lightly into a complex narrative fabric. But while it attains a significant degree of apparent impartiality by relieving both the loyalists and the ministry of much of the blame that had been heaped on them, it does not explain, in terms that are compatible with its explanation of the creative forces at work, why some people opposed the Revolution; it does not make clear why any sensible person could have failed to associate himself with the relentless, unstoppable march forward of American public institutions.

Nor have other twentieth-century historians provided this explanation. Though the crude partisanship of the nineteenth century has been left far behind, more recent writings on the Revolution have made even less of an effort to explain motives, goals, and experience than did their predecessors, however benighted they may have been. Partly this is the result of a kind of scholasticism that at worst sacrifices thought to technique and at best subordinates explanation to the compilation of data within the loosest of descriptive categories. The effect this has had on writings about the loyalists can be seen in the earliest writings of the twentieth century with the publication, in

1901 and 1902, of the first two books entirely devoted to the history of the loyalists. They are doctoral dissertations, one written by Alexander C. Flick, the other by C. H. Van Tyne.[29] Both are based on archival information never used before; both have appendixes containing tables of statutes and persons; and both are entirely descriptive, making only incidental efforts at explaining the larger meaning of the material gathered or the bearing that the loyalists' experiences might be said to have had on the overall history of the Revolution. Such early dissertations initiated an academic style, which may be said to have reached its fulfillment in recent years in statistical compilations, some of which have provided useful information about the loyalists.[30]

Through the first half of the twentieth century, however, it was not such eclectic scholarship that dominated American historiography but the thought of the historians associated with the intellectual trends of the Progressive era—particularly J. Allen Smith, J. F. Jameson, Charles Beard, and A. M. Schlesinger, Sr. Their sophisticated and extremely influential writing stressed social trends and their economic substructures, and their general picture of American history rested conceptually on a view of the American Revolution as the moment when the permanent struggle of American life between the business community and the ordinary people was set in motion. From the beginning the loyalists were involved, as extremists among the conservatives, a group that could now be defined in social and economic terms; and in this sense the loyalists are important to the conclusions of two key works of modern scholarship, Schlesinger's *Colonial Merchants and the American Revolution* (1918) and Jameson's *American Revolution Considered as a Social Movement* (1926). More recently there have been studies in this tradition that attempt to describe the Revolution as a social upheaval by tracing the redistribution of confiscated loyalist property. But all such efforts have proved to be indecisive, for though of course the Revolution had social consequences, in its essence it can only be understood in political and ideological terms, and the reality of the struggle does not appear in abstracted "forces." The Progressives' approach, even

29. *Loyalism in New York during the American Revolution* (N.Y., 1901); *The Loyalists in the American Revolution* (N.Y., 1902).

30. For references to recent writings, especially those relating to the loyalists who resettled in Canada, see Wallace Brown, "The View at Two Hundred Years: The Loyalists of the American Revolution," AAS *Procs.*, 80 (April 1970), 25–47.

more than that of Gipson and the "imperialists," was such as to preclude penetration into what people believed, thought, and felt; what led them to do what they did; what they sought to achieve; the whole world of inner life which shapes the responses people have to events. These, to the Progressives, were not basic elements, and they found a concept by which to write them off systematically. What people said and wrote was not taken to reflect what they believed or felt or thought, but what they hoped would influence others to act as they wished them to. It was all, in a word, *propaganda;* and the more systematic the thought the more likely it was to be propaganda. The use of the written word as the expression of the satisfactions, beliefs, attitudes, perceptions, and aspirations that make up the experience of life was systematically excluded and the entire realm of ideology written off as insincere and ineffective.

Not all recent writers on the loyalists have been constrained by these ideas. Leonard Labaree, for example, in a notable essay on the loyalists and in his *Conservatism in Early American History* dealt with the loyalists' ideas and attitudes as well as with their organization, their numerical strength, their geographic and socioeconomic distribution, and their losses and final dispersal. So too has William Nelson in his survey, *The American Tory,* approached the questions broadly, and Mary Beth Norton has written an extremely informative account of the careers of the loyalists in exile in England.[31] Yet these are general descriptions, and they fail to penetrate deeply into the inner lives of this important segment of the population. They leave one still asking not only what the loyalists' experience tells us about the boundaries of that distant world, about the latent limitations within which everyone involved was obliged to act, but ultimately what the loyalists' experience reveals about the origins and character of the Revolution itself.

31. Labaree, "The Nature of American Loyalism," AAS *Procs.*, n.s., 54 (April 1944), 15–58; *Conservatism in Early American History* (N.Y., 1948), esp. chap. vi; William H. Nelson, *The American Tory* (N.Y., 1961); Mary Beth Norton, *The British-Americans: The Loyalist Exiles in England, 1774–1789* (Boston and Toronto, 1972). See also Wallace Brown, *The King's Friends: The Composition and Motives of the American Loyalist Claimants* (Providence, R.I., 1966), which classifies the loyalists who filed claims with the English government for repayment for their losses and enumerates the property they professed to have lost, and the same author's general survey, *The Good Americans* (N.Y., 1969). Robert M. Calhoon's broad-ranging study, *The Loyalists in Revolutionary America, 1760–1781* (N.Y., 1973), which became available after the present book went to press, centers on questions of perception and motivation, and promises to go well beyond the earlier general descriptions mentioned above.

Note on the Hutchinson Manuscripts

The Hutchinson manuscripts are voluminous, despite the loss, in the Stamp Act riot of August 26, 1765, of the entire collection of papers that Thomas Hutchinson had been gathering up to that time as a foundation for a public archive. The surviving correspondence of Thomas Hutchinson alone includes some fifteen hundred letters or drafts of letters, and it is that extraordinarily complete series of documents, running from the early 1760's until his death in 1780, which, together with the diaries from 1774 to 1780, forms the documentary basis of this book.

The Hutchinson manuscripts are located primarily in two depositories. The first is the Massachusetts Archives, in the State House, Boston. Volumes XXV, XXVI, XVII of that superb but ill-preserved collection contain the bulk of Thomas Hutchinson's correspondence. These are the letters that were found—in circumstances that are described in Chapter IX—in Hutchinson's house in Milton in 1775 and that were used by the Revolutionaries for propaganda purposes. (The complicated history of this collection, from its discovery in 1775 until its final lodging in the Massachusetts Archives, is traced in MHS *Procs.*, 13 [1873–1875], 217–232.) Volume XXV includes four letters of the years before 1760, five of the years 1760–1765, and then a series of some 250 letters, many of them written to Hutchinson, from the years 1765–1773. The letters in volume XXVI, numbering approximately 500, are mainly from Hutchinson and form an almost unbroken series from December

1761 to September 1770. Volume XXVII continues the series, with some 500 letters, dated from September 1770 to early January 1774.

These documents, written for the most part in Hutchinson's hand, are not all finished copies of letters that were sent; some are drafts of letters—frequently much emended drafts—which are occasionally marked "not sent." In a few sub-series—especially the letters written to Israel Williams, Thomas Gage, and the secretary or undersecretaries of state for the colonies—the recipient's copies have survived, and one may note interesting difference between the letterbook drafts in the MA volumes and the letters as finally sent.

These documents are, like the rest of the Massachusetts Archives, wretchedly—disgracefully—preserved, and they would be extremely difficult to use had they not been transcribed by Catherine Barton Mayo. Her typescript copy of the letters, checked and edited for eventual publication by Malcolm Freiberg, was presented to the Massachusetts Historical Society in 1957, and it is available there for the use of scholars.

Most of the rest of the Hutchinson manuscripts are in the Egerton Manuscripts, volumes 2659–2674, in the British Museum. As has been explained in note 24 to the Appendix, the Hutchinson family papers that were taken to, or after 1774 originated in, England were carefully preserved by Thomas Hutchinson's great-grandson, Peter Orlando Hutchinson, who edited and indexed them, largely in preparation for his publication, *The Diary and Letters of His Excellency Thomas Hutchinson;* when that work was finished he sold the papers to the British Museum. P. O. Hutchinson wrote comments in these notebooks as he used them, and from these remarks, and from letters in the MHS, one can reconstruct the picture of this devoted amateur scholar working for years in Sidmouth, England, to preserve the remarkable collection.

The first two volumes, Eg. MSS 2659 and 2660, contain letters from several members of the Hutchinson family, including Thomas, and include much material from the period after his death in 1780. Eg. MSS 2661 is the continuation of Thomas Hutchinson's letterbook, picking up from where MA XXVII leaves off and continuing in an unbroken series until early 1776, when Hutchinson, for the first time in his life, stopped keeping copies of the letters he wrote. There are only a few full letters for the years after that date; except for the separate correspondence with Lord Hardwicke, from November 1774 to December 1779, Add. MSS 34527 in the British Museum, most of what remains of Hutchinson's correspondence after 1776 consists of memoranda only. Eg. MSS 2662–2665 contain Thomas Hutchinson's diaries from June 1774 to May 1780, the month before his death.[1] These diaries are almost all published in full, and accurately, in *Diary and Letters,* where they appear together with excerpts from the Hutchinson family's correspondence, but there are a number of passages—relating primarily to Peggy Hutchinson's illness and to Thomas Hutchinson's condemnation of Thomas Pownall—that were omitted from that publication, though in almost every case the omissions are indicated by asterisks.

Eg. MSS 2666 is Thomas Hutchinson's annotated almanac for the year 1770, probably one of many such notebooks he kept. It contains, as noted in Chapter V, a running commentary on the events of that year, and the writing there forms the basis for passages in Hutchinson's *History of Massachusetts-Bay.* Eg. MSS 2668 is the letters of Thomas Hutchinson's son Elisha to his wife, 1774–1778. Eg. MSS 2670 is Andrew Oliver's letterbook, 1767–1774. Volumes 2672–2673 are Chief Justice Peter Oliver's journal, 1776–1780, and volume 2674 is the diary of Peter Oliver, Jr., 1777–1821.

In addition to the manuscripts in these two primary collections there are letters of Thomas Hutchinson scattered in a number of other repositories. All of Hutchinson's official correspondence with the home authorities in the years of his governorship is among the Colonial Office Papers, Public Record Office, London: CO5/759–763 and 768. These volumes contain the recipient's copies and office duplicates of letters whose drafts or sender's copies are in the MA collection. The CO5 files also contain the enclosures Hutchinson sent along with his dispatches, and they are often extremely valuable material not otherwise available. There are a few Hutchinson

---

1. Eg. MSS, 2664, is really two volumes in one. Hutchinson began the volume in the usual way, with a continuation of his diary beginning with the entry of August 1, 1777. Then after filling 100 pages (to August 1778) in this fashion he turned the volume over, end-to-end, filled the first pages at that end with reading notes and financial accounts, and then began writing, on the third leaf recto of these reversed pages, the family and personal memoir that he called "Hutchinson in America," concluding it on p. 99. There are, therefore, two sets of page numbers in this volume, one beginning at each end and progressing about the same distance toward the center. In referring to the pages of this volume, I have cited the diary entries in normal pagination but I have used the phrase "from end" after the page numbers of the second series, at the back of the volume. Thus "Eg. MSS, 2664, p. 24 from end" means page 24 in the pagination of the memoir that runs from the back toward the front of the volume.

items not found elsewhere among the Gage Papers in the William L. Clements Library at the University of Michigan and the Loudoun Papers at the Henry E. Huntington Library, San Marino, California; microfilm copies in both cases are at the MHS. There are unique copies of other Hutchinson material in the New England Papers (4 volumes, Sparks MSS 10) and the British Papers Relating to the American Revolution (4 volumes, Sparks MSS 43) in the Houghton Library, Harvard University. That Library also has the thirteen volumes of the Francis Bernard Papers (Sparks MSS 4) which, though consisting exclusively of letters written by Governor Bernard, are documents so closely connected with Hutchinson's career that they are in effect an extension of his personal archive.

Index

Index

Index

America, 323, 332–333, 340–341; arrives in London, 353
Hutchinson, William Sanford (TH's son), 24n, 30, 265, 274, 290, 308; TH seeks employment for, 354–356; death of, 373
Hutchinson family, 9ff., 21n, 28ff., 338, 363; closeness of, 30–31, 264, 356, 361–362; marriages with Olivers and Sanfords, 30–31; scattered in 1774, 270; endangered by war, 323, 332–334, 340, 342–343; illnesses of, 352; escapes from Boston to London, 353–354; burden of, on TH, 355

Independence, American, 56, 74, 98, 117, 131, 232, 323n; TH's fear of, 83, 91, 96–97, 199n, 304, 346–347; seen as radicals' goal, 114, 125, 206, 210, 212, 219n, 268, 294, 349–350, 358–359, 377; Franklin's commitment to, 225, 379–380; expressed in Assembly's replies to TH, 279
Independent Chronicle (Boston), 375–376
Ireland, 134, 392

Jackson, Richard, 19, 26, 58–59, 62, 63, 64, 71, 74, 80, 84, 86, 124, 130, 139, 142, 144, 145, 146, 147, 148n, 149, 152, 169, 186, 187, 219n, 250, 282, 326, 347; ideas on Anglo-American relations, 89ff., 97; as colonial agent, 89, 114
Jamaica, 348
James II, 200
Jameson, J. F., *American Revolution Considered as a Social Movement*, 407
Jared Ingersoll (Gipson), 405
Jefferson, Thomas, 173n, 326
Jenkinson, Charles, 282, 285, 317
Jenyns, Soame, 153
Johnstone, George, 347–348
Jones, Thomas, *History of New York*, 384–385n
Journal and Letters (Curwen), 385
Journal of the Times (1768), 124, 157
Judges: tenure of, 92, 303; and law enforcement, 102
Juries, 278. *See also* Grand jury
Justinian, 51

Kennebec Purchase, 44n
King's Friends (Brown), 408n
Kinnoul, Thomas Hay, 8th Earl of, 26n, 143
Knox, William, 189, 282, 304, 345

Labaree, Leonard, *Conservatism*, 408; "Nature of American Loyalism," 408n
Land bank, 133, 138
Law: and morality, 102, 104, 107; nature of, 103
Lechmere, Richard, 4
Lecky, W. E. H., 389n, 398, 400, 404; *History of England*, 391–393, 397n, 402–403; *Historical and Political Essays*, 404
Lee, Arthur, 193n, 197, 203n, 212, 233, 254, 286, 298, 308, 373–374
"Legendary and Myth-Making Process" (Fisher), 397n
Leonard, Daniel, 395
Leslie, Lt. Col. Alexander, 263
Letters from a Farmer in Pennsylvania (Dickinson), 98, 99
Lexington, battle of, 331–332, 334
Liberty: protection of British, 79; growth of, in TH's time, 80; American, protected by Britain, 82; TH's view of limits of, in America, 91–92, 209, 227, 230, 243, 246, 250–251
Life of Washington (Weems), 384
Literary History of the American Revolution (Tyler), 402–403
Livy, 101
Locke, John, 22n, 100, 101
London, *see* England
London, Richard Terrick, Bishop of, 317
London Chronicle, 335
Loudoun, John Campbell, 4th Earl of, 40, 41, 42, 325
Loyalism in New York (Flick), 407
Loyalists: flood into London (1775–6), 344–345, 354; historiography of, 383ff.
Loyalists (Van Tyne), 407
Loyalists in Revolutionary America (Calhoon), 408n
Lycurgan laws, 90
Lyttleton, William Henry, 1st Baron, 348

Mackintosh, Ebenezer, 72
McMaster family, 157n

Pownall, Thomas (*cont.*)
89, 90, 93, 232–233; antagonism with
TH, 5, 14, 42–45, 221n, 320, 368–369;
TH's letters to, 72, 73, 86; and
publication of TH-Whately letters, 225,
231–233, 235, 287–288; counsels Mass.
radicals, 231–232; takes Treasury seat
in Commons, 314, 319–320;
Administration of Colonies, 88–89, 231
Pownallborough, Maine, 44n
Press, freedom of, 120
Preston, Capt. Thomas, 28n, 158, 249
Price, Richard, 336
"Principles of Law and Polity" (Bernard),
86–88
Public Advertiser (London), 214n
Putnam, James, 177

Quakers, 102
Quebec, 332, 341, 354
Quincy, Josiah, Jr., 3, 36, 78, 249, 309,
379; visit to England (1774–5), 318–321

Ramsay, Allan, 76–77, 78, 79
Ramsay, David, 376, 384
Randolph, Edward, 197
Reading, England, 308
Remembrancer (London), 335, 359
Reminiscences (Boucher), 385n
Representation in Parliament, American,
87, 88, 90–91, 351
Rhode Island, 12, 14, 283, 293, 341
Richardson, Ebenezer, 136, 264
Richmond, Charles Lennox, 3d Duke of,
306
Right of the British Legislature (Gray),
212n
Riots, 84–85. *See also* Mobs; Stamp Act
Robertson, William, 19, 27
Robie, Thomas, 177
Robinson, John, 177
Rockingham, Charles Watson-Wentworth,
2d Marquess of, 143, 144, 288, 297, 306–
307, 308, 317
Rockingham Whigs, 282, 307
Rogers, Nathaniel, 131, 135, 149, 157n,
165n, 183, 224n, 226, 227
Rome, George, 224n, 226, 227, 228
Rotch, Joseph, 260
Rowe, John, 72

Royal Society, 235
Royall, Isaac, 72
"Rules by Which a Great Empire"
(Franklin), 237n
Russell, Chambers, 48

Salaries, crown, 118, 120, 121n, 146–148,
165n, 169, 199, 202ff., 259, 265–266, 290,
303
Salem, Mass., 293, 302
Salisbury, England, 353
Salkeld, William, 51
Sandwich, John Montagu, 4th Earl of,
317
Sanford, Grizell (TH's sister-in-law), 30,
353
Sanford family, 10n, 12, 30
Saratoga, 365
Sayward, Jonathan, 129n, 181–182
Scarborough, The, 301
Schlesinger, A. M., Sr., *Colonial
Merchants,* 407
Scotland, rebellion in, 309–310, 311
Selwyn, George, 386
Separation of powers, 53–54, 113, 117–118,
121n
Sewall, Jonathan, 112, 129, 177–178, 198,
312n, 314, 315–316, 332n, 338, 345;
defends TH's letters to Whately, 245–
248, 250
Sewall, Stephen, 47, 49
Sheaffe, Edward, 118, 119
Shelburne, William Petty, 2d Earl of,
119–120, 153, 306, 308, 320
Shirley, Gov. William, 40, 41, 50, 60,
221; his group in politics, 42, 43, 44
Short History of Anglo-Saxon Freedom
(Hosmer), 399–401
Silvester, Richard, 127–128, 178
Slavery, 378
Smith, J. Allen, 407
Smith, William, 4, 93, 94n, 95, 211, 336,
385n
Snider, Christopher, 136, 264
Sons of Liberty, 136n, 178, 227
South Carolina, 263, 293
Sovereignty, 101, 103, 379; indivisibility
of, 77, 94, 97, 201, 209, 231, 297, 299,
311, 346–347, 377
Sparhawk, Nathaniel, 72